Gabriel's Inferno

Books by Sylvain Reynard

GABRIEL'S INFERNO
GABRIEL'S RAPTURE
GABRIEL'S REDEMPTION
THE RAVEN
THE SHADOW

Novella

THE PRINCE

Gabriel's Inferno

SYLVAIN REYNARD

BERKLEY
New York

BERKLEY
An imprint of Penguin Random House LLC
375 Hudson Street, New York, New York 10014

Originally published by Omnific Publishing, www.omnificpublishing.com

ISBN: 9780425265963

Omnific Publishing trade paperback edition / April 2011
Berkley trade paperback edition / September 2012

Printed in the United States of America
7   9   11   13   15   16   14   12   10   8

Cover design by Micha Stone and Amy Brokaw
Book design by Tiffany Estreicher

In memoriam Maiae.
Resurgam.

Dante and Virgil crossing the river Styx.
Engraving from 1870 by Gustave Dore

Prologue

Florence, 1283

T he poet stood next to the bridge and watched as the young woman approached. The world ground to a near standstill as he remarked her wide, dark eyes and elegantly curled brown hair.

At first he didn't recognize her. She was breathtakingly beautiful, her movements sure and graceful. Yet there was something about her face and figure that reminded him of the girl he'd fallen in love with long ago. They'd gone their separate ways, and he had always mourned her, his angel, his muse, his beloved Beatrice. Without her, his life had been lonely and small.

Now his blessedness appeared.

As she approached him with her companions, he bowed his head and body in a chivalrous salute. He had no expectation that his presence would be acknowledged. She was both perfect and untouchable, a brown-eyed angel dressed in resplendent white, while he was older, world-weary and wanting.

She had almost passed him when his downcast eyes caught sight of one of her slippers—a slipper that hesitated just in front of him. His heart beat a furious tattoo as he waited, breathless. A soft and gentle voice broke into his remembrances as she spoke to him kindly. His startled eyes flew to hers. For years and years he'd longed for this moment, dreamed of it even, but never had he imagined encountering her in such a serendipitous fashion. And never had he dared hope he would be greeted so sweetly.

Caught off balance, he mumbled his pleasantries and allowed himself the indulgence of a smile—a smile that was returned to him tenfold by his muse. His heart swelled within him as the love he held for her multiplied and burned like an inferno in his chest.

Alas, their conversation was all too brief before she declared that she must depart. He bowed before her as she swept by, and then straightened to stare at her retreating form. His joy at their reunion was tempered by an emergent sadness as he wondered if he'd ever see her again . . .

Chapter One

" . . . Miss Mitchell?"

Professor Gabriel Emerson's voice carried across the seminar room to the attractive brown-eyed young woman who was seated at the back. Lost in thought, or lost in translation, her head was down as she scribbled furiously in her notebook.

Ten pairs of eyes swung to her, to her pale face and long lashes, her thin white fingers clutching a pen. Then ten pairs of eyes swung back to the professor, who stood perfectly still and began to scowl. His scathing demeanor contrasted sharply with the overall symmetry of his features, his large, expressive eyes, and full mouth. He was ruggedly handsome, but in that moment bitterly severe, which rather ruined the overall pleasing effect of his appearance.

"*Ahem.*" A modest cough to her right caught the woman's attention. She glanced in surprise at the broad-shouldered man sitting next to her. He smiled and flicked his eyes to the front of the room, back to the professor.

She followed his gaze slowly, looking up into a pair of angry, peering blue eyes. She swallowed noisily.

"I expect an answer to my question, Miss Mitchell. *If you'd care to join us.*" His voice was glacial, like his eyes.

The other graduate students shifted in their seats and stole furtive glances at one another. Their expressions said *what crawled up his ass?* But they said nothing. (For it is commonly known that graduate students are loath to confront their professors with respect to anything, let alone rude behavior.)

The young woman opened her mouth minutely and closed it, staring into those unblinking blue eyes, her own eyes wide like a frightened rabbit.

"Is English your first language?" he mocked her.

A raven-haired woman seated at his right hand tried to stifle a laugh, smothering it into an unconvincing cough. All eyes shifted back to the frightened rabbit, whose skin exploded into crimson as she ducked her head, finally escaping the professor's gaze.

"Since Miss Mitchell seems to be carrying on a parallel seminar in a different language, perhaps someone else would be kind enough to answer my question?"

The beauty to his right was only too eager. She turned to face him and beamed as she answered his question in great detail, making a show of herself by gesturing with her hands as she quoted Dante in his original Italian. When she had finished, she smiled acidly at the back of the room, then proceeded to gaze up at the professor and sigh. All that was lacking from her display was a quick leap to the floor and a rubbing of her back on his leg to show that she would be his pet forever. (Not that he would have appreciated the gesture.)

The professor frowned almost imperceptibly at no one in particular and turned his back to write on the board. The frightened rabbit blinked back tears as she continued scribbling, but mercifully she did not cry.

A few minutes later, as the professor droned on and on about the conflict between the Guelfs and the Ghibellines, a small square of folded paper appeared on top of the frightened rabbit's Italian dictionary. At first she didn't notice it, but once again, a soft *ahem* drew her attention to the good-looking man beside her. He smiled more widely this time, almost eagerly, and glanced down at the paper.

She saw it and blinked. Carefully watching the back of the professor as he drew endless circles around endless Italian words, she brought the paper to her lap where she quietly unfolded it.

Emerson is an ass.

No one would have noticed because no one was looking at her, except for the man at her side. As soon as she read those words, a different kind of flush appeared on her face, two pink clouds on the curve of her cheeks, and she smiled. Not enough to show teeth or what could be dimples or a laugh line or two, but a smile nonetheless.

She raised her large eyes to the man next to her and looked at him shyly. A wide, friendly grin spread across his face.

"Something funny, Miss Mitchell?"

Her brown eyes dilated in terror. Her new friend's smile quickly disappeared as he turned to look at the professor.

She knew better now than to look up at the professor's cold blue eyes. Instead, she put her head down and worried her plump lower lip between her teeth, back and forth and back and forth.

"It was my fault, Professor. I was just asking what page we were on," the friendly man interceded on her behalf.

"Hardly an appropriate question from a doctoral student, Paul. But since you asked, we began with the first canto. I trust you can find it without Miss Mitchell's help. Oh, and Miss Mitchell?"

The frightened rabbit's ponytail trembled ever so slightly as she lifted her gaze.

"See me in my office after class."

Chapter Two

At the end of the seminar, Julia Mitchell hastily tucked the folded piece of paper she'd been cradling in her lap into her Italian dictionary, under the entry *asino*.

"Sorry about all that. I'm Paul Norris." The friendly man extended his large paw over the table. She shook it gently, and he marveled at how small her hand was in comparison to his. He could have bruised it just by flexing his palm.

"Hello, Paul. I'm Julia. Julia Mitchell."

"Good to meet you, Julia. I'm sorry The Professor was such a prick. I don't know what's eating him." Paul gave Emerson his preferred title with no little sarcasm.

She reddened slightly and turned back to her books.

"You're new?" he persisted, tilting his head a little as if he was trying to catch her eye.

"Just arrived. From Saint Joseph's University."

He nodded as if that meant something. "And you're here for a master's?"

"Yes." She gestured to the front of the now empty seminar room. "It probably doesn't seem like it, but I'm supposed to be studying to be a Dante specialist."

Paul whistled through his teeth. "So you're here for Emerson?"

She nodded, and he noticed that the veins in her neck began to pulsate slightly as her heart rate quickened. Since he couldn't find an explanation for her reaction, he dismissed it. But he would be reminded of it later.

"He's difficult to work with, so he doesn't have a lot of students. I'm writing my dissertation with him, and there's also Christa Peterson, whom you've already met."

"Christa?" She gave him a questioning look.

"The tart at the front. She's his other PhD student, but her goal is to be the future Mrs. Emerson. She just started the program, and she's already baking him cookies, dropping by his office, leaving telephone messages. It's unbelievable."

Julia nodded again but said nothing.

"Christa doesn't seem to be aware of the strict non-fraternization policy set up by the University of Toronto." Paul rolled his eyes and was rewarded with a very pretty smile. He told himself that he would have to make Julia Mitchell smile more often. But that would need to be postponed, for now.

"You'd better go. He wanted to see you after class, and he'll be waiting."

Julia quickly tossed her things into a shabby L.L. Bean knapsack that she had carried since she was a freshman undergraduate. "Um, I don't know where his office is."

"Turn left on your way out of the seminar room, then make another left. He has the corner office at the end of the hall. Good luck, and I'll see you next class, if not before."

She smiled gratefully and exited the seminar room.

As she rounded the corner, she saw that The Professor's office door was ajar. She stood in front of the opening nervously, wondering if she should knock first or peek her head around. After a moment's deliberation, she opted for the former. Straightening her shoulders, she took a deep breath, held it, and placed her knuckles in front of the wood paneling. That's when she heard him.

"I'm sorry I didn't call you back. I was in my seminar!" an angry voice, all too familiar now, spat aloud. There was a brief silence before he continued. "Because it's the first seminar of the year, asshole, and because the last time I talked to her she said she was fine!"

Julia retreated immediately. It sounded like he was on the telephone, yelling. She didn't want him yelling at her, and so she decided to flee and deal with the consequences later. But a heart-wrenching sob tore from his throat and assaulted her ears. And from that she could not flee.

"Of course I wanted to be there! I loved her. Of course I wanted to be there." Another sob emerged from behind the door. "I don't know what time I'll get there. Tell them I'm coming. I'll go straight to the airport and hop a plane, but I don't know what kind of flight I can get on short notice."

He paused. "I know. Tell them I'm sorry. I'm so sorry . . ." His voice trailed off into a soft, shuddering cry, and Julia heard him hang up the telephone.

Without considering her actions, Julia carefully peeked around the door.

The thirty-something man held his head in his long-fingered hands, leaning his elbows on his desk and crying. She watched as his wide shoulders shook. She heard anguish and sorrow rip out of his chest. And she felt compassion.

She wanted to go to him, to offer condolences and comfort and to put her arms around his neck. She wanted to smooth his hair and tell him that she was sorry. She imagined briefly what it would be like to wipe tears away from those expressive sapphire eyes and see them look at her kindly. She thought about giving him a gentle peck on his cheek, just to reassure him of her sympathy.

But watching him cry as if his heart was broken momentarily froze her, and so she did none of those things. When she finally realized where she was, she quickly disappeared back behind the door, blindly pulled a scrap of paper from her knapsack, and wrote:

I'm sorry.
—Julia Mitchell

Then, not quite knowing what to do, she placed the paper against the doorjamb, trapping it there as she silently pulled his office door shut.

❦ ❦

Julia's shyness was not her primary characteristic. Her best quality, and the one that defined her, was her compassion, a trait that she hadn't inherited from either of her parents. Her father, who was a decent man, tended to be rigid and unyielding. Her mother, who was deceased, had not been compassionate in any way, not even to her only child.

Tom Mitchell was a man of few words, but was well-known and generally liked. He was a custodian at Susquehanna University, and the fire chief of Selinsgrove Borough, Pennsylvania. Since the fire department was entirely volunteer, he and the other fire fighters found themselves on call at all times. He inhabited his role proudly and with much dedication, which meant that he was rarely home, even when he wasn't responding to an emergency. On the evening of Julia's first graduate seminar he called her from the fire station, pleased that she finally decided to answer her cell phone.

"How's it going up there, Jules?" His voice, unsentimental but comforting nevertheless, warmed her like a blanket.

She sighed. "It's fine. The first day was . . . interesting, but fine."

"Those Canadians treating you right?"

"Oh, yes. They're all pretty nice." *It's the Americans who are the bastards. Well, one American.*

Tom cleared his throat once or twice, and Julia caught her breath. She knew from years of experience that he was preparing to say something serious. She wondered what it was.

"Honey, Grace Clark died today."

Julia sat upright on her twin bed and stared into space.

"Did you hear what I said?"

"Yes. Yes, I heard."

"Her cancer came back. They thought she was fine. But it came back, and by the time they found out, it was in her bones and her liver. Richard and the kids are pretty shaken up about it."

Julia bit her lip and stifled a sob.

"I knew you'd take the news hard. She was like a mother to you, and Rachel was such a good friend of yours in high school. Have you heard from her?"

"Um, no. No, I haven't. Why didn't she tell me?"

"I'm not sure when they found out that Grace was sick again. I was over to the house to see everyone earlier today, and Gabriel wasn't even there. That's created quite a problem. I don't know what he's walking into when he arrives. There's a lot of bad blood in that family." Tom cursed softly.

"Are you sending flowers?"

"I guess so. I'm not really good at that sort of thing, but I could ask Deb if she'd help."

Deb Lundy was Tom's girlfriend. Julia rolled her eyes at the mention of Deb's name but kept her negative reaction to herself.

"Ask her, please, to send something from me. Grace loved gardenias. And just have Deb sign the card."

"Will do. Do you need anything?"

"No, I'm fine."

"Do you need any money?"

"No, Dad. I have enough to live on with my scholarship if I'm careful."

Tom paused, and even before he opened his mouth she knew what he was about to say.

"I'm sorry about Harvard. Maybe next year."

Julia straightened her shoulders and forced a smile, even though her father couldn't see it. "Maybe. Talk to you later."

"Bye, honey."

The next morning Julia walked a little more slowly on her way to the university, using her iPod as background noise. In her head, she composed an e-mail of condolence and apology to Rachel, writing and rewriting it as she walked.

The September breeze was warm in Toronto, and she liked it. She liked being near the lake. She liked sunshine and friendliness. She liked tidy streets free of litter. She liked the fact she was in Toronto and not in Selinsgrove or Philadelphia—that she was hundreds of miles away from *him*. She only hoped it would stay that way.

She was still mentally writing the e-mail to Rachel when she stepped into the office of the Department of Italian Studies to check her mailbox. Someone tapped her on the elbow and moved out of her periphery.

She removed her ear buds. "Paul . . . hi."

He smiled down at her, his gaze descending some distance. Julia was petite, especially in sneakers, and the top of her head merely reached the lower edge of his pectorals.

"How was your meeting with Emerson?" His smile faded, and he looked at her with concern.

She bit her lip, a nervous habit that she should stop but was unable to, primarily because she was unaware of it. "Um, I didn't go."

He closed his eyes and leaned his head back. He groaned a little. "That's . . . not good."

Julia tried to clarify the situation. "His office door was closed. I think he was on the phone . . . I'm not sure. So I left a note."

Paul noticed her nervousness and the way her delicately arched eyebrows came together. He felt sorry for her and silently cursed The Professor for being so abrasive. She looked as if she would bruise easily, and Emerson was oblivious to the way his attitude affected his students. So Paul resolved to help her.

"If he was on the telephone, he wouldn't want to be interrupted. Let's hope that's what was going on. Otherwise, I'd say you just took your life into your own hands." He straightened up to his full height and flexed his arms casually. "Let me know if there's any fallout, and I'll see what I can do. If he shouts at me, I can take it. I wouldn't want him to shout at you." *Because from the looks of it, you'd die of shock, Frightened Rabbit.*

Julia appeared as if she wanted to say something but remained silent. She smiled thinly and nodded as if in appreciation. Then she stepped over to the mailboxes and emptied her pigeonhole.

Junk mail, mostly. A few advertisements from the department, including an announcement of a public lecture to be delivered by Professor Gabriel O. Emerson entitled, *Lust in Dante's Inferno: The Deadly Sin against the Self.* Julia read the title over several times before she was able to absorb it into her brain. But once it had been absorbed, she hummed softly to herself.

She hummed as she noticed a second announcement, which mentioned that Professor Emerson's lecture had been cancelled and rescheduled for a later date. And she hummed as she noticed a third announcement, which declared that all of Professor Emerson's seminars, appointments, and meetings had been cancelled until further notice.

And she kept right on humming as she reached back into her pigeonhole for a small square of paper. She unfolded it and read:

I'm sorry.
—*Julia Mitchell*

She continued to hum as she puzzled over what it meant to find her note in her mailbox the day after she'd placed it at Professor Emerson's door. But her humming finally stopped, as did her heart, when she turned the paper over and read the following:

Emerson is an ass.

Chapter Three

There was a time when, in reaction to such an embarrassing event, Julia would have dropped to the floor and pulled herself into a fetal position, possibly staying there forever. But at the age of twenty-three, she was made of sterner stuff. So rather than standing in front of the mailboxes and contemplating how her short academic career had just gone up in flames and been reduced to a pile of ash at her feet, she quietly finished her business at the university and went home.

Pushing all thoughts of her career aside, Julia did four things.

First, she pocketed some cash from the emergency fund that was conveniently located in a Tupperware container underneath her bed.

Second, she walked to the closest liquor store and bought a very large bottle of very cheap tequila.

Third, she went home and wrote a long and apologetic condolence e-mail to Rachel. Purposefully, she neglected to mention where she was living and what she was doing, and she sent the e-mail from her Gmail account rather than her university account.

Fourth, she went shopping. The fourth activity was intended only as a weepy and somewhat heartbroken tribute to both Rachel and Grace, because they had loved expensive things, and Julia was in reality too poor to shop.

Julia couldn't afford to shop when she came to live in Selinsgrove and met Rachel in their junior year of high school. Julia could barely afford to shop now, as she eked out a meager living on a graduate student's stipend, without the eligibility to work outside the university to supplement her income. As an American on a student's visa, she had limited employability.

While she walked slowly past the beautiful shop windows on Bloor

Street, she thought of her old friend and her surrogate mother. She stood in front of the Prada store, envisioning the one and only time Rachel had taken her shopping for couture shoes. Julia still had those black Prada stilettos, tucked in a shoebox in the back of her closet. They'd only been worn once, on the night she'd discovered she'd been betrayed, and although she would have loved to have destroyed them like she destroyed her dress, she couldn't. Rachel had bought them for her as a coming-home present, having had no idea what Julia was actually coming home to.

Then Julia stood for what seemed like forever in front of the Chanel boutique and wept, remembering Grace. How she always greeted Julia with a smile and a hug whenever she came to visit. How when Julia's mother had passed away under tragic circumstances, Grace had told her that she loved her and would love to be her mother, if she'd let her. How Grace had been a better mother to her than Sharon ever had, to Sharon's shame and Julia's embarrassment.

And when all her tears were gone and the stores had closed for the evening, Julia walked back to her apartment slowly and began to beat herself up for having been a bad surrogate daughter, a lousy friend, and an insensitive twit who didn't know better than to check a scrap of paper to see if it was blank before she left it behind with her name on it for someone whose beloved mother had just died.

What must have been running through his mind when he found that note? Heartened by a shot or two or three of tequila, Julia allowed herself to ask some simple questions. *And what must he think of me now?*

She contemplated packing up all of her belongings and boarding a Greyhound bus bound for her hometown of Selinsgrove, just so she wouldn't have to face him. She was ashamed she hadn't realized it was Grace that Professor Emerson had been discussing on the telephone that terrible day. But she hadn't even contemplated the possibility that Grace's cancer had returned let alone that she had passed away. And Julia had been so upset about having gotten off on the wrong foot with The Professor. His hostility was shocking. But even more shocking was his face as he cried. All she had thought about in that terrible moment was comforting him, and that thought alone had distracted her from considering the source of his grief.

It wasn't enough that he'd just had his heart ripped out by hearing that Grace had died, without having an opportunity to say good-bye or to tell her that he loved her. It wasn't enough that someone, probably his brother Scott, had effectively torn into him for not coming home. No, after having been destroyed by grief and crying like a child, he'd had the delightful experience of opening his office door to escape to the airport and finding her note of consolation. And what Paul had written on the other side.

Lovely.

Julia was surprised that The Professor hadn't had her dismissed from the program on the spot. *Perhaps he remembers me.* One more shot of tequila enabled Julia to formulate that thought, but to think no further, as she passed out on the floor.

❈ ❈

Two weeks later, Julia found herself in a slightly better state as she checked her mailbox in the department. Yes, it was as if she was waiting on death row with no hope of commutation. No, she hadn't dropped out of school and gone home.

It was true that she blushed like a schoolgirl and was painfully shy. But Julia was stubborn. She was tenacious. And she wanted very much to study Dante, and if that meant invoking an unidentified co-conspirator in order to escape the death penalty, she was willing to do so.

She just hadn't revealed that fact to Paul. Yet.

"Julianne? Can you come here for a minute?" Mrs. Jenkins, the lovely and elderly administrative assistant, called over her desk.

Julia obediently walked toward her.

"Have you had some sort of problem with Professor Emerson?"

"I, um, I . . . don't know." She flushed and began to bite viciously on the inside of her cheek.

"I received two urgent e-mails this morning asking me to set up an appointment for you to see him as soon as he returns. I never do this for the professors. They prefer to schedule their own appointments. For some reason, he insisted that I schedule a meeting with you and have the appointment documented in your file."

Julia nodded and removed her calendar from her knapsack, trying hard not to imagine the things he had said about her in his e-mails.

Mrs. Jenkins looked at her expectantly. "So tomorrow then?"

Julia's face fell. "Tomorrow?"

"He arrives tonight, and he wants to meet you at four o'clock tomorrow afternoon in his office. Can you be there? I have to e-mail him back to confirm."

Julia nodded and noted the appointment in her calendar, pretending that the notation was necessary.

"He didn't say what it was about, but he said it was serious. I wonder what that means . . ." Mrs. Jenkins trailed off absently.

Julia concluded her business at the university and went home to pack with the help of Señorita Tequila.

❀❀

By the following morning, most of Julia's clothes were packed into two large suitcases. Not willing to admit defeat to herself (or to the tequila), she decided not to pack everything, and thus found herself twiddling her thumbs anxiously and in need of a distraction. So she did the one thing any self-respecting, procrastinating graduate student would do in such a situation besides drink and carouse with other procrastinating graduate students—she cleaned her apartment.

It didn't take very long. But by the time she was finished, everything was in perfect order, lightly scented with lemon, and scrupulously clean. Julia took more than a little pride in her achievement and packed her knapsack, head held high.

Meanwhile, Professor Emerson was stomping through the halls of the department, leaving graduate students and faculty colleagues spinning in his wake. He was in a foul mood, and no one had the courage to trifle with him.

These days he was ill tempered to begin with, but his fractious disposition had been exacerbated by stress and lack of sleep. He had been cursed by the gods of Air Canada and consequently seated next to a father and his two-year-old child on his flight back from Philadelphia. The child screamed and wet himself (and Professor Emerson), while the father slept soundly. In the semi-darkness of the airplane, Professor Emerson had reflected on the justice of government-enforced sterilization on lax parents as he mopped urine from his Armani trousers.

Julia arrived promptly for her four o'clock appointment with Professor Emerson and was delighted to find that his door was closed. Her delight soon left her when she realized that The Professor was inside his office growling at Paul.

When Paul emerged ten minutes later, still standing tall at six foot three but visibly shaken, Julia's eyes darted to the fire exit. Five steps and she'd be free behind a swinging door, running to escape the police for illegally sounding a fire alarm. It seemed like a tempting proposition.

Paul caught her eye and shook his head, mouthing a few choice expletives about The Professor, before smiling. "Would you like to have coffee with me sometime?"

Julia looked up at him in surprise. She was already off kilter because of her appointment, so without thinking much about it, she agreed.

He smiled and leaned toward her. "It would be easier if I had your number."

She blushed and quickly took out a piece of paper, checked it to be sure it was free of any other writing, and hastily scribbled her cell phone number on it.

He took the piece of paper, glanced at it, and patted her arm. "Give him hell, Rabbit."

Julia didn't have time to ask him why he thought her nickname was or even should be Rabbit, because an attractive but impatient voice was already calling her.

"*Now*, Miss Mitchell."

She walked into his office and stood uncertainly just inside the door.

Professor Emerson looked tired. There were purplish circles underneath his eyes, and he was very pale, which somehow made him look thinner. As he pored over a file, his tongue flicked out and slowly licked his lower lip.

Julia stared, transfixed by his sensual mouth. After a moment, through a great effort, she dragged her gaze away from his lips to look at his glasses. She hadn't seen them before; perhaps he only wore them when his eyes were tired. But today, his penetrating sapphire eyes were partially hidden behind a pair of black Prada glasses. The black frames contrasted sharply with the warm brown of his hair and the blue of his eyes, making the glasses a focal point on his face. She realized immediately that not only had she never seen a professor as attractive as he before, she had never encountered a professor who was so studiously put together. He could have appeared in an advertising campaign for Prada, something no professor had ever done before.

(For it must be noted that university professors are not usually admired for their fashion sense.)

She knew him well enough to know that he was mercurial. She knew him well enough to know that he was, at least recently, a stickler for politeness and decorum. She knew it would probably be all right if she sat down in one of his comfy leather club chairs without his invitation, especially if he remembered her. But given the way he had addressed her, she stood.

"Please be seated, Miss Mitchell." His voice was cold and flinty, and he gestured to an uncomfortable-looking metal chair, instead.

Julia sighed and walked over to the stiff Ikea chair that sat just in front of one of his massive built-in bookcases. She wished he had given her permission to sit elsewhere but elected not to quibble with him.

"Move the chair in front of my desk. I won't crane my neck in order to see you."

She stood and did as she was told, nervously dropping her knapsack on the floor. She winced and blushed from head to foot as several of the smaller contents of her bag spilled out, including a tampon that rolled under Professor Emerson's desk and came to a stop an inch from his leather briefcase.

Maybe he won't notice it until after I'm gone.

Embarrassed, Julia crouched down and began to gather up the other contents of her knapsack. She had just finished when the strap on her very old bag snapped and everything she was carrying crashed to the floor with a loud bang. She kneeled quickly as papers, pens, her iPod, cell phone, and a green apple skidded across the floor and onto The Professor's beautiful Persian rug.

Oh, gods of all graduate students and eternal screw-ups, kill me now. Please.

"Are you a comedian, Miss Mitchell?"

Julia's spine stiffened at the sarcasm, and she glanced up at his face. What she saw nearly made her burst into tears.

How could someone with an angelic name be so cruel? How could a voice so melodic be so harsh? She was momentarily lost in the frozen depths of his eyes, longing for the time when they had looked down at her with kindness. But rather than give in to her despair, she breathed deeply and decided that she had better get used to the way he was now, even though it was a grave and painful disappointment.

Mutely, she shook her head and went back to filling her now broken knapsack.

"I expect an answer when I ask a question. Surely you've learned your lesson by now?" He studied her quickly, then glanced back at the file in his hands. "Perhaps you're not that bright."

"I beg your pardon, Dr. Emerson." The sound of Julia's voice surprised even her. It was soft but steely. She wasn't sure where her courage had come from, but she silently thanked the gods of graduate students for coming to her aid . . . just in case.

"It's *Professor* Emerson," he snapped. "Doctors are a dime a dozen. Even chiropractors and podiatrists refer to themselves as 'doctors.'"

Sufficiently chastened, Julia tried to zip up her broken knapsack. Unfortunately, the zipper was broken now too. She held her breath as she pulled on it, trying to coax it back to life with unspoken curses.

"Would you stop fussing with that ridiculous abomination of a bag and sit in a chair like a human being?"

She could see that he was beyond furious now, so she placed her ridiculous abomination on the floor and sat quietly in the uncomfortable chair. She folded her hands, just to keep from wringing them, and waited.

"You must think you're a comedian. I'm sure you thought *this* was funny." He threw a piece of paper which landed just shy of her sneakers.

Bending down to pick it up, she realized it was a photocopy of the terrible note she'd left for him the day Grace died.

"I can explain. It was a mistake. I didn't write both . . ."

"I'm not interested in your excuses! I asked you to come to the last appointment, and you didn't, did you?"

"But you were on the telephone. The door was closed and . . ."

"The door wasn't closed!" He tossed something at her that looked like a business card. "I suppose this was meant to be funny too?"

Julia picked up the discarded item and gasped. It was a small condolence card, the kind one would send with flowers:

I'm so sorry for your loss.
Please accept my sympathy.
With love,
—Julia Mitchell

She glanced over and saw that he was practically spitting he was so angry. She blinked rapidly as she tried to find the words to explain herself.

"It's not what you think. I wanted to say that I was sorry and . . ."

"Hadn't you already done that with the note you left?"

"But this was supposed to be for your family, who . . ."

"Leave my family out of it!" He turned his body away from her and closed his eyes, removing his glasses so that he could rub his face with both hands.

Julia had been evicted from the realm of the surprised and relocated right into the land of the astonished. *No one had explained.* He had completely misunderstood her card, and no one had set him straight. With a sick feeling in the pit of her stomach, she began to puzzle over what that meant.

Oblivious to her musings, The Professor appeared to calm himself through a Herculean effort, then closed the file and dropped it contemptuously on his desk. He glared at her.

"I see that you came here on scholarship to study Dante. I'm the only professor in this department who is currently supervising theses in that field. Since this—" he gestured between the two of them "—is not going to work, you'll have to change your thesis topic and find another supervisor. Or transfer to another department, or better yet, another university. I'll inform the director of your program of my decision, effective immediately. Now, if you'll excuse me."

He swiveled in his chair toward his laptop and began typing furiously.

Julia was stunned. While she was sitting there, silently absorbing not only his tirade but also his conclusion, The Professor spoke, not even bothering to lift his eyes in her direction. "That is all, Miss Mitchell."

She didn't argue with him for truly, there was no point. She dragged herself to her feet, still dazed, and picked up her offending knapsack. She cradled it to her chest, somewhat uncertainly, and slowly exited his office, looking very much like a zombie.

As she exited the building and crossed to the other side of Bloor Street, Julia realized that she'd chosen the wrong day to leave home without a jacket. The temperature had dropped, and the heavens had opened. Her thin, long-sleeved T-shirt was soaked only five steps outside of the department. She hadn't thought to bring an umbrella, so she faced the prospect of walking three long city-blocks in wind and cold and rain to get to her apartment.

Oh, gods of bad karma and thunderstorms, have mercy upon me.

As she walked, Julia took some comfort in the realization that her ridiculous abomination of a knapsack was currently serving the very proper purpose of covering her wet and possibly see-through T-shirt and cotton bra. *Take that, Professor Emerson.*

As she walked, she contemplated what had just happened in his office. She had prepared herself by packing two suitcases the night before, just in case. But she had sincerely believed that he would remember. She had believed that he would be kind to her. But he wasn't.

He hadn't allowed her to explain the colossal fuck-uppery that was the note. He had misunderstood her flowers and card. And he'd effectively dismissed her from the program. It was all over. Now she would have to return to Tom's little house in Selinsgrove in disgrace . . . and *he* would discover that she had returned and laugh at her. *They* would laugh at her together. Stupid Julia. Thought she'd leave Selinsgrove and try to make something of herself. Thought she could go to graduate school and become a professor . . . Who was she kidding? It was all over now, at least for this academic year.

Julia looked down at the destroyed and now soaked knapsack as if it were an infant and hugged it tightly to her chest. After her horrid display of gracelessness and ineptitude, she didn't even have her dignity anymore. And to lose it all in front of him, after all these years, well, it really was too much to bear.

She thought of the lone tampon underneath his desk and knew that when he leaned down to pick up his briefcase at five o'clock her humiliation would be complete. At least she wouldn't be there to witness his shocked and disgusted reaction. She envisioned him having a cow upon the discovery, literally—lying down on the beautiful Persian rug that graced his office and painfully and loudly giving birth to a calf.

About two blocks from her apartment, Julia's long, brown hair was plastered to her head in stringy sheets. Her sneakers squished-squashed with every step. Rain poured off of her as if she were beneath a downspout. Cars and buses whooshed by, and she didn't even bother trying to get out of the way as tidal waves of dirty water crashed over her from the busy street. Like life's disappointments, she simply accepted it.

At that moment another car approached, this one slowing down appropriately so that she wouldn't be soaked by its splash. It was a new-looking, black Jaguar.

The Jaguar slowed down even more and came to a stop. As Julia walked by, she saw the passenger door open and a masculine voice called out, "Get in."

She hesitated; surely the driver wasn't calling to her. She looked around, but she was the only one foolish enough to be walking in a torrential downpour. Curious, she took a step closer.

She knew better than to get into a car with a stranger, even in a Canadian city. But as she looked into the driver's seat and saw two piercing blue eyes stare back at her, she walked slowly toward him.

"You'll catch pneumonia and die. Get in. I'll drive you home." His voice was softer now, the fire gone. This was almost the voice that she remembered.

So for the sake of memory and for no other reason, she climbed into the passenger's seat and pulled the door closed, silently apologizing to the gods of Jaguars for fouling their pristine black leather interior and immaculate car mats.

She paused as the strains of Chopin's *Nocturne* 9, Op. No. 2 filled her ears, and she smiled to herself. She had always liked that tune.

She turned to face the driver. "Thank you very much, Professor Emerson."

Chapter Four

Professor Emerson had taken a wrong turn. His life, perhaps, could be described as a series of wrong turns, but this one was entirely accidental. He'd been reading on his iPhone—an angry e-mail from his brother—while he was driving his Jaguar through a thunderstorm in the middle of rush hour in downtown Toronto. Consequently, he turned left rather than right onto Bloor Street from Queen's Park. This meant that he was headed in the opposite direction of his apartment building.

There was no possibility of a u-turn on Bloor during rush hour, and there was so much traffic he had a difficult time pulling over so that he could make a right and turn around. This was how he came upon a very wet and pathetic-looking Miss Mitchell, walking dejectedly down the street as if she were a homeless person, and how in a fit of guilt he came to invite her into his car, which was his pride and joy.

"I'm sorry I'm ruining your upholstery," she offered hesitantly.

Professor Emerson's fingers tightened on the steering wheel. "I have someone who cleans it when it's soiled."

Julia bowed her head, for his response hurt. Implicitly, he had compared her to dirt, but of course, that's what he thought she was now. Dirt beneath his feet.

"Where do you live?" he asked, seeking to engage her in polite and safe conversation for the duration of what he hoped would be a short time together.

"On Madison. It's just up there on the right." She pointed some distance in front of them.

"I know where Madison is," he snapped.

Watching him out of the corner of her eye, Julia cringed toward the passenger window. She slowly turned her head to look outside and drew her lower lip roughly between her teeth.

Professor Emerson cursed under his breath. Even beneath the tangle of wet, dark hair she was pretty—a brown-eyed angel in jeans and sneakers. His mind halted at the inward sound of his description. The term *brown-eyed angel* seemed oddly familiar, but since he couldn't think of the source for that reference he put the thought aside.

"What number on Madison?" He softened his voice, so much so that Julia could barely hear him.

"Forty-five."

He nodded and shortly pulled the car in front of the three-story, red brick house that had been converted into apartments.

"Thank you," she murmured, and in a flash she dove for the door handle to make her escape.

"Wait," he commanded, reaching into the backseat to retrieve a large, black umbrella.

She waited and was stunned to see The Professor walk around the car to open the door for her, wait with an open umbrella while she and her abomination exited the Jaguar, and march her up the sidewalk and the front steps of her building.

"Thank you," she said again as she pulled on her book bag zipper, trying to open it so she could find her keys.

The Professor tried to hide his distaste at the sight of the abomination, but said nothing. He watched as she struggled with the zipper, then watched her face as she grew very red and upset over the fact that the zipper wouldn't open. He remembered her expression as she knelt on his Persian rug, and it occurred to him that this current trouble was probably his fault.

Without saying a word, he grabbed the book bag out of her hands and shoved the now closed umbrella at her. He ripped open the zipper and held the bag out, inviting her to stick her hand inside to retrieve her keys.

She found the keys, but she was nervous, so she dropped them. When she picked them up her hands were shaking so badly she had troubling locating the correct key on her key ring.

Having lost all patience, The Professor snatched the key ring away from her and began trying keys in the lock. When he'd successfully opened the door, he allowed her to enter before returning her keys.

She took the repellant book bag from him and murmured her thanks.

"I'll walk you to your apartment," he announced, following her through the hallway. "A homeless person once accosted me in the lobby of my building. One can't be too careful."

Julia silently prayed to the gods of studio apartments, begging them to help her locate her apartment key swiftly. They answered her prayer. As she was about to slip behind the door and close it firmly but not unkindly in his face, she stopped. Then, as if she'd known him for years, she smiled up at him and politely asked if he would like a cup of tea.

Despite being surprised by her invitation, Professor Emerson found himself standing in her apartment before he had the opportunity to consider whether it was a good idea. As he looked around the small and squalid space, he quickly concluded that it wasn't.

"May I take your coat, Professor?" Julia's cheerful little voice distracted him.

"Where would you put it?" he sniffed, noticing primly that she did not seem to have a closet or a hall tree near the door.

Her eyes dropped to the floor, and she ducked her head.

The Professor watched her chew her lip nervously and instantly regretted his rudeness.

"Forgive me," he said, handing her his Burberry trench coat of which he was inordinately proud. "And thank you."

Julia hung his coat up carefully on a hook that was attached to the back of her door and hastily placed her knapsack on the hardwood. "Come in and be comfortable. I'll make tea."

Professor Emerson walked to one of only two chairs in the apartment and sat down, trying for her sake to hide his distaste. The apartment was smaller than his guest bathroom and included a small bed, which was pushed up against a wall, a card table and two chairs, a small Ikea bookshelf, and a chest of drawers. There was a small closet and a bathroom, but no kitchen.

His eyes roamed around the room, looking for evidence of any kind of culinary activity until they finally settled on a microwave and a hot plate that were perched somewhat precariously on top of a dresser. A small refrigerator sat on the floor nearby.

"I have an electric kettle," Julia said brightly, as if she was announcing the fact that she had a diamond from Tiffany's.

He noticed the water that was continuing to stream off her, then he began to notice the clothes that were under the water, and then he began to notice what was under her clothes, because it was cold . . . and he hastily and somewhat huskily suggested that she forego making tea in order to dry herself.

Once again her head tipped down, and she flushed before ducking into the bathroom and grabbing a towel. She emerged a few seconds later with a purple towel wrapped around her upper body over her wet clothes and a second towel in her hand. She moved as if she was going to crawl across the floor to clean up the trail of water she'd scattered from the door to the center of the room, but The Professor stood up and stopped her.

"Allow me," he said. "You should change into some dry clothes before you catch pneumonia."

"And die," she added, more to herself than to him as she disappeared into her closet, trying not to trip over two large suitcases.

The Professor wondered briefly why she hadn't unpacked yet but dismissed the answer as unimportant.

He frowned as he cleaned the water from the worn and scratched hardwood. When he'd finished, he looked at the walls and noticed that they had probably been white once, but were now a dingy cream color and were blistered and peeling. He inspected the ceiling and found several large water stains and what he thought might be the beginning of mold in one of the corners. He shuddered, wondering why on earth a nice girl like Miss Mitchell would live in such a terrible place. Although he had to admit that the apartment was very clean and quite tidy. Unusually so.

"How much is your rent?" he asked, wincing slightly as he accordioned his six foot two frame in order to perch once again on the vile thing that masqueraded as a folding chair.

"Eight hundred a month, utilities included," she called to him just before she entered the bathroom.

Professor Emerson thought with some regret of the Armani trousers he had disposed of after the flight back from Pennsylvania. He couldn't bear the notion of wearing something that had been soaked in urine, even if it had been cleaned, so he'd just thrown them out. But the money Paulina had spent on those trousers would have paid Miss Mitchell's rent for an entire month. And then some.

Looking around the small studio, it was both painfully and pathetically clear that she had tried to make it into a home, such as it was. A large print of Henry Holiday's painting, *Dante meets Beatrice at Ponte Santa Trinita*, hung to the side of her bed. The Professor imagined her reclining on her pillow, her long, shiny hair cascading around her face, gazing over at Dante before she fell asleep. He dutifully put that thought aside and reflected on how strange it was that they both owned that painting. He peered at it and noticed with surprise that Julia bore a remarkable resemblance to Beatrice—a resemblance that had previously gone unnoticed. The thought twisted in his mind like a corkscrew, but he refused to dwell on it.

He noticed other smaller pictures of various Italian scenes on the peeling walls of the apartment: a drawing of the Duomo in Florence, a sketch of St. Mark's in Venice, a black-and-white photograph of the dome of St. Peter's in Rome. He saw a row of potted herbs gracing the window sill along with a single cutting from a philodendron that she was apparently trying to nurse into a full grown plant. He observed that the curtains were pretty—a sheer lilac that matched the bedspread and its cushions. And her bookshelf boasted many volumes in both English and Italian. The Professor scanned the titles quickly and was but mildly impressed with her amateurish collection. But in short, the studio was old, tiny, in poor repair, and kitchen-less, and Professor Emerson would not have permitted his dog to live in a place like this, had he had one.

Julia reappeared in what looked like an exercise uniform—a black hoodie and yoga pants. She'd knotted and twisted her lovely hair and fastened it near the top of her head with a clip of some sort. Even in such casual garb he noticed that she was very attractive—extremely attractive and dare he say it, sylphlike.

"I have English Breakfast or Lady Grey," she spoke over her shoulder, descending to her hands and knees in order to snake the plug from the electric kettle back to the outlet that was underneath the dresser.

The Professor regarded her as she kneeled, just as she had in his office, and silently shook his head. She was without arrogance or selfish pride, which he knew was a good thing, but it pained him to see her constantly on her knees, although he couldn't exactly say why.

"English Breakfast. Why do you live here?"

Julia stood up quickly in response to the sharpness of his tone. She kept her back to him as she located a large, brown teapot and two surprisingly beautiful china teacups with matching saucers.

"This is a quiet street in a nice neighborhood. I don't have a car, and I needed to be able to walk to school." She paused as she placed a small silver teaspoon on each of the saucers. "This was one of the nicer apartments I looked at in my price range." She placed the elegant teacups on the card table without looking at him and returned to the dresser.

"Why didn't you move into the graduate student residence on Charles Street?"

Julia dropped something. The Professor couldn't see what it was.

"I was expecting to go to a different university, but it didn't work out. By the time I decided to come here, the residence was full."

"And where were you going to go?"

She began to worry her lower lip between her teeth, back and forth.

"Miss Mitchell?"

"Harvard."

Professor Emerson just about fell off his very uncomfortable chair. "Harvard? What the hell are you doing here?"

Julia smothered a secret smile as if she knew the reason behind his anger. "Toronto is the Harvard of the north."

"Don't be coy, Miss Mitchell. I asked you a question."

"Yes, Professor. And I know that you always expect an answer to your questions." She arched an eyebrow, and he looked away. "My father couldn't afford the contribution he was expected to make to my education, so the fellowship they offered me was not enough, and the living expenses were much more in Cambridge than in Toronto. I already have thousands of dollars of student loans from Saint Joseph's University, so I decided not to add to them. That's why I'm here."

She returned to her hands and knees to unplug the now boiling kettle as The Professor shook his head in shock.

"That wasn't in the file Mrs. Jenkins gave me," he protested. "You should have said something."

Julia ignored him and began to measure loose tea into the teapot.

He leaned forward in his chair, gesturing wildly. "This is a terrible place to live—there isn't even a proper kitchen. What do you eat here?"

She placed the teapot and a small, silver tea strainer on the card table and sat down on the other folding chair. She began to wring her hands.

"I eat lots of vegetables. I can make soup and couscous on the hot plate. Couscous is very nutritious." Her voice shook a little, but she tried to sound cheerful.

"You can't live on that kind of rubbish—a dog is better fed!"

Julia ducked her head and blushed deeply, suddenly blinking back tears.

The Professor looked at her for a moment, then finally saw her. As he regarded the tortured expression that marred her lovely features, he slowly began to realize that he, Professor Gabriel O. Emerson, was a self-absorbed bastard. He had shamed her for being poor. But there was no shame in being poor. He had been poor once too, very poor. She was a smart, attractive woman who was also a student. There was no shame in that. But he'd come into her little home that she had tried to make comfortable because she had no other place to go, and he had said it wasn't fit for a dog. He had made her feel worthless and stupid when she was neither. What would Grace say if she could hear him now?

Professor Emerson was an ass. But at least now he knew it.

"Forgive me," he began haltingly. "I don't know what's gotten into me." He closed his eyes and began to rub them.

"You've just lost your mother." Julia's gentle voice was startlingly forgiving.

A switch inside him flipped. "I shouldn't be here." He stood up quickly. "I need to go."

Julia followed him to the front door. She picked up his umbrella and handed him his trench coat. Then she stood with downcast eyes and flaming cheeks, waiting for him to leave. She felt regret for having shown him her home, since it was clearly so far beneath him. Whereas a few hours earlier she had taken pride in her small but clean hobbit hole, now she was mortified. Not to mention the fact that being humiliated again in front of him made matters so much worse.

He nodded at her, or at something, muttered under his breath, and exited her apartment.

Julia leaned her back against the closed door and finally allowed herself to weep.

Knock. Knock.

She knew who it was. She simply didn't want to answer the door.

Please gods of overpriced, not-fit-for-a-dog hobbit holes, just let him leave me in peace. Julia's silent and spontaneous prayer went unanswered.

Knock. Knock. Knock.

She quickly wiped her face and opened the door, but only a crack.

He blinked at her like a Christmas tree, somehow having a difficult time registering the fact that she had clearly been crying in between his departure and his return.

She cleared her throat and looked down at his Italian-made wing-tipped shoes, which he shuffled slightly.

"When was the last time you had a steak?"

Julia laughed and shook her head. She couldn't remember.

"Well, you're going to have one tonight. I'm starving, and you're joining me for dinner."

She allowed herself the luxury of a small but wicked smile. "Are you sure, Professor? I thought *this*—" she mimicked his gesture from earlier "—was not going to work."

He reddened slightly. "Never mind about that now. Except . . ." His eyes wandered to her clothes, resting perhaps a little too long on the curves of her lovely breasts.

Julia lowered her gaze. "I could change."

"That would be best. See that you dress appropriately."

She looked up at him with a very hurt expression. "I may be poor, but I have a few nice things. None of them are immodest, if you're worried I might embarrass you by looking cheap."

The Professor reddened again as he kicked himself, inwardly. "I just meant . . . appropriate for a restaurant where I will have to wear a jacket and tie." He hazarded a small smile as a means of apology.

Julia's eyes traveled over his button down and sweater, perhaps lingering a little too long on the planes of his lovely pectorals. "I'll agree on one condition."

"You're really not in a position to argue."

"Then good-bye, Professor."

"Wait." He stuck his expensive Italian shoe in between the door and the doorjamb, wedging it open. And he didn't even worry about the scuffs that would result. "Let's hear it."

She cocked her head to one side and regarded him mutely before she spoke. "Tell me why, after everything you've said to me, I should join you for dinner."

He looked at her blankly. Then he blushed to the roots of his hair and began to stammer. "I—um . . . that is, I think . . . you could say that we . . . or you . . ."

Julia lifted a single eyebrow and slowly began to close the door on his foot.

"Wait." His hand shot out to hold the door and to provide some relief for his now injured right foot. "Because what Paul wrote was correct: *Emerson is an ass*. But at least now he knows it."

In that instant she smiled up at him, and he found himself smiling back in spite of himself. She really was very pretty when she smiled. He would have to see to it that she smiled more often, purely for aesthetic reasons.

"I'll wait for you here." Not wishing to give her a chance to demur, he reached out and pulled her apartment door closed.

Inside her apartment, Julia closed her eyes and groaned.

Chapter Five

Professor Emerson paced the hallway for a few minutes, then leaned up against a wall and scrubbed at his face with his hands. He did not know how he got there or what had propelled him to behave in such a way, but he was about to be caught in a clusterfuck of epic proportions. He'd been unprofessional to Miss Mitchell in his office, perilously close to harassing her verbally. He'd picked her up in his car, without a chaperone, and entered her apartment. All of these behaviors were highly irregular.

If it had been Miss Peterson who he'd picked up, she probably would have leaned over and undone his zipper with her teeth while he was driving. The Professor shuddered at the thought. Now he was about to take Miss Mitchell to dinner, for *steak*, no less. If that didn't violate the non-fraternization policy set up by the university, he didn't know what would.

He took a long and cleansing breath. Miss Mitchell was a Calamity Jane, a vortex of vexation. She'd had a remarkable string of misadventures, starting with her inability to go to Harvard, and things seemed to fall apart in her wake—including his calm and collected disposition. Although he was sorry she was living in deplorable circumstances, he was not going to risk his career to help her. She would be well within her rights to go to the chairman of his department tomorrow and file a harassment complaint against him. He could not let that happen.

He crossed the hall in two long strides and raised his hand to knock on her door. He was going to offer some feeble excuse, which would be better than just disappearing. But he stopped as soon as he heard footsteps from inside.

Miss Mitchell opened her door and stood, eyes downcast, in a simple but elegant V-necked black dress that fell to her knees. The Professor's eyes raked over her gentle curves and down to her surprisingly long and very shapely legs. And her shoes . . . she couldn't have known this, but Professor Emerson had a thing for women in exquisite high-heeled shoes. He swallowed noisily as he took in her breathtaking and obviously designer black stilettos. The Professor wanted to touch them . . .

"*Ahem.*" Julia coughed slightly, and he reluctantly dragged his eyes up from her shoes to her face. She was staring at him with an amused expression.

She had pinned her hair up, but several of the curls had escaped and were falling delicately around her face. She wore a little makeup, her porcelain skin pale but luminous, with two delicious swathes of pink on her cheeks. And her eyelashes seemed even darker and longer than he remembered.

Miss Julianne Mitchell was *attractive*.

She shrugged into a navy blue trench coat and quickly locked her apartment door. The Professor gestured to her to lead the way and followed her mutely through the hall. Once outside the front door, he opened his umbrella and stood somewhat awkwardly.

Julia looked up at him, puzzled.

"It would be easier for me to cover both of us if you took my arm." He offered her the crook of his left arm, which was holding the umbrella. "If you don't mind," he added.

Julia took his arm and looked up at him with a soft expression.

They drove in silence down to the harbor front, a place that Julia had heard of but not yet explored. Before The Professor gave his keys to the restaurant's valet, he asked Julia to hand him his tie from the glove compartment. She obliged, smiling to herself at the fact that he kept a boxed and immaculate silk tie in his car.

When she moved toward him, he caught a whiff of her scent and closed his eyes, just for a second. "Vanilla," he murmured.

"What?" she asked, not quite having heard him.

"Nothing."

He pulled off his sweater, and she was rewarded momentarily with the sight of his chest and a few curls of dark hair through the open buttons at his neck. Professor Emerson was sexy. He had an attractive face, and Julia believed that underneath his clothes he would be just as attractive. She tried very hard not to think about that too much, for her own sake.

But that didn't stop her from watching in mute but rapt admiration as he effortlessly tied his tie without a mirror. Alas, the tie was crooked.

"I can't seem to . . . I can't see." He fussed as he tried to straighten his tie, but to no avail.

"May I?" she offered shyly, not willing to touch him without his consent.

"Thank you."

Julia's deft fingers quickly straightened and smoothed his tie, and she lightly traced the top of his collar back to the nape of his neck, where she tugged the top of the collar down so as to cover the tie at the back. By the time she withdrew her hand, she was breathing rapidly and very red in the face.

The Professor was oblivious to her reaction because he was too busy thinking about the strange familiarity of her fingertips, and wondering why Paulina's fingers never felt familiar. He removed his jacket from the hanger that hung behind his seat and quickly put it on. Then with a smile and a nod, they exited the car.

Harbour Sixty Steakhouse was a landmark in Toronto, a famous and very expensive restaurant popular with CEOs, politicians, and various other impressive personages. Professor Emerson ate there because their steak was superior to any other he had tried, and he was impatient with mediocrity. So it never occurred to him to take Miss Mitchell anywhere else.

Antonio, the maître d', greeted him warmly with a firm handshake and a torrent of Italian.

The Professor responded equally warmly, also in Italian.

"And who is the beauty?" Antonio kissed the back of Julia's hands while he chattered away to her in very descriptive Italian about her eyes, her hair, and her skin.

Julia flushed and thanked him, shyly but determinedly answering him in his own language.

Miss Mitchell had a lovely voice, it was true, but Miss Mitchell speaking *Italian* was something celestial. Her ruby mouth opening and closing, the delicate way she almost sang the words, her tongue peeking out to wet her lips from time to time . . . Professor Emerson had to remind himself to close his mouth after it had dropped open.

Antonio was so surprised and pleased at her response that he kissed her cheeks not just once but twice and quickly led them to the back of the restaurant where he provided them with his best and most romantic table for two. The Professor hovered over his chair reluctantly as he realized what Antonio was doing. He'd sat at that table before, not long ago, but with someone else. This was a mistake and one he needed to correct, but just as he cleared his throat to offer a clarification, Antonio asked Julia if she would accept a bottle of a very special vintage from his family's vineyard in Tuscany.

Julia thanked him profusely, but explained that *Il Professore* might have other preferences. He sat down quickly, and not wanting to offend, said that he would be delighted with whatever Antonio offered. Antonio beamed and quickly withdrew.

"Since we're in public, I think it would it be best if you didn't refer to me as Professor Emerson."

Julia smiled brightly and nodded.

"So just address me as Mr. Emerson."

Mr. Emerson was too busy looking at the menu to see the way that Julia's eyes widened before her gaze fell.

"You have a Tuscan accent," he remarked absently, still not looking at her.

"Yes."

"How did you come by that?"

"I spent my junior year in Florence."

"Your Italian is fairly advanced for only a junior year abroad."

"I began studying it in high school."

He looked across the small and intimate table and saw that she actively avoided his eyes. She was studying the menu as if it were an exam, worrying her lovely lower lip between her teeth.

"You are invited, Miss Mitchell."

Her eyes darted to his with a questioning look.

"You are my guest. Order whatever you like, but please order some meat." He felt the need to add that qualification since the express purpose of their dinner was to provide her with something more fortifying than couscous.

"I don't know what to choose."

"I could order for you, if you prefer."

She nodded and closed her menu, still worrying her lip back and forth.

Antonio returned just then and proudly displayed a bottle of Chianti with a handwritten label. Julia smiled as he opened the bottle and poured a little into her glass.

Mr. Emerson watched, almost breathless, as she swirled the wine in her glass expertly, then lifted it so that she could examine it more closely in the candlelight. She brought the glass to her nose, closed her eyes, and sniffed. Then she placed the glass to her plump lips and tasted the wine, holding it in her mouth for a while before swallowing. She opened her eyes, smiled even more widely, and thanked Antonio for his precious gift.

Antonio beamed, complimented Mr. Emerson on his choice of dining companion a little too enthusiastically, and filled both of their glasses with his favorite wine.

Meanwhile, Mr. Emerson had been adjusting himself under the table because the sight of Miss Mitchell tasting wine was the most erotic thing he'd ever witnessed. She was not merely attractive; she was beautiful, like an angel or a muse. And she wasn't merely beautiful; she was sensual and hypnotic, but also innocent. Her pretty eyes reflected a depth of feeling and radiant purity that he had never noticed before.

He had to drag his eyes away from her as he adjusted himself once more for good measure, suddenly feeling dirty and more than a little ashamed of the reaction she was eliciting from him. A reaction that he would need to attend to later that evening. When he was alone. And surrounded by the scent of vanilla.

He ordered their meals, making sure that he requested the largest possible portions of filet mignon. When Miss Mitchell protested, he dismissed her concern with a wave of his hand, remarking that she would be able to take her leftovers home with her. If Mr. Emerson had his way, this meal would feed her for a couple of days.

He wondered what she would eat after her leftovers were exhausted but refused to allow himself to dwell on the problem. This was a one-time event, and only because he'd shouted at her and shamed her. After this, things between them would be strictly professional. And she would be left to face future calamities alone.

For her part, Julia was happy to be with him. She wanted to be able to talk to him, to *really* talk to him, to ask him about his family and the funeral. She wanted to comfort him over the loss of his mother. She wanted to tell him secrets and have him whisper secrets to her in return. But with his eyes determinedly but somewhat distantly fixed on her, she knew she could not have what she wanted. So she smiled and fidgeted with the silverware, hoping that he wouldn't find her nervousness and its desperate outlets annoying.

"Why did you start studying Italian in high school?"

Julia gasped. Her eyes grew wide, and her beautiful red mouth hung open.

Mr. Emerson's eyebrows furrowed at her reaction. It was completely out of proportion to his question; he hadn't asked her for her bra size. His eyes dropped involuntarily to the swell of her breasts and returned to her eyes. He reddened as a number and a cup size miraculously entered his head.

"Um, I became interested in Italian literature. In Dante and Beatrice." She folded and refolded the linen napkin in her lap, a few loose curls hanging forward around her oval-shaped face.

He thought of the painting in her apartment and her extraordinary resemblance to Beatrice. Once again, the thought twisted in his mind tauntingly, and once again he pushed it aside.

"Those are remarkable interests for a young girl," he prompted, allowing himself to memorize her beauty.

"I had . . . a friend who introduced me to them." She sounded pained and more than a little sad.

He realized he was treading very closely to an old wound, and so he quickly retraced his steps, trying to find more comfortable ground to venture upon.

"Antonio is very taken with you."

Julia looked up and smiled prettily. "He's very kind."

"You blossom under kindness, don't you? Like a rose." The words escaped his lips before he had time to consider them, and by the time they were pronounced and Julia had looked at him with no little warmth, it was far too late to retract them.

That did it. Professor Emerson began focusing his attention on his glass of wine; his features clouded, and his demeanor grew very cold. Julia observed the change, but accepted it and made no further attempt at conversation.

Throughout the meal the clearly charmed Antonio spent more time than was necessary at their table, chatting in Italian with the beautiful Julianne and inviting her to join his family at the Italian-Canadian Club for dinner next Sunday. She accepted his invitation graciously and was rewarded later with tiramisu, espresso, biscotti, grappa, and finally, a small chocolate Baci, in leisurely succession. Professor Emerson was not rewarded with these delights, and so he just sat there, brooding, as he watched Miss Mitchell enjoy herself.

By the end of the evening, Antonio had pressed something that resembled a large food hamper into her hands and would not allow her to refuse it. He kissed her cheeks several times after he helped her with her coat, then he begged The Professor to bring her back to them soon and often.

Professor Emerson straightened his shoulders and fixed Antonio with a stony glare. "That isn't possible." Turning on his heel, he exited the restaurant, leaving Julia and her heavy food hamper trailing dejectedly behind him.

As he watched the mismatched couple depart, Antonio wondered why The Professor would bring such a lovely creature to a romantic place and sit stoically without speaking to her, looking all the while as if he were in pain.

When they arrived at Miss Mitchell's apartment, Professor Emerson obligingly opened her door for her and removed the hamper from the backseat of the Jaguar. He peered into it curiously, moving a few things around so he could analyze its contents.

"Wine, olive oil, balsamic vinegar, biscotti, a jar of homemade marinara made by Antonio's wife, leftovers. You're going to be very well fed for the next little while."

"Thanks to you." Julia smiled, holding her hand out for the hamper.

"This is heavy. I'll carry it for you." He escorted her to the front porch of the building and waited while she unlocked the door. Then he handed her the food.

She began to examine her shoes, and her cheeks grew warm as she thought of what she needed to say.

"Thank you, Professor Emerson, for a nice evening. It was really generous of you to . . ."

"Miss Mitchell," he interrupted, "let's not make this more awkward than it already is. I apologize for my . . . previous rudeness. My only excuse is, ah, reasons of a rather private nature. So let's just shake hands and move forward."

He held out his hand, and she took it. He shook her hand, trying very hard not to bruise her, and absolutely ignoring the thrill that coursed through his veins at the feel of her soft and delicate skin against his.

"Good night, Miss Mitchell."

"Good night, Professor Emerson."

And with that, she disappeared into her building, leaving The Professor on slightly better terms than she had that afternoon.

An hour or so later, Julia sat on her bed staring at the photograph she always kept under her pillow. She gazed at it for a very long time, trying to decide if she should destroy it, leave it where it always was, or put it away in a drawer. She'd always loved this picture. She loved the smile on his face. It was the most beautiful picture she'd ever seen, but it also hurt her terribly to look at it.

She gazed up at the lovely painting that hung over her bed and fought back tears. She did not know what she had expected from her Dante, but she definitely hadn't received it. So with the wisdom that comes only from having experienced a broken heart, she resolved to let him go once and for all.

She thought of her now crammed makeshift pantry and the kindness Antonio had shown her. She thought of the voice mails she'd received from Paul, how he had expressed concern at leaving her alone with The Professor and begged her to call him at any hour to tell him she was all right.

She padded over to her dresser, opened the top drawer, and placed the photograph reverently but determinedly at the very back, underneath the sexy underwear that she never wore. And with the contrast between the three men well fixed in her mind, she went back to bed, closed her eyes, and dreamed of a neglected apple orchard.

Chapter Six

O n Friday, Julia received an official form in her mailbox indicating
that Professor Emerson had agreed to be her thesis supervisor.
She was staring at the form in amazement, wondering why he had reversed his decision, when Paul came up behind her.

"Ready to go?"

She greeted him with a smile as she placed the form in her crudely
mended knapsack. They exited the building and began walking down
Bloor Street to the nearest Starbucks, which was only about half a block
away.

"I want to ask you about your meeting with Emerson, but before I
do that, there's something I need to tell you." Paul sounded serious.

Julia looked over at him with an expression that resembled anxiety.

"Don't be scared, Rabbit. It's not going to hurt." He patted her arm.
Paul's heart was almost as big as he was, and so he was very sensitive to
the pain of others.

"I know about what happened with our note."

Julia closed her eyes and cursed. "Paul, I'm so sorry about that. I
was going to tell you that I screwed up and wrote on your note, but I
didn't get a chance. I didn't tell him it was your handwriting."

Paul pressed his hand against her upper arm to stop her. "I know
that. *I* told him."

She looked up at him in astonishment. "Why would you do that?"

As he probed the depths of Rabbit's large brown eyes, he knew, without doubt, that he would do anything to keep someone from hurting her.
Even if it meant his academic career. Even if it meant dragging Emerson
out behind the Department of Italian Studies and giving him the serious
ass kicking that he and his pretentious posterior so richly deserved.

"Mrs. Jenkins told me Emerson was hauling you in, and I figured he was going to chew you out. I found a copy of our note in a pile of photocopying he left for me." He shrugged. "Occupational hazard of being a research assistant to a total dick."

Paul tugged Julia slightly to persuade her to keep walking but waited to continue their conversation until he had purchased her a very large sugar-free vanilla latté. Once she'd settled in a purple velvet armchair, like a cat, and he had satisfied himself that she was both warm and comfortable, he turned to her with a sympathetic expression.

"I know it was an accident. You were so shaken up after that first seminar. I should have walked you to his office myself. Honestly, Julia, I've never seen him act the way he did that day. He can be kind of uppity and touchy about things, but he's never been so aggressive with a female student before. It was painful to watch."

Julia sipped her coffee and waited for him to continue.

"So when I found a copy of our note with the junk he left for me, I knew he was going to rake you over the coals. I found out what time your appointment was and scheduled a meeting with him before it. Then I confessed that I'd written the note. I even lied and tried to say I'd forged your signature as a joke, but he didn't buy it."

"You did all that for me?"

Paul smiled and casually flexed his substantial arms. "I was trying to be a human shield. I thought if he shouted at me and got it out of his system, he'd have nothing left for you." He studied her expression thoughtfully. "But it didn't work, did it?"

She looked at him in gratitude. "No one has ever done something like that for me before. I really owe you one."

"Don't mention it. I only wish he'd taken his anger out on me. What did he say to you?"

She focused all of her attention on her coffee and acted as if she hadn't heard the question.

"That bad, huh?" Paul rubbed his chin thoughtfully. "Well, it must have blown over because he was polite to you in the last seminar."

Julia snickered. "Sure. But he wouldn't let me answer any questions, even when I put my hand up. He was too busy letting Christa Peterson do all the talking."

Paul observed her sudden flash of indignation with amusement. "Don't worry about her. She's in for some trouble with Emerson over her dissertation proposal. He doesn't like the direction she's taking. He told me."

"That's terrible. Does she know?"

He shrugged. "She should be able to figure it out. But who knows? She's so focused on seducing him that she's letting her work slide. It's embarrassing."

Julia noted all of this and tucked it into her memory for future reference. She sat back in her chair, relaxed, and enjoyed the rest of her afternoon with Paul, who was charming and thoughtful and made her glad she was in Toronto. At five o'clock, her stomach rumbled, and she clutched at it awkwardly.

Paul laughed and smiled in order to ease her embarrassment. She was so cute about everything, including the way her stomach growled. "Do you like Thai food?"

"I do. There was a great place in Philadelphia I used to go to with . . ." She caught herself before she said his name out loud. That restaurant had been the place she'd always gone with *him*. She silently wondered if *they* were going there now, eating at her table, laughing at the menu, mocking her . . .

Paul cleared his throat to gently bring her back to him.

"Sorry." She ducked her head and rummaged in her knapsack for nothing in particular.

"There's a great Thai place down the street. It's a few blocks away, so it would be a bit of a walk. But the food is really good. If you don't have plans, let me take you to dinner."

His nervousness was telegraphed only in the slow and subtle tapping of his right foot, which Julia detected out of the corner of her eye, just visible over the edge of the coffee table. She looked up into his warm, dark eyes and thought briefly about how kindness was worth so much more in the world than passion, and she said *yes* before she could even contemplate saying *no*.

He smiled as if her acceptance gave him more than a secret delight, and picked up her knapsack, effortlessly swinging it to his shoulder.

"This is too heavy a burden for you." He said, gazing into her eyes, choosing every word carefully. "Let me carry it for a while."

Julia smiled at her toes and followed him outside.

⁂

Professor Emerson was walking home from work. It was a short walk, although on inclement days and days on which he had evening engagements, he drove.

While he traveled, he thought about the lecture that he was going to deliver at the university, on lust in Dante. Lust was a sin that he found himself thinking of often and with much enjoyment. In fact, the thought of lust and its myriad satisfactions was so tantalizing, Professor Emerson found himself pulling his trench coat closed so the slightly spectacular sight of the front of his trousers would not attract untoward attention.

That's when he saw her. He stopped, staring across the street at the attractive brunette.

Calamity Julianne.

Except she was not alone. Paul was holding her abomination of a book bag and walking with her. They were chatting easily and laughing and strolling dangerously close to one another.

Carrying her books now, are we? How very adolescent of you, Paul.

Professor Emerson watched as the couple's hands brushed against each other, drawing a small but warm smile from Miss Mitchell. A growl rumbled low in Emerson's throat, and his lips curled back from his teeth.

What the hell was that? he thought.

Professor Emerson took a moment to collect himself, and as he leaned against the window of the Louis Vuitton boutique, he tried to figure out what the hell had just happened. He was a rational agent. He wore clothes to cover his nakedness, he drove a car, and he ate with a knife and a fork and a linen napkin. He was gainfully employed in a job that required intellectual ability and acuity. He controlled his sexual urges through various civilized means and would never take a woman against her will.

Nevertheless, as he stared at Miss Mitchell and Paul, he realized that he was an animal. Something primitive. Something feral. And something made him want to go over there and rip Paul's hands from his body and carry Miss Mitchell off. To kiss her senseless, move his lips to her neck, and claim her.

What the fuck?

The thought scared the living hell out of The Professor. In addition to being an ass and a pompous prick, he was a knuckle-dragging, potentially mouth-breathing Neanderthal who felt some proprietary ownership over a younger woman he barely knew and who hated him. Not to mention the fact that she was his student.

He needed to go home, lie down, and breathe until he calmed the fuck down. Then he was going to need something else, something stronger to calm his urges. As Professor Emerson continued his journey home, dragging himself painfully away from the sight of the two young people together, he pulled out his iPhone and quickly pressed a few buttons.

A woman answered on the third ring. "Hello?"

"Hello, it's me. Can I see you tonight?"

❋ ❋

The following Wednesday, Julia was walking out of the department building after Emerson's seminar when she heard a familiar voice call to her.

"Julia? Julia Mitchell, is that you?"

She whipped around and was drawn into a hug that was so tight she thought she'd choke.

"Rachel," she managed as she fought for air.

The thin, blond-haired girl squealed loudly and hugged Julia again. "I've missed you. I can't believe it has been so long! What are you doing here?"

"Rachel, I'm so sorry. I'm sorry for everything and for your mom and . . . everything."

Two friends were quiet in their shared sorrow and held one another for a long time.

"I'm sorry I missed the funeral. How's your dad?" Julia asked, wiping away tears.

"He's lost without her. We all are. He's on a leave of absence from Susquehanna right now, trying to sort some things out. I'm on leave too, but I had to get away. Why didn't you tell me you were here?" Rachel reproached her, tearfully.

Julia's eyes shifted uncomfortably from her friend to Professor Emerson, who had just exited the building and was gaping at her like a codfish.

"I wasn't sure I'd be staying. The first couple weeks have been really, um, rough."

Rachel, who by all accounts was very intelligent, noticed the strange and somewhat conflicted energy radiating between her adopted brother and her friend, but for the moment she overlooked it.

"I was just telling Gabriel that I'm going to cook for him tonight. Come home with us."

Julia's eyes grew wide and round, and she looked mildly panicked.

Gabriel cleared his throat. "Ah, Rachel, I'm sure Miss Mitchell is busy and has other plans."

Julia caught his look, pregnant with meaning, and began to nod obediently.

Rachel whirled around. *"Miss Mitchell?* She was my best friend in high school, and we've been friends ever since. Didn't you know that?" Rachel searched her brother's eyes and saw nothing, not even a glimmer of recognition. "I forgot that you two never met. Regardless, your attitude is a bit much. Do me a favor and lose the pole from your keister."

She whirled back around to see Julia swallowing her tongue. Or at least that's what it looked like she was doing, as she almost turned blue and began to cough.

"We should meet for lunch, instead. I'm sure The Profess—your brother wants you all to himself." Julia forced a smile, conscious of the fact that Gabriel was staring daggers at her over his sister's head.

Rachel narrowed her eyes. "He's *Gabriel*, Julia. What's wrong with you two?"

"She's my student. There are rules." Gabriel's tone began to grow increasingly cool and unfriendly.

"She's my friend, *Gabriel*. And I say screw the rules!" Rachel looked between her brother and her friend and saw Julia gazing down at her shoes and Gabriel scowling at both of them. "Will someone please tell me what's going on?"

When neither Julia nor Gabriel replied, Rachel crossed her arms in front of her chest and narrowed her eyes. She considered briefly Julia's remark about the first weeks of university being rough and came to one swift conclusion.

"Gabriel Owen Emerson, have you been an ass to Julia?"

Julia smothered a laugh, and Gabriel frowned. Despite their collective silence, either reaction would have been enough to tell Rachel that her suspicion was correct.

"Well, I don't have time for this nonsense. You two will just have to kiss and make up. I'm only here for a week, and I expect to spend lots of time with both of you." Rachel grabbed each of them by the arm and dragged them toward the Jaguar.

Rachel Clark was nothing like her adopted brother. She was an assistant to the press secretary of the Mayor of Philadelphia, which sounded important but really wasn't. In fact, the majority of her days were spent either scouring local newspapers for any mention of the mayor or photocopying press releases. On especially auspicious days, she was permitted to update the mayor's blog. In appearance, Rachel was fine-featured and willowy, with straight, long hair, freckles, and gray eyes. She was also very outgoing, which sometimes exasperated her much older, introverted brother.

Gabriel kept his lips firmly pressed together during the drive to his condo, as the two women chatted in the backseat like a couple of high school girls, giggling and reminiscing. He didn't relish spending an evening with both of them, but his sister was suffering at the moment, and he wasn't about to do anything to add to her suffering.

Soon the two-thirds-happy trio was riding the elevator in the Manulife Building, an impressive luxury high-rise on Bloor Street. As they exited the elevator on the top floor, Julia noticed that there were only four doors opening onto the hallway.

Wow. These apartments must be huge.

Once Julia entered the condo and followed Gabriel through the small foyer into the central and open-concept living space, she realized why his sensibilities had been so offended by her studio. His spacious apartment boasted floor-to-ceiling windows, which were hung with dramatic ice-blue silk curtains, facing south to the CN tower and over Lake Ontario. The floors were a rich, dark hardwood, with Persian rugs adorning them, and the walls were light taupe.

His living room furniture looked as if it had been chosen from Restoration Hardware, and ranged from a large chocolate brown leather sofa with nail-head detailing, to two matching leather club chairs, to a red velvet, wing-backed chair that was angled next to the fireplace.

Julia looked at the lovely red chair and its matching ottoman with more than a little envy. It would be the perfect place to sit on a rainy day while sipping a cup of tea and reading a favorite book. Not that she would ever have that opportunity.

The fireplace had a gas insert, and Gabriel had suspended a flat plasma screen television over the mantle as if it were a painting. Various pieces of art, oil paintings, and sculpture adorned the walls and some of the furniture. He had museum quality pieces of Roman glass and Greek pottery interspersed with reproductions of famous sculptures, including the *Venus de Milo* and Bernini's *Apollo and Daphne*. In fact, thought Julia, he had entirely too many sculptures, all of them female nudes.

But there were no personal photographs. Julia considered it a good deal more than strange that there were black-and-white pictures of Paris, Rome, London, Florence, Venice, and Oxford, but no photos of the Clarks, not even of Grace.

In the next room, near the large and formal dining table, stood an ebony sideboard. Julia took in its richness and expanse appreciatively. It was bare except for a large crystal vase and an ornate silver tray that held various decanters containing amber-colored liquids, an ice chest, and old-fashioned crystal glasses. Silver ice tongs completed the vignette, angled across a stack of small, square white linen napkins with the initials *G. O. E.* embroidered on them. Julia giggled to herself when she envisioned what those napkins would look like if Gabriel's last name had been, say, *Davidson*.

In short, Professor Emerson's apartment was aesthetically pleasing, tastefully decorated, scrupulously clean, intentionally masculine, and very, very cold. Julia wondered briefly if he ever brought women home to this frigid space, then she tried very hard not to imagine what he would do to them when he brought them here. Perhaps he had a room for such purposes so that they wouldn't soil his precious things . . . She ran a hand across the cold, black granite countertop in the kitchen and shivered.

Rachel immediately preheated the oven and washed her hands. "Gabriel, why don't you give Julia the grand tour while I start dinner."

Julia clutched her knapsack to her chest, unwilling to put so offensive an item on his furniture. Gabriel took it out of her hands and placed it on the floor under a small table. She smiled at him in appreciation, and he found himself smiling back at her.

He didn't want to give Miss Mitchell a tour of his condo. And he certainly wasn't about to show her his bedroom and the black-and-white photos that adorned those walls. But with Rachel there to remind him of his obligations as a (reluctantly) gracious host, he didn't see a way out of giving a tour of the guest rooms.

So that is how he came to be standing in his study, which had been a third bedroom, but which he had converted into a comfortable working library by installing dark wood bookshelves from floor to ceiling. Julia gaped at all the books—titles new and rare and mostly hard-covered in Italian, Latin, French, English, and German. The room, like the rest of his condo, was intentionally masculine. The same ice-blue curtains, the same dark hardwood, with an antique Persian rug centered in the room.

Gabriel stood behind his ornate and rather large oak desk. "Do you like it?" He gestured to his library.

"Very much," said Julia. "It's beautiful."

She reached out to stroke the velvet of the red wing-back, the mate to the chair she had admired by the fireplace. But she didn't think he'd like that. Professor Emerson was the sort to object to his things being handled, and so she stopped herself just in time. He'd probably snap at her for soiling it with her grubby little fingers.

"That's my favorite chair. It's quite comfortable, if you'd like to try it."

Julia smiled as if he'd given her a present and eagerly sat in it, pulling her legs under herself and curling up like a kitten.

Gabriel could swear that he heard her purring. He smiled at the sight of her, momentarily relaxed and almost happy over such a trivial event. On a whim, he decided to show her one of his most valuable things.

"Here's something for you to see." He waved her over, and she came to stand in front of his desk.

He opened a drawer and withdrew two sets of white cotton gloves.

"Put these on." He handed her a pair, which she accepted mutely, copying his movements as he pulled them over his long fingers.

"This is one of my most precious possessions," he explained, withdrawing a large wooden box from a now unlocked drawer. He placed the box on his desk, and for one horrible moment Julia was afraid of what she might find inside.

A shrunken head? Perhaps from a former graduate student?

He opened the box and withdrew what looked like a book. When he opened it, it became evident that it was a series of stiff paper sleeves accordioned together, each labeled in Italian. He leafed through it carefully until he found the sleeve he wanted, then he removed something, cradling it in both hands.

Julia gasped at the sight of it.

Gabriel smiled with pride. "Do you recognize it?"

"Of course! But this . . . this can't be the *original?*"

He chuckled softly. "Sadly, no. That would be beyond the reach of my small fortune. The originals date from the fifteenth century. These are reproductions, from the sixteenth century."

He held in his hand a copy of a famous illustration of Dante and Beatrice and the fixed stars of Paradise, the original having been drawn in pen and ink by Sandro Botticelli. The illustration was about fifteen inches by twenty inches and even though it was only ink on parchment, the detail was breathtaking.

"How did you get this? I didn't know there were any copies."

"Not only are they copies, they were probably done by a former student of Botticelli's. But this set is *complete*. Botticelli prepared one hundred illustrations of *The Divine Comedy*, but only ninety-two of them survived. I have the full complement."

Julia's eyes grew wide and round, shining in excitement. "You're kidding."

Gabriel laughed. "No, I'm not."

"I went to see the originals when they were on loan to the Uffizi Gallery in Florence. The Vatican has eight, I think, and the rest are owned by a museum in Berlin."

"Quite. I thought you'd appreciate them."

"But I've never seen the remaining eight."

"No one has. Let me show you."

Time flew as Gabriel showed Julia his treasures, and she was very quiet in her admiration until Rachel's voice called to them from the hall.

"Gabriel, get Julia a drink, would you? And stop boring her with your antique crap!"

He rolled his eyes, and Julia giggled.

"How did you get them? Why aren't they in a museum?" she asked as she watched him store his illustrations in their respective sleeves.

He pressed his lips together. "They aren't in a museum because I refuse to give them up. And no one knows I have them but my lawyer, my insurance agent, and now you."

He set his jaw as if he was shutting down all further discussion, so Julia decided not to press him.

It was probable that the illustrations had been stolen from a museum and that Gabriel had purchased them on the black market. That would explain his reticence in revealing their existence to the world. Julia shivered when she realized that she had seen what less than half a dozen people in the world had seen. And they were so breathtakingly beautiful—a true masterpiece.

"Gabriel . . ." Rachel stood in the doorway, scolding him.

"Fine, fine. What would you like to drink, Miss Mitchell?" They exited the study, and he walked to the wine refrigerator in the kitchen.

"Gabriel!"

"Julianne?"

She started at the unfamiliar name as it dropped from his lips. Rachel noticed her strange reaction and disappeared into a cabinet searching for her brother's pots and pans.

"Anything would be fine, thank you Prof—Gabriel." Julia closed her eyes at the pleasure of finally being able to pronounce his name to him. Then she settled herself on one of the elegant stools at the breakfast bar.

Gabriel removed a bottle of Chianti and set it on the counter. "I'll let it come up to room temperature," he explained to no one in particular. He excused himself and disappeared, presumably to change into more casual clothes.

"Julia," Rachel hissed, putting a pile of vegetables into one side of the double sink. "What's going on with you and Gabriel?"

"You need to ask him that."

"I plan on it. But why is he acting so weird? And why didn't you just tell him who you were?"

Julia looked as if she was about to burst into tears. "I thought he'd remember me. But he doesn't." Her voice shook, and she looked down into her lap.

Rachel was puzzled by her friend's words and by her overly emotional response and immediately flew to her side to press her into a hug. "Don't you worry. I'm here now, and I'll straighten him out. He has a heart, somewhere, underneath everything else. I know, I saw it once. Now help me wash some vegetables. The lamb is already in the oven."

When Gabriel returned, he eagerly opened the wine, smiling to himself wickedly. He was in for a treat, and he knew it. He knew how Julianne looked when she tasted wine, and now he would have a repeat of her erotic performance from the other night. He felt himself twitch more than once in anticipation and wished that he had a video camera secretly placed in his condo somewhere. It would probably be too obvious to pull his camera out and take snapshots of her.

He showed her the bottle first, noting with approval the impressed expression that passed across her face when she read the label. He'd brought this special vintage back from Tuscany, and it would have pained him to waste it on an undiscerning palate. He poured a little into her glass and stood back, watching, and trying very hard not to grin.

Just as before, Julia swirled the wine slowly. She examined it in the halogen light. She closed her eyes and sniffed. Then she wrapped her kissable lips around the rim of the goblet and tasted it slowly, holding the wine in her mouth for a moment or two before swallowing.

Gabriel sighed, watching her as the wine traveled down her long and elegant throat.

When Julia opened her eyes, she saw Gabriel swaying slightly in front of her, his blue eyes darkened, his breath somewhat affected, and the front of his charcoal gray trousers . . . She frowned at him. Hard. "Are you all right?"

He passed a hand over his eyes and willed himself into submission. "Yes. Sorry." He poured a large glass for her and one for himself and began to sip it sensuously, watching her intently over the rim of his glass.

"You're probably starving, Gabriel. I know what a beast you turn into when you're hungry." Rachel spoke over her shoulder as she stirred some kind of sauce on the stove.

"What are we having with the lamb?" He was watching Julia like a hawk as she brought her wineglass up to her luscious mouth once again and took a large swallow.

Rachel placed a box on the breakfast bar. "Couscous!"

Julia spat out her wine, drenching Gabriel and his white shirt. In shock at her sudden expectoration, she dropped the wineglass, dousing herself and his hardwood floor in the process. The crystal goblet shattered on impact at the foot of her barstool.

Gabriel began shaking the wine droplets off of his expensive dress shirt and cursed. Loudly. Julia dropped to her knees and swiftly tried to pick up the scattered glass shards with her bare hands.

"Stop," he said quietly, peering down at her over the edge of the breakfast bar.

Julia continued her desperate mission, tears escaping her eyes.

"*Stop*," he said more loudly, walking around the counter.

She transferred some of the glass shards to her other hand and tried picking up the remainder piece by piece, crawling on the floor pathetically like a wounded puppy that was dragging a broken paw.

"Stop! For God's sake, woman, *stop*. You'll shred yourself to ribbons." Gabriel towered menacingly, his anger descending on her from on high like the wrath of God.

He pulled her to her feet by her shoulders and forced her to dump the glass from her hands into a bowl on the countertop, before guiding her down the hall and into the guest washroom.

"Sit," he ordered.

Julia sat on the top of the closed toilet and heaved a subdued but shuddering sob.

"Hold out your hands."

Her hands were stained with red wine and some small trickles of blood. A few crystals of glass sparkled on her palm amongst the cuts. Gabriel cursed a few times and shook his head as he opened the medicine cabinet. "You don't listen very well, do you?"

Julia blinked at her tears, sorry that she couldn't wipe them away with her hands.

"And you don't do what you're told." He looked over at her and abruptly stopped.

He didn't know why he stopped, and if you had asked him why afterward, he would have shrugged and given you no explanation. But once he stopped what he was doing and saw the poor little creature that was huddled in a corner crying, he felt . . . something. Something other than annoyance or anger or guilt or sexual arousal. He felt *compassion* for her. And he felt sorry that he'd made her cry.

He leaned over and began to wipe her tears away very tenderly with his fingertips. He noticed the hum that came from her mouth as soon as he touched her, and he noticed once again that her skin felt very familiar. And when he'd wiped away her tears, he cupped her pale face in his hands, tilting her chin upward . . . then retreated quickly and began cleaning her wounds.

"Thank you," she murmured, noting the care with which he removed the glass from her hands. He used tweezers, meticulously searching out even the smallest fragment from her skin.

"Don't mention it."

When all the glass had been removed, he poured iodine onto some cotton balls.

"This is going to sting."

He watched as she steeled herself for his touch, and he winced slightly. He did not relish the thought of hurting her. And she was so soft and so fragile. It took him a full minute and a half to work up the courage to put the iodine on her cuts, and all the time she was sitting there, wide-eyed and biting her lip, waiting for him to just do it already.

"There," he said gruffly, as he wiped away the last of the blood. "You're all better."

"I'm sorry I broke your glass. I know it was crystal." Her soft voice interrupted his reverie as he returned his first-aid implements to the medicine cabinet.

He waved a hand at her. "I have dozens. There's a crystal shop downstairs. I'll pick up another if I need it."

"I'd like to replace it."

"You couldn't afford it." The words escaped his mouth without him realizing it. He watched in horror as Julia's face first reddened then grew pale. Her head went down, of course, and she started chewing at the inside of her cheek.

"Miss Mitchell, I wouldn't dream of taking your money. It would violate the rules of hospitality."

And we couldn't have that, thought Julia.

"But I've stained your shirt. Please let me pay for the dry cleaning."

Gabriel stared down at his lovely but obviously ruined white shirt and cursed inside his head. He'd liked this shirt. Paulina had bought it for him in London. And there was no way Julia's spittle mingled with Chianti would ever come out.

"I have several of these as well," he lied smoothly. "And I'm sure the stains will come out. Rachel will help me."

Julia raked her upper teeth across her lower lip back and forth and back and forth.

Gabriel saw the movement, and it made him rather queasy, like a kind of seasickness, but her lips were so red and inviting he couldn't look away. It was a bit like watching a car wreck while standing on the deck of a ship.

He leaned over and patted the back of her hand. "Accidents happen. They're no one's fault." He smiled and was rewarded with a very pretty smile in return as she released her lower lip.

Look at her. She does blossom under kindness. Just like a rose, opening her petals.

"Is she all right?" Rachel asked, suddenly appearing beside them.

Gabriel withdrew his hand quickly and sighed. "Yes. But apparently Julianne hates couscous." He winked at her slyly and watched as the flush spread from her cheeks and over the surface of her porcelain skin. She truly was a brown-eyed angel.

"That's fine. I'll make rice pilaf instead." Rachel disappeared, and Gabriel followed, leaving Julia to stop her heart from trying to escape out of her chest.

While Rachel packed away the disdained grains into the refrigerator, Gabriel went to his bedroom to change his soiled shirt, depositing it with more than a little regret in the garbage. Then he joined his sister in the kitchen to clean up the broken glass and wine from the floor.

"There are a couple of things I need to tell you about Julia," she began, speaking over her shoulder.

Gabriel walked the glass shards to the garbage bin. "I'd rather not hear it."

"What's wrong with you? She's my friend, for crying out loud!"

"And she's *my* student. I shouldn't know anything about her personal life. Her friendship with you already presents a conflict of interest that I was unaware of."

Rachel squared her shoulders and shook her head stubbornly, her gray eyes darkening. "You know what? I don't care! I love her a lot and Mom did, too. So you remember that the next time you're tempted to shout at her.

"*She's been broken*, you jackass. That's why she hasn't kept in touch with me this past year. And now she's *finally* crawled out of her shell, a shell I might add, that I thought she would *never* leave, and you're forcing her back into it with your . . . your arrogance and condescension! So drop the Mr. Rochester-Mr. Darcy-Heathcliff British stuck-uppity bullshit and treat her like the treasure she is! Or I'm coming back here and putting a pump in your ass!"

Gabriel straightened his spine and cast her a withering stare. "By 'pump,' I take it you're referring to a lady's shoe?"

She didn't back down. Or flinch. In fact, she grew taller. And almost menacing.

"Fine, Rachel."

"Good. It's hard for me to believe that you didn't recognize her name, after all the times I told you about how much she loved Dante. I mean, how many Dante enthusiasts from Selinsgrove do you know?"

He leaned over to her and placed a kiss across her furrowed brow. "Go easy on me, Rach. I try not to think about anything connected with Selinsgrove if I can help it."

Her anger melted at his words, and she hugged her brother tightly. "I know."

A few hours and another bottle of expensive Chianti later, Julia stood up to leave. "Thanks for dinner. I should be getting home."

"We'll drive you," Rachel volunteered, disappearing to find her coat.

Gabriel frowned and excused himself to go after her.

"It's all right. I can walk. It's not far," Julia called to the siblings.

"No way. It's dark out, and I don't care how safe Toronto is. Besides, it's raining," Rachel shouted before finding herself engaged in a heated discussion with Gabriel.

Julia walked toward the door so that she wouldn't have to hear him say that he didn't want to drive her home. But the siblings reappeared shortly, and the three of them walked down the hall to the elevator. Just as the elevator was arriving, Rachel's cell phone rang.

"It's Aaron." She hugged Julia tightly. "I've been trying to get hold of him all day, and he's been in meetings. Let's go to lunch. No need to worry, big brother, I have your spare key!"

Rachel strolled back to the apartment, leaving a scowling Gabriel and an uncomfortable Julia to take the elevator down to the garage.

"Were you ever going to tell me who you are?" His voice was slightly accusing.

Julia shook her head and hugged her ridiculous knapsack more tightly.

He looked at her book bag and decided then and there that it had to go. If he had to see that hideous thing one more time, he was going to lose it. And Paul had touched it, which meant that it was polluted. She'd have to throw it away.

Gabriel led her to his parking space, and she immediately walked to the passenger's side of the Jaguar.

He pressed a button and the Range Rover next to the Jaguar chirped. "Um, let's take this one instead. The four-wheel drive is better in the rain. I don't like taking the Jaguar out in weather like this if I don't have to."

Julia tried to hide her look of surprise at Gabriel's embarrassment of riches, especially when he opened her door and helped her in. As she settled herself in her seat, she wondered if he'd felt the connection that passed between them when he touched her arm. Of course, he had.

"You let me make an ass out of myself." He scowled as he drove out of the garage.

You did that all by yourself, thank you. Julia's unspoken thought shimmered between them, and she briefly wondered how good The Professor was at reading nonverbal cues.

"I would have treated you differently. I would have treated you better, if I'd known."

"Would you? Really? And found some other student to rip apart? If that's the case, I'm glad your anger was directed at me. Then you couldn't take it out on anyone else."

Gabriel gave her a cold look. "This doesn't change anything. I'm glad you're Rachel's friend, but you're still my student, which means we need to be professional, Miss Mitchell. And you will be careful how you speak to me now and in the future."

"Yes, Professor Emerson."

He searched her face for any sign of sarcasm but saw none. Her shoulders were hunched, and her head was down. He'd made his little rose wither. Any blossoming had now been completely undone.

Your little rose? What the hell, Emerson!

"Rachel is very glad you're here. Did you know that she was engaged?"

Julia shook her head. "Was? Not anymore?"

"Aaron Webster asked her to marry him, and she said yes, but that was before Grace . . ." He exhaled slowly. "Rachel doesn't feel like planning a wedding now, so she's called it off. That's why she's here."

"Oh, no, I'm so sorry. Poor Rachel." She exhaled slowly. "Poor Aaron! I loved him."

Gabriel frowned. "They're still together. Aaron loves her, obviously, and agreed she needed some time away. There was a lot of . . . fighting at my parents' house when I was home. She came to see me to get away. Which is laughable, really, since I'm the black sheep of the family and she's the favorite."

Julia nodded as if she understood.

"I have a problem with anger, Miss Mitchell. I have a bad temper. I have trouble controlling it, and when I lose my temper I can be very destructive."

Her eyes widened at his declaration, and her mouth opened slightly, but she did not speak.

"It would be . . . inadvisable for me to lose my temper around someone like you. It would be very damaging, for both of us." His declaration was so honest and so frightening, the words burned into her like fire.

"Wrath is one of the seven deadly sins," she remarked, turning away from him to gaze out the window, trying to alleviate the burning sensation in her middle.

He laughed bitterly. "Remarkably, I have all seven; don't bother counting. Pride, envy, wrath, sloth, avarice, gluttony, *lust.*"

She lifted an eyebrow but did not turn around. "Somehow, I doubt that."

"I don't expect you to understand. You're only a magnet for mishap, Miss Mitchell, while I am a magnet for sin."

Now she turned to face him. He smiled at her with a look of resignation, and she offered him a sympathetic look in return.

"Sin isn't something that is attracted to a human being, Professor. It's the other way round."

"Not in my experience. Sin seems to find me even when I'm not looking for it. And I'm not very good at resisting temptation."

He glanced at her, then returned his eyes to the road.

"Your friendship with Rachel explains why you sent gardenias. And why you signed the card the way you did."

"I'm sorry about Grace. I loved her too."

He looked into her eyes. They were kind and open, yet he saw traces of sadness and incalculable loss.

"I realize that now," he admitted.

"You have satellite radio?" She gestured to the console as he switched on the radio and pressed one of the preset buttons.

"Yes. I usually listen to one of the jazz stations, but it depends on my mood."

Julia reached out a tentative finger to the radio but withdrew her hand.

Gabriel smiled at her reticence, remembering the way she purred when he gave her permission to curl up in his favorite chair. He wanted to make her purr again.

"It's all right. You can choose something."

She ran through the pre-sets, smiling at his choices, which included the French CBC station and BBC News, until she came to the last one, which was labeled Nine Inch Nails.

"There's an entire station devoted to them?" She sounded incredulous.

"Yes." Gabriel squirmed a little, as if she had uncovered an embarrassing secret.

"And you like them?"

"When I'm in a particular mood."

Julia pressed the button for the jazz station.

Gabriel felt rather than observed her visceral reaction. He did not understand it but decided not to probe it.

Julia hated Nine Inch Nails. She changed the station whenever they came on the radio. If a song of theirs was playing somewhere, she left the room or the building. The sounds of their music and especially Trent Reznor's voice creeped her the hell out, although she never told anyone why.

She first heard them in a club back in Philadelphia. She was dancing with *him*, and *he* was grinding all over her. She hadn't minded at first; that's how *he* always was, but then that song came on, and as soon as the music began, Julia felt mildly ill. It was the strange sequence in the opening bars, then it was the voice, then it was the lyrics about fucking like an animal, and the look on his face as *he* brought his forehead to hers and whispered it to her, staring straight into her soul.

Whatever Julia's religious beliefs and her half-hearted attempts to pray to lesser gods and deities, at that moment she'd believed that she heard the voice of the Devil. Lucifer himself held her in his arms and whispered to her. And the very idea, coupled with his words, frightened her.

Julia had wrenched herself from *him* and fled to the ladies' washroom, looking at the pale and shaking girl in the mirror, wondering what the hell had just happened. She did not know why *he* had spoken to her like that or why *he* had chosen that moment to confess. Nevertheless, she knew *him* well enough to know that the repeated lyric was a confession of his deepest and perhaps darkest intentions and not just a mindless repetition.

But Julia didn't want to be fucked like an animal; she wanted to be loved. She would have foresworn sex forever if she thought it would guarantee her the kind of love that was the stuff of poetry and myth. That was the kind of affection she craved desperately but didn't actually believe that she deserved. She wanted to be someone's muse—to be worshipped and adored, body and soul. She wanted to play Beatrice to a dashing and noble Dante and to inhabit Paradise with him forever. And to live a life that would rival the beauty of Botticelli's illustrations.

And that is why at the age of twenty-three, Julia Mitchell was still a virgin, with the photograph of the man who ruined her for others tucked in the back of her underwear drawer. For the past six years, she'd slept with his picture under her pillow. No man had ever come close to comparing to him; no feelings of affection had ever approximated the love and devotion he inspired in her. Their entire relationship was based on a single night, a night she relived in her memories over and over again . . .

Chapter Seven

Julia parked her bike next to the Clarks' large white home and walked to the front porch. She never knocked when she visited them, so she skipped up the stairs and pulled the screen door open. What she found inside shocked her.

The glass coffee table in the living room was smashed, blood spattered on the carpet. Chairs and cushions were strewn about, and Rachel and Aaron sat huddled together on the sofa in the center of the room. Rachel was sobbing.

Julia stood there, gaping in horror. "What happened?"

"Gabriel," said Aaron.

"Gabriel? Is he hurt?"

"He's fine!" Rachel laughed almost hysterically. "He's been home less than twenty-four hours, and he's already gotten into a shoving match with my dad, made my mom cry twice, and sent Scott to the hospital."

Aaron continued rubbing his girlfriend's back in order to comfort her, a grim expression on his face.

Julia gasped. "Why?"

"Who knows? No one ever knows what's going on with him. He got into an argument with Dad, Mom stepped in between them, and Gabriel shoved her. Scott said he'd kill him if he ever touched her again. So Gabriel threw a punch and broke his nose."

Julia gazed down at the pieces of glass that were now embedded with blood in the carpet. A dozen or so cookies, crumbled now, were scattered in and around the glass along with the remains of what appeared to be a couple of cups of coffee.

"And this?" She pointed at the macabre mess.

"Gabriel pushed Scott through the coffee table. Scott and Dad are at the hospital, Mom is locked in her room, and I'm spending the night at Aaron's."

Rachel began to drag her boyfriend to the front door.

Julia stood frozen to the spot, unable to move. "Maybe I'll try to talk to your mom."

"I can't stay in this house another minute. My family has just been destroyed." With that, Rachel fled with Aaron.

Julia intended to climb the stairs to find Grace, but she heard a noise coming from the direction of the kitchen, so she quietly padded to the back of the house. Through the open back door she could see someone sitting on the porch, swinging a beer bottle to his lips. A shock of brown hair shone in the fading sunlight. Julia recognized him from Rachel's photographs.

Before she had time to think about it, her feet walked out the back door, and she found herself sitting some distance from him on a chaise lounge, her knees drawn up under her chin. She wrapped her arms around her legs and looked over at him.

He ignored her.

Julia traced his appearance with her eyes, hoping to burn the vision into her memory. He was far better-looking in person. She looked at his blue and bloodshot eyes, which were startling under his brown brows. She followed the angle of his high cheekbones, his straight, noble nose, and the squareness of his jaw, noting the two or three days' growth of beard that shadowed his skin and the kiss of a dimple. Her eyes came to rest on his full lips, noticing the curve and fullness of the lower one before she was able to drag her gaze reluctantly to look at his bruises.

Gabriel had bruises and blood on his right hand and something purple on his left cheek. Scott's fist had met its mark, but surprisingly, Gabriel was still conscious.

"You're a bit late for the six o'clock show. It ended thirty minutes ago." His voice was gentle and almost as pleasing as his features. Julia thought momentarily about what it would be like to hear that voice pronounce her name.

She shivered.

"There's a blanket right here." He gestured to a large, plaid wool blanket that was bunched up near his hip. Without looking at her, he patted it.

Julia watched him warily. Satisfied that his anger had cooled, she walked over to him and sat on a nearby stool, still keeping a healthy distance between them. She wondered how fast he could run. And how fast she could run if he was chasing her.

He handed her the blanket.

"Thank you," she murmured, pulling it around her shoulders.

Out of the corner of her eye, she took in his figure and noted how he had folded his considerable height casually into an Adirondack chair. His shoulders appeared broader in his black leather jacket, the planes of his pectorals visible underneath the fabric of his tight black T-shirt. His long legs filled out his black jeans well, and Julia noticed that he seemed taller and heavier than he'd looked in his sister's old pictures.

She wanted to say something. She wanted to ask him why he'd gone berserk on the nicest family she'd ever met. But she was too shy and too scared of him to do that. So she asked him if he had a bottle opener instead.

He frowned at her before pulling one out of his back pocket and passing it over. She thanked him and continued to sit there quietly. He turned to the half-empty case of beer behind him, chose a bottle, and held it in front of her.

"Allow me," he said, seeing her now and smiling. He took the opener back, uncapping her beer with one swift movement and clanking their bottles together. "Cheers."

Julia sipped her drink politely, trying not to choke as the strange, yeasty flavor entered her mouth. She hummed unconsciously and waited.

"Ever had a beer before?" Gabriel grinned.

She shook her head.

"Then I'm glad I'm your first."

She blushed and hid her face behind her long mahogany hair.

"What are you doing here?" He wore a curious expression.

Julia paused, wondering how best to put it. "I was invited to dinner." *I was hoping to finally meet you.*

Gabriel laughed. "I guess I ruined that. Well, Miss Brown Eyes, add that charge to my tab."

"Will you tell me what happened?" She kept her voice quiet and tried not to let it shake.

"Will you tell me why you haven't run away yet?" His blue eyes found hers, and he looked at her sharply.

She ducked her head again, hoping the act of submission would cool his sudden flare of anger. Sitting with Gabriel after what happened was a stupid thing to do. He was drunk, and there was no one to rescue her if he decided to get violent. Now was her chance to leave.

Inexplicably, however, Gabriel's arm reached out to close the gap between them. He pushed her hair behind her shoulders, his fingers tangling in the waves slowly, very slowly, before he withdrew. A connection of sorts flowed from his fingers and into her hair. Julia absorbed the sensation and hummed again softly, forgetting his question entirely.

"You smell like vanilla," he remarked, shifting his body so that he could stare at her properly.

"It's my shampoo."

He finished his beer and opened another, taking a long pull from the bottle before he turned to her again.

"It wasn't supposed to be like this."

"They love you, you know. You're all they talk about."

"The prodigal son. Or perhaps, a demon. *The demon Gabriel.*" He laughed bitterly and finished his beer in almost one swallow. He opened another.

"They were so happy you were coming home. That's why your mother invited me to dinner."

"She isn't my mother. And maybe Grace invited you because she knew I needed a brown-eyed angel to watch over me."

Gabriel leaned closer so that he could cup her cheek. Julia inhaled sharply as his touch surprised her, his large, blue eyes gazing at her in intoxicated surprise. He moved the pad of his thumb across her blush and hesitated, almost as if he was absorbing the heat from her skin. When he withdrew his hand, Julia almost cried out at the loss.

He placed his bottle down on the porch and stood up quickly. "The sun is setting. Would you like to go for a walk?"

She bit her lip. She knew she shouldn't. But this was Gabriel from the photograph and possibly her one and only chance to see him and spend time in his presence. After what had happened earlier, she doubted he'd be coming home again. At least, not for a long, long time.

She placed the blanket to one side and stood up.

"Bring the blanket," he said, and when she'd scooped it up under her arm, he took her smaller hand in his.

She gasped. A tingling sensation began at the tips of her fingers and traveled slowly through her arm until it reached her shoulder and skated to her heart, causing it to beat much faster.

He brought his head closer to hers. "Have you ever held a boy's hand before?" She shook her head, and he laughed softly. "Then I'm glad I'm your first."

They walked slowly into the woods, quickly disappearing from view of the Clarks' house. Julia liked the way her hand fit in his and the way his long fingers curved across the back of hers. He held her gently but securely, squeezing her from time to time, perhaps to reassure her of his presence. Julia began to think that this was the way holding hands with someone was supposed to feel. Not that she had any experience.

She'd only ventured into these woods a time or two before and always with Rachel. She knew that if something went wrong, she'd most likely get lost trying to find her way home. She pushed such thoughts to the back of her mind and focused her attention entirely on what it felt like to hold the enigmatic Gabriel's warm, strong hand.

"I used to spend a lot of time here. It's very peaceful. Up ahead there's an old apple orchard. Has Rachel shown it to you?"

Julia shook her head.

Gabriel gazed down at her with what looked like a serious expression. "You're awfully quiet. You can talk to me. I promise I won't bite." He flashed her one of his winning smiles, one Julia recognized from Rachel's photographs.

"Why did you come home?"

He ignored Julia's question and kept walking, but she noticed that he began to grip her hand more tightly. She tightened her grip on his as well to signal to him that she was not afraid. Even though she was.

"I didn't want to come home, not like this. I lost something, and I've been drunk for weeks."

Gabriel's honesty surprised her.

"But if you lost something, maybe you can try to find it."

He narrowed his eyes. "What I lost is lost forever."

He began walking more quickly, and Julia had to hasten her strides just to keep up with him.

"I came home for money. That's how desperate and absolutely fucked I am." Gabriel's voice softened, and Julia felt him shudder. "I was fucked up even before I destroyed everything and everyone. Before you ever arrived."

"I'm so sorry."

He shrugged and began to drag her to the left. "We're almost there."

Through an opening in the trees they entered a small clearing that was carpeted in thick grass. Wildflowers and weeds and old rotting stumps littered the expanse of green. The air was quiet and vibrated with peace. And at the edge of the open area stood several aged apple trees, weary-looking and worn.

"This is it." He gestured widely. "This is Paradise."

He pulled Julia to a large rock that stood inexplicably at the edge of the clearing and lifted her by her waist so that she was perched on top of it. Then he climbed to her side. Julia shivered. The rock was cold in the shade of the setting sun and was already sending chills through her thin jeans.

Gabriel shrugged out of his jacket and placed it around her shoulders. "You'll catch pneumonia and die," he said absently, placing an arm around her and drawing her close to his side. His body heat radiated from his bare arms and his T-shirt, warming her immediately.

She inhaled deeply and sighed with contentment, marveling at how well she fit under the crook of his arm. As if she'd been made for him.

"You're Beatrice."

"Beatrice?"

"Dante's Beatrice."

Julia flushed. "I don't know who that is."

Gabriel chuckled to himself, his breath warm against her face as he nuzzled her ear with his nose. "Didn't they tell you? Didn't they tell you the prodigal son is writing his book on Dante and Beatrice?"

When Julia didn't answer, he brought his lips to the top of her head and brushed a gentle kiss against her hair. "Dante was a poet. Beatrice was his muse. He met her when she was very young, and he loved her from afar his whole life. Beatrice was his guide through Paradise."

Julia's eyes were closed as she listened to his voice, inhaling the scent that clung to his skin. He smelled of musk and sweat and beer, but Julia ignored those distractions and focused on the scent that was Gabriel, something very masculine and potentially dangerous.

"There's a painting by an artist named Holiday. You look like his Beatrice." Gabriel reached down and brought her pale fingers to his lips, kissing her skin reverently.

"Your family loves you. You should make up with them." Julia's own words surprised her, but he only pulled her in more closely.

"They aren't my family. Not really. And it's too late anyway, Beatrice."

Julia started at the name and realized that the beer had definitely caught up with him. But she didn't move her head from resting on his shoulder. A short while later he was rubbing his hand up and down her arm, trying to attract her attention.

"You haven't had your dinner."

She shook her head. "No, I haven't."

"Shall I feed you?"

Though it made her sad to do so, she lifted her head from his shoulder. He smiled at her and walked over to one of the remaining apple trees. He studied the boughs of hanging fruit and chose the largest, ripest red apple before picking a smaller one. He put the smaller one in his pocket as he walked back to her.

"Beatrice." He smiled and handed her the apple.

Julia stared at it entranced, as if it were a treasure.

Gabriel laughed and moved his hands, extending the fruit in his right palm, the way a child would hold a sugar cube to a pony. Julia took the apple and brought it immediately to her lips, taking a firm bite.

He watched her chew; he watched her swallow. Then in silent satisfaction, he resumed his former position, his arm tight around her waist.

He pressed her head gently to his shoulder and began eating the smaller apple that he had hidden in his pocket.

They sat very still as the sun set, and just before the orchard was covered in darkness, Gabriel took the blanket from under Julia's arm and spread it like a bed on the grass.

"Come, Beatrice." He held his hand out to her.

Julia knew it would be a very foolish thing to take his hand and to sit with him on the blanket. But she didn't care. She'd developed a crush on him the first time Rachel had shown his photograph to her, and Julia had stolen it. Now that he was here, real, breathing, alive, in flesh, all she could do was take his hand.

"Have you ever lain next to a boy and looked up at the stars?" He pulled her down to the blanket and watched her as they lay on their backs.

"No."

Gabriel threaded his fingers through hers and placed the connection that was theirs on top of his heart. She could feel it beating slowly beneath her touch, and she took comfort in its steady rhythm.

"You're beautiful, Beatrice. Like a brown-eyed angel."

Julia turned her head so she could look at him and smiled. "I think you're beautiful." She shyly began to run her fingers along his jaw, marveling at the way the stubble felt under her hand.

He smiled at her touch and closed his eyes. She traced his features gently for a long time, until her arm began to grow tired.

He opened his eyes. "Thank you."

Julia smiled and squeezed his hand, feeling his heart leap at her movement.

"Have you ever been kissed by a boy?"

She blushed deeply and shook her head.

"Then I'm glad I'm your first." Gabriel propped himself up on his side and leaned over. His eyes shone gently, and he smiled down at her.

Julia managed to close her eyes before his perfect mouth found hers. She floated.

Gabriel's lips were warm and inviting, and he spread them over her mouth carefully, as if he were worried he might bruise her. Not knowing how to kiss and still slightly wary, Julia kept her mouth closed. Gabriel brought his hand up to cup the curve of her cheek, caressing the skin with his thumb as his lips moved softly over hers.

This kiss was not what she expected.

She had expected him to be careless or slightly rough. She had expected his kiss to be desperate and urgent and perhaps for his fingertips to trail along her skin and down her body to places she wasn't ready to let him touch. But he kept his hands where they were, one caressing the small of her back and the other at her cheek. His kiss was tender and sweet—the kind of kiss she imagined a lover giving his beloved after a long absence.

Gabriel kissed Julia as if he knew her, as if she belonged to him. His kiss was passionate and full of emotion, as if every fiber of his being had melted and spread itself on his lips only to be given to her. Her heart skidded in her chest at the thought. She had never dared to hope for such a first kiss. Somehow, as the pressure of his lips lessened, she felt like bursting into tears, knowing that she'd never be kissed like that again. He'd ruined her for anyone else. Forever.

Gabriel sighed deeply as he released her and pressed his lips gently to her forehead.

"Open your eyes."

Julia looked up into a pair of blue orbs that were startlingly clear and very emotional, but she could not decipher the emotions. He smiled and pressed his lips to her forehead again before rolling onto his back and gazing up at the stars.

"What are you thinking?" She shifted herself so that she was curled up at his side, close to but not touching him with her body.

"I was thinking about how I waited for you. I waited and waited, and you never came." He smiled at her sadly.

"I'm sorry, Gabriel."

"You're here now. *Apparuit iam beatitudo vestra.*"

"I don't know what that means." She sounded shy.

"It means *now your blessedness appears*. But really, it should be *now my blessedness appears*. Now that you're here." He pulled her closer, snaking his arm beneath her neck and down to her waist where he splayed his hand, fingers wide, at the small of her back. "For the rest of my life, I'll dream of hearing your voice breathe my name."

Julia smiled at herself in the darkness.

"Have you ever fallen asleep in the arms of a boy before, Beatrice?"

She shook her head.

"Then I'm glad I'm your first." He pulled her so that her head rested on his chest near his heart, and her delicate body molded perfectly to his side. "Like Adam's rib," he whispered into her hair.

"Do you have to leave?" she whispered back, running her hands hesitantly over his chest, up and down and back and forth.

"Yes, but not tonight."

"Will you come back?" Her voice was almost a whimper.

Gabriel sighed deeply. "I'm going to be thrown out of Paradise tomorrow, Beatrice. Our only hope is that you find me afterward. Look for me in Hell."

He gently rolled her onto her back and placed his hands on either side of her hips, hovering over her—eyes wide—staring longingly and intensely down into her very soul.

And then he brought his lips to hers . . .

Chapter Eight

Rachel sat at Gabriel's breakfast bar Thursday morning, drinking a latté and poring over French *Vogue*. It was not her normal reading material. Rachel's nightstand in Philadelphia was covered with books about politics, public relations, economics, and sociology, all in the hope that someday one of her superiors would ask for her opinion, rather than asking her to photocopy someone else's. Now that she was on a leave of absence from her job, such as it was, she had time to read beyond mayoral politics.

She was feeling better this morning. Much better. Her conversation with Aaron the night before had gone well. Although he continued to be disappointed that the wedding was off, he told her over and over again that he would rather have her than a wedding.

"We don't have to get married right away. We can delay the wedding until you've finished grieving. But I still want you, Rachel. I'll always want you. As my wife, as my lover . . . Right now, I'll take whatever I can get, because I love you. Come back to me."

Aaron's words burned through the haze of depression and grief that clouded Rachel's mind. And suddenly, everything was clear. She'd thought she was running away from Scott and her father and the ghost of her mother. But perhaps she was running from Aaron too, and to hear him voice those words . . . as if it was possible for her to leave him. As if she could even contemplate staying away from him.

His statement had almost broken Rachel's heart and made her realize how much she truly wanted to be his wife. And how determined she was not to make him wait too long to be her husband while she sorted herself out. Life was too short to be miserable. Her mother had taught her that.

Gabriel entered the kitchen wearing his glasses, kissed the top of her head, and slid a wad of bills in front of her. She glanced at the cash suspiciously and flipped through it, her eyes widening.

"What's this for?"

He cleared his throat and sat down next to her. "Aren't you going shopping with Julianne?"

She rolled her eyes. "It's *Julia*, Gabriel. And no, we aren't. She's working on some project all day with a guy named Paul. Then he's taking her to dinner."

Angelfucker, thought Gabriel. The expletive sprang into his mind, unbidden and uncensored, and he tensed, rumbling low in his chest.

Rachel slid the money back to him and returned to her magazine.

He placed the cash in front of her again. "Take it."

"Why?"

"Buy something for your friend."

Rachel's eyes narrowed. "Why? This is a lot of money."

"I know," he said quietly.

"This is five hundred dollars. I know you have money to waste, but jeepers, Gabriel, that's a bit much."

"Have you seen her apartment?"

"No. Have you?"

He shifted on his bar stool. "Just for a moment. She was caught in the rain, and I drove her home and . . ."

"And?" Rachel draped an arm over his shoulder and leaned toward him with a delicious grin. "Spill."

Gabriel pushed her arm off his shoulder and glared. "It wasn't like that. But I saw her place briefly while I was dropping her off, and it's awful. She doesn't even have a kitchen, for God's sake."

"No kitchen? What the hell?"

"The girl is as poor as a church mouse. Not to mention the fact that she carries around this loathsome excuse for a book bag. Spend all the money on buying her a decent briefcase, I don't care. But do something. Because if I see that knapsack one more time, I'm going to burn it."

Gabriel raked his hands through his chestnut hair and finally kept them there, hunching his tall frame over the breakfast bar. With the power of perception only possessed by a sister, Rachel regarded him carefully. Gabriel appeared to be the ideal poker player: impassive, unemotional, cold. Oh, so very cold. Not merely cool, like a breeze, or water from a stream in the autumn, but *cold*. Cold like a rock against your skin in the shade of the setting sun. Rachel believed that his coldness was his worst character flaw—his ability to say and do things without regard for the feelings of others, including his family.

Despite his failings, Gabriel was her favorite. And as the baby of the family and ten years younger, she was his favorite too. He'd never fought with her the way he'd fought with Scott or their father. He'd always and only protected her—loved her, even. At his worst, there was no possibility of Gabriel intentionally hurting Rachel. She'd only been hurt by watching him hurt everyone else. Especially himself.

She knew that upon closer inspection Gabriel would make a lousy poker player. He had too many tells, too many ways he revealed his inner turmoil. He shut his eyes when he was close to losing his temper. He rubbed his face when he was frustrated. He paced when he was distressed or afraid. Rachel watched him begin to pace and wondered what he was afraid of.

"Why are you so worried about her? You weren't that friendly when she was here for dinner. You won't call her *Julia*."

"She's my student. I have to be professional."

"Professionally mean?"

Gabriel stood still and scowled.

"Fine. I'll take the money for Julia, and I'll buy her a briefcase. *But I'd rather buy her shoes*."

Gabriel sat back on his bar stool. "Shoes?"

"Yes. What if we were to buy her something to wear? She likes pretty things, she just can't afford them. And she's cute, don't you think?"

Gabriel twitched beneath his gray wool trousers. He brought his thighs closer together to hide the disturbing fact from his sister.

"Spend the money on whatever you like, but you must replace the book bag."

"Good! I'll buy her something fabulous. But I'll probably need more money . . . and we should take her somewhere special so she can show off her new clothes." Rachel batted her eyes playfully at her older brother.

Without argument or negotiation, he removed a business card from his wallet, picked up his Montblanc fountain pen, and slowly unscrewed the cap.

"Do normal people still use those kinds of pens, or just medievalists?" She leaned over inquisitively. "I'm surprised you're not using a quill."

Gabriel frowned. "This is a *Meisterstück* 149," he said, as if that should mean something.

Rachel rolled her eyes as he used his sparkling eighteen-karat gold nib to write a brief note on the back of his business card in a confident but old-fashioned hand. Her brother was beyond pretentious.

"There." He slid the business card across the counter. "I have an account at Holt Renfrew. Show this to the concierge, and he will direct you to Hilary, my personal shopper. She'll place everything on my account. Don't go completely mad, Rachel, and you can keep the cash for yourself. Happy Birthday, six months in advance."

She leaned over to press a light kiss to his cheek. "Thank you. What's Holt Renfrew?"

"The Canadian Saks Fifth Avenue—they have everything. But you must replace the book bag. That's all I care about. The rest are just . . . inconsequential details." His voice sounded gruff all of a sudden.

"Fine. But I want you to explain why you're so agitated about an L.L. Bean knapsack. All the undergrads had one. I had one, for crying out loud. Before I grew up and discovered Longchamp."

"I don't know." Gabriel removed his glasses and began rubbing his eyes.

"Hmmm. Should I add lingerie to my shopping list? Do you like her—like her?" Rachel grinned annoyingly.

He snorted. "How old are we, Rachel? Remember, she's my student. It isn't about romance—it's about penance."

"Penance?"

"Penance. For sin. My sin."

Rachel snorted. "You really are medieval. What sin have you committed against Julia? Apart from being a jackass! You don't even know her . . ."

He replaced his glasses, shifting uncomfortably in his seat. He was twitching at the mere *thought* of sin and Miss Mitchell. Together. In the same room. With him. And nothing else . . . except perhaps a pair of couture stilettos . . . which he could finally touch . . .

"Gabriel? I'm waiting."

"I don't need to confess my sins to you, Rachel. I just need to atone for them." He snatched the magazine out of her hand.

She set her teeth. "How good is your French? And your knowledge of women's fashion?"

Gabriel glanced down to find the magazine open to a photo of an airbrushed and spread-eagled model wearing a *très petite* white bikini. His eyes widened.

Rachel crossed her arms in annoyance and glared at him. "Don't bark at me. I'm not one of your students, and I'm not going to put up with your shit."

He sighed and began to rub his eyes again, minutely adjusting his glasses to do so.

"I'm sorry," he muttered, returning the magazine, but not before he gave the model one more serious look, purely for research purposes, *bien sûr.*

"Why are you wound up so tight? Are you having girl troubles? Do you even have a girl right now? When was the last time you had one? And by the way, what's with those photos in your . . ."

He interrupted her quickly. "I'm not having this conversation with you. I don't ask who you're fucking."

Rachel bit back an angry response and took a very deep breath. "I'm going to forgive you for that remark, even though it was insensitive and crass. When you're down on your knees making your penance, include the sin of envy, will you?

"You know I've only ever been with Aaron. And I think you know that what we do together goes way beyond *what you said.* What's wrong with you?"

Gabriel muttered an apology and refused to make eye contact. But his warning shot across the bow had accomplished what he wished it to, and that was to divert her attention from one of her questions. So he felt no remorse. Not really.

Rachel toyed with her brother's business card for a moment as she tried to calm down.

"If you don't like Julia, then you must feel sorry for her. Why? Is it just because she's poor?"

"I don't know." He sighed and shook his head.

"Julia brings out the protective side in people. She was always a little sad and a little lost. Although make no mistake, she has steel in her bones. She survived an alcoholic mother and a boyfriend who . . ."

Gabriel's blue eyes shifted to hers with interest. "Who?" he prompted.

"You said you didn't want to know about her personal life. It's too bad, really. If you and she weren't in a professional relationship, you might have liked her. You might have been friends."

She smiled at him, testing the waters, but Gabriel kept his eyes on the breakfast bar and began rubbing his chin absently.

Rachel drummed her fingers on the countertop. "Do you want me to tell her the briefcase and the shoes are from you?"

"Of course not! I could get fired for that. Someone will jump to the wrong conclusion, and I'll be hauled in before the judicial committee."

"I thought you were tenured."

"It doesn't matter," he muttered.

"So you want to spend all of this money on Julia, and you don't care if she knows that they gifts are from you? It's a bit like *Cyrano de Bergerac*, don't you think? I guess your French is better than I thought."

He stood up, effectively ignoring her, and walked over to the large espresso machine on one of the counters. He began the somewhat laborious process of making the perfect espresso, keeping his back to his annoying sister.

She sighed. "All right. You want to do something nice for Julia. You can call it penance, if you like, but maybe it's just kindness. And it's doubly kind, because you want to do it in secret and not embarrass her or make her feel like she owes you something. I'm impressed. Sort of."

"*I want her petals to open,*" Gabriel breathed softly.

Rachel dismissed his admission as incoherent mumbling, because she couldn't believe that he'd said what she in fact heard. It was too bizarre. "Don't you think you should treat Julia as an adult and tell her the gifts are from you? Let her make her own decision about whether she should accept them or not?"

"She wouldn't accept them if she knew they were from me. She hates me."

Rachel laughed. "Julia is not the type of girl to hate people. She's far too forgiving for that. Although if she hates you, you probably deserve it. But you're right—she doesn't accept charity. She would never let me buy things for her except on very special occasions."

"Then tell her it's for a backlog of Christmas presents from you. Or tell her it's from Grace." A meaningful look passed between the siblings.

Rachel's eyes filled with tears. "Mom was the only person Julia would accept charity from, because she thought of Mom as her mother."

Gabriel was at her side in an instant and wrapped her in his arms, trying to comfort her as best he could.

In his heart, he knew exactly what he was doing by persuading his sister to buy some pretty, girlish things for Miss Mitchell. He was paving hell with energy—buying an indulgence, forgiveness for sin. He'd never reacted this way to a woman before. But no, Gabriel wouldn't indulge himself with that line of thought. That would serve no purpose, no purpose at all.

He knew he lived in hell. He accepted it. He rarely complained. But truth be told, he desperately wished he could make his escape. Unfortunately, he had no Virgil and no Beatrice to come to his aid. His prayers went unanswered, and his plans for reform were almost always thwarted by something or other. Usually a woman wearing four-inch heels and long blond hair, who would scratch long fingernails down his back while screaming his name, over and over and over again . . .

Given his current state of affairs, the best that he could do to reform himself would be to take the old man's blood money and lavish it on a brown-eyed angel. An angel who couldn't afford an apartment with a kitchen, and who would blossom a little when her best friend gave her a pretty dress and a new pair of shoes.

Gabriel wanted to do more than buy her a briefcase, although he would never admit what he truly wanted; he wanted to make Julianne smile.

While the siblings were discussing penance, forgiveness, and ridiculous abominations of book bags, Paul was waiting for Julia just outside the entrance to Robarts Library, the largest on the campus of the University of Toronto. Although Julia could only guess at this, in the short time in which he had known her Paul had grown quite fond of her.

He was used to having lots of friends, many of them women. And he'd dated his share of both well-adjusted and troubled girls. His most recent relationship had run its course. Allison wanted to stay in Vermont, and be a schoolteacher. He wanted to move to Toronto and study to become a professor. After two years of a long-distance relationship, it was not meant to be. But there was no malice—no slashing of tires or burning of photographs. They were friends, even, and Paul was proud of that fact.

But now that Paul had met Rabbit, he began to appreciate how a relationship with someone with whom he shared common interests and common career goals could be very exciting and very fulfilling.

Paul was old-fashioned. He believed in courting a woman. He believed in taking his time. And so he was perfectly content only to build a friendship with the beautiful and shy Rabbit until he knew her well enough to express his feelings. And until he was confident of her regard for him. He was determined to spend time with her and treat her properly and pay her a lot of attention, so that if someone else came along in the meantime and tried to muscle in on him, he'd be close enough to tell that individual to *back the fuck off.*

Julia was sorry that she would miss out on shopping with Rachel, but she'd already promised Paul that she would spend the day with him at the library. She needed to get started on her thesis proposal now that Professor Emerson had agreed to be her supervisor. She felt more than a strong motivation to perform well in his class and to dazzle him with her proposal, although she knew based upon his previous behavior that she was likely to do neither.

"Hi." Paul greeted her warmly and immediately slipped her heavy knapsack off her shoulder and transferred it to his. He barely felt its weight on his massive shoulder.

Julia smiled up at him, relieved to be unburdened for a little while. "Thanks for agreeing to be my guide. The last time I was in here I got lost. I ended up in an obscure section on the fourth floor that was entirely devoted to maps." She shivered.

Paul laughed. "It's a huge library. I'll show you the Dante collection on the ninth floor and take you to my office."

He held the door open for her, and Julia floated by, feeling very much like a princess. Paul had excellent manners, and he did not use them as a weapon. Julia considered how some people, who-would-not-be-named, used manners to intimidate and to control, while others, like Paul, used them to honor and to make others feel special. Very special, indeed.

"You have an office?" she asked, as they flashed their student ID cards at the security guard who sat by the elevators.

"Sort of." He held the elevator door open, waiting for Julia to enter before he joined her. "My study carrel is next to the Dante section."

"Can I apply for a carrel?"

Paul grimaced. "They're like gold. It's almost impossible to get one, especially as an MA student."

He read the question in her eyes and hastened to add, "I think MA students are just as important as PhD students. But there aren't enough carrels to go around. The one I have isn't even mine—it's Emerson's."

If Paul hadn't allowed Julia to push the button for the ninth floor, he would have seen her skin turn slightly green and heard her sharp intake of breath. But he didn't.

Once they arrived on the ninth floor, he patiently guided her through the Dante collection, showing her both the primary and secondary sources. And he watched with delight as she trailed her hand across the spines of the books lovingly, as if she were greeting old friends.

"Julia, would you mind if I asked you a personal question?"

She stood very still, fingering a *quarto* volume that had a tattered leather binding. She inhaled its scent deeply to keep herself calm and nodded.

"Emerson asked me to pull your file from Mrs. Jenkins and—"

She turned her head to face him, eyes large and unblinking. *Oh no*, she thought.

He held his hands up to reassure her. "I didn't read it. Don't worry." He chuckled softly. "There's nothing too personal in those files anyway. Apparently, he wanted to remove something he'd put in there. But it was what he did afterward that surprised me."

Julia raised her eyebrows, waiting for him to spit it out.

"He telephoned Greg Matthews, the chair of the Department of Romance Languages and Literatures at Harvard."

She blinked slowly as she reflected on what he said. "How do you know?"

"I was dropping off some photocopying, and I overheard Emerson on the telephone. He was asking Matthews about you."

"Why would he do that?"

"That's what I wanted to ask you. He demanded to know why they didn't have generous enough funding for their MA students. He's an alumnus of that department, you know. Matthews was the chair when he completed his PhD."

Holy shit. He was checking up on me? Of course. He wouldn't believe I actually got into Harvard, just like him. Julia closed her eyes, her fingers clutching the bookshelf for support.

"I couldn't hear everything that Matthews was saying. But I heard Emerson."

She kept her eyes closed and waited for the other shoe to drop. She only hoped that Paul would drop it quickly and not directly on her toes.

"I didn't know that you got into Harvard, Julia. That's pretty amazing. Emerson asked if you'd really been accepted into their program and how highly you were ranked in their admissions pool."

"Of course," she mumbled. "I'm from a small town in Pennsylvania. I went to a Jesuit university of about seven thousand students. How could I get into Harvard?"

Paul frowned. *Poor Rabbit. That sick fucker really did a number on her. I should seriously kick his ass. And then I should go to work on him . . .*

"What's wrong with Catholic schools? I did my undergrad at St. Mike's in Vermont, and I got a great education. They had a Dante specialist in the English Department and a Florentine specialist in History."

Julia nodded as if she heard him. But she hadn't really.

"Listen, you haven't heard the whole story yet. The point is that Matthews tried to persuade him to send you back for your PhD. Said you were very highly ranked. That's pretty good, considering the source. I applied to that department and was rejected outright." He smiled somewhat half-heartedly, not knowing how she would react to that piece of information. "So if it isn't too personal, why didn't you go to Harvard?"

"I didn't want to come here," she whispered, her voice low and guilty. "I knew he was here. But I had no other choice. I have thousands of dollars in student loans from Saint Joseph's . . . I just couldn't afford to go to Harvard. I was hoping to finish my MA quickly and go to Harvard next year. If I win a larger fellowship, I won't have to borrow money for my PhD."

Paul nodded reassuringly, and as Julia distracted herself by turning around to examine the books more carefully, he regarded her, entirely oblivious to the small piece of information she had unknowingly revealed. The piece of information that told him much more than why she hadn't gone to Harvard.

As he watched her opening and closing the dusty volumes, her eyes widening and a smile playing across her lovely lips, he realized that the nickname *Rabbit* was an even better fit than he'd initially thought. For yes, she was very much like a rabbit one might find in a meadow or some such place. But she was also very much like *The Velveteen Rabbit*.

Paul would never have spoken such words aloud, and if you'd asked him if he knew the book, he would have lied while looking you straight in the eye. But Allison had loved that book, and early in their relationship she had demanded that he read it so that he could understand her properly. And Paul, all two hundred plus pounds of Vermont farm boy, had read the damn thing surreptitiously because he loved her.

Although he wouldn't admit it, he loved that story too.

In looking at Rabbit, he had the feeling that she was waiting desperately to become Real. Waiting to be loved, even. And the waiting had taken its toll on her. Not on her outward appearance, which was very attractive (although Paul would have said she was clearly too thin and too pale, something a good deal of Vermont milk and dairy products could have improved). Not that, but on her soul, which he thought was beautiful but sad.

Paul wasn't even sure he believed in souls until he met Rabbit. And now that he knew her, he had to believe. He hoped privately that some day she would become what she wanted to be, that someone would love her and she would transform from a frightened rabbit into something else. Something bolder. Something happy.

Not wanting to indulge himself in too many literary flights of fancy, Paul swiftly decided that he needed to distract Rabbit from her sorrows, and so he smiled at her again. Then he led her to a door that had a brass nameplate on it that said in very elegant cursive script: *Professor Gabriel O. Emerson, Department of Italian Studies.*

Julia noticed with interest that none of the other doors had brass nameplates on them. She also noticed that Paul had taped an index card with his own name on it underneath the nameplate. She imagined Professor Emerson coming along and ripping the card off out of spite. Then she noticed Paul's full name: *Paul V. Norris, MA.*

"What does the *V* stand for?" She crooked a finger at the homemade sign.

Paul looked uncomfortable. "I don't like using my middle name."

"I don't use mine either. And I can understand if you don't want to tell me." She smiled, turning her gaze expectantly at the locked door.

"You'll laugh."

"I doubt it. My last name is *Mitchell*. It's nothing to be proud of."

"I think it's nice."

Julia reddened but only slightly.

Paul sighed. "Promise you won't tell anyone?"

"Of course. And I'll tell you my middle name: it's Helen."

"That's beautiful too." He drew a deep breath and closed his eyes. Then he waited. When he could hold his breath no longer, and his lungs were clamoring for oxygen, he exhaled quickly. "*Virgil.*"

She stared incredulously. "Virgil?"

"Yes." He opened his eyes and studied her for a minute, worried she was going to laugh at him.

"You're studying to be a Dante specialist, and your middle name is *Virgil*? Are you kidding?"

"It's a family name. My great-grandfather was named Virgil . . . He never read Dante, trust me. He was a dairy farmer in Essex, Vermont."

Julia smiled her admiration. "I think Virgil is a beautiful name. And it's a great honor to be named after a noble poet."

"Just like it's a great honor to be named after Helen of Troy, *Julia*

Helen. And very fitting too." His eyes grew soft, and he gazed at her admiringly.

She looked away, embarrassed.

Paul cleared his throat as a means of lessening the sudden tension between them. "Emerson never uses this carrel—except to drop things off for me. But it belongs to him, and he pays for it."

"They aren't free?"

Paul shook his head and unlocked the door. "No. But they're totally worth it because they're air conditioned and heated, they have wireless internet access, and you can store books in here without checking them out at the circulation desk. So if there is anything you need—even if it's reference material that you can't check out—you can store it in here."

Julia looked at the small but comfortable space as if it were the Promised Land, her eyes wide as they wandered over the large built-in workspace, comfortable chairs and floor-to-ceiling bookshelves. A small window offered a very nice view of the downtown skyline and the CN tower. She wondered how much it would cost to live in a carrel rather than in her not-fit-for-a-dog hobbit hole.

"In fact," said Paul, clearing some papers off one of the bookshelves, "I'll give you this shelf. And you can have my extra key."

He fished around and came up with a spare key, writing a number down on a piece of paper. "That's the number on the door, in case you have trouble finding it again, and here's the key."

Julia stood, gaping. "I can't. He hates me, and he won't like this."

"Fuck him."

Her eyes widened in surprise.

"I'm sorry. I don't usually cuss—that much. At least, not in front of girls. I mean, *women.*"

She nodded, but that was not *exactly* why she was surprised.

"Emerson is never here. You can store your books, and he'll think they're mine. If you don't want him to catch you, you don't have to work in here. Just drop by when I'm around—I'm here a lot. Then if he sees you, he'll think we're working together. Or something."

He smiled sheepishly. He really wanted to *key* her—to know that she could drop by at any time. To see her things on his shelf . . . to study and to work next to her.

But Julia didn't want to be *keyed*.

"Please." He took her pale hand in his and gently opened her fingers. He felt her hesitate, and so he ran his thumb across the back of her hand just to reassure her. He pressed the key and the paper into her palm and closed her fingers, taking great care not to press too hard lest he bruise her. He knew that Emerson had bruised her enough.

"Real isn't what you are; it's something that happens. And right now, you need something good to happen to you."

Julia started at his words, for he had no idea how true they were. *Is he paraphrasing from . . . ? Impossible.*

She looked up into his eyes. They were warm and friendly. She didn't see anything calculating or crude. She didn't see anything underhanded or harsh. Maybe he truly liked her. Or maybe he simply felt sorry for her. Whatever his mysterious motivations, in that instant Julia chose to believe that the universe was not entirely dark and disappointing and that there were still vestiges of goodness and virtue, and so she accepted the key with a bowed head.

"Don't cry, little Rabbit."

Paul reached out to stroke away a tear that had not yet fallen. But he thought better of it and placed his hand at his side.

Julia turned away, ashamed of the sudden and intense rush of emotions she was having, over being *keyed* of all things, and having him cite beloved children's literature to her. As she frantically looked for something, anything, to distract herself, her eyes alighted on a CD that was sitting by its lonesome on one of the bookshelves. She picked it up. *Mozart's Requiem.*

"Do you like Mozart?" she asked, turning the jewel case over in her hand.

Paul averted his eyes.

She was surprised. She moved as if to put the CD case back, worried she had embarrassed him by going through his personal effects, but he stopped her.

"It's all right, you can look at it. But it's not mine. It's Emerson's."

Once again, Julia felt cold all over and slightly sick.

Paul saw her reaction this time and started speaking very quickly. "Don't tell anyone, but I stole it."

Her eyebrows lifted.

"I know—it's terrible. But he was playing *one track* from the damn thing over and *over* and over again in his office, while I was cataloging part of his personal library. *Lacrimosa, lacrimosa, lacri*-fuckin'-*mosa*. I couldn't take it anymore! It's so damned depressing. So I stole it from his office and hid it here. Problem solved."

Julia laughed. She closed her eyes and laughed.

He smiled with relief at her reaction.

"You didn't do a very good job of hiding it. I found it in what, thirty seconds?" She giggled and tried to hand him the CD.

He cautiously pushed her long hair back behind her shoulders so he could have an unobstructed view of her face. "Why don't you hide it at your place, instead?"

Instinctively, she stiffened and took a step backward.

Paul watched her head go down and her teeth clamp on to her lower lip. He wondered what he'd done . . . should he not have touched her? Was she worried that Emerson would find out she had his CD?

"Julia?" His voice was quiet, and he made no move toward her. "I'm sorry. Did I do something wrong?"

"No. It's nothing." She glanced at him nervously and placed the CD on the shelf. "I love Mozart's *Requiem*, and *Lacrimosa* is my favorite part. I didn't know he liked it too. I'm just . . . um . . . surprised."

"Borrow it." He placed it in her hand. "If Emerson asks, I'll say I have it. But at least if you borrow it you can upload it to your iPod and give it back to me on Monday."

Julia looked at the cd. "I don't know . . ."

"I've had it all week, and he hasn't been looking for it. Maybe his mood has shifted. He started listening to it after he got home from Philadelphia. Not sure why . . ."

Julia impulsively slid the CD into her decrepit knapsack. "Thanks."

He smiled. "Anything for you, Julia."

He wanted to hold her hand. Or at least to squeeze it for an instant. But she was skittish, he could see, and so he gave her a wide berth as he led her into the hallway so that he could continue giving her a tour of the library.

"Uh, the Toronto Film Festival is on this weekend. I have a couple of

tickets to some films on Saturday. Would you like to join me?" He tried
to sound casual as he led her to the elevators.

"What films?"

"One is French and the other is German. I prefer European films."
He smiled half-heartedly. "I could trade the tickets for something more
local . . ."

Julia shook her head. "I like European films too. As long as they're
subtitled. My French is almost nonexistent, and I only know how to
swear in German."

Paul pressed the button for the elevator and turning, gave her a very
long, very studious look. Then he grinned mischievously. "You can
swear in German? How did you come by that?"

"I lived in the International House at Saint Joseph's. One of the exchange students was from Frankfurt, and she really liked to swear—a
lot. By the end of the semester, we were all swearing in German. It was
kind of a res hall thing." She turned a light shade of pink and shuffled
her sneakers.

Julia knew that Paul was a doctoral student, which meant that he'd
already taken language courses in French and in German, in all prob-
ability. No doubt he would make fun of her amateur linguistic skills, as
Christa had after a seminar. She waited for a snide remark or a dismissive wave of the hand.

But he only smiled and held the elevator door open for her. "My
German is terrible. Maybe you can teach me to swear in it—that would
be an improvement."

Julia turned to him and smiled back. Widely this time. "Maybe.
And I'd like to go to the movies with you on Saturday. Thanks for inviting me."

"No problem."

He was pleased with himself. The lovely Julia was coming to the
Film Festival with him, and afterward, there would be dinner. He had
yet to introduce her to his favorite Indian restaurant. Or perhaps he
should do that tonight and take her to Chinatown after the double feature. Then he would take her to Greg's for homemade ice cream . . . and
invite her to accompany him to the Art Gallery of Ontario to see Frank
Gehry's architectural addition next weekend.

As they continued their tour, Paul resolved in his heart to be patient. Very, very patient. And cautious, whenever he reached out a tentative hand to offer her a carrot or to gently stroke her soft fur with his fingers. Or else he knew he would frighten Rabbit away, and he wouldn't have the opportunity to help her become Real.

⁂

The next morning Julia sat on her narrow bed with her old laptop, working on her thesis proposal and listening to Mozart. Professor Emerson's choice of music surprised her. How could he go from listening to Nine Inch Nails to *this*? Was he only listening to it because of Grace? Or was there some other reason he was torturing himself by repeating the same depressing track over and over again?

Julia closed her eyes and concentrated on the words to *Lacrimosa*, sung loudly and hauntingly by the multi-voice choir in Latin . . .

> *Day of Weeping,*
> *on which will rise from ashes guilty man for judgment.*
> *So have mercy, O Lord, on this man.*
> *Compassionate Lord Jesus, grant them rest.*
> *Amen.*

What is wrong with Gabriel that he listens to this over and over again? And what does it say about me that I can't help but feel close to him when I listen to it? All I've done is replace his photograph with his CD—I'm just not sleeping with it under my pillow.

I am one sick puppy.

Julia shook her head and tried to concentrate on her thesis proposal, distracting herself from the sound of classical weeping with thoughts of Paul and the previous day's activities.

He'd been very helpful. In addition to giving her a key to The Professor's carrel, he'd offered advice about how best to structure her thesis proposal, and he'd made her laugh more than once—more than she had laughed in a very, very long time. He was a gentleman; he opened doors and carried her ugly, heavy knapsack. He was chivalrous, and Julia could not help but like him. It was nice to be around someone who was

both handsome and sweet—an oft overlooked and frequently rare combination. She was grateful for his guidance, as well. For truly, who better than Virgil, who had shepherded Dante through the Inferno, to
guide her through her thesis proposal?

She wanted her proposal to impress Professor Emerson, to make
him realize that she was a capable student and somewhat intelligent.
Even then she knew he would likely disagree with her on both points,
no matter what Professor Greg Matthews of Harvard had said about
her. And she'd be lying if she said that she wasn't trying to subliminally
jar Emerson into remembering her.

She wondered what was worse—that Gabriel had forgotten her? Or
that Gabriel had become Professor Emerson? Julia was sickened by the
second arm of the disjunction, and so she refused to even consider it—
much. She would far rather Gabriel had forgotten her but remained the
sweet and tender man she kissed in the old orchard, than for him to
become Professor Emerson, with all of his vices, and still remember her.

Julia's thesis proposal was straightforward. She was interested in a
comparison between the courtly love manifested in the chaste relationship between Dante and Beatrice, and the passionate lust manifested
in the adulterous relationship between Paolo and Francesca, two characters Dante placed in the circle of the lustful in *The Inferno*. Julia
wanted to discuss the virtues and drawbacks of chastity, a subject she
had more than a passing interest in, and compare it with the subliminal
eroticism of *The Divine Comedy*.

As she worked on her proposal, she found herself staring back and
forth between Holiday's painting, which hung over her bed, and a postcard with the image of Rodin's sculpture *The Kiss*. Rodin had sculpted
Paolo and Francesca in such a way that their lips weren't touching; nevertheless, the sculpture was sensual and erotic, and Julia had not purchased a replica of it when she visited *Musée Rodin* in Paris because she
found it too arousing. And too heartbreaking.

She had settled for a postcard and taped it to her wall.

In addition to her *boulangerie* and *fromagerie* French, she knew
enough of the language to realize that the title of Rodin's sculpture, *Le
Baiser* in French, was part of its subversion. For *baiser* in French could
mean either the innocence of a kiss or the animalistic quality of a fuck.

One could say *le baiser* and refer to a kiss, but if one said, *Baise-moi*, one was begging to be fucked. Both innocence and begging were wrapped up in the embrace of these two lovers whose lips never touched: frozen together, yet separated for all eternity. Julia wanted to free them from their frozen embrace, and she secretly hoped her thesis would allow her to do so.

From time to time over the years, Julia had indulged herself in thinking about the old orchard behind the Clarks' house, in reliving her first kiss with Gabriel and some of what came afterward, but mostly she did so in her dreams. She rarely, if ever, thought of the morning after and its tears and hysterics. It was far too painful a memory. It was a memory of betrayal she revisited only in her nightmares . . . and unfortunately for her, that was all too often. It was the reason she had never sought him out.

Just then, her cell phone rang, interrupting her homework.

"Hey, Julia. Do you have plans tonight?" It was Rachel. Julia could hear Gabriel talking gruffly in the background.

Immediately she hit the *mute* button on her computer so that he wouldn't hear Mozart over the telephone. She waited with bated breath to see if he had heard . . .

"Julia? Are you still there?"

"Yes, I'm here."

From the sounds of Gabriel's muttering, Julia couldn't tell if he was angry or simply complaining. Not that either behavior would have surprised her.

"What's wrong? Are you okay?"

"Yes, fine. Um, no plans. No plans tonight." Julia bit her lip as a wave of relief washed over her. He hadn't heard the CD. Or so it seemed.

"Good. I want to go to a club."

"Oh, come on. You know I hate those places. I can't dance, and it's always too loud."

Rachel laughed heartily. "Funny you should say that. Gabriel said almost the same thing. Minus the dancing part. He *thinks* he can dance—he just refuses."

Julia sat up very straight on her bed. "Gabriel would come with us?"

"I have to fly home in two days. He's taking me somewhere nice for dinner, then I want to go to a club. He isn't happy about it, but he didn't say no. I thought it would be fun if you joined us after dinner. So how about it?"

Julia shut her eyes. "I'd love to, Rachel. But I don't have anything to wear. Sorry."

Rachel giggled. "Wear a little black dress. Something simple. I'm sure you own something that would work."

At that instant, the doorbell rang, interrupting the call.

"Hang on, Rachel, someone is at my door." Julia walked out into the hall, noticing a deliveryman standing outside the front door to the building.

She opened the door. "Yes?"

"Delivery for Julia Mitchell. You her?"

She nodded and signed for what turned out to be a very large rectangular parcel.

"Thanks," she mumbled, sticking the parcel under her arm and shifting her cell phone to her ear. "Rachel, you still there?"

Rachel sounded as if she was laughing. "Yes. What was that?"

"Some kind of delivery. For me."

"Well, what is it?"

"I don't know. It's a big box."

"Open it."

Julia locked her apartment door behind her and put the box on her bed. She propped her phone between her ear and her shoulder so that she could still talk while she opened the package.

"The box has a label on it—Holt Renfrew. I don't why someone would send me a present . . . Rachel, you didn't!"

Julia could hear peals of laughter over the phone.

She opened the box and found a beautiful violet-colored, single-shouldered cocktail dress with crisscross panels. Julia didn't recognize the name on the label, *Badgley Mischka*, but it was probably one of the most feminine dresses she'd ever seen.

Nestled in a shoebox next to the dress she discovered a pair of black patent leather Christian Louboutins. She looked incredulously at the red soles and the very high heels. The shoes had a pretty velvet bow on each toe, and Julia knew that they were probably worth about a month's rent, at least. Tucked into the corner of the box, almost as an after-thought, was a small beaded handbag.

Julia felt momentarily like Cinderella.

"Do you like everything? The sales clerk put it all together. I just asked to look at purple dresses." Julia could hear Rachel's hesitance over the phone.

"It's beautiful, Rachel. All of it. Wait a minute, how did you know what sizes to buy?"

"I didn't. You looked as if you were the same size as you were in col-lege, but I had to guess. So you'll have to try the dress on and see if it fits."

"But it's too much. The shoes alone . . . I just can't . . ."

"Julia, please. I'm so glad we're friends again. Apart from running into you and being able to get close to Gabriel, nothing good has happened to me since my mom got sick. Please, don't take this away from me too."

Rachel really knows how to lay on a guilt trip.

Julia inhaled slowly. "I don't know . . ."

"It's not my money. It's family money. Since Mom died . . ." Rachel trailed off, hoping that her friend would derive her own (erroneous) conclusion.

And that's exactly what Julia did. "Your mom would have wanted you to spend her money on yourself."

"She wanted everyone she loved to be happy, and that included you. And she didn't have much of a chance to spoil you after . . . after what happened. I'm sure she knows we're talking again and she's smiling down on us. Make her happy for me, Julia."

Now she felt tears pricking at the back of her eyes. And Rachel felt guilty for being so manipulative. Gabriel felt neither tears nor guilt and wished that the two girls would settle things already so that he could use his own damn telephone to make a call.

"Could I pay for part of it? Could I pay for the shoes—over time?"

Gabriel must have heard Julia, because she could hear his cursings and loud protestations in the background. He was muttering some-thing about a mouse and a church. Whatever that meant.

"Gabriel! Let me handle this," said Rachel.

Julia could hear bits and pieces of an argument that was brewing between the two siblings.

"If that's what you want, that's fine. *(Gabriel, stop it.)* But it's our last night out together, and I want you to come with us. So wear it and join us, and we'll work the money out later. Much later. Like when I'm back in Philadelphia. And living on social security."

Julia sighed deeply and offered a silent prayer of thanks to Grace, who had always been good to her. "Thanks, Rachel. I owe you one. Again."

Rachel squealed. "Gabriel! Julia is coming too!"

Julia held the phone away from her ear so she couldn't hear her friend shrieking.

"Be ready around nine—we'll pick you up at your place. Gabriel says he knows how to get there."

"That's pretty late, are you sure?"

"Please! Gabriel chose the club, and he says it doesn't even open until nine. We're going to be early as it is. Just spend some time getting ready, and we'll see you tonight. You're going to look hot!"

And with that Julia ended her phone call and began to admire her beautiful new dress. Rachel shared her mother's generous and charitable spirit. It was too bad some of that spirit hadn't rubbed off on Gabriel . . .

She wondered how she was ever going to be able to dance in those sexy and dangerous shoes. She contemplated the exciting and slightly frightening prospect of dancing with a certain Professor.

But Rachel said he doesn't dance. Figures.

In a fit of inspiration, Julia walked over to her dresser and cautiously opened her underwear drawer. Without looking at the photograph that was hidden at the back, she quickly withdrew a small and sexy string of cloth that could charitably be termed *underwear* if and only if one thought that anything worn underneath one's clothes counted as underwear.

Julia held the string in the palm of her hand (for that is how tiny it was) and meditated on it as if it were an image of the Buddha. And in a snap decision, she decided that she would wear it, hoping that like a talisman or a charm it would give her the courage and the confidence to do what she needed to do. What she wanted to do. And that was to remind Dante of how much he had lost when he abandoned her.

There was to be no more *lacrimosa* for Beatrice.

Chapter Nine

Lobby was an upscale martini bar and lounge on Bloor Street. Gabriel, in true Dantean fashion, always referred to the club as *The Vestibule*, because he deluded himself that its inhabitants resembled the virtuous pagans who spent eternity in Dante's vision of Limbo. In reality, however, Lobby and its patrons had far more in common with the various circles of Hell.

Gabriel did not want to bring Julianne there, let alone Rachel, for Lobby was his hunting ground, the place he always went to feed his hungers. Too many people knew him there, or knew of him, and he was afraid of what they might say—of what might slip unbidden from blood-red lips.

But he felt comfortable at Lobby, confident that he could control the environment. There was no way in hell he was taking Rachel and Julianne into an environment that he could not control. For this one night, he would be Beowulf instead of Dante, warrior instead of poet. He would carry his sword unsheathed in his hand, and he would slay Grendel and all of his relatives if they even *looked* in the direction of his precious charges. Although he saw the sheer hypocrisy of it, he swallowed it whole to make Rachel happy.

When Rachel and Julia dutifully followed him out of the cab and toward the front door of Lobby, they were met by a long line of people who were waiting to get into the club. Gabriel disdained the line and approached the bouncer, a large, bald African-Canadian, who wore diamonds in his ears. He shook Gabriel's hand and greeted him formally. "Mr. Emerson."

"Ethan, I'd like you to meet my sister, Rachel, and her friend Julianne." Gabriel gestured to the young women, and Ethan smiled and nodded, stepping aside to let them in.

"What was that about?" Julia whispered to Rachel as they entered a modern and tastefully decorated black-and-white space.

"Gabriel is on the VIP list, apparently. Don't ask." Rachel wrinkled her nose.

Gabriel led them to the back of the club, to an exclusive area he had reserved known as the White Lounge, imaginatively named because of its monochromatic decor. The two friends sat on a low, white banquette, lounging comfortably on the ermine-covered cushions. From their perch, they could see the dance floor that was located like a hub at the entrances to the private lounges. At the moment, no one was dancing.

Rachel gave her protégé an admiring glance. "Julia looks beautiful, doesn't she, Gabriel? Really gorgeous."

Julia blushed an abnormal shade of crimson and began fidgeting with the hem of her dress. "Rachel, please," she whispered

"What? Isn't she beautiful?" Rachel frowned over at her brother, who was shooting her a warning glance.

"You both look fine," he said, admitting nothing and shifting his legs as if he were in pain.

Julia shook her head minutely and cursed under her breath, wondering why she cared so much about his opinions and why it was so difficult for him to be nice. Next to her, Rachel shrugged. It was Gabriel's money. And if he didn't worry about throwing away almost two thousand dollars to make Julia look *fine*, who was she to object? Except that his obvious lack of enthusiasm was an indictment of her ability to elicit a reaction from him. So she rose to the challenge.

"Hey, Julia . . ." she began, making sure Gabriel was listening and watching him out of the corner of her gray eyes, "how was your date with Paul?"

Julia's skin maintained its current shade of red. "It was very nice. He's a real gentleman. Very old-fashioned."

She resisted the urge to turn to Gabriel to see if he was listening. She needn't have bothered. Rachel was doing enough watching for both of them.

"And he took you to dinner?"

"Yes. To the Nataraj, his favorite Indian restaurant. Tomorrow he's taking me to a double-feature at the Film Festival and afterward to Chinatown."

"Is he cute?"

Julia squirmed. "If a rugby player could be termed *cute*. But he's handsome and kind. He treats me like a princess."

"*Angelfucker.*"

Rachel and Julia turned to Gabriel, not quite sure they heard what they thought they heard. Julia's eyebrows went up, and frowning, she looked away.

Satisfied that she'd provoked a reaction from her brother commensurate with his most recent infraction, Rachel turned in her seat to check her makeup in the mirror behind them. She was dabbing her rose-colored Chanel-coated lips when she suddenly stopped, staring at someone who was walking in their direction.

"Gabriel, that woman is totally eye-fucking you! What the hell?"

As if in response to Rachel's exclamation, an artificially blond-haired waitress approached them immediately.

"Mr. Emerson! It's so good to see you again." The waitress leaned down, exposing the top of her moderately endowed cleavage and resting a finely manicured hand on his shoulder, her coral-colored nails gleaming in the low light.

Julia scowled in spite of herself and wondered if the waitress planned on doing something to Gabriel with those fingernails, or if she was just flashing them to scare other women away.

The woman nodded at them. "My name is Alicia, and I'll be your server."

"Start a tab for me, please. Drinks for the three of us are on me and one for Ethan and yourself, of course." Gabriel placed a folded bill in her hand, effectively freeing his shoulder from her touch.

She smiled faintly and palmed it.

"Ladies?" she asked, keeping her eyes fixed on Gabriel and smiling provocatively, the tip of her tongue just poking out between her coral-colored lips.

"A Cosmo for me," said Rachel.

Julia froze.

"What would you like?" Rachel nudged her.

"I ... don't know," Julia stammered, wondering what she could order that wouldn't embarrass her. In a place like Lobby she couldn't exactly order a beer or start doing shots of tequila, which were her usual poisons.

"Two Cosmos, then." Rachel turned back to her friend. "You'll love them—they're great."

"A double shot of Laphroaig twenty-five-year-old, neat, please. And ask the bartender for a small shot glass of spring water, non-sparkling," Gabriel instructed without making eye contact with the waitress.

The waitress left, and Rachel began to laugh. "Big brother, only you could make ordering a drink sound pretentious."

Julia giggled, if only because she liked the sight of Gabriel's irritation at his sister's characterization.

"What's Laphroaig?" she asked.

"A single malt Scotch whisky."

"And the spring water?"

"Just a drop or two to open up the taste. I'll let you try it when it arrives." He hazarded a small smile in her direction, and she turned away, looking down at her lovely shoes.

He followed her gaze and found himself entranced by her beautiful high heels. Rachel had no idea how fine a purchase they'd been. It was worth every penny just to see Miss Mitchell's lovely legs, arched and lengthened by those exquisite shoes. He shifted uncomfortably in his seat, hoping the movement would successfully dislodge his advancing arousal from its current trap.

It didn't.

"I guess you can wait for the drinks, Gabriel. Julia and I are going to dance."

Before Julia could protest, Rachel had pulled her onto the dance floor, motioned to the DJ for him to turn the music up, and proceeded to dance with enthusiasm.

Julia, on the other hand, was uncomfortable. She could see that Gabriel had moved so that he could stare at her, leaning back on the banquette and watching, eyes intense and unblinking. She wondered if he'd noticed the fact that she wasn't wearing traditional panties underneath her dress.

Is that something men notice? Panty lines?

She was unable to look away as his eyes leisurely smoothed over her from head to foot, resting longer than necessary on her shapely bare legs and her red-soled heels.

"I can't dance in these shoes," Julia protested in her friend's ear.

"Bullshit. Just move your body and let your feet take a rest. And you look great, by the way. My brother is an idiot."

Julia turned her back on her professor and began to dance, closing her eyes and letting the music take her. It was a remarkable feeling. As soon as she forgot about him and his penetrating blue eyes, she was actually able to enjoy herself. Marginally.

I wonder if he can see vestiges of my thong through the fabric of my dress. Scratch that. I hope he can see it. I hope it tortures him. Enjoy the view, Professor, because that's all you're ever going to get.

When the song ended, Rachel approached the DJ with a smile, asking what his plans were for the next few musical choices. Whatever he said must have pleased her, because she pumped a fist in the air in a very unladylike manner and almost let out a yell.

"Awesome!" she cried, crossing the floor to return to Julia, grabbing her hands and swinging her around.

Now that Julia and Rachel were dancing (and obviously enjoying themselves), a number of people from various adjoining lounges decided to join them, including a very handsome blond-haired man.

"Hi," he offered, edging in closer to Julia and moving in time to the music.

"Hi," she managed, feeling somewhat conspicuous.

She thought about that old line, about how women associate dancing with sex. This man, whoever he was, would no doubt be excellent at the latter, because he certainly very heterosexually excelled at the former. It was breathtaking, actually.

"I haven't seen you here before." He smiled.

Julia noticed he had very white teeth and that his eyes were bright blue, as blue as a cornflower. She momentarily forgot to answer him as she focused on the startling color of his eyes.

"I'm Brad. What's your name?" He leaned forward, his ear almost brushing against her lips in order to hear her response over the pulsing music.

She blinked a little at his nearness. "Julia."

"Pleased to meet you, Julia. That's a beautiful name."

She indicated that she'd heard him, and sent a desperate look to Rachel, hoping she would come to her rescue. But Rachel was too busy dancing with her eyes closed, because apparently she loved the current song.

"Can I buy you a drink? My friends and I have a table up front." He gestured vaguely, but Julia did not follow his gesture.

"Thanks, but I'm with my friend."

He smiled, undeterred, and moved closer. "Bring your friend with you. You have the most beautiful eyes. I couldn't live with myself if I let you get away and didn't ask for your number."

"Um . . . I don't know . . ."

"Let me at least give you mine."

Julia's eyes darted in Rachel's direction, which was a bad decision because it prevented her from seeing Brad move toward her. She ended up stepping right on his toes, which made him wince in pain and pushed her off balance.

He caught her before she hit the floor and held her close to his chest while she found her feet. She had to admit, he had a muscular chest, and surprisingly strong arms for someone who wore a suit.

"Easy there, beautiful. I'm sorry I cut you off like that. Are you all right?" He kept his left hand on her arm and moved his right so that he could brush the curls out of her eyes. He looked down at her and smiled.

"I'm fine. Thank you for not letting me fall."

"I'd be a fool to let you go, Julia."

She noticed obliquely that his smile was not creepy. He seemed nice, even. His suit told her that he'd come to the club after work and that he probably worked downtown for a large company—someplace where they still demanded that young men wear suits and ties. And really shiny black shoes.

He was confident, she thought, but not arrogant. And his words, though carefully chosen, did not seem calculated. He was, perhaps, the kind of person who she could imagine dating for a little while, but she doubted that they would have much in common. Certainly, dancing was not something she wanted to do again in the near future. Although dancing with him . . .

She was far too shy to extend the conversation any further. She opened her mouth to speak her regrets, but just then someone grabbed her other arm and effectively body-checked Brad out of the way. Something sent a shock wave rippling across the surface of her skin, and she knew immediately whose long, cool fingers wrapped around her bare upper arm.

"Are you all right?" Gabriel asked, speaking and looking only at Julia. His calm and concerned tone totally belied the inexplicable anger in his eyes.

His anger confused her, so she didn't answer. She looked dumbfounded, which Brad noticed immediately.

"Is this asshole hurting you?" he asked, straightening his shoulders as he scowled at Gabriel. He made a move forward, looking rather menacing.

Julia shook her head in response, still somewhat shocked.

"She's with me," snarled Gabriel, not even bothering to turn his head in Brad's direction.

He retreated slightly, for Gabriel's snarl was very fierce.

"Come," he commanded, pulling her away from the dance floor and back to their seats.

Julia gave Brad an apologetic glance over her shoulder and left willingly.

Gabriel handed her a drink as he tried to catch his breath. He was surprised at himself and his eagerness to come to Julia's rescue before he'd even considered the repercussions.

While she sipped her Cosmopolitan and tried to process what had just happened, Gabriel turned to her, clutching his now half-empty glass. "You need to be more careful. These places can be very dangerous for girls like you, and you, my dear, are a calamity waiting to happen."

She clenched her teeth. "I was fine. And he was nice!"

"He put his hands on you."

"So what? We were *dancing*, and he kept me from hitting the floor when I tripped! I didn't hear *you* asking me to dance."

Gabriel reclined against the banquette and regarded her with a slow and sinuous smile. "That would rather defeat the purpose of *watching*, don't you think?"

She tossed her hair and looked away from the Scotch-brightened sapphire of his eyes. She saw Brad trying to catch her eye from the dance floor, and she tried to indicate with her body that she and Gabriel were not together. A flash of understanding lit Brad's eyes, and he nodded, before disappearing.

"I promised you a taste." Gabriel slid closer to Julia and held his glass close to her lips.

"No." She sniffed, turning sideways.

"I insist." His voice grew more forceful.

Julia sighed and tried to take the glass out of his hand, but he held it fast.

"Let me feed you," he whispered, his tone suddenly husky.

He sounded like sex. Or at least, what Julia imagined sex would sound like if it was sitting on a white banquette with shining blue eyes and an arrogant jaw, trying to press a cold glass up to her mouth.

Oh my, Gabriel. Oh my, Gabriel. Oh my, Gabriel. Oh ... my ... Gabriel.

"I can feed myself," she breathed uncertainly.

"Of course you can. But why should you, when I'm here to do it for you?" he countered, smiling in such a way as to show his perfect teeth.

Julia didn't want to drop his precious Scotch by accident, so she allowed him to press his drink against the curve of her lower lip, which he did slowly and sensuously. She closed her eyes and momentarily fixated on the feel of the cold, smooth glass against her flesh. He tipped his drink gently, until the smoky liquid penetrated her parted lips and flowed into her open and awaiting mouth.

She was surprised that he was being so forward with her, so sensual. But she was even more surprised when the Scotch lit her mouth on fire, scorching her. She swallowed quickly.

"That's awful!" she sputtered. "It tastes like a campfire!"

He moved backward and analyzed her face. She was flushed now and animated.

"That's the peat. It's an acquired taste. You might decide it's a taste you *want* to acquire, once you've tried it a few times." He smirked at her, half of his mouth curling up.

She shook her head while she coughed. "I doubt it. And by the way, I'm a big girl, and I can take care of myself. So unless I ask for help, please leave me be."

"Nonsense." He gestured vaguely to the dance floor. "Grendel and his relatives would devour you given half a chance, and don't bother arguing with me."

"I beg your pardon! Who do you think you are?"

"Someone who recognizes naïveté and innocence when he sees it. Now sip your drink slowly like a good little girl, and stop acting like you belong in a place like this." Gabriel glared at her darkly and finished his Scotch in one swallow. *"Calamity Julianne."*

"What's that supposed to mean, 'naïveté and innocence'? Exactly what are you trying to say, Gabriel?"

"Do I need to spell it out for you?"

He grimaced and dropped his voice to a whisper, leaning toward her. Julia's eyes rolled back in her head in spite of herself as his warm breath skimmed down her naked neck.

"You blush like a teenager, Julianne. And I can sense your innocence. It's more than obvious that you're still a virgin. So stop pretending to be anything else."

"You! You—!" Julia jerked her ear away from him as she tried to think of a bad enough word in English. Sadly, she lapsed into Italian. *"Stronzo!"*

At first Gabriel looked furious, then his face softened and he laughed—a throw-your-head-back, close-your-eyes, and grasp-your-belly kind of laugh.

Julia was furious. She sat there seething, drinking her Cosmo very quickly, and wondering how it was that Gabriel knew the truth about her and from so short a reacquaintance. Surely Rachel hadn't . . . She shook her head. Rachel wouldn't. That information was personal, and she wouldn't have spoken it aloud to anyone but Aaron. And Aaron was too much of a gentleman to repeat something like that, ever.

While Gabriel grinned, Julia bemoaned the fact that he'd effectively ruined an opportunity to meet someone who looked like he was nice. Julia probably wouldn't have given Brad her number because she didn't do that sort of thing, but she wanted it to be her decision and not her Professor's. He really was a prick. And it was time he changed.

A few minutes later, their artificially blond-haired waitress came over and handed Julia a small gold box. "This is for you."

"I'm sorry, there must be some mistake. I didn't order this."

"Obviously, dear. One of the guys at the bankers' table sent it. And I was supposed to tell you that you'll be breaking a heart if you send it back." She smiled seductively at Gabriel. "Can I freshen your drink, Mr. Emerson?"

"I think we're fresh enough over here, thank you." He kept his eyes fixed on Julia, watching as she turned the small box over in her hand. In it she found a business card and a single, gold foil-wrapped truffle. On the business card, she read:

Brad Curtis, MBA
Vice-President, Capital Markets
The Bank of Montreal
55 Bloor Street West, Fifth Floor
Toronto, Ontario
Tel. 416-555-2525

She turned the card over and read the words that were written in a very confident hand:

Julia,
Sorry we got off on the wrong foot.
The chocolate reminds me of your beautiful eyes,
Brad.
Please call me: 416-555-1491

Julia turned the card over, and a smile spread across her oval face. He'd made a joke. He hadn't thought her extreme awkwardness was a reason to reject her. And he hadn't called her a *virgin* as if it were a curse word. He'd admired her eyes and thought she was attractive.

She carefully unwrapped the truffle and popped it into her mouth. *Heaven.* How did he know she loved expensive chocolates? It had to be fate. She closed her eyes and savored the intense, dark taste, licking her lips to make sure she didn't miss anything. An involuntary groan escaped her mouth.

Why couldn't I have met someone like him my freshman year at Saint Joseph's?

Meanwhile, Gabriel was gnawing through the knuckles of his right hand like a crazed animal. Once again, the sight of Miss Mitchell enjoying life's little pleasures was one of the most erotic things he'd ever witnessed. The way her eyes grew wide at the sight of the truffle, the flush that painted her pretty cheeks in anticipation of tasting it, the way she moaned with a half-open mouth, and the way her tongue darted out to pick up the traces of cocoa that clung to her ruby lips . . . it really was too much.

So of course, he had to ruin it.

"You didn't just eat that, did you?"

Julia whipped her head around. She'd forgotten Gabriel was there, enmeshed as she was in her own chocolate-induced haze of pseudo-orgasmic ecstasy.

"It was delicious."

"He could have drugged you. Don't you know not to take candy from strangers, little girl?"

"I suppose it's all right to accept *apples*, Gabriel?"

He narrowed his eyes at her *non sequitur*. He was missing something.

"And I'm not a little girl," she huffed.

"Then stop acting like one. You aren't going to keep that, are you?" He gestured to the box that was now poking out of Julia's tiny handbag.

"Why not? He seemed nice."

"You'd do that? You'd pick up a man in a bar?"

Her eyebrows knit together, and her lower lip began to tremble. "I wasn't *picking him up!* And I'm sure you've *never* picked up a woman in a bar before—and taken her home with you, which, I might add, I've *never* done. Not that it's even a shred of your business, *Professor.*"

Gabriel's face grew very red. He couldn't contradict her; he wouldn't be that hypocritical. But something about what had just transpired between Miss Mitchell and Grendel-the-blond-banker really rankled him, although he didn't know why. He quickly waved to the waitress to order another Scotch.

For her part, Julia ordered another Cosmopolitan, willing the fruity but potent mixture to help her forget the cruel but captivating man who sat achingly near to her, but whom she could never have.

When Rachel returned, collapsing in exhaustion on the banquette, Julia stood up and excused herself. She entered the back hallway in search of the ladies' room. Gabriel's arrogance and condescension truly infuriated her. He didn't want her, but now he didn't want anyone else to have her either. What was his problem?

She was so fixated on Gabriel that she didn't see a man standing in the hallway. She ran right into him, springing backward and careening dangerously toward the floor. Luckily, the man caught her.

"Thank you," she murmured, looking up into the amused face of Ethan, the bouncer.

"No problem." He released her immediately.

"I was looking for the ladies' room."

He pointed with his cell phone. "Other direction." Returning to the text he'd been composing before she ran into him, he cursed. "Damn it."

"Did I break something?"

Ethan shook his head. "No. I'm just having . . . text trouble."

Julia smiled sympathetically. "I'm sorry."

"So am I." He eyed her appraisingly. "I'm impressed. Emerson doesn't usually *arrive* with a lady."

"Why not?"

Ethan snorted. "Are you serious? Look around you. How many couples do you think arrived together?"

"Oh," she said. "Is he here a lot?"

Ethan looked at her carefully, wondering how much he should reveal. "You should probably ask him that."

She looked ill.

When he saw her expression, he tried to comfort her. "Hey, he's here with you tonight. That says something, doesn't it?"

She looked down at her hands and fidgeted with her fingernails. "Um, he isn't really *with* me. I'm just an old friend of his sister."

She looked so sad, with those big brown eyes and that trembling lower lip, Ethan tried to think of something to distract her.

"Julianne, you don't happen to speak Italian do you?"

She smiled. "Um, it's Julia, actually. And yes, I do. I'm studying Italian at university."

Ethan's expression instantly brightened. "Could you help me text something to my girlfriend? She's Italian. I'd like to impress her."

"Gabriel's Italian is better than mine. You should ask him."

Ethan shot her a look. "Are you kidding? I don't want him anywhere near my woman. I see how women react to him here. They're all over him."

Julia felt ill once again, but she pushed her revulsion aside. "Sure, I'll translate whatever you want."

Ethan handed her his phone, and she began entering his words in Italian. She giggled slightly at some of the more intimate sounding phrases, but on the whole Julia was impressed that Ethan, for all his toughness and rough edges, cared enough about his girlfriend to tell her how much he loved her and to reassure her that he was keeping the women of Lobby at bay. She was just finishing the text when someone came up behind them.

"Ahem."

Julia looked up into a familiar pair of angry blue eyes.

"Mr. Emerson," said Ethan.

"Ethan," Gabriel growled.

Julia wasn't sure her ears were working. It sounded like Gabriel had rumbled low in his chest like an animal, but that was impossible.

She pressed *send* on the phone and handed it back to Ethan. "There you are. Now we're all set."

"Thanks, Julia. I'll send a drink over to you." Ethan nodded at Gabriel and disappeared around a corner.

Julia began to walk toward the restroom.

"Where do you think you're going?" Gabriel followed her.

"To the ladies' room. What's it to you?"

He shot out his hand and grasped her wrist, grazing the pad of his thumb across the veins that were pulsating underneath her pale skin. She gasped.

He moved her until they were hidden in a long, dark corridor, pushing her against a wall. He continued to hold her wrist, drinking in the feel of her quickening pulse beneath his fingers and placing his other hand on the wall next to her shoulder. She was trapped.

Gabriel took a moment to inhale her vanilla scent and licked his lips, but his eyes were far from happy. "Why did you give him your number? He lives with a woman, you know. Now he's buying you drinks and calling you *Julia?*"

"That's my name, Professor! You're the only one who doesn't use it. And at this point, even if you wanted to use it, I wouldn't let you. I think you should have to call me *Miss Mitchell* forever. And I didn't give him my number."

"You entered your number into his phone. Do you really put yourself out there with multiple men at the same time?"

Julia shook her head, too angry to respond, and tried to duck under his elbow, but he caught her around the waist.

"Dance with me."

She snickered. "Not a chance in hell."

"Don't be so difficult."

"I'm just getting started being difficult with you, Professor."

"*Watch it.*" He sounded ominous.

Julia waited a moment for the chill his tone gave her to travel up and down her spine. "Why don't you just stick a knife into my heart and get it over with?" she whispered, looking him straight in the eye. "Haven't you hurt me enough?"

Gabriel released her immediately and reeled back. "*Julianne.*" Her name rolled off his tongue as something between a reproach and a question. His eyebrows furrowed, and he looked very upset. Not angry, but upset. Wounded, perhaps.

"Am I so evil?" His voice was low, just above a whisper.

Julia shook her head no, and her shoulders sagged.

"I have no wish to hurt you. Far from it." He looked down at her intentionally submissive posture, and his eyes quickly sought her mouth. He watched her lower lip push out slightly and tremble. Her eyes darted around anxiously.

She's frightened, you asshole. Ease up!

"You mentioned before that I hadn't asked you to dance. Well, now I'm asking." He softened his voice considerably. "Julianne, will you do me the honor of dancing with me? Please?"

He flashed a winning smile and tilted his head a little . . . a signature seductive move. But it didn't have the effect he desired, for Julia would not lift her head. He reached out to smooth his fingers gently across her wrist, as if he was trying to apologize to her skin. (Not that her skin would have accepted his apology.)

Julia clutched at her neck instinctively, suddenly feeling as if she was experiencing physical whiplash from his emotional caprice. Gabriel gazed at the hand that fluttered against her milk-white throat, and once again he saw her blue veins quiver with every heartbeat.

Like a hummingbird, he thought. *So tiny. So fragile. Be careful . . .*

She swallowed noisily and eagerly searched out an exit.

"Please," he repeated, his eyes shining in the darkness.

"I can't dance."

"You were just dancing."

"Not slow dancing. I'll step on your toes and injure you with these heels. Or I'll trip and end up on the floor, and you'll be humiliated. You're already angry with me . . ." Her lower lip began to tremble more noticeably.

He took a step closer, and she pressed herself more tightly against the wall, almost as if she was trying to disappear through it in order to escape him. He took her hand and regally lifted it to his lips. Then with a smile firmly on his face, he inched forward, leaning down and bringing his mouth to her ear. Julia's skin vibrated with his nearness and the feel of his breath across her skin.

"Julianne, how could I stay angry with someone so sweet? I promise I won't become cross or humiliated. You'll be able to dance with me." His whisper was bracing and soft, sexual and seductive, Scotch and peppermint. *"Come."*

He took her hand in his, and the same familiar spark coursed across her skin. As he waited for her to respond, he felt her still beneath his touch, and he wondered at the strange reaction she was having to him. It seemed as if his charm was actually working, even though she'd been shaking a moment before.

"Please, Professor," she breathed, fixating on his shirt front, unwilling to meet his gaze.

"I thought we were supposed to be Gabriel and Julianne tonight."

"You don't really want to dance with me. It's just the Scotch talking."

His eyebrows shot up, and he had to bite back a harsh retort. She was pushing his buttons, almost as if she knew exactly which buttons to push and when.

"One slow dance. That's all I ask."

"Why would you want to dance with a virgin?" she whispered, suddenly fascinated by the bows on her shoes.

His spine stiffened. "Not just any virgin, but *you*, Julianne I thought you might want to dance with someone who wasn't about to molest you on the dance floor and take liberties with you in front of a club full of sexually aggressive men."

She appeared skeptical but said nothing.

"I'm trying to keep the wolves at bay," he said, his voice low.

A lion in charge of wolves, she thought. *How convenient.*

He hadn't made a joke; he was looking at her seriously, his intense blue eyes boring into hers.

"One dance with me and they'll know enough to leave you alone. That should be an improvement over the current state of affairs." He smiled faintly. "If I'm very lucky, no one will bother you for the rest of the evening, and I won't have to guard my charge so closely."

She bristled at his characterization but relented, realizing that at this stage of his life he was used to getting his way—always.

It wasn't always that way, though, was it Gabriel?

"What shall we dance to?" He persuaded her to reenter the lounge, placing a hand on her lower back. "I'll request whatever you want. How about Nine Inch Nails? Maybe a little *Closer?*"

He grinned in order to indicate that he was kidding. But Julia wasn't looking at his face, she was watching the floor so she didn't trip and embarrass herself and The Professor. Nevertheless, as soon as the name of *that song* left his lips, she froze.

He nearly ran into the back of her she stopped so suddenly. Through the tips of his fingers he felt the marked coolness of her body and immediately and fiercely regretted ever suggesting that song. He moved to regard her face, and what he saw troubled him deeply.

"Julianne, look at me."

Her breathing paused.

"Please," he added.

Obediently, she raised her wide brown eyes to his and looked up at him through her long eyelashes. He saw fear and radical unease on her face, and something inside of him twisted.

"It was a joke. And in poor taste. Forgive me. I would never request that song for a dance with you. It would be the worst form of blasphemy, to expose someone like you to words like that."

Julia's eyelashes fluttered in her confusion.

"I know I've been a bit of a—*stronzo* tonight. But I'll choose something nice. I promise."

Unwilling to release her for fear she might bolt, Gabriel brought her to the DJ's booth and slipped him a bill, whispering his request. The DJ nodded and smiled, saluting Julia before he searched for the requested song.

Gabriel walked her to the dance floor and pulled her in close—but not too close. He noticed that her hands, which were so much smaller than his, had begun to sweat. It didn't occur to him that perhaps she was having this reaction because of the song he mentioned. No, his only thought was that she was completely averse to him, and he'd made matters worse by being insulting and overbearing with her when all he really wanted to do was save her from the wolves that had descended to sniff at her skirts.

Why the hell do I care? She isn't a child. She isn't even a friend.

He felt her shiver, and again he regretted being harsh with her. She was a delicate little thing and clearly quite sensitive. He shouldn't have mentioned the fact that he'd observed that she was a virgin. That was a boorish thing to do. Grace would have been appalled at his lack of gentility, and rightly so.

Perhaps he could make it up to the beautiful Julianne by dancing with her nicely and showing that he could act like a gentleman, after all. Gabriel placed his hand at the small of her back and flexed it. Immediately, he felt her breathing quicken.

"Relax," he whispered, his lips brushing against the skin of her cheek accidentally.

He brought their bodies close together, making sure that she could feel his chest against hers. Strong and hard met gentle and soft, as they brushed against one another through their clothing. Gabriel was now on his best behavior.

Julia didn't recognize the song he'd requested. The vocalist was singing in Spanish, and the words were unfamiliar, although she recognized the phrase *besame mucho* and knew that it translated as *kiss me a lot*. The arrangement itself was slow Latin jazz, and they swayed to it gently, Gabriel moving her across the dance floor like an expert. The fact that he'd chosen such an overtly romantic song made her blush.

I kissed you a lot, Gabriel, for one glorious evening. But you don't remember. I wonder if you'd remember me if I kissed you . . .

She felt his pinky graze the top of her barely there panties through her dress, and she wondered if he knew what lay beneath his finger. The thought that perhaps he did made her skin explode in heat. She hid her eyes by keeping them determinedly fixed on the buttons of his shirt.

"It would be better if you looked me in the eye. It will be easier for you to follow my lead."

She found him smiling down at her, a wide and genuine smile that she hadn't seen in years. Her heart fluttered, and she beamed back at him, dropping her guard (but not her special panties) for only an instant.

Gabriel's smile slipped. "Your face is familiar. Are you sure Rachel never introduced us during one of my visits home?"

Julia's eyes brightened with what looked like hope. "She didn't introduce us, no, but we . . ."

"I could have sworn I'd met you before." He wrinkled his forehead in confusion.

"Gabriel?" she prompted, trying to reveal the truth with her eyes.

He exhaled slowly, shaking his head. "No, I guess we haven't. But you remind me of Beatrice, from Holiday's painting. Isn't it funny that you own it?"

If Gabriel had known what to look for, or if he'd been better at reading her, he would have seen that she appeared slightly ill and any hope on her face disappeared.

She bit her lip absently. "A—friend told me about that painting. That's why I bought it."

"Your friend has good taste."

Something about her answer displeased him, but he dismissed his displeasure as derivative of the fact that she was so tense in his arms. He sighed and brought their foreheads together, his warm breath on her face. He smelled of Laphroaig and something distinctively Gabrielian and potentially dangerous.

"Julianne, I promise I won't bite. You don't have to be anxious."

She stiffened, even though she knew he was trying to put her at ease. But he'd upset her countless times, and she was fatigued by it. She was not some marionette on a string that he could toy with for his own mercurial amusement, just because some blond-haired banker sent her a truffle. It seemed that this dance was simply an opportunity for him to declare his superiority.

"I don't think this is very professional," she began, her eyes suddenly afire.

His smile slid off his face, and his eyes flashed to hers. "No, it isn't, Miss Mitchell. I'm not being professional with you, at all. I suppose it's no excuse for me to claim that I wanted to dance with the prettiest girl in the club?"

Her lovely red mouth opened slightly, then he watched her press her lips together.

"I don't believe you."

"What, that you're easily the most beautiful woman here? With all due respect to my sister? Or that I, cold-hearted bastard that I am, would want to dance with you to something sweet?"

"Don't make fun of me," she snapped.

"I'm not, *Julianne.*"

He flexed his arm across her lower spine, and she gasped because it did something to her on the inside. He knew it, of course, and had expected a reaction. What he did not know was that he'd touched her there before, that he'd been the first man to ever touch her there. And her skin had never quite recovered from his absence.

He watched her subsequent irritation with no little amusement. "When you aren't frowning at me, and your eyes are large and soft, you look very pretty. You're attractive at all times, but in those moments, you look like an angel. It's almost as if you are . . . you look like . . ."

A sudden flash of recognition passed over his face, and Julia stopped dancing.

She squeezed his hand and looked up into his eyes, willing him to remember. "What, Gabriel? Do I look like someone?"

The expression on his face vanished as quickly as it appeared, and he shook his head, smiling at her indulgently. "Just a passing fancy. Don't worry, Miss Mitchell, the dance is almost over. Then you'll be free of me."

"I only wish I could be," she mumbled.

"What's that?" He brought his forehead close to hers again.

Without thinking about how intimate the action would be, he released her hand and slowly pushed a lock of her hair aside, the backs of his fingers trailing across the skin at her neck much longer than necessary.

"You're lovely," he whispered.

"I feel like Cinderella. Rachel bought my dress and my shoes." Julia changed the subject quickly.

He withdrew his hand. "Do you really feel like Cinderella?"

She nodded.

"It takes so little to make you happy," he said, more to himself than to her. "Your dress is lovely. Rachel must have known your favorite color."

"How did you know that purple is my favorite color?"

"Your apartment is covered in it."

She grimaced in memory of his one and only visit to her hobbit hole.

He wanted to make her look at him—only at him. "Your shoes are exquisite." His eyes traveled from where the top of her head lined up with his chin and down to her feet.

She shrugged. "I'm worried I'll fall."

"I won't let you."

"Rachel is very generous."

"She is. As was Grace."

Julia nodded.

"But not me." His remark came out almost as a question, and his eyes sought hers.

"I never said that. In fact, I think that you can be very generous, when you want to."

"When I want to?"

"Yes. I was hungry, and you fed me." *Twice*, thought Julia.

"You were *hungry?*" Gabriel's voice was rough, horrified, and he stopped dancing immediately. *"You're going* hungry?" His eyes hardened into two icy blue jewels, and his voice cooled to the temperature of water gliding over a glacier.

"Not starving, Professor, just a little hungry—for steak. And apples." She glanced up at him shyly, hoping to soothe his sudden show of temper.

Gabriel was far too upset to notice the remark about apples. His very stomach was lodged in his throat as he contemplated the reality of graduate student poverty—a reality he was all too familiar with—and the poor and hungry Miss Mitchell. No wonder she was so pale and so thin.

"Tell me the truth. Do you have enough money to live on or not? I will go to the chair of my department on Monday and have him increase your fellowship if you tell me you need it. I'll give you my American Express card tonight, for God's sake. I won't have you hungry. I won't."

Julia was momentarily silent, for his reaction astonished her.

"I'm fine, Professor. I have enough money if I'm careful. My apartment makes cooking a problem, but I promise you, I'm not starving."

Gabriel slowly began dancing again, leading her gently across the floor.

He looked down at her lovely shoes. "Will you be selling those to buy groceries? Or to pay your rent?"

"Of course not! They came from Grace, sort of. I would never, ever, part with them. No matter what."

"Will you promise that if ever you are desperate for money, you'll come to me? For Grace's sake?"

Julia averted her eyes, choosing to remain silent.

He sighed and lowered his voice. "I know I don't deserve your trust, but I'm asking for it only in this one respect. Will you promise?"

She took a deep breath and held it. "Is it very important to you?"

"In the extreme. Yes."

She exhaled noisily. "Then yes, I promise."

"Thank you." He exhaled in relief.

"Rachel and Grace were always good to me, especially after my mother died."

"When did your mother die?"

"My senior year of high school. I was already living with my dad in Selinsgrove by then. She was in St. Louis."

"I'm sorry."

"Thank you." She moved her mouth as if she was going to say something further, but stopped.

"It's all right," he whispered. "You can say it." He gazed into her eyes encouragingly, and for a moment Julia forgot what she'd wanted to say. But she recovered herself.

"Um, I was just going to say that if you ever need someone to talk to—about Grace, I mean. I know Rachel is going back to Philadelphia. But I'll be here, um, obviously. Not that it would be very professional, but I'll be around. Um. Yeah, that's it."

She avoided his eyes, and he felt her whole body tense as if she was steeling herself for something awful to happen.

What have I done to this poor girl? She's terrified I'll lash out at her or something.

Gabriel knew that he deserved her wariness, and so he resolved to lavish her with kindness . . . at least until the song ended and they inhabited their professional roles once again. Then he would be distant, but gentle.

"Julianne, look at me. You know, I don't have any prohibitions against people looking me in the eye."

She glanced up at him hesitantly.

"That's a very kind offer. Thank you. I don't like to talk about certain things, but I'll keep you in mind." He smiled at her again, and this time the smile remained. "You have both charity and kindness, two of the most important of the heavenly virtues. In fact, I'm sure you have all seven."

Especially chastity, they each thought to themselves, independently. *And he thinks chastity is something to ridicule*, thought Julia.

"I haven't really danced like this before," she said wistfully.

"Then I'm glad I'm your first." He squeezed her hand warmly.

Julia froze.

"Julianne? What's wrong?"

Her eyes glazed over, and her skin grew very cold. Gabriel watched as the virulent blush that had spread across her cheeks not two minutes earlier faded completely, and her skin became a translucent white, like rice paper. She wouldn't look at him, and when he flexed his hand against her lower back, it was as if she couldn't even feel it.

When Julia came out of her trance or shock or whatever it was, he tried to get her to talk to him, but she was too shaken to do so. He had no idea what had happened, so he waved to Rachel and asked her to take Julia to the ladies' room. Then he went to the bar and ordered a double, downing it quickly before they returned.

Gabriel made an executive decision and decided it was time for them to go home. Miss Mitchell was clearly unwell, and *The Vestibule* was no place for her, even under normal circumstances. He knew that at a certain point in the evening the men would become drunk and grabby and the women would become drunk and horny. He didn't want his baby sister and the beautiful and virginal Miss Mitchell exposed to either type of behavior. So he settled his tab and asked Ethan to provide them with two taxis, with the full intention of paying the taxi driver for Miss Mitchell's cab and instructing him to wait outside her residence to see that she entered safely.

Alas for poor Gabriel, Rachel had a plan of her own.

"Good night, Julia! I'll meet you back at your place, Gabriel. Thanks for seeing her home personally!" Rachel hurled herself into one of the cabs, slamming the door behind her, and handed the cabbie a twenty so that he would peel out before Gabriel could take a single step.

He was now pissed in a very different sense, since it was obvious what his sister was trying to do. Nevertheless, she was less likely to run into some ne'er-do-well in the lobby of the Manulife Building with security on duty than Miss Mitchell was on Madison Avenue. So he couldn't fault her judgment.

Gabriel helped Julia into the cab and climbed in after her. When they stopped in front of her building, he waved her money aside and instructed the cabbie to wait for him. He escorted Julia to the front door of her building and stood in the soft porch light while she tried to find her keys.

She dropped them, of course, because she was still shaky after what happened at the club. Gabriel picked them up, trying keys in the lock until he successfully opened the door. He returned her key ring and brushed a finger across the back of her hand. Then he stood staring down at her with a funny look on his face.

Julia inhaled sharply and began to talk to his black pointed-toe shoes (which were a tad too fashionable even for Gabriel), because she could not say what needed to be said and look into his beautiful but cold eyes.

"Professor Emerson, I want to thank you for opening doors for me and for asking me to dance. I'm sure it was demeaning to have to behave that way to a student. I know that you're only tolerating me because Rachel is here, and that when she's gone everything will go back to normal. And I promise I won't say anything—to anyone. I'm really good at keeping secrets.

"I'm going to request another thesis director. I know you don't think I'm very bright, and you only changed your mind because you felt sorry for me because of my apartment. It's clear from what you said tonight that you think I'm beneath you, and that it pains you to have to talk to a stupid little virgin. Good-bye."

With a heavy heart, Julia turned to walk into the building.

Gabriel moved to block her path.

"Are you quite finished?" His voice grew very harsh.

She met his gaze, wide-eyed and trembling.

"You've delivered your speech; I believe courtesy demands that I be given an opportunity to respond to your remarks. So if you please . . ." He moved out of the doorway and stood, staring down at her with an expression of nearly concealed fury.

"I open doors for you because that is how a lady is supposed to be treated, and you are, after all, a lady, Miss Mitchell. I haven't always behaved like a gentleman, but Grace tried her best.

"As for Rachel, she's a sweet girl, but sentimental. She'd have me reciting sonnets under your window like a teenage boy. So let's leave my sister out of this, shall we?

"As for you, if Grace adopted you like she adopted me, that tells me she saw something very special in you. She had a way of healing people through her love. Unfortunately, in your case, as in mine, she probably arrived a little too late."

Julia raised her eyebrows at this last statement, wondering silently what it meant, but she did not have the courage to ask him.

"I asked you to dance because I wanted your company. Your mind is good, and your personality is charming. If you want another director, that's your prerogative. But frankly, I'm disappointed. I never thought of you as a quitter.

"If you think I do things for you out of pity, then you don't know me very well. I am a selfish and self-absorbed bastard who barely notices the concerns of other human beings. Damn your little speech, damn your low self-esteem, and damn the program." He huffed in frustration, trying hard not to raise his voice. "Your virginity is not something to be ashamed of, and it's certainly none of my business. I just wanted to make you smile and . . ."

Gabriel's voice trailed off as his hand found Julia's chin. He lifted her face gently, and their eyes met.

He found himself moving toward her, his face approaching hers, their lips inches apart. So close that she could feel his warm breath on her face.

Scotch and peppermint . . .

They both inhaled deeply, drinking in one another's scent. She closed her eyes, and her tongue darted out quickly to wet her lower lip. She waited.

"*Facilis descensus Averni,*" he whispered, his ominous and preternatural words striking her very soul. "'The descent to Hell is easy.'"

Gabriel stood up very straight, released her chin, and strode to the taxi, slamming the car door behind him.

Julia opened her eyes to see the cab pull away. She leaned against the door for support, her legs turning to jelly.

Chapter Ten

While Julia was at Lobby, there were moments when she was convinced that Gabriel remembered her. But those moments were fleeting and ethereal, and they'd disappeared like cobwebs blown away by the wind. So Julia, because she was an honest young woman, began to doubt herself.

Perhaps her first encounter with Gabriel had been a dream. Perhaps she'd fallen in love with his photograph and imagined the events that occurred after Rachel and Aaron fled. Perhaps she had fallen asleep in the orchard alone, the sad recipient of the desperate and lonely illusion of a young girl from a broken home who had never felt loved before.

It was possible.

When everyone in the whole world believes one thing and you are the only one who believes differently, it's very tempting to assimilate. All Julia would have to do would be to forget, to deny, to suppress. Then she would be just like everyone else.

But Julia was stronger than that. No, she had not been prepared to call Gabriel out publicly about exposing her virginity, for that would be to draw too much attention to a fact that she was partially ashamed of. And no, she was unwilling to force him to acknowledge her or the night they shared together, for Julia had a fairly pure heart, and she did not like to force anyone to do anything.

When she saw the confusion on Gabriel's face while they were dancing and realized that his mind wouldn't allow him to remember, she withdrew. She was worried what a sudden strong realization might do to him, and fearful that his mind might shatter like Grace's glass coffee table, she chose to do nothing.

Julia was a good person. And sometimes goodness doesn't tell everything it knows. Sometimes goodness waits for the appropriate time and does the best it can with what it has.

Professor Emerson was not the man that she'd fallen in love with in the orchard. In fact, Julia concluded that there was something seriously wrong with The Professor. He was not just dark or depressed, but *disturbed*. And she worried that he had alcoholic tendencies, familiar as she was with the alcoholism of her mother. But because she was good, she would not break him the way she had been broken, by forcing him to look at something he did not want to see.

She would have done anything for Gabriel, the man she spent the night with in the woods, if he'd given her even a single indication that he wanted her. She would have descended to Hell and searched for him, looking until she found him. She would have stormed the gates and dragged him back. She would have been Sam to his Frodo and followed him into the bowels of Mount Doom.

But he was not her Gabriel. Her Gabriel was dead. Gone. Leaving behind only vestiges of him in the body of a harsh and tortured clone. Gabriel had almost broken Julia's heart once. She was determined she would not let him break her heart for the second time.

Before Rachel left Toronto to return to Aaron and the dystopia that was her family, she insisted on seeing Julia's studio apartment. Julia had been putting her off for days, and Gabriel himself had discouraged his sister from simply showing up unannounced. He knew that as soon as she saw where her friend was living she'd pack Julia up personally and force her to move into a nicer place, preferably Gabriel's guest room.

(One can only imagine Gabriel's reaction to that suggestion, but it ran along the lines of *no fucking way*.)

So on Sunday afternoon, Rachel arrived on Julia's doorstep in order to have tea and say her good-byes before Gabriel took her to the airport.

Julia was nervous. She had the cardinal virtue of fortitude, like a stubborn medieval saint, and so she was unlikely to mind various discomforts or slights. Consequently, she hadn't thought her little hobbit hole was really that bad when she signed the lease. It was safe, and it was clean, and she could afford it. But believing that and showing her apartment to Rachel were two different things.

"I need to warn you that it's small. But remember, I'm living on a grad student's income and it's fixed. I can't get a job up here because I don't have a work permit. And I can't afford to live in Gabriel's building or anywhere even half as nice," Julia explained as she ushered her friend into her apartment. Rachel nodded and placed a large square box on the bed.

Gabriel had warned her how tiny the apartment was. He'd told her not to make a scene, for Gabriel still nursed a secret regret over his appalling behavior during his one and only visit to Julia's apartment.

But still, nothing her brother or her friend told her quite prepared Rachel for what she saw behind Julia's closed door. The space was small, old, and everything in it was second-hand or cheap, apart from the simple curtains, bedding, and anything Julia had brought with her from home. To her credit, Rachel walked through the studio first, which only took about five steps, and looked at the closet, inspected the bathroom, and stood in the kitchen "area" looking at a pathetic little hot plate and an old decrepit microwave. Then she put her hands over her face and burst into tears.

Julia stood rooted to the spot, not quite knowing what to do. Rachel was disturbed by ugliness, she knew, but Julia had tried to make her studio pretty and had used her favorite shades of purple to do so. Surely Rachel could appreciate that.

Rachel came to herself a few moments later, wiping her tears and giggling.

"I'm sorry. It's hormones and lack of sleep, and I've been emotional because of Mom. Then there's everything with my dad, and Aaron, and the wedding. Oh, Julia, I just wish I could take you home with me and you could live with us in Philadelphia. We have so much space. And our kitchen is bigger than your entire apartment!"

Julia hugged her friend tightly until she cracked a smile.

"Gabriel said you're very particular about your tea. He was impressed with how you made it. And you know *nothing* ever impresses him. So I'm going to curl up on your lovely lilac bed and learn how you do it." Rachel plopped herself down on top of Julia's comforter, holding the large square box on her lap and trying to be cheerful for the sake of her friend.

Julia was surprised that Gabriel even remembered the tea since he'd been so busy criticizing her eating habits during his visit. But she pushed such thoughts aside and focused her attention on making Rachel feel at home and helping her forget her troubles. Soon they were both perched on her bed, holding their china teacups and nibbling on chocolate truffles that Julia had purchased as a celebratory treat with part of her emergency fund.

Rachel traced the rim of her cup with a single finger. "There's something I need to tell you about Gabriel."

"I don't want to hear it."

Rachel looked over at Julia and frowned. "Why not?"

"Because he's my professor. It's—safer if we pretend not to know each other. Trust me."

Rachel shook her head. "He said something similar to me, you know. But I'm going to tell you what I told him, *I don't care*. He's my brother, and I love him. And there are a few things you should know."

Julia sighed in acquiescence.

"He'd kill me if he knew that I was telling you this, but I think it will make his attitude easier to understand. Did Mom ever tell you how she came to adopt him?"

"She only talked about happy things: how proud she was of him, how well he did at Princeton and Oxford. She never talked about his childhood."

"Mom found him when he was nine years old, wandering around the hospital in Sunbury. He'd been traveling with his mother, who was a crazy alcoholic, and she got sick. They ended up in Sunbury, and his mother died, of pneumonia I think. Anyway, Mom found Gabriel, and he didn't have a dollar to his name. He couldn't even buy a drink from the vending machine. She was even more upset when she tracked down his mother's relatives and they told her to keep him. He knew that his family didn't want him. And despite everything my parents did, I don't think he ever felt at home with us. He never became a Clark."

Julia thought of Gabriel as a scared and hungry little boy and fought back tears. She imagined his eyes, large and blue in his pale but angelic face. His shock of brown hair spiked and unruly. Dirty clothes and a crazy mother. Julia knew what it was like to have an alcoholic mother. She knew what it was like to cry herself to sleep at night wishing someone, anyone, would love her. She and Gabriel had more in common than she cared to admit. Much, much more.

"I'm sorry, Rachel. I didn't know."

"I'm not excusing his rudeness. I'm just telling you who he is. Did you know that after his horrible fight with Scott, Mom lit a candle every night and placed it in one of the windows? She thought that if Gabriel happened to be in Selinsgrove and saw the candle, he would know that she was waiting for him, that she loved him, and he'd walk up the front steps and come in."

Julia shook her head. She hadn't known that, but she believed it. That's just who Grace was—charity unbound.

"He pretends to be whole, but he's been broken. And deep down, he hates himself. I told him to treat you nicely, so I think his behavior will improve. Let me know if it doesn't and I'll deal with him."

Julia snorted. "He ignores me, mostly. I'm a lowly grad student, and he doesn't let me forget it."

"I find that difficult to believe. I doubt very much that he would stare so intensely at a 'lowly' grad student."

Julia busied herself with her chocolate. "He stares at me?" She was trying very hard to sound relaxed, but her voice sounded unnatural, shaky even.

"He stares at you all the time. Haven't you noticed? I caught him looking at you over dinner the other night and when we were at the club. Every time you took a drink, actually. And when I winked at him, he scowled." Rachel looked at her friend thoughtfully. "I see the two of you together, and I feel like I'm missing something . . . He knew that I was going shopping this week, and he not only encouraged me, he gave me money."

"So? That's nice. That's what big brothers are for. What did you buy?"

"The money was for you, not me."

Julia frowned and turned sideways on the bed, cross-legged, so that she could face her friend. "Why the hell would he do that?"

"You tell me." Rachel cocked her head to one side.

"I don't know. He's been rude to me since I got here."

"Well, he gave me some money and told me to buy you a gift. He was very specific. So here it is." Rachel placed the box in Julia's lap.

"I don't want it." She tried to hand it back, but Rachel refused.

"At least open it and see what it is."

Julia shook her head, but Rachel insisted. So she opened the box. In it she found a very nice chocolate-brown, Italian-made leather messenger bag. She held the bag up by its strap and looked at it. The label said *Fendi.*

Holy crap, thought Julia.

"Well? What do you think?"

"I don't—know," she stammered, staring at the beautiful and classic bag in astonishment.

Rachel took it from her and began rummaging through it, muttering about its internal stitching, numerous compartments, and overall quality workmanship. "See how perfect it is? It's functional and feminine, since it's a messenger bag and not a briefcase, and it's Italian. And we both know that you and Gabriel have a thing . . . for Italy," she added, after a pause that was designed to elicit some kind of reaction.

Julia's telltale flush and immediate nervousness told Rachel all she needed to know, but she chose not to embarrass her friend any further. "I'm not supposed to tell you it's from him. He was very explicit. Of course, I ignored him." She chuckled.

"Your brother wants me to have this because he doesn't like looking at my ratty old knapsack. Its very existence offends his patrician sensibilities, so he thinks he can use you to persuade me to get rid of it. But I'm not going to. It's an L.L. Bean, damn it, and they offer a lifetime guarantee. I'll send it back to Maine, and they'll replace it. He can take his messenger bag and shove it up his I'm-too-good-for-domestic-items ass."

Rachel was stunned momentarily. "It's not as if he'll miss the money. He has piles of it."

"Professors don't make that much money."

"That's right. He inherited it."

"From Grace?"

"No, from his biological father. A number of years ago a lawyer tracked Gabriel down and told him his father had died and left him a lot of money. I'm not sure he even knew his father's name before that. Gabriel refused the inheritance at first, but later changed his mind."

"Why?"

"I don't know. It was after his fight with Scott. I didn't talk to Gabriel after that for a very long time. But as far as the money is concerned, I think he's trying to spend it faster than it accumulates interest. So don't think of this as a gift from Gabriel—think of it as him sticking it to his old man. He *wants* to give money away. And he wants you to have something nice. He told me so."

Julia shook her head. "I can't accept it. I don't care where it came from or why."

Rachel gave her friend a pained look. "Please, Julia. Gabriel has been on the outs with all of us for so long. He's finally letting me back into his life. I don't think I can lose him now after everything . . ." Her face crumpled, and she looked very upset.

"I'm sorry, but it's too much. He's my professor—he'll get in trouble!"

Rachel clutched Julia's hand. "Will you tell on him?"

"Of course not."

"Good, because you're supposed to think this is a belated birthday gift from me or Mom." Rachel's eyes widened as she realized her mistake. "Oh God, Julia, your birthday. I forgot. I'm so sorry."

Julia clenched her teeth a little. "I don't really celebrate it anymore. It's just too hard . . . I can't . . ."

"Do you ever hear from *him?*"

Julia immediately felt ill. "Only when *he's* drunk or pissed off about something. But I changed my cell phone number when I moved here so he couldn't call me."

"Bastard," said Rachel. "Well, I wasn't supposed to tell you the messenger bag was from Gabriel, but I just couldn't lie to you. I know how much it hurts you when people lie, and I wasn't going to do that."

The two friends exchanged a meaningful look. Julia contemplated this one gift from Gabriel and all of its implications, spoken and unspoken. She didn't want to receive a gift from him. He'd rejected her, plain and simple. Could she have this bag in her little hobbit hole? Could she use it, carry it to school, knowing all the while that it was from him? Knowing that he'd be staring at her smugly, thinking that he'd done her some kind of service? Not for Gabriel. Not for all the tea in China.

Rachel saw what Julia was about to do even before the words had formed in the back of her mind. "If you don't accept the bag, he'll know something went wrong. He'll blame me, instead."

Julia silently cursed him. *Oh gods of all pretentious pole-in-keister Dante specialists, send him a rash on* il pene. *Please. Something extra itchy.*

But for Rachel, Julia would do anything. "Fine. I'll do this for you. But will you please tell Gabriel not to buy me any more stuff? I'm starting to feel like one of those kids on the UNICEF box at Halloween."

Rachel gave her friend a nod and a smile and bit into a chocolate. She licked the cocoa from her lips and closed her eyes. It was good.

Julia hugged the briefcase to her chest, like a shield, and inhaled the lovely leather scent. *Gabriel wanted me to have a present. He must feel something for me, even if it's only pity. And now I have something of his besides a photograph . . . something I'll own forever.*

She waited a moment before delicately changing the subject. "Will you tell me what happened at the funeral? I sent a card with some flowers, and Gabriel saw them, but he had no idea why I sent them."

"I heard about that. I saw the gardenias, and Scott said they were from you, but the card disappeared before I had a chance to explain it to Gabriel. I was a wreck. My brothers were fighting, and I was trying to keep them away from each other before someone went through a window. Or a coffee table."

Julia thought of shattered glass and blood on a white carpet, and she shivered. "Why are they always fighting?"

Rachel sighed. "It never used to be that way. Gabriel changed when he went to Harvard . . ." Her voice trailed off mysteriously.

Julia didn't feel comfortable pressing her, so she kept silent.

"As you know, Gabriel didn't come home again for years after his fight with Scott, and when he did, he would only stay a few days. He insisted on sleeping at a hotel, and that broke Mom's heart. Scott won't let Gabriel forget it—all the stuff he put Mom through." Rachel chewed another truffle thoughtfully.

"Scott looked up to Gabriel. It really hurt him when things went sour. Now they barely speak to one another, and when they do . . ." She shuddered. "I don't know what I would have done without Aaron. I'd probably have run away and never come back."

"Even a dysfunctional family is better than no family at all," Julia said softly.

Rachel looked sad. "Well, that's what we are now. We were the Clarks—now we are a *dysfunctional family*. A dead mother, a grief-stricken father, a hotheaded black sheep, and a pig-headed brother called Scott. I guess I'm the partridge in the pear tree."

"Does Scott have a girlfriend?"

"He was dating a woman in his office, but they broke up right before Mom got sick."

"I'm sorry."

Rachel sighed. "My family is like a Dickensian novel, Julia. No, it's worse. We're a twisted mix of Arthur Miller and John Steinbeck, with a bit of Dostoyevsky and Tolstoy thrown in."

"Is it really that bad?"

"Yes, because I have the feeling there are elements of Thomas Hardy lurking below the surface. And you know how much I hate him. Mind-fucking bastard."

Julia thought about this and hoped for her friend's sake that the Hardy novel approximating the Rachel Clark experience was more *Mayor of Casterbridge* than *Tess of the D'Urbervilles* or, God forbid, *Jude the Obscure*.

(Unfortunately, Julia did not pause to consider which Hardy novel best described her own experiences . . .)

"With Mom gone, everything is in upheaval. Dad is talking about retiring and selling the house. He wants to move to Philadelphia to be closer to me and to Scott. When he asked Gabriel if he minded if he sold the house, Gabriel flipped out and wandered off into the woods. We didn't see him again for hours."

Julia inhaled sharply and began to fidget with her messenger bag.

Rachel was too busy placing her teacup on the card table and walking to the bathroom to notice, but something she said had upset Julia deeply. By the time Rachel returned, Julia had calmed herself through no little effort and was adding hot water to the teapot.

Rachel fixed her friend with a concerned look. "What did Gabriel say that bothered you so much when you were dancing with him? And by the way, my Spanish is rusty but *Besame Mucho* is a pretty hot song! Did you even listen to the lyrics?"

Julia focused her attention on her tea and tried very hard not to hyperventilate. She knew she was going to have to lie to Rachel, and it was not a decision she took lightly. "All we talked about is the fact that he knew I was a virgin."

"Bastard! Why the hell does he do things like that?" Rachel shook her head. "You just wait, I'll get him. He has these photos in his bedroom, and I'm going to . . ."

"Don't bother. It's true. Why should I try to hide it?" She bit her lip. "I just can't figure out how he knew. It's not as if I bring it up in polite conversation: *Good afternoon, Professor Emerson. My name is Miss Mitchell, and I'm a virgin from Selinsgrove, Pennsylvania. Pleased to meet you.*"

Rachel waved her hand dismissively. "Think about it. He's never exactly been in want of female companionship. I'm sure you seem different to him; you were probably the only girl at the club, apart from me, who wasn't in heat."

Julia looked disgusted, and rightly so, but didn't comment.

"When you came off the dance floor you looked as if you'd seen a ghost. Like how I imagined you would have looked the night you saw Si—"

"Please, Rachel. Don't. I can't talk about that night. I can't even think about it."

"I could run him over with my car for what *he* did to you. I still might do that. Is *he* in Philadelphia? Give me his address."

"Please," Julia begged, hugging her arms protectively across her chest.

Rachel pulled her friend into a warm embrace. "Don't you worry. You're going to be happy someday. You're going to fall in love with a beautiful boy, and he's going to love you back so much it will hurt. And you're going to get married and have a baby girl and live happily ever after. In New England, I think. At least, that's the story I'd write for you, if I could."

"I hope your story comes true. I'd like to believe something like that is possible, even for me. Otherwise, I just don't know . . ."

Rachel smiled. "You, of all people, deserve a happy ending. Despite everything that happened to you, you aren't bitter. You aren't cold. You've just retreated a little and been shy, and that's okay. If I were a fairy godmother, I would give you your heart's desire in an instant. And I would wipe away your tears and tell you not to cry. I wish Gabriel had taken a page from your book, Miss Julia. He could have learned a thing or two from you about how to deal with heartbreak."

Rachel released her friend, looking at her closely before she spoke again. "I know that it's a lot to ask, but will you look out for Gabriel?"

Julia leaned over the teapot on purpose, refilling their cups so that Rachel couldn't see her face. "Gabriel has nothing but contempt for me. He's merely tolerating me for your sake."

"That's not true. Believe me, that is simply not true. I've seen how he looks at you. He can be . . . cold. But apart from his biological parents, I don't think he's ever hated anyone, other than himself. Not even Scott during their worst fight."

Julia shrugged. "There's nothing I can do."

"I'm not asking you to do anything, really. Just keep your eyes open. And if you see him . . . starting to act strangely, or if he's in trouble, I want you to call me. Day or night."

Julia wore an incredulous expression.

"I'm serious, Julia. With Mom gone, I'm worried that his darkness is going to return. And I can't lose him again. Sometimes I feel as if he's standing on the edge of a very high cliff, and the slightest movement, the slightest breath of wind, will push him over the edge. I can't let that happen."

Julia's eyebrows knitted together, and she nodded. "All I can do, I will do."

Rachel closed her eyes and exhaled. "I feel so much better knowing that you're around. You can be his guardian angel." She laughed softly. "Maybe some of your good luck will rub off on him."

"I have nothing but bad luck, and you, of all people, should know it."

"You've met Paul. He sounds nice."

Julia smiled.

Rachel was pleased by her friend's smile. "Paul doesn't seem to be the type who'd mind if you were a—*you know*. Not that there's anything wrong with that."

Julia laughed. "You can say it, Rachel—it's not a curse word. And no, I don't think Paul would mind that I'm a virgin. But we don't talk about such things."

Shortly thereafter, Rachel hugged Julia good-bye and climbed into a cab so that she could return to her brother's apartment.

"When I finally work through the monumental pile of issues that I have to deal with, I'm planning a wedding. And I'm expecting you to be my maid of honor."

Julia felt tears form at the corners of her eyes. "Of course. Just name the date. And I'll help you plan it too, if you need some help."

Rachel blew her a kiss out the open window. "I was dreading this trip, but I'm so happy I came. At least two broken pieces of my life are coming back together. And if Gabriel gives you any shit, any shit at all, you call me, and I'll hop a plane!"

With Rachel's departure, Julia and Gabriel were forced to part company with their solid and secure St. Lucy. But in true saint-like fashion, she had accomplished all of her tasks before she returned home, and she had planted seeds that would soon blossom, in unexpected ways.

Chapter Eleven

L ate Tuesday afternoon, Julia and Paul sat in the Bloor Street Star-bucks enjoying their respective coffee drinks, curled up together on a purple velvet loveseat and talking. They were sitting close but not too close. Close enough that Paul could admire her beauty, far enough away that Julia could watch his large, kind eyes and not feel overly nervous. Or crowded.

"Do you like Nine Inch Nails?" she asked, cupping her coffee in two hands.

Paul was taken aback by her question. "Uh, no. No, I don't." He shrugged. "Trent Reznor twists my head around. Unless he's singing backup for Tori Amos. Why, do you?"

Julia shivered. "Absolutely not."

He pulled a CD out of his briefcase and handed it to her. "I like this kind of stuff. Music I can write my dissertation to."

"I've never heard of Hem before," she mused, turning the jewel case over in her hand.

"They have a song I think you'll like. It's called *Half Acre*. They used to play it on an insurance ad on television, so you might have heard it before. It's beautiful. And no one yells at you or screams or tells you he wants to fu—" Paul stopped suddenly and reddened. He was trying very hard to watch his language around her but having only marginal success.

She tried to hand the CD back to him, but he refused. "I bought it for you. *Rabbit Songs* for the Rabbit."

"Thanks, but I can't."

He seemed offended. And hurt. "Why not?"

"I just can't. But thank you anyway."

Paul looked down at Julia's new messenger bag, resting at her feet. He squinted.

"You accepted a nice briefcase from someone. Early Christmas present from a boyfriend?"

"I don't have a boyfriend," she admitted uncomfortably. "My best friend's mother wanted me to have the briefcase. She passed away recently."

"I'm so sorry, Rabbit. I didn't know."

Paul reached over and patted Julia's hand, placing the CD on the loveseat between them. He noticed that she didn't move away. In fact, she rummaged in her bag to find Professor Emerson's CD and returned it to Paul with her other hand, while still allowing him to cradle her fingers in his own.

"What can I do to persuade you to accept my gift?" He hid his face from her as he placed Emerson's Mozart in his book bag.

"Nothing. I've received too many gifts in the last little while. I'm all stocked up."

Paul straightened up and smiled. "Let me try to convince you, then. You have such small, small hands. Smaller than the rain's." He moved their hands together, back and forth, holding her hand up toward the halogen light. It looked diminutive encased in his.

Julia looked at him curiously. "That's pretty. Did you just make it up?"

Paul leaned his head back against the loveseat and held her hand more closely, his thumb fingering her lifeline, almost as if he were trying to read her palm with the tips of his fingers.

"No. I'm paraphrasing from *somewhere i have never travelled*, by E. E. Cummings. You haven't heard it before?"

"No, but I'd like to." Julia sounded very shy all of a sudden.

"Then I'll have to read it to you some time." Paul gazed into her dark eyes with a hopeful smile.

"I'd like that."

"It isn't Dante, but it's beautiful." His thumb found the center of her lifeline and pressed it ever so gently. "The poem reminds me of you. You are where I've never traveled: your fragility and your small, small hands."

Julia leaned forward to hide her sudden flush of color and sipped her coffee. But she allowed him to continue caressing her palm, sweetly. The movement of her coffee to her lips caused her ancient purple sweater to slip off her shoulder somewhat provocatively, revealing about two inches of a white-cotton bra strap and a rounded curve of alabaster skin.

Paul immediately released her hand and gently pulled the sweater to cover the innocent-looking strap, averting his eyes as he did so and pressing his hand to her shoulder in order to make the sweater stay.

"There," he said softly. "All better now." Then he retreated ever so quickly so as not to overstay his welcome, tentatively curling his fingers over hers again, still worried she might withdraw at any moment.

Julia watched what he was doing breathlessly, as if it occurred in slow motion. Something about his movement touched her deeply. It was an intimate act but very chaste; he *covered* her. He covered the smallest most innocent part of her, away from prying and possibly lecherous eyes, and in so doing telegraphed his regard and his respect. Virgil was honoring her.

In that one act, that one gallant and chivalrous act, Paul had made his way into her heart. Not all the way, but to the Vestibule, so to speak. If his movement represented the contents of his soul, then Julia believed that he would not mind that she was a virgin, and that upon knowing, his acceptance would cover her gently.

He would not ridicule or expose her. He would keep whatever secrets she held between the two of them alone. He would not treat her like an animal to be fucked and violated. He would not wish to share her.

So she did something impetuous—she leaned over and kissed him, but shyly and chastely. There was no rush of blood, no humming, no explosion of fire across her skin. His lips were soft, and he responded hesitantly. Julia felt his surprise in the quick clenching of his jaw. He tensed beneath her lips, no doubt in shock at her boldness. She was sorry for that.

She was sorry his lips were not Gabriel's. And this kiss was not like those.

In almost half a heartbeat, a great wave of sadness washed over her as she cursed herself for having tasted of something long ago that she could never have after or again. For in partaking of that first taste, she was absolutely ruined. The tasting of the apple was knowledge itself, and now she knew.

Julia pulled back before Paul had a chance to reject her, wondering how she'd managed to be so forward. Wondering what he would think of her now. *I've just kissed my only Toronto friend good-bye*, she thought. *Damn it.*

"Little Rabbit." Paul gave her a tender look and immediately brought his fingertips up to caress her cheek. His touch wasn't electric, but it was light and soothing. Even his skin was kind.

He put his arms around her and drew her against his chest so he could stroke her hair and whisper something sweet in her ear . . . something to reassure her . . . something to remove the mixture of confusion and pain he read on her face. His soft whisperings were interrupted by the arrival of a great-winged harpy, wearing four-inch heels and crimson lipstick and carrying two paper cups.

"Well, isn't this cozy." A voice, cold and steely, interrupted the couple's soft moment, and Julia looked up into the harsh brown eyes of Christa Peterson.

Julia sat up quickly and tried to move away from Paul, but he held her fast. "Christa," he greeted her flatly.

"Slumming with MA students, Paul? How very democratic of you," she said, ignoring Julia pointedly.

"Be careful, Christa." His tone held a warning. "Two fisted, today? That's a bit much. Pulling an all-nighter?" He pointed to the cups she was holding, one in each hand.

"You have no idea," she purred. "One is for me and one for Gabriel, of course. Oh, I'm sorry, I didn't see you there, Julianne. I guess he's still *Professor Emerson* to you." Christa cackled like an old chicken.

Julia raised an eyebrow but resisted the urge to set Christa straight or to smack that smug smile off her face. For Julia was a lady. And she liked how Paul's arm felt about her shoulders and was unwilling to move. At least, not yet.

"You've never called him *Gabriel* to his face, Christa. I dare you to do it the next time you see him."

Christa's eyes hardened, and she glared at Paul. Then she smiled. *"You dare me?* That's funny. Is that a Vermont thing? Something farmers say to one another when they're shoveling manure? After my meeting with Gabriel, we'll probably head over to Lobby for drinks. He likes to go there after work. I'm sure we'll be exchanging more than, ah . . . *names* this evening." Her tongue peeked out from between her lips, and she began licking the curve of one of them languorously.

Julia heaved.

"And he'll take you there?" Paul appeared skeptical.

"He will. Oh, he will."

Julia gagged and silently swallowed back her stomach contents. For the thought of Gabriel with this . . . *Emerson whore* was nauseating in the extreme. Even the waitress at Lobby would be better for him than Christa.

"You're not his type," Julia muttered.

"Pardon?"

She looked up into narrowed and suspicious eyes, and she weighed her options for the slimmest of seconds. And decided caution was the better part of valor.

"I said—*don't believe the hype."*

"About what?"

"About Lobby. It's not that great."

Christa shot Julia a frosty smile. "As if the doorman would let you in. Lobby is an exclusive club."

She looked Julia up and down as if she were a less-than-prized animal. As if she were an old, half-blind, forgotten pony at a petting zoo. Julia suddenly felt very self-conscious and ugly. Tears pricked at her eyes, but she fought them back bravely.

Paul noticed exactly what Miss Peterson was doing in measuring Julia and finding her wanting. He felt her shiver in reaction to Christa's feline claw sharpening. So although it pained him to do so, he released Julia's shoulders and sat forward on the loveseat, flexing his arms.

Don't make me stand up, bitch, he thought.

"Why wouldn't they let Julia in, Christa? They only admit working girls now?"

Christa turned very red. "What would you know about it, Paul?

You're practically a monk! Or perhaps that's what monks do—they pay for it." She shot a meaningful glance at Julia's precious new messenger bag.

"Christa, you're going to shut your mouth right now, or I'm going to stand up. And then all chivalry goes out the window." Paul glared at her and silently reminded himself that he could not strike a woman. And that Christa was, in fact, a woman, and not an anorexic sow in heat. Paul would never have compared Christa to a cow, for he thought cows were noble creatures. (Especially Holsteins.)

"Don't get your panties in a twist," she snapped. "I'm sure there are multiple explanations. Maybe Lobby wouldn't let her in because of her IQ. Gabriel says you're not that bright, Julianne."

Christa smiled triumphantly as Julia ducked her head, feeling very small indeed. Paul shifted his weight to the soles of his feet. He wasn't going to hit Christa; he was simply going to shut her up. And maybe drag her to the exit or something. He needn't have bothered.

"Oh, really? And what else does *Gabriel* say?"

The three graduate students turned slowly *en masse* to look up at the blue-eyed Dante specialist who had sidled up to them silently. None of them were exactly sure how much he'd heard or how long he'd been standing there. But his eyes sparked, and Julia could feel his anger radiating toward Christa. It billowed like a cloud. But thankfully, it did not billow in her direction. This time.

By the pricking of my thumbs, something wicked this way comes, thought Paul.

"Paul." Gabriel nodded coolly, his eyes flickering to the now noticeable space in between Julianne and his research assistant. *The Angelfucker. That's right—hands off the angel, asshole.*

"Miss Mitchell, how nice to see you again." Gabriel smiled somewhat stiffly. "You're looking *smart*, as always."

Yes, brown-eyed angel, I heard what she said to you. Don't worry, I'll fix her.

"Miss Peterson." Now Gabriel's voice was cold, and he gestured to her to follow him as if she were a dog. *You looked at Julianne as if she were trash. You won't be doing that again. I'll make sure of it.*

Julia watched as he refused the coffee Christa bought for him and walked to the counter to order something else. She saw Christa's shoulders trembling with rage.

Paul turned to Julia and sighed. "Now, where were we?"

She inhaled deeply and took a minute to focus before she did what she knew she needed to do. "I shouldn't have kissed you. I'm sorry." She looked down at her leather messenger bag, feeling very uncomfortable.

"I'm not sorry. I'm only sorry that you're sorry." Paul brought his face close to hers and smiled. "But it's all right. I'm not upset or anything."

"I don't know what happened. I'm not usually like that—to just kiss someone."

"I'm not *just someone*, am I?" He looked at her inquisitively. "I've wanted to kiss you for the longest time. Ever since that first seminar, I think. But that would have been too soon."

He tried to persuade her to look at him, but she looked away. She looked toward another table and its two quarreling occupants. She sighed.

"Julia, the kiss doesn't have to change anything. Think of it as a moment between friends. It doesn't have to happen again, unless you want it to." He searched her face, worriedly. "Would that make it better? If we left it like that?"

She nodded and squirmed. "I'm sorry, Paul. You've been nothing but nice to me."

"You don't owe me anything. I'm not looking for payment, here. I'm nice to you because I want to be. That's why I bought you the CD. That's why the poem reminds me of you. You inspire me." He leaned closer so that he could whisper in her ear, acutely aware of the fact that a pair of angry sapphire eyes was suddenly focused on him. "Please don't feel obligated to do anything that you don't want to do. I'll be your friend no matter what." He paused. "It was a friendly little kiss, instead of a hug. But from now on, we can stick to hugs, if you want. And one day, if you want more . . ."

"I'm not ready," she breathed, somewhat surprised that she found honest words to say and found them so quickly.

"I know that. That's why I didn't kiss you back much, even though I wanted to. But it was very nice. Thank you. I know you're careful about who you let yourself get close to. I feel honored that you kissed me."

He patted her hand and smiled at her again. She opened her mouth to say something, but he beat her to it.

"I could break Christa's neck for what she said to you. I won't bother talking to her next time." His eyes darted to The Professor's table where he noticed with some relief that the angry sapphire eyes were now fixated on Christa, who was bowing her head and close to tears.

Julia shrugged. "I don't care."

"I care. I saw how she was looking at you. And I felt your reaction: you cringed. You fucking *cringed*, Julia. Why didn't you tell her to go to hell?"

"I don't do things like that if I can help it. I try not to lower myself to her level. Sometimes, I just feel so . . . so surprised that someone is being nasty to me, I can't think. I'm speechless."

"People are . . . nasty to you?" Paul began to get angry.

"Sometimes."

"Emerson?" he whispered.

"He's coming around. You saw him just then—he was nice."

Paul nodded reluctantly. *Professor Dick-erson.*

Julia fidgeted with her hands. "I don't mean to be all . . . St. Francis of Assisi or something, but anyone can shout obscenities. Why should I become like her? Why not think that sometimes—just sometimes— you can overcome evil with silence? And let people hear their hatefulness in their own ears, without distraction. Maybe goodness is enough to expose evil for what it really is, sometimes. Rather than trying to stop evil with more evil. Not that I'm good. I don't think that I'm good." She paused and looked over at Paul. "I'm not making any sense."

He simply smiled. "Of course you're making sense. We talked about this in my Aquinas seminar—evil is its own punishment. Look at Christa. Do you think she's happy? How could she be, behaving like that? Some people are so self-absorbed and deluded that all the shouting in the world wouldn't be enough to convince them of their own shortcomings."

"Or jog their memory," Julia mumbled, gazing over at the other table and shaking her head.

The next day, she found herself in the Department of Italian Studies checking her mailbox before the Dante seminar. She was listening to the CD that Paul had given to her, which she'd finally agreed to accept and upload to her iPod. He was right; she'd fallen in love with the album immediately. And she found that she could write her thesis proposal while listening to his music much better than while listening to Mozart. *Lacrimosa* was far too depressing.

After days of finding nothing in her pigeonhole, she finally received some mail. Three pieces of mail, actually.

The first was an announcement of the rescheduling of Professor Emerson's lecture, *Lust in Dante's* Inferno: *The Deadly Sin against the Self.* Julia made note of the new date and planned on asking Paul if he would accompany her to the lecture.

The second piece of mail was a small cream-colored envelope. Julia opened it and was surprised to find that it contained a Starbucks gift card. It had been personalized, she saw, and the image on the card was a large lightbulb. The text emblazoned across it read: *You are very bright, Julianne.*

Julia looked at the back of the card and saw that the value was one hundred dollars. *Holy shit*, she thought. *That's a lot of coffee.* It was obvious who had sent it to her and why. Nevertheless, she was very, very surprised. Until she withdrew the third piece of mail.

The third piece was a long, sleek envelope, which she quickly opened. It was from the chair of the Department of Italian Studies congratulating her on winning a bursary. She read no further than the amount, which was five thousand dollars per semester, payable on top of her regular graduate student stipend.

O gods of all really poor graduate students with very small hobbit-hole-not-fit-for-a-dog apartments, thank you, thank you, thank you!

"Julianne, are you all right?" The voice of Mrs. Jenkins, comforting and gentle, wafted over her shocked body.

She stumbled uncertainly to Mrs. Jenkins' desk and wordlessly handed her the award letter.

"Oh yes, I heard about this." She grinned amiably. "It's amazing, isn't it? These bursaries are few and far between, and suddenly on Monday morning we received a call saying that some foundation had donated thousands of dollars for this award."

Julia nodded, still in shock.

Mrs. Jenkins glanced down at the letter. "I wonder who he is."

"Who he is?"

"The person the bursary is named after."

"I didn't read that far."

Mrs. Jenkins held the letter up and pointed to a block of bold print. "It says that you are the recipient of the *M. P. Emerson Bursary*. I was just wondering who M. P. Emerson is. I wonder if he's a relative of Professor Emerson. Although *Emerson* is a common enough name. It's probably just a coincidence."

Chapter Twelve

Professor Emerson saw light spilling from underneath the door of his library carrel, but since Paul had pasted brown craft paper over the narrow window in the door, Gabriel couldn't peer inside. He was surprised to find Paul working so late on a Thursday night. It was ten-thirty in the evening, and the library would be closing in thirty minutes.

Gabriel fished around in his pocket for his keys and opened the door without knocking. What he saw inside completely floored him. Curled up in a chair was Miss Mitchell, her head resting on folded arms that were poised elegantly on the desktop. Her eyes were closed, her mouth partially open but not quite smiling. Her cheeks were flushed with sleep, her chest rising and falling slowly, soothingly, like the waves of the ocean against a quiet beach. He stood in the doorway entranced, thinking that the simple sound of her breathing would make an excellent relaxation CD. One he could imagine falling asleep to again and again.

Her laptop was open, and Gabriel saw her screen saver, which was a slide show of hand-drawn illustrations of what looked like a children's story—something with animals—including a funny-looking white bunny with long ears that fell to its feet. The strains of music filled the air, and Gabriel realized that the sound was coming from her computer. He saw a CD with a rabbit on it. Gabriel began to wonder why Miss Mitchell was so obsessed with bunnies.

Perhaps she has an Easter fetish? Gabriel was halfway through a very elaborate imagining of what an Easter fetish might include before he came to his senses. He quickly entered the carrel and closed the door behind him, taking care to lock it. It would not be good for the two of them to be caught together like this.

He regarded her peaceful form, not wishing to disturb her or to intrude upon what looked like a very pleasant dream. Now she was smiling. He located the book he was seeking, preparing to leave her in peace, when his eyes alighted on a small notebook that lay just out of reach of her fingers.

Gabriel, he read. *My Gabriel.*

The sight of his name written lovingly, albeit randomly, several times in her notebook beckoned to him like a soft Siren call and sent a thrill coursing up and down his back. He was momentarily frozen, his hand hovering in midair.

Of course, it was possible that she was writing about another Gabriel. It seemed too incredible for her to be writing about him and calling him her own.

Gazing at her, he knew that if he stayed everything would change. He knew that if he touched her, he wouldn't be able to resist the urge—the undeniable and primal urge—to claim the beautiful and pure Miss Mitchell. She was there, waiting for him, calling to him, her vanilla scent heavy in the small, too warm space.

My Gabriel. He imagined her voice laving across his name the way a lover's tongue moves across the skin . . . His mind traveled at light speed as he envisioned pulling her into his arms. Kissing her, embracing her. Lifting her onto the desk and pressing himself between her knees, her hands tugging at his hair, his sweater, his shirt, undoing his bow tie and flinging it to the floor.

His fingers would explore her wavy hair and trace gentle lines across her neck, causing every space, every pore, to explode into scarlet—his nose nuzzling her cheek, her ear, her perfect milk-white throat. He would feel her pulse at her neck and find himself strangely calmed by the gentle rhythm, and he would feel connected to the beating of her heart, especially as it would begin to quicken beneath his touch. He would wonder if they were close enough, would their hearts beat synchronously . . . or was that simply a poet's fancy?

She would be shy at first. But he would be gently insistent, whispering words of sweet seduction into her hair. He would tell her whatever she wanted to hear, and she would believe it. His hands would drop from her shoulders and inch over her lovely and innocent curves, marveling at her receptivity as she blossomed under his touch.

For no man would have touched her like that before. Eventually, she would be eager and responsive to him. Oh, so responsive. They would kiss, and it would be electric—intense—explosive. Their tongues would tangle and tango together desperately, as if they had never kissed before.

She would be wearing too many clothes. He'd want to tease her out of them and spread feather-light kisses against every inch of perfect porcelain skin. Especially her lovely throat and its metro of bluish veins. She would blush like Eve, but he would kiss away her nervousness. Soon she would be naked and open before him, thinking only of him and his rapt admiration, and not the feel of the carrel air against pale, pink flesh.

He would praise her with oaths and odes and soft murmurings of sweet pet names, and she would not feel shame. *Honey, sweet girl, dear, my lovely* . . . He would make her believe in his adoration, and her belief would not be entirely false.

Eventually the teasing and tingling would be too much, and he'd lean her back gently, cradling the back of her head in his hand. He'd keep his hand there throughout, for he would be worried he might hurt her. He would not have her head banging against the desk like an unloved toy.

He was not a cruel lover. He would not be rough or indifferent. He would be erotic, passionate but gentle. For he knew what she was. And he would wish her to be pleased as much as he, her first time. But he desired her spread out beneath him, breathless and inviting, her eyes wide and unblinking, blazing with desire.

His other hand would flex across her lower back, the sweet expanse of arched skin, and he'd gaze into her large and liquid eyes as she gasped and moaned. He would make her moan. Only him.

She'd bite her lip, her eyes half-closed as he slid toward her, willing her with whispered words to *relax* as she gave herself to him. It would go easier for her that way, the first time. He would still and not rush. He would pause and not tear. He would stop, perhaps?

His beautiful, perfect brown-eyed angel . . . her chest rising and falling quickly, the flush of her cheeks blooming across her entire body. She would be a rose in his eyes, and she would flower beneath him. For he would be kind, and she would open. He would watch entranced, almost as if it were occurring in slow motion . . . sight, scent, sound, taste, touch . . . as she transformed from maiden to matron through loss of maidenhead, all because of him. All because of him.

Maidenhead? There would be blood. For the price of sin was always blood. And a little death.

Gabriel's heart stopped. It lay silent for half a beat then thudded double time as a new awareness crashed over him. Metaphysical poetry, long forgotten from his days at Magdalen College, sprang to his lips. For in that instant, he saw very clearly that he, Professor Gabriel O. Emerson, would-be seducer of the lovely and innocent Julianne, was a flea.

The words of John Donne echoed in his ears:

Mark but this flea, and mark in this,
How little that which thou deniest me is;
It suck'd me first, and now sucks thee,
And in this flea our two bloods mingled be
Thou know'st that this cannot be said
A sin, nor shame, nor loss of maidenhead;
Yet this enjoys before it woo,
And pamper'd swells with one blood made of two;
And this, alas! is more than we would do.

He knew why his subconscious mind chose that moment to foist Donne's poetry upon him; the poem was an argument for seduction. Donne spoke to his prospective lover, a virgin, and argued that her loss of virginity was less consequential than the swatting of a flea. She should give herself to him quickly, without a second thought. Without hesitation. Without regret.

As soon as the words presented themselves, Gabriel knew that they were perfect for him. Perfect for what he was contemplating doing to her. Perfect for his own self-justification.

Tasting. Taking. Sucking. Sinning. Draining. Abandoning.

She was pure. She was innocent. He wanted her.

Facilis descensus Averni.

But he would not be the one to make her bleed. He could not, would not, make another girl bleed for the rest of his life. All thoughts of seduction and mad, passionate fucking on desks and chairs, against walls and bookshelves and windows, immediately gave way. He would not take her. He would not mark her and claim what he had no right to claim.

Gabriel Emerson was a trite and only semi-repentant sinner. Preoccupied with the fairer sex and his own physical pleasure, he knew he was governed by lust. Never did that thirst give way to something more, something approximating love. Nevertheless, despite these and other moral failings, despite his constant inability to resist temptation, Gabriel still had one last moral principle that governed his behavior. One line he would not cross.

Professor Emerson did not seduce virgins. He did not take virginity, ever, even if it was freely offered. He did not slake his thirst with innocence; he fed only on those who had already tasted and who in tasting, wanted more. And he was not about to violate his last and only moral principle for an hour or two of salacious satisfaction with a delectable graduate student in his study carrel. Even a fallen angel had his principles.

Gabriel would leave her virtue intact. He would leave her as he found her, the blushing brown-eyed angel, surrounded by bunnies, curled up like a kitten in her little chair. She would sleep unruffled, unkissed, untouched, and unmolested. His hand tightened on the doorknob, and just as he was about to unlock the door, he heard the sounds of stirring behind him.

He sighed and hung his head. He wasn't foregoing a night of pleasure with her out of hatred but out of love—for the goodness he craved and wished his life had been. And perhaps out of love for the memory of his former self, before all the sin and vice took root and grew, like a patch of thorns turning and twisting and choking out his virtues. Gabriel's hand left the doorknob, and he drew in a very deep breath. He straightened his shoulders and closed his eyes, wondering what he would say to her.

He slowly turned around and saw Miss Mitchell groan slightly and stretch. Her eyelids fluttered, and she stifled a yawn with the fan of her hand.

But her eyes flew open when she saw Professor Emerson standing by the door. Startled, she let out a yelp and flew backward out of her chair and against the wall. She cowered in confusion, and it almost broke Gabriel's heart. (Which would have at least proven that he had one.)

"Ssssshhhhh. Julianne, it's just me." He held his hands aloft in complete surrender. He tried to smile disarmingly.

Julia was stunned. She'd been dreaming of him moments before. And now he was here. She rubbed her eyes. He was still there, staring. She pinched the skin on her arm between her fingers. He was still there.

Holy shit. He caught me.

"It's just me, Julianne. Are you all right?"

She blinked rapidly and began rubbing her eyes again. "I . . . don't know."

"How long have you been here?" He lowered his hands.

"Um . . . I . . . don't know." She was trying to wake up and remember all at the same time.

"Is Paul with you?"

"No."

Somehow, Gabriel felt relieved. "How did you get in? This is my carrel."

Julia's eyes flew to his, measuring his reaction. *I am in so much trouble. And so is Paul. Emerson will evict him now.*

She moved forward rapidly, knocking the chair over in the process and tipping over a stack of books that had been resting near her hands. A ream of loose notebook paper was thrown aloft by the general upheaval and began falling about her like massive, pinstriped snowflakes. Gabriel thought that she looked like an angel—an angel in a child's snow globe, with whiteness fluttering all around her.

Beautiful, he thought.

She began to scramble, trying to put everything back in order. She was repeating an apology over and over again like a decade of the Rosary, mumbling something about borrowing Paul's key. She was sorry. So very, very sorry.

In one stride, Gabriel was next to her, his hand gently but firmly on her shoulder. "It's all right. You are welcome to be here. Be still."

Julia closed her eyes and willed herself and her heartbeat to slow. It was very difficult to do; she was so afraid he would lose his temper and banish Paul from his precious carrel. Forever.

Gabriel inhaled sharply, and her eyes flew open, glazing over at his touch.

He brought his head close to her face and peered down at her. "Julianne? You've gone pale. Are you unwell?"

He didn't know what to do. Why was she acting so strangely? Perhaps she was weak from hunger or not quite awake. The room was very warm. Too warm. She'd left the heater on. He caught her just as she swooned, wrapping her tightly and pulling her into his chest. She was not unconscious, at least, not yet.

"Julianne?" He pushed the hair out of her eyes and brushed the back of his hand across her cheek.

She murmured something, and he realized she hadn't fainted, but was leaning against him as if she didn't have the strength to stand. He held her to keep her from hitting the upturned chair or the floor.

"Are you okay?"

He began to move her so that she could sit down, but she clung to him, wrapping her arms about his neck without hesitation. He liked the feel of her pressed against him, so he hugged her tightly and leaned down to sniff her hair, somewhat surreptitiously. *Vanilla.* Her little body pressed against his perfectly, as if their shapes were ideal complements. It was astonishing.

"What happened?" she mumbled against his sweater, which was a brilliant green calculated to contrast with the blue of his eyes.

"I'm not sure. I think you grew light-headed because you stood up too quickly. And it's hot in here."

She smiled weakly, a smile that melted his heart.

Julia desperately wanted to kiss him. He was close. So very, very close. Two inches and those lips would be hers . . . again. And his eyes were soft and warm . . . and he was being sweet with her . . .

He pulled back from her minutely, testing her to see if she was going to fall over. When she didn't, he placed her gently on top of the desk before righting the chair. Then he withdrew to the door of the carrel and straightened his tie.

"I don't mind if you use the carrel—not at all. I was just surprised to find you here. In fact, I'm glad Paul suggested you use it. There's no problem." He smiled to put her at ease, watching as she grasped the surface of the desk for support. "I was looking for a book Paul borrowed." He held the volume aloft and turned to look at Julia again.

Moving slowly but carefully, she stood up and began to stack books on the desk and pick up the white sheets of paper that had drifted to the floor.

"Were you supposed to meet Paul tonight?"

"He's gone to a graduate student conference at Princeton. He's presenting a paper tomorrow." She looked over at him cautiously, and when she saw that his head was cocked to one side and he was still smiling, she relaxed. Marginally.

"Princeton. Yes, of course. I forgot. That's a very fine briefcase you have." He smiled at her knowingly, gesturing to the bag that was propped up against the wall.

Julia blushed, trying very hard to keep her secret knowledge secret.

"But there appears to be something alive in there. I can see a pair of ears poking out of one of the zippers."

She whirled around. Gabriel was right; two little brown ears could be seen sticking out of the briefcase, almost as if she had tried to smuggle a pet into the library. Julia blushed even more deeply.

"May I?" He gestured to the briefcase, but made no move as he waited for her permission.

Hesitantly, she pulled the stuffed toy out of the briefcase and handed it to him, biting her lip in embarrassment.

Clearly Miss Mitchell has a bunny fetish.

Gabriel held the toy rabbit between his thumb and forefinger, gazing at it curiously as if he didn't know what it was. Or as if, in a fit of temper, it might decide to emulate the behavior of the famous rabbit in *Monty Python and the Holy Grail* and go right for his throat. Gabriel placed a hand to his neck as a precaution and resisted the sudden and overwhelming urge to say *Ni.*

The toy was brown, of course, and soft, made of velvet or something.

It had long ears and short limbs and very pleasant-looking whiskers. It stood straight up, looking rather stiff. It looked familiar to him, strangely enough. Something Grace would have owned and loved. Something from a childhood he never had.

Around its neck someone had tied a very sloppy bow out of pink ribbon. Gabriel measured the bow with his eyes and came to the conclusion that someone who was either slightly handicapped (no disrespect intended), or perhaps who had very large hands and lacked the fine motor skills of someone who was gifted with manual dexterity (such as himself), had tied the bow, such as it was. And there was a card.

Not wishing to embarrass her further, he smiled and let his eyes dart momentarily to the card, just so he could catch a glimpse of it:

R,
Someone to keep you company while I'm away.
See you when I get back.
Yours,
Paul.

The Angelfucker strikes again, Gabriel growled to himself.

He handed the bunny back to Julia. "It's very—ah—nice."

"Thank you."

"But who is *R?*"

Julia turned away as she placed Paul's latest gift back into her briefcase, taking great care not to catch the bunny's ears in the teeth of the zipper. "It's one of my nicknames."

"But why that letter? Why not something that begins with *B?*"

Julia frowned at him. *Like what? Bitch? Badass? Bovine? Bunny?*

"*Beautiful,*" said Gabriel. Then he blushed, for the word had slipped out by mistake. "So you've been asleep here for hours, with *Rabbit Songs* and a pet rabbit to keep you company? I didn't realize you were a bunny lover."

Julia seemed embarrassed. He couldn't help himself; the characterization was obvious, if a little flirtatious.

"I like your choice in music."

"Thank you." She quickly turned off her ancient laptop and placed it carefully in her briefcase with the CD.

"The library is closing shortly. What would you have done if I hadn't arrived?"

She looked around, slightly confused. "I don't know."

"If no one noticed that the carrel light was on when they checked this floor, you could have been locked in the library all night. Without any food." His smile slid off his face at the mere idea. "What are you going to do to ensure that doesn't happen in the future?"

She looked around quickly. "Set the alarm on Paul's clock?"

He nodded as if that answer satisfied him. But it didn't. "Are you hungry?"

"I should be going, Professor. I'm sorry I've intruded on your personal space."

If only you knew how true your words were, Julianne.

"Miss Mitchell, stop." He took a step closer as she picked up her new briefcase with one hand and cleared the desk of debris with the other. "Have you had your dinner?"

"No."

Gabriel's eyebrows knitted together like thunderous clouds.

"When did you have lunch?"

"At noon."

He scowled. "That was almost eleven hours ago. What did you have?"

"A hot dog from the cart in front of the library."

Gabriel cursed. "You can't live on that kind of rubbish. And I wouldn't eat street meat *ever*. You promised you'd tell me if you were going hungry—and now you're fainting on me."

He glanced at his white-gold Rolex Day-Date. "It's too late to take you for steak—Harbour Sixty is closed. Why don't you join me for dinner somewhere else? I was caught up working on my lecture, and I haven't eaten either."

Julia stared at him. "Are you sure?"

His expression hardened. "Miss Mitchell, I am not the kind of person who makes idle invitations. If I invite you to dinner, then I'm sure. Now are you coming or not?"

"I'm not dressed for dinner, thank you very much." Her voice was satin over steel, and she arched an eyebrow at him. She had gotten over her initial shock at being surprised in his carrel and was now fully awake and fully annoyed at his tone.

His eyes passed over her slowly, pausing to regard her lovely figure and then resting for a long time on her sneakers. He despised sneakers on women, for they were a waste of a perfectly good podiatric opportunity. He cleared his throat. "You look fine. I think the color of your blouse brings out the blush in your skin and the butterscotch flecks in your eyes. You look nice, actually." He smiled at her a little too warmly and looked away.

I have butterscotch in my eyes? Since when? And since when has he looked at them long enough to notice?

"There is a little place near my building that I frequent during the week, especially on late nights. I'll buy you dinner, and we can talk about your thesis proposal, informally, of course. How's that?"

"Thank you, Professor."

Their eyes did not meet for long, but they met, and warm and somewhat hesitant smiles were exchanged on both sides.

He waited patiently for her to put everything in order before he stood aside and waved his hand toward the hallway. "After you."

She thanked him, and as she was passing, he reached out his hand and grasped the handle of her messenger bag, brushing against one of her fingers. Julia pulled back instinctively, dropping the bag.

Thankfully, he caught it. "This is a very fine briefcase. I think I should like to carry it for a little while. If you don't mind." He smirked at her, and she blushed.

"Thank you," she murmured. "I really like it. It's perfect."

Gabriel made no attempt to engage her in conversation until they were at the restaurant, Caffé Volo on Yonge Street. The Caffé was a quiet but friendly establishment that boasted perhaps the longest and best beer list in Toronto. It also had a very fine Italian chef, and so their food was some of the finest simple Italian fare on offer in the neighborhood. The restaurant itself was small, only ten tables, which were supplemented in the summer by a patio. The décor was rustic and included antiques, such as reclaimed church pews and old harvest tables. It gave

Julia the impression of something like a German weinkeller, like the restaurant Vinum that she had visited with friends when she was in Frankfurt.

Gabriel liked it because they sold a particular kind of Trappist Ale that he preferred, Chimay Première, and it pleased him to have pizza in the Neapolitan style to pair with that beer. (As ever, he was impatient with mediocrity.) Since Gabriel was a frequent patron of Caffé Volo and more than somewhat persnickety, he was offered the best seating, which was a quiet table for two tucked into a corner near the large picture window that looked out on the madness that was Yonge Street at night.

Transvestites, university students, frat boys, policemen, happy gay couples, happy straight couples, celebrities slumming, yuppies walking their pretentious pets, eco-friendly activists, street persons, buskers, possible gang members, Russian mafia, a wayward professor or Member of Provincial Parliament or two or four, etc. It was a myriad of fascinating human behavior, it was live, and it was free.

Julia settled cautiously into her seat, which was a converted church pew, and pulled the lambskin rug that the waiter had draped over the back of the pew tightly around her.

"Are you cold? I'll ask Christopher to seat us near the fireplace." Gabriel moved to signal to the waiter, but Julia stopped him.

"I like to people watch," she said shyly.

"Me too," he admitted. "But you look like a Yeti."

Julia reddened.

"Forgive me," he hastened to add. "But surely we can do better than a lambskin rug that has been God knows where. It probably used to grace the floor of Christopher's apartment. And who knows what kind of shenanigans went down on it."

Did he just use the word shenanigans *in a sentence?*

And with that, Professor Emerson gracefully pulled his British-racing-green cashmere sweater over his pretentious bow tie and head and handed it to her. Julia accepted it and moved the objectionable Yeti-like carpet to one side. She gently pulled on his generously sized sweater.

"Better?" he smiled, trying to smooth his now mussed hair.

"Better." She smiled, feeling much warmer and very comfortable, blanketed in the warmth and scent that was Gabriel. She folded up the cuffs considerably because his arms were much longer than hers.

"Did you go to Lobby on Tuesday?" she asked.

"No. Now, why don't you tell me about your proposal?" His tone immediately became businesslike and professorial.

Thankfully, Christopher interrupted them at that moment to take their order, which gave Julia precious minutes to gather her thoughts.

"Their Caesar salads are quite good, as are their Neapolitan pizzas. But they are both a bit large for one person. Are you the type to share?" Gabriel asked.

Julia's mouth dropped open.

"I mean, would you share with me, please? Or you could order whatever you like. Perhaps you don't want salad and pizza." Gabriel frowned, trying very hard not to be an overbearing, domineering professor for at least five minutes.

Christopher tapped his foot quietly, for he did not want The Professor to notice his impatience. He'd seen The Professor when he was irritated and did not wish to witness a repeat performance. Although perhaps he would behave differently now that he had female companionship (which was Christopher's professional prescription for any kind of personality disorder, small or large).

"I'd like to share pizza and a salad with you. Thank you." Julia's quiet voice ended the deliberations.

Gabriel placed the order, and shortly thereafter Christopher appeared with their Chimays, which Gabriel had insisted Julia try.

"Cheers," he said, clinking his glass to hers.

"*Prost*," she replied.

She sipped the beer slowly, unable to forget her first beer and who it was with. That beer had been a domestic lager. This beer was reddish brown and sweet and malty all at once. She liked it a great deal and hummed her approval.

"It's over ten dollars a bottle," she whispered, not wishing to embarrass Gabriel or herself with loud incredulity.

"But it's the best. And wouldn't you rather drink one bottle of this rather than two bottles of Budweiser, which really is like drinking appalling bath water?"

I can only assume that all bath water would be appalling to drink, Professor Emerson, but I'll take your word for it. Sicko.

"Well? Let's hear it," he prompted. "What are you thinking? I can see the wheels turning in that little mind of yours. So out with it." He crossed his arms in front of his chest and grinned, as if her little mind gave him no end of secret, condescending amusement.

Julia bristled. She didn't like the fact that he'd used the diminutive *little* in referring to her mind, for it seemed to signify his contempt for her intellectual ability. So she decided to strike back.

"I'm glad I have a chance to speak to you privately," she began, withdrawing two envelopes from her messenger bag. "I can't accept these." She slid the Starbucks gift card and the bursary award letter across the table.

Gabriel glanced at both items, recognized them immediately, and scowled. "What makes you think these are from me?" He pushed them back across the table.

"The powers of deduction. You're the only one who calls me *Julianne*. You're the only one with a bank account large enough to fund a bursary." She returned the envelopes.

He paused for a moment. Was he really the only one who called Julianne by her proper name? What was everyone else calling her?

Julia.

"You must accept them." He slid the papers over to her once again.

"No, I mustn't. Gifts make me very uncomfortable, and the Starbucks card is too much. Not to mention the bursary. I will never be able to repay you, and I owe your family too much already. I can't accept them." She pushed them back.

"You *can* accept them, and you *will*. The gift card is inconsequential; I spend more than that on coffee in a month. I need to show you, in some tangible way, that I respect your intelligence. I said something in an unguarded moment that Miss Peterson took and twisted. So, it isn't even a gift—it's more like restitution. I maligned you; now I'm praising you. You must accept it, or this injustice will remain unresolved between us, and I won't believe you've forgiven me for my verbal indiscretion in front of one of your peers." He slid the envelopes across the table and glared at her for good measure.

Julia began to stare at his fancy hand-knotted bow tie in order to distract herself from the blazing blue of his eyes. She wondered how he'd managed to make the tie so straight and even. *Perhaps he hired a professional bow tie-tier, just for that purpose. Someone with artificially blond hair and high heels. And very long fingernails.*

She slid the Starbucks card back toward him defiantly. And to her great surprise, his face hardened and he pocketed it.

"I won't play gift card ping-pong with you all evening," he snapped. "But the bursary can't be returned. The money isn't from me. I simply alerted Mr. Randall, the director of the philanthropic organization, of your accomplishments."

"And poverty," Julia muttered.

"If you have something to say to me, Miss Mitchell, please do me the courtesy of speaking at an audible level." His eyes flashed to hers.

Her eyes flashed back. "I don't think this is very *professional*, Professor Emerson. You're passing me thousands of dollars through a bursary, however you managed to do it. It looks like you're trying to buy me."

Gabriel inhaled sharply and counted to ten just to avert a verbal explosion. "Buy you? Believe me, Miss Mitchell, nothing could have been further from my mind! I am deeply offended at being so maligned. If I wanted you at all, I certainly wouldn't have to buy you."

Julia's eyebrows shot up, and she glared at him. Harshly. *"Watch it."*

He squirmed under her glare, which was a rare experience for him. She reveled in it.

"That is not what I meant. I meant I would never *want* to treat you like a commodity. And you are not the type of girl who could be bought, are you?"

Julia eyed him frostily before looking away. She shook her head and began staring at the doorway, wondering if she should make her escape.

"Why do you do that?" he whispered, after a few minutes.

"Do what?"

"Provoke me."

"I don't . . . I . . . I'm not provoking you. I'm stating a fact."

"Nevertheless, it *is* extremely provocative. Every time I try to have a conversation with you like a normal person, you provoke me."

"You are my professor."

"Yes, and your best friend's older brother. Can't we just be Gabriel and Julianne for an evening? Can't we have a pleasant conversation and an even more pleasant dinner and all the rest? It might not seem obvious to you, but I'm trying to be human here." He closed his eyes in frustration.

"You are?" It was an innocent question asked in good faith. Julia clapped a hand over her mouth as she realized how it sounded aloud.

Gabriel's dark blue eyes opened slowly, like the dragon in the Tolkien story, but he did not take the bait of her impertinence. And he did not breathe fire. Yet.

"You wish to be professional, so act like it. A normal graduate student would receive an award letter, be profoundly grateful for her good fortune, and accept the money. So act *professionally*, Miss Mitchell. I could have hidden my connection to the bursary from you, but I chose to treat you like an adult. I chose to respect your intelligence and not engage in deception. Nevertheless, I took great care to hide my connection to the bursary from our department. The philanthropic organization does not have my name attached to it publicly, so it can't be traced back to me. And *Emerson* is an extremely common name. So no one will believe you if you reveal that I'm behind the bursary."

He withdrew his iPhone from his pocket, opened up the notepad application, and began writing with his finger.

"I wasn't going to complain . . ." Julia began.

"You might have said *thank you*."

"Thank you, Professor Emerson. But think of it from my point of view—I don't want to play Héloïse to your Abelard." She looked down at her silverware and began adjusting the pieces until they were all lined up symmetrically.

Gabriel quickly remembered seeing her do that once before, when they were dining at Harbour Sixty. He placed his phone on the table and looked over at her with a pained expression, made doubly painful by the guilt he felt over what had almost happened in his study carrel. Yes, he'd come close to succumbing to Miss Mitchell's considerable charms, and risking Abelard's fate, for Rachel would no doubt castrate him if she discovered he'd seduced her friend. Miraculously, however, his self-control proved to be superior to that of Abelard. "I would *never* seduce a student."

"Then thank you," she murmured. "And thank you for the *gesture* of the bursary, even though I can't promise to accept it. I know it's only a small amount to you, but it would have meant airline tickets home for Thanksgiving and Christmas and spring break and Easter. And money for many more extras than I can afford now. Including steak, on occasion."

"Why would you use it for airline tickets? I would have thought you'd use it to secure a better apartment."

"I don't think I can get out of my lease. And anyway, going home to see my dad is important to me. He's the only family I have. And I would have liked to see Richard before he sells the house and moves to Philadelphia."

Actually, it would be worth it to accept the bursary so I could visit Richard and the orchard. I wonder if my favorite apple tree is still there I wonder if anyone would notice if I carved my initials into the trunk . . .

Gabriel scowled obliquely, for a number of reasons. "You wouldn't have gone home otherwise?"

She shook her head. "Dad wanted to fly me home for Christmas, rather than taking Greyhound. But the prices on Air Canada are outrageous. I would have been ashamed to accept a ticket from him."

"Never be ashamed to accept a gift when there are no strings attached."

"You sound like Grace. She used to talk like that."

He shifted in his seat and involuntarily scratched at the back of his neck. "Where do you think I learned about generosity? Not from my biological mother."

Julia looked at Gabriel, meeting his gaze without blushing or blinking. Then she sighed and put the award letter back in her bag, resolving to spend more time thinking about how best to deal with it once she was no longer in The Professor's magnetic presence. For she saw that arguing with him would get her nowhere. And in that respect, as in several others, he was exactly like Peter Abelard, sexy, smart, and seductive.

He peered over at her. "But despite all I've tried to do, which isn't much I'll admit, you're still going hungry?"

"Gabriel, I have a tenuous relationship with my stomach. I forget to eat when I'm busy or preoccupied or—or sad. It's not about the money— it's just the way things are. Please don't trouble yourself." She readjusted her cutlery once again for good measure.

"So . . . you're sad?"

She sipped her beer slowly and ignored his question.

"Does Dante make you unhappy?"

"Sometimes," she whispered.

"And other times?"

She looked up at him, and a sweet smile spread across her face. "I can't help myself—he makes me deliriously happy. Sometimes when I'm studying *The Divine Comedy*, I feel as if I'm doing what I was always meant to do. Like I found my passion, my vocation. I'm not that shy little girl from Selinsgrove anymore. I can do this, I'm good at it, and it makes me feel . . . important."

It was too much. Too much information. The quickly drunk beer, the rush of blood to the head, his scent clinging and heavy in her nose from his sweater. She should never have said all those words to him, of all people.

But he only watched her somewhat warmly, which surprised her. "You are shy, it's true," he murmured. "But that's certainly not a vice." He cleared his throat. "I'm envious of your enthusiasm for Dante. I used to feel that way. But for me, it was a long time ago. Too long." He smiled at her again and looked away.

Julia leaned across the table and lowered her voice. "Who is M. P. Emerson?"

Startled blue eyes flew to hers, burning with laser-like intensity. "I'd prefer not to talk about it."

His tone wasn't harsh, but it was very, very cold, and Julia realized she'd touched upon a nerve so injured, so raw, it was still vibrating with pain. It took her a moment to collect herself, and before she had fully considered the prudence of her question, she spoke. "Are you trying to be my friend? Is that what you were trying to communicate to me with the bursary?"

Gabriel frowned. "Did Rachel put you up to this?"

"No. Why?"

"She thinks we should be friends. But I'll tell you what I told her—it's impossible."

Julia felt a lump grow in her throat, and she swallowed noisily. "Why?"

"We exist under the red flag of professionalism. Professors can't be friends with their students. And even if we were just Julianne and Gabriel sharing a pizza, you shouldn't want to be friends with me. I am a magnet for sin, and you are not." He smiled sadly. "So you see, it's hopeless. *Abandon hope all ye who enter.*"

"I don't like to think of anything as hopeless," she whispered to her silverware.

"Aristotle said that friendship is only possible between *two* virtuous people. Therefore, friendship between us is impossible."

"No one is truly virtuous."

"You are." Gabriel's blue eyes burned into hers with something akin to passion and admiration.

"Rachel said you were on the VIP list at Lobby." Julia changed the subject again swiftly, still not considering her words.

"That's true."

"She made a mystery of it. Why?"

Gabriel scowled. "Why do you think?"

"I don't know. That's why I asked."

He fixed her with his gaze and dropped his voice. "I go there regularly, hence the VIP status. Although I haven't been there much of late."

"Why do you go? You don't like to dance. Is it just to drink?" Julia looked around at the simple but comfortable interior of the Caffé. "Here is as good a place to drink as any. I think it's much nicer here. It's *gemütlich*—cozy." *And there doesn't appear to be a single Emerson whore in sight.*

"No, Miss Mitchell, in general I do not go to *The Vestibule* to drink."

"Then why do you go?"

"Isn't it obvious?" He frowned. Then he shook his head. "Perhaps not to someone like you."

"What's that supposed to mean? *Someone like me?*"

"It means that you don't know what you're asking me," he spat, staring angrily. "Otherwise you wouldn't make me say it! You want to know why I go there? I'll tell you why I go there. I go there to find women to *fuck*, Miss Mitchell." He was pissed now and glaring at her. "Happy now?" he growled.

Julia drew a deep breath and held it. When she could hold it no more she shook her head and exhaled. "No," she said quietly, looking down at her hands. "Why would that make me happy? It makes me sick to my stomach, actually. Really, really sick. You have no idea."

Gabriel sighed deeply and placed both hands at the back of his neck. He wasn't cross with her; he was cross with himself. And he felt ashamed. Part of him wanted to repel her intentionally—to stand naked in front of her, hiding nothing—so that she would see him for what he really was, a dark, sinister creature exposed by her virtue. Then she would walk away.

Perhaps his subconscious was already trying to do that with these ridiculous, unprofessional outbursts. For he should never in a thousand years have said what he just said to a graduate student, especially a female graduate student, even if it was the truth. She was undoing him slowly, bit by bit, and he did not understand how.

Gabriel's blue eyes found hers. And across his pale and handsome face, Julia read remorse.

"Forgive me. I know I've disgusted you." He spoke very quietly. "But believe me when I tell you that that is a very good reaction for you to have. You *should* be repulsed by me. Every time I'm near you, I *corrupt* you."

"I don't feel corrupted."

He gazed at her sadly. "Only because you don't know what it means. And by the time you realize it, it will be too late. Adam and Eve didn't realize what they'd lost until they were thrown out of Paradise."

"I know something about that," Julia mumbled. "And I didn't learn it by reading Milton."

Just then Christopher brought their pizza, effectively ending their awkward exchange. Gabriel played the part of the host, serving Julia her salad and pizza first and taking great care to make sure that she received more shaved parmesan and croutons than he did. And it wasn't because he didn't like those items; he liked them both a great deal.

While they were eating and Julia was thinking back to their first silent meal together, a song began to play over the stereo system that was so sweet, she put her fork down in order to listen.

Gabriel heard the song too and softly began to sing to himself, almost under his breath, something about heaven and hell and virtue and vice.

Julia was struck by the eerie relevance of the words. But then Gabriel stopped, suddenly unsure of himself, and began focusing his attention on his pizza. She glanced over at him with a dropped jaw. She didn't know that he could sing. And to hear his perfect mouth and voice sing those words . . .

"That's a beautiful song. Who is it by?"

"It's called *You and Me* by Matthew Barber, a local musician. Did you catch that line—the one about *virtue and vice?* I guess we know which term applies to each of us."

"It's beautiful but sad."

"I've always had a terrible weakness for beautiful but sad things." He looked at her carefully before turning away. "I suppose we should begin discussing your thesis proposal now, Miss Mitchell."

Julia saw that his professional mask was firmly in place once again. She took a deep breath and began describing her project, invoking the names of Paolo and Francesca and Dante and Beatrice, when she was interrupted by Gabriel's phone.

The ring tone sounded like the clanging of Big Ben. He lifted a finger to indicate Julia should pause while he glanced down at his iPhone's screen. Something disturbing flew across his face.

"I have to take this. I'm sorry." Gabriel stood up and answered his phone in one swift motion. "Paulina?"

He walked into the next room, but Julia could still hear him. "What's wrong? Where are you?" His voice grew muffled.

Julia busied herself with her beer and her dinner, wondering who Paulina was. She had never heard the name before. Gabriel had looked deeply troubled when he saw whatever it was that he saw on the phone's screen.

Is M. P. Emerson—Paulina? Is she his ex-wife? Or is M. P. a code for something and he's just messing with me?

Gabriel returned about fifteen minutes later. He did not sit down. He was agitated in the extreme, pale-faced and almost shaking.

"I have to go. I'm sorry. I paid for dinner, and I asked Christopher to find you a taxi when you finish."

"I can walk." Julia leaned over to pick up her messenger bag.

He held his hand out to stop her. "Absolutely not. Not late at night on Yonge Street by yourself. Here." He pushed a folded bill across the table. "For the cab and in case you want more to eat and drink. Please stay and finish your dinner. And take the leftovers home, will you?"

"I can't take your money." She moved as if to hand him back the bill, and he gave her a tremulous look.

"Please, Julianne. Not now." He was rubbing his eyes with one hand.

She felt sorry for him so she decided not to argue.

"I'm sorry I have to leave you. I . . ."

He was sorry, very sorry, about something. He was in anguish, groaning involuntarily. Without thinking about it, she slipped her hand into his, a movement of compassion and solidarity. She was surprised when he didn't flinch or throw her hand back at her.

He squeezed her fingers immediately, as if he was grateful for the contact. He opened his eyes and looked down at her and slowly began to move his fingers across the back of her hand, caressing her lightly. It was all so comfortable and sweet. As if he'd done it a thousand times. As if she belonged to him. He pulled her hand upward, close to his mouth, and stared at their connection.

"*Here's the smell of blood still; all the perfumes of Arabia will not sweeten this little hand,*" he whispered. Gabriel kissed her hand reverently, but it was his own hand he was staring at. "Goodnight, Julianne. I'll see you on Wednesday—if I'm still here."

Julia nodded and watched him walk outside and break into a run as soon as his feet hit the sidewalk. It was only after he was gone that she realized she was still wearing his precious cashmere sweater and that tucked into the fifty dollar bill he had left her was the Starbucks gift card, with a note written on the back of the envelope:

J,

You didn't think I would give up this easily, did you?

Never be ashamed to accept a gift when there are no strings attached.

There are no strings here.

Yours,

Gabriel

Chapter Thirteen

By the next morning, Julia still hadn't decided what to do about the bursary. She was not in a hurry to do anything that would expose Gabriel's generosity to the suspicious minds of the university's administration, as she knew that would be dangerous for him.

And she was not in a hurry to do anything that would expose herself as anything other than a serious graduate student, so she was reticent to go to the chair of their department and explain that she wasn't interested in the bursary. For the bursary would contribute an impressive line to her curriculum vitae, and serious graduate students were supposed to care about those things more than they cared about silly little things like personal pride.

In classical terms, Miss Mitchell found herself caught between the Scylla of protecting Gabriel and herself and the Charybdis of holding fast to her pride. Unfortunately for her pride, the true peril aligned with her rejection of the bursary; the peril could be avoided if she just took the money. She did not like that. Not one little bit. Especially against the backdrop of Rachel's generosity in buying her a dress and shoes and Gabriel's not so secret attempt at replacing her book bag.

She neglected to mention to him that she'd returned her knapsack to L.L. Bean and was eagerly awaiting its replacement. And she fully intended to use it when it arrived, just to reassert her independence.

Friday afternoon, impatient for answers, Julia sent a short text to Rachel, telling her about the bursary and asking if she knew who M. P. Emerson was.

Rachel texted her back immediately:

J: G did what? Never heard of foundation. Never heard of MPE.
MP = G's bio-mother? Grandmother? luv, R.
P.S. A says hi and thanks

Julia puzzled over Rachel's text, but was persuaded by her suggestion. M. P. must have been Gabriel's grandmother, for she couldn't
imagine him naming a bursary for someone he hated. And she was
pretty sure Gabriel harbored hatred for his biological mother.

Although it was possible, Julia thought, that if Gabriel was secretive
even with Rachel, that there were many things he could have kept from
her. So in a fit of boldness, which was brought on by a shot or two of
tequila, Julia sent another text asking if Gabriel had a girlfriend in Toronto who she could ask about the bursary. And she immediately received the following response in her e-mail inbox:

> Julia!
> Okay, screw texting—the buttons are too small.
> Gabriel has NEVER had a girlfriend, as far as I know. He
> never brought anyone home to meet Mom and Dad, even when
> he was in high school. Scott accused him of being gay once. But
> Scott has no gaydar.
> Did you see how Gabriel's apartment was decorated? And the
> photos in his bedroom? Wait. Did you see those?? No girlfriend
> locally—for sure. I think just screw-buddies. Although he acted
> weird when I asked. He's 33 for God's sake—being a player isn't
> cute anymore.
> Are you sure he didn't make M. P. Emerson up? I'll ask Scott
> and get back to you. I don't want to upset my dad by asking—he's
> a mess and . . . you know.
> Aaron and I are on our way to the Queen Charlotte Islands to
> stay in a log cabin for two weeks. No internet. No cell phones.
> Just us—peace, quiet, and an outdoor Jacuzzi.
> Please keep Gabriel from falling off the cliff until I get back.
> Love, R.
>
> P.S. Aaron wants to say hi personally. Take it away, honey.

Hello, Julia. It's Aaron.

Thank you for taking such good care of my fiancée while she was in Canada. She came back a different person, and I know it wasn't because of Gabriel.

We all missed you at the funeral—would love to see you at Thanksgiving. If you aren't planning on coming home, would you reconsider? It's going to be rough without Grace. Richard (and Rachel) need their family around them, and that means you too.

I have frequent flyer miles—I could send you a ticket.

Think about it.

Love you, girlie,

Aaron.

Julia wiped away a tear at the sweetness that was Aaron, feeling happy and relieved that he and his fiancée were still very much in love. What Julia would not give to be loved like that . . .

She wondered why Aaron's offer of frequent flyer miles leaped off her screen as something other than charity, why she was instantly considering his very kind offer. Then it occurred to her—Grace was right. When there are no strings attached and a gift is given out of love, or friendship, which is a kind of love, there was no shame in accepting it. If Julia accepted Aaron's gift, she could still be part of Richard's first Thanksgiving without Grace and give the Emerson bursary back.

In thinking about Grace, Julia wondered if a small prayer to Grace for both herself and Gabriel would be efficacious, for Grace was a true saint, a heavenly mother, and one that would no doubt send help to her children. So while St. Lucy went on vacation with her beloved Aaron, Julia turned her attention upward and begged for her heavenly mother's intercession in all of their lives, lighting a candle in the window of her small studio on a lonely Friday night in Grace's memory. And before she crawled into her single bed with her velveteen rabbit, she resolved to accept Aaron's gift graciously, as evidence of her own newfound openness to charity and her ability to swallow her pride when appropriate. Which meant, not surprisingly, that her deadly sin was not so deadly.

❋ ❋

In Paul's absence, Julia found herself spending a long Saturday at the library, working on her thesis proposal in Professor Emerson's carrel. Part of her secretly hoped that The Professor would surprise her again, but he didn't. And his words came back to her, *"I'll see you Wednesday. If I'm still here."*

Julia realized that despite what Rachel said, it was more than possible that Gabriel had a girlfriend named Paulina. Julia remembered that Gabriel had assigned the chimes of Big Ben to Paulina's ring tone. Was Paulina in London? Was she English? Or was there something about the chimes that Gabriel thought was important? Julia looked up Big Ben on Wikipedia, but did not find anything particularly illuminating.

(Wikipedia can be like that.)

She wasn't naïve, despite what Gabriel thought of her. She knew he wasn't a virgin and that he hadn't been when she first met him. Still, knowing it and having it flaunted in front of her face were two very different things.

Her thoughts drifted to Gabriel and Paulina or some nameless, faceless girl, skin against skin, their bodies entwined. She saw Gabriel kissing the girl's lips and exploring her body with his mouth, his hands, his eyes. She saw Gabriel giving and receiving physical pleasure from some tall, perfect, blonde. She imagined Gabriel in ecstasy, screaming the girl's name, gazing deeply into her eyes as his body climaxed. She thought of Gabriel becoming one with some other soul, belonging in this way to some other girl. Would she love Gabriel? Be kind to Gabriel? Would she want him to be a better man, or just want him for his body, his passion, his animalistic nature? Would she even care that behind those beautiful eyes was the soul of a man long gone, wounded now and in need of both redemption and repair? Or would she want to drag him deeper down, ensnaring him with her body and her fingernails?

The thought of Gabriel taking another girl, any girl, to his bed, perchance to his soul, wounded her deeply. But somehow, the thought that there was another girl who warmed his bed for more than just one night was absolutely devastating—because she had wanted to be his girl, forever.

However sad and sordid her imaginings were, they didn't stop her from somewhat pathetically wearing his green cashmere sweater to the library and hugging her arms across her chest, just to embrace herself with his softness and his scent. For that seemed to be the closest she was ever going to come to having his body next to hers.

In Professor Emerson's carrel, Julia put away Paul's CD in favor of listening to Yael Naim. Julia loved the song *Far Far*, although she had no idea how apt Yael's words were. Julia had spent most of her life waiting for good things to happen, keeping her hopes and dreams to herself. But soon there would come a day when she would have to make something happen.

She found the music soothing and distracting, and it enabled her to make a lot of progress on her thesis proposal as she worked away until the library's close.

Leaving the library, she placed her earbuds firmly in her ears and disdained the hot dog cart outside in favor of a liquid dinner. She purchased a very large mango smoothie and began to walk home, sipping her meal and thinking. Because she was deep in thought, wondering where Gabriel was and what he was doing, she almost missed Ethan, who waved at her as she came across the long line-up in front of Lobby.

"Hey, Ethan." She smiled as she took the earbuds out of her ears.

He gestured to her to come closer. "Hi, Julia. Thanks again for helping with my text to Raphaela. She really liked it." If Ethan could have blushed, he would have; his dark eyes sparkled, and he smiled widely. "She's teaching me Italian now."

Julia grinned, happy that he and his girlfriend were happy. "So, how are things tonight? Lots of people?" She glanced at the long line.

"I'm about to let some more people in, but I have to take someone out first."

"Really? That sounds ominous."

He shook his head. "Your friend is in there drinking his ass off. The bartender is refusing to serve him, which means I need to put him in a cab and send him home."

Julia's eyebrows shot up in surprise. *Gabriel's here? What about Paulina?*

"The last time I tried to throw him out he took a swing at me. Right now, I'm just waiting for one of the other bouncers to replace me on the line. I'm going to have to go in to remove him and probably take back-up." He looked at Julia appraisingly. "Unless you can persuade him to come out peaceably."

Julia shook her head violently. "Are you kidding? He won't listen to me. I'm not even his friend."

"That's not the impression I got when you were in here, but I get it. It's cool." He shrugged nonchalantly and looked at his watch.

Julia sipped her smoothie and began thinking about her promise to Rachel. She wondered if this constituted a case in which she was morally obligated to watch out for Gabriel. *What if I walk away and he ends up in jail? He tried to be nice to me this week. I can't ignore that—it would be bad karma.*

"Um, I could try to talk to him. See if he'll come out on his own," she suggested somewhat hesitantly. "I don't want him to get arrested."

"Neither do I. We like our VIPs to stay happy. But he has been throwing back doubles since he got here, and they can't serve him anymore. Maybe he'll listen to the voice of reason and agree to go home and sleep it off." Ethan moved the velvet rope so that she could walk in.

"I'm not really dressed for it." Julia looked down at her sneakers and ripped jeans and Gabriel's heavenly scented but too large sweater.

"You're fine. But listen, if he's too far gone, or if you're just not up to it, come right back. He can be a handful when he's drunk."

Julia knew exactly what Gabriel could be like when he was drunk, but she reminded herself that he had been sweet to her that night so long ago.

She walked into the club, hoping no one would recognize her. She quickly pulled her hair out of its ponytail and draped it around her face, using it as a veil to hide from inquisitive eyes. She prayed desperately to the gods of Manhattan-style martini bars to keep Brad Curtis, MBA, away from her tonight. She didn't want to run into him looking like this. She pulled her navy-surplus peacoat closed and buttoned all the buttons, because she didn't want Gabriel to see that she was wearing his sweater—still.

It didn't take long to find him. He was sitting at the bar, talking to an attractive woman whose back was to Julia. He was staring not at the brunette, whose hand was tangled in his hair and who was pulling him toward her by his tie, but at his empty Scotch glass. He didn't look happy, but that probably had more to do with his drinking companion than anything else.

From her vantage point several feet away, Julia saw that the Emerson whore who was practically sitting on his lap, her cleavage hovering in front of his mouth, was none other than Christa Peterson. *Holy shit. Is he planning on going home with* her?

Julia knew without a doubt that this was an instance in which she needed to watch out for Gabriel. If he slept with Christa, not only would he be violating the non-fraternization policy and putting his academic career at risk, he would likely end up embroiled in a nasty personal situation with the hoping-to-be-future-Mrs. Emerson. It was more than possible that Christa was trying to seduce him in order to exact revenge for what had transpired in Starbucks earlier that week— actions Gabriel had taken on Julia's behalf.

In either case, Julia was not going to allow the seduction to proceed. Not for one damn minute.

Hands off the Precious, Gollum.

She turned on her heel and walked back outside, coming up behind Ethan and whispering in his ear. "I need your help. He's with a girl who he shouldn't go home with. She's one of his students, so I need to separate them before you put him in a cab."

Ethan shrugged. "I'm not sure what I can do about that. That's his business."

"What if one of the waiters spilled a drink on her and sent her to the ladies' room? Then maybe I could talk Gabriel into coming outside."

"Do you think you can convince him?"

Julia blinked as she took a moment to consider it. "I don't know. If we separate them, I'll have a better chance. I doubt he can form a coherent thought with her plastic boobs in his face."

O gods of all graduate-students-trying-really-hard-to-do-a-good-thing- for-an-old-friend, help me pry that Emerson whore off his dick. Please.

He laughed. "A bit cloak and dagger, don't you think? But all right, I'm sure the bartender can help us out. He has a sense of humor. If Emerson gives you any trouble, ask the bartender to call me. Okay?"

"Okay."

Ethan made a call on his cell phone, and within two minutes, he was signaling to Julia to go after Gabriel. She took a deep breath, squared her shoulders, and walked back into the club. Gabriel was laughing. Something had struck him as funny, and he was howling, head thrown back, hands clutching his stomach.

Julia had to admit that he was even more handsome when he was smiling. He was wearing a pale-green dress shirt with the top two buttons open, revealing chest hair that was poking out like a few blades of grass over the snowy white of his T-shirt. Mercifully, he'd gotten out of the fifties and lost the bow tie; the silk tie he was wearing was striped black on black and hanging loosely around his neck. He was wearing a pair of black dress pants that fit him snugly and very shiny black shoes that were far too pointy.

In short, he was drunk, but he was perfect.

"Professor?"

He stopped laughing and turned to Julia, a wide smile spreading across his face. He seemed very happy to see her. *Too* happy.

"Miss Mitchell! To what do I owe this unexpected delight?" He took her hand in his and pressed it to his lips, holding it there for several seconds.

Julia couldn't help but frown. He didn't seem drunk, but he was being friendly, flirtatious even, so he must be drunk.

(Or he must have received a personality transplant from someone charming like, say, Daniel Craig.)

"Could you help me flag a cab? I need to get home." Julia withdrew her hand, wincing at the lameness of her excuse.

"Anything for you, Miss Mitchell. And I do mean *anything*. May I buy you a drink first?" He smiled as he peeled off a few bills and handed them to the bartender.

"Um, no. I have one." She held out her smoothie and waved it under his nose.

The bartender glared at her garish takeout cup but settled Gabriel's tab and then went about his business.

"Why are you drinking that? Does it pair well with couscous?" Gabriel chuckled.

Julia bit her lip.

He stopped chuckling immediately and frowned, somewhat roughly tugging at her lip with his thumb until he'd loosened it from her teeth. "Stop that. I don't want you to bleed." He pulled his thumb back and brought his face closer to hers—too close, actually. "I made a joke about couscous."

Julia was still trying to catch her breath after the flash of heat that she experienced having his thumb in between her lips.

"It wasn't funny, was it? It's rude to make fun of someone's poverty. And you are a sweet little girl."

Julia clenched her teeth, wondering just how much of his condescending attitude she could take before she decided to leave him (and his dick) in Christa's clutches.

"Professor, I . . ."

"I was just talking to someone. You know her—she's a real vixen." Gabriel's drunken gaze lazily swept the room before coming to rest again on Julia. "She's gone now. I'm glad. She's a nasty bitch."

Julia nodded. And smiled.

"She looked at you as if you were trash, but I fixed her. She bothers you again, and I drop her as a student. You'll be fine, now."

He brought his face close to hers again and licked his red and perfect lips slowly, *very* slowly. "You shouldn't be in a place like this. It's past your bedtime, isn't it? You should be asleep in your little purple bed, curled up like a kitten. A pretty little kitten with big brown eyes. I'd like to pet you."

Julia's eyebrows shot up. *Where the hell does he get this stuff?*

"Um, I really need to go home. Now. Would you come outside and help me hail a cab? Please, Professor?" Julia gestured vaguely toward the exit, trying to place some distance between the two of them.

He grabbed his trench coat immediately. "I'm sorry. I left you to find your way home unescorted on Thursday. I won't do that again. Let's get you home, little kitten."

He held out his arm in a very proper and old-fashioned way, and she took it, wondering who exactly was leading whom. When they got outside, Ethan was standing next to a cab, holding the rear passenger door open.

"Miss Mitchell," Gabriel breathed, placing his hand at the small of her back, gently moving her toward the open door of the taxi.

"On second thought, I can walk," she protested, trying to move out of the way.

But Gabriel was insistent and so was Ethan, probably because he was trying to get both of them out of there before Gabriel decided he didn't want to leave and decked him. So for the sake of time and to avoid Christa, the Gollum who could reappear at any moment and try to snatch back the Precious, Julia crawled into the cab and slid over to the far side.

Gabriel climbed in after her. She held her nose slightly so she wouldn't get an inhalant high from all the Scotch he'd imbibed. Ethan handed a few bills to the driver and closed the door behind them, waving at Julia as the cab sped away.

"Manulife Building," said Gabriel to the cabbie.

Julia was just about to correct The Professor and give the cabbie her address when Gabriel interrupted her. "You didn't come into *The Vestibule* for a drink." He was looking at her clothes, his eyes resting somewhat hungrily on the flesh at her knees, exposed underneath her ripped jeans.

"Bad luck. I was in the wrong place at the wrong time."

"Hardly," he breathed, a smile playing at the corners of his lips. "I would say you have extremely *good* luck. And now that I've seen you, so have I."

She sighed. It was too late to ask the cabbie to turn around now; they were driving in the opposite direction. She was going to have to see to it that The Professor made it inside safely before she could walk home. She shook her head and took a long sip from her smoothie.

"Were you spying on me?" His eyes shifted to hers suspiciously. "For Rachel?"

"Of course not. I was on my way home from the library when I saw you through the window."

"You saw me and decided to come and talk to me?" He sounded surprised.

"Yes," Julia lied.

"Why?"

"I only know two people in Toronto, Professor. You're one of them."

"That's a shame. I suppose Paul is the other one."

Julia eyed him cautiously but said nothing.

"*Angelfucker.*"

She frowned. "Why do you keep calling him that?"

"Because that's what he is, Miss Mitchell. Or rather, what he *hopes* he will become. Over my dead body. You tell him that—tell him he fucks with the angel at his peril."

Julia arched an eyebrow at his eccentric and obviously medieval profanity and its attendant explanation. She'd seen him drunk before, of course, and knew that his drunkenness vacillated between moments of absolute clarity and complete lunacy.

How exactly does one fuck with an angel? Angels are immaterial, spiritual creatures. They don't have genitalia. Gabriel, you are one sick Dante specialist.

They arrived shortly at his apartment building, and the two of them exited the cab. It wasn't that far for Julia to walk home—only about four city blocks. And she didn't have any cash to spare for a cab, anyway. So she smiled at Gabriel, bade him a good night, and patted herself on the back for doing Rachel a favor. Then she and her smoothie began the long solitary walk home.

"I've lost my keys," he called after her, patting the pockets of his trousers and leaning precariously against a faux potted palm. "But I've found my glasses!" He held the black Prada frames aloft.

Julia closed her eyes and drew breath. She wanted to leave him there. She wanted to pass along the responsibility for his well-being to some other Good Samaritan, preferably, a passing homeless person. But when she looked over at Gabriel's confused face and saw him beginning to tilt to one side as if he was going to fall over and take the poor potted palm with him (a potted palm that had never harmed anyone), she knew that he needed her help. He was Grace's little boy once, and she couldn't just abandon him. And she knew deep within her heart that kindness, no matter how small, was never wasted.

He can't even find his keys, for the love of Dante. She deposited her half-empty smoothie in a garbage can with a sigh.

"Let's go." She placed an arm around his waist, flinching slightly as he wrapped his arm around her shoulder and gave her a squeeze that was almost too friendly.

They listed into the lobby like a galleon, waving at the concierge, who recognized Gabriel and buzzed them into the building. Once they made it to the elevator, the Scotch seemed to hit Gabriel even harder. He stood with his eyes closed, his head lolling backward, and he groaned from time to time. Julia took the opportunity to search his pockets for his keys, which she found quickly and easily once she wrested his prized Burberry trench coat away from him.

"You picked me up, you naughty little kitty. I thought you didn't go home with men you met in bars."

Even while drunk, Professor Emerson was still an ass.

"I'm not *picking you up*, Professor. *I'm dropping you off*. And if you keep that up, I'm going to drop *you*," Julia muttered in a fit of irritation.

It took several attempts for her to find the key to his apartment, and when she did, she helped him in and pulled the key out of the lock. Her goal was to leave him there, assuming he'd be fine on his own, but he started mumbling about feeling sick. She envisioned him choking on his own vomit and dying on a bathroom floor alone and friendless like a faded rock star, so she decided to stay long enough to get him to the bedroom and to see that he didn't throw up (and die). She put his keys and his coat on the hall table. And she quickly took off her own coat and placed it on top of her briefcase.

Gabriel was leaning up against the wall with his eyes closed, which meant that he wasn't going to notice that she was still wearing his sweater, like a teenage girl with a crush.

"Come on, Professor." Julia pulled his arm around her shoulder and grabbed his waist again, trying to ease him down the hall.

"Where are you taking me?" He opened his eyes and looked around.

"To bed."

Gabriel began to laugh. He planted his feet and leaned up against the wall, gazing down at her.

"What's so funny?"

"You, Miss Mitchell," he breathed, his voice suddenly husky. "You're taking me to bed, but you haven't even kissed me yet. Don't you think we should *start* with kissing and maybe some canoodling on the couch for a couple of evenings? *Then* work up to bed? I haven't even had a chance to pet you, you naughty little kitty. And you are a virgin, aren't you?"

Julia bristled, especially at the last remark. "You've never canoodled a day in your life. And I'm not taking you to *bed*, you idiot, I'm taking you to your *bedroom* so you can sleep it off. Now come on. And cut the chitchat."

"Kiss me, Julianne. Kiss me good night." Gabriel's eyes grew wide as he fixated on her. He dropped his voice to a satin whisper. "Then I'll go to bed like a good little boy. And maybe, if you're a very good kitten, I'll let you join me."

Julia caught her breath. He didn't look drunk now. He looked remarkably lucid, and his eyes were caressing her, touching her, spending longer than was appropriate on the expanse of her chest. He began licking his lips.

Here comes the seductive smile . . . in five, four, three, two, one . . . swoon. (It was a good thing that in her current mood she was swoon-proof.)

Julia let go of him instantly and backed up, averting her eyes, for in truth, looking into the radiance of *that* smile was like staring into the sun. He pushed off the wall and took a step toward her. Now she was trapped. Her back was against the other wall, and he was still coming closer.

Julia's eyes grew larger. He was stalking her. And he looked hungry.

"Please, don't. Please don't . . . hurt me," she whimpered.

A furrow appeared between Gabriel's eyebrows. He reached out, and soft hands cupped her face gently, tilting her so that she was staring straight into his bold, shining eyes.

"Never." And with that he brought his lips to hers.

As soon as they connected, skin against skin, Julia lost all ability to think and simply drowned in feeling. She had never felt more embodied than at the moment, never felt as if she existed less in her head. His mouth barely moved over hers. It was warm, and his lips were wet and surprisingly soft. She didn't know if he was kissing her like that because he was drunk or for some other reason, but it was as if their lips were frozen together. As if their connection, so intense and real, could not be broken even for a second. Julia dared not move her mouth for fear he would release her and she would never be kissed by him again.

He pressed into her firmly but gently, while his hands tenderly floated across her cheeks. He did not open his mouth. But the feeling that surged between them was more powerful than ever. Julia's blood sang in her ears, and she felt herself flush and grow hot as she pressed forward against his chest, closing the gap between them and winding her arms around his back. She could feel the muscles underneath his shirt. She could almost feel his heart beating against her own chest. But he was so gentle, so tender. His mouth left her wanting more—much, much more.

She wasn't sure how long they kissed, but by the time he released her Julia's head was spinning. It was transcendent. It was emotional. The momentary fulfillment of her heart's deepest longing. Memories and dreams of the orchard came flooding back. They were not the stuff of her imagination—the spark, the attraction, was real and so stirring to her soul. She had not imagined it, but she wondered if he felt it too. Or perhaps he was immune to those kinds of feelings now.

"Beautiful Julianne," he murmured as he staggered backward. "Sweet like candy."

Gabriel licked his lips as if he was savoring her taste, and whatever lucidity he had suddenly disappeared. He shut his eyes and collapsed against the wall, close to passing out.

When she finally regained her senses, which took more than a minute, she managed to half-drag him into his bedroom. And all would have been well. All would have been well if he hadn't opened up his mouth at that moment and vomited all over her. And all over his beautiful and expensive British-racing-green cashmere sweater, which was no longer green by the time he was finished with it.

Julia gasped and heaved at the sight and smell, for she had a very queasy stomach. *It's even in my hair. Oh gods of all Good Samaritans, make haste to help me!*

"I'm sorry, Julianne. I'm sorry I was a bad boy." Gabriel's voice was like a child's.

She held her breath and shook her head. "It's all right. Come on." She pulled him into the master bathroom and was able to position him on his knees over the toilet before the next volcanic stomach eruption.

While he vomited, she held a hand to her nose and tried to distract herself by taking stock of his elegant and spacious bathroom. Large two-person or more bathtub? Check. Large two-person or more shower with decadent tropical rain showerheads? Double check. Large fluffy white towels perfect for picking up puke? Check, check, and check.

When Gabriel finished, she handed him a small but absorbent hand towel to wipe his mouth. He groaned loudly and ignored her offer. So she leaned over and gently swiped the towel over his face before giving him a sip of water to swish around his mouth.

She stared at him. Despite the train wreck that was her own family and her overall skittishness about marriage, she had thought from time to time about what it would be like to have a baby—a little boy or girl who would look like Julia and her husband. As she gazed down at a very sick Gabriel, she imagined what it would be like to be a mother and to care for her ill child. Gabriel's vulnerability tugged on her heartstrings, for she'd never seen it before except that once, when he cried in his office over Grace.

Grace would be happy that I'm taking care of her son.

"Will you be all right for a minute?" Julia asked, pushing his soft hair out of his eyes.

He groaned again, eyes closed, and she took that as an indication that he would be fine. But Julia had a difficult time letting him go. So while he sat there, moaning, she petted him a little, stroking his hair and chattering to him as if he were a baby.

"It's all right, Gabriel. It's all right. All I ever wanted was to be nice to you . . . to care for you a little . . . even if you never cared for me."

When she was satisfied that she could leave him alone for a few minutes, she went into his bedroom and quickly began looking through his chest of drawers for something, anything, that she could change into. She resisted the impulse to rummage through his underwear in search of a prize that she could take home (or sell on eBay) and grabbed the first pair of boxer shorts she could find. They were black and decorated with the shield of Magdalen College and looked as if they would be too small for Gabriel's finely shaped derrière.

Even Gabriel's underwear is pretentious, thought Julia as she searched for a T-shirt.

She went to the guest washroom and quickly stripped off her fouled clothes, hopped into the shower just to rinse the vomit out of her hair and the stench from her skin, then changed into his things.

Afterward, she tried to tackle the disaster that was Gabriel's cashmere sweater. She cleaned it as best she could, soaking it a little in the sink. Finally, she placed it on the marble countertop to air dry. He'd have to have it dry-cleaned (or burned). Julia took the rest of her clothes, put them in the washer, and returned to the master bathroom.

Gabriel was sitting with his back against the wall, his knees up to his chest and his face in his hands. He was still moaning.

Julia quickly cleaned the toilet and kneeled beside him. She didn't like the idea of leaving him in vomit-soaked clothes, but she didn't like the idea of undressing him either. He'd probably accuse her of sexual harassment or something, and she didn't want to deal with a drunk and angry Professor Emerson. Or a sober and angry Professor Emerson. For like a dragon, he could turn on you in a second if he thought you were pulling his tail.

"Gabriel, you've thrown up all over yourself. Do you understand? Do you want to stay like this or . . ." She let her voice trail off.

He shook his head with some semblance of understanding and tried to remove his tie. Of course, with his eyes closed he had little success. So Julia gently loosened the tie and slowly pulled it over his head. She blotted it with water as best she could, leaving it on the counter. He would have to dry clean it too.

While her back was turned, he began undoing the buttons of his shirt. However, it was much more difficult than he anticipated, and so he cursed and tugged at the buttons, almost tearing them off in the process.

Julia sighed. "Here, let me." She kneeled beside him once again, brushed his long fingers aside, and quickly unfastened the buttons.

He shrugged out of his dress shirt and immediately pulled his T-shirt over his head. Because he was disoriented he was unable to free his head from the shirt, so he just sat there with it wrapped over his hair like a turban.

It really was quite funny. Julia stifled a laugh, wishing she had her cell phone close at hand so she could take a picture of him. She would have loved to have used that shot as her screensaver. Or her avatar, should she ever have need of one. She gently freed his face from his shirt and sat back on her heels, gasping.

Gabriel's naked chest was stunning. Indeed, his entire upper body was a study in perfection. He had large, muscular arms, broad shoulders, and excellently toned pectorals. He'd always seemed to have a slender build, Julia thought, especially when his physique was masked by sweaters or jackets. But there was nothing slender about Gabriel now. Absolutely nothing.

And Gabriel had a tattoo. This surprised her greatly. She'd seen photos of Gabriel and Scott with their shirts off—pictures from summer vacations taken before she moved to Selinsgrove. But she could have sworn that Gabriel did not have a tattoo in those pictures. So the tattoo was recent, within the last six or seven years.

The tattoo was over his left pectoral, above the nipple and spreading over to his sternum. The image was of a winged medieval dragon that was wrapped around an oversized heart, crushing it between its two front feet. The heart was lifelike, not stylized, and the dragon's claws dug into its flesh so deeply that blood seeped from its wounds.

Julia gaped openmouthed at the dark and disturbing image. The dragon was green and black with a coiled, barbed tail and large fluttering wings. Its mouth was open and breathing fire. But what captured her attention was the black lettering across the surface of the heart. She was able to make out the letters *m a i a*. Maia. Or was it m.a.i.a.—an acronym?

Julia had no idea who Maia was or what m.a.i.a. was. She'd never heard the name from Rachel or any of the Clarks. It seemed to her to be completely out of character for Gabriel, the Gabriel she barely knew once and the one she was only beginning to know again, to have a tattoo at all, let alone one so large and haunting.

He has a tattoo like that underneath his clothes and he wears a bow tie? With a sweater?

Julia wondered what other surprises lurked across the surface of his skin, and her eyes wandered a little lower. Even in a seated position, she couldn't help but notice his well-defined abdominal muscles and the deep V that extended from his hips to down beneath the waistband of his wool trousers.

Holy crap. Professor Emerson must work out—a lot. Could I take a photo of his abs—and his V—for my screen saver?

Julia blushed and turned away. She was being bad, ogling The Professor. She wouldn't have wanted anyone to do that to her, especially at a low moment. So feeling more than slightly guilty, she gathered up his soiled clothes and the towel that she used to clean up the sick that had dripped onto the Persian rug in his bedroom, and took them to the laundry room. She quickly placed everything in the washer, filled it with detergent, and started a wash. Then she passed through the kitchen to fetch a glass and a pitcher of filtered water from the refrigerator.

In her absence, Gabriel had managed to stagger to the imposing silk-draped bed that was in the center of the room. He was now seated on the edge, barefoot and clad only in a pair of black boxer briefs, his hair sticking out of his head in all directions.

Holy cow.

Although there was probably nothing hotter in the universe than the sight of a half-naked Gabriel sitting on his bed (except perhaps for the surface of the sun), Julia averted her eyes and placed the water on his nightstand. She wanted to ask him how he was, but she thought maybe she should give him a moment. So she stood back and let her eyes roam around the room. And what she saw astounded her.

Gabriel's penchant for black-and-white photographs was more noticeable here, for every wall but one was adorned with pairs, each extremely large and hung in imposing black frames. However, it was the content of the pictures that Julia found surprising.

The photos were erotic. Pictures of naked, primarily female forms, although sometimes a female and male together, with the faces and genitalia either absent or in shadow. Tastefully posed, they were quite beautiful, and Julia would not have said that they were filthy. But they were highly sensual and amative, much more sophisticated than average pornography and far more arousing.

One showed a couple from the side, facing one another and straddling a bench of some kind. Their torsos were pressed together, his hands in her long, fair hair. Julia blushed as she wondered if the photo was taken before, during, or after the beautiful couple made love, for she couldn't tell.

Another was of a woman's back and a pair of man's hands, one of which embraced her middle back and the other cupping her bottom. A tattoo ran across her right hip, but the writing was in Arabic, Julia surmised, so she couldn't read it.

But it was the two larger photos that hung over the bed that caught her attention.

One of them depicted a woman lying on her stomach. A man's form floated over hers, almost like a dark angel, pressing a kiss to a shoulder blade and splaying his left hand across her lower back. It reminded Julia of Rodin's sculpture, *The Angel's Kiss*, so she wondered if the photographer had been inspired by that work.

The other photo took Julia's breath away, for it was the most overtly erotic, and she was instantly repulsed by its rawness and aggression. It was the side view of a woman lying on her stomach, with only her length from mid-torso to knee visible. Hovering above her was part of a male form. His hand was planted white-knuckled on her left hip and bottom cheek, his hips pressed tightly against the curve of her backside. The man had an attractive gluteus maximus in profile and long, elegant fingers. Julia was disturbed by the photo and immediately looked away in embarrassment.

Why would someone have a photo of that *hanging on his wall?* She shook her head. From gazing at the photographs, one point was abundantly clear: *Professor Emerson is a back man.*

Given his décor and his choice of artwork, Gabriel's bedroom appeared to have one purpose and one purpose only, and that was to serve as a cauldron of seething lust. She knew based upon what she'd observed, that he must have intended it to be so, despite its obvious and palpable coldness—a coldness that was in keeping with the overall glacial atmosphere of his entire apartment. In this taupe-walled space, a chill emanated from the photographs, the ice-blue silk of his bed coverings and curtains, and the sparseness of the all-black furniture of the room, dominated by an oversized bed with an ornately carved and high-posted headboard and a low and equally intricate footboard.

Medieval, thought Julia. *How fitting.*

But the photographs were soon supplanted in her attention by something else, something even more surprising. She stared in shock at the painting on the far wall, her jaw dropping open.

On the wall opposite Gabriel's large and medieval bed, and strangely out of place among the black-and-white erotica, was a Pre-Raphaelite oil painting in brilliant and glorious color. It was a full-scale reproduction of Henry Holiday's painting of Dante and Beatrice, the same painting that hung over her own bed.

Julia's eyes darted from the painting, to Gabriel, and back to the painting again. He could see the painting from his bed. She imagined him falling asleep at night, every night, looking at Beatrice's face. It was the last thing he would see at night and the first thing he would see in the morning. Julia hadn't known that he owned that painting. He was the reason why she owned it; was she, by any chance, the reason why he did?

She began to tremble at the thought. No matter who came into his bedroom, no matter which girl Gabriel brought home to warm his bed, Beatrice was always there. Beatrice was ever present.

But he didn't remember that she was Beatrice.

Julia shook her head to suppress those thoughts and gently persuaded Gabriel to lie down. She covered him with the sheet and the silk duvet, tucking the edges under his arms, across his chest. She sat down on the bed next to him, watching him as he looked at her.

"I was listening to music," he whispered, as if he was continuing a conversation.

She frowned in confusion. "What kind of music?"

"*Hurt*. Johnny Cash. Over and over."

"Why do you listen to that?"

"To remember."

"Oh, Gabriel. Why?" Julia blinked back tears, for that was the one Trent Reznor song she could listen to without heaving, but it always made her weep.

He didn't answer.

She leaned over him. "Gabriel? Sweetheart, don't listen to that kind of music anymore, okay? No more *Lacrimosa* or Nine Inch Nails. Walk out of the darkness and toward the light."

"Where's the light?" he mumbled.

Julia exhaled deeply. "Why do you drink so much?"

"To forget," he said, closing his eyes and resting back on the pillow.

With his eyes closed, she was able to admire him. She surmised that he would have been sweet-looking as a teenager—all big sapphire eyes and kissable lips and sexy brown hair. He might have been shy instead of angry or sad. He might have been noble and good. If Julia and he had been closer in age, he might have kissed her on her father's porch, taken her to the prom, and made love to her for the first time on a blanket under the stars, in the old orchard behind his parents' house. She might have been his first, in some more perfect universe.

Julia contemplated how much pain a human soul, her soul, could bear without shriveling completely, and she turned to go. A warm hand darted out to catch her.

"Don't leave me," he breathed. His eyes were only half open, and they pleaded with her. "Please, Julianne."

He knew who she was, but somehow he still wanted her to stay. And the way his eyes and his voice grew desperate . . . she could not deny him when he looked like that.

She wrapped her hand in his and sat beside him again. "I'm not going to leave you. Just sleep now. There's light all around you. So much light."

A smiled played on his perfect lips, and she heard him sigh; the grip with which he held her hand loosened. She took a deep breath, held it, and ghosted a finger over his eyebrows. When he didn't flinch or open his eyes, she softly stroked them, one by one. Her mother had done this when Julia wasn't able to sleep as a child. But that was ever so long ago, long before her mother neglected her in order to pursue other, more important interests.

Gabriel was still smiling, and so Julia bravely moved her hand to his hair. Feeling the unruly strands running though her fingers reminded her of a day she'd spent on a farm in Tuscany during her year abroad. An Italian boy had taken her out to a field, and they had walked together, her hand floating over the tops of the grasses. Gabriel's hair was feather light and soft against her hand, like the whispering Italian grass.

She began to stroke his hair, the way Grace must have done at one time. He allowed her fingertips to trail down the side of his face, tracing his angular jaw and rubbing gently against his stubble. She touched the merest hint of a dimple in his chin and began to move the back of her hand against his high and noble cheekbones. She would never again be this close to him; if he were awake, he wouldn't let her. He'd have bitten her hand, she was sure, and gone for her throat.

His perfect chest rose and fell with his now regular breathing. He seemed to have fallen asleep.

She stared at his neck, the muscles in his shoulders and the tops of his arms, his collarbone, and the tops of his pectorals. If he had been pale, he would have looked like a Roman statue carved in cold, white marble. But the merest hint of a tan left over from the summer made his skin glow almost gold in the lamplight.

Julia pressed a kiss against two of her fingers and placed those fingers tenderly against his slightly parted lips. "*Ti amo, Dante. Eccomi Beatrice.* I love you, Dante. Here I am, Beatrice."

Just then, Gabriel's telephone rang.

She jumped in surprise. The phone was ringing very loudly. Gabriel was beginning to move, the horrible noise piercing his rest. So Julia answered it.

"Hello?"

"Who the hell is this?" a woman's voice, shocked and shrill, demanded.

"This is Gabriel Emerson's residence. Who is *this?*"

"This is Paulina. Put Gabriel on the phone!"

Julia's heart thudded twice and skipped a beat before beginning to race. She stood up, taking the cordless receiver with her, and walked into the bathroom, closing the door.

"He can't come to the phone right now. Is it an emergency?"

"What do you mean *he can't?* Tell him it's Paulina and I want to speak to him."

"Um, he's indisposed."

"Indisposed? Listen, you little slut, roll Gabriel over and put the phone in his hand. I'm calling from the—"

"He can't talk to you right now. Please call back tomorrow." Julia pressed the *end* button, interrupting Paulina's torrent of furious words, feeling thoroughly disgusted.

She's more demanding than a casual lover. She must be his mistress—and she's going to be pissed that I answered the phone. Maybe she'll be so pissed she'll break up with him.

Julia cringed at her continued misfortune and removed the towel from her hair, hanging it up to dry. She returned to the bedroom and placed the telephone on its cradle. She intended to leave Gabriel to his dreams and sleep in the guest room, because she'd promised that she wouldn't abandon him.

Suddenly, two blue eyes opened wide and began to stare right through her.

"Beatrice," he whispered, reaching out his hand.

Julia shuddered convulsively.

"*Beatrice,*" he whispered again, gazing into her eyes with unblinking recognition.

"Gabriel?" She stifled a sob.

Chapter Fourteen

His eyes closed, but only for a second, and a slow, sweet smile spread across his face. His eyes grew soft and very warm. "You found me."

Julia chewed at the inside of her cheek, willing herself not to burst into tears at the sound of his voice. This was the voice she remembered. And she'd waited to hear it for so long. She had waited for him to return to her for so, so long.

"Beatrice." He clasped her wrist, pulling her toward him. He shifted slightly on the bed to accommodate her, enveloping her in his arms as she rested her head on his naked chest. "I thought you'd forgotten me."

"Never," she choked out as the tears began to flow uncontrollably. "I thought of you every day."

"Don't cry. You found me."

Gabriel closed his eyes and turned his head, his breathing beginning to regulate again. Julia lay very still, not wanting her sobs to disturb him, trying desperately not to shake the bed as she let her grief and relief wash over her. Tears traveled in small rivers down her pale cheeks and onto the expanse of tanned and tattooed skin that lay beneath her head.

Her Gabriel had remembered her. Her Gabriel had finally returned.

"Beatrice," his arm tightened around her waist as he moved to whisper against her hair, still damp from the shower. "Don't cry." With his brilliant blue eyes closed, Gabriel pressed his lips to her forehead, once, twice, thrice.

"I missed you. So much," she whispered, her lips moving against his tattoo.

"You found me," he murmured. "I should have waited. *I love you.*"

Now Julia wept harder, clinging to him as if she were drowning and he was her savior. She kissed the skin of his chest lightly and ran her fingers up and down his abdomen.

In response, Gabriel's fingertips traced the goose-pimpled flesh of her arms before slipping under the loose fabric of her T-shirt. He feathered his fingers across her skin until his hand finally stilled against her lower back. He sighed deeply and seemed to pass into his dreamland once again.

"I love you, Gabriel. So much it hurts," she said, her hand coming to rest over his gently beating heart. She whispered Dante's own words back to him, somewhat changed:

Love hath so long possess'd me for his own
And made his lordship so familiar
That he, who at first irk'd me, is now grown
Unto my heart as its best secrets are.
And thus, when he in such sore wise doth mar
My life that all its strength seems gone from it.
Mine inmost being then feels thoroughly quit
Of anguish, and all evil keeps afar.
Love also gathers to such power in me
That my sighs speak, each one a grievous thing.
Always soliciting
My Gabriel's salutation piteously.
Whenever he beholds me, it is so,
Who is more sweet than any words can show.

When all her tears were dry, Julia placed a few tentative kisses against Gabriel's stilled, soft lips and fell into a deep and dreamless sleep in the arms of her beloved.

❀ ❀

When she awoke, it was shortly past seven in the morning. Gabriel was still sound asleep. In fact, he was snoring, and from the looks of it neither of them had moved all night. It was probably the most peaceful sleep she'd ever had, but one.

She didn't want to move. She didn't want to be separated from him, not by one inch. She wanted to lie in his arms forever and pretend as if they had never been apart.

He recognized me. He loves me. Finally.

She had never felt loved before. Not really. Oh *he* had mumbled it, and her mother had shouted it but only when drunk, so the words never entered Julia's consciousness. Or heart. She never believed them because their actions had showed their words to be false. But she believed Gabriel.

So on this morning, the first morning ever, Julia felt loved. She smiled so widely she thought her face would break. She pressed her lips to Gabriel's neck and nuzzled against his stubbled skin. He moaned softly and his arm tightened against her, but his regular and deep breathing told her that he was still very much asleep.

Julia had enough experience with alcoholics to know that Gabriel would be hungover and probably cranky when he woke up. So she wasn't in a hurry to wake him. She was silently grateful that last night, at least, Gabriel had been a harmless, flirtatious drunk. That kind of drunk she could handle. It was the other kind that frightened her.

She spent about an hour drinking in his scent and his warmth, reveling in their closeness, skimming her hands tentatively over his upper body. Apart from the evening she spent with him in the woods, these moments were the happiest of her life. But eventually, she had to get up.

She stealthily crawled out from under his arm and padded to the master bathroom, closing the door behind her. She noticed a bottle of Aramis cologne sitting on his vanity. She picked it up, opened it, and sniffed. It wasn't the scent that she remembered from the orchard. His scent then had been more natural, wilder even.

This is the new scent of Gabriel. And just like him—it's breathtaking. And now he's mine . . .

She brushed her teeth, twisted her now curly hair up into a messy knot, and walked into the kitchen to find a rubber band or a pencil with which to hold it. Her hair thus affixed, she floated into the laundry room and transferred the clean but damp clothes to the dryer. She couldn't go home until her clothes were dry. But she had no intention of leaving now that he remembered her.

What about Paulina? Or m.a.i.a.*?* Julia pushed those questions aside, simply because they were irrelevant. Gabriel loved her. Of course, he would let Paulina go.

What about the fact that he's my Professor? And what if he's an alcoholic?

She had promised herself long ago that she would never get involved with an alcoholic. But rather than face that possibility head-on, she actively suppressed all the little, niggling doubts that were bubbling to the surface, for truly, she wanted to believe that their love would conquer all.

"Let me not to the marriage of true minds admit impediments," she thought, citing Shakespeare as a talisman against her fears. She believed Gabriel's vices were borne out of loneliness and despair. But now that they had found each other once again, their love would be enough to rescue both of them from their respective darknesses. Together they would be far stronger and far healthier than they had been separately.

As Julia pondered these things in her heart, she went through the cupboards of Gabriel's excellently stocked kitchen. She wasn't sure if he would want breakfast, given his hangover. Sharon had always eschewed food in favor of a breakfast libation such as a Seabreeze, which Julia had (sadly) learned to make with aplomb at age eight. Nevertheless, after she finished her own breakfast of scrambled eggs, bacon, and coffee, she prepared the same for Gabriel.

Not knowing if he would need the hair of the dog that bit him, but wanting to give him that option, she made him a Walters cocktail. She found the recipe in his bartender's guide, having chosen (she hoped correctly) the decanter on top of the sideboard that held his least favorite Scotch, not wanting to sully his finest single malt with juice.

In sum, Julia was ecstatic at having the opportunity to spoil Gabriel a little, and so she took extra care as she prepared his breakfast tray. She clipped a few small sprigs of parsley from his countertop herb garden for a garnish, which she placed alongside the orange sections that she'd cut up and fanned next to the bacon. She even wrapped his silverware in a linen napkin, which she folded somewhat clumsily into the shape of a pocket. She wished she was clever enough to make something more substantial than a pocket, a peacock perhaps, or a fan, and she decided to investigate those options the next time she was on her computer. Martha Stewart would know. Martha Stewart always knew.

Then Julia bravely walked into Gabriel's study and found a pad of paper and a fountain pen on top of his large, wooden desk. She wrote a note:

> *October 2009*
> *Dear Gabriel,*
> *I'd given up hope,*
> *until you looked into my eyes last night and finally saw me.*
> *Apparuit iam beatitudo vestra.*
> *Now your blessedness appears.*
> *Your Beatrice*

Julia propped the note up against the wineglass she used for his orange juice. Not willing to wake him just yet, she placed the entire tray, cocktail and all, in his large and half-empty refrigerator. Then she leaned up against its door and sighed with satisfaction.

Knock. Knock. Knock.

Julia's domestic goddess routine was suddenly interrupted by someone banging on the front door.

Holy shit, she thought. *Could that be—?*

At first she didn't know what to do. Should she wait and see if Paulina let herself in with a key? Or should she run back to Gabriel's arms and hide? After waiting a minute or so her curiosity got the best of her, and she found herself tiptoeing quietly to the front door.

O gods of all just-been-reunited-with-my-soul-mate-after-a-really-painful-six-friggin'-years-graduate-students, please don't let my soul mate's (soon to be) ex-mistress mess things up. Please.

Julia took a deep breath and gazed through the peephole. The hallway was empty. Out of the corner of her eye, she saw something on the ground. Hesitantly, she opened the door just a crack and darted a nervous hand out toward the something, exhaling deeply in relief when her hand closed on the Saturday morning *Globe and Mail.*

Smiling again, and relieved that her blissful reunion with Gabriel had not been ruined by his erstwhile mistress, Julia picked up the paper and hastily locked the door. Still smiling, she poured herself a glass of orange juice and curled up in the red velvet wing-backed chair that was angled next to the fireplace, with her bare feet resting on the matching ottoman. She sighed in contentment.

If you had asked her over two weeks ago when she was visiting Gabriel's apartment with Rachel if she ever thought she'd be sitting in his precious chair on a Sunday morning, she would have said *no*. She hadn't thought it possible, even with Grace's saintly intercession. But now that she was here, she was very, very happy.

She settled in for a leisurely morning of orange juice and the Saturday paper and decided that her felicity deserved Cuban music, more specifically, a little bit of *Buena Vista Social Club*. As she listened to *Pueblo Nuevo* on her iPod, she perused the Arts section of Gabriel's newspaper. An exhibition of Florentine art was coming to the Royal Ontario Museum on loan from the Uffizi Gallery. Maybe Gabriel wouldn't mind taking her to see it. On a *date*.

Yes, they'd missed out on her high school prom and all the fancy parties at Saint Joseph's University. But Julia was sure that all the wasted time and lost opportunity would now be returned to her tenfold to fill as she wished with Gabriel. Happily, she leaped to her feet as the trumpet player in her ears began playing a few bars of *Stormy Weather* as a counterpoint to the Cuban melody. Julia sang loudly, too loudly, dancing with her orange juice in Gabriel's pretentious underwear, blissfully unaware of the half-naked man who was striding up behind her.

"What the hell are you doing?"

"*Aaaagggghhhhhh!*"

Julia yelped and jumped about a foot in reaction to the harsh, angry voice. She quickly took her earbuds out of her ears and turned around. And what she saw crushed her.

"I asked you a question!" Gabriel snapped, his eyes transformed to blackish-blue pools. "What the fuck are you doing in *my* underwear, jumping around *my* living room?"

Crack.

Was that the sound of Julia's heart snapping in two? Or just the final nail in the coffin in which her dead love rested, but not in peace?

Perhaps it was his tone of voice, angry and commanding. Perhaps it was the fact that in that one question she realized that he no longer viewed her as Beatrice, and all her realized hopes and dreams just fucking *died* in their infancy. But whatever the true explanation, Julia's iPod and orange juice slipped through her fingers. The glass promptly shattered, sending her old iPod skating through an ever expanding pool of liquid sunshine at her feet.

Julia stared at the disaster beneath her for a few seconds, trying to wrap her mind around it. It was as if she didn't understand how glass could shatter and make such a mess, something in the shape of a glittering starburst. Eventually, she dropped to her knees to pick up the glass and began repeating two questions over and over in her head.

Why is he so angry with me? Why doesn't he remember?

A tall and shirtless Gabriel looked down at her. He was clad only in his underwear, which made him look slightly sexy and slightly ridiculous. His fists were clenched, and Julia saw the tendons standing out in his magnificent arms.

"Don't you remember what happened last night, Gabriel?"

"No, thankfully I don't. And get up! You're on your knees more than the average whore." He spoke through clenched teeth, glaring at her servile form.

Julia's head popped up. She searched his eyes, noting his complete and utter lack of memory and his irritation. He might as well have run her through with a sword. She felt the blade pierce and enter her heart, and she felt her heart begin to hemorrhage slowly.

Just like his tattoo, she thought. *He's the dragon; I'm the bleeding heart.*

In that instant of silent realization, the most remarkable thing happened. Something inside of her, six years in the making, finally, *finally* snapped.

"I'll have to take you at your word about the behavior of whores, Emerson. Only you would know," she growled.

Then, when that snide remark didn't quite heal the ache in the now expanding fissure in her heart, she boldly forgot about cleaning up her mess and leaped to her feet. And promptly lost her temper.

"Don't you *dare* speak to me like that, you lousy drunk!" she snarled.

"Who the *fuck* do you think you are? After everything I did for you last night? I should have let Gollum have you! I should have let you fuck her brains out in front of everyone on top of the bar at Lobby!"

"What are you talking about?"

She leaned toward him, eyes flashing, cheeks flushed, and lips trembling. She shook with anger as the adrenaline coursed through her veins. She wanted to hit him. She wanted to wipe that expression off his face with her fists. She wanted to pull his hair out in handfuls and leave him bald. Forever.

Gabriel inhaled her scent, erotic and inviting, and licked his lips involuntarily. But that was the wrong thing to do in front of a woman as angry as Miss Mitchell.

She tossed her head in fury and stomped down the hall, muttering various and sundry exotic expletives in both English and Italian. And when she came to the end of them, she switched to German, a sure sign that she was in a towering rage.

"*Hau ab! Verpiss dich!*" she spat from the laundry room.

Gabriel slowly began rubbing his eyes, for in addition to suffering from one of the worst hangover headaches of his life, he was slightly enjoying the sight of Miss Mitchell in his T-shirt and boxer shorts, passionately angry and shouting at him in a multiplicity of Western European languages. It was the second most erotic thing he had ever witnessed. And it was entirely beside the point.

"How did you learn to swear in German?" He followed the sound of her cursing *auf Deutsch* to the laundry room where she was removing her now semi-dry clothes from the dryer.

"Bite me, Gabriel!"

He was distracted at that moment by a black lace bra that was reclining provocatively but somewhat casually on top of the dryer. He gazed at it and realized that the number and cup size that popped into his head the night he'd taken her to Harbour Sixty for dinner were absolutely correct. Gabriel silently congratulated himself.

He dragged his eyes up to meet hers. There were sparks in them, luminescent butterscotch in dark chocolate, like a glittering sundae.

"What are you doing?"

"What does it look like I'm doing? I'm getting the hell out of here before I take one of your stupid bow ties and strangle you with it!"

Gabriel frowned, for he had always thought that those ties were smart. "Who is Gollum?"

"Christa-fucking-Peterson."

Gabriel's eyebrows shot up. *Christa? I guess she is Gollum-like. If you squint.*

"Forget about Christa. I don't care about her. Did you have sex with me?" He crossed his arms and his voice grew serious.

"In your dreams, Gabriel!"

"That is not a denial, Miss Mitchell." He put his hand on her arm and forced her to stop what she was doing. "And don't tell me it wouldn't have formed part of your dreams too."

"Get your hands off me, you arrogant bastard!" Julia pulled away so forcefully she almost fell backward. "Of course, you would have to be drunk to want to fuck *me.*"

Gabriel reddened. "Stop it. Who said anything about fucking?"

"What else would you do? I'm the crazy little whore who's down on my knees every five seconds. Whatever happened, consider yourself lucky you don't remember it! I'm sure it was more than forgettable."

Gabriel's hand grabbed her chin and held it firmly, lifting it so her face was inches from his. "I said *stop it.*" His eyes flashed back at hers, and in them Julia read a serious warning. "You are not a whore. And don't ever speak about yourself like that again." His tone slid across her skin like an ice cube.

He let her go and took a very large step back, his chest heaving and his eyes burning. He closed his eyes hard and began to breathe deeply, very deeply. Even in his shadowy, soused thinking he knew that things had escalated far beyond what was warranted. He needed to calm the fuck down fast, and then he needed to calm her down before she did something rash.

The look in her eyes said it all; he'd cornered her like an animal. She was angry and hurt and frightened and sad—a furious, wounded kitten with claws drawn and tears glistening at the corners of her eyes. He had done this. He had done this to her, a brown-eyed angel, when he compared her to a whore and failed to remember whatever happened between them last night.

You must have seduced her if she's acting like this . . . Emerson, you are a grade A asshole. And you just kissed your career good-bye.

While Gabriel was thinking, and thinking slowly, Julia saw an opportunity and took it. Cursing him loudly, she grabbed her clothes from the dryer and ran into the guest room, slamming and locking the door behind her.

She pulled off his boxer shorts, dropping them disdainfully on the floor, and quickly pulled on her damp socks and jeans. When she realized that she'd left her bra on top of the dryer she decided she'd just leave without it. *He can add that to his collection. Bastard.* She decided not to change out of his T-shirt since it was less revealing than her own. And if he demanded his T-shirt back, she'd scratch his eyes out.

Julia stood with her ear against the door, listening for any sound of movement in the hallway. Her lack of clarity on this point gave her a few precious moments to think.

She'd lost her temper and been stupid. She knew what Gabriel could be like; she'd seen the shattered coffee table and the blood spattered on Grace's carpet. Although she was positive that her Gabriel would never, ever strike her, she had no idea what Professor Emerson would do when provoked.

But he'd made her so angry. And she'd never had the chance to rage against him before. It was as if all of her pent-up anger was screaming to get out. She had to push back; she had to get him out of her system once and for all. She'd wasted her life pining for someone who wasn't real, some temporary alcoholic apparition, and today it was finally going to stop.

You've yelled and cursed at him. Just get the hell out before he decides to get physical.

While Julia was getting dressed, Gabriel was stumbling to the kitchen in order to find something to remove the Scotch-woven cobwebs from his mind. He opened the door to the refrigerator and leaned against it, bathed in its brilliant fluorescence.

His blue eyes glanced over the fridge's contents until they found a large white tray. A very pretty, large white tray. A very pretty, very feminine, large white tray with food, orange juice, and what appeared to be a cocktail on it.

And was that . . . ? *She even* garnished *the plate, for God's sake.*

Gabriel stared. Miss Mitchell seemed to be a kindly person, but what were the chances that she made him breakfast for any reason other than the fact that he'd taken her to bed? The tray, in all of its garnished glory, seemed to be evidence of his seduction, and for that reason it sickened him.

Nevertheless, he was grateful that she'd prepared him a cocktail, as he gulped it greedily. It was precisely the antidote his pounding head needed, and in a few moments he felt some measure of relief.

Lazily, his eyes alighted on the note that was propped up against the orange juice. He scanned the writing slowly, not quite understanding why Miss Mitchell would choose to address him in such a manner. He read the note again and again, his focus finally coming to rest on these words:

Apparuit iam beatitudo vestra.
Now your blessedness appears.
Your Beatrice

He thrust the note aside in irritation. If it didn't confirm their tryst, it was evidence of a crush. No wonder it had been so easy to charm her out of her virginity. Students were intrigued by figures of authority and developed inappropriate attachments to them. In Julianne's case, she viewed him through the characters of her research, i.e., she was Beatrice to his Dante. A simple but forbidden crush. A crush he'd indulged in a selfish, drunken haze. Now he'd lost his appetite. *What will Rachel say when she finds out?*

Cursing his own lack of self-control, he walked past the closed guestroom door on the way to his bedroom. Flashes of the previous evening danced before his eyes. He remembered kissing Julianne in his hallway and the feel of her skin beneath his hands. He remembered earnestly desiring her, the sweetness of her lips, her warm breath in his face, the way she trembled under his touch. Even though he couldn't remember the act itself, or the pleasure of her nakedness, he remembered looking up into her face while he was lying in bed. He felt her hand against his cheek as she pleaded with him to walk toward the light. She had the face of an angel. A beautiful, brown-eyed angel.

She came to my rescue, and see how I treated her. I took her virginity, and I don't even remember it. She deserved better. Much, much better.

He emitted the groan of a tortured soul as he pulled on a pair of jeans and an old T-shirt and hunted around for his glasses. Just as he was about to exit the bedroom, he stopped, his gaze inexplicably drawn to the oil painting on the front wall.

Beatrice.

He moved so that he was but inches from her lovely face, her white figure familiar and comforting. His brown-eyed angel. A glimpse of the impossible drifted before his eyes, but like a wisp of smoke it vanished. He was hungover and not thinking clearly.

Julia quietly unlocked the door and peered into the hall. It was empty. She tiptoed toward the kitchen, shoved her feet into her sneakers, grabbed her things, and ran to the front door. Gabriel was waiting for her.

Scheisse.

"You can't leave until I get some answers."

Julia swallowed thickly. "Let me go. Or I'll call the cops."

"You call the cops, I'll tell them you broke in here."

"You tell them that, I'll tell them that you kept me here against my will and that you hurt me." She was speaking without thinking again, which wasn't smart. And now she was threatening him with a falsehood. Anything they did together had been consensual and chaste and sweet—and absolutely, absolutely ruined. But Gabriel didn't know that.

"Please, Julianne. Tell me I didn't—" His eyes grew large and round, and his face contorted in pain. "Please tell me I wasn't . . . rough with you." Gabriel turned almost green in his revulsion and raised a shaking hand to his glasses. "How badly did I hurt you?"

Julia debated how long she should leave him on the proverbial hook but decided hastily to un-bait him. She closed her eyes and groaned. "You didn't hurt me. Not physically, at least. You just wanted someone to put you to bed and keep you company. You begged me to stay, actually, but just as a friend. You were more of a gentleman to me last night than you were this morning, which is saying something. I think I like you better when you're drunk."

"Never think that, Julianne." He shook his head at her and sighed. "And I'm still drunk. I'm simply relieved that I wasn't your first."

She inhaled sharply, and Gabriel watched as a pained expression marred her lovely features.

"But your clothes . . ." He stared down at her chest, at her nipples that were poking prettily from underneath his black T-shirt. He tried not to ogle her, but failed.

"Is this some kind of joke?" she snapped. "Do you honestly not remember?"

"I have gaps in my memory—when I drink sometimes I can't tell . . ." He began mumbling incoherently.

Julia reached the end of her patience. "You threw up on me. That's why I was in your clothes. And for no other reason, believe me."

A look of relief and pained acknowledgment passed across his face. "I'm sorry," he said. "And I apologize for insulting you. I didn't mean what I said earlier, truly I didn't. I was shocked to find you here and the way you were dressed, I thought that we . . ." He made a vague hand gesture.

"Bullshit."

Gabriel glared, forcing himself to keep his temper. "If anyone connected with the university found out that you stayed here, I could be in a lot of trouble. We both could."

"I won't tell anyone, Gabriel. I'm not stupid, despite what you think of me."

He frowned. "I know you aren't stupid. But if Paul or Christa found out, then I . . ."

"Is that all you care about? Covering your own ass? Well, don't worry, I covered it for you. I pried Christa off your dick last night before you had a chance to consummate your professor-student relationship. You should be thanking me!"

Gabriel's face hardened, and he pressed his lips together. "*Thank you*, Miss Mitchell. But if someone sees you leaving here . . ."

Julia threw her hands up in frustration. He really was incredibly dense.

"If anyone sees me, I'll say I was on my knees for your next door neighbor, making money to buy couscous. I'm sure it's believable."

In a flash Gabriel's hand was on her chin again, more forcefully this time. "Stop it. I warned you about saying things like that."

Julia froze, but only for a second, before jerking out of his grasp. "Don't touch me," she hissed. She tried to move past him, praying he wasn't going to retaliate by hitting her, but he put his hand on the doorknob and braced himself against the door.

"Damn it! *Just stop.*" He raised his hand, hoping to still her.

Instinctively, she ducked and reeled backward. Gabriel saw her movement for what it was and instantly felt ill.

"Julianne, please." He lowered his voice to the softest whisper and pleaded with his eyes. "I'm not going to hit you. I just want to talk to you."

He placed a hand to his head and grimaced. "I've done terrible things when I wasn't in my right mind. I was afraid I'd treated you badly last night. I lashed out, but I'm only angry with myself.

"I think very highly of you. Very highly. How could I not? You are . . . beautiful and innocent and sweet. I don't like seeing you crawling on floors as if you were an animal or a fucking slave. Leave the bloody glass where it is—I don't care. Do you remember the self-deprecating words you said to me when I took you home after *The Vestibule?* Those words have haunted me. So have mercy on me and stop denigrating yourself. I can't take it."

He cleared his throat, twice. "I don't remember everything that happened with Miss Peterson, but I apologize. I was a fool, and you came to my rescue. *Thank you.*"

He slowly adjusted his glasses. "What happened last night cannot happen again. I apologize for kissing you. I'm sure that was a disgusting experience, some slobbering drunk putting his mouth all over you. Forgive me."

The air left Julia's body in a loud gasp. Gabriel's apology hurt. For from the sound of it, he didn't remember the kiss the way she did. And that upset her, greatly.

"Oh, that," she said coolly. "I'd forgotten all about it. It was nothing."

Gabriel raised his eyebrows. For some reason, his expression dark-

ened and he frowned. "Nothing? It was a good deal more than nothing."
He stared for a moment or two, wondering if he should bring up the
note she left on his tray.

"You're upset. I'm still drunk. Let's end this before it escalates any
further." His voice was clipped and suddenly cold. "Good-bye, Miss
Mitchell."

He unlocked the door and held it open.

"Gabriel?" She paused once she entered the hallway, turning to look
up at him.

"Yes?"

"I need to tell you something."

"Proceed." He sounded grim.

"Paulina called last night, while you were—unavailable. And I answered the phone."

He removed his glasses and began rubbing his eyes. "Shit. What did
she say?"

"She called me a slut and told me to roll you over and hand you the
phone. I said you were indisposed."

"Did she say why she was calling?"

"No."

"Did you tell her who you are? Your name?"

Julia shook her head.

"*Thank God,*" he muttered.

She frowned. She'd expected him to apologize for Paulina. But he
didn't. In fact, he seemed entirely unfazed by her behavior, as if he were
more concerned about Julia upsetting *her* than the other way round.

She must be his mistress.

Julia fixed him with a stony gaze, as her body began to vibrate with
anger. "You begged me to come after you—to look for you in Hell.
That's exactly where I found you. And you can stay there forever, for all
I care."

He stepped back, replacing his glasses, his eyes narrowing into slits.
"What are you talking about?"

"Nothing. I'm done, Professor Emerson." She turned on her heel and
walked to the elevator.

Confused, he watched her walk away, his thoughts hazy and unfocused. After a moment he jogged after her. "Why did you write that ridiculous note?"

She felt as if he'd stabbed a dagger into her heart. She straightened her shoulders and tried to steady her voice. "What note?"

"You know damned well what note! The note you left in my fridge."

Julia shrugged dramatically.

He grabbed her elbow and spun her around. "Is this a game to you?"

"Of course not! Let me go." She pulled her arm away from him and began punching the down button for the elevator, willing it to come to her rescue. She was humiliated and angry, feeling silly and oh so small. She couldn't get away from him fast enough, even if she ran down the stairs.

He moved a step closer. "Why did you sign the note the way you did?"

"Why do you care?"

He heard the elevator approaching and knew that he had mere seconds to get answers to his questions. He closed his eyes, her previous words thundering in his ears. *She looked for him in Hell.* He'd begged the brown-eyed angel to come looking for him. Of course, she hadn't. Hallucinations don't respond to begging.

What if Beatrice wasn't a hallucination? What if . . . He felt something like fear begin to creep across his skin. Once again, the impossible floated before his eyes. If he concentrated, he could see her in his memory, but her face was blurry.

The ringing of a bell signaled the arrival of the elevator.

His eyes snapped open.

She stepped through the open door and shook her head at him, at his confusion, and at the intoxication that still swam in his eyes. Everything hinged on this. She could tell him or she could keep secret what happened between them just as she always had. Just as she had for six fucking years.

As the door slowly began to close, she saw a wave of realization wash over him.

"*Beatrice?*" he whispered.

"Yes," she said, moving so she could maintain eye contact with him until the last possible second. "I'm Beatrice. You were my first kiss. I fell asleep in your arms in your precious orchard."

Gabriel sprang forward to stop the elevator door from closing. "Beatrice! Wait!"

He was too late. The door closed at the sound of her name. He pressed the button furiously, hoping to reopen the doors.

"I'm not Beatrice anymore." As the elevator began its slow but unstoppable descent, Julia burst into tears.

Gabriel pressed his forehead and palms against the cold steel of the elevator door.

What have I done?

Chapter Fifteen

Old Mr. Krangel looked out his peephole into the hallway and saw nothing out of the ordinary. He'd heard voices, a man and a woman arguing, but couldn't see anyone. He'd even heard a name—*Beatrice*. But he was unaware of any tenant called Beatrice on the floor. And now the hall appeared to be empty.

He'd already ventured out once that morning; he'd had to return his anonymous neighbor's Saturday paper, which had been delivered to his door by mistake. The Krangels didn't take the Saturday paper, but Mrs. Krangel suffered from dementia and had picked it up and hid it in the apartment the day before.

Slightly annoyed at having his Sunday morning thus interrupted by a *kemfn* in the hallway, Mr. Krangel opened his door and stuck his aged head out. Not fifty feet away, he saw a man leaning against the closed elevator door. His shoulders were shaking.

Mr. Krangel was immediately embarrassed by the pathetic sight before him but was momentarily mesmerized.

He didn't recognize the man, and he wasn't about to introduce himself. Surely a grown man who would waltz about the thirtieth floor of an apartment building barefoot and casually dressed and . . . doing whatever it was he was doing, was not the kind of person he wished to know. Men from his generation *never* cried. Of course, they never took their socks off in hallways, either. Unless they were—*odd*. Or lived in California.

Mr. Krangel retreated quickly, closed and locked his door, and called the concierge downstairs to report a barefoot crying man out in the hallway who had just had a screaming *kemfn* with a woman called Beatrice.

It took five tiresome minutes to explain to the concierge what a *kemfn* was. Mr. Krangel vocally lamented this fact, choosing to place the blame on the Toronto District School Board and their narrow, waspish curriculum.

❀ ❀

It was late October, and the weather in Toronto was already cool. Julia was without something warm under her coat as she slowly and miserably walked home, because she'd left Professor Emerson's fouled sweater behind. She hugged her arms tightly across her chest, wiping away angry and resigned tears.

People passed her on the street and gave her sympathetic glances. Canadians could be like that—quietly sympathetic but politely distant. Julia was grateful for their sympathy and even more grateful that no one stopped to ask why she was crying. For her story was both too long and too utterly fucked up to tell.

Julia never asked herself why bad things happen to good people, for she already knew the answer: bad things happen to everyone. Not that this was an excuse or a justification for wronging another human being. Still, all humans had this shared experience—that of suffering. No human being left this world without shedding a tear, or feeling pain, or wading into the sea of sorrow. Why should her life be any different? Why should she expect special, favored treatment? Even Mother Teresa suffered, and she was a saint.

Julia did not regret looking after The Professor while he was drunk, even though her good deed had not gone unpunished. For if you truly believe that kindness is never wasted, you have to hold tightly to that belief even when the kindness is thrown back in your face.

She was ashamed that she'd been so stupid, so foolish, so naïve as to think that he would remember her after a drunken binge and that they could return to the way things were (but never were, really) that one night in the orchard. Julia knew that she'd been swept up into the romantic fancy of a fairy tale, without any thought of what the *real* world, and the real Gabriel, was like.

But it was *real—the old spark was there. When he kissed me, when he touched me, the electricity was still there. He had to have felt it—it wasn't all in my head.* Julia quickly pushed those thoughts aside, willing herself to stick to her new, non-Emerson diet. *It's time to grow up. No more fairy tales. He didn't care enough to remember you back in September, and he has Paulina, now.*

When she entered her little hobbit hole, she took a long shower and changed into her oldest and softest flannel pajamas—pajamas that were pale pink with images of rubber duckies on them. She threw Gabriel's T-shirt to the back of her closet where it hopefully would be forgotten. She curled up on her twin bed, clutching her velveteen rabbit, and fell asleep, physically and emotionally spent.

While Julia was sleeping, Gabriel was warring with his hangover and fighting the urge to dive into a bottle of Scotch and never resurface. He hadn't gone after her. He hadn't run for the stairwell and stumbled down thirty flights to meet her at the lobby. He hadn't taken the next elevator and raced to the street to catch her.

No, he'd stumbled back to his apartment and slumped into a chair, so he could wallow in nausea and self-loathing. He cursed the roughness with which he'd treated her, not just this morning, but since his first seminar back in September. A roughness made worse by the fact that she had suffered saint-like in silence, all the while knowing exactly who and what she was to him.

How could I have been so blind?

He thought of the first time he'd seen her. He'd returned to Selinsgrove in depression and despair. But God had intervened, a genuine *deus ex machina*. God sent him an angel to rescue him from Hell—a delicate, brown-eyed angel in jeans and sneakers with a beautiful face and a pure soul. She comforted him in his darkness and gave him hope. She seemed to cherish a sincere affection for him despite his failings.

She saved me.

As if that salvation wasn't enough, the angel appeared to him a second time, the very day he'd cruelly lost the other strong force of goodness in his life, Grace. The angel sat in his Dante seminar, reminding him of truth, beauty, and goodness. And he responded by snapping at her and threatening to push her out of the program. Then this morning, he was cruel and compared her to a whore.

I'm the Angelfucker now. I've fucked over the brown-eyed angel. Ga-

briel cursed the irony of his name as he walked to the kitchen to retrieve her note.

Holding her beautiful, fragile message in his hand, he saw his own
ugliness—not an ugliness of body but of soul. Julianne's note, and even
her breakfast tray, confronted Gabriel's sin in a manner that was stark,
convicting, and absolutely unrelenting.

She could not have known this, but in that moment her words from
a week ago rang true. Sometimes people, when left alone, can hear their
own hatefulness for themselves. Sometimes goodness is enough to expose evil for what it really is.

Gabriel dropped her note onto the counter and buried his face in
his hands.

❋ ❋

When Julia finally awoke it was after ten o'clock in the evening. She
yawned and stretched, and after making a very sad bowl of instant oat-
meal and barely being able to choke down a third of it, she decided to
check her voice mail.

She'd turned her cell phone off when she arrived at Gabriel's the
night before because she was expecting a call from Paul. She was not in
a mood to speak with him, then or now, even though she knew he
would likely cheer her. She just wanted to be left alone to lick her
wounds, like a puppy that had been kicked repeatedly.

So it was with a heavy heart that she checked her messages, scroll-
ing through to listen to the oldest ones first, frowning when she realized that her inbox was full. Julia's inbox was never full, for the only
people who ever called her were her father, Rachel, and Paul, and their
messages were always short.

*"Hi Julia, it's me. It's Saturday night and the conference went well. I'm
bringing you back something from Princeton. It's small, so don't worry.
You're probably at the library, working. Call me later. [Pregnant pause . . .]
I miss you."*

Julia sighed and deleted the first message from Paul and moved to
his next one.

*"Hey, Julia. It's me again. It's Sunday morning, and I should be
home sometime tonight. Do you want to meet me for a late dinner?*

There's a great sushi place over by your apartment. Call me. Miss you, little Rabbit."

Julia deleted Paul's second message and quickly texted him, saying she'd come down with the flu and was catching up on her sleep. She'd call him when she was feeling better, and she hoped he'd arrived home safely. She did not tell him that she missed him.

The next message was from a local number that she didn't recognize.

"Julianne . . . um, Julia. It's Gabriel. I . . . Please don't hang up. I know I'm the last person you want to hear from, but I'm calling to grovel. In fact, I'm standing outside your building in the rain. I was worried about you, and I wanted to be sure you got home safely.

"I wish we could go back to this morning, and I could tell you that I've never seen anything more beautiful than the sight of you in my living room, happy and dancing. That I'm incredibly lucky that you rescued me and stayed with me all night. That I'm an idiot and a fuck-up, and I don't deserve your kindness. At all. I know I hurt you, Julia, and I'm sorry.

[Deep inhale and exhale.] "I should never have let you go this morning—not like that. I should have run after you and begged you to stay. I fucked up, Julia. I fucked up.

"I should have humiliated myself in person, which is what I'm trying to do now. Please come outside so I can apologize. Actually, don't come outside—you'll catch pneumonia. Just come to the front door and listen to me through the glass. I'm going to stand here and wait for you. Here is my cell number . . ."

Julia scowled and deleted his message, not even bothering to save his number. Still wearing her rubber duckie pajamas, she opened her apartment door and walked across the hall. She had no intention of listening to Gabriel; she just wanted to find out if he was still waiting outside in the cold, dark rain.

She pressed her nose against the glass in the front door, smudging it, and peered outside into the inky blackness. It was no longer raining. And there was no Professor to be found. She wondered how long he'd waited. She wondered if he'd walked to her apartment without an umbrella. Her spine stiffened, and she told herself that she didn't care.

Let him catch pneumonia. Serves him right.

Before she turned to go, she noticed a large bouquet of purple hyacinths leaning up against one of the pillars on the porch. It had a large, pink bow attached to it and something that looked like a Hallmark card resting in the middle of it. The envelope read *Julia*.

Oh really, Professor Emerson? I didn't know that Hallmark's greeting cards included the "something for the girl/graduate student I cussed out after telling her I wanted to pet her and later puking on her." Julia turned on her heel and went back to her apartment, shaking her head and muttering.

Curling up on her bed with her laptop, she decided to perform an internet search on purple hyacinths, just in case Gabriel (or his florist) was trying to send her a subliminal message. On a horticultural website, she read the following: *Purple hyacinths symbolize sorrow, the request for forgiveness, or an apology.*

Yeah, well if you hadn't been such a bastard to me, Gabriel, you wouldn't have to buy hyacinths to beg for my forgiveness. Jackass. Still shaking her head in irritation, Julia put her laptop aside and checked her last and final voice message. It was from Gabriel, and he'd left it a few minutes ago.

"Julia, I wanted to say this in person, but I can't wait. I can't wait.

"I wasn't calling you a whore this morning. I swear. It was a terrible comparison, and I never should have said it, but I wasn't calling you a whore. I was objecting to seeing you on your knees. It really . . . upsets me. Every time. You should be worshipped and adored and treated with dignity. Never on your knees. Never on your knees, Julia, for anyone. No matter what you think of me, that's the truth.

"I should have apologized immediately for what Paulina said to you. I just finished setting her straight, and I want to pass on her apology. She's sorry. She and I have a . . . um . . . (cough) . . . it's complicated. You can probably imagine why she jumped to that conclusion, and it has to do only with me and my previous—ah—behavior, and nothing to do with you. I'm really sorry she insulted you. It won't happen again, I promise.

"Thank you for making me breakfast this morning. Um . . . [very long pause] seeing the tray you prepared really did something to me. I can't put it into words. Julia, no one has ever done anything like that for me before. No one. Not Grace, not a friend, not a lover, no one. I . . . you've been

nothing but good and kind and giving. And I've been nothing but selfish and cruel. [Clears throat . . .]

[Voice is husky now.] "Please, Julia, we need to talk about your note. I am holding your note in the palm of my hand, and I'm not going to let it go. But there are some things I need to explain to you, serious things, and I'm not comfortable doing that over the phone. I'm sorry for what happened this morning. It's all my fault, and I want to fix it. Please tell me how to fix this, and I'll fix it. Call me."

Once again, Julia deleted his message, and once again, she made no attempt to save his number. She turned her phone off, placed it with her laptop on her card table, and went back to bed, trying to put Gabriel's sad and tortured voice out of her mind.

The next day and the day after that, Julia didn't leave her apartment. In fact, she spent all her time in various flannel pajama sets, trying to distract herself with loud music and a series of well-worn paperbacks by Alexander McCall Smith. His Edinburgh stories were her favorite because they were cheerful, slightly mysterious, and smart. She found his writing comforting and more than soothing to her soul. The stories tended to make her hungry for Scottish things like porridge and Walker's shortbread and Isle of Mull cheddar (not necessarily in that order).

Although she had had a truly scarring experience with Gabriel, hard on the heels of spending the night in his arms, she was more determined than ever that she would not let him break her. She'd been broken before; *he* had broken her. And she'd sworn in her heart that she would never allow her spirit to be broken again. By anyone.

So she made the following three decisions:

First, she was not going to drop Emerson's class, because she needed a Dante seminar to demonstrate her competency.

Second, she was not going to quit school and return to Selinsgrove a coward.

Third, she was going to find herself another thesis director and file the paperwork behind Emerson's back, as soon as possible.

Near midnight Tuesday, she finally turned her cell phone on to check her messages. Once again, her inbox was full. She rolled her eyes when she discovered, not surprisingly, that the first message was from Gabriel. It had arrived Monday morning.

"Julianne . . . I left something for you last night on your front porch. Did you see it? Did you read the card? Please read it.

"By the way, I had to call Paul Norris in order to get your cell phone number. I made up some excuse about needing to speak with you about your thesis, in case he asks you about it.

"Did you know that you forgot your iPod? I've been listening to it. I was surprised to find that you are a fan of Arcade Fire. I've been listening to Intervention, although I'm more than surprised that someone as well-adjusted and happy as you would listen to such a tragic song. I'd like to be able to return your iPod in person.

"I'd like you to talk to me. Scream at me. Curse me. Throw things in my face. Anything but silence, Julianne. Please. [Large sigh . . .] Just a few moments of your time, that's all I ask. Call me."

Julia deleted his message and promptly walked herself and her Scottish tartan flannel pajamas out to the front porch. She picked up the card that was attached to the bouquet, ripped it into a hundred pieces, and threw the pieces over the railing and into the grass. She picked up the now withered purple hyacinths and threw them over the railing too. Then she inhaled the cold night air deeply and ran back inside, slamming the front door behind her.

Once she'd calmed down, she listened to the next message, which was also from Gabriel. He'd called her that afternoon.

"Julianne, did you know that Rachel is on some Godforsaken Canadian island? With no access to either a cell phone or her e-mail? I had to call Richard, for God's sake, when she wouldn't answer her phone. I was trying to track her down so she can track you down since you are refusing to respond to my messages.

"I'm worried about you. I checked around and no one, not even Paul, has seen you for days. I'm going to send you an e-mail, but it's going to be formal because the university has access to my e-mail account. I'm hoping you get this message before you read it, otherwise you'll think I'm being an ass again. But I'm not. I just have to sound like one in an official e-mail. If you reply to me, keep in mind anyone from the administration can read those e-mails. So be careful what you say.

"I'll see you at my seminar tomorrow. If you aren't there, I'm going to call your father and ask him to find you. For all I know, you're already on

a bus on your way back to Selinsgrove. Call me, please. I've had to re-
strain myself from coming over every day since Sunday.

[Long pause . . .] "I just want to know that you're all right. Two words,
Julia. Just text me two words—tell me you're okay. That's all I'm asking."

Julia quickly turned on her computer and checked her university
e-mail account. There, sitting in her inbox like a dirty bomb, was the
following message from Professor Gabriel O. Emerson:

> Dear Miss Mitchell,
> I need to speak to you concerning a matter of some urgency.
> Please contact me as soon as possible. You may telephone
> me at the following number: 416-555-0739 (cell).
> Regards,
> Prof. Gabriel O. Emerson,
> Associate Professor
> Department of Italian Studies/
> Centre for Medieval Studies
> University of Toronto

Julia deleted the e-mail and the voice mail without a second thought,
and she typed a quick e-mail to Paul, explaining that she was too sick
to attend Professor Emerson's seminar the following afternoon and asking Paul to pass that information to The Professor. She thanked Paul for
his several e-mails, apologized for not answering sooner, and asked if
he'd like to accompany her to the Royal Ontario Museum to see the
Florentine art exhibit when she had recovered her health.

The following day, she spent the better part of the afternoon composing an exploratory e-mail to Professor Jennifer Leaming of the Department of Philosophy. Professor Leaming was an Aquinas specialist
who also had an interest in Dante. Although Julia didn't know her personally, Paul had taken a class with her and liked her a great deal. She
was young, funny, and very popular with her students—the complete
opposite of Professor Emerson. Julia was hoping Professor Leaming
would consider directing her master's thesis, and she stated this hope
as a mere possibility in her e-mail.

Julia wanted to consult Paul about the switch and take his advice, but she couldn't. She knew he would assume that Emerson dropped her and would likely confront him about it. So she sent the e-mail to Professor Leaming and hoped that she would receive it graciously and respond quickly.

Later that evening, Julia checked her voice mail and once again, there was a message waiting from Gabriel.

"Julianne, it's Wednesday evening. I missed you in my seminar. You brighten a room, you know, just by being in it. I'm sorry I never said that to you before.

"Paul said you've been sick. Can I bring you some chicken soup? Ice cream? Orange juice? I could have those items delivered. You wouldn't have to see me. Please let me help you. I feel terrible knowing that you're in your apartment, alone and sick, and there's nothing I can do.

"At least I know that you're safe and not on a Greyhound bus somewhere. [Pauses—clears throat.]

"I remember kissing you. You kissed me back. You kissed me back, Julia, I know you did. Didn't you feel it? There is something between us. Or at least, there was.

"Please, we need to talk. You can't expect me to uncover your true identity and not have the chance to talk to you about it. I need to explain a few things. More than a few things, all right? Just call me back. All I'm asking for is one conversation. I think you owe me that."

The tone of Gabriel's voice in his messages had grown increasingly desperate. Julia turned off her phone, deliberately suppressing her own innate empathy. She knew the university had access to Gabriel's e-mail, but she didn't care. His messages needed to stop; she would never be able to move on if he kept bothering her. And he didn't appear to be giving up any time soon.

So Julia typed an e-mail and sent it to his university address, pouring all of her hurt and anger into every single word:

Dr. Emerson,
Stop harassing me.
I don't want you anymore. I don't even want to know you. If you don't leave me alone, I will be forced to file a harassment complaint against you. And if you call my father, I will do just that. Immediately.

If you think I'm going to let an insignificant thing like this drive
me from the program, then you are very much mistaken. I need a
new thesis director, not a bus ticket home.

Regards,

Miss Julia. H. Mitchell,

Lowly Graduate Student,

On-Knees-More-Than-The-Average-Whore.

P.S. I will be returning the M. P. Emerson bursary next week.
Congratulations, Professor Abelard. No one has ever made me
feel as cheap as you did Sunday morning.

Julia pressed *send* without proofreading her message, and in a fit of
rebellion, she took two shots of tequila and began to play the song *All
the Pretty Faces* by The Killers. At a high volume. On repeat.

It was a Bridget Jones moment if there ever was one.

Julia grabbed a hairbrush from the bathroom and began singing
into it as if it were a microphone and dancing about the room in her
now penguin-decorated flannel pajamas, looking more than slightly
ridiculous. And feeling strangely . . . dangerous, daring, and defiant.

In the days after Julia sent her angry e-mail, all contact from Professor Emerson ceased. Every day she somehow expected to hear from
him, but every day there was nothing. Until the following Tuesday,
when she received another voice mail.

*"Julianne, you're angry and hurt—I understand that. But don't let your
anger prevent you from keeping something you earned by being the top
master's student in this year's admissions pool.*

*"Please don't deprive yourself of money you could use to go home and
visit your father just because I was an ass.*

*"I'm sorry I made you feel cheap. I'm sure when you called me Abelard
you didn't mean it as a compliment. But Abelard truly cared for Héloïse,
and I care for you. So in that sense, there is a similarity. He also hurt her,
as I have hurt you. But he was deeply sorry for having injured her. Have
you read his letters to her? Read the sixth letter and see if it alters your
perception of him . . . and me.*

"The bursary was never awarded before because I never found someone

who was special enough to receive it, until I found you. If you give it back, the money will just sit in the Foundation's bank account benefiting no one. I'm not going to allow anyone else to have that money because it's yours.

"I was trying to bring goodness out of evil. But I failed in doing that just like I've failed in everything else. Everything I touch becomes contaminated or destroyed . . . [Long pause . . .]

"There is one thing I can do for you and that's find you another thesis advisor. Professor Katherine Picton is a friend of mine, and although she's retired, she has agreed to meet with you to discuss the possibility of directing your project. This will be a tremendous opportunity, in more ways than one. She asked me to have you contact her directly via e-mail, as soon as possible, at K Picton at U Toronto dot C A.

"I know it's officially too late for you to drop my seminar, but I'm sure that's what you want. I will approach one of my colleagues and see if she will supervise a reading course with you, which will enable you to have enough credits to graduate, even if you drop my class. I'll sign the drop form and work it out for you with the School of Graduate Studies. Just tell Paul what you want to do and ask him to pass on the message. I know you don't want to talk to me.

[Clears throat.] "Paul is a good man.

[Muttering . . .] "Audentes fortuna iuvat.

[Pause—voice drops to almost a whisper.] "I'm sorry you don't want to know me anymore. I will spend the rest of my life regretting the fact that I wasted my second chance to know you. And I will always be conscious of your absence.

"But I won't bother you again. [Clears throat twice.]

"Good-bye, Julianne." [Long, long pause before Gabriel finally hangs up.]

Julia was stunned. She sat, openmouthed, with her phone in her hand, trying to wrap her mind around his message. She listened to it again and again, puzzling out the words, but the only part she readily believed was the quote from Virgil, *Fortune favors the brave.*

Only The Professor could use an apologetic voice mail as an occasion to reassert his academic prowess and give Julia an impromptu lecture on Peter Abelard. Julia moved past her annoyance, deciding *not* to follow his suggestion and read Abelard's letters. Instead, she turned her attention to the more interesting part of his message, his mention of Katherine Picton.

Professor Picton was a seventy-year-old, Oxford-educated Dante specialist who had taught at Cambridge and Yale before she was lured to the University of Toronto by an endowed chair in Italian Studies. She was known to be severe, demanding, and brilliant, and her erudition rivaled that of Mark Musa. Julia's career would be greatly advanced if she were to write a successful thesis under Professor Picton's supervision, and she knew it. Professor Picton could send Julia anywhere for her doctorate, Oxford, Cambridge, Harvard . . .

Gabriel was single-handedly giving Julia the biggest career opportunity of her life, gift-wrapped with a bright, shiny bow—an opportunity worth far more than a messenger bag or the M. P. Emerson bursary. But what were the strings attached to this gift?

Atonement, Julia thought. *He's trying to make up for every wrong he has ever done me.*

Gabriel was asking Katherine Picton to do him a favor, for Julia. Emeritus professors rarely, if ever, directed doctoral dissertations, let alone masters' theses. This was a tremendous favor that would have required Gabriel to call in all of his markers with Katherine.

All for me.

After she contemplated this new information from all angles, Julia pushed everything aside to focus on the single question that filled her heart with shameful dread.

Gabriel is telling me good-bye?

She listened to the message three more times, and with more than a little self-criticism, she cried herself to sleep. For despite all her defiance, there was a flame in her that recognized its twin in Gabriel. And that flame could not be extinguished, unless Julia was willing to extinguish a part of herself.

Early the next morning, she called Paul under the pretence of making plans to meet him before Emerson's seminar. She hoped that he would tell her that Emerson had gotten sick or mysteriously left for England or taken ill with swine flu and cancelled his seminar for the rest of the semester. Sadly, he had done none of those things.

Julia decided that she would continue attending the Dante seminar, just in case Gabriel had trouble finding her a reading course as a substitute. Indeed, if Professor Picton became her thesis advisor, Julia was confident she could tolerate being in Emerson's seminar for the five remaining weeks of the semester. So that afternoon, she wandered into the office of the department in order to check her mailbox before she was supposed to meet Paul.

She was somewhat intrigued to find a large, padded envelope in her pigeonhole. Removing it, she noticed that there wasn't a name on it. It was not addressed to her, nor was there a return address or any marking of any kind on the envelope.

She slid her finger through the adhesive, opening it quickly. What she saw inside shocked her. Nestled inside the padded manila envelope, like the feathers of a raven, was a black lace bra. *Her* black lace bra. Her black lace bra that she'd left, unfortunately, on top of Gabriel's dryer.

That bastard.

Julia was so angry her body began to shake. How dare he return it to her mailbox? Anyone, *anyone*, could have been standing next to her when she opened it. *Is he trying to humiliate me? Or does he think this is funny?* (Julia didn't notice that her iPod was also enclosed.)

"Hey, gorgeous."

She jumped about a foot off the floor and shrieked.

"Whoa, I didn't mean to scare you."

She looked up into Paul's kind, dark eyes and saw him staring down at her with a puzzled expression.

"You're jumpy today. What's that?" He pointed to her envelope, hands still raised.

"Junk mail." She stuffed the envelope into her new L.L. Bean knapsack and forced a smile. "Ready for Emerson's seminar? I think it's going to be a good one."

"I don't think so. He's in a foul mood again. I need to warn you not to mess with him today—he's been out of sorts for two weeks." Paul's face took on a very serious expression. "I don't want a repeat of what happened the last time he was like this."

Julia tossed her hair and grinned. *Actually, I think that you need to tell Emerson not to mess with* me. *I've got a lot of rage, a black bra, and I'm wearing a thong. He's the one in trouble, not me.*

"I'm so glad you're feeling better. I was really worried about you." Paul reached out to take her hand in his, spreading wide her palm and placing something cold in it. He closed her fingers in on themselves and squeezed gently. Julia withdrew her hand and uncurled her fingers. Resting on her palm was a beautiful silver key ring, with a striped *P* that swung like a pendulum from the ring itself.

"Now, please don't say you won't accept it. I know you don't have a nice key ring, and I wanted you to know I was thinking about you while I was gone. So please don't give it back."

Julia's cheeks ripened into a rosy pink. "I'm not going to give it back," she said. "I don't want to be the kind of person who flings kindness back in someone's face. I know what that feels like." She looked around quickly, making sure that they were alone. "Thank you, Paul. I missed you too."

She stepped closer to him and hesitantly put her arms around his barrel chest, clutching the key ring in between her fingers. She pressed her cheek against the buttons of his shirt and hugged him.

"Thank you," she sighed, as his long, muscular arms engulfed her.

He brought his lips to the top of her head and pressed them cautiously to her hair. "You're welcome, Rabbit."

Unbeknownst to them, a certain temperamental blue-eyed Dante specialist had just walked through the door, eager to discover if a certain item had been received by its owner. He froze as he witnessed the young couple in front of him, murmuring to each other and locked in an embrace.

And the Angelfucker makes his move.

"But who has been flinging kindness back in your face?" Paul asked, oblivious to the dragon who was standing behind him, silently breathing fire.

Julia was mute and unconsciously hugged him more tightly.

"Tell me, Rabbit, and I'll fix him. Her. Whomever." Paul's lips moved against Julia's hair. "You know that you're special to me, right? If you ever need anything, you just have to ask. Anything at all. Okay?"

She sighed against his chest. "I know."

The blue-eyed dragon turned on his heel and abruptly departed, cursing about a *Rabbitfucker* as he disappeared down the hallway.

Julia broke free first. "Thanks, Paul. And thanks for this." She held the key ring up and smiled.

I could look at that smile forever, he thought. "You're welcome. My pleasure."

Shortly thereafter, they entered the seminar room. Julia studiously avoided making eye contact with Gabriel, laughing softly at one of Paul's jokes. His hand pressed familiarly to her lower back as he guided her to their seats. At the front of the seminar room, Gabriel seethed, his long white fingers gripping the edge of the lectern and not letting go.

Hands off her back, Rabbitfucker.

The Professor stared with hostility at Paul until he was suddenly distracted by Julia's book bag. He wondered how she'd been able to transform it so effectively from its previous putrid state and why she wasn't using his gift, instead. The thought tortured him.

Did Rachel tell her the bag was from me?

He fidgeted slightly with his bow tie, purposefully drawing attention to it. He'd worn it as a sign of his own self-mortification. He'd worn it to attract her attention. But she didn't seem to notice, and she certainly wasn't looking at him. Instead, she was whispering and laughing with Paul, her dark hair long and flowing, her cheeks slightly pink and her mouth . . . Julia was even more beautiful now than in his memory.

"Miss Mitchell, I need to speak with you after class, please." Gabriel smiled in her direction and looked down at his shiny shoes, shuffling his feet. He was about to begin his seminar when a small but determined voice from the back of the classroom interrupted him.

"I'm sorry, Professor, I can't. I have an urgent appointment afterward that cannot be delayed." Julia looked over at Paul and winked.

Gabriel slowly raised his head and stared at her. Ten graduate students inhaled as one and began to move backward in their chairs, fearful that he might explode, or that a dagger from his eye might fly out and gut them. She was baiting him. And he knew it. Her tone, her physical proximity to Paul, the way she flicked her hair behind her shoulder with one hand . . .

Gabriel was distracted momentarily by the curve of her neck, her delicate skin, the scent of vanilla that either wafted toward him or came to him only in memory. He wanted to say something, to demand that she speak with him, but he knew that he couldn't. If he lost his temper now, she would only retreat further from his grasp, and he would lose her. He could not let that happen.

Gabriel blinked. Rapidly.

"Of course, Miss Mitchell. These things happen. Please e-mail me to set up an appointment." He tried to smile, but found that he couldn't; only one-half of his mouth would curl up, making him look as if he'd been stricken with palsy.

Julia shifted her gaze to stare back at him, her eyes empty. She did not blush. She did not blink. She just looked . . . vacant.

Gabriel noticed her expression, which he'd never seen before, and began to panic. *I'm trying to be nice to her, and she looks at me as if I wasn't there. Is it really so surprising that I can be cordial? That I can keep my temper?*

Paul dropped his hand below the table and quickly but gently squeezed Julia's arm at the elbow. His touch distracted her so she looked at him, and he shook his head, his eyes flickering to the front of the room and back to her.

She seemed to be awakened from her reverie. "Of course, Professor. Another time." For good measure, she averted her eyes and waited without expression for the class to begin.

Gabriel's mind was racing. If he couldn't speak with her today, he would have to go days and perhaps weeks without explaining. He couldn't wait that long. Their separation was eating away at him. The longer he waited, the less receptive she was going to be to his explanation. He had to do something. He had to find some way of communicating with her. Immediately.

"Um, I've decided that rather than have a normal seminar today, I will deliver a lecture. I'll be examining the relationship between Dante and Beatrice. In particular, what transpired when Dante met Beatrice the second time and she rejected him."

Julia stifled a gasp and looked up at him in horror.

"I'm sorry to have to do this," his voice took on a conciliatory tone, "but I was left with no other choice. A misunderstanding has emerged that must be dealt with before it's too late." His eyes met hers for mere seconds, and he lowered his gaze to his notes. Of course, his notes were of no use for this particular lecture.

Julia's heart raced. *Oh, no. He wouldn't. . . .*

Gabriel inhaled deeply and began. "Beatrice represents many things for Dante. Most importantly, an ideal of womanhood and femininity. Beatrice is beautiful. She's intelligent and charming. She has all of the character qualities Dante believes are essential to the ideal woman.

"He first encounters her when they are both very young, too young for any kind of relationship. Rather than sully their love with any kind of pedestrian or tawdry entanglement, he chooses to adore her reverently but distantly, in deference to her age and experience.

"Time passes. He meets Beatrice again. She has matured into a talented young lady; she is even more gifted and beautiful. Now his feelings for her are much stronger, even though he is married to someone else. He pours his affection into writing poetry and pens several sonnets for Beatrice, but none for his wife.

"Dante does not know Beatrice. He has little contact with her. Even so, he adores her from afar. After she dies at the age of twenty-four, he celebrates her in his writings.

"In *The Divine Comedy*, Dante's most famous work, Beatrice helps to persuade Virgil to guide Dante through Hell because she, as one of the redeemed in Paradise, is unable to descend into Hell to rescue him. Once Virgil sees Dante safely through Hell, she joins him and guides him through Purgatory and into Paradise.

"In my lecture today, I wish to pose the following question: where was Beatrice and what was she doing in between her two meetings with Dante?

"He waited for her for years. She knew where he lived. She knew his family; she was friendly, very friendly, with them. If she cared about him, why didn't she write to him? Why did she make no attempt to contact him? I think the answer is obvious: their relationship was entirely one-sided. Dante cared for Beatrice, but Beatrice cared *nothing* for Dante."

Julia almost fell off her chair.

All of the graduate students were following his lecture diligently and taking copious notes, although Paul, Julia, and Christa, who were familiar with Dante, found precious little that was new in his lecture. With the exception of the last full paragraph, which had nothing whatsoever to do with Dante Alighieri and Beatrice Portinari, at all.

Gabriel's eyes wandered to Julia's and lingered there almost a beat too long, before he turned to Christa, smiling flirtatiously. Julia fumed. He was doing that on purpose—purposefully looking at her and then focusing all of his attention on Christa-the-Gollum, just so she could see how easily she would be replaced.

Fine. If he wants to play the jealousy game, bring it.

Julia began to tap her notebook with her pen just loud enough to be distracting. When Gabriel's narrowed eyes darted around to look for the noise and landed on her left hand, she slid her right hand closer to Paul and gave his hand a squeeze. He looked over at her with a heart-melting smile, and she gazed up into his eyes through her eyelashes. She parted her lips, exposing her teeth, and gave Paul the loveliest, sweetest smile she could muster.

A half-groan, half-cough from the front of the room caused Paul to rip his eyes away from her and stare straight at the very angry face of Professor Emerson. Paul withdrew his hand from Julia's immediately.

Smirking now, and still continuing his lecture without fumbling a word, Gabriel began to write on the board. More than one graduate student reacted in shock when they saw what he had written:

In real life, Beatrice was only too happy to leave Dante in Hell because she couldn't be bothered to keep her promise.

Julia was the last person to look up because she was still huffing about what had just happened. By the time she saw the board, Gabriel was leaning his back against it with his arms folded and a very smug expression on his face. Julia determined then and there that even if he had her expelled, that smug expression was going to be wiped off his face. Immediately.

She put her hand up and waited until he called on her. "That's really arrogant and self-serving, Professor."

Paul tightened his fingers on her arm, slightly tugging at her. "Are you crazy?" he whispered.

Julia ignored him and continued. "Why blame Beatrice? She's the victim in all of this. Dante met her when she was under eighteen. It wasn't possible for them to be together, unless he's a pedophile. Are you telling us that Dante is a pedophile, Professor?"

One of the female students gasped.

Gabriel scowled. "Of course not! He has true affection for her, and this affection is undiminished even during their separation. If she had ever had the courage to ask him, he would have told her that. Unequivocally."

Julia moved her head to one side and narrowed her eyes. "That's a bit difficult to believe. Everything in Dante's later life seems to revolve around sex. He can't relate to women in any other way. And he's certainly not sitting at home alone on Friday and Saturday nights waiting for Beatrice. So he must not have cared for her."

Gabriel's face grew very red, and he unfolded his arms, taking a step in her direction. Paul immediately put his hand up, trying to distract The Professor, but Gabriel ignored him and came a step closer.

"He is a man, after all, and needs . . . uh . . . companionship. And if it makes it any more palatable, those women were just *helpful friends.* Nothing more. His draw to Beatrice is undiminished. He simply despaired of waiting for her, since it was obvious that he was never going to see her again. And that's her fault, not his."

She smiled sweetly as she prepared her knife. "If that's affection, I'll take hatred. And just what were these *friends* so *helpful* with, Professor? Hmmmm? They're not friends—they're *pelvic affiliates.* Wouldn't a friend want the other person to have a good life? A happy life? And not be clawing after fleeting pleasure like a randy old sex addict?"

Julia saw Gabriel wince, but she ignored his reaction and plowed ahead. "It's commonly known that Dante's dalliances were anonymous and tawdry. He tended to pick up women at the *meat market,* I believe, and when he was finished, he simply threw them away. That doesn't sound like someone who would appeal to Beatrice. Not to mention the fact that he has a mistress named Paulina."

Immediately, ten pairs of eyes swung inquisitively to Julia. She flushed a deep red but continued, somewhat flustered. "I—I found something once by a woman from Philadelphia who unearthed evidence of their relationship. If Beatrice lacked affection for Dante and rejected him later in life, it was completely justified. Dante was a self-absorbed, cruel, and arrogant man-whore who treated women like toys for his own personal amusement."

Now at this point, both Christa and Paul were wondering what in the holy hell had just happened to their Dante seminar, for neither of them knew anything about a female Dante expert from Philadelphia or a mistress named Paulina. They silently pledged to spend more time in the library from now on.

Gabriel glared at the back of the room. "I believe I'm somewhat familiar with the *woman* you're talking about, but she isn't from Philadelphia. She's from some podunk village in rural Pennsylvania. And she doesn't know what she's talking about, so she should refrain from pronouncing judgment."

Julia's cheeks flamed. "That's an *ad hominem* objection. Her place of origin doesn't diminish her credibility. And Dante and his family were from a podunk village too. Not that Dante would ever admit it."

Gabriel's shoulders shook slightly as he tried to control himself. "I'd hardly call the Florence of the fourteenth century *podunk*. And with respect to the mistress, that's just shoddy research. In fact, I'll go further. That woman's head is filled with nothing more than appalling rubbish, and she doesn't have a shred of evidence for her conjectures."

"I wouldn't dismiss her evidence out of hand, Professor, unless you're prepared to discuss it in detail. And you haven't given us an argument, just an abusive attack," she countered, arching an eyebrow at him and trembling slightly.

Paul took her hand underneath the table and squeezed. "Stop," he whispered, so low only she could hear. "Right now."

Gabriel's face reddened again, and he began to breathe through his mouth. "If that woman wanted to know how Dante truly felt about Beatrice, she knew where to find the answer. Then she wouldn't be shooting her mouth off about things she knew absolutely *nothing* about. And making herself and Dante look ridiculous. *In public.*"

Christa looked from Professor Emerson to Julia and back again.

Something wasn't right. Something was definitely wrong, but she couldn't put her finger on what it was. She was determined to find out.

Gabriel turned back to the board and began writing, trying to calm himself down:

Dante thought it was a dream.

"The language that Dante uses about his first meeting with Beatrice has a dreamlike quality. For various—ah—*personal reasons,* he doesn't trust his senses. He's not sure who she is. In fact, one theory is that Dante thought Beatrice was an angel.

"So later in life, Beatrice is completely out of order in assuming that he remembered everything from their first meeting and in holding that fact against him and not giving him the opportunity to explain himself. Clearly, if he thought that Beatrice was an angel, he would have no hope that she would return.

"Dante would have explained all of this to her, if she hadn't rejected him before he had the chance. So once again, her lack of clarity on this point is her fault. Not his."

Christa's hand shot up, and Gabriel reluctantly nodded at her, growing very tense as he waited for her to speak.

But Julia spoke first. "The discussion of their first meeting is patently irrelevant, since Dante must have recognized her when he saw her the second time, dream or not. So why did he pretend not to?"

"He wasn't pretending. She was familiar to him, but she was all grown up, he was confused, and he was upset about other things in life." Gabriel's voice grew pained.

"I'm sure that's what he told himself so he could sleep at night, when he wasn't on an alcoholic bender in the *lobbies* of downtown Florence."

"Julia, that's enough." Paul raised his voice above a whisper.

Christa was about to interject something when Gabriel held out his hand to silence her.

"That has nothing to do with it!" He inhaled and exhaled quickly as he tried in vain to keep his emotions in check. He dropped his voice and stared only at her, ignoring the way Paul shifted his body so that he could come between The Professor and Julia if need be.

"Haven't you ever been lonely, Miss Mitchell? Haven't you ever ached for companionship, even if it's only carnal and temporary? Sometimes it's all you can get. And so you take it and you're grateful for it, while recognizing it for what it is, *because you have no other choice.* Instead of being so high-handed and self-righteous in your assessment of Dante's lifestyle, you should try having a little compassion." Gabriel snapped his mouth shut as he realized he had revealed far more than he had ever intended. Julia stared back at him coolly and waited for him to continue.

"Dante was haunted by his memory of Beatrice. And that made things worse, not better, for no one ever measured up to her. No one was beautiful enough, no one was pure enough, no one made him feel the way she did. He always wanted her—he just despaired of ever finding her again. Believe me, if she had presented herself earlier and told him who she was, he would have dropped everything and everyone for her. Immediately." Gabriel's eyes grew desperate as they bore into Julia's deep brown eyes.

"What was he supposed to do, Miss Mitchell? Hmmmm? Enlighten us. Beatrice rejected him. He only had one thing of value left and that was his career. When she threatened that, what else could he do? He had to let her go, but that was *her choice*, not his."

Julia smiled sweetly at his tirade, and he knew that he was in for it.

"Your lecture has been *very* illuminating, Professor. But I still have one more question. So you're saying that Paulina is not Dante's mistress? That she's just a fuck buddy?"

A very loud popping sound echoed across the seminar room. Each graduate student gazed in complete and utter shock as they realized that Professor Emerson had snapped the whiteboard marker in two. Black ink spread across his fingers like a starless night, and his eyes ignited into an angry blue fire.

That's it. That's fucking it, he thought.

Paul pulled Julia into his side protectively, curving his body around her as he watched The Professor's shoulders begin to shake with rage.

"Class is dismissed. In my office, Miss Mitchell. Now!" Professor Emerson angrily shoved his notes and his books into his briefcase and exited the seminar room, slamming the door behind him.

Chapter Sixteen

The graduate students sat in the now silent seminar room, stunned. Since the majority of the students weren't Dante specialists, they quickly dismissed the altercation as an entertaining (albeit aberrant) internecine debate. Academics could be passionate about their subject matter; everyone knew it. Some, like Julia and The Professor, were more passionate than others. Today's seminar was a train wreck, of course, but not entirely surprising. Not, thought Paul, as bizarre as some of the things that happened the previous semester in Professor Singer's Medieval Torture Methods seminar . . . which turned out to be surprisingly *hands-on . . .*

As the students slowly realized that the steel-cage death match they'd just witnessed was over, and that there would be no second round (or popcorn), they began filing out, with the exception of Christa, Paul, and Julia.

Christa fixed Julia with narrowed eyes and went after The Professor like a codependent duckling.

Paul closed his eyes and groaned. "Are you suicidal?"

Julia seemed to be shaking herself awake from a dream. "What?"

"Why did you provoke him like that? He's looking for a reason to get rid of you!"

She was only now able to grasp the gravity of her predicament. It was as if she'd been another person, spewing venom and anger, without any thought about the audience. And now that she'd vented she felt deflated, like a lonely and empty balloon left after a child's birthday party. She slowly began packing her things and tried to steel herself for what she knew would be a very, *very* unpleasant conversation in The Professor's office.

"I don't think you should go," said Paul.

"I don't want to go."

"Then don't. Send him an e-mail. Tell him you're sick—and you're sorry."

Julia thought about that for a moment. It was very, very tempting. But she knew that her only chance at saving her career would be to *woman up* and take her punishment, and try to piece her personal life together afterward. If that was even possible.

"If I don't go to his office, he'll be even angrier. He could kick me out. And I need this class, or I won't be able to graduate in May."

"Then I'm going with you. Better yet, I'll speak with him first." Paul drew himself up to his full height and flexed his arms.

"No, you need to stay out of this. I'm going to go and apologize and let him yell at me. And when he has his pound of flesh, he'll let me go."

"*The quality of mercy is not strained*," muttered Paul. "Not that he would know anything about that. What were you fighting about, anyway? Dante didn't have a mistress called Paulina."

Julia blinked rapidly. "I found an article about Pia de' Tolomei. Paulina was one of her nicknames."

"Pia de' Tolomei wasn't one of Dante's mistresses. There were rumors of mistresses and illegitimate children, so you weren't completely wrong. But I'm sorry, Julia, Emerson is right—no one believes that Pia was Dante's mistress. No one."

Julia chewed the inside of her cheek thoughtfully. "But he wouldn't let me explain. And I just kind of . . . snapped."

"You snapped, all right. If it were anyone else, I'd be cheering you on thinking that he got what was coming to him. *The uptight prick*. But in your case, I knew he'd overreact." Paul shook his head. "Let me talk to him."

"You're writing your dissertation with him, you can't have him angry with you. If it's too much, I'll leave. And I'll file a harassment complaint."

Paul gazed down at her with a very worried expression. "I don't feel right about this. He's furious."

"What can he do? He's the big bad Professor, I'm the little grad student. He has all the power."

"Power does funny things to people."

"What's that supposed to mean?"

Paul stuck his head outside the door of the seminar room in order to check the hallway.

"Emerson is a twisted fuck. He was involved with Professor Singer and that means that he . . ." Paul stopped suddenly and shook his head.

"That means that he—what?"

"If he has been harassing you, or trying to get you to *do things*, let me know and I'll help you. We can file a complaint."

Julia gazed at him blankly. "There's nothing sinister going on here. He's just a crusty professor who doesn't like to be contradicted. I'm going to eat humble pie in his office, and hopefully, he won't make me drop his class."

"I hope you're right. He's always been professional with his students. But with you, things are different."

Paul walked Julia to The Professor's office and without warning, knocked on the door.

Professor Emerson opened the door quickly, his eyes still an angry, sparking lapis. "What do you want?" he spat, shooting daggers at Julia.

"Just a minute of your time," said Paul mildly.

"Not now. Tomorrow."

"But Professor, I . . ."

"Tomorrow, Mr. Norris. Don't push me."

Paul gave Julia a very worried look and mouthed the words, "I'm sorry."

The Professor waited until Paul had disappeared around the corner before stepping aside to let Julia in. He closed the door behind her and walked over to the window.

Abandon hope all ye who enter here . . .

The Professor's office was dark, illuminated only by his desk lamp. He'd drawn the blinds and was now leaning as far away from her as possible and rubbing his eyes with his inky fingers.

Julia moved her knapsack in front of her like a shield, clasping it with two hands. When he didn't speak, she busied herself by glancing around the room. Her eyes alighted on a chair—the very uncomfortable Ikea chair that she sat on back in September during her first ill-fated meeting with The Professor. The chair had been smashed to bits and was lying in small, bent pieces that were scattered across the Persian carpet.

Julia's eyes slowly moved from the pieces to The Professor and back again. *He smashed a chair. He smashed a* metal *chair.*

His eyes opened, and she saw a strange and dangerous calmness in their blue depths. Here was the dragon in his den. And she was unarmed.

"If you were anyone else I'd have you expelled."

Julia shook as soon as she heard the tone of his voice. It was deceptively calm and soft, like silk brushing across bare skin. But the undertone was steel and ice.

"That was the most disgusting display of infantile behavior I have ever witnessed. Your disrespectful attitude is absolutely unacceptable. On top of that, I can't even begin to express the anger I have over what you said about Paulina. You are *never* to speak about her again. Do I make myself clear?"

Julia swallowed hard but was too upset to answer.

"I said *do I make myself clear?*" he growled.

"Yes."

"My self-control is tenuous at best. You would do well not to push it. And I expect you to fight your own battles and not manipulate Paul into rescuing you from your own stupidity. He has his own problems."

Julia looked at the carpet, avoiding his eyes, which seemed to glow in the darkness.

"I think you *wanted* me to lose my temper. I think you wanted me to get angry and make a scene, so you'd be justified in running away. You wanted me to behave like every other abusive asshole that has knocked you around. Well, I'm not an abusive asshole, and I'm not going to do that."

She glanced over at the twisted wreckage of the chair—(a nice, Swedish chair that had done *nothing* in its short life to hurt anyone)— and looked back at The Professor. But she didn't argue.

His tongue darted out, and he licked his lips. "Is this a game to you? Hmmmm? Playing us off each other like something out of Prokofiev? He's Peter; I'm the Wolf. What does that make you—the duck?"

Julia shook her head.

"What happened in my seminar today will *never* happen again. Do you understand?"

"Yes, Professor."

She clutched at the doorknob behind her. It was locked. "I'll apologize to the class."

"And expose us to even more gossip? You will do no such thing. Why wouldn't you talk to me? One phone call. One meeting. I could have spoken to you through a door, for God's sake. And instead, you finally choose to talk to me in the middle of *my* fucking graduate seminar!"

"You put a bra in my mailbox . . . I thought—"

"Use your head!" he snapped. "If I'd mailed it to you, there would have been a paper trail. That would have been far more incriminating. And I wasn't about to leave your iPod on your porch in the middle of a rainstorm."

Julia was confused by his apparent *non sequitur* but decided not to question him.

"I started this clusterfuck by changing my lecture, but you finished it, Julianne, and you finished it with the equivalent of a hydrogen bomb. You are *not* going to drop my class. Clear? You are *not* going to drop out of the program. And we're going to pretend this debacle never happened and hope that the other students are too wrapped up in their own lives to notice anything."

Gabriel fixed her with an impassive look. "Come." He pointed to a space on the carpet.

She took a few steps forward.

"Have you returned the bursary?"

"Not yet. The chair of Italian Studies has swine flu."

"But you've made an appointment?"

"Yes."

"So you made an appointment with him, but you didn't have the courtesy to send me a two word text message when I was desperate to know how you were," he growled.

Julia blinked.

"You're going to cancel that appointment."

"But I don't want the money, and . . ."

"You will cancel the appointment, you will take the money, and you

will keep your mouth shut. You've made the mess; I have to clean it up."
He glared at her darkly. "Understood?"

Julia held her breath and nodded rather reluctantly.

"The e-mail you sent me was disgraceful, a real slap in the face after
all the messages I left you. Did you even listen to my voice mails? Or
did you just delete them?"

"I listened to them."

"You listened to them, but you didn't believe them. And you sure as
hell didn't answer them. You used the word *harassment* in your e-mail
to me. What the fuck did you hope to accomplish by that?"

"Um—I don't know."

Gabriel closed the gap between them, standing only inches from
her. "It's quite possible that your e-mail has been red-flagged by someone already. Even if I erase that e-mail, and I did, someone could still
find it. E-mails are forever, Julianne. You are never going to e-mail me
again. Is that clear?"

"Yes."

"You seem to be the only person capable of pushing all of my buttons, and I do mean all of them."

Julia glanced over at the door, wishing she could fling it open and
escape.

"Look at me," he breathed.

When she met his eyes he continued. "I'm going to have to do some
damage control. I just handled Christa, and now I'm going to have to
deal with Paul, thanks to you. Christa is a menace, but Paul was a good
research assistant."

Was *a good research assistant?*

"Please don't fire Paul. It's my fault he came to you. I'll make sure he
doesn't say anything," she pleaded.

"Is he who you want?" Gabriel's tone grew glacial.

Julia fidgeted with her book bag.

"*Answer me.*"

"I tried."

"And?"

"And nothing."

"It doesn't look like nothing when I see you in his arms in front of the mailboxes. It doesn't look like nothing when he knocks on my door, like a knight, ready to fight me to protect you. Why can't you tell me what you want, Julianne? Or do you only answer to *Rabbit?*" Gabriel's voice dripped with sarcasm.

Julia's eyes widened in surprise, but she said nothing. She didn't know what to say.

"Fine. I give up." He waved his hand contemptuously at the door. "Paul can have you."

It took a moment for Julia's brain to tell her feet to walk toward the door, but eventually it did. She walked with lowered head and hunched shoulders, looking remarkably like a butterfly that had had its wings torn off. But she'd kept her spot in his class, and she hadn't been expelled. Small consolation for some of the other losses she had just suffered.

Gabriel stood motionless as she fumbled with the door. A whimper escaped her lips as she struggled with the lock. He stepped behind her and reached an arm around her waist to unlock the door, brushing against her left hip. When she didn't flinch, he leaned closer, bringing his lips to her ear.

"So all of this agony was for nothing?"

She could feel the heat of his body behind her. It radiated from his chest to her shoulder blades. The silk of his bow tie brushed against her hair, penetrating it, until it grazed across the surface of her neck, causing it to explode into goose-pimples.

"You exposed us to malicious gossip for nothing?"

"You were cruel."

"So were you."

"You hurt me."

"And you hurt me. Is revenge everything you dreamed it might be?" Gabriel continued whispering, his warm breath huffing across her cheek. "You've transformed from a rabbit into a furious kitten. Well, you scratched me deeply today, my kitten. You drew blood with every word. Are you happy now? Now that you've humiliated me in front of my students by reciting all my secret sins? It was a true bonfire of the vanities, with you lighting the flame."

He brought his lips even closer to her ear, and the air from his mouth caused her to shiver. *"You're a coward."*

"I am not a coward."

"You're the one who's leaving."

"You're sending me to him."

"Like hell I am! Do you do everything people tell you to do? Where's my furious kitten now?"

"I'm just a student, Professor Emerson. You're the one with all the power. You could—destroy me."

"Bullshit. Is that what you think? That this is a power trip?" Gabriel pulled her book bag from her tense and twisted fingers and cast it aside. He spun her around and grasped her face, moving his hands to the curves of her cheeks. "You think I'd destroy you? After our history?"

"I'm not the one with the memory problem. You think I'm happy? You think this is what I want? I'm *miserable*. To finally see you after all these years and to see you like this? I don't even recognize you!"

"You never gave me a chance. How the hell would I know what you want, Julianne, when you won't fucking talk to me? You tell me nothing!"

"Shouting at me won't persuade me to talk to you!"

His mouth collided with hers, passionately but briefly, until he tore himself from her lips to whisper in her ear. "Talk to me." His lower lip trailed temptingly along her earlobe.

She was silent as she felt the energy between them shift, like a serpent circling back on itself, swallowing itself whole, anger and passion feeding off one another.

"Tell me that you want me, or get out."

When she didn't answer, Gabriel slowly withdrew. She felt ill from the loss of contact and didn't even think about the words as they tumbled impetuously from her lips. "I never wanted anyone else."

He stared into her eyes before he initiated the kiss. Lips met tightly, warm breath against warm breath, mouths wet and slick. Gabriel's right hand smoothed across Julia's cheek and slowly past her ear, before moving to the nape of her neck. As his mouth engulfed hers, he began to rub his thumbs across the surface of her skin, coaxing her to relax. Their lips floated together, sliding and smoothing. After a moment or two, he tilted her head back slightly—a silent plea.

Open for me.

Julia wasn't breathing. How could she when the sensation was so intense? The taste of peppermint, the scent of Aramis, the way his breath consumed her. When she didn't respond to his plea, Gabriel's tongue slowly emerged, hesitantly exploring her lower lip, before curving over it and coaxing it backward dexterously into his mouth. Julia inhaled sharply at the strange but intimate sensation.

He pulled her lip between his, tugging and teasing. It was all so new, yet strangely familiar. Lips, teeth, the gentle play of tongue. Passion remained, but anger gave way to a bracing electricity that burned and crackled around them, as Julia answered his invitation and opened to him.

Her jaw was tense. He could feel it. Gabriel slipped his left hand from her cheekbone to the curve of her jaw and began stroking, willing her to loosen. As she relaxed under his fingers, he grew bolder. The tip of his tongue rolled over her lower lip as he tugged on it with his mouth, and slowly his tongue touched hers. There were timid introductions as their tongues met first as friends, shy and soft, then as lovers, sensual and erotic, as the heat exploded in their mouths and the dance of the two became a tango of one.

It was better than Gabriel imagined—so much better than in his dreams or imagination. She was real. *Beatrice* was real. As he pressed his lips to hers and explored her mouth, he could say in those moments that she was his, body and soul. If only for those moments.

So sweet, thought Julia. *So warm.*

She tugged Gabriel closer, her tentative hands tangling in his hair, pulling him until she was sandwiched tightly between him and the door, her petite frame pressed up against his tall, muscular one. Gabriel moved his right hand to cup the back of her head, protecting it with his knuckles while he groaned loudly against her mouth.

He groaned because of me.

The groan was loud, feral, and erotic. Julia would remember that sound and the way it vibrated against her lips, echoing into her mouth, for the rest of her life. She felt the blood course through her, hot and thick, as her skin bloomed under his touch. She had never wanted anything more than to feel his arms around her and his lips against hers.

There was no Paul. No Christa. No university. Just them.

Gabriel's lips enveloped her, owned her. A fire ignited inside as their bodies moved together, soft curves against unyielding steel. Julia inhaled frantically, but it wasn't enough. Her head grew light.

Gabriel swore he could feel her heartbeat through his shirt they were so tightly bound together. His left hand trailed under the hem of her blouse to inch toward the bare skin of her lower back. He moaned again as his fingers spread across that valley, claiming it. He didn't need to see it to know that it was beautiful and precious.

Until . . . Julia began to gasp, her breathing labored and uneven. Gabriel did not want to stop. He wanted to continue, to carry her to his desk and lay her back so they could finish what they started. He wanted to explore every inch of her and gaze deeply into her dark eyes as her body gave up its secrets. But prudence took hold, and he slowed his movements even as his body ached at the mere thought of separation.

He held her tightly, still protecting her head, and pressed three chaste kisses against her open mouth. He brushed his lips, angel-soft, all the way down her neck to where it met her shoulder. One more kiss under the ear, with a flick of his tongue, more of a promise than a farewell, and Gabriel stopped.

He slid his hands down her arms and brought them to rest on her hips. He traced intricate patterns with his thumbs, willing her to open her eyes. He swore he could hear their heartbeats, echoing a frantic but almost synchronous rhythm in the silence of his office. She did this to him. She bewitched him, blood and flesh. He gazed down at her in wonder and brushed his lips once more against her parted mouth. She did not respond. Gabriel peered at her closely, slightly panicked.

"Julia? Darling? Are you all right?"

His heart halted as she collapsed in his arms.

She hadn't fainted. Not really. She'd just been overcome by sensation and sense and lack of proper food. But she knew that he was holding her tightly in his arms. And she knew that he was whispering kindly in her ear.

Gabriel stroked her face with his fingertips. When this elicited no response, he pressed his lips to her forehead. "Beatrice?"

Julia's eyes popped open. "Why are you calling me that?"

"Because that's your name," he murmured, stroking her hair now. "Are you all right?"

She breathed in and out quite deeply. "I think so."

He kissed her forehead again.

Julia suddenly remembered Gabriel's fury and his strangely glowing blue eyes. "This is wrong. You're my professor. I'm in so much trouble." She tried to wrest herself from his arms, but he would not let her go. She leaned against the door.

"What have I done?" She lifted a trembling hand to her forehead.

Gabriel frowned darkly and released her. "You disappoint me, Julianne. I'm not one to kiss and tell. I'm going to protect you, I promise." He picked up her knapsack and put it over his shoulder, grabbing his briefcase in one hand and wrapping his other arm around her waist, drawing her to him. "Come with me."

"Paul is waiting."

"Fuck Paul."

Julia's eyelids fluttered.

"You're nothing more than a pet to him."

"I'm not a pet—I'm his friend. He's my only friend in Toronto."

"I'd like to be your friend," Gabriel said, gazing down at her. "And I'm going to keep my little friend very close to make sure she doesn't run away again."

"This is—complicated. And dangerous." Julia willed herself to forget the feeling of his lips on hers and to focus on their insurmountable problems. But it was impossible, especially since the memory of the sounds he made while kissing her still echoed in her ears.

Groan.

"You didn't seem to think that it was complicated and dangerous when you pranced around my apartment in my underwear. You didn't think it was complicated when you left a breakfast tray in my refrigerator with something that could only be described as a love letter. Why is everything more complicated now that I've kissed you?"

"Because we've been—outed."

Gabriel's expression hardened. "No, we haven't. Apart from the e-mail, the only public evidence is an argument, which is open to interpretation. The burden of proof is on our antagonists. We'll deny everything."

"Is that what you want to do?"

"What's our alternative? Besides, at the time of the seminar there was no relationship."

He bent over to pick up a key ring from the floor. "Are these yours?"

She held out her hand. "Yes."

"*P* as in Princeton? Or *P* as in Paul?" Gabriel mocked, as he dangled the keys in front of her.

Julia grabbed the keys out of his hand with a grimace and shoved them into the knapsack he was holding.

He smiled at her reaction. "Wait here while I check to see if Paul has his gun out, waiting to shoot the wolf to save the duck."

He quickly peered into the empty hallway. "Hurry up. We'll take the stairs." He pulled Julia swiftly through the door and locked it behind them.

"Are you okay to walk? We can take the short cut through Victoria College and walk up Charles Street. Or I could call a cab," he whispered, as he opened the door to the stairwell for her.

"Where are you taking me?"

"Home."

She relaxed minutely.

"Home . . . *with me*," he clarified, bringing his face closer to hers.

"I thought I pushed all of your buttons."

Gabriel pulled his face back and straightened up to his full height.

"You do. All of them. But it's six o'clock, and you're fainting from hunger. There's no way in hell I'm taking you somewhere public after what happened. And I can't cook you a proper dinner at your place."

"But you're still angry. I can see it in your eyes."

"I'm sure you're angry with me too. But hopefully, we'll get over it. Right now, every time I look at you all I can think about is kissing you." Gabriel released her and began to lead her down the stairs.

"Paul could take me home."

"I told you—fuck Paul. You're *my* Beatrice. You belong with *me*."

"Gabriel, I'm not anyone's Beatrice. The delusions have to stop."

He placed a hand on her arm to stop her. "Neither of us has a monopoly on delusions. Our only hope is to take time to discover who we really are and decide if that's a reality we both can live with.

"I've had enough vexation with you to last a lifetime, and I'm putting an end to it tonight. We're going to sit down and have the conversation I wanted to have with you ten days ago. I'm not letting you out of my sight until that's happened. End of discussion."

With one look at the resolve on his face, Julia realized there was no point in arguing. As he led her through a side door and behind the building, she pulled out her cell phone and guiltily sent Paul a text. She told him she was okay, that she was too embarrassed to talk about it, and was already on her way home.

Paul had been hovering by the elevators, staying out of sight as he waited for Julia to come out. He'd walked by The Professor's door once or twice but hadn't heard anything. He didn't want to antagonize Emerson by waiting outside his door.

As soon as he received her text, he immediately ran back to the office. He knocked on Emerson's door, but no one answered. Paul ran to the stairwell and flew down the stairs hoping that he could catch her.

❀ ❀

Gabriel followed Julia into his apartment. "Did you eat lunch?"

"I don't remember."

"Julianne! What about breakfast?"

"I had coffee . . ."

He swore under his breath. "You need to take better care of yourself. No wonder you're so pale. Come."

He led her to the red velvet wing-back chair in the living room and made her sit down, gently lifting her feet and placing them on top of the ottoman.

"I don't need to sit down over here. I could sit in the kitchen, with you."

Gabriel glared at her mildly as he turned on the gas fireplace. He let his hand pass over her head, brushing back her hair.

"Kittens should be curled up in a chair by the fire on a day like today. You're safer here than on one of the bar stools. I'm going to make dinner, but I need to step out and pick up a few things. Will you be all right by yourself?"

"Of course, Gabriel. I'm not an invalid."

"If you feel scorched, flip the switch and the inferno will go out."

He leaned over and pressed a kiss on top of her hair before walking to the front door. "Promise me you won't leave before I come back," he called.

"I promise." Julia wondered if he was really that worried about losing her.

She thought back to what had happened in the lecture and the events in his office. She wondered if it was lack of food that made her light-headed, or Gabriel's kiss. It wouldn't have been the first time that he'd affected her this way . . .

Julia closed her eyes just for a moment as the dull roar of the fire hummed in her ears, and she fell fast asleep.

The sound of a woman's voice, passionate and soulful, floated through the air. Julia recognized the song before she opened her eyes. Gabriel was playing Edith Piaf, *Non, je ne regrette rien*. It was an extraordinary choice.

Julia opened her eyes to find Gabriel smiling down on her, looking very much like a troubled angel—an angel with dark hair, a mouth made for sin, and piercing blue eyes. He'd changed into a black button-down shirt and a pair of black trousers, his shirtsleeves pushed up to expose muscled forearms.

"Julianne?" He smiled and offered her his hand.

She took it, and he led her into the dining room. Gabriel had set his formal dining table with a white linen tablecloth and lit the candles in an ornate silver candelabra. She saw two place settings of china, crystal, and silver, and a bottle of what appeared to be champagne.

Veuve Clicquot Ponsardin vintage 2002, she read on the label.

"Are you pleased?" He stood behind her and rubbed her arms with his hands.

"It's beautiful," she managed, eyeing the expensive champagne with suspicion.

"Then allow me." He pulled her chair out and handed her a white linen napkin. "I've tried a second time with the flowers. Please don't destroy them like you did the last ones."

Gabriel smiled wryly as he gestured to a tall, modern glass vase that held an arrangement of purple hyacinths.

"If you're good, I'll let you read the card," he whispered, as he poured her a glass of champagne. Without waiting to watch her taste it, he disappeared into the kitchen.

With a quick look over her shoulder to be sure she wasn't being watched, Julia removed the card that was nestled among the flowers. In it she read:

My Dear Julianne,
If you wish to know how I feel about you,
just ask me.
Yours,
Gabriel

Smug bastard, Julia thought before she hastily replaced the card.

As she sat there, annoyed, a number of different things caught her attention. Gabriel had chosen Edith Piaf for mood music; she was now singing *La Vie en Rose*. The tablecloth, the place settings, the champagne, the flowers . . . he hadn't gone to such trouble for Rachel.

All the arguing and passion in his office had lit their bodies on fire. And the way he'd kissed her . . . Julia had never been kissed like that before, even by him. She shivered in remembrance, solely from pleasure. It was a new feeling, but not an unwelcome one.

Foreplay.

She knew that he'd struggled to stop kissing her, as if he were at war with himself. The tension between them had been palpable, almost concrete. She knew that he was a very sexual man who was never in want of female companionship, by his own admission. Now that he had tasted her while sober, he wanted *her*. It was overwhelming to be desired by such a tempting, sensual creature. She felt like Psyche being desired by Cupid. And she could not deny the attraction she felt for him, or the way she fluttered with longing when he kissed her.

But Julia did not share, which made all other romantic or sexual considerations moot. She decided to wait until after the salad course to tell him that.

When Gabriel sat next to her at the head of the table, he picked up his water glass and toasted their evening. As they clinked their glasses together, Julia realized he wasn't drinking champagne.

"No *Veuve Clicquot?*" she asked, sipping away incredulously.

He smiled at her and shook his head. *"Non, seulement de l'eau ce soir. Mon ange."*

Julia rolled her eyes at Gabriel's French, but it wasn't because his pronunciation was faulty.

"You will probably find this difficult to believe, but I don't drink all the time. Nevertheless, I don't expect you to finish this bottle by yourself. We'll save it for Mimosas for breakfast."

Julia's eyebrows shot up. *Breakfast? You're awfully sure of yourself, Casanova.*

"I searched my collection for a vintage from 2003 but had to make due with 2002."

It took a moment for Julia to realize the significance of the year, and when the realization hit her she blushed and looked down at her hands. Gabriel watched her over his salad but said nothing. He'd hoped for a more vocal reaction, but he surmised rather quickly that she was overwhelmed by the tumult of the day.

She's nervous; she's quivering, and her face is flushed.

Gabriel reached over to stroke the skin at her wrist from time to time, just to reassure her. Whenever their eyes met he would stop whatever he was doing and smile at her encouragingly, hoping that she'd engage him in conversation. But she would only duck her head and look down at her plate—until the strains of a certain song filled their ears.

Besame, besame mucho . . .

Gabriel watched Julia carefully. When she reacted to the music, as well as turning a deeper shade of rose, he winked.

"Do you remember this song?"

"Yes."

"How is your Spanish?" He gazed at her expectantly.

"Nonexistent."

"That's a pity. The words are very beautiful." He smiled at her somewhat sadly, and she looked away.

When Gabriel wasn't singing, he was watching her, the movement of her eyes, the fidgeting of her hands, the blush of her skin. And when the song was over he smiled, stood up, and pressed a long kiss to the top of her head.

He cleared their dishes, topped up her champagne flute, and served their entrées, *spaghetti con limone* with capers and tiger shrimp. It was a rare treat and one of Julia's favorites, so it surprised her that he made it. Maybe Rachel had . . .

She shook her head. This was between her and Gabriel. Period. Except for the specter of Paulina, who was haunting them both . . .

"You aren't the same man you were in the orchard," Julia announced flatly, the champagne making her bold.

Gabriel rested his fork on his plate, his eyebrows knitting together. "You're right—I'm much better."

Julia laughed bitterly. "Impossible! He was kind to me and very, very gentle. He would never have been as cold and indifferent as you have been."

"You don't know what you're talking about." His eyes flashed to hers. "I've never lied to you. Why would I start now?"

A flush of anger started in her cheeks and spread across her face. "I won't let your darkness consume me."

Gabriel was puzzled by her sudden hostility and was sorely tempted to call her out on it. Surprisingly, however, he cocked his head to one side. She watched as he wet his finger in Perrier and began running it around the rim of his water glass, smoothly and sensuously. Soon the crystal goblet was singing in their ears.

Suddenly, Gabriel stopped. "You think darkness can consume light? That's an interesting theory. Let's see if it works." He waved his hand at the candelabra. "There. I just threw some of my darkness at those candles. See how successful it was?"

He smirked and returned to his meal.

"You know what I'm talking about! Don't be so damned condescending."

Gabriel's eyes darkened. "I have no wish to *consume* you, but I won't lie and say that I'm not attracted to your luminosity. If I am the darkness, then you are the stars. In fact, I'm quite taken by *la luce della tua umilitate.*"

"I won't let you fuck me."

Now he sat back in his chair with a look of shock and disgust on his face. He silently resolved that she'd drunk her last glass of champagne.

"I'm sorry, did I ask you to?" His voice was smooth and unruffled, which made Julia even more upset.

Liar. Liar. Beautiful blue eyes on fire.

He grinned at her impertinently, watching her face over the rim of his glass. He wiped his lips with his napkin and brought his face inches from hers. "If I were to ask you to do anything, Miss Mitchell, it wouldn't be that." He smiled, sat back in his seat, and almost cheerfully finished his dinner without another word.

Julia seethed. She knew he was staring at her; she could feel his eyes on her face, her mouth, her shoulders, which were shaking. Nothing escaped those piercing blue eyes. She felt as if he could read her soul, and still he did not look away.

"Julianne," he said at last. He moved his hand underneath the table to catch her wrist and pull it out of her lap, brushing the top of her thigh as he did so.

His voice was gentle and smooth, and Julia felt the warmth of his touch travel all the way to her toes.

"Look at me."

She tried to withdraw her hand, but he held her fast.

"Look at me when I'm speaking to you."

Julia slowly raised her eyes to his. They were softer and less ominous than his tone, but remarkably intense.

"I would never, ever, fuck you. Clear? One doesn't fuck an angel."

"Then what does someone like you do with an angel?" Her voice trembled slightly.

"Someone like me would cherish her. Try to get to know her and puzzle her out. Start by being . . . friends, perhaps."

She squirmed under his grasp. "Friends with benefits?"

"Julianne . . ." Gabriel's voice held a warning in it. He released her hand and stared at her momentarily. "Is it too much to believe that I *want* to know you? That I want to take my time?"

"Yes."

He bit back a curse. "This is new for me, Julianne. Your prejudice is warranted to some degree, but don't deliberately try my patience."

"We both know that professors are never friends with their students."

"We could be," he whispered, gently pushing her hair back behind her shoulder and allowing his fingertips to graze the exposed curve of her neck. "If that's what you want."

She didn't know how to react to this stunning utterance, so she angled away from him.

"I don't seduce virgins, Julia. Your virtue is safe with me." And with that, he cleared the dinner dishes and disappeared into the kitchen.

Julia finished her champagne in two quick swallows.

He's a liar. If I hadn't said no, he'd have flashed his signature smile and had me naked and spread-eagled before my panties even hit the floor. And he'd probably demand that we reproduce one of the poses from his black-and-white photographs. Then Paulina would call right in the middle of it.

Gabriel returned and hastily removed her glass and the bottle of champagne. A few minutes later, he brought her an espresso served with a small twist of lemon rind. Julia was surprised. It was difficult to imagine him zesting his own lemons, but nevertheless, there it was—perfect and fresh lemon rind.

"Thank you, Gabriel. Espresso Roma is my favorite."

He looked at her smugly. "I thought it was time we switched you to something non-alcoholic before you threw up on me."

Julia scowled. She felt fine. She felt slightly less inhibited but still in command of her faculties. *She thought.* "What did you write in the card? The one you left on my porch?"

Gabriel stiffened. "So you didn't read it?"

"I was upset."

He shrugged. "Then I suppose it's a good thing you didn't." He turned on his heel and disappeared.

Julia sipped her espresso slowly, trying to guess what he'd written. It must have been something sufficiently intimate for him to be so out of sorts. She wondered if the pieces of the card were still in the flowerbed in front of her building and if she would be able to piece them together.

A few minutes later, Gabriel returned with a single piece of choco-late cake and one fork. "Dessert?" He moved his chair so that he was sitting closer to her—too close, actually.

"Julianne," his voice sang in her ear, "I know you're partial to choco-late. I bought this to please you."

He held the fork under her nose, just so she could pick up the scent. She licked her lips involuntarily. It smelled divine. She reached out to take the fork from him, but he snatched it out from underneath her hand. "No. You need to let me feed you."

"I'm not a child."

"Then stop acting like one. *Trust me*. Please."

Julia turned her face and shook her head, resisting the urge to watch as he brought the fork up to his own mouth and darted his tongue out to catch some of the frosting.

"*Mmmmmm*. You know, the act of feeding someone is the ultimate act of care and affection . . . sharing yourself with someone else through food." He held another mouthful of cake under her nose. "Think about it. We are fed in the Eucharist, by our mothers when we are infants, by our parents as children, by friends at dinner parties, by a lover when we feast on one another's bodies . . . and on occasion, on one another's souls. Don't you *want* me to feed you? You don't want to feast on my body, but at least feast on my cake."

Gabriel chuckled. When Julia didn't answer, he turned his full at-tention to his dessert. She scowled. If he thought this disgusting display of food porn was going to get her attention and maybe make her a little hot and bothered until she was putty in his hands . . .

. . . *he was right.*

The sight of Gabriel eating chocolate cake was perhaps the most erotic thing she'd ever witnessed. He savored every morsel, licking his lips and laving his tongue suggestively across the fork after every bite. He closed his eyes and groaned from time to time, making feral, throaty noises that were achingly familiar. He moved slowly and sinuously toward the plate, the tendons in his arms clearly visible, extending for-ward and moving backward, his eyes burning into hers with every gentle and obvious rhythm.

Before he'd even come to the last bite, Julia felt the room begin to grow stiflingly warm. Her cheeks were flushed, her breathing labored, and she felt little beads of sweat beginning to form on her forehead. And lower down . . .

What is he doing to me? It feels just like . . .

"Last chance, Julia." He made the fork dance before her eyes.

She tried to resist. She tried to turn away, but somehow when she opened her mouth to refuse, he slid the fork past her lips and into her mouth.

"Mmmmmm," he hummed, smiling widely and showing all of his white, perfect teeth. "That's my good little kitten."

Julia blushed more deeply and ran her fingers across her lips, gathering up the last of the crumbs. He was right, the cake was delicious.

"Now that wasn't so bad, was it? See how nice it is to be cared for?" he whispered. "See how nice it is to be cared for . . . by me?"

She was beginning to wonder if she even had a chance at resisting seduction. All thoughts of what he said about her virtue miraculously flew out of her head.

Gabriel reached out and grasped her wrist, drawing her fingers to his mouth. "You left some chocolate behind," he purred, looking up at her through his eyelashes. "May I?"

Julia inhaled sharply. She didn't quite know what he was going to do, so she said nothing.

He grinned wickedly at her silent acquiescence before drawing her fingers into his mouth, one by one, sucking them slowly and swirling his tongue unhurriedly around the tips.

Julia bit her lip to suppress a moan as her skin exploded into flames. *Holy fuck, Gabriel.* When he finished, she closed her eyes and wiped the sweat from her forehead.

Gabriel regarded her silently for what seemed like an age. "You're exhausted," he announced suddenly, blowing the candles out. "Time for bed."

She opened her eyes as he bent over her. "What about our conversation?"

"We've done enough talking for today. Our conversation is going to be a long one, and we should approach it when both of our heads are clear."

"Please, Gabriel. Don't do this." Her voice grew low and desperate.

"One night. Spend the night with me, and if you want to leave tomorrow, I won't stop you."

He picked her up carefully and pulled her tightly to his chest.

Julia said nothing, the last of her self-control ebbing out of her. She was spent. He'd worn her down and her resistance was decimated. Perhaps it was the champagne. Perhaps it was the drama of the day and their explosive encounter in his office. No matter the explanation, she couldn't resist him anymore. Her heart was already beating a fevered pace, her insides melting at the heat that floated across her body. And further down, near her womb, came the not so subtle fluttering of desire.

He will consume me, body and soul.

In her dreams, it was always Gabriel to whom she gave her virginity. But not like this. Not with such hopelessness in the pit of her stomach and whatever illegible emotion that flashed in his eyes.

He carried her down the hall to his bedroom and tenderly placed her in the center of his large, medieval bed. He lit a few candles and placed them around the room, on the nightstands, the dresser, and the credenza underneath the painting of Dante and Beatrice. Then he turned out all the lights and disappeared into the bathroom.

Julia took this opportunity to examine his black-and-white photographs. But they were gone. The walls were bare, with the exception of the Holiday reproduction and six hooks and bits of wire that testified to the previous presence of the now absent pictures.

Why did he remove them? And when?

Julia was glad they were gone. She was afraid of how they might look in the flickering candlelight, their images glowing raw and Satanic in the semi-darkness, depicting her soon to be sealed fate. Naked, nameless, faceless, soulless. She only hoped the most aggressive one, the sixth photo, would not be what he had in mind for her first time.

Is that what he would want? Is that what he would demand? Tearing her clothes off, shoving her onto her stomach, pushing into her from behind . . . not even looking into her eyes as he took her virginity, no kisses, no love-making, nothing but aggression and domination. Julia only knew of his sexual predilections from the photographs, and the fact that he'd described what he did to women as *fucking*.

Her breathing began to speed as panic washed over her. She heard an old voice in her head taunting her about fucking like animals.

Gabriel returned wearing a hunter green T-shirt and a pair of Black Watch tartan pajama bottoms. He deposited a glass of water on the nightstand next to one of the candles, pulled the covers back, and lifted Julia so that he could place her under the sheets.

She flinched, but he pretended not to notice and reclined on his side by her legs, drawing them close to his chest. He undid her sneakers and pulled off her socks, tenderly caressing the soles of her feet and her toes, making her moan in spite of herself.

"Relax, Julianne. Don't fight it. This is supposed to be nice." He murmured from time to time, more to himself than to her, and at one point Julia thought she heard him say *la sua immagine*. But she couldn't be sure. His voice was low, like a whisper or a prayer.

She silently wondered if he was referring to her or to Beatrice, and which debauched gods he was addressing. Just as silently, she begged them to aid in her escape, instead.

Please don't let him consume me.

"I seem to recall that you liked my Magdalen College boxer shorts. They're in the top drawer, if you'd care to borrow them. They don't fit me anymore."

Julia sniffled. "Your pictures . . . the ones you used to have on the wall. Is that what you want?"

Gabriel's hands stilled against her feet. "What are you talking about?"

Her eyes darted nervously to where the sixth photograph had hung and back to Gabriel. His face morphed rapidly from surprise into horror.

"Of course not! What do you take me for?" His voice was a tragic, offended whisper. "You're here, you're tired. I don't want to run the risk of losing you again before we talk." He smiled minutely. "I want to make you a breakfast tray with parsley and orange sections, not take your virginity. And certainly not like that." He seemed disgusted. "I'm not a barbarian."

When she didn't respond, he slipped her feet under the covers. He tucked her in as if she were a child and pressed a light kiss to her forehead, smoothing her hair back from her face.

"Let's try to forgive one another, shall we? We've both been hurt, and we've both wasted so many years. Let's not waste any more time jumping to conclusions."

He stood up and rubbed his eyes with the heels of his hands. "It's quite possible you won't want me tomorrow, anyway," he muttered. Then he stood to attention and gave her a small smile. "Call me if you need anything."

While Julia tossed and turned alone, she heard Gabriel playing the stereo, softly but fluidly. She didn't recognize the music, but with the sounds of arpeggios imitating waterfalls she eventually fell into a light sleep.

Later that night, Gabriel was lying on his back in the guest bed, his arm crooked over his face. He was hovering in between wakefulness and dreaming when he felt a slight shift at his left. A warm body moved toward him, gently tugging at the covers.

The body crawled in beside him and molded itself to his side. He felt long, soft curls whisper across his now naked chest. He heard a small, contented sigh as an arm slid across the ridges of his abdominal muscles, eventually resting on top of them. Gabriel pressed a gentle kiss to the forehead that was placed above his tattoo and slid his arm around the shoulders and down to the lower back, hesitantly moving his fingers under the T-shirt until they came in contact with soft, smooth skin. And dimples just above the waistband of a pair of boxers that were far too large.

The warm body sighed again and pressed soft lips to the stubble at his neck. "I tried to stay away . . ." Julia's voice was hesitant, " . . . but I couldn't."

"I tried not to lick chocolate off your fingers. But I couldn't." Gabriel's voice was playful but there was a note of underlying sadness.

She hummed unconsciously at his remark. "Why did you remove the photographs in your bedroom?"

He squirmed in her arms. "Because I was ashamed."

"You weren't before."

"That was before I decided to bring an angel to my bed."

Lazy but curious hands caressed naked skin, exploring gently but chastely. Sighs commingled in the dark as two souls breathed as one. Two heartbeats synchronized when they recognized one another. And two troubled, conflicted minds finally came to rest.

Just as Gabriel was drifting off, he thought he heard her talking in her sleep; not words, just utterances that grew progressively more panicked, culminating in her breathless release of a name he'd not heard before.

"Simon."

Chapter Seventeen

When Julia awoke, she yawned and stretched, reaching her hand out and . . . nothing. Gabriel was gone and his side of the bed was cold. A feeling of unease washed over her. The feeling was old; she'd felt it before. It made her momentarily nauseated.

She swung her legs to the floor and saw a small note on the bedside table, propped up against a wine goblet, which was filled with water floating with lemon slices. The note was written with a fountain pen:

> Lovely Julianne,
> I've gone to pick up something special for breakfast.
> Please use the washroom in the master bedroom; it's better.
> I've laid out some personal items for you there.
> You can also choose whatever you need from my dresser and my closet.
> Please stay.
> Yours,
> Gabriel.
>
> P.S. Forgive my boldness, but you asleep in my arms this morning was by far the most beautiful sight I have ever seen.

Wow. How does he do that? she thought, flushing scarlet. The Professor certainly had a way with words . . . and flowers and music and chocolate cake . . . She placed a hand to her forehead as she tried to collect herself. Chocolate cake was her new favorite dessert. And the memory of her fingertips in his warm mouth and the way that his tongue artfully . . .

Focus, Julia. You need to take a shower. Preferably, a cold one.

She quickly drank the water he'd left for her and tapped the note against her teeth. The last time she'd slept in his bed she'd had a very rude awakening in his living room. Although he'd been tender with her last night, she worried he might snap at her this morning.

She opened the door to the guest room and stuck her head out, eager to discern any signs of life. When she was satisfied that she was alone, she walked quietly to the master bedroom and closed the door behind her. She retrieved her clothes and entered his large bathroom, making sure to lock the door.

Gabriel had left another note with a wine goblet filled with orange juice. It was garnished with an orange slice. *Clearly, Gabriel has a thing for garnishes*, she thought.

On the note, she read:

> Julianne,
> I hope you'll find everything you need here.
> If not, Rachel stocked the vanity in the guest
> washroom with a number of different items. Please help
> yourself.
> My clothes are at your disposal.
> Please choose a sweater as the weather has turned cold
> today.
> Yours,
> Gabriel

Julia sipped the orange juice as she examined the items before her. Laid out on the vanity with military precision was a new toothbrush in its packaging, toothpaste, a new disposable razor (which she examined with an arched eyebrow), various feminine-looking toiletries from a company called Bliss, which were all scented with vanilla and bergamot, and a lavender-colored mesh shower sponge that was commonly referred to as a *poof*.

Had Gabriel asked Rachel to purchase these items for his guests? Or was Gabriel the kind of man who kept random unused shower poofs on hand for just such occasions? Perhaps he followed a color-code: lavender for virgins, red for Paulina, black for Professor Singer, green for the Emerson whores . . . Julia doubted the lavender one had ever been used before.

A virgin poof for a virgin . . . how fitting.

Julia stopped herself. Gabriel had asked for forgiveness and tried, gently, to suggest that she refrain from jumping to conclusions about him. And here she was, jumping to conclusions over a shower poof.

Looking around, she found a white, Turkish cotton bathrobe hanging on the back of the door and a pair of ladies' bedroom slippers by the bathtub. They were far too large for her and would have been far too large for Rachel's feet too. This time Julia limited her negative reaction to a roll of the eyes.

It took more than a few minutes for her to figure out how to operate his very fancy shower, for it had multiple settings for body sprays, water pressures, and temperatures, and was extremely complicated. Julia was only interested in the large and central tropical rain shower, which was, of course, controlled by the last lever she pulled.

While she surrounded herself in vanilla and bergamot and tried not to think of Cream Earl Grey tea, Julia asked herself some very serious questions. She suspected that Gabriel would want to have their conversation as soon as possible. It was going to be painful. And what was she going to do afterward? Try to be friends with him? For what purpose?

She realized that if she focused on the future, she'd never be able to address the past, at least not adequately. So she was determined to focus solely on their past interactions, including his rudeness and condescension this semester. He needed to explain himself, and she needed to listen without jumping to conclusions. Then she would tell him exactly what she thought about him.

Yes, it was going to be painful for both of them. It saddened her to realize that she had never had a healthy romantic relationship, when one of the things she wanted most in life was to enjoy affection and love. And Gabriel, despite the fact that he came from a good albeit adopted family and was intelligent, handsome, and wealthy, was probably incapable of having a healthy romantic relationship at all.

Her mother's relationships were far from healthy or normal, and Julia had seen too many of them from an early age, an endless parade of myriad dysfunctions. In contrast, her father's relationship with Deb Lundy was normal enough, if not a little on the casual side. They cared for one another, Julia thought, but their care was cool and small, like a distant star.

Gabriel's love would burn hot like the sun, if he was even capable of loving someone. It's obvious he prefers sex to love, or maybe he just conflates the two. What's worse—thinking sex is love, or thinking that the two can be separated from one another and preferring sex?

Julia allowed the warm water of the shower to pour over her, trying to take her mind away from the inexplicable draw she felt toward him. *What I would not give to have even a part of the happiness that Grace and Richard had. They had the ideal marriage. They always spoke kindly to one another. And they were so much in love . . .*

Julia exited the shower and was soon clad only in Gabriel's bathrobe with a thick, white towel wrapped around her curling hair. At least, she thought it was Gabriel's bathrobe. It didn't smell like him. She pulled on the slippers and went hunting in the bedroom for some clothes. She found a pair of socks, a white undershirt, and a pair of Princeton boxer shorts in his dresser, all of which looked like they would fit her somewhat. Walking over to Gabriel's large and immaculate walk-in closet, she flipped on the light switch. Row upon row of meticulously organized clothes met her on three sides.

She moved to the far wall and began going through a pile of sweaters and cardigans, almost all cashmere by Loro Piana, neatly arranged between wooden dividers on a shelf. She quickly found the British-racing-green sweater that she'd borrowed before and noticed with satisfaction that it had apparently been returned to its formerly pristine condition. She boldly held the sweater to her nose and inhaled, smiling with pleasure as she realized that it smelled of Aramis and Gabriel. He must have worn it after it had come back from the dry cleaner.

Just then, something shiny caught her eye. Leaning up against the wall and half-hidden behind the hangers of sports coats and suit jackets were Gabriel's black-and-white framed photographs. She recognized the top photograph as the fifth one, the one that had been over the bed. It was gently erotic and almost tender.

He shouldn't have been ashamed of this one. Julia wished her back was that beautiful. And part of her wished that Gabriel would look at her the way the man in the photograph looked at the woman. Just once.

She quickly returned to the bathroom and regarded her face in the mirror. She looked tired. She was pale, as usual, with dark circles under her eyes. Those eyes were glassy, and her veins showed at her neck. She looked ill, actually, after a couple of weeks of drama and lack of sleep, and the contrast between her pale skin and her dark hair wasn't helping matters. Nor was the fact that Rachel had not thought to leave cosmetics behind for Gabriel's overnight guests. Clearly, it was an oversight on her part.

After dressing, Julia ventured into the kitchen. Gabriel was nowhere to be found. She stuffed her dirty clothes into her knapsack and pulled out her phone and the padded envelope. Plopping herself on one of the bar stools she quickly checked her voice mail. Five messages from Paul were waiting, each more urgent than the last, culminating with a message in which he said he was standing outside her building on Madison Avenue and ringing her doorbell.

Scheisse. There was no way she could explain what had happened. But she couldn't ignore Paul either, so she quickly manufactured an excuse and texted it to him:

> Paul, hi. Sorry. Didn't hear doorbell. Broken? Emerson scolded me but won't have to drop class (phew). Have to find new advisor. Working on it. Chat later & thanks, Julia

She hoped her message would be enough to occupy him until she constructed a better explanation. She supposed she would have to speak to Gabriel about that so that they could get their story straight.

Something Gabriel had said yesterday made her curious about the contents of the envelope he'd left for her in her mailbox. Opening it, in addition to her black lace bra she found her iPod. She pulled it out, placed the earbuds in her ears, and scrolled through the music to the

Recently Added Songs section, where she discovered that Gabriel had made two additions.

The first song was *Prospero's Speech* by Loreena McKennitt. With surprise, Julia listened to the haunting female voice sing words from Shakespeare's *The Tempest*:

> *But release me from my bands*
> *With the help of your good hands:*
> *Gentle breath of yours my sails*
> *Must fill, or else my project fails,*
> *Which was to please. Now I want*
> *Spirits to enforce, art to enchant,*
> *And my ending is despair,*
> *Unless I be relieved by prayer,*
> *Which pierces so that it assaults*
> *Mercy itself and frees all faults.*
> *As you from your crimes would pardon'd be,*
> *Let your indulgence set me free.*

Julia listened to the song twice more, stunned by both the language and the music. She had known long ago that Gabriel was intense; Grace had said so. And Julia had experienced his intensity during their first encounter, when he'd gazed into her eyes as if she was the first woman he had ever seen.

"Julianne?"

She let out a small cry and clapped a hand over her mouth. Gabriel was standing in front of her with three small bags in one hand and a bouquet of purple irises in the other. Staring, she removed the earbuds from her ears. He eyed her iPod curiously and smiled.

Julia smiled back. In response, he leaned toward her, his eyes locked on hers, and lightly pressed his lips to her left cheek and then to her right. She thought he was approaching her mouth, so when he touched her cheek she felt disappointed. Nevertheless, a spark surged from his lips, causing her heart to speed. She blushed and looked down at her hands.

"Good morning, Julianne. I'm glad you stayed. How did you sleep?" Gabriel's voice was gentle.

"I slept well—later on."

He reached behind her to place the groceries and flowers on the breakfast bar.

"As did I." He made no move to touch her but followed her gaze to her fingers.

Julia shivered slightly as she thought of what he had done to her fingers the night before.

"Are you cold?"

"No."

"You're quivering." Gabriel's eyebrows knit together, creating a furrow in between them. "Am I making you nervous?"

"A little."

He withdrew to the kitchen and began unpacking the groceries.

"What did you buy?" she asked, gesturing to the bags.

"Pastries and a baguette. There's a French bakery around the corner that makes the best *pain au chocolat* in the city. Also, some cheese from the cheese shop downstairs, fruit, and a surprise."

"A surprise?"

"Yes." He smiled and waited.

She wrinkled her nose. "Will you tell me what the surprise is?"

"If I tell you, it won't be a surprise."

She rolled her eyes, and he laughed at her.

"*Baci,*" he said.

Julia paused. *Kisses?*

Gabriel saw her reaction and realized the *double entendre* had not been understood. He pulled something from one of the grocery bags and placed it in the center of his right palm, holding it out to her as one might hold out an apple to tempt a horse.

The similarity was not lost on Julia, who looked at the small, foil-wrapped chocolate with an upturned nose.

"I thought you liked them," he said, a tinge of hurt coloring his voice. "When Antonio gave you one, you said they were your favorite."

"They are. But I'm not supposed to take chocolates from men, remember? I think you gave me an order to that effect when we were at

Lobby with Rachel." Julia took the proffered chocolate and eagerly unwrapped it, popping it into her mouth.

"I don't order you around."

She gaped at him while she chewed and swallowed her chocolate.
"Are you kidding?"

"No."

"What planet are you from? *Hello, my name is Gabriel, and I'm from
the planet of bossy-no-self-awareness.*"

He frowned. "Very amusing, Julianne." He cleared his throat and
searched her eyes. "Be serious for a moment. You think I order you
around?"

"Gabriel, you do nothing *but*. You only have one form of direct address, and it's the imperative; *do this, do that, come here*. On top of all
that, like Paul, you seem to think I belong in a zoo. Or a children's book."

At the mere mention of Paul's name Gabriel's frown deepened into
a scowl. "Someone had to attend to our situation yesterday. I was trying
to protect both of us. And I asked you to talk to me, Julianne. I tried to
talk to you for days, but you spurned me."

"What was I supposed to do? You're an emotional roller coaster, and
I wanted to climb off. I never know whether you're going to be sweet
and whisper something that takes my breath away or say something so
fucking *mean* it breaks my . . ." She stopped herself.

Gabriel cleared his throat. "I apologize for being mean. There's no
excuse for that."

She muttered something under her breath as he stared at her.

"I find you—difficult to talk to sometimes. I never know what you're
thinking, and you're only forthcoming when you're furious. Like now."

She sniffed. "I'm not furious."

"Then I need you to talk to me a little." His voice was soft again.

He took a risk and began running his fingers through her long,
damp curls. "You smell like vanilla," he whispered.

"It's your shampoo."

"So you think I'm bossy?"

"Yes."

Gabriel sighed. "It's habit, I suppose. Years of living alone have
made me boorish, and I'm out of practice with being considerate. But

I'll try to watch how I speak to you in future. As for Paul and the pet names, it's insulting that he refers to you as a rabbit. Rabbits end up as entrées, so that needs to stop. But what about *kitten?* I thought that was rather . . . sweet."

"Not when you're twenty-three and petite and trying to be taken seriously in Academia."

"What about when you're twenty-three and *beautiful* and someone who's thirty-three and a professional academic says it to you because actually, he thinks you're seriously *sexy?*"

Julia pulled away. "Don't make fun of me, Gabriel. That's mean."

"I would never make fun of you." He gave her a serious look. "Julianne, look at me."

She kept her eyes on the floor.

He waited somewhat impatiently until she met his gaze again. "I would never make fun of you. And certainly not about something like that."

She grimaced and looked away.

"But perhaps *kitten* is a lover's word."

Julia reddened as he continued unpacking the groceries. At length, he turned to her. "It meant a great deal to me to fall asleep with you in my arms last night. Thank you."

She avoided his eyes.

"Look at me, please," he breathed.

Their eyes met, and Julia was surprised at Gabriel's expression. He looked *worried.* "Are you ashamed of coming to my bed?"

She shook her head.

"It reminded me of our first night together."

"Me too," she whispered.

"I'm sorry I wasn't there when you woke up this morning. I was awake at dawn. The sight of you sound asleep reminded me of da Vinci's *La Scapigliata.* You looked very serene with your head resting on my shoulder. And very, very beautiful." He reached across the breakfast bar and tenderly pressed a kiss to her forehead. "So you slept—well?"

"Too well. Why did you light candles in your bedroom?"

He ran his thumb across one of her eyebrows. "You'd already told me what you thought about the darkness. I wanted you to see Holiday's painting and me. I didn't know how you'd feel about staying the night. I was worried you'd run."

"That was, um, considerate of you. Thank you."

His hand stilled against her cheek as his blue eyes pierced into hers, scorching her. "I am a good lover, Julianne, in all senses of the word."

When he withdrew, she tried, almost in vain, to catch her breath. "Tell me why you disliked me so much."

"I didn't dislike you. I was distracted and short-tempered during the first seminar. You seemed familiar to me. I asked you a question so you'd show me your face. When you ignored me, I lost my temper. I'm not used to being ignored."

She chewed her lip slightly.

"I realize that isn't an excuse—I'm just offering an explanation. Simply looking at you elicited very strong feelings. I didn't know where they were coming from, and I resented them. My resentment quickly spiraled into something vicious. But my rudeness to you was absolutely inexcusable." Gabriel reached over to free her lip from her teeth. "I was punished for it afterward. Scott telephoned to tell me Grace had died, and that she died whispering my name because I wasn't there. He told me her deathbed distress was my fault . . ."

Julia took his hand in hers and without thinking, kissed it. "I'm so sorry."

Now he brought his lips to hers and pressed them together tightly. They remained still for a few moments until he began shifting his weight from foot to foot.

"I'm hungry," she murmured, interpreting his signal.

"Shall I feed you?"

Julia nodded, growing a good deal too warm as she recalled how he had fed her the night before.

"Latté or espresso?" He turned to the espresso machine.

"Latté, please."

She stood for a moment, watching him, before taking a closer look at the irises he'd purchased.

"Could you put those in water, please? There's a crystal vase on top of the sideboard in the dining room. You can move the hyacinths from last night or leave them where they are."

She walked over to the buffet, admiring its ebony beauty once again, and fetched the empty vase. "I heard your music last night. It was beautiful."

"I find classical music soothing. I hope I didn't disturb you."

"You didn't. Why did you choose irises?"

"*Fleur-de-lis*," he said simply, placing her latté, which he had poured into a bowl in the Parisian style, in front of her. "And I know your favorite color is purple."

"They're my favorite flower," she remarked shyly, more to herself than to him.

"Mine too, probably because they symbolize Florence. But for you, I think the association has a deeper meaning." He winked at her impertinently and began preparing breakfast.

Julia huffed slightly. She knew what he was referring to: the iris was a symbol of Mary in the Middle Ages and so it became associated with virginity. In giving her irises, Gabriel was saluting her purity. Which was a strange thing for a would-be lover to do, she had to admit.

Maybe he was serious about being friends, after all.

Taking the flowers and her coffee with her, she went to the dining room. She sat down and sipped her drink, trying to plan what to say to him.

He joined her shortly, bringing her breakfast and seating himself in the chair next to her at the head of the table.

"*Buon appetito.*"

Julia quickly concluded that she was eating better at Gabriel's than she had ever eaten, outside of Italy. In front of her sat a plate of fresh fruit, *pain au chocolat*, and sliced baguette and cheese, most notably Brie, Mimolette, and Gorgonzola. He'd even decorated their plates with parsley and orange sections.

He held up his champagne flute and waited until she did the same. "These are Bellinis, not Mimosas. I thought you'd prefer it."

They clinked their glasses together, and Julia took a sip. *It tastes like a sparkling peach*, she thought. It was so much better than orange juice. Although she wondered why he'd decided to drink again.

"You're very good at this," she said.

"Good at what?"

"Seductive food play. I'm sure your overnight guests don't want to leave."

Gabriel placed his fork down somewhat roughly on his plate and wiped his lips with his linen napkin. "I am not in the habit of *entertaining* overnight guests. And certainly never like this." He glared at her. "I thought it would be obvious that *you* are different—that I'm treating you differently." He shook his head. "Perhaps not."

"You said we'd talk," she injected, changing the subject.

"Yes." He gazed at her for a moment. "I have some questions I would like to ask, and I have some things to say."

"I didn't agree to an inquisition."

"This is hardly an inquisition. A few questions, primarily because when I first met you I was not entirely lucid. So forgive me if I wish to have a clearer idea of what actually happened." Gabriel's tone was slightly sarcastic.

She speared a strawberry with her fork and bolted it. *Fine. Let him ask questions. I have a few to ask as well, and they won't be pretty.*

"Before we begin, I think we should agree to some ground rules. I'd like to speak to you about the past before we discuss the present or the future. Is that all right?"

"Agreed."

"And I promise that what you say to me will be kept strictly confidential. I hope that you will extend the same courtesy to me."

"Of course."

"Are there any ground rules you'd like to establish?"

"Um, just that we tell one another the truth."

"Absolutely. Now, how old were you when we first met?"

"I'm the same age as Rachel," she began, evasively, and when he looked at her sharply she added, "seventeen."

"*Seventeen?*"

Gabriel cursed several times and took a lengthy drink of his Bellini. He was clearly rattled by her revelation, which more than surprised her. "Why did you come to see me that night?"

"I didn't. I was invited to dinner, but when I arrived Rachel and Aaron were flying out the door. I heard a noise and found you on the porch."

Gabriel seemed to think about this for a moment. "You knew who I was?"

"They talked about you all the time."

"Did you know how fucked up I was?"

"No. No one ever said anything bad about you, at least not in front of me. Even afterward. They only said nice things."

"What happened the morning after?"

This was the part that Julia didn't want to talk about. She ignored his question and began eating her pastry, knowing he wouldn't expect her to answer when her mouth was full.

"This is important, Julianne. I want to know what happened. My memory of the next morning is a little fuzzy."

Her eyes flashed to his, and she swallowed hard.

"Really? Well, let me enlighten you. I woke up before sunrise, alone, in the middle of the woods. *You left me there*. I was terrified, so I grabbed the blanket and took off. But I couldn't remember the path we took, and it was still dark. I wandered around in hysterics for almost *two hours* until I finally found my way back to your parents' house." Julia started to shake. "I didn't think I'd ever find my way back."

"That's where you went," he breathed.

"What are you talking about?"

"I didn't leave you."

"What do you call it then?"

"I must have woken up shortly before you did. You were asleep in my arms, and I didn't want to wake you, but I had to—relieve myself. So I wandered off. Then I stopped for a smoke and picked a few apples for our breakfast. When I returned, you were gone. I went back to the house but you weren't there. I assumed you'd left, and I went upstairs to crash in my old bedroom."

"You assumed I'd left?"

"Yes." He gazed at her steadily.

"I called your name, Gabriel! I shouted for you."

"I didn't hear you. I was hungover, and maybe I wandered a little too far away."

"You didn't smoke when you were with me," she sounded skeptical.

"No, I didn't. And I quit soon afterward."

"Why didn't you try to find me?"

Guilt clouded his eyes, and he looked away.

"My family woke me up, demanding that I deal with the aftermath of the night before. When I asked where Beatrice was, Richard told me I was delusional."

"What about Rachel?"

"I left before she returned. She refused to speak to me for months."

"Don't lie to me, Gabriel. I brought your jacket back. I folded it and put it on top of the blanket and set it on the porch. That was a clue. And didn't someone see my bike?"

"I don't know what they saw. Grace gave me my jacket, and no one mentioned you or your name, not that I would have recognized it. It was as if you were a ghost."

"How could you have thought it was a dream? You weren't that drunk."

He closed his eyes and clenched his fists. Julia watched the tendons stand out on his arms, rippling up and down.

Gabriel opened his eyes, but kept them fixed on the table. "Because I was hungover and confused, and I was strung out on coke."

Slam.

That was the sound of Julia's fairy tale crashing into the unyielding wall of reality. Her eyes widened, and she inhaled sharply.

"Didn't Rachel ever tell you what precipitated the fight? Richard knew when he picked me up at the airport in Harrisburg that I was on something. He searched my room before dinner and found my stash. When he confronted me, I snapped."

Julia closed her eyes and put her head in her hands.

He sat very still, waiting for her to speak.

"Cocaine," she whispered.

Gabriel squirmed in his chair. "Yes."

"I spent the night in the woods, alone, with a twenty-seven-year-old coke head who was strung out and drunk. What a stupid, stupid girl."

He clenched his teeth. "Julianne, you are *not* stupid. I'm the fuck-up. I should have known better than to lead you out there in my condition."

She exhaled slowly and her shoulders began to shudder.

"Look at me, Julianne."

She shook her head.

"I saw your father that morning."

Julia peered over at him. "You did?"

"You know what it's like to live in a small town. The gossip started when Richard brought Scott to the hospital and neither of them would explain how he got hurt. Your father caught wind of it and came over to see if he could help."

"He never mentioned it."

"Richard and Grace were embarrassed. I'm sure your father wanted to protect them from small-town gossip. Since no one but you and I knew what happened between us . . ." His voice trailed off, and he shook his head. "Why didn't you tell Rachel?"

"I was traumatized. And humiliated."

Gabriel winced. He reached over to take her hand in his, his eyes burning into hers. "Don't you remember what happened between us?"

Julia threw his hand back.

"Of course I remember! That's the reason I've been so screwed up. Sometimes I'd think back to that night and I'd believe what you said. I'd try to convince myself that you must have had a reason for leaving.

"Other times, all I could think about was how you abandoned me, and I'd have nightmares about being lost in the woods. But do you know what the sickest thing is? I hoped that you would come back. For years I hoped you'd show up on my doorstep and tell me you wanted me. That you meant what you'd said about being glad you'd found me. How pathetic is that?"

"That is *not* pathetic. I agree that it looked like I abandoned you, but I swear I didn't. And believe me, if I had thought for one moment that you were real and living in Selinsgrove, I would have shown up on your doorstep." He cleared his throat, and Julia felt the reverberation of his knee bouncing up and down underneath the table. "I am an addict. This is who I am. I have a need to control things and people, and that need will never go away."

"Are you on something now?"

"Of course not! You think I'd do that do you?"

"If you're an addict, you're an addict. Whether I'm here or not makes no difference."

"It makes a difference to me."

"Addictive personalities can latch on to anything: drugs, alcohol, sex, people . . . what if you become addicted to me?"

"I am already addicted to you, Beatrice. Only you're far more dangerous than cocaine."

Julia's eyebrows shot up in surprise.

He reached over to take her hand again, stroking the veins that stood out against her pale, thin wrist. "I'm confessing to you now. I'm destructive. I'm moody. I have a bad temper. Some of that has to do with my addiction and some of that has to do with my—past.

"Was it wrong of me to think so highly of you that my only explanation for your existence was that you were either the product of a desperate mind or the crown of God's creation?"

His words and his face were so intense that Julia had to pull away. The combination of his voice and the feel of his long cool fingers stroking her veins . . . She was worried her skin would catch fire and she would disintegrate into a pile of ash. "Are you still doing drugs?"

"No."

"Recreationally?"

"No. After my disgusting behavior in Selinsgrove, Grace convinced me to get help. I was planning to kill myself—I just needed some money to settle my affairs. My night with you changed all that. When they told me there was no one called Beatrice, I assumed you were a hallucination or an angel. And in either case, I thought someone, God perhaps, had shown mercy to me and sent you to save me. *Lo seme di felicità messo de Dio nell' anima ben posta.*"

Julia closed her eyes at the sound of Dante's words from the *Convivio. The seed of felicity sent by God into a well-disposed soul.*

Gabriel cleared his throat. "Scott agreed not to press charges if I went into treatment immediately. So Richard drove me to Philadelphia that same day and checked me into a hospital. After I went through my initial detox, he took me back to Boston and put me in rehab so that I would be close to my . . . job." He shifted in his chair.

Julia opened her eyes, a troubled look on her face.

"Why did you want to kill yourself, Gabriel?"

"I can't tell you."

"Why not?"

"I don't know what would happen if I brought those old demons back, Beatrice."

"Are you still suicidal?"

He cleared his throat. "No. Part of my depression was caused by the drugs. Part of it was caused by—other factors in my life that I have tried to deal with. But you know as well as I that a suicidal person is a person who has lost hope. I found my hope when I found you."

His eyes blazed intensely, and Julia decided to change the subject. "Your mother was an alcoholic?"

"Yes."

"What about your father?"

"I don't speak of him."

"Rachel told me about the money."

"That's the only good thing that ever came out of him," Gabriel growled.

"That's not true," Julia said quietly.

"Why not?"

"Because he made you, that's why."

Gabriel's face immediately softened, and he pressed his lips to the back of her hand.

"Was your father an alcoholic?" she asked.

"I don't know. He was the CEO of a company in New York and died of a heart attack. I didn't care to discover anything else about him."

"Are you an alcoholic?"

"No."

Julia carefully folded her linen napkin with shaking fingers and pushed her chair back from the table. "I'm glad you're not doing drugs, and I'm glad you're in recovery. But I won't get involved with an alcoholic. Life is too short to be bound to that kind of misery."

He stared at her steadily, searching her eyes. "I agree. But if you were to spend time with me, you would realize that I am not an alcoholic. And I pledge not to get drunk anymore. It's unfortunate that I've only gotten drunk once in the past six months and you happened to witness it."

"My mother went in and out of recovery several times, and she never stuck with it. What happens if you start doing drugs again? Not to mention the fact that you have this delusional vision of Beatrice. I'm not her, Gabriel. You want an ideal, or a drug-induced misperception, not me."

"I've been clean for six years. I didn't just get out of recovery. Nevertheless, I know that I am deeply, deeply flawed. But I want to know you, just you, as you are. I want you to be yourself, and yes, Julianne, I know you're more than just a dream. Your reality is far more beautiful and alluring than any dream. I'd choose you over the dream any time."

A tear slid down her cheek, which she wiped away hastily. "You don't know me. You never knew me. You held Dante's Beatrice in your arms that night, the image from his writings and from Holiday's painting, not me."

Gabriel shook his head. "What I felt was real. What I did was real."

"You thought it was real, but that's part of the illusion."

"It was real, Julia. It was everything. As soon as I touched you I knew . . . and when I touched you again . . . *I remembered you*. My body remembered you. It was only my conscious mind that had forgotten."

"I'm not that little girl anymore. And the woman I am you despised on sight."

"That is not true. You've grown into a lovely young woman."

"You want a pet kitten."

"No, Beatrice."

She spoke through clenched teeth. "Stop calling me that."

"I'm sorry, Julianne. I know that I hurt you. I know I have a dark side. Will you let me show you that I can be good? Very, very good?"

"It's too late. I can't." Though it pained her to do so, she walked to the front door, grabbing her knapsack and her coat on the way.

"What about last night?" he asked, striding after her. "Did that mean nothing to you?"

"What should it have meant? Tell me!" She hugged her knapsack close to her chest and backed up against the wall.

He placed his hands on either side of her shoulders and leaned closer. "Do I have to explain it? Didn't you feel it?"

He brought his face to hers, his lips inches from her mouth. She could feel his warm breath on her skin. She shivered.

"Feel what?"

"Your body and mine together. You came to *me* last night, Julianne. You came to my bed. Why did you do that? Why did you tell me you couldn't stay away? Because we're soul mates, just like Aristophanes described—one soul in two bodies. You're my missing half. You're my *bashert.*"

"*Bashert?* Do you even know what that means? *Bashert* is *bashert*, Gabriel; *destiny is destiny.* It can mean anything you want, and it doesn't have to mean me."

He smiled at her widely. "Your linguistic knowledge constantly surprises me."

"I know that word."

"Of course, my lovely. Because you're smart." He brought his fingertips lightly to her neck, stroking up and down.

"Gabriel—stop it." She pushed him away so she could think clearly. "You're clean, but you're still an addict. I am the child of an alcoholic. I won't let this happen."

"I don't deserve you. I know that. *Conosco i segni dell'antica fiamma.* I felt it the first time I took your hand. The first time I kissed you. And it was all there last night—every feeling, every memory, every sensation I had before was there. It was real. Look at me and tell me it meant nothing to you, and I will let you go."

She closed her eyes to block out his pleadings, his assertion that he knew *the signs of the ancient flame.*

"You can't do it, can you? Your skin remembers me, and so does your heart. You told them to forget, but they can't. Remember me, Beatrice. Remember your first."

His lips met her neck, and she felt her pulse begin to race under his touch. Her body was a traitor; it would not lie. It would not listen to reason. He could have asked her anything in this position, and she would have agreed to it. The thought made her desperate.

"Please, Gabriel."

"Please, what?" he whispered, trailing angel soft kisses up and down her neck, finally pausing so he could feel her lifeblood flow under his mouth.

"Please let me go."

"I can't." He tugged her knapsack and her coat out of her hands and dropped them to the floor.

"I don't trust you."

"I know."

"You'll shatter me, Gabriel, and that will be the end of me."

"Never."

He brought his hands to cup her face, and just as she closed her eyes, he paused. Julia waited, expecting the smooth wetness of his lips to connect with hers, but they didn't. She waited. Then she opened her eyes.

Gabriel's eyes were large, soft and warm, and staring down at her. He smiled. He began by stroking her face, gentle caresses here and there, exploring every curve, every line, as if he was memorizing it. He moved to her neck, using a single fingertip from his right hand to travel back and forth. Julia shivered.

He brought his lips to her ear. "Relax, my darling." He nibbled her earlobe and nuzzled her neck enticingly. "Let me show you what I can do when I take it slow."

Holding her face in his hands, he brushed his lips to her forehead, her nose, her cheeks, her chin. Only when she closed her eyes a second time did he cover her mouth with his lips. By then, Julia was already breathless.

As soon as their lips met, there was a rush of blood and heat and energy. But Gabriel was careful and would not speed. His lips matched hers, moving back and forth, their skin humming with the soft friction. But he did not open his mouth. His hands moved to her hair, tangling gently, massaging her scalp and floating downward.

Julia was less gentle as she grabbed at the back of his head, tugging and twining his hair around her fingers. Their mouths continued to press together, smoothing over every inch. His tongue peeked out, and he drew it languorously across her upper lip, tasting her tentatively before sucking her lower lip between his.

It was tempting. It was teasing. It was the slowest kiss he'd ever given. And it made his heart beat quickly. When she moaned against his mouth, he tilted her head back so that she would open for him. But he would not rush. He waited for her jaw to soften, and when she could wait no more and her own tongue hesitantly came out to meet his, only then did he allow himself to accept her invitation.

She would have responded at a fevered pace, but Gabriel controlled the kiss, and he wished to kiss her softly. Gently. Leisurely. It took half an age for his hands to travel from her face down the sides of her neck so that they were kneading her shoulders. And another half an age for those same hands to slide down her spine and under her clothes to find bare skin. All this time he was slowly exploring her mouth as if he'd never have a second chance.

He gasped and groaned when his hands slipped and found the dimples he'd discovered the night before. He already thought of them as uncharted territory, found first by his explorations, even though he had no right, no right at all to claim her.

His fingers glided across her skin as Julia whimpered and clung to him. Her helpless sounds were more erotic than any wanton moan that had ever filled his ears. It pierced and enflamed him. Then he was pressing up against her, returning soft, delicate curves with sinew and steel, subtly switching places so it was his back that flattened against the wall, for he was unwilling to trap her, to make her feel like she'd been cornered. Instead, he let her corner him.

Julia was breathing his breath, hot and moist inside her mouth. He was her oxygen. She couldn't stop kissing long enough to truly inhale, and her head began to float. It made the feel of his lips more intense, so she didn't fight it. She just gave in, licking and sucking and moving . . .

Gabriel retreated minutely, breaking the kiss.

He let his thumbs trace the curve of the naked skin at her waist. She inhaled quickly, and he hugged her close, wrapping his arms around her and feeling her breasts pressed up against him.

"You need to become accustomed to my lips, Julia, because I intend to kiss you a lot." He kissed her hair and smiled down at her, looking truly happy.

When she eventually found her voice, it shook. "Gabriel, I make no promises. I agree to nothing. One kiss doesn't change that."

His smile disappeared, but he continued to hold her closely. He reached out a finger and pushed some of the hair back from her face.

"Just give me a chance. We can take it slowly and try to heal one another."

"Last night you spoke of being friends. Friends don't kiss like that."

He chuckled. "We can be friends. We can follow the model of courtly love, if you wish. I'll just have to remember that the next time I kiss you. And so will you."

Julia looked away. "I don't trust you enough to be anything else. And even if I did, you've got the wrong girl. You will be sorely disappointed with me."

"What are you talking about?"

"You will never be satisfied only with me, and you will leave once you realize that. So have mercy on me and choose someone more sexually compatible before one of us ends up hurt."

She watched as the color in his face deepened and his eyes began to blaze. She waited for him to explode.

"What did he do to you?"

That was not the question she expected. "I don't know what you're talking about."

Gabriel looked at her carefully, measuring her expression. He stood away from the wall and drew himself up to his full height, straightening his shoulders. "I don't know what he did to make you think so little of yourself, but *I* am not *him*. Didn't our night in the orchard demonstrate that our connection is not based on sex?" He stroked her hair for a moment with a gentleness that belied the fierceness of his tone. "I could kill him for doing this to you," he whispered, "for crushing your spirit.

"I won't deny that I've indulged myself and been far from monogamous. But I want something more, something real. And I know you want that too. What are the chances that your next boyfriend will be a virgin? Almost nil. Your self-esteem will be an issue with anyone you date, not just me. And any man who would leave you because you were sexually inexperienced is not worth missing. You have to have faith, Julia, and you have to have hope. Even if you don't have any hope for us, you have to have hope for yourself. Otherwise, you will never let anyone love you."

"You don't even know me."

"I know more about you than you think and the rest I wish to learn. Teach me, Beatrice. I'll enroll in your university as your student. Teach me how to care for you."

"Please, Gabriel. Be serious!"

"I am serious. There are a lot of things that we don't know about each other. Things I am looking forward to finding out and exploring."

"I won't be shared."

He growled. "I am not in the habit of sharing what's precious to me. I'm not going to allow another man to put his hands on you, and that includes Paul and any other Angelfucker out there."

"I won't share you, either."

"Me?"

"Yes."

"Well, that goes without saying."

"No, it doesn't."

"What's that supposed to mean?" he huffed.

"I would expect you not to sleep with anyone else, even while I'm still—deciding. As a demonstration of good faith."

"Done."

Julia laughed. "You say it as if it were easy! You're willing to give up all of your female companions just like that in order to pursue the *possibility* of something with me? I don't believe you."

"I'm gaining more, much more than I am losing, believe me. And I intend to make you see that, over and over and over again." He leaned over and kissed her cheek.

"Paulina . . ." she whispered.

Gabriel continued kissing her, moving down to where her neck curved into her shoulder. "Don't worry about her."

"I won't share you with her."

"You won't have to." He sounded impatient.

"Is Paulina your wife?"

He pulled back and fixed her with a stony look. "Of course not. What do you take me for?"

"Ex-wife?"

"Julianne, stop it. No, she is not my ex-wife. End of conversation."

"I want to know about her."

"No."

"Why not?"

"For reasons I'd rather not discuss. I told you I'm not sleeping with her, and I won't. That should be enough for you."

"What about m-a-i-a?"

His face grew harsh. "No."

"I saw the tattoo on your chest, Gabriel. I saw the letters."

He crossed his arms. "I can't."

"Then I can't, either." She reached down to pick up her knapsack and coat.

He stopped her. "Julianne, tell me who made you feel so insecure about yourself and your sexual abilities. Was it Simon?"

She cringed.

"Tell me."

"Don't say his name around me."

"You said it. You said his name in your sleep. You sounded upset. Tell me."

"No."

"Why not?"

"Because it makes me sick," she whispered, silently pleading with him to change the subject.

An insight, dark and disturbing, slowly took hold of Gabriel's mind. And once it took hold, he could not rid himself of it.

"Julianne, he didn't . . . force you, did he?"

She hung her head. "No, Gabriel. I'm a virgin."

He paused for a moment, exhaling slowly. "You would be a virgin even if he had forced you. You would be a virgin to me."

His voice was so pained and so sincere, her heart almost snapped under the weight of it.

"That's very noble of you. But I wasn't raped."

He closed his eyes for a second and sighed deeply. "We both have secrets we don't want to tell. I won't lie to you, but I can't tell you everything. Not today. And based on the look in your eyes, I know you're keeping some very painful secrets from me. But I accept that. I'm not going to pressure you to talk about them." He put his arm around her waist and pulled her flush against him.

"So we're going to keep secrets from each other?" She sounded puzzled.

"For now, yes."

"There's still the fact that I'm your student."

He kissed her again to prevent her from saying anything further. "That's another secret we'll have to keep. But darling, I don't want to have the rest of our conversation in this damned hallway. Please come back to the table and finish your breakfast. We can talk over coffee or we can just eat in silence. But please don't leave. Please."

Julia's eyes darted toward the door. "I need to know how you feel about me, Gabriel," she began uncertainly. "I need to know that this isn't a game for you. Do you even like me at all? The real me?"

He gave her a puzzled look. "Of course I like you. And I would like to win your affection. Where we go from there is up to you."

She reached uncertain fingers to stroke his hair. He closed his eyes and relaxed into her touch, inhaling and exhaling deeply. When she was finished, he opened his eyes, and Julia saw hunger in them.

He smiled, and the hunger was replaced by something else.

Hope. The sight of hope on Gabriel's face made her tears come.

"This isn't how I imagined it," she wept, wiping her face with the back of her hand. "Finding you again is so different from what I dreamed. And you aren't who I thought you were."

"I know." He wrapped himself around her and softly kissed her forehead.

"I had a crush on you when I was seventeen, Gabriel. My first real crush. And it wasn't even you. I've wasted my whole life on a delusion."

"I'm sorry I disappointed you. I wish I was the knight rather than the dragon. But I'm not." He pulled back to stare deeply into her eyes. "Everything is up to you. You can rescue me or banish me with a single word."

Julia pressed her face against his chest and wondered if she ever had a choice.

Chapter Eighteen

Paul, hi. Sorry. Didn't hear doorbell. Broken? Emerson scolded
me but won't have to drop class. (phew) Have to find new advisor.
Working on it. Chat later & thanks, Julia

Paul stared in confusion at the text message he'd just received from
Julia. A broken doorbell? That seemed *convenient*. He didn't know
whether she was giving him the brush off because she was embarrassed
about her altercation with Emerson or for some other reason. In either
case, he didn't have time to track her down and find out; Emerson had
e-mailed him with a list of books that he wanted checked out of the library and delivered to his office before one o'clock.

Paul sent Julia a short reply saying he was glad she was all right and
walked quickly from his apartment to Robarts Library, shaking his
head.

❄❄

Julia sat facing backward on the leather sofa, resting her chin on her
folded arms. The view through Gabriel's floor-to-ceiling windows was
remarkable. From her position she could see much of downtown and
part of Lake Ontario. The trees of the city had changed color and were
now dappled in gold and yellow and brilliant orange and red. They reminded Julia of some of the Canadian landscapes Paul had taken her to
see at the Art Gallery of Ontario.

She'd volunteered to help Gabriel clean up after breakfast, but he
wouldn't hear of it. He'd kissed her forehead and asked her to relax, as
if relaxing was even an option. Gazing at the Toronto skyline enabled
her to focus on something beautiful while she replayed her conversa-

tion with him over and over in her head, trying to match it with their previous encounters.

How had she been so blind? And why had the Clarks hidden Gabriel's addiction from her? They'd always treated her as if she was a member of the family. But not even Rachel had ever breathed a word about it, unless one considered what she said recently about his darkness. Did the Clarks always speak in extended metaphors like metaphysical poets? Julia would have needed a literary criticism class in order to interpret their allusions.

Gabriel leaned up against the fireplace, staring at her. She appeared remarkably at home perched on his sofa, looking out his window like a cat. But her tense shoulders telegraphed worry. He sat next to her, purposefully leaving a healthy gap between them. When she made no move to inch closer to him or even to look at him, he extended his hand.

"Please." He smiled.

Julia took his hand reluctantly and found herself pulled to his side. He wrapped both arms around her and kissed her hair. "That's better."

She sighed and closed her eyes.

"Comfortable?" he asked.

"Yes."

Gabriel felt her body relax. After all they'd discussed, he was surprised that she could relax with him. "When was the last time someone held you like this?" He began stroking her hair absentmindedly, when in reality he was anything but.

"Last night."

He chuckled. "I seem to remember that. But before?"

"I don't remember." Julia's tone was defensive, so he elected not to press her.

She's probably starved for physical affection. Alcoholic mothers don't have the wherewithal to look after their children. And that Simon character probably didn't hold her—unless he was trying to take her clothes off.

The mere idea made him furious—that someone would treat her with so little care. He knew that something about their physical connection calmed her, as it did him. And that led him to believe that she had little experience with positive physical contact.

"Is this all right? Holding you like this?" he whispered against her hair.

"Yes."

"Good." And for effect, he traced the hairline around her face, brushing a wisp of hair back from her cheek. "So beautiful," he whispered. "So lovely."

They sat like that for some time until Julia decided to ask a question that she'd been wondering about. "The photo that you had over the bed, where the man is kissing the woman's shoulder . . . where did you find it?"

Gabriel pressed his lips together. "I didn't."

"Then where—"

"Does it matter?"

"If you don't want to tell me, that's fine. I saw it in the closet when I was looking for a sweater. It's very beautiful." She tried to move away from him, but he held her fast.

"Do you really think it's beautiful?" His voice grew soft, and he lifted her chin so he could gaze into her eyes.

"Yes," she breathed.

"And the others?"

"Not so much."

Gabriel appeared smug. "I made them."

"You made them?" She pulled back in surprise.

"Yes."

"But they're . . ."

"Erotic?"

"Yes." He smiled wryly. "Is it difficult to believe that I could take a beautiful and erotic photograph, Miss Mitchell?"

"I didn't know you were a photographer. And those aren't regular photographs."

"I'm not much of one, really. But they turned out nicely, I think. I have others."

Julia's jaw dropped. *Others?* "And the women?"

He shifted next to her.

"The women are, or rather were, friends of mine."

"Models?"

"No."

Julia crinkled her face in confusion until the answer finally dawned on her. And with eyebrows raised, she gave Gabriel a very surprised look.

He sighed and began rubbing his eyes. "Yes, I'm sure it was in poor taste to display them. And it was certainly in poor taste to subject you to them when they're personal in that way. That's why I felt it necessary to remove them before I brought you into my bedroom. But the photos were taken with their consent. In a few cases they begged, actually. You'll notice that I'm in more than one of them too, so I was far from simply a prurient observer."

She forgot her question about which photograph was of Paulina and drew back in complete and utter astonishment. "That's you?"

"Yes."

"The one I was asking you about, that's you?"

His eyebrows knit together. "Don't act so surprised. I thought you found me attractive."

"But you're naked in that photo." Feeling very flustered, Julia began waving a hand furiously in front of her face, fanning her heated skin.

Gabriel laughed heartily and drew her closer. "I am naked in *all* those photos." His voice oozed sex as he crooned in her ear. "That photo was my favorite too, even though in the end I didn't like the woman very much." He smiled a slow, smoldering grin and kissed the top of her head. "I'd like to take your picture."

"I don't think so."

"You're beautiful, Julianne. A photo of you—of your smile or your profile or your elegant neck—would be far lovelier than any of the art I own, including Holiday's painting."

She shook her head.

"I'll ask you again someday. Now, how about a reservation tonight at Scaramouche? It's one of my favorite restaurants."

"I don't think dinner out is a good idea." Julia was still trying to catch her breath.

"Why not?"

"Didn't you say we shouldn't be seen in public?"

Gabriel frowned. "But I know the owner. I can reserve the chef's table where we'd be away from prying eyes. Unless you'd rather go to Harbour Sixty to see Antonio. He has been pestering me to bring you back."

"Really?"

"Really. He told me all about the meal you shared with him and his family at the Italian-Canadian Club."

"Antonio was very kind to me."

Gabriel nodded and moved as if to kiss her, but she placed a hand on his chest.

"I can't go to dinner with you tonight. I have a meeting with Katherine Picton tomorrow and I'm not ready for it."

"Tomorrow?"

"She invited me to tea at her house. She kind of scares me."

"Wait till you meet her. She looks like someone's grandmother, but don't let that fool you—she's brilliant and definitely no-nonsense. She'll expect you to address her as Professor Picton, and she doesn't do small talk or speak of anything personal."

"Only pretentious Oxonians prefer to be addressed as Professor," murmured Julia.

He frowned until she winked at him.

"She's very formal, but she's a hell of an academic, and if you can work with her, it will be very good for you. Just be on your best behavior, and I'm sure she'll take to you. As much as she is capable of doing."

Julia shivered, and Gabriel responded by tightening his arms about her.

"Don't worry, she'll be interested in your proposal. I'm sure she will want you to change it, but if I were you, I would accept her corrections without argument. She knows what she's doing."

"I'm sure she has more important things to do during her retirement than supervise graduate students."

"She owed me a favor. I told her I had a brilliant student who I didn't feel comfortable supervising because she was a friend of my family, and Katherine agreed to meet you. She's pretty skeptical about today's youth— she doesn't think they're as talented or as hard-working as they were when she was in graduate school. So she didn't promise me anything."

"You didn't have to do that for me."

Gabriel wound a lock of her hair around one of his fingers. "I wanted to do something nice. I'm sorry you weren't able to go to Harvard."

Julia looked down at her hands. "It led me back to you, didn't it?"

He smiled, even with his eyes. "Yes, it did."

After an intense moment, he shifted his body so he could check his Rolex. He groaned.

"What is it?" she asked.

"I have to go. I have a meeting."

"I should go too."

She climbed off the couch and walked quickly to her knapsack, slinging it over her shoulder and searching for her coat.

Gabriel crossed the room in three strides and put his hands on her shoulders. "Stay. I won't be long, and I'll come right back."

She brought her lip between her teeth and grazed on it thoughtfully.

He poked his thumb in between her teeth and her lip, effectively freeing her scraped flesh. "Don't. It troubles me when you do that."

He withdrew his thumb quickly lest she misread his intention, but not before accidentally making contact with her tongue. It was difficult to tell whose accident it had been.

"What's your meeting about?"

Gabriel began rubbing at his eyes. "It's with Christa. It's going to be unpleasant. But it would go much easier if I knew that you would be here waiting for me."

"I have so much work to do, and I have to call Paul. Apparently he went to my apartment last night to check on me." Julia's speech quickened. "I sent him a text telling him I was fine. I said I wasn't going to have to drop your class, but that I had to find a new director. I don't know how I'm going to explain having Katherine Picton as my advisor."

Gabriel fumed. "You don't owe him an explanation. Tell him it's none of his business."

"He's a friend."

"Then mention something about a connection between your Harvard application and Katherine. She's a friend of Greg Matthews."

Julia nodded and began buttoning up her coat.

"Wait." He walked over to his study and disappeared for a few minutes. When he returned, he pressed an old hardcover book into her hands.

She read the title, *The Figure of Beatrice: A Study in Dante* by Charles Williams.

"I want you to have this."

"Gabriel, I want you to stop giving me things." She held it out to him.

"You will impress Katherine if you are familiar with this book. She's a fan of Dorothy L. Sayers, and Sayers borrowed a lot of her insights on *The Divine Comedy* from Williams." He cleared his throat. "There are no strings here, Julianne. And no shame."

She stared at the volume and smoothed her hand over its old binding.

"At least take it until she agrees to be your advisor."

"Thank you."

"You're welcome. Now, we need to talk about something else."

She looked up at him nervously.

"It would be much easier if you weren't my student, but you are. At least for now."

She inhaled sharply.

Gabriel rubbed his eyes. "Sorry. That didn't come out right. What I mean is, I can't be your thesis supervisor, obviously. But that still leaves the problem of the Dante seminar."

"Dropping your class would prevent me from graduating in May. You said in your voice mail messages that you could find me a reading course as a substitute, but that won't help me. I need a Dante seminar for my specialization and my thesis."

"The non-fraternization policy covers students in a faculty member's classes, not just students under thesis supervision. That means that I cannot have a relationship with you while you're my student. Next semester, of course, is entirely different. You won't be my student anymore."

She knew this. The Declaration of Graduate Student Rights and Responsibilities had said as much. Faculty were not allowed to sleep with their current students, that much was clear. And graduate students were not allowed to sleep with supervising faculty members. Or else . . .

Of course, Julia wasn't planning on sleeping with Gabriel. She wondered if he remembered that.

"I won't lose you again," he whispered. "And I won't keep you from doing what you came here to do. So we're going to have to figure something out. In the meantime, I will have a conversation with my lawyer."

"Your lawyer?"

"A preemptive, privileged conversation about what I can expect from the university if I intend to date one of my students while she is in my class."

Julia placed a trembling hand on his sleeve. "Do you want to lose your job?"

"Of course not," he said roughly.

"I've already jeopardized your career once. I won't do it again. We'll have to stay away from one another, and when the semester is over we can talk about this again. You might change your mind, you know, and decide you don't want me." She looked down at her sneakers and nervously wiggled her toes.

"That is not going to happen, Julianne."

"We're still getting to know one another. Maybe five weeks of friendship is just what we need."

"Friends go to dinner. How about tomorrow night?"

She shook her head forcefully. "Why don't you call me? I promise I'll answer my phone."

Gabriel frowned. "So when will I see you again?"

"At your seminar next Wednesday."

"That's too far off."

"That's just the way it is, Professor." Julia gave him a half-smile and walked toward the door.

"Aren't you forgetting something?"

She quickly checked her knapsack to make sure she had her keys. "I don't think so."

He stalked toward her, his eyes momentarily dark. "No kiss goodbye for poor, lonely Gabriel?" he whispered, his voice intentionally seductive.

Julia gulped. "Friends don't kiss the way you do."

He came closer, until her back was pressed up against the front door. "Just a friendly peck. Scout's honor."

"Were you ever a Boy Scout?"

"No."

Gabriel brought his hand up slowly so as not to spook her and gently caressed her cheek. He smiled at her disarmingly, and she found herself smiling back. He pressed his lips to hers, firmly but lightly, and held them there.

Julia waited for him to do something, to open his mouth, to move, anything, but he didn't. He was frozen still, applying gentle pressure to her lips, until he pulled back and gave her a small smile.

"That wasn't so bad, was it?" He chuckled as he traced her jaw line with the tip of his finger.

She shook her head. "Good-bye, Gabriel."

As the front door closed behind her, he leaned up against the wall and rubbed his eyes, muttering to no one in particular.

❧❦

After Gabriel returned home from a very unpleasant and slightly colorful meeting with Christa, he grabbed a Perrier from the refrigerator and dialed the number of John Green, his lawyer. Gabriel hadn't had need of John's services for quite some time, and he preferred to keep it that way. John had some shady clients, but he was the best, and Gabriel knew it, especially when it came to Canadian criminal law. However, John was not a specialist in employment law, which he pointed out to Gabriel more than once during their thirty minute conversation.

"I need to warn you, if observing the non-fraternization policy is a term of your employment, you violate it at your peril and at the peril of your job. So let me ask you a question—are you sleeping with her?"

"No," said Gabriel tersely.

"Good. Don't start now. In fact, my professional advice to you is to keep your distance from this girl until you hear from me. How old is she?"

"Pardon?"

"The girl, Gabriel, the twinkie."

"Call her that again and I take my business elsewhere."

John paused. Gabriel was a tough son of a bitch, he knew, and a bit of a brawler. And John didn't have the energy for a telephone altercation.

"Let me rephrase—the young lady in question, how old is she?"

"Twenty-three."

John breathed a sigh of a relief. "Good. At least we aren't dealing with a minor."

"Once again, I'll pretend I didn't hear that."

"Listen, Emerson, I'm your lawyer. Let me do my job. I can't give you a professional opinion on your situation until I know all the facts. One of my partners sued the University of Toronto last year; I'll get her to bring me up to speed. But for now, my advice to you is to steer clear of this girl, but whatever you do, don't sleep with her. Do you understand?"

"Yes."

"And let me be even more explicit. Don't engage in any kind of sexual activity with her, at all. We don't want to be drawn into a Clintonian debate about what constitutes sexual relations. Do nothing with her; it doesn't matter if the activity is consensual."

"What if we're involved romantically, but not sexually?"

John paused for a moment and began cleaning his ear out with the tip of his baby finger. "I didn't quite catch that."

"I said, what if I'm seeing her socially but there is no sexual contact."

John laughed loudly. "Are you kidding me with this, Emerson? I don't believe you, and I get paid to. No one else will believe you, either."

"That's not the point. The point is, if I am not engaging in sexual activity with my student, does our relationship violate the policy?"

"No one is going to believe that you're having a relationship with a student that does not involve sex, especially given your reputation. Of course, the onus is on the employer to provide evidence of the relationship, unless your chiquita files a complaint against you or someone catches the two of you in a compromising situation. Or she ends up pregnant."

"That isn't going to happen."

"Everyone says that, Emerson."

Gabriel cleared his throat. "Yes, but in this case, it would be beyond the realm of possibility. For more than one reason."

John rolled his eyes and decided not to give The Professor a biology lesson. "Nevertheless, if you were caught, and there was no sexual contact, you'd likely face only a reprimand for an improper relationship. But I can't state for certain without reading the policy, and I need to know from my partner what kind of precedents the university has set up for itself."

"Thank you."

"It's your ass and not mine if something blows up here, so be careful. I get paid either way." John cleared his throat. "And Gabriel?"

"Yes?"

"I would stay out of trouble for the next little while. No girls, no fist fights, no public drunkenness, or anything of the sort. Any lawsuit with the university will expose your past, remember that. Let's try to keep the past in the past, okay?"

"All right, John."

And with that, Gabriel hung up the phone and grabbed his keys, deciding to work out his frustration at his fencing club.

※ ※

When Julia returned to her apartment, she eagerly searched the now hibernating flower bed for any fragments of Gabriel's card. Sadly, all she found were a few ripped pieces, far from enough to reconstruct his note.

She spent most of the day skimming Charles Williams' book, making notes that she hoped would help with her meeting with Katherine. She had to admit, Gabriel's foresight on this point was almost providential. Williams had a mastery of Dante that offered her a lot of suggestions for her thesis.

Before she went to sleep, she sat on her bed listening to her iPod and thinking about Gabriel. He'd uploaded two songs for her; the second song was *Dante's Prayer*, also by Loreena McKennitt. It was a profoundly moving piece, and listening to it made Julia weep. She fell asleep that night with the photograph from her underwear drawer under her pillow once again, while she pondered a number of things.

Gabriel was a drug addict. She knew without doubt that if his addiction ever overtook him, it would overtake her as well, dragging her down to depths she did not wish to inhabit.

Furthermore, any relationship with Gabriel had the potential to taint both their careers. Once their connection was discovered, he'd be the gifted young professor who'd tapped a piece of ass he found in one of his seminars, making him the subject of tantalizing innuendo at faculty cocktail parties. She would be the young slut who spread her legs to get her degree because she wasn't smart enough to do it any other way. It didn't really matter if they waited until the semester was over or not, the gossip would tarnish them both.

Finally, she had fallen in love with Gabriel Emerson when she was seventeen. Perhaps it could be explained by their intense connection, or the way he looked at her, or the feelings he invoked when she was in her arms. Whatever the true basis for her crush, she had fallen for him and fallen hard. She tried to suppress her feelings when he didn't come home; she tried to kill them by developing feelings for someone else. But snuggled in his arms the night before, a wave of emotion had crashed over her, and all her little defenses were carried out to sea like a toppled sandcastle. The love she had for Gabriel was still there, a small flame burning brightly that not all the water in the ocean could extinguish.

So perhaps it was the case that she had no choice now because she had made her choice then. She'd made her choice when he asked for her hand and she'd offered it without question. Once he touched her, she knew she was his. Afterward, he had always been there in the shadows, like a ghost who would not leave. And now the ghost had decided that he wanted her.

But Julia believed that he would never, ever love her.

❋ ❋

The next morning, she checked her cell phone and was surprised to find a message from Gabriel. He'd called after she'd fallen asleep,

"Julianne, you promised you'd answer your phone. [Sigh.] I'm assuming all is well and that you're in the shower or something. Call me when you get this message.

"I'm sorry I couldn't take you to dinner this evening, but I would like to have dinner with you tomorrow night. Can we at least talk about it? [Pause . . .] Call me, principessa. *Please."*

Julia immediately saved his number on her phone, but entered his name as "Dante Alighieri." When she called him back, she reached his voice mail.

"Hello, it's me. Um, I'm sorry I didn't get your message last night. I fell asleep. Of course it would be nice to see you, but I think dinner is too risky. I want to get to know you again, Gabriel, and I'm hoping we can find some safe way to do that. Sorry I missed your call. I'll talk to you later."

She spent most of Friday working on her thesis proposal. She kept her cell phone on, just in case. But Gabriel didn't call her. She did, however, receive a call from Paul. Their conversation was cut short because he was interrupted in his study carrel by Professor Emerson. Since Emerson seemed in a much better mood, Paul had only a slight reticence in believing that he'd gone easy on Julia. And Julia did her best to eliminate that reticence. Crisis averted.

After her very interesting meeting with Katherine, Julia came home and fed herself a modest meal of cream of tomato soup. After dinner, she showered and wrapped herself in a purple towel that barely covered her from breasts to bottom, wandering over to her closet to choose a pair of flannel pajamas to wear to bed. In view of the chill in the late October air and the proximity to Halloween, she decided that jack-o'-lantern pajamas were in order.

Tap, tap, tap.

Startled, Julia yelped. A muffled voice from outside her window started speaking rather loudly, and the tapping noise continued in earnest. She ran to the window, threw back the curtain, and looked down into the worried face of Gabriel.

"You scared the hell out of me!" she screeched, unlocking the ancient window and trying with one hand to pull it upward while anxiously clutching her towel with the other.

"You wouldn't answer your phone. Or the doorbell. I thought something was wrong. I walked into the backyard and saw your lights were on."

Gabriel noticed that she was struggling and slid his fingers underneath the window. "Let me do this." With one movement, he lifted the window and proceeded to hand her a couple of paper bags.

"What's this?"

"Dinner. Now stand back, it's cold out here." He placed his hands on the windowsill, trying to hoist himself up.

"What are you doing?"

"I'm crawling through your window. What does it look like I'm doing?"

"I could let you in the front door like a normal human being," she protested, putting the paper bags on her card table.

Gabriel eyed her somewhat hungrily as he swung his legs through the window. "Not undressed like that you can't." He closed the window tightly, locked it, and pulled the curtain closed. "You should put some clothes on."

Julia trembled as he reached out a finger to stroke the skin of her bare shoulder.

Smooth, soft, wet, and warm, he thought.

She wrapped the towel more tightly around herself as he averted his eyes. She was barely covered and damp from the shower, and the sight of the two together . . . he twitched. More than once.

"Please get dressed now, Julianne." His voice was low and rough.

She reacted to what she thought was his embarrassment and immediately began backing up.

"I'll change in the bathroom," she mumbled, hurriedly searching for a yoga outfit and her old shearling slippers.

"Why don't you have the heat on?" he called as she darted into the bathroom.

"It *is* on."

"Hardly. It's almost the same temperature in here as it is outside. And walking around in a towel will make you sick."

Julia closed the door behind her, ending their conversation.

Gabriel adjusted himself and looked around for a thermostat, but of course, there wasn't one. He was soon on his hands and knees wrestling with the aged radiator that was the only source of heat in the main room of the apartment. *How can she live like this? It's freezing in here.*

When Julia exited the bathroom, she found Gabriel still in his dress coat, kneeling in front of her radiator as if it were an altar. She giggled. "You're on your knees more than the average professor."

He shot her a look. "Very amusing, Julianne. This radiator is useless. Do you have a space heater?"

"There's an electric baseboard heater in the bathroom. But I don't use it."

He shook his head as he got to his feet and strode past her. He cranked up the heat and made sure to leave the bathroom door wide open.

"Just let me warm the apartment up a little. Your hair is wet, and you're going to catch cold. I should make you some tea," he offered, hanging his coat up on the back of her front door.

"I could do that," she said softly.

"Allow me." He pressed a kiss to her forehead and picked up the electric kettle, filled it with water from the bathroom faucet, and got down on hands and knees to plug it in underneath the dresser.

Julia tried very hard not to stare at the way his black wool trousers clung to his really very fine derrière as he plugged in the kettle. To distract herself, she compared his current behavior with the way he had behaved during his last visit to her little hobbit hole. It was as if there were two Gabriels, and she was only now being visited by the nice one. *This newer model is just as handsome but infinitely more attractive.*

"Now," he said, looking around. "I need to warm you up."

Gabriel fixed his eyes on her and pulled her into a hug, rubbing his hands up and down her back. "Are you all right?"

"Yes."

"Why don't you answer your phone?"

"I answer it. Just not while I'm asleep or in the shower."

"I was worried. You didn't answer last night, and you didn't answer about an hour ago."

"I was washing my hair."

Gabriel buried his face against her neck, inhaling her scent. *Vanilla.*

"Julianne," he began, bringing his left hand to touch her face.

She blinked rapidly. "Yes?"

He grew silent.

She looked at him in surprise. His eyes were dark, and he was staring at her intensely.

He leaned over and began feathering his lips up and down the left side of her neck, beginning just under her ear lobe and ending at her collarbone. A flash of want flared in Julia's stomach and lower down. His lips were barely floating over the surface of her skin and making every drop of blood in her body rush to that space. His touch had never felt so erotic, so affectionate.

Up and down and up and down, he worshipped the curve of her neck, now and then darting his tongue out to taste her skin. Now and then he withdrew his lips so that he could nuzzle her gently with his nose or his chin, the slightest hint of stubble subtly scratching across her flesh. He fluttered his mouth with soft kisses down to the hollow at the center of her throat and pressed his lips there firmly, beginning his sojourn up and down the right side of her neck.

Julia moaned and closed her eyes, sliding her arms up his back to trail her hands in his hair. Her fingertips moved without conscious thought, stroking the edge of his hairline just above his shirt collar.

"Mmmmmmmm," she breathed.

"Does this please you?" he whispered, continuing his gentle kissing.

She murmured her appreciation.

"I want to bring you pleasure, Julianne. More than you know."

He paid special attention to the skin around her ear and just under her jaw line, teasing her slightly with his tongue. "Tell me if I'm pleasing you."

She barely heard the question, focused as she was on the myriad sensations that coursed through her body and the warmth that fanned across her flesh. She no longer felt cold. She no longer felt anything but him.

"You please me, Gabriel," she whispered dazedly.

"This is a declaration of desire," he breathed against her ear, making her quiver. "If we were lovers, I would kiss you like this to signal my intention to take you to bed. And you can only imagine the delights that await you there. But at this moment, I can only declare that I burn for you. I won't let myself touch your lips for fear that I wouldn't be able to stop."

Julia moaned even louder, and Gabriel continued, moving her hair away from her shoulders so he could expand his exploration. He poured out the lightest of kisses, covering her neck until he finally took the edge of her earlobe in his mouth and drew on it slightly, tracing the edge delicately with his tongue.

"If I were to taste your mouth now, I couldn't answer for the consequences. So I can only adore this beautiful neck. I know that in a few seconds I will have to pull away, before the temptation becomes too much. It's too much already. You have no idea how much I want you." Gabriel's voice was raspy, and he seemed to be breathing rather fast.

Julia felt her legs grow weak, and she started to sway . . . And that's when the electric kettle began to whistle at them. Gabriel pressed a chaste kiss to her cheeks and went to make tea, while Julia sat down shakily on one of the chairs. Her heart was thumping so loudly she thought she was having a heart attack. She leaned her head forward, holding it in her upturned hands.

If I'm this unglued while he's kissing me, what am I going to be like when he . . .

"What kind of tea, darling?" Gabriel's voice held only the smallest edge of amusement as he watched her try to catch her breath.

Of course, the only reason why he was able to catch his breath so quickly was because he'd walked away. And he was far more skilled than she at hiding his feelings, except upon visual inspection.

"Lady Grey. It's in the tin by the teapot." Julia's voice was shaky.

"I'm not a tea drinker, so it won't be as good as yours. But hopefully it will be potable."

She arched an eyebrow at his choice of adjectives, but politely thanked him when he placed the pot of tea, teacup, and saucer in front of her.

"I bought a few things for dinner. Have you eaten yet?"

"I had soup."

"Julianne." He sat next to her and gave her a scolding look. "Soup isn't a meal."

"Yes, I believe I've heard that before."

She rolled her eyes, and Gabriel laughed.

The first items he took from the bag were a bottle of wine and a Rabbit corkscrew.

"Do you have wineglasses?"

"Yes." Julia stumbled over to her small kitchen area to fetch them. She still had questions about Gabriel's relationship to alcohol, especially in light of his past. But she had decided to give him the benefit of the doubt, for the present.

When she returned to the table, she read the wine label: *Serego Alighieri Vaio Armaron Amarone* 2000.

"Is that who I think it is?" She extended a finger toward the bottle.

Gabriel took her hand and pressed his lips to her palm. "Yes. Dante's son bought the vineyard in the fourteenth century, and the Masi family still produce wine from it." He sat back in his folding chair and regarded her quietly. She seemed awestruck.

"I didn't know his family had a vineyard."

"It's a very good wine. Although in light of our past, perhaps you find the choice overly sentimental?"

She shook her head. "No. No, I don't."

"I had to work late, but I wanted to have dinner with you, so I went to Pusateri's and ordered takeout. There's manicotti, Caesar salad, and a loaf of bread. How's that?"

Julia looked at the array of food set in front of her and immediately felt hungry. "What are these?" She pointed to a cellophane package of cookies that had a reindeer on the label.

Gabriel grinned. "Lime cookies from the Dancing Deer Baking Company. They're my favorite. Why don't you let me look after this while you dry your hair and drink your tea?"

He reached out his hand to run it through Julia's long, wet curls.

"Why do you keep feeding me?"

His hand stilled. "I told you, I like giving you pleasure." He withdrew his hand, his expression quizzical. "This is how a man acts when he is interested in a woman, Julianne. He's attentive and anticipatory." He flashed her a wicked grin. "Perhaps I'm trying to indicate that if I am this attentive with respect to sating your culinary longings, I'll be even more attentive with respect to satisfying other—ah—appetites."

Julia flushed immediately, and Gabriel touched her cheek with his hand. "Your skin is lovely," he breathed. "Like a rose in first bloom." He gazed at her admiringly. "Rachel stopped blushing when she started sleeping with Aaron."

"How do you know?"

"As I recall, we all noticed it. One minute she was reading *The Little Prince* and the next she was buying lingerie."

Julia chewed at her lip thoughtfully. "I loved that book."

"We need to see with our hearts and not our eyes," said Gabriel.

"Exactly," she murmured. "I like the part when the fox talks to the prince about the process of taming. And the fox decides that he wants to be tamed, to be the prince's fox, even though doing so will make him vulnerable."

"Julianne, I think you should dry your hair now."

He removed his hand from her face and stood up quickly, turning his back on her allegedly so that he could prepare dinner, leaving Julia to wonder what had so disquieted him.

※ ※

After dinner, they found themselves sitting on her bed as if it were a sofa. Gabriel propped up some pillows against the wall and leaned back, putting his arm around her waist.

"I'm sorry it's so uncomfortable," she apologized meekly.

"It isn't uncomfortable."

"I know you hate this place. It's small and cold and—" She gestured to the room with a wave of her hand.

"I will regret forever what I said to you when you were kind enough to invite me in. I don't hate this place. How could I?" He interlaced his fingers with hers. "This is where you are."

"Thank you."

"Thank you for making everything beautiful just by being."

She smiled as he brought their hands up to his mouth and kissed each of her fingers tenderly, one by one.

"Now tell me about your meeting with Katherine."

Julia had to wait a moment until her fingers stopped tingling before she began. "She was exactly as you described. But she was very happy

I'd read Charles Williams. I think that warmed her up a little. She agreed to be my advisor."

"And what did she think of your proposal?"

"Um, she thought it was derivative and so she suggested that rather than comparing courtly love and lust, I should compare aspects of the friendship between Virgil and Dante with the theme of courtly love. So rather than discussing lust and love, I'll be discussing love and friendship."

"Are you happy with that?"

"I think so. We decided that I should take Professor Leaming's Aquinas seminar next semester because it's going to be on love and friendship."

Gabriel nodded. "I know Jennifer Leaming. She's quite good."

Julia fidgeted with the duvet.

He placed his hand over hers. "What?"

"Nothing."

"No hiding, Julianne. What is it?"

"I e-mailed Professor Leaming a week ago to ask if she would be my director. That was before you and I had our, um, conversation."

Gabriel's eyes grew momentarily cold. "And what did she say?"

"She didn't."

"Jennifer is very busy. She's untenured, and I doubt she has time to supervise graduate students outside of the Philosophy Department." He paused. "When I told you I would find you another director, did you not believe me?"

Julia squirmed. "I believed you."

"Then why did you feel the need to go behind my back?"

"I wanted to see if I could fix it on my own."

Gabriel pressed his mouth into a hard line. "And how did that work out?"

"It didn't."

"Sooner or later you are going to have to trust me. Particularly about things having to do with the university. Or this isn't going to work."

She nodded, chewing the inside of her mouth slightly. "Tell me about your meeting with Christa."

"I'd rather not. She's a pest."

Julia tried in vain to smother a smile.

"She's far too busy trying to rescue her dissertation proposal to trouble us. I won't accept her project as it is, which means she has to find another supervisor. And as you know, I'm the only professor supervising theses on Dante at the moment."

"So Christa is out?"

"I told her today that I would give her until December eighteenth to turn in an acceptable proposal. And that was a gift. So don't worry about her anymore. Her academic future hangs by a thread, and I'm holding the end of it."

Good, thought Julia.

"I had an interesting conversation with my lawyer today."

She took another sip of wine and waited for him to continue.

"He said that he's going to look into the non-fraternization policy, but he strongly warned against any kind of romantic relationship with you while you're in my class."

She reddened. "Does that include kissing?"

"Assuredly, but he pointed out that the university is concerned primarily with sexual activity. So as long as we're chaste and discreet this semester, I don't think we'll have a problem."

Julia reddened even further and looked down into her wineglass.

"So you'll have to keep your hands to yourself, Miss Mitchell, until I've turned your grade in. After that, well . . ." He grinned at her suggestively.

"You can't be kissing me one minute and grading my essay the next."

"At this point, I couldn't be objective about your work even if I tried. I'll have Katherine grade it."

"Won't she find that peculiar?"

He smiled. "I'll make an excuse. And I'll buy her a bottle of sixteen-year-old Lagavulin. It would resurrect the dead."

"You're still proposing fraternization—of a sort."

Gabriel cupped her face in his hands. "But it's less serious than an affair and therefore puts us at much lower risk with the administration. I have my lawyer looking at all the loopholes."

"I don't want to be a loophole."

"I don't view you as one. Do you want me to stay away for five weeks and not see you at all? Not hold your hand or put my arms about you? Is that what you want?"

Julia thought for a moment, and the idea made her ill. She shook her head.

"I'd like to continue to see you, as friends of course. You're still deciding if you can trust me, and we're still getting to know one another. What the university doesn't know won't hurt us." Gabriel took her wineglass and placed it alongside his on the card table. When he returned, he pulled her so that she was almost sitting in his lap.

"We can pretend we're both in high school and living in Selinsgrove. We've just begun dating, and because we're good little teenagers and slightly old-fashioned, we've taken a vow of chastity."

"You've given this a lot of thought."

"I have a vivid and detailed imagination when it comes to you," he whispered. "And maybe I wish we'd been teenagers together."

"So this is headed toward an affair?"

Gabriel was quiet for a moment.

"I had in mind something less tawdry. But Julianne, much of what our relationship will or won't be rests entirely with you."

She nodded to indicate that she'd heard him, and they both fell silent. Eventually she closed her eyes, breathing in his scent and feeling strangely calmed by the regular rhythm of his heartbeat. Gabriel stroked her hair and whispered to her in Italian.

"Julianne?"

Silence.

"Julia?" He leaned down only to discover that she'd fallen asleep. He didn't want to wake her. But he also didn't want to leave without saying good-bye, and he wanted her to lock the door behind him.

He lifted her carefully and placed her underneath the sheets and comforter, hoping that she would wake up. But she didn't. Gabriel regarded her little form, the way her chest rose and fell with her gentle breathing, her lips slightly parted. She was pretty. She was sweet.

He couldn't remember the last time he'd spent a chaste evening with a beautiful woman who wasn't a relative. A chaste evening that was fraught with desire and passion and an overwhelming need . . . He wanted her.

But the old interior conflict loomed large in his mind. He did not wish to corrupt her, to make her like him. He did not want to make her vulnerable or cause her to bleed in any sense. He seriously doubted his ability to be involved with her physically and not lose control, for the mere sight of her in a towel had almost shattered his resolve.

This is what comes of years of unbridled lust—now you don't even have the ability to court her like a gentleman. You want to make love to this girl without lapsing into fucking, but can you? Can you be sexually involved with her without treating her like a pretty toy that has been constructed solely for your carnal satisfaction? Can you love without sin?

Gabriel's thoughts troubled him as he stared at the rosy-cheeked lamb that trusted him enough to fall asleep in his arms, oblivious to the passion that boiled in his veins. He emptied his pockets and turned off his iPhone before heading to the washroom. He turned down the baseboard heater, as promised, and quickly stripped to his T-shirt and boxer briefs. He took a moment to inventory Julia's shampoo and bath products, committing their names to memory so that he could be sure to stock his bathroom for her next visit. He definitely preferred vanilla to any other scent. *Although vanilla and chocolate . . .*

He turned out the lights and climbed into her twin bed. It was far too small for two persons; in truth, it made Gabriel almost nostalgic for the residence hall beds at Princeton or Magdalen College. Almost. Those beds were barely tolerable for sleeping and certainly far from ideal for any kind of sexual activity. It was fortunate that such activity was off the menu for this evening.

As Gabriel rolled to his side, his hand fastened on a small, smooth piece of paper that was wedged underneath the pillow. He retrieved it and held it up against the sliver of moonlight that was streaming in from behind the curtain. What he saw more than surprised him for in his hand was an old photograph of him from his Princeton days. He recognized the varsity rowing jersey he was wearing.

How did she get this? How long has she had it? He slid the photo back under the pillow, the ends of his mouth turning up in wonder. Something akin to hope began to warm his insides.

He'd never been a fan of spooning; it was an act far too intimate for him. But tonight it was what he wanted. He curved his body around hers and stretched his left arm over her waist, placing a light hand on her stomach. They fit together perfectly. Gabriel sighed with contentment at the soft warmth of the young woman he treasured in his arms, his nose buried in long, soft, vanilla-scented hair.

❉ ❉

Sometime around three o'clock in the morning, Julia opened her eyes. A strong arm tightened its hold on her, and the scent that was Gabriel's filled her head. She was wrapped in his arms, his chest against her back. Although he'd moved seemingly in reaction to her anxiety, the sound of his breathing indicated that he was still asleep.

Julia looked at him in the darkness. How many years had she waited just to be sleeping at his side once again? She shifted slowly, so that she was lying on her back. With his eyes closed and a look of peace on his face, he looked much younger. Almost like a boy—a gentle boy with brown hair and pink lips who smiled sweetly in his sleep. Julia sighed her aesthetic appreciation.

His eyes flickered open. It took a moment for him to be able to focus on her in the dark, but when he did, he leaned over to press his lips against hers.

"Are you all right?" he whispered against her mouth.

"You're still here."

"I won't leave you again without saying good-bye. Can't you sleep?"

"I thought this was a dream."

Gabriel smiled at her in the darkness. "Only for me."

"You're gorgeous, Gabriel. You always were, you know."

"Nature's cruelty—the fallen angel retains his beauty. But I'm ugly on the inside."

She kissed him back firmly, trying to convey the truth of the words she was about to speak before they were audible. "Someone who is ugly on the inside wouldn't have bought me a messenger bag and kept his generosity a secret."

Gabriel stared at her. "How long have you known?"

"Rachel told me."

"And did it make you more likely to accept it, or less likely?"

"At the time, only half and half."

"I noticed you don't use it anymore," he whispered, reaching up to push the hair back from her face.

"I'll use it again."

"So you like it?"

"Very much. Thank you."

He nuzzled his nose lightly against hers and smiled. "You were merely beautiful at seventeen, Julianne. You're stunning now."

"Everyone is pretty enough in the dark," she whispered.

"No, they are not." He kissed her before pulling back abruptly, willing himself to stop.

She rested her head on his chest and closed her eyes, listening to the steady beat of his heart and trying not to drink too deeply of the energy that charged between them.

"It just occurred to me, Julia, that I only seem to get honest answers out of you whenever we share a bed."

She blushed, and even though it was dark, Gabriel knew it. He chuckled softly. "Why do you think that is?"

"When we're in bed, you're gentle with me. I feel . . . safe."

"I don't know how safe it is to be with me, Julianne, but I promise that I will try to be gentle with you always. Especially in bed."

She hugged him tightly and nodded against his chest, as if she understood the full implication of what he was saying. But she didn't. How could she?

"Are you going home for Thanksgiving?"

"Yes. I need to call my father to give him the good news."

"I promised Richard I'd come home. Would you . . . consider flying out with me?"

"I'd like that."

"Good." He sighed and rubbed at his eyes. "It isn't going to be a pleasant holiday."

"I don't like Thanksgiving. But Grace always made it nice."

"Wasn't it nice with your family?"

Julia squirmed. "We didn't really celebrate it."

"Why not?"

"I did all the cooking unless my mother was in recovery. And whenever I tried to do something special . . ." She shook her head.

Gabriel tightened his arms around her. "Tell me," he whispered.

"You don't want to hear this."

She tried to turn away from him, but he held her fast. "I didn't mean to upset you. I'm just trying to know you."

The tone of Gabriel's voice was such that it tugged at her, more powerfully than his words or his arms. She drew a deep breath.

"During my last Thanksgiving in St. Louis, Sharon was on a bender with one of the boyfriends. But stupid me, I decided to cook a Martha Stewart recipe for stuffed roast chicken, twice-baked potatoes, and vegetables." She stopped.

"I'm sure it was delicious," he prompted.

"I never found out."

"Why?"

"I kind of had an accident."

"Julianne?" He tried to lift her chin so that he could look into her eyes, but she wouldn't look at him. "What happened?"

"We didn't have a kitchen table. So I set up a card table in the living room and set it for three. It was stupid, really. I shouldn't have bothered. I put all the food on a tray to carry it to the table, and the boyfriend stuck out his foot and tripped me."

"On purpose?"

"He saw me coming."

Gabriel seethed with instantaneous anger, his hands curling into fists.

"I went flying. The dishes shattered. Food was everywhere."

"How badly were you hurt?" he asked with clenched teeth.

"I don't remember." Julia's voice instantly cooled.

"Did your mother help you?"

She shook her head.

Gabriel growled, low in his throat.

"They laughed. I must have looked pathetic on my hands and knees, crying, covered in gravy. The chicken skidded across the tiles and under one of the chairs." She paused thoughtfully. "I was on my knees for a while. You would have had a stroke if you'd seen me."

Gabriel stifled the urge to ram his fist through the wall behind his head. "I wouldn't have had a stroke. I would have beaten him and been sorely pressed not to horsewhip her."

Julia traced his fist with one of her fingers. "They got bored and went into her bedroom to fuck. They didn't even bother to close the door. That was my last Thanksgiving with Sharon."

"Your mother sounds like Anne Sexton."

"Sharon never wrote poetry."

"My God, Julia." Gabriel unclenched his fists and hugged her close.

"I cleaned up so that they wouldn't get mad at me, and I hopped on a bus. I rode around aimlessly until I saw a Salvation Army mission. They were advertising a Thanksgiving meal for the homeless. I asked if I could volunteer in the kitchen, and they put me to work."

"That's how you spent Thanksgiving?"

She shrugged. "I couldn't go home, and the people at the mission were friendly. After the guests were served, I had a turkey dinner with the volunteers. They even sent me home with leftovers. And pie." Julia paused thoughtfully. "No one ever baked me a pie."

He cleared his throat. "Julianne, why didn't your father take you away from her?"

"It wasn't always bad." She began fidgeting with his T-shirt, gathering the soft cotton in between her fingers and tugging slightly.

"Ouch. Careful." Gabriel chuckled. "You're pulling out what few chest hairs I have."

"Sorry." Julia nervously smoothed the cotton with her fingers. "Um, my dad lived with us until I was four, when my mom kicked him out. He went back to live in Selinsgrove, where he grew up. He used to call me on Sundays. I was talking to him one day, and I let slip the fact that one of the boyfriends had wandered into my room the night before, naked, thinking my room was the bathroom." She cleared her throat and began speaking quickly, so Gabriel wouldn't have a chance to ask *that question*.

"Dad freaked out, wanting to know if the boyfriend had touched me. He hadn't. He wanted to speak to my mom, and when I explained that

I wasn't supposed to bother her when one of the boyfriends was over, he told me to go into my room and lock the door. Of course, I didn't have a lock. First thing the next morning, Dad showed up to take me to Selinsgrove. I guess it was a good thing the boyfriend was gone by the time he arrived. I think my father would have killed him."

"So you left?"

"Yes. Dad told Sharon that if she didn't get rid of the boyfriends and get off the alcohol, he was going to take me away from her permanently. She agreed to go into rehab, and I went to live with him."

"How old were you?"

"Eight."

"Why didn't you stay with him?"

"He was never home. He had a day job that was very busy and sometimes he had to work weekends. Plus, he was a volunteer with the fire department. When school finished for the year, he sent me back to St. Louis. Sharon was out of rehab by then and working in a nail salon. He thought I'd be fine."

"But you came back?"

She hesitated.

"You can tell me, Julianne." He squeezed her tightly and waited, softly stroking her hair. "It's all right."

She swallowed. Hard. "The summer before I turned seventeen, Dad brought me back."

"Why?"

"Um, Sharon hit me. I fell against the corner of the kitchen counter, hitting my head. I called my dad from the hospital and said that if he didn't come and get me I was going to run away. And that was it. I never saw my mother again."

"Do you have a scar?"

She took his hand and brought it up to the back of her head, pressing his fingers against a raised line of flesh where hair no longer grew.

"I'm sorry for this." He traced it a few times and pressed his lips against it. "I'm sorry that those things happened to you. If I could, I'd beat them all senseless . . . starting with the bastard who is your father."

"I was pretty lucky, actually. Sharon only hit me once."

"Nothing you have told me sounds even remotely lucky."

"I'm lucky now. No one hits me here. And I have a friend who feeds me."

Gabriel shook his head and cursed. "You should have been cuddled and adored and treated like a princess. That's what Rachel had."

"I don't believe in fairy tales," she breathed.

"I'd like to make you believe." He leaned over and kissed her forehead.

"Reality is better than fantasy, Gabriel."

"Not if reality *is* the fantasy."

She shook her head, but smiled. "Can I ask you something?"

"Of course."

Her smile faded. "Do you have any scars?"

Gabriel's face was impassive. "You can't hit something that you don't know is there."

Julia leaned up and pressed her cheek into the crook of his neck. "I'm sorry."

"It's difficult to know what's worse—being hit or being ignored. I guess it depends on what kind of pain you prefer."

"I'm so sorry, Gabriel. I didn't know."

She took his hand in hers and wrapped their fingers together. Taking a deep breath, she asked, "Are you going to go home now?"

"Not unless you want me to leave." He stroked her hair again, carefully avoiding the place where the flesh was raised.

She rested her head on his shoulder and sighed. "I want you to stay with me."

"Then I'll stay."

Julia fell asleep while Gabriel remained awake contemplating the scars she had shown him, wondering with queasiness and anger about the scars she had not revealed.

"Julia?" he whispered. Her regular breathing and lack of response indicated that she was sleeping.

"I won't let anyone hurt you." He kissed her cheek softly. "Least of all myself."

Chapter Nineteen

Julia awoke the next morning to the sounds of the shower. She was trying to work out how someone other than she could be in her washroom when the sounds stopped and a tall, brown-haired man wrapped in a small, purple towel came through the door. Her eyes widened in surprise, and she gasped, clapping a hand over her open mouth.

"Good morning," said Gabriel, clutching the towel that was slung low on his hips with one hand while grabbing his clothes with the other.

Julia stared. And she wasn't staring at his face.

Regardless of what she was staring at, his hair was wet and sticking out in unruly spikes from his head. Beads of water clung to his shoulders and chest and glistened off the surface of his tattoo. The contours of sinew, muscle and veins, symmetry and balance, idealized proportion, and classical lines would be breathtaking even to the casual observer. But Julia was anything but a casual observer, for she had spent the entire night with this very body in her bed, spooning her close and playing with her hair. And this body was attached to a damn fine mind and a very deep, passionate soul.

Nevertheless, Julia was staring at his physical form, and thus the term *aquatic demi-god* flitted through her consciousness.

Gabriel grinned. "*I said good morning*, Julianne."

She closed her mouth. "Um, good morning."

He walked over and leaned down, pressing a firm but gentle opened-mouth kiss against her lips. A few droplets of water splashed around her on the sheets. "Did you sleep well?"

She nodded slowly, feeling a good deal too warm.

"You're not saying much." He straightened up and smirked at her.

"You're half-naked."

"Right. Would you prefer me wholly naked?" He shifted the towel provocatively on his hips and grinned.

Julia nearly expired in shock.

"I'm just kidding, sweetheart." He kissed her again, with a furrowed brow.

A discomforting thought occurred to him. He retreated backward with a very serious expression on his face. "I forgot about what happened to you in St. Louis. When you were little," he clarified. "I'm sorry to barge in on you like this. I wasn't thinking."

Julia looked over at him with mute appreciation. She smiled shyly. "It's all right. You're just distracting. You seem happy this morning."

He grinned. "Sharing a bed with you agrees with me. Can I make you breakfast?"

"Um, sure. But you know I don't have a kitchen."

"I'm a resourceful man." Gabriel smiled at her genuinely, his warmth enough to overcome her embarrassment about her cooking facilities.

Just before he closed the bathroom door behind him, she was treated to the barest glimpse of the most beautiful gluteus maximus muscles as Gabriel dropped his purple towel.

Julia gaped like a codfish.

※ ※

The following evening, Rachel returned to Philadelphia from her romantic holiday with Aaron and promptly checked her voice mail. After a frantic call to her father, she immediately telephoned Gabriel and left a message.

"What the hell is going on up there, Gabriel? What did you do to Julia? She only disappeared once in her life and that was when she was completely humiliated by her ex! So what the fuck did you do to her? I swear to God I'm hopping on a plane. Call me . . .

"By the way, Dad says hi and he's glad you called. Would it kill you to call him once a week? He has decided to go back to work because he can't stand being home alone. And by the way, he put the house up for sale."

Then, more than slightly worried about her best friend, Rachel called Julia and left a message on her voice mail, as well.

"Julia, what did Gabriel do? He was raving like a lunatic on my voice

mail. He isn't answering his phone, so I can't get his side of the story. Not that I expect the truth from him. Anyway, I hope that you're all right, and I'm really sorry. Whatever he did, please don't disappear on me again. Not when this is our last Thanksgiving in the house. My dad put it up for sale. Aaron still wants to get you a ticket, so call me, okay? Love you."

Afterward, Rachel returned to her normal life in Philadelphia, anxiously awaiting news from her brother and her best friend. And quietly planning a wedding.

After Gabriel convinced his sister not to fly to Toronto in order to kick his ass, and he spoke to Richard about taking the house off the market, he promptly left a message on Julia's voice mail, which he connected with while she was talking to her father:

"You never seem to answer your phone. [Fumes slightly . . .] Do you have call waiting? Would you order it, please? I don't care what it costs. I'll pay for it. But I'm tired of leaving messages. [Deep breath.] I'm assuming you've heard from Rachel. She's furious with me, but I think I've been able to convince her that you and I had an academic misunderstanding and have since kissed and made up. [Chuckle.] Well, I left out the kissing part.

"Maybe you can call and reassure her before she fulfills her threat to get on an airplane. [Sigh . . . deep breath.] Julianne, I enjoyed waking up next to you yesterday. More than I can say on an answering machine. Tell me I'll be able to wake up next to you again soon. [Lowered, smoldering voice . . .] I'm sitting in front of the fireplace wishing you were here, wrapped in my arms. Call me, principessa."

❋❋

Meanwhile, Julia was talking to her father.

"I'm glad you're coming home, Jules. I'll be on call, but we'll be able to spend some time together . . ." Tom's voice trailed off into a cough as he tried to clear his throat.

"Good. Rachel wants me to visit her too. She's getting married, and I think she needs some help with the preparations, now that Grace is gone."

"Deb invited me over for dinner with her and her kids. I'm sure she'd set an extra place for you."

"No way in hell," Julia muttered.

"What's that?"

"Sorry, Dad. It would be nice to see Deb but there's no way I'm going over there. No way."

Tom paused uncomfortably. "I don't need to, either. I, um, see Deb all the time."

Julia rolled her eyes.

"What time should I pick you up at the airport?"

"Actually, Gabriel Emerson is living in Toronto. He mentioned something about going home that weekend. I'll see if I can catch a ride with the Clarks from Philadelphia, if we fly in at the same time."

Tom was quiet for a moment or two. "Gabriel is there?"

"He teaches at the university. I have a class with him."

"You never told me that. Jules, you need to stay away from him."

"Why?"

"Because he's trouble."

"Why do you say that?"

Tom cleared his throat again. "He never came home to see his mother when she was dying. Never spends time with his family. I don't trust him, and I sure as hell wouldn't trust him with my daughter."

"Dad, he's Rachel's brother. She knows I'm coming home for Thanksgiving. She'll probably pick us up at the airport, anyway."

"Whatever you do, don't carry anything for him on the airplane and don't accept anything from him that looks suspicious. You'll be going through customs."

"What's that supposed to mean?"

"It means I'm keeping an eye out for you. Can't I do that with my only daughter?"

Julia stifled the urge to say something cruel or rude in response. "I'll buy my ticket and let you know what's happening."

"Fine. Talk to you later."

And with that, Julia's largely uninformative conversation with Thomas Mitchell of Selinsgrove came to an end.

She spent the next hour reassuring Rachel that yes, she was fine and no, Gabriel was (perhaps surprisingly) no longer being an ass. She also convinced Aaron that she had enough money from her scholarship to purchase a flight. She mentioned her father's scheduling conflict and promised that she would join the Clarks for Thanksgiving dinner Thursday night.

More than slightly exhausted, she spent another hour persuading Gabriel that it was not a good idea for them to share a bed every evening, especially when there was the possibility that someone connected with the university could see them entering or leaving one another's apartments. He had acquiesced, albeit grumpily, while exacting a promise for another sleepover before seven days had elapsed.

Julia did not want to be the cause of Gabriel losing his job, so she was determined to limit the possibilities that they might be seen together. She was also determined not to spend every night in his bed, for she knew where that would lead. She was still struggling to trust him, her reticence more than reasonable given the fact that he had only changed his disposition toward her recently. And he'd all but admitted that his passion for her was teetering on the edge of his control.

Julia did not want to be persuaded into doing things she was not ready to do. She didn't want to give him part of herself and return to her apartment feeling used and lonely, as she had so many times with *him*. No, Gabriel was not *him*. But that fact made her no less cautious, although she wanted to trust him.

Despite her self-protection, Julia slept far more peacefully with Gabriel than without him, and every day she didn't see him her heart ached.

❧ ❧

Monday afternoon found Julia answering her doorbell. A delivery person stood outside, holding a large, white box. She signed for it, and when she returned to her studio, she opened a card that was attached to the box. The card had the initials *G. O. E.* embossed on the top and was handwritten:

Dear Julianne,
Thank you for sharing yourself with me Friday night.
You have the heart of a lion.

I would dearly like to tame you, slowly,
but without the tears or the good-bye.
Yours,
Gabriel

P.S. I have a new, private e-mail account at your
disposal:
goe777@gmail.com

Julia opened the box and was immediately captivated by a beautiful fragrance. Inside, she was stunned to find a large glass bowl filled with water. Suspended on the surface of the water were seven gardenias. She carefully removed the bowl from its packaging and placed it on her card table, inhaling deeply as the perfume began to permeate the room.

She re-read Gabriel's note and eagerly opened her laptop so that she could send him a quick e-mail from her Gmail account:

> Dear Gabriel,
> Thank you for the gardenias; they're lovely.
> Thank you for your card.
> Thank you for listening.
> Looking forward to seeing you soon,
> Julia
> XO

❀ ❀

On Wednesday afternoon, Julia met Paul by the mailboxes before Professor Emerson's seminar. They exchanged pleasantries and chatted briefly before they were somewhat rudely interrupted by Julia's cell phone. The call was (miraculously) from Dante Alighieri, so of course, she answered it.

"I have to take this," she murmured to Paul apologetically before she walked into the hall.

"Hello?"

"Julianne."

She smiled widely at the sound of his voice. "Hello."

"Will you join me for dinner?"

She looked around quickly to ensure that she was alone. "Um, what did you have in mind?"

"Dinner at my place. I haven't seen you since Saturday. I'm beginning to think you only want e-mail correspondence now that you have my new address." Gabriel chuckled.

Julia breathed deeply, glad that he wasn't irritated with her. "I've been getting ready for my next meeting with Katherine. You've been working on your lecture, so . . ."

"I need to see you."

"I want to see you too. But we'll see each other in a few minutes."

"I need to speak to you about that. We're going to have to pretend as if nothing happened in my last seminar. I'll probably ignore you, just for effect. I wanted to tell you in advance so that I wouldn't upset you." He paused for a moment. "Of course, all I want to do is touch you, but we need to keep up appearances."

"I understand."

"Julianne . . ." he began, dropping his voice, "I don't like this any more than you do. But I would like to have you join me for dinner tonight, so I can make it up to you. After, we can spend a quiet evening by the fire enjoying one another's company. Before bed."

Julia's cheeks immediately flamed with color. "I'd like to, but I was planning on working all evening. I haven't finished the revisions Katherine asked for, and I meet with her tomorrow afternoon. She's very demanding."

He began muttering under his breath.

"I'm sorry, Gabriel, but I want to make her happy."

"What about making me happy?"

"I . . ." Julia was at a loss for words.

He fumed slightly. "Will you promise to see me Friday night, instead?"

"After your lecture?"

"I'll be going to dinner. I'd like you to meet me at my place after that."

"Won't that be too late?"

"Not for what I have in mind. You promised, you know."

Julia smiled at the thought of the new, mature sleepover she had only recently discovered.

"So will I see you Friday night?" He dropped his voice to a seductive whisper.

"Yes. I'll have to come up with an excuse to give Paul. We're going to the lecture together."

Silence rippled on the other end of the telephone line.

"Hello?" Julia moved to a different location in the hallway, hoping her movement would improve her reception. "Are you still there?"

"I'm here." Gabriel's tone was suddenly glacial.

Scheisse, she thought.

He was silent for another moment before he resumed speaking. "Did we or did we not have an arrangement that excluded sharing?"

Double Scheisse.

"Um, of course."

"I've kept up my end of that arrangement."

"Gabriel, please—"

He cut her off. "Tell me that I misunderstood what you just told me."

"We're friends. He asked me to go with him to your lecture. I didn't think it was wrong."

"Do you want me seeing other women as friends? Going to public events with them?"

"No," she whispered.

"Then extend me the same courtesy."

"Please don't be cross with me."

Her request was met with silence.

"He's the only friend I have. Being a grad student in a strange city is very . . . lonely."

"I thought I was your friend."

"Of course you are. But I need someone to talk to about school and things."

"Anything to do with the university should be discussed with me."

"Please don't make me give up the one friend I have, apart from you. Then I really will be isolated, since I can't be with you all the time."

Gabriel flinched. "Have you told him you're seeing someone?"

Julia gulped. "No. I thought it was a secret."

"Come on, Julianne. You're smarter than that." He sighed loudly. "Fine. I'll concede that you need a friend, but he needs to realize that you are no longer available. He's far too invested as it is, and that could create a problem for us."

"I'll tell him I have a new boyfriend. We're supposed to go to the museum in two weeks to see—"

Gabriel growled into the phone. "No, you are not. I'll take you."

"In public? How can you?"

"Let me worry about that. So I suppose he'll be carrying your books to class in a few minutes?" His tone became sarcastic.

"Please, Gabriel."

He exhaled deeply into the phone. "All right. Let's forget about this. But I will have my eye on him. As for Friday, I'll give you a key, or I'll call the concierge and he will let you in."

"Okay."

"See you in a few minutes."

❄✾❄

When Julia and Paul arrived at the seminar room, The Professor was already there. He glanced at them, scowled at Paul, and turned his attention to his lecture notes. However, he noticed with satisfaction that Julia was using her messenger bag. The thought pleased him a great deal.

The rest of the graduate students, including Christa, looked from Julia to The Professor and back again about three or four times. It was almost like watching a volley at Wimbledon.

Julia sat in her usual chair next to Paul and immediately adopted a deferential posture.

"Don't be nervous. He's been in a good mood all week. I don't think he'll bother you today." Paul leaned in closely, far too closely, to whisper in her ear. "He must have gotten laid last weekend, more than once."

Professor Emerson coughed loudly at the front of the room until Paul moved away from Julia.

For her part, Julia was flustered over Paul's remark. She kept her head down, writing copious notes in her notebook. It was a good distraction, for it stopped her from thinking about Saturday morning and what

Gabriel looked like under his clothes, *wet from the shower, dropping a small, purple towel* . . .

The Professor barely looked at her and never called on her to comment or to answer a question. In sum, the lecture was a colossal disappointment from an entertainment perspective and left more than one graduate student wanting. Christa, however, was delighted that the course of the universe had finally corrected itself and all was (almost) as it should be.

"You are all invited to the lecture I will be delivering on lust in Dante's *Inferno* at Victoria College on Friday afternoon at three o'clock. I'll see you next week. Class dismissed." The Professor quickly packed up his things and exited the seminar room without so much as a backward glance.

Paul leaned over to Julia. "Can I walk you home? We could grab some Thai food on the way."

"It would be nice for you to walk me home. But I'm probably going to work right through dinner. And there's something I need to tell you . . ."

❦ ❦

On Friday morning, Julia stood in the entrance to her rather small closet wondering what she should wear. She knew that Gabriel would not be pleased when he saw her sitting with Paul. She knew that she would be meeting Gabriel at his apartment later that evening and sleeping over. She had already packed her messenger bag in preparation for her visit.

She wanted to make a good impression. She wanted Gabriel to notice her amongst all the other women and think that she looked pretty, so for the first time that semester, Julia decided to dress up for school. She wore a black dress with black opaque stockings and knee-length, high-heeled, black leather boots that Rachel had persuaded her to buy a few years ago. She wore simple jewelry—pearl stud earrings that had belonged to her Grandma Mitchell—and she wrapped a dark purple pashmina around her neck, fearful that her modest cleavage would turn out to be too much for a daytime lecture.

Julia and Paul were almost the first to arrive at the large lecture hall.

They quickly chose seats near the back, on the aisle, so as not to be too conspicuous. Faculty members usually took the best seats near the front, and graduate students would not dare to meddle with that convention.

As soon as Julia stepped into the room she felt his presence. A strange tension hummed between them, even at a distance. She felt his eyes on her too, and knew that he was staring. She knew that his stare would quickly morph into a scowl. A sly glance to the front of the room confirmed her suspicions. He was glaring at Paul as he placed a hand to her lower back, guiding her to their seats.

Gabriel gave Julia a quick half-smile as his eyes raked over her form, resting a beat too long on the heels of her boots. Turning away, he continued his conversation with one of the other professors.

Julia took a few moments to admire Gabriel's appearance. He was breathtaking, as usual, dressed in a very handsome black Armani suit with a white French-cuffed shirt and a black silk tie. He was wearing his glasses and a pair of black dress shoes that, mercifully, were not pointy. Surprisingly, however, he wore a vest under his suit, and as his jacket was unbuttoned, Julia saw the fob of a gold watch dangling from one of the buttons of his vest, with the chain leading to a pocket.

"Look at him. A vest and a pocket watch?" muttered Paul, shaking his head. "How old is this guy? I bet he has a personal portrait in his attic that's aging rather rapidly."

Julia smothered a smile, but said nothing.

"Do you know what he had me do yesterday?"

She shook her head.

"I had to pack some of his precious pens in a crate, insure it, and ship it to a fountain pen infirmary. Can you believe that?"

"What's a fountain pen infirmary?"

"Some repair shop for sick fountain pens that caters to even sicker fuckers who have way too much money. And too much time on their hands. Or in their pockets."

Julia snickered and switched off her cell phone.

❈ ❈

Having recovered from the swine flu, Professor Jeremy H. Martin, the chair of Italian Studies, welcomed a crowd of about one hundred people and offered a glowing description of Professor Emerson's research and accomplishments. Julia watched as Gabriel shifted uncomfortably in his chair, as if all the high praise and fine words displeased him. His eyes found hers, and she smiled encouragingly. She watched as his shoulders visibly relaxed.

Professor Martin was proud of Professor Emerson, and he had no qualms about making that fact known. To him, Gabriel had been one of the most promising hires of the Department and had truly lived up to his potential. He'd been tenured early on the strength of the publication of his first book by Oxford University Press, and was well on his way to becoming another Katherine Picton. Or so Professor Martin hoped.

After a thinnish round of applause, Gabriel took center stage, spreading his notes on the lectern and double-checking the readiness of his PowerPoint presentation. He took a moment to scan the crowd— Professor Martin was smiling in anticipation, Miss Peterson had slithered forward and was slyly fingering her plunging neckline, while his faculty colleagues sat quietly, seemingly interested in the topic of his lecture.

One striking exception was seated in the very front row. This professor had no interest in his research or his academic prowess. No, her interests were far more profligate, and it seemed to Gabriel that she was flaunting them now, her pink tongue darting out to moisten crimson lips. She was twisted. Predatory. And Gabriel was made very uncomfortable by the fact that she was staring at him with serpentine eyes, while sitting in the same room as Julia. He knew that his past lurked around every corner, but God help him if the two women ever met.

Dragging his eyes away from the blond professor, he forced a smile at the audience. He quickly sought out Julia's pretty face and drew strength from her warm expression, and then he began.

"The title of my lecture is *Lust in Dante's* Inferno: *The Deadly Sin against the Self.* Immediately, one might wonder why lust would be a sin against the self since it is always directed toward another—the use of another human being for personal, sexual gratification."

A muffled snort reached Gabriel's ears from the front row, but he ignored it, his reaction telegraphed by a noticeable tightening of his expression.

"Dante's notions of sin are shaped largely by the writings of St. Thomas Aquinas. In his famous *Summa Theologiae*, Aquinas argues that any evil action or sin is a form of self-destruction. He assumes that human beings have a nature that is supposed to be rational and good. Aquinas conceives of this nature, that of the rational animal, as being created by God specifically to pursue goodness, more specifically, the virtues.

"When a human being departs from this natural purpose, she injures herself, for she does what she was not intended to do. She wars against herself and her nature."

Miss Peterson leaned forward, as if she were paying rapt attention.

"Why does Aquinas hold this peculiar view of sin?

"One reason is because he accepts Boethius' assertion that goodness and being are convertible. In other words, anything that exists has some goodness in it because God made it. And no matter how marred or broken or sinful that being is, it still maintains some goodness so long as it exists."

Gabriel pressed a button, and his first slide appeared on the screen to his left. Julia recognized it as Botticelli's illustration of Lucifer.

"According to this view, no one, not even Lucifer encased in ice at the bottom of Dante's *Inferno*, is wholly evil. Evil can only feed off of goodness like a parasite; if all the goodness of a creature were eliminated, the creature in question would no longer exist."

Gabriel felt a pair of cunning eyes fixate on him, mocking him and his silly recognition of concepts so bourgeois as *good* and *evil*.

He cleared his throat. "It's a foreign way of thinking to many of us— the idea that even a fallen angel condemned to live out his days in the *Inferno* has some goodness left in him." His eyes wandered over to Julia's where they rested just long enough for her to see something pleading in them. "Goodness that begs to be recognized, despite the fallen angel's sad and desperate addiction to sin."

Another Botticelli illustration, one of Dante and Beatrice and the fixed stars of Paradise, was displayed on the screen. Julia recognized it as the same scene Gabriel had showed her from his private collection.

"Against the backdrop of good and evil, consider the characters of Dante and Beatrice. They have a relationship that typifies courtly love.

In the context of *The Divine Comedy*, Beatrice is connected with Virgil. She appeals to him to guide her beloved Dante through Hell because she is unable to travel there, owing to her permanent residence in Paradise. In making the connection between Beatrice and Virgil, Dante is expressing his notion that courtly love is tied to reason rather than passion."

At the mention of Beatrice, Julia began to fidget, keeping her face down lest it give anything away. Paul noticed her movements and misreading them, took her hand in his, squeezing it gently. They were seated too far away for Gabriel to see what was going on, but he observed that Paul had turned toward Julia, his hand disappearing near her lap. The sight distracted him momentarily.

He coughed, and Julia's eyes flew to his as she hastily withdrew her hand.

"But what of lust? If love is the rabbit, then lust is the wolf. Dante says so explicitly when he identifies lust as a sin of wolf-like incontinence—a sin in which passion overtakes reason."

At this remark, Christa slid to the very edge of her seat, leaning forward just enough so that her cleavage was visible from the podium. Unfortunately for her, Gabriel was too busy posting the next slide, Rodin's sculpture *Le Baisir*, to notice.

"Dante places Paolo and Francesca in the Circle of the Lustful. Surprisingly, the story of their downfall is linked with the courtly love tradition. At the time of their lustful indulgence, they were engaged in reading about the adultery between Lancelot and Queen Guinevere." Gabriel grinned mischievously. "Perhaps this was the medieval equivalent of porn-fueled foreplay."

Polite laughter echoed across the lecture hall.

"In the case of Paolo and Francesca, passion overtook reason, which should have told them that since one of them was joined to another, they should keep their hands to themselves."

Gabriel glared meaningfully at Paul. But Paul thought the glare was directed elsewhere, possibly to Julia or one of the women sitting in front of him, so he did nothing. At Paul's lack of reaction, Gabriel's blue eyes grew green like a dragon's. All that was lacking from his display was the breathing of fire.

"Perhaps this is similar to the proprietary relationship that exists between a couple when they are courting. If someone else were to start indulging in some of the special delights that should be reserved for the courting couple, no doubt anger and jealousy would result." Gabriel's voice grew sharp.

Julia flinched and shifted slightly to her left, away from Paul.

"But the fact that Dante sees in Lancelot and Guinevere and Paolo and Francesca a corruption of the courtly love tradition shows that he recognizes the very real dangers facing his attachment to Beatrice. If Dante's passion were to overtake his reason, it would ruin their lives and expose them to scandal. So the fate of Paolo and Francesca is a very personal warning to Dante for him to keep his affection for Beatrice chaste. Which is no easy task given her great beauty and allurements, and the depth and degree of his desire for her."

Julia blushed.

"Let me be clear, despite the fact that they were separated from one another for years, Dante aches for her. He wants her, and he wants all of her. His chastity is made all the more virtuous because of the strength and desperation of his desire."

While he paused, the serpentine eyes followed Gabriel's gaze back to Julia before making eye contact with him. He glared in response and continued.

"In Dante's philosophy, lust is a misplaced love, but a kind of love nonetheless. For this reason, it is the least evil of the seven deadly sins, and that is why Dante locates the Circle of the Lustful just underneath Limbo. Lust deals with the greatest of earthly pleasures . . ."

Gabriel's eyes darted in Julia's direction, and she stared back at him, transfixed.

"Sex is properly understood to be not only physical, but spiritual—an ecstatic union of two bodies and two souls, meant to mimic the joy and ecstasy of union with the Divine in Paradise. Two bodies joined together in pleasure. Two souls joined through the connection between two bodies and the whole-hearted, enthusiastic, selfless giving of the entire self."

Julia tried not to squirm in her seat as she recalled how she felt the other night when Gabriel's mouth sucked her fingers, one by one, cleaning them of chocolate cake. The room began to feel more than a little warm, and several people shifted in their seats.

"It's pedantic perhaps to point out that if one holds back and doesn't give one's entire self during intercourse, orgasm will be eluded. The result is tension, frustration, and an unhappy partner. The moment of orgasm is a foretaste of absolute transcendence and wholehearted, rapturous pleasure. The kind of pleasure in which all of one's deepest urges and longings are wholly and heart-stoppingly satisfied."

Gabriel smiled to himself as Julia crossed and uncrossed her legs, reveling in her reaction as he paused to take a sip of water.

"The idea of shared orgasm, one partner's ecstasy tripping the other's, highlights the shared intimacy of physical and spiritual union. Panting, twisting, touching, yearning, giving, and finally and most gloriously, coming."

Gabriel paused as he struggled not to gaze at Julia, and thus draw attention to her flushed and downcast face. He cleared his throat and smirked slightly. "Does anyone feel faint?"

Cheerful but reserved laughter echoed around the hall, and Christa lifted her hair away from her neck and fanned herself with a copy of Gabriel's book.

"I believe my words have illustrated Dante's thesis, namely, that lust is powerful enough to distract the mind, which is the faculty of reason, and prompt it to focus on earthly, carnal concerns rather than rising above to contemplate the heavenly concerns, namely, God. No doubt some of you would rather be rushing home to your lover's embrace than remaining here to listen to the rest of my dry lecture."

He chuckled, absolutely ignoring the professor in the front row who exposed a small but obscene object from her purse in order to taunt him.

"In contrast to lust, which is a mortal sin, is love. Aquinas argues that a lover is related to his beloved as if his beloved were a part of himself."

At this, Gabriel's expression softened and a sweet smile spread across his face.

"The joys and beauty of sexual intimacy, expressed in the unifying act of sexual intercourse, are the natural outgrowth of love. In this case, as should be clear, sex is not identical with lust. Hence the modern distinction made in contemporary parlance between, forgive my vulgarity, fucking and making love. But sex is not identical with love either, as the courtly love tradition demonstrates. One can love one's friend chastely and passionately without engaging in sexual intercourse with her.

"In Dante's *Paradiso*, lust is transformed into charity, the truest, purest manifestation of love. In Paradise, the soul is free from longing, for all her desires are satisfied, and she is filled with joy. She no longer has guilt over her previous sins but enjoys absolute freedom and fulfillment. However, time prevents me from giving a more complete discussion of Paradise.

"In Dante's *Divine Comedy*, we find the dichotomy of lust and charity and a powerful manifestation of the chastity of courtly love, as typified by the relationship between Dante and Beatrice. This ideal of courtly love is perhaps best expressed in the words of Beatrice, herself, '*Apparuit iam beatitudo vestra.*' That is, '*Now your blessedness appears.*' Truer words were never spoken. Thank you."

The lecture hall erupted in polite applause and low murmurings of approval. The Professor then began to field questions from the audience. In typical fashion, full-time faculty members were the first to speak, while graduate students waited patiently for their turn.

(For Academia, like Europe in the Middle Ages, was organized under a class system.)

Julia sat very still, trying to absorb what she thought she'd heard during Gabriel's lecture. She was repeating some of his more profound statements to herself when Paul leaned over to whisper in her ear.

"Watch this. Emerson is going to ignore Christa."

From their vantage point, they couldn't see Christa's cleavage (which was a mercy). She was still leaning forward, now with her hand in the air, trying to gain The Professor's attention. He seemed to pass over her deliberately, pointing at other questioners and offering reasoned responses. Eventually, Professor Martin stood up in order to indicate that question period had come to an end. Only then did Christa lower her hand, a scowl darkening her fine features.

Another round of applause was given and received, and Gabriel stepped off the platform. He was greeted immediately by an average-sized brunette, who looked like she was a professor in her mid to late thirties. The two shook hands.

Paul snorted. "Did you see that? He wasn't going to allow Christa to ask a question in an open forum. He's worried she'll stand up and throw her bra at him, or hold up an 'I heart Emerson' poster."

Julia giggled and watched as the brunette professor chatted with Gabriel before stepping aside to speak to someone else.

"I was surprised no one corrected Emerson on his mistake." Paul scratched at his sideburns thoughtfully.

"What mistake?"

"He attributed *'Apparuit iam beatitudo vestra'* to Beatrice, but we all know it was Dante. He says those words in the second section of *La Vita Nuova*, when he meets Beatrice for the first time."

Julia knew this, of course, but would never have commented on it. So she remained silent.

Paul shrugged. "I'm sure it was a slip of the tongue. He can quote those texts from memory in Italian and English. I just thought it was funny that Professor Perfect made a very public mistake and no one corrected him." He chuckled to himself. "Maybe that was why Christa put up her hand."

Julia nodded. She knew that Gabriel's error had been intentional. But she would tell no one, especially not Paul.

His eyes passed over her admiringly. "You look pretty today. You always look pretty, but today you're just—glowing." His face morphed into a serious expression. "I hope I'm not stepping on your boyfriend's toes by telling you that. What was his name again?"

"Owen."

"Well, I can see it in your eyes. You're obviously glad to be back together with him. After weeks of seeing you sad, I'm happy that you're happy."

"Thank you," she murmured.

"So why the dress?"

She peered around the room. "I didn't know if people dressed up for these occasions. I knew all the professors would be here, and I wanted to look nice."

Paul laughed. "Most academic women don't care about fashion." He shook his head and gently touched her hand. "I hope your ex treats you right this time. Or I'll have to go to Philadelphia and kick his ass."

At this point, Julia was only half-listening as she saw a petite blond professor greet Gabriel with a kiss on both cheeks.

She raised her eyebrows in surprise.

And you gave me a hard time about Paul, Professor. I thought we weren't sharing . . .

Paul muttered something under his breath.

"What's wrong?" she asked.

"Well, the lecture was great. You can see why I came here to work with him." Paul glanced meaningfully at Gabriel. "But look at them."

As if on cue, the blond threw her head back and laughed uproariously, while Emerson gave her a tight smile. She was less than five feet tall, with flaxen hair that was pulled back tightly into a severe-looking bun. She wore Armani glasses that were both squarish and red and an expensive-looking black suit highlighted by a tight pencil skirt that barely grazed her knees. Julia noted also that the woman wore black pumps that were very high and fishnet stockings that would have netted only the tiniest of fish.

The woman was beautiful, but she seemed rather out of place amongst all of the other professional academics. And there was something about her presence that was decidedly aggressive.

"That's Professor Singer." Paul grimaced.

"The blonde?"

"Yes. The dark-haired woman to her left is Professor Leaming. She's great. You need to meet her. But stay away from Singer. She's a dragon lady."

Julia's stomach flipped as she watched Professor Singer grip Gabriel's forearm in a far too familiar fashion, digging her talons into his suit jacket while she stood on tiptoe to whisper something in his ear. His expression remained utterly impassive.

"Why do you say that?" Julia asked.

"Have you seen her website?"

"No."

"Consider yourself lucky. You'd be shocked by what she's in to. They call her *Professor Pain*."

Julia reluctantly dragged her eyes away from the sickening display that was The Professors Pain and Emerson show and began wringing her hands. She wondered if Professor Pain's first name was Paulina.

Disgusted by the display, she grabbed her coat and stood up. "I guess it's time for us to leave."

"I'll walk you home." Paul chivalrously helped her with her coat.

They left their seats and were just about to walk toward the exit when Professor Martin, the chair of Italian Studies, caught Paul's eye, motioning him to come over.

"I'll just be a minute. Wait for me."

Julia sat back down, fingering her coat buttons as a distraction.

Gabriel wasn't looking at her at all, and from his body language she suspected that he was avoiding her. Paul had a brief exchange with the chair before turning around and pointing in her direction. The chair nodded and patted Paul on the back. By the time he returned, Paul was beaming.

"Well, you'll never guess what that was about."

Julia lifted her eyebrows.

"We've been invited to the faculty dinner in honor of Emerson's lecture."

"You're kidding."

"No. Apparently, there's money in the budget to buy dinner for a couple of graduate students, and the chair decided to invite me. When I told him I was here with you, he invited you to come as my guest." He winked at her. "Poor Christa isn't on the list. Looks like this is your lucky day."

At that moment, Gabriel's eyes met Julia's from behind Paul's back. Gabriel was upset, angry even, and he was shaking his head at her. His eyes flicked over to Paul and back to her, and again he shook his head.

Julia pursed her lips stubbornly. *How can Gabriel be jealous of Paul when Professor Pain is all over him? Talk about a double standard.*

"We don't have to go, if you don't want to." Paul cleared his throat. "I know Emerson has been a jerk to you. You probably don't want to celebrate his latest success over paella."

"It would be rude to turn down the invitation when it came from the chair," Julia said slowly.

"You're probably right. I promise we'll have fun. We're going to Segovia, which is a great restaurant. But dinner isn't until seven. Would you like to go to Starbucks? Or somewhere else?" Paul extended his hand to help her to her feet.

"Starbucks is fine."

Within a few minutes of exiting the building, Julia finally found the courage to ask a question that had been troubling her.

"Do you know Professor Singer well?" She tried to sound casual.

"No. I stay away from her." Paul cursed more than once. "I wish I could *unsee* the e-mails she sent to Emerson. They're burned into my brain."

"What's her first name?"

"Ann."

Chapter Twenty

Julia treated Paul to a coffee that she paid for surreptitiously with a Starbucks gift card—a card that had a picture of a lightbulb on it. When they eventually crossed the threshold of Segovia, they were met by a very pleasant-looking Spaniard who identified himself as the owner. Much to his delight, Paul responded in Spanish.

Segovia's interior featured sunny yellow walls on which were painted images from Picasso's drawing of Don Quixote and Sancho Panza. A classical guitarist sat in a corner playing arrangements by Maestro Segovia. And nearby, a series of long tables had been placed in a square in the very center of the room, marking the reserved space for the faculty dinner. Its geometric configuration made it inevitable that all guests would sit facing one another. Julia did not relish the idea of facing Professor Pain, and if she thought she could have escaped without insulting or drawing undue attention from Professor Martin, she would have.

Paul chose seats on one of the far corners of the table; for once again, he was conscious of the class system and knew that his place was not one of honor. While he discussed the menu with the waiter *en Español*, Julia silently mused about Gabriel's jealousy and stealthily turned on her cell phone so that she could text him. But there was a text already waiting for her:

> Don't come to dinner. Give Paul an excuse.
> Wait for me at my place; the concierge will admit you.
> I'll explain later. Please do as I ask.—G

Julia stared at the screen blankly until Paul nudged her. "Would you like a drink?"

"Um, it's probably out of season for sangria, but I'd love some if they have it."

"Our sangria is excellent," said the waiter before leaving to place their drink orders with the bartender.

Julia gave Paul an apologetic look. "I have a text from Owen. I'm sorry to be rude."

"No worries," said Paul, busying himself with the menu while she quickly prepared a reply:

> My phone was off. It's too late, I'm already here.
> You have nothing to be jealous of—I'm going home with you.
> You'll have me in your bed until morning.—J

She deposited her phone in her messenger bag, praying silently that Gabriel would not be too cross. Oh gods of all overprotective and jealous (fill in appropriate description of Gabriel and our relationship here), please don't let him make a scene. Not in front of his colleagues.

Unfortunately for Julia and whoever was texting her, the messenger bag muffled the sound of an incoming message, which arrived shortly thereafter.

Within twenty minutes, the rest of the guests filtered in. Professor Leaming and some of the other professors were seated beside Paul. On the far end, Gabriel was sandwiched in between Professors Martin and Singer.

At the sight of Gabriel and his seatmates, Julia began sipping her sangria a little too eagerly, hoping she'd be able to get a refill to alleviate the tension that crackled in the air. The sangria was delicious and packed with lots of citrus fruit, which pleased her greatly.

"Are you cold?" Paul gestured to the purple pashmina that was wound around her neck in a very chic manner.

"Not really." She slowly removed the scarf and placed it on top of her bag.

Paul politely averted his eyes as the delicate pale flesh of Julia's neck and décolletage became visible. She was beautiful, and her body, although small, was blessed with generous breasts that provided her with very handsome, proportional cleavage.

As soon as she removed her pashmina, a pair of jealous blue eyes darted across the table, hungrily taking in her newly exposed skin before making a hasty retreat.

"Paul, what's up with Professor Singer?" Julia kept her voice low behind her wineglass.

He saw Singer sitting far too close to Emerson, and he watched as Emerson subtly moved his chair away from her. She moved her chair closer in response. But Julia missed the exchange.

"She and Emerson had an affair. Looks like they're back at it." Paul snickered. "I guess we discovered the reason for his good mood this week."

Julia's eyes widened, and she felt ill.

"So she was his—girlfriend?"

Paul moved his chair closer so that Professor Leaming couldn't overhear their conversation. Of course, the fact that a flamenco dancer had appeared and was now dancing to the loud strains of a classical guitar made his task much easier.

"Just a minute." He passed a tapas plate to Julia. "Try these. It's chorizo and Manchego cheese, and crostini with Cabrales, a Spanish blue cheese."

She helped herself, nibbling on the appetizers while she waited anxiously for an answer.

"Singer doesn't have boyfriends. She's into pain. And control. You know . . ." His voice trailed off suggestively.

Julia blinked in disbelief.

"Did you ever see *Pulp Fiction?*" he asked.

She shook her head. "I don't like Quentin Tarantino. He's too dark."

"Then let's just say that she likes to get medieval . . . in her personal life . . . on people's asses. And she isn't shy about letting people know it. She researches that stuff and posts her publications online."

Julia swallowed a piece of chorizo quickly. "So that means that he—"

"Is a sick fucker like she is. But he's a hell of a researcher, as you saw this afternoon. I try not to think about what goes on in his personal life. I think that lovers should be gentle with one another. Not that love enters into what they're doing."

Paul surveyed the room cautiously before whispering in Julia's ear.

"I think if you care enough about someone to have sex with them, then you should care enough to respect them and not treat them as an object. You should be responsible and careful and never, ever hurt them. Even if they're fucked up enough to beg you to."

Julia shivered and took a very large sip of her second sangria.

He leaned back in his chair. "I can't relate to someone wanting pain at all, let alone during sex. Sex is supposed to be about pleasure and affection. Do you think Dante would have tied Beatrice up and worked her over with a whip?"

Julia hesitated, then shook her head.

"When I was an undergraduate at St. Mike's, I took a course on the Philosophy of Sex, Love, and Friendship. We talked about consent. You know how everyone says that as long as an activity is between two consenting adults, it's okay? Our professor asked us if we thought a human being could consent to an injustice, such as selling himself into slavery."

"No one wants to be a slave."

"They do in Professor Pain's world. Some people sell themselves into sexual slavery—voluntarily. So is slavery okay if the slave wants to be a slave? Can someone who is in their right mind consent to slavery, or are they simply irrational because they want to be a slave?"

Julia began to feel more than slightly uncomfortable having this particular conversation so close to Professor Pain and Gabriel, so she tipped back the last of her sangria and swiftly changed the subject.

"What's your dissertation topic, Paul? I don't think you ever told me."

He chuckled. "Pleasure and the beatific vision. It's a comparison between the deadly sins associated with pleasure—lust, gluttony, and greed—and the pleasure of the beatific vision in Paradise. Emerson is a great dissertation advisor, but like I said, I stay out of his personal life. Even though he'd probably be a hell of a case study for the Second Circle of the Inferno."

"I can't understand why everyone just doesn't want kindness," Julia mused, more to herself than to Paul. "Life is painful enough."

"That's the world we live in." He offered her a sincere smile. "I hope your boyfriend is kind to you. Just be grateful you found someone who isn't into the sick shit."

At that moment they were interrupted by the waiter, so Paul didn't see the color drain out of Julia's cheeks and lips. She involuntarily peeked over at Gabriel and saw Singer whispering in his ear again.

Gabriel's eyes remained stubbornly fixed on the table in front of him, teeth clenched and jaw set. He picked up his glass of wine, sipped it, and set it down again, all while Julia stared.

Look at me, Gabriel. Roll your eyes, rub your face, scowl . . . something, anything. Show me this is all a misunderstanding. Show me Paul is wrong.

"Julia?" Paul's voice interrupted her thoughts. "Do you want to share the paella *Valenciana* with me? They only make it for two. It's very good." Now he noticed Julia's paleness and the fact that her fingers were trembling. "Hey, are you okay?"

She rubbed her forehead. "Yeah. The paella is fine."

"Maybe you should go easy on the sangria. You haven't had much to eat, and you're starting to look sick."

He was worried that he'd shocked her with his salacious revelations, revelations that he had no right to offer to a fellow graduate student. So he changed the subject by telling her stories of his last trip to Spain and his fascination with Gaudi's architecture. She nodded as if on cue and even asked questions from time to time, but her mind was far away, trying to sort out who exactly she'd shared a bed with a week ago—the fallen angel who still had goodness in him or someone much, much darker.

She noticed that Professor Singer's left hand was suddenly hidden from view. She couldn't bring herself to meet Gabriel's eyes. But that didn't stop Professor Singer from noticing Julia. Their eyes met just as Gabriel appeared to push her hand away under the table. Embarrassed, Julia turned to Paul, while Singer wore a look of inquisitive amusement that slowly morphed into an unblinking, fascinated stare.

Eager to escape the sordid spectacle she thought she'd witnessed, Julia made a feeble excuse to Paul about not feeling well and left the table. She climbed the staircase to the second floor and quickly located the restroom. Examining her features in the mirror, she tried to process what he'd told her. Her thoughts were a sordid jumble of words and dark images, while her heart bled.

Why would anyone want to be hit? Gabriel and Ann . . . pain . . .

control . . . Ann's fingers in Gabriel's lap . . . Ann hitting Gabriel . . . Gabriel hitting Ann.

Julia found herself leaning against the counter as she fought a wave of nausea. She wasn't sure how long she stood there, eyes closed, before someone pushed through the door.

"Hello there." Professor Singer smiled widely, showing rows of shiny teeth.

Julia marveled at how the light glinting off the professor's glasses tricked the brain into thinking that her green eyes were glowing red.

"I'm Professor Singer. It's a pleasure to meet you." She extended her hand, and Julia took it reluctantly, mumbling a response.

The professor's hand was cold but far from lifeless. She gripped Julia firmly and for far too long. When she released her, she trailed a finger down Julia's lifeline as if she were intentionally measuring her. The act made Julia shiver.

Ann cocked her head to one side and narrowed her eyes. "I thought you were expecting me. Do I make you nervous?"

Julia frowned. "No, I came up here to wash my hands. I think I'm getting the flu."

"That's a pity." The professor smiled more widely and took a step closer. "You seem healthy enough. You have lovely skin."

"Thank you." Julia's eyes darted toward the door, eager to make an escape.

"Not at all. Not at all. Are you wearing lipstick, or is that the natural shade of your lips?" She leaned forward at the waist and peered far too closely at Julia's ripe, open mouth, their faces mere inches from one another.

Julia took a step backward. "Um, it's my natural color."

Ann took another step forward. "Extraordinary. You know, of course, that the natural shade of the lip is repeated across a woman's body in more intimate places. Your color is so pleasing on your mouth. I'm sure it's breathtaking elsewhere."

Julia's jaw dropped open.

"Look at yourself in the mirror. How could I not have noticed you downstairs? And fortunately, you noticed me too." Ann took another step forward and dropped her voice. "Do you like to watch?" she whispered. "Did you like watching what I was doing to him under the table?"

Julia reddened. "I don't know what you're talking about."

"Flesh changes color, you know, in response to increased blood flow. Like now." She smiled, exposing her teeth. "I've embarrassed or aroused you, so your cheeks have grown flushed and so have your lips. But you're flushed elsewhere, aren't you?" She dropped her voice still further. "And lower down, I'm sure you're begging to be stroked and teased . . ." She licked her lips and smiled. "My little pink pearl. I think you want me to tease you. You'd make such a pretty pet."

Julia stared defiantly. "I'm not interested in being anyone's pet."

That made Professor Singer back up. Julia's sudden show of spirit was wholly unexpected.

"I'm a human being, not an animal. Leave me alone." Julia did not know where in holy hell she found the nerve to dispute with Professor Singer, but she found it.

Ann laughed. "Human beings *are* animals, my dear. We share the same physiology, the same reactions to stimuli, the same needs for food, drink, and sex. Some of us are just more intelligent."

Julia glared down at her. "I'm intelligent enough to know what an animal is. And I am not interested in being fucked like one. Excuse me."

She sidestepped the professor quickly, heading for the door.

"If you change your mind, come and find me," Ann purred.

"Not a chance in hell," spat Julia. She fled, inhaling and exhaling very quickly as she began to jog down the hall.

A quick pair of footsteps followed close behind. She let out a shriek as someone pulled her into a darkened room, closing and locking the door behind them. She pushed against a hard chest roughly before someone grabbed her wrists.

"Julianne."

It was too dark to see his face, but she recognized his voice and the strange sensation that hummed up and down her arms in reaction to his touch. She stopped struggling.

"Please turn on the light. I—I'm claustrophobic." Her voice sounded to Gabriel's ears like that of a frightened child.

He released her and pulled out his iPhone, holding it up like a lamp.

"Is this better?" Gabriel suppressed the urge to ask what light had to do with claustrophobia as he wrapped an arm around her trembling shoulders and pressed his lips to her forehead. "Julianne?"

She took a moment to examine their surroundings and realized that they were in a broom closet.

"Julianne?" he repeated, trying to capture her attention. "I saw Ann follow you. Are you all right?"

"No."

"What did she do?"

"She said I'd make a good pet," Julia whispered, her eyes downcast.

Gabriel scowled darkly. "Did she touch you?"

She closed her eyes and wiped a few beads of sweat from her forehead. "Just my hand."

He quickly dimmed the light on his phone so that they were only partially illuminated, for he was worried that Ann might see the light under the door.

"This is what I was afraid might happen. Why didn't you do as I asked?"

"I told you, I didn't get your text until it was too late. I didn't expect to be hit on at a faculty dinner, by a professor who wasn't you."

Gabriel growled. "She was watching you across the table and was probably excited by your shyness, not to mention your beauty. Having you in the same room as her is the equivalent of dangling a lamb in front of a wolf." He shook his head and cursed. "I tried to keep you away from her."

Julia searched his eyes. "You weren't keeping me away because you're jealous?"

Gabriel let out a sharp exhalation. "Of course I'm jealous. Jealousy is a new emotion for me, Julianne. I'm not practiced in the art of dealing with it. But I would have begged Paul to take you to dinner somewhere, anywhere, just to keep you away from her."

"Were you involved with Professor Singer?"

His expression darkened, and he pressed his lips into a thin line. "This is not the place to discuss that."

Julia shook her head as her nausea returned. She'd hoped that Paul was mistaken. But Gabriel's reaction told her otherwise.

"How could you?"

"You're shaking. Are you going to be sick?"

"Why won't you answer my question?"

Gabriel spoke through his teeth. "Julianne, your comfort and well-being is my only concern at this moment. I won't answer any questions until I am satisfied that you are all right. Although if you throw up, I promise to hold your hair." He smirked slightly.

"I'm not going to throw up," she murmured. "Unfortunately, she's not the first woman to come on to me. I'm more upset about the fact that you're hiding something."

Gabriel's eyebrows furrowed at her admission, but he quickly pushed his concern aside. "Julianne, trust me when I tell you that you do not want to know more about her. Your mind should remain un-polluted."

"But it's okay for her to molest you under the table? That's how she noticed me, Gabriel. She caught me staring."

A muscle jumped in his jaw, and Julia saw sparks in his eyes.

"She's goading me. And for obvious reasons, I can't react and cause a scene. I was hoping she'd ignore you and focus all of her twisted attention on me. Clearly, I was wrong."

"Why did I have to find out from Paul that you were involved with her?"

"Paul said that?"

She nodded.

Gabriel swore an oath and began rubbing his eyes forcefully, as if he were blotting out a repulsive image. "I didn't expect her to attend my lecture. We don't share the same values or research interests. Today is the first time I've seen her in months. She's part of my past—a past I will not repeat. Not if I live forever."

"Paul said she likes pain. Were you—violent together?"

He clenched his fists at his sides, the tendons in his arms humming in contraction.

"Yes. I'd like to tell you that she was the wicked temptress and I was lured into an entanglement with her, but that isn't what happened. Nevertheless, I am not going to explain the dark contours of her world to you. Not even a single thought of yours belongs there. But I'll tell you that during one of my—encounters with her, she did something that caused me to lose my temper. And I gave her a taste of her own medicine. That act alone terminated our interactions, and I was immediately flung out of her house."

"She hit you?"

"More than once," rasped Gabriel grimly. "That was the point."

"*Gabriel.*" His name came out as something akin to a sob, and his heart was instantly pierced. "How could you? How could you let her touch you, let alone hurt you?"

He encircled her with his arms and squeezed her tightly. "Julianne, you do not want to hear this. Please forget what Paul said. Forget all about her."

"I can't. I can't forget what you said in your lecture this afternoon. Your description of the act of making love was really beautiful, but that's not what you want. Or maybe you think it's impossible for lovers to be like that."

Gabriel's eyes bored into hers. "Of course it's what I want. Of course I think it's possible. I've just never experienced it." He cleared his throat. "You aren't the only virgin in this relationship."

She looked at him in surprise. "Then why would you want someone to hurt you? Haven't you been hurt enough?"

His face wore a pained expression.

"Gabriel, your life is like a series of locked, secret rooms. I have no idea what lurks behind those doors. And you won't tell me. I have to find out about your ex-girlfriend from your research assistant!"

"She was never my girlfriend. And I asked you about Simon, and you wouldn't tell me anything. So far we are even."

Julia winced.

"I told you about my mother."

Gabriel sighed. "Yes, you did. And hearing what happened to you in St. Louis hurt me far more than I can say. More than Ann and her parlor tricks." He shook his head. "You're right. I should have told you about her."

He shifted his weight from one foot to the other, and Julia heard his fists slide into the pockets of his trousers. "I thought that when I told you, you'd be so repulsed that you'd run. You'd realize I truly am a devil."

"You're no devil. You're a fallen angel who still has goodness left in him. A fallen angel who aspires to make love with a woman and treat her with tenderness," whispered Julia. She closed her eyes. "Hearing about Professor Singer from you would have been far better than finding out like this. Or having it flaunted in front of me when you wouldn't even look in my direction."

"I wear tremendous shame, Julianne, which is something you know precious little about."

"You aren't the only sinner in this closet, Gabriel." She opened her eyes and inhaled slowly. "Which is why I can't hold your past sins against you. Do you still want her?"

"Of course not!" His demeanor immediately shifted to outrage. "We did not have a *relationship*, Julianne—we had a couple of encounters. It was over a year ago, and I haven't been involved with her since." He sighed deeply. "If you insist, I'll tell you more, but I can't do it now. Can you give me until after dinner to explain? Please?"

She chewed her lip pensively.

Gabriel gently pressed his mouth to hers, tugging her lip free with his own and slowly releasing her. "Please don't hurt yourself. It upsets me."

"I could say the same to you."

His shoulders slumped forward, and he groaned a little.

"I will give you until after dinner only if you promise not to let her touch you."

"Gladly."

Julia exhaled deeply. "Thank you."

"So you'll stay?"

She shook her head. "I can't sit across the table from her and eat paella. She makes me sick."

"I'll take you home."

"You're the guest of honor. You can't leave."

Gabriel ran his fingers through his hair as he thought for a moment. "At least let me call a taxi for you. I'll try to extricate myself as soon as possible. My concierge will let you in." He reached into his pocket and pulled out a money clip.

She waved his hand aside. "I have my own money."

"Let me give you my credit card so you can order dinner and have it delivered."

"I can't eat."

He sighed and rubbed at his eyes.

She turned to leave, but Gabriel reached out and grasped her elbow.

"Wait." He stared down at her, his voice pleading. "When I saw you walk into the lecture hall, my heart leaped. My heart leaped, Julianne. You've never looked more beautiful. You looked . . . happy." He swallowed noisily. "I'm sorry I killed that look. I'm sorry I didn't tell you the truth. Do you think . . . you might be able to forgive me?"

"You didn't sin against me, Gabriel." Her eyes slowly began to fill with tears. "I'm trying to figure out how deeply rooted your taste for pain is and what that means for us. I feel like I have no idea who you really are, and that hurts."

With that, she exited the closet.

❁❁

The Fates favored Julia on her return to the dinner party. While she fetched her things and made her excuses, Ann was still ensconced in the ladies' room. A second female professor was missing from the table.

One look at Julia's pale face and teary eyes convinced Paul not to try to persuade her to stay. And when she offered an obviously fictitious explanation about having a migraine, he didn't question her until they were standing outside the restaurant.

"Singer followed you to the bathroom, didn't she?"

Julia chewed on her lip and nodded.

He shook his head. "She's a predator. A dangerous predator. I should have warned you. Are you okay?"

"I'm fine. But I have to go home. I'm sorry about the paella."

"Fuck the paella. All I care about is you." He winced slightly. "If you want to file a complaint against her, I'll take you to the judicial committee's office on Monday."

"What's that?"

"It's the office that handles allegations of misconduct against faculty and staff. If you want to tell the judicial committee what happened with Singer, I'll help you."

Julia shook her head. "There weren't any witnesses. It would be my word against hers. I'm going to try to forget what happened, unless she approaches me again."

"It's your decision, but you should know that I filed a complaint against her last year. Even though it was her word against mine, my harassment complaint is still in her file. She stays away from me now. It was the best decision I ever made."

Her smiled faded. "I don't think I want to do that, but I'll consider it. And I'm sorry that happened to you."

"Don't worry about me. Have a nice weekend and try to forget about this. If you need to talk, you've got my number. I'll see you next week." Paul offered an encouraging look and waved as the taxi pulled away.

While Virgil's words rang in Julia's ears, she checked her cell phone. She found a text message that had been sent shortly before the professors arrived at Segovia:

Stay away from Prof. Singer.
Stay close to Paul—she despises him.
Be careful.—G

Too little, too late, Julia thought ruefully.

When she entered Gabriel's apartment she quickly turned on the fireplace, hoping to dispel the darkness that she felt creeping around her heart. But it didn't seem to help. Truly, all she wanted to do was go home and pull the bed covers over her head. But she knew better than to hide from reality now.

She didn't want to snoop, but she found herself in Gabriel's bedroom, kneeling on the floor of his closet. She was searching for his black-and-white photographs, wondering if Professor Singer was in one of them. She certainly had the correct hair color. But the pictures were gone. She examined every inch of his closet and looked around his bedroom and even under his bed. The photos had been removed.

Hanging on the wall in their stead were six pieces of art, some abstract, some renaissance, one by Tom Thomson, but all beautiful and strangely . . . peaceful. Gabriel had redecorated.

She stood in front of his dresser admiring the reproduction of Botticelli's *Primavera* that was displayed over it when her gaze alighted on an eight-by-ten picture in a dark frame. It was of a man and a woman dancing. The man was tall, attractive, elegant, and commanding, and he was looking down at the woman with an intense, almost heated gaze.

The woman was petite, blushing and staring at the buttons of his shirt. She was wearing a purple dress that was so vibrant it seemed to diminish all the other colors in the picture.

How did he get a photo of the two of us dancing at Lobby?

Rachel, she thought.

Julia quickly placed the picture back and exited the bedroom, being sure to leave everything exactly as she found it.

Chapter Twenty-one

While Julia waited at his apartment, Gabriel played the chameleon, blending into his environment. He was charming and gracious to his colleagues, but all the while, his insides churned and his mind raced. He had to force himself to eat and to decline libation upon libation. Gabriel was convinced that he would be returning to an empty apartment. Julianne was going to run.

It wasn't surprising—he knew it would happen eventually. He just hadn't thought it would be *this* secret that would separate them. He was unworthy of her for many reasons, reasons he'd hid like a coward. It wasn't a question of love, for Gabriel did not believe that she could ever love him. He was unlovable. Nonetheless, he'd hoped to be able to court her long enough for their affection and friendship to bind them together, even in the face of some of his darkness. Now it was too late.

When he finally arrived home, he was surprised to find her asleep on the sofa, her face a picture of perfect peace. He tried valiantly to be still, to resist the urge to touch, but he couldn't. He reached out and softly stroked her long, silken hair, murmuring sad Italian words.

He needed music. At that moment, he felt the need for melody and lyric to soothe his agony. But the only song he could think of that would match this moment was Gary Jules' cover of *Mad World*. And Gabriel didn't want to be listening to that song when Julianne left him.

Suddenly, her eyes fluttered open. She saw that Gabriel was no longer wearing his suit jacket and tie and had released the top three buttons of his shirt. He'd also removed his cufflinks and rolled up his sleeves.

He smiled but his expression was cautious. "I didn't mean to wake you."

"It's fine. I just dozed off." She yawned and sat up slowly.

"You can go back to sleep."

"I don't think that's a good idea."

"Did you eat something?"

She shook her head.

"Will you eat something now? I could make you an omelet."

"My stomach is in knots."

He was irritated but refused to argue, for he knew a much bigger argument was on the horizon. "I have a present for you."

"Gabriel, a present is the last thing I need right now."

"I disagree. But it can wait." He shifted uncomfortably on the sofa, never taking his eyes off of her. "You're wearing a scarf and sitting by a roaring fire, yet you're so pale. Are you cold?"

"No." Julia reached up to remove her pashmina, but Gabriel's long, slender fingers caught her hand.

"May I?"

She withdrew her hand and nodded warily.

Gabriel moved closer, and Julia shut her eyes as his scent washed over her. He gently unwound the scarf from her neck with both hands and placed it on the sofa between them. Then he reached out to trail the knuckles of one hand down the column of her throat.

"You are so lovely," he murmured. "No wonder all eyes were on you this evening."

She tensed at his words, and he pulled back, stifling a groan.

Her eyes found her feet, and she realized that she'd been so distracted she hadn't bothered to remove her boots. But he hadn't complained.

"I'm sorry for putting my boots on your couch. I'll take them off." She fingered one of the zippers, but Gabriel moved quickly to kneel on the carpet.

"What are you doing?" Her eyes widened in confusion.

"I've been admiring your boots. Very much." He lightly grazed her high heels with his hands.

"Rachel helped me choose them. She has great taste, but the heels are always too high."

He regarded her seductively. "Your heels could never be too high.

But let me free you." At the sound of his voice, husky and adoring, Julia's heart skipped a beat.

His hands hovered over her knees, where the tops of the zippers rested. "May I?"

She acquiesced and held her breath.

Reverently, he unzipped her boot and gently ran his fingers down her calf to her ankle, freeing her. He repeated this procedure on the other leg, placing the boots next to the sofa. Then he lifted her right foot and began to massage it lightly with both hands. Julia moaned in spite of herself and bit her lip sharply in embarrassment.

"It's all right to voice your pleasure, Julianne," he encouraged. "It reassures me that I don't repulse you completely."

"You don't repulse me. But I don't like seeing you on your knees," she whispered.

His pleased expression faded. "When a man kneels before a woman, it's a gesture of chivalry. When a woman kneels before a man, it's unseemly."

Julia moaned once again involuntarily. "How did you learn to do this?"

He gave her a puzzled look.

"How did you learn to massage feet?" she clarified, flushing more deeply.

He sighed. "A friend."

Probably a black-and-white photograph friend, thought Julia.

"Yes," said Gabriel, as if he'd anticipated her question. "I would like to extend my attention to the rest of your body, but I don't think a full massage would be possible for us, at least not now." His eyes darkened slightly as their eyes met.

He switched his attention to her other foot and lowered his eyes. "I already hunger for your body, Julianne. I'm not strong enough to touch you chastely, not if you were laid out before me wrapped only in a bed sheet."

They sat in silence for a few moments while Gabriel tended to Julia's feet. At length, he sat back on his heels, running light fingertips up and down her stockings.

"I'll drive you home, if you wish, and we can talk tomorrow. Or you

can stay here. You could sleep in my room, and I'll take the guestroom."
He searched her eyes uncertainly.

"I don't want to prolong this," she offered. "So I'd like to talk, if that's
all right."

"That's fine. Can I offer you something to drink?" Gabriel motioned
toward the kitchen. "I can open a bottle of wine. Or fix you a cocktail."
He gazed at her intensely. "Please let me do something for you."

A flame ignited in Julia's middle, flaring up and passing over her.
But she suppressed it. "Water, please. I need a clear head."

He stood up and walked to the kitchen. Julia heard him wash his
hands followed by the sounds of the refrigerator and freezer doors
opening and closing. He returned to her with a tall glass filled with Perrier, ice, and pieces of lime.

"Um, Gabriel, would you excuse me for a minute?"

"Take as long as you need. Come to the fire when you're ready." He
attempted a smile, but his face was too tense to make it genuine.

She disappeared with her drink, and Gabriel assumed she was using
this opportunity to steel herself for the next revelation from his miserable, damned existence. Or maybe she was going to lock herself in the
bathroom and demand to speak to him through the door. Not that he
would blame her.

Julia's mind was traveling at light speed. She didn't know what Gabriel was going to say. She didn't know how she would respond. It was
quite possible that she would learn things that would make it impossible for their relationship to continue, and the thought crushed her. For
no matter what he'd done or with whom, she loved him. The thought of
losing him again, after the joy of reconnecting, was agonizing.

Gabriel sat in his red velvet chair staring vacantly into the fireplace.
Dressed as he was and brooding, he looked very much like a character
out of one of the Brontës' novels. As Julia approached him, she silently
prayed to Charlotte that Gabriel would be one of her ilk and not of her
sister Emily's.

*Pardon me, Miss Charlotte, but Heathcliff terrifies me. Please don't let
Gabriel be a Heathcliff. (No offense to you, Miss Emily.) Please.*

From where Julia stood, he could not see her. She cleared her throat
to alert him of her presence.

He gestured to the fire. "Come warm yourself."

She made as if to sit on the carpet in front of the fire, but his hand shot out to stop her. He forced a smile.

"Please. Sit on my lap. Or the ottoman or the sofa."

He still doesn't like me on the floor, Julia thought. She hadn't objected to the idea of sitting at the hearth. But the mere idea more than offended him. Not willing to argue over such a trivial thing, she eschewed his lap for the ottoman and sat quietly, gazing at the blue and orange flames. He was no longer The Professor in her mind; he was Gabriel, her professor, her beloved.

Gabriel shifted in his chair, wondering why she wanted to be so far away from him. *Because she knows what you are now and she's afraid.*

"Why don't you like me on my knees?" she asked, breaking the silence.

"Perhaps in light of tonight's conversation, you can divine the reason. A reason multiplied and strengthened by what you told me at your apartment." He paused and looked at her pointedly. "You're far too humble as it is, and people take advantage of your sweet nature."

"Graduate students have to pay their dues. Everyone knows that."

"Being a student has nothing to do with it."

"You will always be the gifted professor, and I will always be your student," she remarked quietly.

"You forget that I met you long before you were a student and I was a professor. And you won't be a student forever. I shall sit in the front row when you deliver your first lecture. As for your prejudice against professors, *if you prick us, do we not bleed?*"

"And if you wrong us, shall we not revenge?" Julia countered.

Gabriel sat back in his chair and indulged himself in an appreciative smile. "See? Who is the teacher now, Professor Mitchell? I only claim the advantages of age and experience."

"Age doesn't necessarily make you wiser."

"Of course not. You're young, but you're industrious and bright and at the very beginning of what promises to be a long and brilliant career. Perhaps I haven't done enough to show my admiration for your mind."

She fell silent, pretending to be mesmerized by the dancing, licking flames.

He cleared his throat. "Ann didn't hurt me, Julianne. I hardly think of her, and when I do, it's with regret. She left no scars."

Julia turned her troubled eyes to look into his. They were a lively, earnest navy. "Not all scars mark the skin. Why did you choose her, of all people?"

He shrugged, turning away to peer at the fire. "Why do human beings do anything? Because they're searching for happiness. She promised raw, intense pleasure, and I needed the diversion."

"You let her hurt you because you were bored?" Julia felt instantly ill.

Gabriel's features hardened. "I don't expect you to understand. But at the time, I needed a distraction. It was either pain or alcohol, and I was not about to do anything that might get back to Richard and Grace. I tried . . . interacting with women, but my liaisons quickly lost their luster. Perpetually available but mindless orgasms can become tiresome, Julianne."

I'll remember that, she thought.

"The way Professor Singer was with you at the lecture . . . then at dinner . . . she doesn't behave like a woman scorned."

"She despises weakness. And she can't accept failure. It was a harsh blow to her reputation and her massive ego when she tried to control me and failed. She isn't about to advertise her failure."

"Did you care for her at all?"

"Hardly. She's a soulless, heartless succubus."

Julia looked back at the fire and pursed her lips.

"I was not about to jump into something with Ann without testing it. And we never got beyond the test. In other words, although we . . . interacted, I was not involved with her in the strict sense."

"You'll have to excuse me if I don't own the specific vocabulary that would allow me to understand what you're trying to say."

"I'm trying to explain this to you without tainting more of your innocence than is absolutely necessary. Do not require me to be explicit." His tone was suddenly cold.

"Do you still want what she offers?"

"No. It was a disaster."

"With someone else?"

"No."

"But what about the next time the darkness comes? What will you do?"

Gabriel stared at her. "I thought I'd made myself clear. You dispel the darkness, Beatrice." He cleared his throat. "Julianne."

"Tell me she isn't in one of your photographs."

"Absolutely not. Those pictures were of women I actually liked."

"Why were you thrown out of her house?"

He gritted his teeth. "I did something that in her world is absolutely unacceptable. And I won't lie and say that I didn't enjoy the look on her face when I gave her a taste of her own medicine. Even though I broke one of my most sacred rules in doing so."

Julia shuddered. "Then why is she still after you?"

"I represent her failure, her inability to control. And I possess certain skills."

She flushed uncomfortably.

"Ann was also interested in my pugilistic abilities. When she learned that I was a boxer and a member of Oxford's Fencing Club, she wouldn't leave me alone. We share those hobbies, unfortunately."

Julia fingered the scar that was hidden underneath her hair.

"I can't be with someone who hits, Gabriel. Not out of anger, not for pleasure, not for any reason."

"And you shouldn't. It is not in my nature to be violent with women, but rather, to be seductive. Ann was an exception. And if you knew the circumstances, I think you'd forgive me."

"I can't be with someone who wants to be hit, either. Violence frightens me, Gabriel. Please understand this."

"I do. I understand. I thought that what Ann offered would help me deal with my problems." He shook his head sadly. "Julianne, nothing was as painful as the moment in which I had to look you in the eye and admit my sordid entanglement with her. I wish for your sake I had no past. I wish I was as good as you."

Julia looked down at her hands, which were twisting in her lap. "The thought of someone hurting you . . . treating you like an animal . . ." Her voice began to tremble as her eyes slowly filled with tears. "I don't care if you had sex with her. I don't care if she didn't leave any marks. I can't bear the thought of someone hurting you, especially because you wanted them to."

Gabriel pressed his lips together but said nothing.

"The mere thought of someone hitting you makes me sick."

He clenched his jaw as he watched two lone tears slide down her cheeks.

"You should be with someone who will be kind to you." She wiped her face with the back of her hand. "Promise me you'll never go back to her. Or to someone like her."

Gabriel gazed at her sharply. "I promised that you wouldn't have to share me. I keep my promises."

She shook her head. "I meant—ever. After me. Promise."

He growled. "You say it as if it's a foregone conclusion that there will be an after."

She wiped away another tear. "Promise me you won't let anyone abuse you in order to punish yourself. No matter what happens."

He gritted his teeth.

"Promise me, Gabriel. I will never ask you for anything else, but promise me this."

His eyes narrowed, and he measured her carefully. Then, seemingly satisfied, he nodded. "I promise."

Julia's body relaxed, and she hung her head, physically and emotionally exhausted.

He'd been watching her closely, the alternating flush and paleness of her skin, the way she'd fidgeted and pulled at her dress. It hurt him more than he thought possible to see her so upset. And the sight of her tears . . .

The brown-eyed angel was weeping over the demon. The angel wept because she was grieved at the mere thought of someone hurting him.

Without a word, he pulled her onto his lap. He pressed her head gently against his chest, wrapping his arms around her. "No more weeping. I've seen enough tears from you to last a lifetime," he whispered, pressing his lips to her ear. "And I'm not worth a single one."

He sighed with regret. "I've done a very selfish thing in pursuing you, Julianne. You should be with someone your own age who is your equal in goodness. Not with some twisted Caliban like me."

"There are moments when you are my equal in innocence."

"When? Tell me."

"When you hold me in your arms. When you stroke my hair," she whispered. "When we're in bed."

His face took on a pained expression. "If you don't want me, all you have to do is say so, and I'll disappear from your life forever. I don't want you to be afraid of what might happen if you reject me. I promise I'll let you go, if that's what you want."

Julia was quiet, for she did not know what to say.

"I know that I am controlling and, as you put it, commanding." Gabriel's voice was low and strained. "But I would never do to you what she does. I won't harm you, Julianne. I could never harm you." He lightly trailed his fingertips up and down the exposed flesh of her arm, feeling the skin goose-pimple underneath his words as much as beneath his touch.

"I was more worried about what Ann did to you."

"No one has worried about me for some time."

"Your family does. And I did too, you know, even before I came to Toronto. I thought of you every day."

He pressed a gentle kiss to her lips, and Julia reciprocated softly.

"My past indiscretions notwithstanding, my tastes run to inflicting mad, passionate pleasure on my lovers and not pain, I assure you. Someday I'd like to show you that side of me. Slowly, of course."

Julia chewed at the inside of her mouth, trying to find the right words.

"I need to tell you something."

"Yes?"

"I am—not as innocent as you think I am."

"What's that supposed to be mean?" he snapped.

She raked her upper lip with her teeth nervously.

"Sorry. You took me by surprise." Gabriel rubbed at his eyes.

"I had a boyfriend."

He frowned. "I know that."

"We, um, did things."

His eyebrows shot up. "What kinds of things?" His question emerged before he could consider it, but he soon thought better of it. "Don't answer that. I don't want to know."

"I am not as innocent as I was when you first met me, which means that you have, um . . . an idealized and false perception of me."

He considered her admission for a moment. He wanted to know the specifics, but he was worried about what she might say. The thought of someone else, of *him*, coaxing pleasure out of her, or even touching her, infuriated him. He was far from certain that he could handle whatever confession she was burning to make.

"You were my first kiss. The first to hold my hand," she admitted.

"I'm glad." He took her hand in his and pressed his lips against it. "I wish I had been all your firsts."

"He didn't take them all." Julia closed her mouth quickly. She hadn't meant to say that.

Her use of the word *take* made Gabriel think murderous thoughts. If he ever found himself in the same room as *him* he would rip his throat out with his bare hands.

"When you didn't come back, I started dating someone. In Philadelphia. And things, uh, happened."

"Did you want those things to happen?"

Julia squirmed. "He was my boyfriend. He was—impatient sometimes."

"That's what I thought. He was a manipulative bastard who seduced you."

"I have a free will. I didn't have to give in."

Gabriel was thoughtful for a moment. *Jealousy—the idea of her hands and her lips wrapped around someone else—or someone else's mouth on her. Her body . . .* "I have no right to ask this, but I will. Did you love him?"

"No."

He tried to hide his secret relief at her answer by lifting her chin. "Don't ever touch me or let me touch you unless you truly want me. That's a promise I'd like to exact from you right now."

She blinked at him in surprise.

"I know what I can be like. So far I've kept my passions in check. But I've been forward with you, I know, and on more than one occasion I've made you uncomfortable. It would trouble me to discover that things progressed between us solely because you felt coerced."

"I promise, Gabriel."

He nodded at her and pressed his lips to her forehead. "Julianne, why won't you let me call you Beatrice?"

"It made me sad that you never wanted to know my name."

He gazed at her intensely. "I want more than that. I want to know the real you."

She smiled.

"So do you still want me? Or would you rather I let you go?" He tried to keep his voice steady.

"Of course I still want you."

He kissed her softly before placing her on her feet and leading her to the kitchen. When she was comfortably seated on one of the bar stools, he walked over to the counter and picked up a large, silver dome. He grinned at her, his eyes glinting mischievously as he placed the plate in front of her.

"Homemade apple pie," Gabriel announced, removing the dome with a flourish.

"Pie?"

"You said no one ever baked a pie for you before. Now someone has."

Julia stared at the dessert incredulously. "You made this?"

"Not exactly. My housekeeper did. Are you pleased?"

"You had someone bake a pie for me?"

"Well, I had hoped you'd share it. But if you insist on eating the entire thing by yourself . . ." He chuckled.

Julia covered her mouth with her hand and closed her eyes.

"Julianne?"

When she didn't respond he started speaking very quickly. "You said you liked pie. When you told me about growing up in St. Louis, you said no one had ever baked you a pie. I thought . . ." He stopped, suddenly very unsure of himself.

Her shoulders shook as she silently cried.

"Julia? What's wrong?" His voice was frantic as he watched her cry again. He walked around the counter and enveloped her shaking figure in his arms. "What did I do?"

"I'm sorry." She found her voice.

"Sweetheart, don't be sorry. Just tell me what I did so I can fix it."

"You didn't do anything wrong." She wiped her tears. "No one has ever done something like this for me before." She gave him a half-smile. "I didn't know you had a present waiting here for me."

"I didn't mean to upset you. I was trying to make you happy."

"They're happy tears. Sort of." Julia giggled half-heartedly.

He hugged her one more time and released her, smoothing her hair back behind her shoulders. "I think someone needs dessert."

Gabriel cut a large serving of pie and held a fork in front of her. "I'd like to feed you. But I'll understand if you'd rather I didn't."

Julia opened her mouth immediately, and Gabriel fed her a small piece.

"Mmmmmm. It's really good," she said with her mouth full and grinned as she brushed the crumbs from her lips.

"I'm glad."

"I didn't know you had a housekeeper."

"She's only here twice a week."

"And she cooks?"

"Sometimes. I go through stages. Obsessions, really, but you knew that already." He tapped her nose with his finger. "This was her grand-mother's recipe. I won't tell you what she put in the crust to make it flaky." He winked at her.

"What about you? No pie?" she asked.

"I'd rather watch you enjoy yourself. But this isn't a proper dinner. I wish you'd let me cook for you."

"My dad always eats a slice of cheese with his apple pie. I'd have some cheese if you have it."

Gabriel appeared puzzled by her request but immediately rum-maged in the refrigerator and soon presented her with a substantial piece of aged Vermont white cheddar.

"Perfect," she murmured.

After she'd finished her pie, she sat quietly, wondering if she should go home. She really didn't want to, but perhaps after so many tears and so much drama he wouldn't want her to stay.

"You didn't respond to my note," he said after a protracted silence. "The note I sent with the gardenias."

"I wrote an e-mail."

"But you left something out."

Julia paused. "I didn't know what to say about the taming part."

"You told me the dialogue with the fox was your favorite. I thought it would be clear."

"I know what the fox meant. But you . . ." She shook her head.

"Then I'll tell you. I don't expect you to trust me, but I would like to earn your trust. Maybe once you trust me with your mind, you'll begin to trust me with your body. That's the sort of taming I have in mind. I want to pay close attention to you . . . *to your wants, needs, and desires* . . . and take my time attending to them."

"How will you tame me?"

"By showing you with my actions that I am worthy of trust. And by doing this."

Gabriel stood in front of her and clasped her face in his hands, bringing his mouth inches from hers. She closed her eyes and held her breath, waiting for their lips to meet.

But they didn't.

Warm air from between Gabriel's curled and parted lips floated across her mouth. Her tongue peeked out, slowly wetting her lower lip in anticipation. The feel of his breath across the wetness caused a shiver to shoot down her spine.

"You're trembling," he whispered, pushing more warm breath across her mouth.

Julia felt herself blush against his hands, the warmth traveling across her face and down her neck.

"I can feel you flushing, your skin blossoming in heat and color."

He stroked her eyebrows, and she opened her eyes, staring into large, dark-blue pools.

"Your pupils are dilated." He smiled against her mouth, barely grazing her lips. "And I can hear your breathing speed. You know what that means."

Julia searched his eyes. *"He* said I was frigid." She sounded ashamed. "Cold like snow. It made him angry."

"Only a boy who knew nothing about women could be so blind and so ridiculous. Never think that about yourself, Julianne. I know for a fact that it's far from true." His lips curved into a seductive smile. "I can tell when you're aroused, like now. I can see it in your eyes. I can feel it on your skin. I can—sense it."

Gabriel traced a single finger across her eyebrows to relax them. "Please don't be embarrassed. I'm not. It's tantalizing and very erotic."

She closed her eyes and inhaled his scent—Aramis and peppermint and blessed Gabriel.

He chuckled. "I think you're telling me that you enjoy my cologne." He leaned down so that her nose was able to skim his neck. The scent of Aramis was stronger there.

"What are you doing?"

"I'm building desire, Julianne. Now tell me what you want. You're flushed, your heart is beating rapidly, and I can hear your breathing accelerate. *What do you desire?*" He cupped her face in his hands again and brought his mouth close to hers. Close, but still not touching.

"I want to kiss," she breathed.

He smiled. "I want to kiss too."

She waited. And still he would not move.

"Julianne," he blew across her lips.

She opened her eyes.

"Take what you want."

She inhaled sharply.

"If you don't initiate on occasion, I'll conclude that you don't want me. That I'm being demanding. After a night like tonight, the only person doing the demanding should be you." Gabriel's eyes were wide and dark, and they pierced her.

She didn't need another invitation. Surprising both of them, she wrapped her arms around his neck and tugged him forward. When their lips met, his hands trailed down to her lower back, and he imagined caressing her naked flesh. She teased his bottom lip and drew it into her mouth, copying an act he'd performed with her before. She was less skilled, but he was no less pleased.

Her unhurried ardor enticed him, and within a moment, he felt his skin heat and his heart race. For as his tongue expertly explored her mouth, he wished nothing more than to part her modest knees with one of his own and press himself against her. And sweep her into his bedroom to *fraternize* . . .

He pulled away, placing his hands on her bare forearms. "I have to stop." He leaned his forehead against hers and exhaled deeply.

"I'm sorry."

He pressed his lips to her forehead. "Never apologize for acting on your desires. You're beautiful and sensual. And very, very arousing. I can enjoy you without becoming more intimate, but I can't kiss you again. Not right now."

They stood frozen, holding each other for several minutes, until Gabriel opened his eyes and stroked her cheek.

"Whatever you want, Julianne. Tonight, I'm yours. Do you want me to take you home? Do you want to stay?"

She nuzzled his jaw with her nose. "I'd like to stay."

"Then I think it's time for bed." He extended his hand and helped her to her feet.

"Doesn't it seem strange to you? Sharing a bed with me?"

"I want you in my arms and in my bed every night."

Julia was quiet for a moment as she picked up her messenger bag.

"Does that bother you?" He frowned.

"No. Maybe it should."

"I've missed you this week."

"I missed you too."

"I sleep better when you're in my arms." He smiled at her warmly. "But it's your choice where you sleep tonight."

"I'd like to share your bed," said Julia shyly. "If you'd let me."

"I'd never deny you that." He led her down the hallway to his bedroom.

She sat on the bed, and he picked up the framed photograph from on top of the dresser.

"You have a picture of me under your pillow. I thought I should return the favor." Gabriel smirked as he handed her the photograph.

Julia racked her brain to try to remember when he could have found the old photo she had of him.

"How did you get this?"

"I should be asking you where you obtained a picture of me from my days on Princeton's rowing team." Gabriel untucked and unbuttoned his dress shirt, exposing the tight T-shirt that clung to his chest.

Julia grew embarrassed and looked away, silently ruing the day men decided to wear undershirts. Watching him undress was even sexier than watching him in a purple towel that was far too small.

"Um, Rachel had it on her bulletin board. And the first time I saw it, I took it."

He leaned down to lift her face up so that he could examine her expression. "You took it? You mean, you stole it."

"I know I shouldn't have. But you had this wonderful smile. I was seventeen and stupid, Gabriel."

"Stupid or smitten?"

Julia rested her eyes on the floor. "I think you know."

"Rachel took pictures with her phone while she was visiting. This one is my favorite, which is why I framed it." He examined her closely. "Don't you like it?"

She seemed flustered. "You look nice."

He took the photo out of her hand and carefully placed it on top of the dresser. "What are you thinking? Tell me."

"The way you looked at me while we were dancing . . . I don't understand."

"You're a beautiful woman. Why wouldn't I look at you?"

"It's the way you looked at me."

"I look at you like that all the time." He kissed her softly. "I'm looking at you like that right now." He brushed her hair back from her face. "I'll be back in a few minutes."

After changing into what would serve as her pajamas, she stood in the doorway of the bathroom, backlit in white light.

"Stop," said Gabriel. He had returned to the room during her absence and was lying in bed, staring at her.

Julia looked down at her clothes and fidgeted. She hadn't known what to wear. Most of her pajamas were too juvenile to wear in front of him, and she didn't own any lingerie for sleeping. Not that she would have been brave enough to wear lingerie to bed with him. So at this moment, she was clad in a dark blue T-shirt, which was large enough to hide her chest, and a pair of athletic shorts that had Saint Joseph's University's logo on the front.

"You're exquisite."

She made a face and reached over to switch off the light.

"Wait. Standing there, in the light, you look like an angel."

She nodded to indicate that she'd heard him before silently joining him.

Gabriel immediately pulled her into a warm embrace, and as he did so, she realized he was wearing a T-shirt and shorts too.

They were quite a pair. But now their naked legs could tangle together blissfully under the sheets. He kissed her tenderly and leaned back on the pillow, sighing in pleasure as she rested her head on his chest, wrapping her arm around his waist.

"I'm sorry you're lonely, Julianne."

She appeared puzzled by his *non sequitur*.

"Earlier this week when we were talking on the phone, you mentioned that you feel isolated, that you don't have any friends."

She winced in remembrance.

"What if I were to buy you a kitten or a rabbit? Someone to keep you company at your apartment."

"Gabriel, I appreciate the thought, but you can't just throw money at my problems."

"I know that. But I can spend money to try to make you smile." He kissed her again.

"Kindness is worth more than all the money in the world."

"You shall have that. And much, much more."

"That's all I want."

"Stay for the weekend. Here. With me."

She hesitated only for an instant. "Okay," she whispered.

He seemed relieved. "How about a fish? They're the new companion animal."

She laughed. "I don't think so. I can barely look after myself, let alone another poor creature."

He lifted her chin so that they could see one another. "Then let me look after you," he whispered, eyes intense and unblinking.

"You could have any woman you want, Gabriel."

He furrowed his eyebrows. "I only want you."

She rested her head against his chest and smiled.

"Being without you, Julianne, is like enduring an endless night without stars."

Chapter Twenty-two

Two almost lovers were tangled around each other, their naked legs entwined in a large bed under an ice-blue silk duvet and white Frette sheets. The woman mumbled in her sleep, moving fitfully, while the man remained still, enjoying the pleasure of her company.

He could have lost her. Lying next to her, he was conscious of the fact that their evening could have ended very differently. She didn't have to forgive him. She didn't have to accept him. But she did. Perhaps he could dare to hope . . .

"Gabriel?"

He didn't answer, for he thought she was still asleep. It was three o'clock in the morning, and the bedroom was shrouded in darkness, a darkness made visible by the lights of the city's skyline diffused through the blinds.

She rolled over so that she could see his face. "Gabriel?" she whispered. "Are you awake?"

"Yes. It's all right, darling, go back to sleep." He kissed her lightly and stroked her hair.

She propped herself up on one elbow. "I'm wide awake now."

"So am I."

"Can I—talk to you?"

He quickly mimicked her position. "Of course. Is something wrong?"

"Are you happier now than you were before?"

Gabriel looked at her for a moment and gently tapped her nose with his finger. "Why the deep question in the middle of the night?"

"You said you weren't happy last year. I was wondering if you are happy now."

"Happiness is something I know precious little about. You?"

Julia twisted the edge of the bed sheet in her hand. "I try to be happy. I try to focus on the little things and find pleasure in them. Your pie made me happy."

"If I'd known the pie would make you happy, I would have given it to you sooner."

"Why aren't you happy now?"

"I bartered my birthright for a bowl of pottage."

"You're quoting scripture?" Julia was incredulous.

Gabriel bristled. "I'm not a pagan, Julianne. I was brought up Episcopalian. Richard and Grace were very devout. Didn't you know that?"

She nodded. She'd forgotten.

His face took on a remarkably serious expression. "I still believe, even though I don't live like it. I know that makes me a hypocrite."

"All believers are hypocrites because none of us live up to our beliefs. I believe too, but I'm not very good. I only go to Mass when I'm sad, or at Christmas and Easter." She reached her hand out to find his and clasped him tightly. "If you still believe, you must have hope. You must believe that happiness is possible for you too."

He released her hand and rolled onto his back, gazing up at the ceiling. "I lost my soul, Julianne."

"What do you mean?"

"You're looking at one of those precious few who have committed *the sin unto death*."

"How?"

Gabriel sighed. "My name is the bitterest irony. I'm closer to a devil than an angel, and I'm beyond redemption because I've done unforgivable things."

"You mean—with Professor Singer?"

He laughed bitterly. "Would that those were my only sins. But no, Julianne, I've done worse. Please just accept what I say."

She inched closer. Her delicate features creased with worry, and her eyebrows knitted together. She took her time considering the words he had not said, while he trailed repentant fingers up and down her arm.

"I know that keeping secrets from you is hurtful. I know that I won't be able to keep them from you forever. Please, just give me a little time."

He exhaled slowly and lowered his voice. "I promise I won't make love to you without telling you who I am first."

"It's a bit soon to discuss that, don't you think?"

He frowned and searched her eyes. "Is it?"

"Gabriel, we're just getting to know one another. And there have already been a few surprises."

He winced. "You need to know my intentions. I don't intend to seduce you, then leave. I don't intend to save some of my secrets until after I make you wholly mine. I'm trying to be good."

Gabriel's vow was made in good faith. He wanted her, he wanted all of her, but he realized while he lay awake that night that he couldn't take her virginity before he'd revealed his true self. Although her ultimate reaction to Ann had taught him to hope, he was still afraid that his revelations would drive her away. She could do better. Nevertheless, the thought of Julianne with someone else made his heart stutter.

"Do you have a conscience?"

"What kind of question is that?" he growled.

"Do you believe that there's a difference between right and wrong?"

"Of course!"

"Do you know the difference?"

Gabriel scrubbed at his face with both hands and kept them there. "Julianne, I am not a sociopath. Knowing isn't the problem—doing is the problem."

"Then you haven't lost your soul. Only a creature with a soul can tell the difference between right and wrong. Yes, you've made mistakes, but you feel guilt. You feel remorse. And if you still have your soul, you haven't lost your chance at redemption."

Gabriel smiled sadly and kissed her. "You sound like Grace."

"Grace was very wise."

"And so are you, Miss Mitchell. Apparently," he gently mocked her.

"Actually, I am. With a little bit of help from Aquinas, Professor."

He reached over and pulled up her T-shirt slightly so that he could softly tickle her naked flesh.

"Ah! Gabriel! Stop it!" She giggled and writhed, trying to get away from him.

He continued for a moment, just to give himself the pleasure of hearing her laughter ring out in the darkened space. Then he let her go. "Thank you, Julianne." He caressed her cheek. "You almost make me believe it."

She placed her arm around his waist, snuggling into his side and inhaling his scent gleefully. "You always smell good."

"You can thank Rachel and Grace. They started buying me Aramis a long time ago. I kept on buying it out of habit." He grinned. "Do you think I should try something else?"

"Not if Grace bought it for you."

Gabriel's smile faded, but he pressed a kiss to her forehead nonetheless. "I suppose it's a good thing she didn't buy Brut."

Julia laughed.

They lay very still for a few minutes, before she whispered close to his ear. "There is something I'd like to tell you."

Gabriel pursed his lips slightly and nodded.

In spite of the dark, she looked away shyly. "You could have had me in the orchard. I would have let you."

He traced her cheek with a single fingertip. "I know."

"You know?"

"I am practiced at reading a woman's body, Julianne. That night you were very *receptive*."

She was surprised. "So you knew then that I—?"

"Yes."

"But you didn't . . ."

"No."

"Will you tell me why?"

He paused thoughtfully. "I didn't think it was right. And I was so happy to have found you and to have you in my arms . . . it was enough. It was everything."

Julia leaned over and pressed her lips to his neck. "It was perfect."

"When we go home for Thanksgiving, I'd like to take you back to the orchard. Will you come with me?"

"Of course." She pressed a kiss just shy of his tattoo, for she knew he flinched whenever she touched him there.

"Kiss me," he whispered.

She complied, pressing parted lips and open mouth to his, tasting him for as long as he would have her. Until he sighed and moved away. She was saddened by the sudden loss of contact, and an old worry reared its head.

Gabriel felt her tense. "Don't confuse my restraint with a lack of desire, Julianne. I burn for you." He moved her gently so that she was on her side and spooned behind her, burying his face in her hair. "I'm glad you're here," he whispered.

Julia wanted to tell him that she slept better with him than without him. She wanted to tell him that she would like to sleep with him every night and that she earnestly desired him.

But she didn't.

❀ ❀

When she awoke the next morning, she was alone. She glanced at the old-fashioned clock Gabriel kept on his nightstand and was stunned to discover that it was already noon. She'd slept far too long.

He'd left her a continental breakfast and a note that was propped up against a wineglass filled with orange juice. Julia began eating the *pain au chocolat* as she read his note:

FROM THE DESK OF PROFESSOR GABRIEL O. EMERSON

> *Darling,*
> *You were sound asleep, so I didn't want to wake you.*
> *I've gone to run some errands.*
> *Call me when you wake up.*
> *I was very grateful to have you in my arms all night*
> *and for your words . . .*
> *If I have a soul, it's yours,*
> *Gabriel*

Julia smiled widely and took her time eating her breakfast. Gabriel sounded happy, and that made her happy too. She freshened herself up in the washroom and was about to exit the bedroom when she tripped over something. Righting herself with a curse, she saw that the offending speed bump was in reality three white shopping bags with the words

Holt Renfrew emblazoned on them. She pushed them aside almost wrathfully, and walked to the kitchen.

She was surprised to find Gabriel sitting at the breakfast bar, drinking coffee and reading a newspaper. He was wearing a pale blue button-down shirt that highlighted the blueness of his eyes, and black casual pants. He wore his glasses, and he looked handsome, as always. Julia felt underdressed in her T-shirt and shorts.

"Why, hello there." Gabriel folded his paper and put his cup down. He opened his arms wide, beckoning her.

She stepped in between his parted knees, and he embraced her warmly.

"How did you sleep?" he whispered in her hair.

"Really well."

He kissed her softly. "You must have been tired. How do you feel?" He looked at her with concern.

"I'm fine."

"I can make you lunch, if you wish."

"Have you eaten?"

"Something small with my first coffee. I was waiting to have lunch with you."

He kissed her again, more deeply this time. Julia shyly slid her arms up his back and into his hair. Gabriel reacted by nibbling on her lower lip and pulling away with a smirk.

"Part of me was worried you wouldn't be here when I woke up."

"I'm not going anywhere, Gabriel. My feet are still aching from walking everywhere in those heels yesterday. I don't think I could make it home even if I wanted to."

"I can fix that. With a little help from a hot bath." He moved his eyebrows suggestively.

Julia flushed and changed the subject. "How long did you want me to stay?"

"Forever."

"Gabriel, be serious." She shook her head, smiling.

"Till Monday morning."

"I only have clothes for today. I'll have to go home and pick up a few things."

He smiled at her indulgently. "I'll take you home, if you insist. Or I'll lend you the Range Rover. But before you go, there are a couple of things waiting for you in the bedroom. Perhaps a trip home will be unnecessary."

"What things?"

He waved his hands. "Things someone might need if they were staying at a friend's house."

"And where did they come from?"

"The store where Rachel bought your messenger bag."

"So they were expensive." Julia frowned and crossed her arms in front of her chest.

"You are my guest. The rules of hospitality require that I satisfy *all* your needs." He sounded husky, his tongue peeking out to swipe across his lower lip.

Through a great force of effort, Julia ignored his mouth. "It feels . . . illicit if you are buying me clothes."

"What are you talking about?" Now he sounded cross.

"Like I'm some—"

"Stop it." He released her immediately, and his eyes darkened.

She stared back at him, bracing for the deluge to come.

"Julianne, why do you have this aversion to generosity?"

"I don't."

"Yes, you do. Do you think I'm trying to bribe you into having sex with me?"

Her face reddened. "Of course not."

"Do you think I'm buying you things because I expect you to pay for them in sexual trade?"

"No."

"Then what's the problem?"

"I don't want to owe you."

"Owe me? So now I'm a medieval moneylender who charges interest, and if you don't pay on time, I'll take a pound of your flesh."

"I don't think that," she whispered.

"Then what do you think?"

"I think that I want to stand on my own two feet. You're a professor, and I'm a student and—"

"We discussed that last night. A present from a friend does nothing to inhibit your free will or your personal autonomy," he fumed. "I didn't want you to have to go home. Our time together is short enough as it is. I walked across the street to the store and had my personal shopper assist me in picking out a few things. I was trying to be nice. But since you don't want them, I'll see that they are returned."

He stood up and deposited his coffee cup in the kitchen. Then he walked right past her without saying a word and disappeared into his study.

That could have gone better, thought Julia.

She nibbled at her nails with her teeth, not knowing what to do. On the one hand, she wanted to be independent and not play the part of the poor helpless bird with the broken wing. On the other hand, she had a kind heart and did not like to cause other creatures pain. She had seen Gabriel's eyes. Behind his sudden show of temper, he was hurt. Deeply.

I didn't mean to hurt him . . .

Gabriel was so forceful, so strong, she hadn't realized that he could be so sensitive. And over something that seemed as inconsequential as a few gifts. Perhaps she was the only one who ever saw his sensitivity. That made the fact that she'd hurt him all the more painful.

She poured herself a glass of water and drank it slowly, trying to give him some space and herself a few minutes to think. As she approached his study, the telephone rang. She stuck her head through the doorway and peered over at him.

Gabriel was sitting behind his desk, shuffling papers while he spoke on the phone. He glanced over at her, pointed at the telephone, and mouthed the name *Richard*.

She nodded and walked over to his desk, picked up a pen that did not look expensive, and wrote on a piece of paper: *Forgive me*. She showed him the paper and his eyes met hers. He nodded stiffly.

I'm going to take a shower. Can we talk afterward?

He read her note and nodded again.

Thank you for being so thoughtful. I'm sorry.

Now Gabriel reached out his hand to grasp Julia's wrist. He pressed his lips to the center of her palm before releasing her with a squeeze.

She returned to the bedroom, closing the door behind her. Immediately, she placed the shopping bags on the bed and reluctantly began to unpack them.

In the first bag, she found women's clothes, all in her size. Gabriel had purchased a classic black pencil skirt, black flat-front Theory pants, a white cotton dress shirt with a shirttail and French cuffs, and a Santorini blue silk blouse. A pair of argyle patterned stockings, trouser socks, and black pointed-toe ankle boots completed the ensemble. It was like a small, essential collection from a single designer. Not to be ungrateful, but she would have been happy with a pair of jeans, a long-sleeved T-shirt, and sneakers.

In the second bag she was shocked to find lingerie. Gabriel had purchased an elegant and obviously expensive purple silk bathrobe and matching nightgown, which was ankle length and had a ruffled V-neckline. Julia was simultaneously surprised and pleased at the modesty and sophistication of the gown, for truly it was an item that she would feel comfortable wearing to bed with him even at this stage in their relationship. At the bottom of the bag she found a pair of purple satin mules with kitten heels. Julia surmised that they were a health hazard masquerading as sexy bedroom slippers.

Clearly, Gabriel has a thing for heels . . . in all kinds of women's footwear.

The third and final bag contained underwear. Julia's cheeks flushed red as she unwrapped three lace demi-bras, each with matching panties, all by a French designer. One set was champagne-colored, one was ice blue, and the other was pale pink. The panties were all boy shorts made of lace. Julia blushed even more deeply when she imagined Gabriel combing through racks of racy and expensive underwear, settling on items that were attractive and elegant, purchasing exactly the right sizes.

Oh gods of all really generous (boyfriends? friends?), thank you for steering him away from the really provocative items . . . for now.

She was overwhelmed. She was slightly embarrassed. But everything was so beautiful, so delicate, so perfect. *He might not love me, but he cares about making me happy,* she thought.

Clutching the champagne-colored underwear, white shirt, and black pants, she entered Gabriel's washroom and took a shower. Not only was her lavender poof waiting for her, but miraculously her own brand of shampoo, conditioner, and body wash were also present. Gabriel, in his own obsessive way, had thought of everything.

She was proudly wearing her new robe and towel drying her hair when she heard a knock at the door.

"Come in."

Gabriel peeked his head around the door. "Are you sure?" He eyed her wet hair, and then his eyes wandered down her flowing purple robe to her bare feet and returned to rest on the naked flesh at her neck.

"I'm decent. It's all right."

Gabriel strode toward her, his eyes dark and hungry. "*You* may be decent, but I'm not."

Julia smiled at him appreciatively, and he smiled in return, his hunger checked somewhat.

He leaned against the countertop of the vanity and placed his hands in his pockets. "I'm sorry."

"Me too."

"I overreacted."

"So did I."

"Let's make up."

"Please," she said.

"That was easy." Gabriel chuckled and took the towel out of her hands, tossing it aside. He pulled her into his arms and hugged her tightly. "Do you like your robe?" He fingered the silk hesitantly.

"It's beautiful."

"I'll send the rest back."

"No. I like everything. And I like them even more because you picked them. Thank you."

Gabriel's kisses could be light and sweet, like the kisses given by a boy to his first love. But not at this moment. Now he pressed his lips to hers until her lips parted and gave her a long, heated kiss before retreating. He ran the back of his hand up and down the curve of her cheek.

"I would have chosen jeans, but Hilary, my personal shopper, persuaded me that it's very difficult to buy jeans for another person. If you'd rather wear something more casual, I'll take you to buy something else."

"I don't need another pair of jeans."

"You should know that I chose everything except the underwear. Hilary picked them." He saw surprise on her face and hastened to explain. "I didn't want to embarrass you."

"Too late," she mumbled, somewhat disappointed at his revelation.

"Julianne, I need to explain something." His eyes grew serious, and she felt a chill of some kind travel across the surface of his skin. He shifted his weight once or twice as he seemed to search for the right words.

"My father was a married man with a family when he became involved with my mother. He seduced her, used her like a whore, and abandoned her. It grieves me that you could think I'm treating you the same way. Of course, given my track record, your reaction is not surprising but—"

"Gabriel, I don't think that. It's just that I don't like feeling as if I need to be looked after."

He stared at her closely. "I want to look after you but not because you need it. Of course you can look after yourself. You've been doing a damn good job of it since you were a little girl. But you don't have to be alone anymore. You have me now.

"I want to spoil you and make extravagant gestures because I care for you." He moved uncomfortably. "I can't say everything I feel. All I can do is show you. So when you won't let me . . ." He shrugged, a pained look on his face.

"I never thought of it like that," she said quietly.

"Every time I do something for you, I'm trying to demonstrate the words I cannot say." He traced his thumbs across the curve of her cheekbones. "Don't deprive me of this. Please."

Julia answered him by raising herself up on tiptoe and pressing herself tightly against his chest, wrapping her arms around his neck and plundering his mouth with her own. It was all hunger and promise and giving and need.

Gabriel gave to her, the tension of his jaw fully palpable as he concentrated his entire being on this one, perfect mouth. When they broke apart, they were both panting.

He rested his chin on her shoulder. "Thank you," he whispered.

"It's hard for me to depend on someone else."

"I know."

"It would be easier if you included me in your plans, rather than making decisions for me. I'd feel more like your—partner. Not that that's what we are." Her cheeks pinked up.

He kissed her again. "I want us to be partners, Julianne. What you ask for is fair. I just get carried away sometimes, especially with you."

She nodded against his chest, and when he cleared his throat, she pulled back so that she could see his eyes.

"About a year before he died, my father had an attack of conscience and added me to his will. He must have thought that by giving me the same share in his estate as his legitimate children, he could expiate his sins. You're looking at a living, breathing indulgence."

"I'm so sorry, Gabriel."

"I didn't want the money. But because of the investments he left me, I have more money now than I had when he died. No matter how fast I spend it, I will never be rid of it. I will never be rid of him. So you mustn't think about how much things cost. The cost is inconsequential."

"Why did you accept the inheritance?"

He released her so that he could rub his eyes behind his glasses. "Richard and Grace mortgaged their house to pay for my mistakes. I owed money for drugs, which meant that I was in danger, and there were other things . . ."

"I didn't know."

"Your father knew."

"Dad? How?"

"Richard was determined to save me. When I confessed how much trouble I was in, he decided to go to all of the people I owed money to and pay them off. Fortunately, he called your father first."

"Why would he do that?"

"Because your father knew a private investigator who had connections in Boston."

Julia's eyes widened in recognition. "My uncle Jack."

Gabriel frowned. "I didn't know he was your uncle. Richard was so naïve. He didn't realize that I owed money to some very shady characters who could have taken the money and killed him. Tom arranged for your uncle and some of his friends to pay my debts, safely, with Richard's money. When I got out of rehab, I called my father's lawyer in New York and said I'd take my inheritance. I paid off the mortgage, but I never lost the shame. Richard could have been killed because of me."

Julia pressed her cheek to his chest. "You are his son. Of course he wanted to save you. He loves you."

"The prodigal son," Gabriel muttered.

He slid his hands to her hips and changed the subject. "I want you to feel comfortable here. I emptied one of my dresser drawers and made room in the closet for your clothes. I'd like you to leave some things with me so you can come and go as you please. And I'll give you my spare key."

"You want me to leave my clothes here?"

"Well, I'd rather you left yourself here, but I'll settle for your clothes," he grumbled, half-smiling.

Julia reached up to plant a penitent kiss on his pouting lips. "I'll leave some of your gifts here and the next time I'm over, they'll be waiting for me."

He smiled, and his smile morphed into a smirk. "Since we're talking about leaving things here, perhaps you'll leave some pictures."

"You want to take my picture . . . like this?"

"Why not? You're beautiful, Julianne."

Her skin flamed."I don't think I'm ready to have you take erotic pictures of me."

His eyebrows furrowed. "I was thinking more along the lines of some black-and-white photos of your profile, your neck, your face . . ." He began tracing curved patterns on her back, a gentle gesture designed to reassure her of his affection.

"Why?"

"Because I would like to be able to look at you when you aren't here. My apartment is very empty without you."

She pursed her lips thoughtfully.

"Does that trouble you?" He caressed her jaw line slowly.

"No. You can take my picture. But I'd prefer to be fully dressed."

"I don't think my heart could take the sight of you undressed."

She smiled at him, and he laughed.

"Can I ask you something, Gabriel?"

"Of course."

"When you go home for Thanksgiving, will you stay at Richard's or at a hotel?"

"I'll stay at the house with everyone else. Why?"

"Rachel said that you used to stay in a hotel whenever you visited."

"That's right."

"Why?"

He shrugged. "Because I was the black sheep of the family and Scott never let me forget it. It was a relief to have the option of leaving if things became uncomfortable."

"Did you ever bring a girl home?"

"Never."

"Did you ever want to bring someone home?"

"Not before you." He leaned forward to kiss her again. "And if I had my way, you'd be the first girl to share my bed in my parents' house. Unfortunately, I don't think that's going to happen unless I sneak you in after dark."

Julia giggled slightly but was secretly very, very pleased.

"Richard reminded me that I need to book our airline tickets. Why don't you let me make the arrangements and we can work out the money later?"

"I could book my own ticket."

"Of course you could. But I want us to be seated together. We'll have to leave for the airport after my seminar, which means we'll have to take the last flight out of Toronto, around nine o'clock."

"That's late."

"I was going to reserve a hotel room in Philadelphia for Wednesday night, since we'll be arriving close to eleven. Unless you want to drive to Selinsgrove right away."

Julia shook her head. "Why don't we just fly to Harrisburg?"

"The last flight to Harrisburg leaves in the middle of my seminar. Of course, we could leave the day after, if you'd prefer. Then we wouldn't have to stay at a hotel." Gabriel's eyes fixated on hers, measuring her.

"I don't want to lose another day. And it would be nice to stay at a hotel with you." She smiled.

"Good. I'll make the reservations and rent a car."

"What about Rachel and Aaron? Shouldn't we drive with them?"

"They're driving up Wednesday after work. Rachel instructed me that it was my responsibility to see that you arrived home safely. She expects me to be your chauffeur and your bell boy." He winked at her and grinned.

"She knows, doesn't she?"

"Rachel thinks she knows everything." His grin tightened. "Don't worry about it. I'll handle her."

"It isn't Rachel I'm worried about."

"You don't need to worry about anything. We're just two family friends who met in a city far from home. It will be harder on me than it will be on you."

"Why is that?"

"Because I will be in the same room with you without being able to touch you."

She looked down at her bare feet and smiled shyly.

Gabriel took her hand in his and began to stroke it. "When is your birthday?"

"I don't celebrate it."

"Why not?"

"I just don't." Now her voice was defensive.

"Well, I'd like to celebrate it with you. Don't deprive me, Julianne." Gabriel's blue eyes communicated more frustration than annoyance.

Julia thought back to their argument about the clothes and decided that she didn't want to have another fight with him so soon.

"It was September first. You missed it."

"No, I haven't." He wrapped his arms around her and rubbed his cheek against hers.

"Are you free next Saturday? We can celebrate it then."

"What will we be doing?"

"I'll need to make some arrangements, but we'll be going out."

"I don't think it's a good idea for us to go out together—in public."

He frowned. "Let me worry about that. Now, are you accepting my invitation or not?" He slid his hand down to one of the ticklish spots on her side.

"I am accepting with gratitude. Please don't tickle me." She began giggling in anticipation.

Gabriel ignored her plea and began tickling her lightly until she shrieked with laughter. He loved to hear her laugh. And she loved the rare moments when he was playful.

When she finally caught her breath, she began apologizing. "I'm sorry for hurting your feelings earlier. It's no excuse, but yesterday was a rough day, and on top of that, I'm hormonal."

Hormonal? thought Gabriel. *Ohhh* . . . He looked at her with concern. "Are you ill?"

"I'm fine. I get this way a few days before. I'm sure you don't want to hear about it."

"If it makes you sick or upset, of course I want to hear about it. I care for you."

"You might want to mark it on your calendar so you know when to avoid me. That is, if things . . ." she trailed off.

"I'll do no such thing," said Gabriel, stiffly. "I want you, all of you—not just the bits and pieces. And of course things are going to continue." *I hope.*

Julia's revelation presented Gabriel with an interesting situation. It wasn't that he'd forgotten his human biology. It was more like given his lifestyle, it had never been an issue. Hormonal women, or women on their cycles, did not frequent *The Vestibule* looking for sex.

Rarely had he entertained the same woman in his bed more than once. Even then they had not discussed such intimate subjects. He wouldn't mind discussing such intimate subjects with Julianne. He wanted to be able to read her moods, even if they were weepy or short-tempered. The thought both perplexed and pleased him.

"I should let you get dressed. But there's one more thing we have to talk about." Gabriel gave her a serious look, and Julia immediately steeled herself.

"I spoke with my lawyer again."

"And?"

"He advised me to stay away from you. He said that the university has a zero-tolerance policy with respect to fraternization that covers both students and faculty."

"What does that mean?"

"It means that both of us would be at risk if we were to be involved while you're in my class. You could be expelled, under certain conditions."

Julia closed her eyes as a groan escaped her lips. *Why is the universe always conspiring against us?*

"We knew that the policy was in force, and we knew that it was serious. We just need to maintain the status quo and continue being discreet for a couple more weeks. As soon as Katherine turns in your grade for my seminar, we will be free to see one another."

"I'm afraid."

Gabriel reached up to touch her cheek. "What are you afraid of?"

"If anyone sees us together or suspects something, they can file a complaint. Christa wants you, and she hates me. Paul doesn't like how you've treated me, so I'm sure he'd be eager to claim that you've harassed me. And Professor Singer . . ." Julia shivered. She didn't want to consider what Professor Singer thought.

"I'm not going to let them expel you. No matter what. It's never going to come to that."

Julia tried to protest, but he silenced her with his lips, murmuring reassurances into her mouth as he tried to demonstrate how deeply he cared for her without using words.

❀❀

They enjoyed a beautiful day together. They laughed and kissed and spent hours talking. Gabriel took several pictures of Julia in various casual poses until her embarrassment got the best of her and he was forced to put the camera away. He resolved to take a picture or two while she was asleep that evening, for Julianne had the face of an angel when she was at peace. And he knew that a sleeping Julianne would make a captivating subject.

After dinner, they found themselves dancing in front of the fireplace. Gabriel had prepared a compilation of several sultry songs by Sting, but Julia couldn't concentrate on the music. Her head was in a haze as it always was when he kissed her. She was so caught up in the physical feelings and emotions it almost made her dizzy.

His hands were in her hair, tangling and caressing at the nape of her neck. They moved to her shoulders, where they slowly traced the slope of her skin. Then they slid down to her waist, and gently, teasingly, moved slowly upward to the sides of her breasts. Two strong hands gently cupped her breasts, moving and massaging them softly.

Julia pulled back.

Gabriel kept his hands where they were and opened his eyes. He looked puzzled at first. She'd retreated, and he could feel her heart racing against his fingertips.

"Julianne?" he whispered.

She shook her head, her skin flushed and her mouth open. She didn't break eye contact as she moved closer. Gabriel moved his hands a little, just to gauge her reaction. She closed her eyes, and when she opened them he saw something completely new in their brownish depths—heat.

The sight of Julia's sudden and intense arousal hit him sharply, not just in his own heightened state of excitement, but emotionally as well. She'd never looked at him this way before, all anxious and animated, as if no one had ever touched her before.

Gabriel rumbled slightly in his chest at the thought. He motioned to her with his eyes to come in for a kiss, and he melded his lips to hers, caressing her breasts more forcefully and trailing a thumb against the nubs that began to poke through her shirt. Julia gasped in pleasure into his mouth, and that spurred him on further. Soon he was groaning against her lips and pressing their bodies more tightly together.

More! his body ordered him. Closer. Faster. Tighter. More. More. *More.*

"*Ugghhhh,*" he groaned, breaking free from her lips and moving his hands to the safe space of her shoulder blades.

Julia pressed her cheek to the planes of his pectorals, her emotions swirling. Eyes closed, she grew unsteady on her feet, but Gabriel reached down and caught her by the waist.

"How are you?"

"Happy."

"Passion will do that to you." He gave her a half-smile.

"So will your fingers," she whispered.

He placed her in his red chair by the fire. "I need to take a shower."

Julia tried to regain her composure. Gabriel's seductive skills left her heady and wanting, wanting things for which she was not ready. Yet.

Professor Emerson is a breast man, she thought to herself with no little warmth.

After he'd been gone for quite some time, she wondered what had happened to him. She wondered why, all of a sudden, he felt the need to take a second shower. When the answer to her silent question dawned on her, she smiled to herself.

Chapter Twenty-three

Julia's weekend with Gabriel was perhaps one of the happiest of her life. She carried memories of it like talismans all week—through his seminar on Wednesday and Christa's persistent attempts to demean and embarrass her, and through Paul's well-meaning but unwelcome encouragement to file a complaint against Professor Singer.

Gabriel's week was the week from hell. It was difficult for him to keep his eyes off of Julianne in his seminar, and the exertion made him irritable and short-tempered. Christa had almost arrived at the end of his patience, begging for extra meetings in which they could (allegedly) discuss her dissertation proposal. He rejected all her requests with a dismissive wave of his hand, which only made her redouble her efforts.

And Professor Singer . . . she sent an e-mail to Gabriel:

> gabriel,
> It was good to see you again. I've missed our little talks.
> your lecture was technically proficient but I'm disappointed
> that you would present something so closed-minded.
> you used to be adventurous. And free.
> Perhaps the professor doth protest too much . . .
> you need to embrace your true nature
> and undergo a little training.
> I can give you just what you need.
> I can give you **exactly** what you crave,
> Mme. Ann

Gabriel glared at Professor Singer's dominatrix-like provocation, clear even in her lack of capitalization of his name and pronouns. His revulsion at her words and her person clarified for him how much he'd changed since their last encounter. She held no allurement for him, no attraction at all. Perhaps even in the time before Julianne returned to him he'd begun walking toward the light, a journey that had been nurtured and encouraged by her presence. The thought pleased him.

He was careful not to reply to or delete the e-mail. Instead, he did exactly what he had done with her previous correspondence—he printed it and placed it in a file in his office. He was unwilling to launch a complaint against her since their initial involvement had been consensual. But he was not above threatening her with her own words, should the need arise. He only hoped her fascination with him would continue and that she would forget all about Julianne.

In an effort to divert himself, Gabriel spent most of his free time that week either preparing for Julianne's birthday or fencing with the fencing club at the university. Either option was far healthier than his previous habits for blowing off steam.

Every night he would lie awake staring at the ceiling, thinking of Julianne and wishing that her warm, soft body was next to his. He was beginning to have difficulty falling asleep without her, and no amount of tension release (in any form) was eliminating that difficulty. Or his hunger.

It had been a long time since he'd been on a formal date—since Harvard, at least. He cursed himself for his previous foolishness in thinking that his predations at *The Vestibule* were an adequate or preferable substitution for something real. Something pure.

He missed sex, it was true. Sometimes he wondered how he would be able to keep to his regimen of chastity, whether his hunger might overtake him and he'd work his seductive skills on Julianne's sweetness. He had no intention of straying from her. He didn't miss the alienation that came from going home alone from a lover's apartment and washing her traces from his body as if they were contagions. He didn't miss the self-loathing he felt when he reflected on past assignations, conquests of women who he would never have introduced to Grace.

Julianne was different. With her he wanted passion and excitement, but also tenderness and companionship. And that realization, although new, continued to both frighten and excite him.

❀ ❀

On Saturday afternoon, Julia eagerly read and re-read the e-mail that gave her details about her birthday celebration.

> *Happy Birthday, Darling.*
> *Please do me the honor of gracing me with your presence at the Royal Ontario Museum this Saturday evening at six o'clock.*
> *Meet me at the Bloor Street entrance.*
> *I shall be wearing the suit and tie and the incredibly wide smile as you walk through the door.*
> *I look forward to the pleasure of your company with great anticipation.*
> *Yours with affection and deepest longing,*
> *Gabriel*

She complied eagerly, wearing the iris-purple dress that Rachel had bought, along with sheer black stockings and Christian Louboutin heels. It was too far (and too painful) to walk in those shoes from her apartment to the museum, so she took a cab. She arrived promptly at six, her eyes shining and her cheeks pink with excitement.

I'm going on a date with Gabriel. Our first real date.

It almost didn't matter that he'd insisted on celebrating her birthday; the thought of having Gabriel to herself for a romantic evening shoved all apprehension aside. She missed him, despite their furtive texts and e-mails and occasional leisurely phone calls.

The museum had undergone a substantial renovation, and a crystal sculpture shaped like the hull of a ship jutted out of the original stone wall. Julia didn't like the juxtaposition of modern and Victorian; she preferred one or the other. But perhaps she was in the minority.

As she approached the entrance, she discovered that the museum was closed; its posted hours indicated it had been closed for thirty minutes. Nevertheless, she walked up to the door and was surprised that she was greeted immediately by a security guard.

"Miss Mitchell?" he asked.

"Yes."

"Your host is waiting for you in the gift shop."

Julia thanked him and wended her way through the shelves of arti-
facts, toys, and tchotchkes. A tall man, impeccably dressed in a navy
blue pinstripe suit with side vents, stood with his back toward her. As
soon as she saw his form, his broad shoulders, and brown hair, her
heart jumped in her chest. *Will it always be like this? Will I always feel
breathless and weak-kneed whenever I see him?*

She knew the answer even before she approached him. When
he didn't turn around, she cleared her throat. "Professor Emerson, I
presume."

He spun around quickly, and as soon as he saw her, he gasped. "Hello,
gorgeous." He pressed his lips to hers a little too enthusiastically and
peeled her out of her coat.

"Turn around," he said thickly.

Julia slowly spun in a circle.

"You're stunning." He pulled her into his arms and kissed her more
forcefully, tugging her lip in between his and gently exploring her
mouth.

She pulled back, embarrassed. "Gabriel."

He gave her a heated look. "We'll be doing more of that this evening.
We have the entire museum to ourselves. But first . . ." He reached over
to pick up a clear box that had been sitting on a low table nearby. Inside
the box was a large, white orchid.

"For me?"

He smirked. "I'm making up for having missed your prom. May I?"

She beamed up at him.

Gabriel removed the flower and tied it to her wrist a little too com-
petently, winding the white satin ribbon around her in an elaborate
weave.

"It's lovely, Gabriel. Thank you." She kissed him sweetly.

"Come."

She came willingly, but he immediately realized his mistake and
stopped. "I mean, *if you please.*"

She smiled and threaded their fingers together.

They walked over to a large open space where a small, impromptu bar had been set up. Gabriel guided her with his hand at the small of her back.

"How did you arrange this?" she whispered.

"I was one of the donors for the Florentine exhibit. I asked for a private viewing—they gladly complied." He gave her a half-smile that almost caused her to melt into a puddle on the floor just like in the film *Amélie*.

The bartender greeted them warmly. "Miss?" he prompted.

"Do you know how to make a Flirtini?"

"Of course, Miss. Coming right up."

Gabriel's eyebrows went up, and he leaned over to whisper in her ear, "That's an interesting name for a drink. A preview of coming attractions?"

She laughed. "Raspberry vodka, cranberry juice and pineapple. I've never had one before, but I read about it online, and it sounded yummy."

He chuckled, shaking his head.

"Sir?" asked the bartender, handing Julia her drink, garnished with a small slice of pineapple.

"Tonic water with lime, please."

She was surprised. "You aren't drinking?"

"There's a special bottle of wine at my place. I'm waiting for that." He smiled at her.

Julia waited until Gabriel received his drink so they could toast one another.

"You can bring your—what was it—*Flirtini* with you. We're the only guests here."

"I could nurse one of these all night. They're pretty strong."

"We have all the time in the world, Julianne. The entire evening revolves around you . . . your wants, your desires, your needs." He winked at her and led her to an elevator. "The exhibit is on the lower level."

When they entered the elevator, Gabriel turned to her. "Did I tell you how much I missed you this week? The days and nights seemed to last forever."

"I missed you too," she said, shyly.

"You look lovely." He gazed down appraisingly at her high heels. "You are a vision."

"Thank you."

"It's going to take all of my self-control not to spirit you away to the Victorian furniture exhibit so I can make love to you on one of the four-poster beds."

Julia's eyebrows shot up, and giggling slightly, she wondered what kind of reaction that display would elicit.

He breathed a sigh of relief that his unguarded remark hadn't caused her to retreat from him. He would have to be more careful.

He'd been actively involved not only in the financing of the exhibit of many of Florence's treasures, but also in their selection. As they wandered through the several rooms, he offered a few brief words on some of the more impressive items. But mostly they just strolled hand in hand, like a loving couple on a walk, pausing from time to time to embrace or kiss when the mood struck. Which it did, often.

Julia finished her cocktail a bit ahead of schedule, and Gabriel obligingly found a place to leave their glasses. He was happy to have their hands free, finally. She was a Siren for him, an irresistible voice. He stroked her neck, her cheek, her collarbone. He pressed his lips to her hands, her lips, her throat. She was undoing him little by little, and when she smiled or laughed he thought he would catch fire.

They spent quite some time admiring Fra Filippo Lippi's painting *Madonna with the Child and Two Angels*, for it was a piece they both admired. Gabriel stood behind her, his arms wrapped snugly around her waist.

"Do you like it?" he whispered in her ear, resting his chin on her shoulder.

"Very much. I've always loved the serenity on the Virgin's face."

"Me too," said Gabriel, lightly drawing his lips from just under her jaw back to below her earlobe, nuzzling her softly. "Your serenity is very alluring."

Julia's eyes rolled back into her head. "*Mmmmmmmmm*," she moaned aloud.

He chuckled and repeated his movements, allowing the tip of his tongue to move across the surface of her skin. Only a whisper, only a promise, so light she thought it had to be his lips.

"Does that please you?"

She answered him by reaching up to grasp his hair. It was all the encouragement he needed. He turned her around and pressed her to him, moving his arms to the small of her back.

"You are the true work of art," he murmured against her throat. "You are the masterpiece. Happy birthday, Julianne."

She gently tugged on his ear with her lips, then kissed it softly. "Thank you."

He kissed her firmly, begging her silently to open for him. Their tongues moved together, slowly. He was unhurried. It was just the two of them in an almost empty museum. He kissed her lips and her cheeks, walking her to a corner of the room, hesitantly backing her toward the wall.

His eyes were wary. "Is this all right?"

She nodded, breathlessly.

"If you want to stop, just tell me. I won't let things go too far . . . but I need you."

She wrapped her arms around his neck, pulling him in.

He pressed her gently against the wall, molding his body tightly to hers. Every muscle, every plane of his was met by corresponding curves and softness. His hands traveled down her sides and to her hips, hesitating. She pressed herself more tightly to him in response. And all this time, their tongues and lips explored, never satisfied. His long, thin fingers slid to her back and down so that they were cupping her two rounded, delicious curves. He squeezed tentatively, and smiled against her mouth when she moaned.

"You're perfect. Every part of you. But this . . ." He squeezed her again and began kissing her with renewed vigor.

"Are you telling me you like my ass, Professor?"

Gabriel pulled back so that he could see her eyes. "Don't call me that," he half-growled.

"Why not?"

"Because I don't want to think about all the university policies I'm breaking right now."

Her smile disappeared, and Gabriel instantly felt regret.

"And I would never call the beauty of your backside an *ass*—it's far too elegant for that. I would have to create a whole new word just to describe it in all of its glory."

Now Julia laughed, and he squeezed her with both hands for good measure.

Professor Emerson is an ass man.

Her fingertips preferred his hair, stroking and weaving, tugging his face to hers. She could feel his heart beating against her chest. Her breathing stuttered, but she didn't care. She loved him. She'd loved him since she was seventeen. And he'd been so sweet to her. In that instant she would have given him anything and damned the consequences. *What consequences?* Her mind couldn't even name them.

His fingers began to move, stroking her curves and kneading the flesh beneath them. His right hand slid down to cup her thigh, pulling her leg upward. He wrapped her leg around his hip, and she pressed against him, in an erotic tango against a wall. Now he could move. His hips pressed forward, while his hand traveled downward to support the back of her leg. She could feel him hard against her—a delightful pressure and tentative friction.

Julia couldn't stop kissing long enough to consider how she had mastered the art of balance or breathing through Gabriel's mouth. She felt emboldened to remove her hands from his hair, stroking his shoulders and waist before exploring his own delicious curves. Curves she had greatly admired on more than one occasion. Curves that were taut and muscular beneath her fingers. She pulled him more tightly against her, pressing her hands against him in encouragement.

He didn't need to be encouraged. His hands teased up and down her sheer stockings, caressing her thigh. This was heaven. Breathing, panting, straining, kissing, feeling. He met with no resistance. No hesitation.

She accepted him. She wanted him. And her body was soft and warm and oh so receptive.

"Julia, I—we—have to stop." He pulled back.

Her eyes were closed, and her lips were red and pouting. Now he hungered for her mouth even more.

Brushing the hair away from her face, he questioned softly, "Sweetheart?"

Her eyelids fluttered open.

He brought their foreheads together and inhaled her breath, all perfumed and sweetness. With one final caress, he coaxed her leg backward and helped her lower it. She removed her hands regretfully from his derrière. Then, although it pained him, he placed some distance between their bodies, taking her hands in both of his.

"I shouldn't have cornered you like that. Or let things go so far." He shook his head, biting back a curse. "Did I scare you?"

"I didn't say *no*, Gabriel." Her soft voice echoed in the great hall. "And I'm not scared."

"You were frightened of me before. Remember that night when you asked me about one of my photographs . . . the aggressive one . . ." Gabriel's lips pressed together tightly.

"I know you better now."

"Julianne, I would never take anything from you or try to manipulate you into something you don't want. Please believe me."

"I do, Gabriel." She pulled on one of his hands and coaxed him to spread it across her heart, palm flat to her chest, between her breasts. "Feel my heartbeat."

He frowned. "Too fast. Like a hummingbird's wings."

"This is what happens every time I'm near you. When you touch me. I'm the one who's overcome by you, Gabriel. Don't you know that?"

He brushed his thumb against her naked flesh and gently transferred his attention to her swollen lower lip.

"I did this to you. Does it hurt?" he whispered.

"It only aches in your absence."

He pressed his lips to hers reverently. "You're killing me."

She tossed her hair back and grinned. "But it will be a sweet, sweet death."

He laughed and pulled her into a hug. "Let's continue our tour before my contact decides to evict us for indecency. I'll have to speak to him about getting the videotapes from the security cameras."

Videotapes? Security cameras? Scheisse, thought Julianne.

Hmmmmmm. On the other hand . . .

❧❧

By the time they reached Gabriel's apartment, they were laughing and giddy. Their desperation for one another had cooled somewhat, but was still warm and affectionate. Julia was blissfully happy. And they had the whole night together . . .

Gabriel kissed her in the kitchen, insisting that she allow him to do everything.

"But I want to help."

"We'll cook together tomorrow night."

She thought about this for a moment. "I don't know how you'd feel about it, but I have Grace's chicken Kiev recipe. We could make it together." She looked up at him uncertainly.

"Scott used to call it *squirt chicken*." He smiled sadly and kissed her again. "I haven't had it in years. I'd be glad for you to teach me."

That's likely the only thing I'll ever be able to teach you, Gabriel. You are a love god, amongst other things. She brushed his lips with hers and made herself comfortable on the bar stool.

"Tonight's dinner is brought to you by Scaramouche. Since Mohammed cannot come to the mountain, the mountain must come to Mohammed."

"Really?"

"Everything is here, including a very fine Grand Marnier chocolate cake from Patisserie La Cigogne. And I have an extraordinary bottle of wine that I've been saving, which I will allow to breathe before we get started." He winked at her. "I even have candles for the cake."

"Thank you for a lovely evening, Gabriel. It was—the nicest birthday I've ever had."

"It's not over yet," he rasped slightly, his bright blue eyes sparkling. "I haven't given you your present."

Julia blushed deeply and looked down at her hands, wondering if he had meant to sound so sensual. *I wonder what "present" he wants to give me. I know what present I would like. It's official. I am now fantasizing about making love with Gabriel . . .*

Julia's erotic imaginings were interrupted by the ringing of her cell phone. She walked to her purse and checked it reluctantly.

"I don't recognize the number," she mused. "But it's a Philadelphia area code."

She answered the phone. "Hello?"

"Hello, Jules."

Julia inhaled slowly, making a strained vacuuming sound with her lungs. All the color disappeared from her cheeks, and immediately, Gabriel walked over to her, knowing that something was very, very wrong.

"How did you get this number?" she managed before her legs grew rubbery. She stumbled to a chair and sank down.

"That's not a very warm welcome, Julia. You'll have to do better than that."

She razored her lower lip with her teeth, not knowing how to respond.

Her caller sighed dramatically. "Your father gave me your number. I always enjoy talking to him. He's very forthcoming, which is more than I can say for you. You've been a spoiled little brat."

She closed her eyes and began to breathe in and out very fast. Gabriel took her hand to try to lift her to her feet, but she wouldn't move. "What do you want?"

"I'll overlook your bitchiness because I haven't spoken with you in a while. But don't push your luck." He lowered his voice to a near whisper. "I called you because I wanted to see how you were doing in Toronto. Are you still living on Madison Avenue?"

The caller laughed, and Julia placed a hand to her throat.

"Stay away from me. I don't want to talk to you, and I want you to stop calling my dad."

"I wouldn't have to call your dad if you'd responded to my e-mails. Instead, you deleted your account."

"What do you want?" she repeated.

Gabriel frowned his concern and gestured for her to give him the phone. She shook her head.

"I had an interesting conversation with Natalie the other day," the voice said.

"And?"

"She said that you might have a few photographs that belong to me."

"I don't have anything of yours. I left everything behind. I think you know that."

"Maybe. Maybe not. I simply wanted to tell you that it would be very unfortunate if those photos ever ended up in the hands of the press." The voice paused. "I have a video or two of you I could pass around. I wonder what your dad would think if he saw a tape of you on your knees with my—"

As his foul description rang in her ears, Julia made a wheezing noise and dropped the phone. It crashed against the hardwood and skidded toward Gabriel's feet. But by this point, Julia was already running for the guest washroom. The sounds of her dry heaves echoed down the hallway.

Unfortunately for the caller, Gabriel had overhead his final threat. Gabriel picked up the phone and put it to his ear. "Who is this?"

"This is Simon. Who the fuck is this?"

Gabriel hissed involuntarily, and his eyes narrowed into slits.

"This is Julianne's boyfriend. What do you want?"

Simon was silent for a moment.

"Jules doesn't have a boyfriend, asshole. And no one calls her *Julianne*. Put her back on the phone!"

Gabriel growled, the sound rumbling from his chest. "If you know what's good for you, you'll do what she says and leave her alone."

Simon laughed darkly. "You have no idea who you're dealing with. Julia is unstable. She's a very troubled girl, and she needs professional help."

"In that case, it's a good things she's dating a professional."

"A professional what? Asshole? Do you even know who you're talking to? My father is—"

"Listen, motherfucker, you're lucky we aren't in the same room or you'd be spending the evening in surgery trying to have your head reattached to your body. If I find out that you've contacted her again, *in any way*, I'm going to come after you, and not even your father, whoever he is, will be able to make you sentient again. Do you understand? Never contact her again." Gabriel snapped the phone shut and hurled it against the wall. The cell phone broke into several pieces that scattered across the floor.

SYLVAIN REYNARD

He closed his eyes and counted to fifty before he allowed himself to go to her. He'd never been so angry. Or had such murderous thoughts. It was a good thing Julia needed him. Otherwise, he was pretty sure he would have hunted that boy down and killed him.

Gabriel poured a glass of water and carried it to her. She was seated on the cold, ceramic edge of the bathtub in the guest washroom. Her head was down, and her arms were wrapped across her chest, her poor corsage shaking with the trembling of her hand.

What the fuck did he do to her?

When she reached down to tug the hem of her skirt over her knees, the sight of her instinctive attempt to maintain some semblance of modesty made his heart clench.

"Julia?" He handed her the water.

She sipped it slowly, but didn't respond.

He joined her on the edge of the tub, pulling her into his side.

"He told you about when I was with him, didn't he?" Her voice was low, dull.

Gabriel hugged her closer. "He demanded to speak to you, but I told him not to call again."

She looked up at him as a tear slowly leaked from one eye. "He didn't—say things about me?"

"He mumbled incoherently until I threatened him." Gabriel grimaced. "And I wasn't kidding."

"He's really nasty," she whispered.

"Let me worry about him. And if that means flying to Philadelphia to speak to him in person, I'll do it. And he won't like what happens if I have to make that trip."

Julia was only half-listening. Simon made her feel used. Filthy. Pathetic. And she didn't want Gabriel to look at her like that. She didn't want him to know what had happened. Ever.

"Sweetheart, what did he want?"

"He thinks I have some pictures of him, and he wants them back."

"What kind of pictures?"

Julia sniffled. "I don't know. They must be pretty bad if he's so worried."

"Do you have anything like that?"

"No! But he says he has videos of me. Personal videos." She shuddered. "I don't think he does, but what if I'm wrong? What if he fabricates something and sends it to my father? Or posts it online?"

Gabriel swallowed his revulsion as he reached over to wipe her tears away. "He won't do that, unless he's stupid. As long as he thinks you have something potentially damaging to him, he won't act preemptively. I could speak with your father and explain that I heard this miscreant threaten you. Then no matter what he posts online you'll be able to say it's a fabrication created by a stalker."

Julia looked up at him wildly. "You can't. My dad is already upset that I'm traveling to Selinsgrove with you. He can't know we're together."

Gabriel ran his fingers through her hair before he quickly wiped away another tear. "You didn't tell me that. Not that I blame him. But you need to tell him what happened tonight so that he won't give Simon any more information."

Julia nodded.

"I can speak to my lawyer tomorrow. You can file a complaint against him, and we can try to get a restraining order. We can also try to figure out if he actually has videos of you or if he's bluffing."

"I don't want to do anything to antagonize him. You don't understand—he has powerful connections."

Gabriel pressed his lips together. He wanted to push her to take action, or to take action on her behalf, but it was clear that she was traumatized. And he didn't want to add to her distress.

"If he contacts you again, I'll speak with my lawyer and that boy will be introduced to an entirely new level of discomfort. Tomorrow, I'll take you to pick out a new cell phone, and we'll get you a Toronto number. You should tell your father to keep the new number secret."

He lifted her chin so that she would look into his eyes. "He can't touch you. I promise." He smiled widely. "Don't let the glasses and bow ties fool you. I can take care of myself. And I won't let anyone hurt you." He kissed her lips chastely and added a small kiss to her forehead. "When we're home for Thanksgiving, you'll be with me when you aren't with your father. And I'll always be only a phone call away. All right?"

She murmured just to let him know that she'd heard him.

"Julia?"

"Yes?"

He pulled her into a closer embrace. "This was my fault."

She gave him a questioning look.

"If I hadn't left you that morning—if I had come back to Selinsgrove to find you . . ."

She shook her head. "I was only seventeen, Gabriel. Dad would have pulled a gun on you."

"I should have waited."

She sighed, and her face wore a pained look. "You don't know how much I regret not waiting for you. He's why I never celebrate my birthday. And he just ruined it again." She began to cry quietly.

Gabriel kissed away her tears. "Forget about him. It's just us, now. No one else."

Julia wanted to believe him. But unfortunately, she knew that her past was only just now beginning to catch up with her. She trembled in fear when she thought about what the holidays might bring.

Julia had very bad luck when it came to Thanksgiving.

Chapter Twenty-four

On Tuesday evening, Julia had a very tense albeit edited conversation with her father about the previous weekend's events. She called him on her new iPhone, explaining why she had to change her number. He'd been trying in vain to speak to her for three days but had only reached her voice mail. He was annoyed.

"Dad, I had to change my number because Simon called me."

"Oh, really?" Tom's voice was hesitant, which made Julia suspicious.

"Yes, really. He said that you gave him my number. Then he called and harassed me!"

"Son of a bitch," he muttered.

"I'll give you my new number, but I don't want you to share it with anyone, especially Deb. She'll just turn around and give it to Natalie."

Tom continued talking to himself, as he was wont to do. Until he realized there was a person on the other end of the line. "Don't worry about Deb."

"Yes, Dad, I worry about her! Her daughter still talks to Simon. What if she tells him I'm coming home? He could show up at your house!"

"You're overreacting. He isn't going to drive all the way out here. We had a nice conversation last week. He was very polite and simply said that you had a few things that belonged to him. He didn't want to bother you, but I gave him your number and said it would be okay for him to call you."

"I don't have anything of his! And even if I did, you know I don't want to talk to him. He is not a good guy, Dad. He acts one way around you. With me . . ." Julia shook slightly.

"Are you sure it wasn't a misunderstanding?"

"It's pretty difficult to misunderstand threats and harassment, Dad. He doesn't get to talk to me. He doesn't get to be my friend. And no apology will make up for what he did."

Tom sighed into the phone.

"All right, Jules. I'm sorry. I won't give anyone your number. But are you sure you don't want to give him a second chance? He comes from a great family. And everyone makes mistakes."

Julia rolled her eyes so hard they nearly spiraled out of her head and dropped onto the floor. In that instant she wanted to be vindictive. She wanted to ask her father if he would have taken her mother back if he'd seen what she walked in on at age twelve—Sharon bent over the kitchen table by one of the boyfriends. But she was not vindictive, so she didn't.

"Dad, he might be a senator's son but he's a son of a bitch. And what was broken can never be fixed. Trust me."

Tom exhaled loudly. "Okay. When are you coming home?"

"Thursday."

"And you're driving with Rachel and Aaron?"

"That's the plan. Gabriel is coming too." Julia tried to make her lie convincing.

"See to it that you stick close to Aaron and as far as possible from Gabriel."

"Why?"

"Because he's a bad apple. I'm surprised he isn't in jail right now. All I can say is he's lucky he moved to Canada."

Julia shook her head. "If he was a felon, the Canadians wouldn't have granted him a work visa."

"Canadians let anyone in. Including terrorists."

Julia stuck her tongue out at her father's anti-Canadian bias and proceeded to plan her visit with him, hoping against hope that he would keep his promises.

❊❊

After another Dante seminar in which Christa shamelessly flirted with Gabriel, Julia found herself walking home with Paul, who continued to be charming and friendly. They commiserated over Christa's new *sexier-than-thou* wardrobe and *please-let-me-seduce-you-before-you-*

fail-me stiletto boots, before Julia bid him good evening and entered her apartment. She made herself a modest dinner of chicken noodle soup and Lady Grey tea, and admired her birthday presents.

Once Julia's birthday had been so rudely interrupted by Simon, Gabriel poured her a glass of wine and insisted that she relax by the fire while he prepared dinner. After dinner and a candlelit birthday cake, he presented her with gifts before taking her to bed.

He'd stayed awake almost all night, caressing her back and her arms, their legs rubbing together. She'd woken up several times in a nightmare-induced haze, but each time he'd comforted her and held her more tightly. She felt safe with him but worried about how he would react when he found out the truth. If she was ever able to work up the courage to speak the words.

Her iPhone was a gift—of sorts. On Sunday morning, when Gabriel sheepishly held out the broken pieces of her old phone, she'd laughed, for which he'd been grateful. When he explained that he was so angry that Simon had upset her that he'd smashed her phone, she smiled. She graciously accepted his more sophisticated replacement as well as his patient tutelage in learning how to operate the damn thing.

He'd uploaded the photos Rachel took at Lobby, which pleased her greatly. And he helped her enter all her contacts and numbers, although he'd arched an eyebrow when she explained that he needed to enter the name "Dante Alighieri" in conjunction with his own number. He'd also stubbornly insisted on choosing his own ring tone.

Julia's primary birthday gift was a series of digital copies of Gabriel's Botticelli prints. He had them mounted in a special book with her name engraved in gold letters on the cover. Even though they were only copies, the collection was priceless. And he had handwritten a dedication on the flyleaf in his elegant script:

> To my Darling Julianne,
> Happy Birthday.
> May each year be better than the last
> and may you always have happiness.
> With enduring affection,
> Gabriel

She fingered his inscription, tracing the curls of the capital *G*. The illustrations were, without doubt, the finest gift she had ever received.

In addition, Gabriel had given her a small photo album of black-and-white pictures. In some of them, her identity was recognizable. In the rest, the subject was only a glimpse of a face, or a lock of hair against a long, white neck or a laughing girl with her eyes closed. She felt beautiful when Gabriel kissed her and when he touched her. But viewing these photographs made her feel as if Gabriel saw her beauty. He saw and captured it, recording it forever.

Some of the pictures were sexy, some were innocent, and some were sweet. None of them were embarrassing or the kind of photo that would humiliate her if they were sent to her father or posted on the internet. Her favorite was one in which she stood in profile while a hand with long white fingers held up her hair, a man's face in shadow pressing his lips to the nape of her neck. She could have blown that photo up to poster size and tacked it to the wall over her bed, the Holiday painting be damned.

Take that, simple Simon.

❋ ❋

"Why are you calling? Is something wrong? Did you do something to Julia? I swear to God, Gabriel, if you—"

Gabriel held his iPhone away from his ear as his sister expertly berated him. "I didn't do anything to Julia," he interrupted. "Her exboyfriend called her on Saturday, and she went to pieces. I'd like some answers."

"Holy shit. Is she okay?"

"She was very upset. But she won't tell me much."

"Of course not. Why would she talk about it with her professor?"

Gabriel bristled. "We were discussing Thanksgiving and making plans for the trip when that motherfucker interrupted us."

"A bit angry there, Gabriel. Why do you care?"

"Because that bastard, whoever he is, sweet talked her father into divulging her unlisted cell phone number so that he could harass her."

"Shit," said Rachel.

"Quite," said Gabriel. "So before I bring her back to Selinsgrove, where he might possibly pay her a visit, I'd like to know who I'm dealing with."

His sister was silent.

"Rachel? I'm waiting."

"I don't know what you're expecting me to tell you. This is Julia's past. You need to ask her."

"I told you, she won't talk about it."

"Can you blame her? If you know that he's a motherfucker, then you know why she doesn't want to talk about him. She won't even say his name out loud—she's that skittish." Rachel paused for a minute and took a deep breath. "Simon's father is Senator John Talbot."

Gabriel blinked in recognition. "And?"

"Julia met Simon when they were freshmen. He swept her off her feet in the beginning, but I got the impression that he could be difficult. She went to Florence her junior year, and when she came back, they broke up. I didn't see her again until I came to visit you. Aaron hated Simon, so I didn't spend a lot of time around them."

Gabriel fumed. "You didn't answer my question. What kind of difficulties are we talking about? Assault? Infidelity? Emotional abuse?"

"Honestly, I don't know everything. I pieced together a few things from a conversation I had with Natalie, Julia's old roommate. Simon was an arrogant jerk who liked to have Julia on his arm. It's obvious he crushed her spirit. I think we can imagine the rest."

"He said that Julia is disturbed. That she needs professional help."

"The guy is a lying bastard, Gabriel. What did you expect him to say?" Rachel exhaled her frustration. "Julia's biggest problem is *him*. If you want to help her, you should try to make her life easier and not harder. I hope you aren't intimidating her anymore with your pretentious bullshit. She had enough of that with him."

"Actually, we're getting along quite well." He sniffed.

"As well as in the pictures I e-mailed to you?" Rachel giggled wickedly.

"We have a professional relationship."

"You might be fooling everyone else, but you can't fool me. Julia broke down and told me she had a date with someone Saturday night, and coincidentally, you're with her on Saturday when Simon calls. So tell me, Gabriel, did you see Julia after her date or before? And how was it?"

"We'll arrive in Selinsgrove on Thursday. I'll bring Julia to the house." Gabriel's voice was cold.

"Good. I think she needs to tell her dad that she wants to stay with us. If Simon comes to town, he won't look for her there. And Gabriel, thanks for what you did about the house. Dad is so relieved. I think we all are, Scott included."

"It was the least I could do. Bye, Rachel."

"If you hurt her, I'll kill you. Now go cheer her up and *be gentle*. Otherwise you'll never coax her out of her shell. Love you."

"I—bye." Gabriel ended the call somewhat uncomfortably and returned to the task of preparing next week's Dante seminar.

❋❋

With the impending end of term, Julia's workload increased exponentially. In addition to writing her thesis, she needed to complete essays for her seminars, which were due December fourth. On top of everything, she was working on applications to graduate schools for doctoral programs.

She and Gabriel had a vague conversation late one night about her applications. He knew that she wanted to go to Harvard and that she was focusing a great deal of her attention on that application. What he didn't know was that the thought of leaving Toronto, of leaving him, was almost unbearable, and so unbeknownst to him, she completed an application to the University of Toronto, as well.

While Julia was spending most of her days and all of her nights working, Gabriel was wading through a sea of grading and writing his second book. He preferred to spend his evenings with Julia, even if they were both busy, and sometimes he was able to persuade her to work at his apartment. He would occupy his study, and she would spread her papers across the dining room table. But she usually didn't stay at the table very long. Somehow she would always end up in his red velvet chair in front of the fire, chewing the end of a pencil and scribbling something into a notebook.

After seeing each other rarely, it was with much relief that the couple dragged their luggage from Gabriel's apartment to a waiting cab on the day they left for Thanksgiving vacation. As they watched the taxi driver place their bags in the trunk, Julia looked up and saw the autumn wind blowing Gabriel's hair, swirling the strands into his eyes. Without thinking, she reached up and brushed the hair out of his face and pressed her lips to his. She stroked his face tenderly, trying to tell him with her eyes what she was too afraid to say.

Gabriel stared back at her, eyes burning, and grabbed her by the waist. He pulled her into his chest, deepening the kiss and exploring her lower back through her peacoat. She pulled away first, giggling like a schoolgirl as he surreptitiously patted her backside with a smug grin.

"Still trying to find the right adjective," he teased, sneaking in a final tap. "Although *pert* comes to mind."

"Behave," she warned, toying with his hair again.

"I need to get this out of my system," he countered, wiggling his eyebrows at her. "I'm going to have to go cold turkey for three days."

***

Arriving at Pearson Airport, Julia was surprised when Gabriel pulled her into the exclusive line for executive and first class passengers at the Air Canada counter.

"What are we doing?" she whispered.

"Checking in," he whispered back, his lips curling up into a smirk.

"But I only had money for a coach ticket."

He caressed her cheek with his thumb. "I want you to be comfortable. Besides, the last time I flew coach I ended up sitting in urine, and it cost me a pair of expensive trousers."

Julia arched an eyebrow at him.

"I had enough frequent flyer miles for an upgrade, so I bought coach tickets and upgraded them. Technically, you only owe me for the coach fare. Not that I want your money."

Julia gazed at him quizzically. "Urine, Gabriel? I didn't know that Air Canada had a section for the incontinent."

He waved a hand. "Don't ask. But it's not happening to me again. Besides, they'll at least provide us with drinks and something more substantial than pretzels." He kissed her softly, and she smiled.

The flight to Philadelphia was largely uneventful. After disengaging the phone utility, Gabriel continued his tutoring sessions on iPhone 101, showing Julia various applications on his phone and asking her if she wanted the same ones. As she perused his programs, she found the iPod function and scrolled through his music files—Mozart, Chopin, Berlioz, Rachmaninoff, Beethoven, Matthew Barber, Sting, Diana Krall, Loreena McKennitt, Coldplay, U2, Miles Davis, Arcade Fire, Nine Inch Nails . . .

Julia hit a button by mistake and found herself looking at Gabriel's university e-mail account. She glanced at it quickly as she tried to switch to the photo album application, and was stunned to discover that both Professor Singer and a *Paulina Grushcheva* had e-mailed him in the past week. She resisted the urge to read his e-mails and closed the application. Gabriel was peering through his glasses at a journal article, oblivious to what had just occurred.

Why are they e-mailing him? The answer was obvious, but it didn't prevent her from asking herself the question. She nibbled on one of her fingernails distractedly.

Gabriel had uploaded several of the black-and-white photos of her, including some she hadn't seen before. As she scrolled through them, he somehow became aware of what she was doing. Embarrassed, he tried to wrest his phone out of her hand, but she held it fast and began to laugh. Not wanting to give their fellow passengers a show, he moved closer and threatened in a whisper to kiss her senseless.

She gave him back his phone.

Julia snuggled up at Gabriel's side while he put his research away and pulled out a hard-covered volume from his briefcase.

"What's that?" Her soft voice interrupted his thoughts.

He showed her the cover. *The End of the Affair* by Graham Greene. "Is it good?"

"I just started it. He's considered to be a very good writer. He wrote the script for *The Third Man*, which is one of my favorite films."

"The title is depressing."

"It's not what you think." He shifted in his seat. "Well, it is, but it isn't. It's about faith and God and lust . . . I'll lend it to you when I'm finished."

He smirked at her and leaned closer so that he could brush his lips against her ear. "Perhaps I'll read it aloud to you when we're in bed together."

Julia's cheeks pinked up at that remark, but she smiled. "I'd like that."

He pressed a light kiss to her forehead. She snuggled into his side and relaxed. He found himself peering down at her from time to time over the rims of his glasses.

He found it difficult to put into words how he felt when she was near him. How content he felt whenever she touched him, or when they were enjoying the simple pleasures of music or literature or food and wine. She inspired the strangest emotions and desires, such as wanting to read to her, to chastely share a bed with her, to lavish her with gifts both decadent and plain, to protect her from harm, and to ensure that she smiled daily.

Perhaps this is happiness, he thought. *Perhaps this is almost what Richard and Grace had.* The thought intrigued him.

You love her.

Gabriel started suddenly. *Where had that voice come from? Had someone said it aloud?* He looked around quickly, but the other first class passengers were either napping or otherwise engaged. No one was paying any attention to the nervous professor or the beauty who dozed next to him.

It's too soon. It's just not possible. I can't love her. Gabriel shook his head at the voice, wherever it came from, and returned to his book more than a little disquieted.

After arriving in Philadelphia, Gabriel pulled his rented Jeep Grand Cherokee out of the airport's parking garage.

"Which hotel did you choose?" Julia asked, staring out of the window into the darkness.

"The Four Seasons. Do you know it?"

"I know where it is, but I've never stayed there."

"It's very nice. You'll like it."

What Gabriel failed to mention was that he had booked a suite that had a panoramic view of Logan Circle. He also neglected to tell Julia that their room had a beautiful marble bathroom with an exquisite bathtub. Julia noticed the bathtub before she noticed the view. Not to mention the complimentary fruit basket the manager always provided for his most important guests.

"Gabriel," she breathed. "It's beautiful. I'd love to take a bubble bath but . . ."

He smiled at her and gently took her elbow, leading her inside the bathroom.

"You will have complete privacy, and your companion will behave like a gentleman." He paused and a wicked gleam came into his eyes. "Unless you need me to wash your back. In which case, you'll have to blindfold me first."

Julia grinned. "We could use one of your bow ties," she whispered.

Gabriel's mouth dropped open. Then she started laughing, and he realized that she was only teasing him. *Minx.*

As he watched her remove her purple robe and slippers from her suitcase, he quickly realized that there was no way he was going to be able to sit in the living room of the suite while Julianne took a bubble bath. It was a bit too King David for him. So he mumbled an excuse about finding a newspaper and went to the lobby. He decided against sitting at the bar, populated as it was by various hungry-looking women, and instead enjoyed a glass of wine and a sandwich while sitting in an arm chair in a quiet corner. He picked up a copy of *The Philadelphia Inquirer* and spent the next hour dodging the aforementioned women, trying valiantly not to dwell on the beautiful body of the Bathsheba bathing upstairs.

By the time he returned, the scent of vanilla filled the room, and Julia was curled up like a cat on the bed. Her chest rose and fell in a gentle rhythm, her long dark hair spread out across the sage green duvet. She was still wearing her purple robe and her kitten-heeled slippers.

Gabriel watched her sleep for a moment and felt a wave of emotion wash over him. As he tried to sort out his feelings, it occurred to him that the development of their relationship was not being held back solely by the university. It was being held back by him, by his secrets.

And also by hers.

He'd determined that he would not make love to her until he revealed everything. Although it pained him to think of it, he knew that it would be best if he waited until she did the same. That meant that Julianne would have to feel comfortable and safe enough to finally tell him what happened with Simon. Otherwise, he would only ever know part of her and not the whole. And they needed to know all of each other.

It was important to him that they not break the letter of the non-fraternization policy, even though they were breaking it in spirit. On top of that, although he'd fantasized about moving their physical relationship forward, the nature of Simon's threats had put an end to those fantasies.

He knew based upon her receptivity that she would be willing to participate in manual or oral contact before the end of the semester. It would certainly stave off his cravings and satisfy some of his desires, temporarily. But after hearing that Simon might have videotaped a particularly intimate encounter, there was no possibility of Gabriel persuading her to perform that act. He was determined to treat her gently and respectfully, and not speed things along for his own gratification. Although he would not have used this word, Gabriel craved *intimacy* along with sexual contact, and because of what he surmised had happened in Julia's past, he was unwilling to allow anything other than sexual intercourse to be their first connection.

He knew that in making this decision, as in deciding not to make love to her without first revealing his secrets, he was making it less and less likely that such intimacy would ever occur. But he wanted more with her and not less, and certainly not just what her ex-boyfriend had taken from her, a fumble in the dark meant to mimic the true connection one found in sex. Fumbles which had always left Gabriel somehow wanting.

Julianne deserved a man who was willing to give all, in a manner that was tender and patient and focused on union, and not simply to use her to satisfy his physical desires. She deserved to be adored and even worshipped, especially her first time. Gabriel would be damned if he would give her anything less.

He sighed deeply and looked at his watch. It was almost two o'clock in the morning. They both needed sleep. He gently removed her slippers and, picking her up in his arms, tried to pull back the bed covers. Her robe fell open, exposing her elegant neck, collarbone, and one of her breasts. It was perfect. A rosy nipple budded against creamy white skin. So delicate. So round.

Absolutely not what he needed to see at that moment.

Gabriel struggled to place her underneath the sheets while keeping her from being further exposed, then he lightly tugged at her robe until she was covered, completely resisting the urge to take her rosy tip between his fingers. Or his lips. That was one sight he would never forget. Julianne was stunning in clothes, but Julianne without clothes was like Botticelli's Venus.

He walked over to the windows that looked out over Logan Circle and began rummaging through the fruit basket. He poured himself a glass of Perrier and ate an apple, and when he was satisfied that he could control himself, he changed into a T-shirt and pajama bottoms and quietly slipped into bed.

She sighed at the movement and instinctively turned to face him. This one small, simple act made his heart swell. Even in her sleep, she recognized him and wanted him. He pulled her, all covered, into his arms and kissed her goodnight.

As he fell asleep, he thanked God that the end of the semester was only a week away.

❈ ❈

When they arrived in Selinsgrove the following afternoon, they drove immediately to Richard's house. Julia called her father as soon as they pulled into the driveway.

"Jules! Welcome home. How was the flight?"

"It was fine. We had to leave really early, but it's good to be back."

Tom breathed heavily into the phone. "About that, Jules. I already told Richard that I can't join you all. Deb was a little put out that I was bailing on her, and so I said I'd have dinner with her and her kids tonight. Rachel suggested you stay with her so you aren't home alone."

"Oh." Julia looked over at Gabriel, feeling conflicted.

"Deb said you're more than welcome to join us and she'd love to have you there."

"Absolutely not."

Tom sighed. "Then maybe we can meet at Kinfolks restaurant for breakfast tomorrow."

Julia fidgeted with her fingernails, wondering why she always came second or third in her father's life.

"Okay. I'll ask Rachel to drive me. Around nine?"

"Sounds good. Oh, and Jules, give my best to Rachel and Aaron. And stay away from Gabriel."

She flushed furiously. "Bye, Dad."

She disconnected her call and glanced over at Gabriel. "You heard that, didn't you?"

"I did." He took her hand in his and stroked her palm with the pad of his thumb. "We have a few minutes before someone notices we're here. Can I ask how Tom reacted when you told him about Simon? You wouldn't tell me before."

Julia looked down at their conjoined hands and watched as Gabriel touched her.

"Julianne?"

"Sorry. Um, he said he wouldn't give out my number."

Gabriel looked grim. "Did you mention the video?"

"No, and I'm not going to, either."

"He's your father, Julianne. Shouldn't he know what's going on so he can protect you?"

Julia shrugged and looked out the window. "What can he do? It's my word against *his*."

Gabriel stopped stroking her palm. "Is that what your father said?"

"Not exactly."

"Is he going to take this seriously?"

"Simon has him fooled, just like he fools everyone. Dad thinks it's just a misunderstanding."

"Why in God's name would he think this is a misunderstanding? You're his daughter, for Christ's sake!"

"Dad really liked him. And he knows next to nothing about what happened between us."

"Why didn't you tell him?"

Julia turned to Gabriel with a desperate look in her eyes. "Because

I don't want him to know. He wouldn't believe me anyway, and I can't lose another parent."

"Julia, there is no way your father would disown you because you broke up with your boyfriend."

"He's been watching me my whole life to see if I was going to turn out like my mother. I don't want him looking that way at me. He's the only family I have."

Gabriel closed his eyes and rested his head back against the car seat. "If that boy made you do things you didn't want to do, if he assaulted you or took advantage of you, then you need to tell your dad. He needs to know."

Julia exhaled slowly. "It's too late."

Opening his eyes, Gabriel looked at her and cupped her face in both hands. "Julia, listen to me. Some day you are going to have to tell somebody."

She blinked back tears. "I know that."

"I'd like that person to be me."

She nodded as if she understood, but made no promises.

He leaned over and pressed a chaste kiss to her lips. "Come on. Everyone will be waiting."

As soon as they walked through the front door, Julia felt—odd. The furniture was arranged as it always had been. The décor was the same, minus the fresh flowers Grace loved to display in a large vase on one of the side tables. But the instant Julia exited the foyer and gazed around, she realized that the house felt empty, cold, lonesome, even though it was filled with people. Grace had been the heart of the household, and now everyone could feel her absence.

Julia shivered unconsciously, and without warning, Gabriel's right hand flew to the small of her back—a gentle pressure, a reassuring warmth, then it was gone. They hadn't even exchanged glances. She felt his comfort leave her body, and she wondered what it all meant.

"Julia!" Rachel fairly ran from the kitchen. "I'm so glad you're here."

The two friends embraced, and then Rachel hugged Gabriel. Scott, Aaron, and Richard rose from their chairs to take turns greeting the new arrivals.

Julia nervously tried to find the words to tell Richard how sorry she was that she'd missed the funeral, but Rachel interrupted her. "Let's get rid of your coat. I'm making Flirtinis. Gabriel, help yourself. The beer is in the refrigerator."

Julia mumbled something Gabriel didn't catch, and the two women disappeared into the kitchen, leaving the men to return to the football game.

"I hope Gabriel was polite to you during the trip," said Rachel, as she began pouring a number of ingredients into a martini shaker.

"He was. I'm lucky he agreed to drive me, or I'd be hitchhiking. Dad decided to spend the evening with Deb and her kids. I guess I'm staying here tonight." Julia rolled her eyes, still feeling disappointed that her father had chosen his girlfriend over her.

Rachel smiled sympathetically and handed her a Flirtini. "You need a drink. And you can stay the whole weekend, if you want. Why be home alone when you can be here drinking cocktails with me?"

Julia giggled and sipped her drink a little too eagerly while she and Rachel caught up with one another. By the time they were working on their second round of Flirtinis and beginning to get a little naughty in their discussion, the football game ended, thus emancipating the men from the large, flat-screened plasma television in the living room. Grace had banished the unsightly thing to the basement. Richard had since paroled it.

The men joined the ladies in the kitchen, passing around snacks and bottles of beer and giving Rachel absolutely unsolicited advice about her free-range organic turkey.

"You've cooked it too long. It's going to be dry, like that turkey on *National Lampoon's Christmas Vacation*." Scott winked at Julia behind Rachel's back.

"Scott, knock it off, or I'm going to cut you." Rachel opened the door to the Viking range and began basting the turkey, peering anxiously at the meat thermometer.

"It looks beautiful, honey." Aaron pressed a kiss to her cheek as he took the baster out of her hand, slightly worried that she was going to use it to stab her annoying brother.

Scott was the oldest of Grace and Richard's biological children, and thus five years older than Rachel. He was funny, light-hearted, and frequently bawdy. At six foot three, he was an inch taller than Gabriel and somewhat heavier. Like Rachel, he had his father's hair and eyes and a very big heart, except when it came to his adopted brother.

"Julia, it's good to see you again. Rachel tells me that you've been doing well in graduate school." Richard moved to occupy an empty stool next to her.

Julia smiled. Richard was classically handsome, with light-colored hair that had begun to gray and kind eyes. He was a professor of biology at Susquehanna University, and he specialized in human anatomy, more specifically, the neurons of the human brain. Despite his intelligence and charm, he was often the last to speak; his silence had been complemented by Grace's chattiness. Without her, he seemed . . . adrift. Julia could feel his loneliness and see it in the wrinkles at the corner of his eyes. He looked thinner and older.

"I'm really glad to be back, Richard. I'm sorry I wasn't here in September." She gave him a guilty look, and he patted her hand. "My courses are good. I like them."

Julia tried hard not to fidget, especially when she felt a pair of intense blue eyes latch on to her.

"Gabriel tells me you're in his class."

"Yeah, how's that going?" asked Scott. "Can you understand a word he says? Or do you need a translator?"

Scott was only joking, and Julia knew that, but she saw Gabriel flinch out of the corner of her eye.

"It's my favorite class," she said softly. "Professor Emerson's graduate seminar is considered the best of its kind at the university. He gave a lecture in October that had over a hundred people in attendance. They put his picture in the university newspaper."

Rachel's brows went up, and her eyes narrowed as they traveled from Julia to Gabriel and back again.

"*Professor Emerson?* That must be quite a turn-on, Gabe. Do your women call you that too? Must be really hot in the bedroom." Scott laughed uproariously.

"In the first place, Scott, I do not have *women*. And no, the extraordinary *lady* I am seeing does not call me that." Gabriel's voice was cold and unfriendly as he swept out of the room.

"Scott, I asked you to behave yourself." Richard's voice was low but reproving.

"Dad, I was only kidding. He takes himself so seriously—somebody needs to loosen him up. And he's always been a player. So what's the big deal?"

"It sounds like Gabriel has a girlfriend. Let him be happy." Aaron's voice was quiet and surprisingly compassionate.

Richard's face wore a peculiar expression.

"Look you all, this holiday is hard enough without the passive-aggressive bullshit." Rachel's voice was raised over the rest as she stood, hands on hips, scowling at Scott. "Sorry about the language, Dad."

"Why does everything have to revolve around him? Last time I checked, he was only one out of four." Scott was no longer joking.

"Because he's trying! Which is more than I can say about you. Now come over here and drain these goddamned potatoes, so you can start mashing them. Aaron will take the turkey out of the oven, and Julia, would you go and get Gabriel? I'd like him to look through the wine cellar and choose a couple of bottles."

"I can do that," Richard protested. "Maybe we should give him a minute."

"He's had his minute. As long as Scott agrees to behave." She glared at him until he nodded. "Besides, Dad, you need to carve the turkey. *Julia.*"

Rachel angled her head toward the upstairs, and Julia nodded, slipping out of the kitchen. She quickly ascended the staircase and walked down the hall, pausing in front of the half-opened door to Gabriel's old bedroom. She knocked softly.

"Come in." He sounded cross.

Gabriel's room had not been redecorated since his seventeenth birthday, with the exception of the removal of his old band posters and pictures of scantily clad women. A double bed stood in the center of the room, underneath the large picture window that faced the woods. A large antique armoire stood against one of the walls, and three massive bookshelves and an old stereo covered the opposite wall. Almost all the decor was a masculine shade of dark blue, including the area rug.

Julia watched as Gabriel unpacked his suitcase, methodically plac-

ing the folded clothes on top of the bed. When he saw her, he straightened up and smiled.

"Now do you see why I prefer to stay at a hotel?"

"I'm sorry, Gabriel. I should have done something. Said something."

"You need to do what I normally do—just keep quiet and take it." He
dropped what he was holding and was at her side in a moment. "It's a
good thing we agreed to keep our relationship secret. Scott doesn't
think very highly of me, and your reputation would be tarnished by association."

"I don't mind. Let him tarnish me."

He smiled and caressed her cheek. "I mind. I mind a great deal." He
cleared his throat. "Tonight, after everyone has gone to bed, I'd like to
take you for a walk."

"I'd love to."

"At least that will give me something to look forward to." Gabriel
pulled her into a heated embrace. His tongue entered her mouth immediately, his hands resting on her backside, squeezing it without shame.

Julia allowed herself to forget she was in his father's house for a minute before she struggled to back away. "We—can't."

Gabriel had a wild look in his eye. *"But I need you."* He grabbed her
and wound his hands in her hair. "I need you, Julianne. Right now."

Julia's insides liquefied in reaction to the desperation in his words.
He drew his lips down the curve of her neck, nuzzling at the opening
of her shirt so that he could nibble her collarbone. He closed his bedroom door with his foot, and quickly unfastened two buttons of her
blouse, pushing the fabric aside to expose the perfect skin just above
her bra. Squeezing the curves of her backside, he lifted her and pressed
her back against the door, pulling her legs flush around his hips. Julia
gasped at the closeness, at the direct contact between them.

He floated his lips across her upper chest, pausing to dip the tip of
his tongue just under the pale pink lace. Julia threw her head back and
groaned as her hands sought his hair, urging him forward. He responded by tracing a long finger around the perimeter of her demi-cup,
allowing his hand to gently slip inside, while his other hand held the
back of her right thigh.

Her eyes popped open as his warm palm cupped her naked breast, his mouth latched onto the skin at the base of her throat, sucking slightly. Much as it pained her to do so, she pulled his hand away and shifted so that he was forced to release his hold on her neck.

"Gabriel, I'm sorry. We can't." She quickly adjusted her bra. She wriggled slightly, but he did not set her down. Flushing furiously, she avoided the blazing color of his eyes. "I know you're upset. And I'd like to comfort you, but they're all waiting downstairs. Rachel wants you to choose the wine for dinner."

Gabriel gazed at her with new eyes and carefully put her down. She quickly buttoned her blouse and tried to straighten her trousers.

"You think too highly of me."

Julia ran the pointed toe of her ankle boot along the edge of the area rug. "I very much doubt that."

"What I just did was not appropriate or nice. I'm sorry." He traced a finger over the red mark that had bloomed where his mouth had tasted her and pulled her blouse closed, fastening the top button. Now she looked like a Mennonite.

She gazed up into dark, troubled eyes. "Gabriel, you're still tired from yesterday, and this is a stressful holiday. I know you didn't mean anything just now. You feel better when you touch me. And truthfully, so do I." Now she was looking at the floor again.

"Come here," he whispered, reaching to envelope her in a warm embrace. "You're wrong you know, I did mean it. Of course I feel better when I touch you. But I'm sorry to fly at you like that. I wasn't thinking . . ." Gabriel appeared disgusted with himself.

"You didn't hurt me."

He smiled into her hair and pressed a kiss to her forehead. "I will endeavor to be worthy of you. If you weren't here, I'd have left already."

"No, you wouldn't have. Richard needs you. And you would never leave him in need."

A pained look shadowed Gabriel's features. He kissed her once again, more like a friend than a lover, and turned back to his suitcase.

Julia crept out of his room and down the stairs, wondering what would happen during dinner. She paused on the landing to check her appearance in the mirror, hoping that she didn't look as if she had just stolen a sensual moment with her professor.

Chapter Twenty-five

Rachel planned the seating arrangement. She sat in Grace's place at the foot of the table, so she could be near the kitchen, while Richard sat at the head. Scott and Aaron sat on one side, Julia and Gabriel sat on the other. Julia could feel his eyes on her, but he made no move to brush up against her under the table, much to her disappointment.

Rachel stared at Julia's new Mennonite look and glanced over at Gabriel. He ignored his sister by focusing all of his attention on his linen napkin.

Before they began eating, Richard asked his family to hold hands so that he could say grace. A shock passed from Gabriel's hand to Julia's, making her withdraw hastily. Rachel's eagle eyes saw the retreat, but she said nothing, especially since Julia eventually gave Gabriel her hand.

"Our Father, we thank you for this day and for the many gifts you've given us. Thank you for our country, our home, our food. Thank you for my beautiful family and that we can be together, for my lovely wife, the love of my life—"

Six pairs of eyes opened immediately. Five pairs of eyes swung to the head of the table. One pair of gray eyes immediately closed and his hands covered them.

It had been a mistake. Her description had rolled off his tongue as it normally did during family grace. But the effect was dramatic and immediate. Richard's shoulders began to shake.

"Oh my God," mumbled Julia.

Rachel was out of her seat in a flash, wrapping her arms around her father's shoulders, fighting back her own tears. Aaron quickly finished Richard's prayer as if nothing had happened, and at the *Amen* everyone else wiped away a tear or two. They began passing vegetables and turkey and Scott's mashed potatoes.

Except for Gabriel. He sat stoically, hands clenched into fists at his sides as he watched his adoptive father cry. Underneath the table, Julia reached out a tentative hand to Gabriel's knee. And when he didn't flinch, or throw her hand back into her lap, she kept it there. Eventually, he took her hand in his and squeezed it.

Julia felt Gabriel's body begin to relax before they withdrew their hands. For most of the meal, he brought his left foot to entwine with her right, keeping their continued connection secret.

While the family enjoyed a store-bought pumpkin pie, Richard told Julia he was moving to Philadelphia in January in order to start a new job as a researcher in the Neurosciences Center at Temple University Hospital.

"You sold the house?"

Richard's eyes went to Gabriel and returned to Julia. "Yes. I bought a condo near Rachel and Aaron. I'll be able to focus on my research in Philadelphia, and I won't have to teach anymore. I'm not ready to retire yet, but I'd like to do something different."

Julia felt sad that the house was going to be sold, but she said only complimentary things about his plans. *This must be why Gabriel wants to visit the orchard tonight.*

"So, Gabriel, why don't you tell everyone about your upcoming trip to Italy?" Richard smiled in his adopted son's direction.

Several things happened all at once. Rachel and Aaron glanced at Julia. Julia continued eating her pumpkin pie as if nothing had happened, trying valiantly not to appear wooden. And Gabriel sought her hand under the table while he clenched his teeth. Julia could almost hear his jaw snap shut.

"You're going to Italy? Man, I wish I had a cushy trust fund that would let me do that. I would love to go to Italy." Scott winked at Julia.

Richard gazed at Gabriel politely but expectantly. Julia saw a flicker of anger pass over Gabriel's features before it disappeared.

"I've been invited to give a lecture at the Uffizi Gallery in Florence," he announced stiffly.

"When will you go?" asked Rachel.

"The beginning of December."

"How long will you be gone?" asked Aaron.

"A week or two, possibly more. My hosts have several events planned, and I had hoped to do some research for my book while I'm there. But that depends."

Gabriel squeezed Julia's hand under the table, but her hand had gone limp. She remained focused on her pie and chewed thoughtfully. No one noticed that her eyes had become watery. She didn't dare look in Gabriel's direction.

After dinner, the kitchen was crowded as everyone helped clean and put things away. Gabriel tried to speak to Julia alone, but they were constantly interrupted. Finally, he gave up and accompanied Richard out to the back porch while the rest of the family piled onto the couches in the living room to listen to very bad eighties music.

It had been Scott's choice. And when he stood up to dance to *Tainted Love* by Soft Cell, Rachel and Julia mocked him mercilessly. Aaron didn't understand the attraction to eighties music or the humor in Scott's slightly eclectic dance routine, but he smiled politely as he sipped his beer.

When the song was replaced by *Don't You (Forget About Me)*, Julia knew it was time to get another drink. She floated into the kitchen and found herself looking out the window at Gabriel and Richard, who were wearing their winter coats and sitting in two Adirondack chairs on the back porch.

"Hey, Julia." Aaron came up behind her and pulled another beer from the refrigerator. "Corona?"

"Thanks." Julia took the bottle gratefully.

"Lime?" He pointed to a series of lime sections in a bowl on the counter.

After watching her struggle to force the lime into the narrow opening of the bottle, he took pity on her. "Want me to do that?"

"Please."

Aaron was a Corona specialist. He pushed the lime into the bottle, and capping the opening with his thumb, proceeded to tip the bottle upside down, sending the lime to the very bottom. When he righted the bottle, he carefully let the air pressure out at a snail's pace and with a smug look, handed the bottle back to Julia.

"That's the correct way to do it," he said, grinning at her.

She took a quick pull from the bottle and smiled. He was right. It was good. "You're a good man, Aaron." Julia surprised herself by speaking the words aloud.

He reddened but returned her smile. "How are you doing?"

She shrugged. "I'm fine. Grad school is a lot of work, but I seem to be doing well. I'm applying to different doctoral programs for next year. I hope I get in somewhere."

Aaron nodded, and he fixed her with a serious but sympathetic look. "Rachel told me that Simon called. I don't want to upset you, but we're both really worried. Are you okay?"

Julia blinked slightly as she worked through what he'd said, realizing that Gabriel must have told Rachel about the phone call.

"I was scared. Even though I was so far away, he still found me. He wasn't exactly happy with our conversation."

Aaron gently patted her arm. "You're with us. You're part of our family, and we stick together. If he shows up, I'll take care of him. Hell, I've been itching for a fight. What better way to work out your frustration than by teaching someone like him a lesson?" He grinned and took a swig of his beer.

Julia nodded but did not smile. "What's happening with the wedding? Rachel said that you picked a date, but when I asked her about it tonight she clammed up on me."

He shook his head. "Don't say anything to anyone, but we were planning to get married in July. That is, until Rachel saw her dad break down during grace. She pulled me aside after dinner and said that there was no way she could bring up the topic of a wedding now. So we're back to where we were before—engaged with no fixed wedding date." Aaron hung his head a little and wiped at his eyes with the back of one of his hands.

Julia felt sorry for him. "She loves you. She'll marry you. She just wants a happy family and a big, happy wedding. You'll get there."

"What about a happy Aaron?" he muttered, his eyes momentarily hard. He sighed and shook his head. "I didn't mean that. I really didn't mean that. But I love her. I've loved her for years. I never wanted to live together—I wanted to marry her as soon as we graduated high school. But she always wanted to wait. The waiting is killing me, Jules."

"Some people think that marriage is just a piece of paper. Rachel is lucky you think differently."

"It's not just a piece of paper. I want to stand up in front of her and God, and all our friends and make promises to her. I want her to be mine. Not as my girlfriend, but as my wife. I want what Richard and Grace had, but some days I wonder if that's ever going to happen."

Julia shyly put her arm around Aaron's shoulder and gave him a sideways, one-armed hug. "It's going to happen. Don't give up. Once Richard is out of the house and settled in his new life, Rachel will see that it's okay for all of you to be happy again. Being in this house without Grace is hurting everyone. It's so empty here without her."

Aaron nodded and tipped back the rest of his beer. "Scott decided to play a slow song. Rachel will be wanting a dance. Excuse me." He disappeared into the living room, leaving Julia alone with her perfect Corona and her imperfect thoughts.

Meanwhile, Richard and his eldest son sat outside enjoying Gabriel's gifts—Cuban cigars that he'd smuggled from Canada and a bottle of Richard's favorite Scotch, The Glenrothes.

"Grace would never have allowed this in the house," Richard mused, blowing smoke rings toward the inky velvet of the November sky.

"I'm sure no one would mind now."

Richard smiled at his son sadly. "But I would. For her. Thank you, by the way. These are probably the best I've ever had."

"You're welcome."

They clinked glasses and wished one another cheers, falling silent to gaze out at the woods behind the house and up at the delicate strands of stars above.

"Julia looks well. Do you see much of her?"

Gabriel casually flicked the ash from his cigar into the ashtray between them. "She's in my class."

"She's all grown up. She seems more confident." Richard drew thoughtfully on his cigar. "Your university must agree with her."

Gabriel shrugged.

"Grace loved her." Richard watched his son's face fail to register any reaction. "Now that I'm moving, we're going to have to have a family meeting about the furniture and—other things. I know it's going to be uncomfortable, but I think it would be better to have that conversation now rather than waiting until Christmas. You will be home for Christmas, won't you?"

"Yes, I just don't know when. As for the furniture, Rachel and Scott can have everything."

Richard's lips pulled together. "You're part of this family too. Isn't there something you'd like? What about the armoire that Grace inherited from her grandmother? It's always been in your room. Wouldn't you like that?"

Gabriel studied his father for a moment. "I assumed you'd be taking all of Grace's things."

"It's just not possible. There are a few things I can't part with. But as for everything else . . ." He sighed. "Truthfully, this is the most important thing to me." He held up his hand and showed Gabriel his wedding ring.

Gabriel was surprised he was still wearing it, but only for an instant. Something told him that Richard would be wearing it for the rest of his life.

"Grace wanted her jewelry divided up. Rachel went through it yesterday. There are a couple of things sitting on the dressing table in our room for you."

"What about Rachel?"

"She's happy with what Grace wanted her to have, and the same goes for Scott. In fact, they want Julia to have something, if you don't object."

Gabriel rubbed his eyes. "No, I don't object. What did they have in mind?"

"Grace had two sets of pearls. One of them I gave to her, but one of them came from her parents or she bought them herself when she was a student. I'm not sure. Those are the ones that Rachel would like to give to Julia."

"That's fine."

"Good. Before you leave, just be sure to talk to Rachel about the rest of it. You'll want to take them with you."

Gabriel nodded uncomfortably, focusing his attention on his cigar.

"Grace loved you. She didn't believe in favorites, you know. But you were—special. She believed God brought you to her. She just wanted you to be happy."

Gabriel nodded. "I know that."

"Actually, she wanted you to find a nice girl and settle down, have children, and *then* be happy." Richard smiled.

"That isn't going to happen, Richard."

"You don't know that." He reached out an affectionate hand and lightly gripped his son's forearm. "Grace never gave up. Don't you give up, either. If I know anything about Grace, it's that she still loves you, and no doubt she's lighting candles and praying for you, even now. She's just a little closer to the source."

For a moment their eyes met. For a moment, both sapphire and gray were damp with tears.

Pray for me, Grace. How am I ever going to live without you? thought Richard.

The two men blew smoke rings across the porch, silently savoring their Scotch and their memories. But saying nothing more.

When everyone finally decided it was time for bed, they ascended the staircase almost two by two, like animals lumbering to Noah's ark.

Gabriel held Julia back slightly so that they were the last to go up. When everyone had disappeared into his or her respective chambers, he stood outside her bedroom door, gazing down at her with a somewhat hungry look on his face. Julia felt nervous all of a sudden and became fascinated by her feet.

He reached down with one hand and popped the top button of her blouse open, sliding his hand across her neck. "I'm sorry about this." He touched the mark he'd made earlier.

Julia kept her eyes down.

"Julianne, look at me." He coaxed her chin upward with a single finger, gazing at her with troubled eyes. "I didn't mean to mark you. I know you don't belong to me, but if you were mine, I would find a better way of showing it to the world than by turning your beautiful skin red or purple."

Her eyes grew teary. Of course she was his. She had been his since she took his hand long ago and followed him into the woods.

"Wait here a moment." He disappeared into his bedroom, returning with a familiar-looking British-racing-green cashmere sweater. "This is for you." He handed it to her.

She accepted the sweater but gave him a puzzled look.

"I was worried that you wouldn't be warm enough. I thought maybe you could wear this to the woods."

"Thank you. But won't you need it?"

He smiled knowingly. "I have others. And it pleases me to think that something of mine will be so close to you. If I had my way, you'd wear it all weekend." He straightened his shoulders and took a step closer. "Perhaps this is a more humane way of marking you."

Gabriel's eyes shone in the dim light of the hallway. He took another step forward, as if he were about to draw her into an embrace, when Scott came lumbering out of his room, shirtless and wearing only a pair of boxer shorts. His boxer shorts had smiley faces on them.

At the sight of him, but before he could say something, Gabriel abruptly stuck his hand out. "Good night, Julia," he said stiffly, shaking her hand.

Scott snorted loudly and scratched his ass as he walked toward the bathroom. As soon as the bathroom door closed, Gabriel pulled Julia into his arms and kissed her firmly on the lips.

"I'll come to get you in an hour. Dress warmly and wear comfortable shoes." He eyed her high-heeled boots with a sigh. It pained him to bid them *adieu*, but he knew that it was necessary.

"Good night, my—" He stopped abruptly before disappearing into his bedroom, leaving Julia standing alone.

She wondered what he had not said. She wondered if she should tell him that she was his.

Julia went into her room and changed into warmer clothes, wrapping herself in the scent that was Gabriel and his cozy cashmere sweater, which enveloped her like a lover's embrace.

Chapter Twenty-six

Whehen the house was shrouded in darkness and it seemed that everyone else was fast asleep, Gabriel and Julia stood staring at one another in the kitchen.

"I'm not sure you're dressed warmly enough. It's chilly out there." He gestured to her coat.

"Not as cold as Toronto," she laughed.

"I won't keep you outside for long. Look what I found." Gabriel held up a long, wide scarf made of thick white and black stripes. He wrapped it around her neck, expertly looping it at the front. "This is from my old college at Oxford."

Julia smiled. "I like it."

"It suits you. I found something else too." Gabriel held up an old blanket that looked oddly familiar.

Julia reached out her hand to trace the edge of it. "Is that the one?"

"I think so. But it won't be warm enough, so I brought two more." He took her hand and led her out to the porch.

It was colder now and dark, but somehow it seemed as if no time had passed since Julia took Gabriel's hand and followed him into the woods. She inhaled sharply at the memory, and as they crossed the backyard in the inky darkness, she felt her heart beginning to pound in her chest.

Gabriel squeezed her hand. "What's wrong?"

"Nothing."

"You're nervous, I can tell. Talk to me."

He let go of her hand and wrapped his arm around her waist, pulling her close.

She hugged his waist in return. "The last time I was in these woods I got lost. You have to promise that you won't leave me."

"Julianne, I am not going to leave you. You don't understand how important you are to me. I can't even imagine what it would be like to lose you." The pitch of Gabriel's voice changed; it was low, tense.

His declaration took her by surprise.

"If for some reason we get separated, I want you to wait for me. I'll find you, I promise." Gabriel pulled a flashlight out of his pocket, and it shone brightly, illuminating the well-worn path in front of them, which disappeared into the trees.

The woods were spooky at night—a mixture of lush pines and naked trees waiting for spring. Julia clutched at Gabriel's waist more tightly, worried that she might trip over a root or something and go sprawling. When they arrived at the edge of the orchard, he stopped.

It seemed smaller than Julia remembered it. The grassy space looked the same, and the rock and the apple trees were the same, but not as large and significant as they were in her memory. And sadder, as if everything had been forgotten.

Gabriel led her to the spot that was theirs all those years ago and painstakingly spread the old blanket on the ground.

"Who bought Richard's house?" she asked.

"What's that?"

"I was just wondering who bought the house. Tell me it wasn't Mrs. Roberts. She always wanted it."

Gabriel pulled her to sit next to him on the ground and draped them both in blankets. She curled into his side, and he wrapped his arms about her. "I bought it."

"Really? Why?"

"I wasn't going to allow Mrs. Roberts to live here and chop down all the trees."

"So you bought the house because of the orchard?"

"I couldn't stand the idea of someone else owning it and possibly destroying it. Of never being able to come back here."

"So what will you do?"

He shrugged. "My real estate agent will rent it out. I'd like to keep it as a summer house. I don't know. I just couldn't let Richard sell it to a stranger."

"It was very generous of you."

"Money means nothing. I can never repay him."

Julia pressed a kiss to his cheek.

He smiled at her. "Are you comfortable?"

"Yes."

"Are you warm enough?"

She giggled. "You're generating quite a bit of heat, so yes."

"You're too far away."

Even in the moonlight, Julia could see his eyes grow dark. She scooted closer to him and trembled slightly as he placed her sideways on his lap.

"That's better," he whispered, pulling her peacoat up slightly so that he could touch the naked skin of her lower back.

"Can I ask you something?" Julia looked at him pensively.

"Of course."

"Why isn't your last name Clark?"

He sighed. "Emerson was my mother's name. I thought if I changed it, I would be disowning her. And I'm not a Clark. Not really."

They were quiet for a few minutes, each coming to terms with memories and reality. Gabriel continued to caress her back, and she nuzzled up against him. He didn't seem to be in a hurry to start a conversation, so Julia decided to speak first.

"I had a crush on you from the moment I saw your picture. I was so surprised that you noticed me the night I met you—that you wanted me to come with you."

He brushed his lips against hers, just for an instant, fanning the flames that flickered below the surface. "You appeared to me in my darkness. You asked me once why I didn't sleep with you that night. It's so clear to me now; I drank in your goodness, and it satisfied my longings."

Julia would have looked away, embarrassed, but Gabriel's vulnerable gaze kept her there, exploring the depths of two dark shadowy pools.

"I don't remember everything, but I remember thinking that you were very beautiful. Your hair, your face, your mouth. Sonnets could be written about your mouth, Julianne. I ached to kiss it from the moment I saw you."

Julia pressed their chests together and grasped his neck with both hands, urging his mouth forward. She kissed him slowly but with feeling, tugging on his lower lip with her teeth, exploring his mouth with her tongue.

He placed his large hands flush against her back, almost lifting her. She responded by shifting her legs and moving to straddle him. He groaned in her mouth at their sudden and intense connection and held her even more tightly. His hands began to rub against her flesh, gliding up to the edge of her lacy bra strap and then back down again to the waistband of her jeans, teasing and tracing the barriers to her skin. It was so smooth, so soft. He wished he could see it in the moonlight. He wished he could see all of her.

Gabriel pulled away from her mouth when he felt her shiver. "Are you all right, love?"

She started at the unfamiliar term but then a slow smile crept across her face. "More than all right. I . . ." She paused and shook her head.

"What is it?"

"You're very . . . intense."

Without thinking, Gabriel threw his head back and laughed. His chest vibrated with good humor, and Julia almost found herself laughing too. If she hadn't thought he was laughing at her. He reached his thumb up to pull her lower lip from between her teeth.

"If you think my actions are intense, then it's a good thing you don't know what I'm thinking at this moment."

He shifted underneath her, and if she hadn't noticed before, she noticed now. Where their two bodies pressed up against one another there was solidity and heat, the promise of something mysterious and satisfying.

She flushed at the way his body responded to her but didn't break eye contact. "Tell me."

"I want to make love to you because I care about you. I want to worship your naked body with my own and learn all of your secrets. I want to please you, not for minutes, but for hours and even days. I want to see you arch your back in ecstasy and look into your eyes when I make you come." He sighed and shook his head, his gaze heated but resolute. "But not here. It's too cold and it's your first time and there are some things we need to discuss first." He tenderly kissed her forehead, worried that she would interpret his declaration as a rejection.

"I want you to feel safe and comfortable. I want to adore every part of you. And that's going to take time. And—ah—it's going to require more amenities than this field can afford." He smiled at her seductively and cocked an eyebrow at her. "Of course, what I want is of very little consequence. What is at issue is what you want."

"I think my feelings are pretty clear."

"Are they?" His voice sounded unsure.

She leaned up to kiss him but caught his chin instead of his lips. "I wouldn't be here with you in cold weather if I didn't want to be."

"It's still nice to hear."

"Gabriel Emerson, I want you," she breathed. "In fact, I—" She bit down on her lip roughly to keep from saying the four-letter word.

"You can say it," he whispered. "It will be all right. Say what you feel."

"I—I want you to be my first. I'm yours, Gabriel. If you want me."

"I want nothing more."

This time he captured her mouth. His kiss was filled with promise and resolve. The intensity set fire to Julia's insides, stirring and swirling her desires.

Gabriel wanted her. It had always been there in his kiss, but the line between hunger and affection was so easily misread. She was no longer concerned with that line, there was just his body pressed up against hers and their two mouths connected while their hands gently explored one another. In their orchard, which was Paradise, there were only two almost-lovers and no one and nothing else.

As their kisses grew more passionate, Gabriel slowly reclined backward onto the blanket, pulling her until he was flat and she was kneeling on either side of him. Her chest pressed against his, and a pleasant friction arose between their hips. She moved atop him, shamelessly pressing her softness and curves against him. It was like nothing she had ever felt before.

He allowed her to continue, but only for a moment or two. He freed her lips and traced her cheekbones with his thumbs, lightly back and forth, his gaze heated.

"I burn for you, Julianne, but it's more than just a physical hunger. I crave you, all of you." He sighed and shook his head. "I hate to do this, but there are a few things we need to discuss."

Julia's sigh matched his. "Such as?"

"Such as my trip to Italy. I should have told you first."

She sat up slowly. "Professors travel for work. I know that." She dropped her gaze to the blanket beneath them.

Gabriel sat up too. "Julianne." He lifted her chin with a single finger. "Don't hide from me. Tell me what you are thinking."

She twisted her hands together. "I know I don't have any right to be—demanding, but it hurt to find out that Richard knew about your trip before I did."

"You have every right to be demanding. I am your boyfriend. I should have told you first."

"Are you my boyfriend?" she whispered.

"I'm more than that. I am your lover."

Gabriel's words and his voice, low and sensual, sent a shiver up her spine.

"Even though we aren't having sex?"

"Lovers are intimate with one another in many different ways. But you need to know that I desire all intimacy with you and only you. So the term *boyfriend* is inadequate. And I'm very sorry I hurt your feelings. My trip to Italy came up when Richard and I discussed the house because it affected our arrangements.

"I received the invitation from the Uffizi months ago, long before you came to Toronto. I wanted to bring it up, but I was putting it off until we were more—comfortable with one another."

She peered over at him with interest.

"I wanted your Christmas gift to be a trip to Florence. Of course I don't want to go alone. The thought of leaving you behind, of being separated from you—" His voice grew rough. "I was worried you'd refuse, that you would think it was a tool of seduction."

She frowned at him. "Do you really want me to go with you?"

"I'd rather not go if you won't accompany me."

She smiled widely and kissed him. "Then thank you for the invitation. I accept."

Gabriel smiled in relief and buried his face in her hair. "After what happened with the clothes, I was convinced you'd say no. I'll book separate accommodations, if you wish. And I'll book you an open ticket so you can leave if you decide—"

"Gabriel, I said yes. With all my heart. I can think of no one I'd rather visit Florence with, and please let me stay with you." She looked at him shyly. "The semester will be over. We wouldn't be breaking the rules if we were to . . . if you were to decide to take me to your bed and make me yours—"

He cut her off with a searing kiss. "Are you sure? Are you sure you want me to be your first?"

She gazed at him earnestly. "It was always you, Gabriel. I never wanted anyone else. You are the man I've been waiting for."

She initiated a soft kiss that quickly escalated. Within moments she was lying on top of him, their bodies flush together. She was so close to him, to it, to everything. And she'd never wanted to be closer, not even during their tango in the museum.

He pulled back, panting, dragging his lips down her neck. Carefully avoiding her love bite from earlier, he brushed a kiss against her hair. Julia moaned and wrapped his hair around her fingers.

"It's too dangerous, love. I can't kiss you the way I would like to and be able to stop."

Despite his protestation, his hands ran tantalizing courses up and down the curves of her bottom and over the flare of her hips, teasing and pressing into her. Julia tried to kiss him again, but he caught her face with his hand, stroking her gently.

"Too much of that and I'll have you right here," he whispered. "You deserve better. You deserve everything, and that's what I'm going to give to you."

She leaned into his hand.

"Given your decision, there are a few other things we should discuss." Gabriel's voice was no longer playful and sultry. He cleared his throat and took a couple of deliberate deep breaths. "If you choose to go on the pill or if you are on it already, that's fine. But I need to tell you that contraception is unnecessary."

"I don't understand."

"I can't have children, Julianne."

She blinked at him.

"Are children something you always wanted? Maybe I should have brought this up sooner." He shifted somewhat anxiously.

She paused as his revelation began to sink in. "I didn't exactly come from a happy family. There have been times when I thought it might be nice to have a husband and a baby. But I never really thought something like that would work out for me."

"Why not?"

She shrugged and averted her eyes. "I never thought I'd find someone who could love me. I'm not exactly sexy. I'm shy. And weak."

"Oh, Julia." He embraced her and kissed her on both cheeks. "You're wrong. You are incredibly sexy. And you are far from weak."

She fingered the lapel of his leather jacket for a moment. "I'm sorry to hear that you can't have children. Lots of couples have trouble conceiving."

Gabriel stiffened. "Their situations are completely different."

"How so?"

"Their infertility is natural."

Julia noticed Gabriel's eyes narrow as he watched her with a very worried expression.

She raised a hand to his face and gently touched his cheek. "Were you very disappointed when you found out?"

He grasped her wrist and removed her hand from his face. "I was relieved, Julianne. And I didn't find out."

"Then how . . ."

"I made the decision to have myself sterilized when I came out of rehab."

She swallowed hard.

"Oh Gabriel, why?"

"Because someone like me shouldn't reproduce. I told you about my father. I told you what I was like when I was doing drugs. I thought it would be irresponsible to leave open any kind of paternity. So I had it taken care of, and I will not have it reversed. I decided that there would be no children for me. Ever."

He turned his piercing gaze on her. "I didn't account for you, though. And now I almost regret my decision. But really, Julianne, it's better this way. Trust me." His body suddenly tensed, as if he were preparing himself for an onslaught. "You might decide it would be best not to get involved with me now."

"Gabriel, please. I just—need a minute." Julia moved to sit beside him as she tried to process the information he'd just given her.

Gabriel followed suit, tugging on one of the blankets so that it was wrapped around her entirely. She realized that he'd given her a half-admission, that the true secret was the event or events that led to his despair. Those events had to be more than just his upbringing and his drug use.

Does it matter? Is there a secret he could tell that would kill your love for him?

He was as still as a statue in the cascading moonlight, awaiting her response. The minutes seemed like hours to him.

I love him. Nothing he could say could kill that. Nothing.

"I'm so sorry, Gabriel." She flung her arms around his neck. "But I still want you. I realize there might come a time when we need to revisit this conversation, but I'll accept what you've said for now."

At first he was taken aback by her reaction. Then her gentle acceptance overwhelmed him. It made it difficult for him to find the right words.

"Julia, I need to tell you who I am. What I am." He was suddenly insistent.

"I will listen to whatever you have to say, but I still want you. It was always you, Gabriel."

He cupped her face in his hands and kissed her gently, as if his soul was begging to be joined to hers. "It was always you, Julianne. Only you."

He held her and breathed in her comfort. All of a sudden, he could see the future. He had hope. He had faith that maybe, just maybe, when she knew everything, she would look at him with those big, brown eyes and say that she still wanted him.

You love her. Once again the voice came out of nowhere, only this time Gabriel recognized it. And he silently whispered his thanks.

"You seem so far away, love." Julia smiled as she used his new term.

He kissed her softly. "I'm right where I want to be. Perhaps tonight isn't the best night to share all our secrets. But I can't take you to Italy without telling you everything. And I would like you to tell me everything too." He looked into her eyes with a very serious expression. "I can't ask you to bare your body to me without asking you to bare your soul. I want to do the same with you. I hope you understand." With his eyes he tried to express his feelings, how he was thinking only of her in adding this prerequisite.

She nodded slowly in agreement. He pressed their lips together, and Julia sighed, resting her head against his chest and listening to the steady, contented rhythm of his heart. Time passed or stood still. Two almost-lovers entwined beneath a dark November sky, the stars and moonlight their only illumination.

✲✲

The next morning, Julia awoke early and walked down the hallway to take a shower. She dressed and packed her suitcase, knocking on Gabriel's door at eight o'clock. But there was no answer. She pressed the curve of her ear against the door and listened. There was no movement. No sound.

She dragged her rolling bag down the hallway and carried it down the stairs. As she turned the corner into the living room, she saw Richard and Rachel sitting on one of the sofas. Rachel was crying and her father was trying to comfort her.

Their eyes flew to Julia's as she dropped her bag accidentally. She apologized profusely.

"It's all right, Julia," Richard greeted her. "How did you sleep?"

"Well, thank you. Rachel, are you okay?"

Her friend wiped her eyes. "I'm fine."

"Why don't you two talk while I make some breakfast? Rachel likes blueberry pancakes, Julia. How about you?" He stood up and gestured toward the kitchen.

"Thanks, but my dad asked me to meet him at Kinfolks for breakfast at nine."

"I'll drive you. Just let me whip up some pancakes first."

Richard disappeared, and Julia sat next to Rachel on the couch, putting her arm around her friend's shoulders.

"What happened?"

"I had a fight with Aaron. He was moody this morning, so I asked him what was wrong. He starting talking about the wedding and wondering if I was ever going to set a date. When I said I wanted to wait, he wanted to know how long." She threw up her hands in frustration. "I told him what I said before—*I don't know*. Then he asked if I wanted him to let me out of the engagement!"

Julia inhaled sharply in surprise.

"We never fight. But he was so upset that he couldn't even look at me. Then in the middle of our conversation, he just walked out the front door and drove away. I have no idea where he went or if he's even coming back," Rachel sobbed.

Julia hugged her friend tightly. "Of course he's coming back. I'm sure he was upset with himself for fighting with you and went for a drive to cool off."

"Dad overhead us. So of course he wanted to know why I was delaying the wedding." She wiped her eyes with her hands. "He said Aaron was right, I couldn't put my life on hold. He said that Mom would be upset if she knew I was putting things off because of her." Rachel's face crumpled as her eyes filled with more tears.

"Your dad is right—you both deserve to be happy. Aaron loves you so much. He just wants to get married. He's worried you've got cold feet."

"I don't have cold feet. I've loved him forever."

"Then tell him that. He took you to an island to reconnect with you after the funeral. He's been patient about everything. I'm sure he doesn't care when the wedding is, he just wants to set a date."

Rachel sniffled sadly. "I had no idea how upset he was."

"Maybe you should eat some breakfast, then call him. He'll have calmed down by then, and you two can go somewhere and talk. You can't work things out here with so many people around."

Rachel shuddered. "Thank God Scott didn't walk in on us. He would have sided with me and pissed Aaron off even more."

At that moment, the front door opened and closed and a tall, brown-haired man, sweaty from jogging, strolled into the living room. His hair was messy and damp, and he was wearing a black Nike jogging suit. As he approached the two women, he took a pair of earbuds out of his ears and pressed a button on his iPhone.

He looked at Rachel and Julia, frowning darkly. "What happened?"

"Aaron and I had a fight." More tears fell down Rachel's cheeks, leaving Gabriel stricken.

He walked over and pulled her into a hug, pressing a kiss to the top of her head. "I'm sorry, Rach. Where is he?"

"He left."

He subtly shook his head in frustration. It pained him to see his sister cry.

Before he could ask for more details, Richard emerged from the kitchen, announcing that breakfast was served. "And Julia, if you can give me a few minutes, I'll take you to Kinfolks."

Gabriel released Rachel. "What's happening?"

"Julia needs to meet her father at nine."

Gabriel looked at his watch. "It's not even eight-thirty."

"That's okay. I can just have a cup of coffee at the restaurant and wait for him." Julia avoided Gabriel's gaze. She didn't want to be an inconvenience.

"Let me shower and I'll drive you. I have to stop by my real estate agent's house anyway."

Julia nodded and the three of them entered the kitchen while Gabriel went upstairs. Over blueberry pancakes, Rachel produced something from her purse and fastened it around Julia's neck.

She touched the pearl necklace with surprise. "What's this?"

"They were Mom's. We wanted you to have something of hers."

"I can't, Rachel. You should have them."

"I have other things," she said, smiling.

"What about Scott?"

Rachel giggled. "Scott said they weren't his style."

"We wanted you to have them." Richard looked at her kindly.

"Are you sure?"

"Of course!" Rachel hugged her friend, grateful for the opportunity to return her kindness in some tangible way.

Julia was overwhelmed, but she fought back tears for Richard's sake. "Thank you. Thank you both."

He pressed a fatherly kiss to the top of her head. "Grace would have been so happy to see you wearing something of hers."

"I should thank Scott."

Rachel rolled her eyes and stifled a snort. "He won't be up till noon. Aaron and I had to turn the stereo on last night to block out the sounds of him snoring. We could hear him through the walls." She looked up into her father's slightly disapproving face. "Sorry, Dad, but it's the truth. Anyway, just bring your dad to dinner tomorrow night, Julia, and you'll be able to thank Scott then."

Julia nodded, fingering the pearls thoughtfully, marveling at their smooth spherical shape.

❉ ❉

Gabriel and Julia didn't say much on the drive to the restaurant. Almost all the words they needed to speak had already been spoken. They held hands like teenagers in the car. Julia beamed when Gabriel gave her his Magdalen College scarf and said that he wanted her to have it. When they arrived at the restaurant, Tom's truck was nowhere to be found.

"I guess we're lucky." Julia sounded relieved.

"He'll have to be told eventually. I'll tell him, if you wish."

Julia turned her head to see if he was serious. He was. "He told me to stay away from you. He thinks you're a criminal."

"Then you should let me tell him. You've taken enough abuse to last a lifetime."

"Gabriel, my father never abused me. He isn't a bad man. He's just—misguided."

Gabriel rubbed his mouth but said nothing.

"I'm not going to say anything until we're back in Toronto and the semester is over. It will be easier to explain on the phone. But I should go. He'll be here any minute."

Gabriel kissed her lightly, caressing her cheek with the back of his hand. "Call me later."

"I will." She kissed him again and slipped out of the Jeep.

He pulled her luggage out of the back and placed it at her feet, leaning forward to whisper in her ear, "I'm already fantasizing about our first time."

Julia blushed and murmured, "Me too."

Tom Mitchell was a man of few words. He was incredibly average-looking—of medium height and build with medium brown hair and rather medium brown eyes. Despite his failure as a father and whatever failures he had been guilty of as a husband, he was a dedicated volunteer and very active in municipal life. In fact, he enjoyed an excellent reputation amongst the townsfolk of Selinsgrove, and his opinion was frequently sought after in all matters municipal.

To Tom's credit, he and Julia spent an enjoyable day together. The regulars at Kinfolks restaurant welcomed her gladly, and he was able to brag to them about how well she was doing in graduate school and how she was applying to Harvard for her PhD.

He took her for a drive around town to see some of the new building projects, pointing out how Selinsgrove had grown even during her short absence. And he brought her to a first-aid training session that was being hosted at the fire house so that his colleagues could tell her how much her old man talked about her. Afterward, they went grocery shopping, because for various reasons Tom didn't keep a lot of food in the house. Later that afternoon, he skipped the football game so that they could watch an old movie together. Yes, it was the director's cut of *Blade Runner*, but it was a film that they both wanted to see, and they quite enjoyed it.

When it was over, Julia handed him a beer, thus encouraging him to watch football while she made Grace's famous chicken Kiev for dinner. Finally alone, she sent a short text to Gabriel:

G, Just making Grace's chicken Kiev and a lemon meringue pie for Dad.

He's watching football. Hope you're having a great day.
I'll call you around 6:30. Your Julia. XO

A few minutes later, while Julia was in the middle of assembling two casseroles of chicken Kiev, one for that evening and one for Tom to freeze, her iPhone chirped with an incoming text:

My Julia, I've missed you. We're watching football too.
R and A have kissed and made up and set a date.
Richard is something of a miracle worker, I think, or perhaps it was you?
You don't know what it means to me to hear you say that you are mine.
Looking forward to your call. I am yours, Gabriel XO

Julia fairly floated in the kitchen, buoyed as she was by Gabriel's words and the moments they'd shared the previous night. Her dream was going to come true. After years of dreaming, Gabriel was going to be her first.

All the tears and trouble and the humiliation with Simon were now forgotten. She'd waited for the man she loved, and now she was going to have the first time she'd always desired. And in *Florence*, of all places. She had many things to be thankful for, including the string of pearls around her neck. She was pretty sure that Grace had had a hand in everything, and she silently whispered her thanks.

When she was finished with her preparations, Julia placed one of the casseroles of chicken Kiev in the oven and walked the second one down to the basement. Upon opening the freezer, she was surprised to find a lot of pre-made meals, stored in Tupperware or wrapped in tin foil, many of which had little notes on them signed *Love, Deb*.

Julia resisted the urge to gag at the sight of them. Deb Lundy was a nice lady, and she seemed to take good care of Tom. But her daughter Natalie was another story, and Julia couldn't even fathom how upset she would be if Deb and Tom decided to move in together or God forbid, get married. That would be disturbing on more than one level.

Julia pushed all thoughts of Deb and Natalie aside and devoted her full attention to preparing her father's favorite dessert, which was lemon meringue pie. He tended to prefer the pie that was served at Kinfolks, but that didn't stop Julia from making her own.

She was just putting the pie into the oven when the telephone rang. Tom answered it and within seconds was cursing loudly. After a few brief sentences that sounded work-related, he slammed the phone into its cradle and disappeared upstairs. When he returned, he had changed into his uniform.

"Jules, I've got to go."

"What happened?"

"There's a fire over at the bowling alley. The guys are there already, but they think it might be arson."

"At Best Bowl? How?"

"That's what I'm going to find out. I don't know when I'll be back." He was almost to the door when he stopped and hunched his shoulders. "I'm sorry I ruined your dinner. I was looking forward to it. See you later."

Julia watched her father back out of the driveway in his truck and drive away. No doubt Gabriel was already in the middle of dinner with his family, so Julia decided against texting him. She would wait until six-thirty and call him as planned.

When the timer went off, she removed the pie from the oven and inhaled the sweet, citrusy aroma. While she waited for it to cool, she wrapped the chicken Kiev and put it in the refrigerator. It would keep until tomorrow—she'd make a sandwich for dinner.

About fifteen minutes later she heard the front door open and close. She hurriedly grabbed a plate so that she could serve Tom a piece of pie.

"How did you get away so quickly? The pie is ready right now," she called to the hallway.

"I'm glad to hear that, Jules."

At the sound of that voice, the plate slipped through Julia's fingers, smashing on the old linoleum floor beneath her.

Chapter Twenty-seven

Simon walked into the kitchen and paused, leaning against the door-way with his arms folded across his chest. She stared in shock at a handsome face with blue eyes, framed by short blond hair.

Julia shrieked and sprang toward the doorway, trying to run around him. His large hand shot out to the doorjamb, effectively clotheslining her. She grabbed on to his arm to prevent herself from falling backward.

"Please," she begged. "Let me go."

"Is that any way to greet me? After all this time?" He grinned, with-drawing his arm and standing to his full height of five feet, eleven inches.

Julia cowered just inside the doorway, her eyes darting around nervously.

Simon backed her into the kitchen, his medium-sized frame still intimidating. When he'd successfully cornered her, he wrapped his arms around her waist, pulling her into a tight bear hug.

"Simon, put me down." She gasped and squirmed.

He squeezed her more tightly, a wicked grin slicing from ear to ear. "Come on, Jules. Loosen up."

She struggled in his arms. "I have a boyfriend. Let go of me!"

"I don't care if you have a boyfriend."

He brought his face close to hers, and Julia feared that he was going to kiss her. But he didn't. He pressed himself against her and allowed his hands to wander, smirking at her discomfort. Eventually, he pulled back.

"Wow, still a cold fish. I would have thought your boyfriend would have fixed that." His eyes slithered over her lustfully. "At least I know

I'm not missing anything. Although it's still insulting that you'd give it up to him and not to me."

Julia pulled away from him and sped to the front door, opening it and gesturing outside. "Just go. I don't want to talk to you. And Dad will be back any minute."

Simon slowly followed her, like a wolf following a lamb. "Don't lie to me. I know he just left. Seems they had a bit of trouble over at Best Bowl. Someone burned the building to the ground. He'll be gone for hours."

Julia blinked nervously. "How do you know?"

"I heard it on the radio. I was already in the neighborhood, so it seemed like the perfect time to drop by and see you."

She tried to appear calm as she weighed her options. She knew there was no way she could outrun him, and she didn't want to run the risk of angering him by trying. At least if she stayed inside she had a chance of trying to get to her cell phone, which was in the kitchen.

She plastered a fake smile on her face and tried to sound pleasant. "It was nice of you to stop in. But we both know it's over. You found someone else, you're happy with her. Let's leave the past behind, okay?"

She tried to hide her anxiety, and she did a pretty good job of it.

Until he came closer and started running both hands through her long hair, drawing the strands up to his face so that he could sniff them.

"I wasn't happy with her. It wasn't about happiness—it was about sex. And she isn't the kind of girl I could introduce to my parents. You, on the other hand, were at least presentable. Even if you were a disappointment."

"I don't want to talk about this."

He pulled the door out of her grasp and slammed it shut. "I'm not finished. And I don't like being interrupted."

Julia took a cautious step backward. "Sorry, Simon."

"Let's cut the bullshit. You know why I'm here. I want the pictures."

"I told you, I don't have them."

"I don't believe you." He clamped a hand around her neck and yanked her toward him by her necklace.

"Do you really want to play this game with me? I've seen what Nata-

lie has. I know the pictures exist. If you give them to me now, we'll remain friends. But don't push me. I didn't drive three hours to put up
with your shit. I don't care how many strands of pearls you wear, *you
are nothing.*" He began to tug on the necklace, straining the knots between each pearl.

Julia brought her hands up to stop him. "Please don't. This was
Grace's."

"Oh, this was *Grace's.* Excuse me. I spent more money on you in a
week than they're worth." He tugged the necklace again, defiantly.

Julia swallowed hard, and he could feel her throat flutter against his
fingers. "Natalie is lying. I don't know what her motivation is, but I'm
telling you that I left behind all the pictures of you that I had. I have no
reason to lie to you. Please, Simon."

Simon laughed. "You give an impressive performance but that's all
it is—a performance. I know you were mad at me because of what happened, and I think you took something for revenge."

"If that's true, then why haven't I used them? Why didn't I send them
to a newspaper or ask you for money? Why would I be holding on to
them for over a year? It doesn't make sense!"

He crushed her to him and brought his lips to her ear. "You aren't
exactly street smart, Jules. It isn't a stretch for me to believe that you
have something that you don't know how to use. Why don't we move
this conversation upstairs? I can look around for the pictures, and you
can try to put me in a better mood." He drew her earlobe into his
mouth, biting it slightly.

Julia inhaled and exhaled a couple of times, trying to grasp at any
courage she could summon. She looked up into his cold, blue eyes. "I'm
not doing anything until you take your hands off me. Why can't you be
nice?"

Simon's eyes darkened momentarily, and he released her. "Oh, I'll
be nice to you." He started petting her cheek. "But I expect something
in return. If I don't leave here with the pictures, then I'll have to leave
with something else. So you should start thinking about what you can
do to put a smile on my face."

Julia cringed.

"Things have certainly changed, haven't they? I'm really going to enjoy this." He pulled her into his arms and pressed his open, eager mouth to hers.

❀❀

At six-thirty sharp, Gabriel excused himself from the dining room table and walked into the living room, readying himself to receive Julia's call. The call never came.

He checked his voice mail. No messages from Julia. No new texts from Julia. No e-mails, either. At ten minutes to seven, he dialed her cell phone. After a few rings his call went to voice mail.

"Julianne? Are you there? Call me."

He ended the call and used the White Pages application on his iPhone to find Tom's home number. It rang and rang and rang. Then the answering machine came on. He hung up without leaving a message.

Why isn't she answering the phone? Where is she? And where's Tom?

A dreadful suspicion took hold in his mind. Not wanting to waste a single second, Gabriel stormed out the front door without speaking to anyone. He started the Jeep and sped all the way over to Tom's house, trying again and again to reach Julia or Tom on the way. And if a policeman stopped him for speeding, so much the better.

❀❀

Simon's victory was so close he could taste it. He knew that Julia wasn't a strong person, and he was accustomed to using her weakness to his advantage. When she looked him in the eye and pleaded with him to believe that she didn't have the photographs, he believed her. It was far more likely that Natalie was setting her up, trying to deflect attention from her own vindictive game. As he held Julia in his arms once again, he gave up his quest for the pictures. Now he was on an entirely different mission.

Undeterred by the ringing of the telephone in the kitchen, which alternated with a few bars of *Message in a Bottle*, as played by Julia's iPhone, Simon continued kissing her, pulling her so that she was straddling him as he sat on her father's couch.

She was still frigid. She was tolerating his advances, but barely, her arms and body limp. She'd never liked his tongue in her mouth. She'd never really liked anything of his in her mouth, and even now she squirmed in his arms. But her discomfort excited him, and when he slid his tongue over and around hers, he felt his arousal grow and strain against the zipper of his jeans.

He kissed her until she screwed up the courage to push against his chest with her fists, and he knew it was time to move on to other activities. As he began to unbutton her shirt, she struggled.

"Please don't do this," she whimpered. "Please let me go."

"You're going to like it." He chuckled as he leaned around to cup her ass, kneading and groping it while she tried to escape from his lap. "I'm going to make sure you enjoy it. Then I'll let you go."

He dragged his mouth across her jaw line and down to the left side of her neck, sucking on a patch of skin near the middle of her throat, above the pearls. "I don't think you want a repeat of our last fight, do you Julia?"

She trembled.

"Julia?"

"No, Simon."

"Good." Since his eyes were closed, he missed the obvious love bite on the right side of her neck. It wouldn't have mattered. He'd already planned on marking her. A nice bite mark so that her boyfriend back in Canada would see what his little girlfriend had been up to. A mark that would even the score between the two of them. He vacuumed her blood up to the surface of her skin and for good measure, sank his teeth into her.

She cried out in pain.

He licked the skin softly, enjoying her taste, salty and sweet and bloody and Julia. When he was finished, he moved back to admire his handiwork. She'd have to wear a turtleneck to cover it up, and he knew that Julia didn't like turtlenecks. The mark was monstrous, angry and red. It showcased his large ring of teeth. It was perfect.

Julia looked up at him through her impossibly long lashes, and he watched something shift in her eyes. He leaned forward in anticipation and licked his lips. Suddenly her palm connected with his cheek with a vicious slap. In a flash, Julia flew to the staircase to escape to the second floor.

"You fucking bitch!" Simon roared as he followed, easily catching up to her. Just before she reached the top stair, he caught her ankle with both hands and twisted. She collapsed on her knees, shrieking in pain.

"I'm going to teach you a lesson you'll never forget," he said, moving to grab her by the hair.

She howled as he yanked her head backward.

Flailing madly, she kicked at him furiously with her uninjured foot and miraculously made contact with his groin, releasing his grip from her hair and sending him careening down the stairs. She hobbled up to her bedroom and locked the door behind her while he doubled over in pain.

"Wait till I get my hands on you, you bitch!" he shouted, clasping his crotch with both hands.

Julia braced her bedroom door with a chair and tugged on a nearby dresser. Old framed photographs clattered against one another on top of the antique as she tried to move it, while a china doll crashed to the floor. Ignoring the pain in her now injured ankle, she hobbled to the other side of the dresser, pushing it frantically with short, desperate attempts. Simon shouted expletives at her as he wrestled with the door-knob.

Finally, she managed to place the dresser in front of the door. She only hoped she could buy herself enough time to make a phone call before Simon came bursting into her room. She limped over to the telephone that sat on her nightstand, but in her haste she knocked it to the floor.

"Shit!"

She picked up the phone and with trembling fingers, began dialing Gabriel's cell phone. It immediately went to voice mail. As she waited for the beep, Simon's body came hurtling against the door. Julia watched in horror as the old door sagged and began to come away from its hinges.

"Gabriel, please come to my dad's house right away. Simon is here and he's trying to break down the door to my room!"

Simon cursed and growled, pounding relentlessly against the door. Once he smashed his way in he'd tip the dresser over to get to her.

This is it. I'm dead, she thought.

She couldn't imagine a scenario in which she escaped without sustaining serious bodily harm or worse. Realizing that she couldn't wait another second, she dropped the phone and opened the window, preparing to crawl out onto the roof and possibly to jump. Just as she was trying to swing herself over the windowsill, she saw Gabriel's Jeep screech into the driveway. He left the car running and tore across the lawn.

Gabriel shouted her name and Simon swore at him. Light, quick footfalls reverberated from the staircase followed by the sounds of flesh hitting flesh and a torrent of curses. Something heavy fell to the floor. Someone tumbled down the stairs.

Julia crept over to her nearly destroyed door, straining to hear. The noises seemed to have moved outside. When she limped back to her window, she saw Simon lying on the front lawn. He was cursing and holding his nose. She watched breathlessly as he lurched to his feet, blood pouring down his face. In the blink of an eye, blood from Simon's nose mingled with blood from his mouth as Gabriel's right hook split his lip, dislodging a few teeth.

"Asshole!" Simon spat out the teeth and lunged at Gabriel. Despite his obvious impairment, he was able to land a punch on Gabriel's chest.

Gabriel reeled back, winded. Simon took another step forward, eager to capitalize on his opponent's weakness. Gabriel recovered quickly, plowing into Simon's stomach with his right and his left. Simon doubled over in pain and fell to his knees.

Gabriel straightened his shoulders slowly and cracked his neck to one side. He looked remarkably relaxed in his tweed jacket and Oxford shirt. He looked as if he was on his way to a faculty meeting at the university and not presently kicking the ass of a senator's son from Philadelphia.

"Get up," Gabriel said in a voice that made Julia's blood cool.

Simon moaned.

"I said *get up!*" Gabriel stood over him like an avenging angel, beautiful and terrible and absolutely without mercy.

When Simon didn't move, Gabriel grabbed a fistful of his hair, jerking his head back.

"If you even *think* about going near her again, I'll kill you. The only reason you're still alive is because it would upset Julianne to see me go to prison. And I'm not about to leave her alone after what you did to her, you sick motherfucker. If a photograph or a video of someone who even looks like her ends up on the internet or in a newspaper, I'll come after you. I've gone ten rounds with a few Southies in Boston and lived to brag about it. So don't think that I will hesitate to smash your skull in next time."

Gabriel reared back and his left uppercut shattered Simon's jaw. Simon slumped onto the ground and remained perfectly still. Pulling a handkerchief out of the pocket of his wool trousers, Gabriel nonchalantly wiped the blood from his hands. At that moment, Julia appeared at the front door and hobbled out to meet him.

"Julia!" He caught her in his arms as she nearly fell down the stairs. "Are you okay?"

He swung her to the ground carefully, clasping her to his chest.

"Julia?" He pushed her hair back so that he could see her. Her lips were red and swollen, there were scratches on her neck, her eyes were wild and was that . . . a huge *bite* mark?

That animal fucking bit her!

"Are you all right? Did he . . . ?" Gabriel dropped his eyes to her clothing, fearing what he might see. But no, her clothing wasn't ripped, and she was still dressed, mercifully, even though her shirt was unbuttoned.

He closed his eyes and thanked God that he hadn't arrived any later. Who knows what he would have found.

"Come with me," he said firmly, removing his jacket and placing it around her shoulders. He quickly buttoned up her shirt and carried her to the passenger's seat of the Jeep, closing the door behind her.

"What happened?" he asked as he climbed in beside her. Julia was clutching her injured ankle and muttering to herself.

"Julia?" When she didn't respond, he reached over to brush the hair out of her eyes.

She flinched toward her door.

He froze. "Julia, it's me. It's Gabriel. I'm going to take you to the hospital. All right?"

She gave no indication that she'd heard him. And she wasn't shaking or crying. *She's in shock*, he thought. Gabriel pulled out his phone and dialed a number.

"Richard? Something happened to Julia." He paused and looked over at her. "Her old boyfriend appeared, and he attacked her. I'm taking her to the hospital in Sunbury. Yes, you could meet us if you want to. See you there."

Gabriel looked over at Julia, hoping she would make eye contact. "Richard is going to meet us in Sunbury. He's going to call a friend of his who is a doctor."

When Julia didn't respond, he dialed information to find the number of the Selinsgrove Fire Station. He left an urgent message for Tom, explaining what had happened and that he was taking Julia to the hospital.

It's her goddamned father's fault. Why the fuck did he leave her by herself?

"I slapped him." Julia's voice, high and unnatural, broke into his thoughts.

"You what?"

"He kissed me . . . I slapped him. I'm so sorry. I'm so sorry. I'll never do it again. I didn't want to kiss him."

At that terrible moment, Gabriel was grateful that he had to drive her to the hospital. Without his need to care for her, he would have turned around and finished Simon off. Permanently.

She began to say the most bizarre things. She was murmuring about *him* kissing her and something about Natalie, and then something about him, Gabriel, not wanting her anymore because she'd been marked and she was going to be a lousy lay . . .

What the fuck did he do to her?

"Ssshhh, Beatrice. Look at me. Beatrice?"

It took a moment for the old nickname to sink in, but when it did she looked at him, her frantic eyes slowly focusing on his face.

"This isn't your fault. Okay? It isn't your fault that he kissed you."

"I didn't mean to cheat on you. I'm so sorry," she whispered.

The tone of her voice, the panic in her eyes—Gabriel swallowed back bile.

"Julia, you didn't cheat on me. All right? And I'm glad you hit him.

He deserved it and much, much worse." Gabriel shook his head, wondering with horror what had actually happened before his arrival.

❀ ❀

When Richard arrived at the hospital, he found his son and Julia in the waiting room. Gabriel was stroking her hair and speaking to her softly. It was a tender scene, but the level of intimacy between the two of them surprised him. Greatly.

While they waited for Richard's friend to arrive, he gently examined her ankle. She yelped. Richard glanced sideways at Gabriel, who was gnawing on his knuckles in order to control his reactions.

"I don't think your ankle is broken, but it's certainly injured. Gabriel, why don't you get us all a cup of tea and maybe some cookies?"

Gabriel pulled his knuckles out of his mouth. "I won't leave her."

"It will just take a minute. I want to speak to Julia."

Gabriel nodded reluctantly and disappeared in the direction of the cafeteria.

Richard couldn't help but notice her neck. The bite mark was obvious, the love bite less so. His eyes flickered to where his son had stood a moment before. The love bite was old, obviously from a day or two ago. Clearly, things between Gabriel and Julia were more intimate than he thought.

"Grace used to volunteer at this hospital. Did you know that?"

Julia nodded.

"Over the years, she served in a lot of capacities but most of her work was with victims of domestic abuse." He sighed. "She saw a lot of sad cases, some of which involved children. Some of her cases ended in fatalities."

He looked into Julia's eyes. "I will tell you what Grace used to tell her patients. This is not your fault. It doesn't matter what you did or what you didn't do, you did not deserve this. And at this moment, I don't know when I've been more proud of my son."

She looked down at her injured ankle and remained silent.

A moment later, a pleasant-looking Asian gentleman walked up to them.

"Richard," he said, extending his hand.

Richard sprang to his feet, shaking his friend's hand. "Stephen, I'd like to introduce you to Julia Mitchell. She's a friend of the family. Julia, this is Dr. Ling."

Stephen nodded and directed a nurse to help Julia to an examination room. He followed shortly thereafter, assuring Richard that he would treat her as if she were his own daughter.

Knowing that Julia was in good hands, Richard decided to walk to the cafeteria to join his son. As he entered the hallway, he could hear Gabriel arguing with Tom Mitchell. Loudly.

"I think I'm a better judge of character than you are." Tom was in Gabriel's face, trying to physically intimidate him, but Gabriel met him toe to toe.

"Well, clearly you aren't, Mr. Mitchell, or I wouldn't have had to drag that animal out of your house before he raped your daughter in her own fucking bedroom."

"Gentlemen, this is a hospital. Take it outside." Richard was stern as he walked toward them.

Tom acknowledged his friend briefly, then turned back to Gabriel.

"I'm glad Julia is okay. And if you rescued her, then I owe you. But I just got a phone call from a police officer telling me that you beat the shit out of Senator Talbot's son. How do I know you didn't start the whole thing? You're the drug addict!"

"I'll take a drug test." Gabriel's eyes flashed. "I have nothing to hide. Instead of worrying about the senator's son, don't you think you should be a little more concerned about your daughter? Protecting Julianne was *your job*. Your job as a father. And you've been doing a lousy fucking job of it her whole life. Christ, Tom. How could you have sent her back to live with her mother when she was a little girl?"

Tom clenched his fists so hard he nearly burst the blood vessels in his hands. "You don't know what you're talking about, so you need to shut the hell up. You've got some nerve lecturing me about my daughter. You're just a cokehead with a history of violence. I don't want you anywhere near her, or I'll have you arrested."

"I don't know what I'm talking about? Come on, Tom, get your head out of your ass! I'm talking about all those men traipsing in and out of the apartment in St. Louis, fucking your ex-wife in front of your little girl. *And you did absolutely nothing.* In fact, you finally rescue her before she becomes another statistic for child molestation, and then you send her back. Why? Was she a delinquent nine-year-old? Was she too needy? Or were you too busy being volunteer fire chief!"

Tom looked at Gabriel with an expression of utter hatred. It took all of his self-control to keep from either punching Gabriel's lights out or grabbing his hunting rifle from his truck and shooting him. But he wasn't about to do either around the corner from a waiting room full of witnesses. Instead, he swore at Gabriel a few more times and stomped over to the Admissions desk to make arrangements to pay for Julia's hospital bill.

By the time she returned on crutches, Tom had calmed himself. He stood by the door of the emergency room with his hands in his pockets, swimming in guilt.

Gabriel walked to Julia immediately, his eyebrows furrowing when he saw her bandaged ankle. "Are you all right?"

"It isn't broken. Thank you, Gabriel. I don't know what I would have . . ." Julia swallowed her words as tears fell down her face for the first time that evening.

Gabriel put his arm around her shoulder and tenderly kissed her forehead.

Tom watched the exchange between his daughter and the violent but valiant cokehead and walked over to Richard. The two friends spoke for a minute before they shook hands.

"Jules? Do you want to come home? Richard says you're welcome to stay at his place if you'd rather." Tom shuffled his feet uncomfortably.

"I can't go home." Julia pulled away from Gabriel and hugged her father with one arm. He immediately teared up and whispered an apology in her ear before walking out of the hospital.

Richard bade the couple good-bye, leaving Julia to dry her tears.

Gabriel turned to her immediately. "We can pick up your prescriptions on the way back to Richard's. I'm sure Rachel has clothes that you can borrow, or I can lend you something. Unless you'd rather go home and pack your suitcase."

"I can't go back there," she whimpered, curling in on herself.

"You won't have to."

"What about *him?*"

"You don't have to worry about him anymore. The police have already picked him up."

Julia looked into his eyes and almost lost herself in the warmth and concern that radiated from them.

"I love you, Gabriel."

At first he didn't react to her statement, he simply stood there as if he hadn't heard. Then his expression softened. He drew her into his side, crutches and all, and kissed her cheek, saying not a word.

Chapter Twenty-eight

After dinner, Scott had dropped by a friend's house for a visit. When he arrived home, he was shocked to discover two police cruisers in the driveway. Officer Jamie Roberts was interviewing Julia in the living room, while Officer Ron Quinn was interviewing Gabriel in the dining room. Richard had already been questioned.

"Will someone please explain why there are cops in the house? What did Gabriel do now?" Scott stood in the kitchen staring down his sister and their father.

Aaron walked to the refrigerator and pulled out a Samuel Adams. He opened it and handed it to Scott, who drank it gratefully. "Simon Talbot attacked Julia."

Scott almost spat out his beer. "What? Is she okay?"

"He fucking bit her," said Rachel. "And he almost broke her ankle."

"Did he . . ." Scott's voice was matter-of-fact, yet he couldn't bring himself to say the words.

Rachel shook her head. "I asked her. Maybe I shouldn't have, but I did. And she said no."

Everyone breathed a collective sigh of relief.

Scott slammed his beer down on the counter. "Well, where is he? Let's go, Aaron. Someone needs to teach him a lesson."

"Gabriel got to him first. Ron told me that they had to take Simon to the hospital to have his jaw wired shut. Gabriel smashed his face in," Aaron explained.

Scott's eyebrows shot up. "The Professor? Why would he do that?"

Aaron and Rachel exchanged a knowing look.

"I'd still like to pay the asshole a visit." Scott cracked the knuckles on his right hand. "Just to talk to him."

Aaron shook his head. "Listen to yourself. You're a prosecutor; he's the son of a senator. You can't tune the guy up. And besides, Gabriel finished it. They'll take him into custody when the doctors are done with him."

"You still haven't explained why Gabriel would get his pretty little hands dirty for Julia. He barely knows her."

Rachel leaned over the kitchen island toward her brother. "They're a couple."

Scott blinked like a lazy stoplight. "Come again?"

"Just what I said. They're—together."

"Holy shit. What the hell is she doing with him?"

Before anyone could offer a hypothesis, Gabriel walked into the kitchen. He looked at the worried faces of his family and frowned. "Where's Julianne?"

"Still being interviewed." Richard smiled at his oldest son and clapped a hand to his shoulder. "I'm very proud of you, for what you did for Julia. I know we're all grateful you arrived in time."

Gabriel pressed his lips together and nodded uncomfortably.

"Clocking Simon Talbot will earn you a medal. But screwing around with Julia will earn you a beating. You aren't good enough for her. Not by a long shot." Scott put his beer down and cracked his knuckles again.

Gabriel's eyes glinted coldly at his brother. "My personal life is none of your business."

"It is now. What kind of professor screws his students? Don't you get enough tail already?"

Rachel inhaled deeply and slowly moved toward the door, away from the impending titanic clash.

Gabriel's fists clenched at his sides, and he took a step closer to his larger but younger brother. "Speak about Julianne that way again and you and I are going to have more than words."

"All right, you guys, no more Cain and Abel bullshit. There are cops in our living room, and you're scaring your sister." Aaron stepped in between the seething men, placing a light hand on Scott's chest.

"Julia is not the kind of girl that you screw around with and then dump. She's the kind of girl you marry," Scott said over Aaron's shoulder.

"You think I don't know that?" said Gabriel, with evident hostility. "Don't you think she's had her quota of assholes?"

Richard held his hand up. "Scott, that's enough."

He looked at his father curiously.

"Gabriel rescued Julia from her attacker." Richard nodded slightly.

Scott stared at his father as if he'd just told him that the earth was flat. And everyone, except him, already knew it.

Rachel jumped in, eager to change the subject. "By the way, Gabriel, I didn't know you knew Jamie Roberts. Did you go to high school with her?"

"Yes."

"Were you friends?"

"Vaguely."

All eyes swung to Gabriel, who turned on his heel and disappeared.

Richard waited a few minutes for the tension in the air to dissipate before turning his attention to his remaining son. "I'd like a word with you, please." His voice was calm but firm.

The two men climbed the stairs to the second floor and walked into Richard's study. He closed the door behind them.

"Have a seat." He pointed to a chair in front of his desk. "I want to talk to you about your attitude toward your brother."

Scott sat opposite his father and prepared himself for what was to come. Richard only brought his children into the study for the most serious of conversations.

He gestured to a reproduction of Rembrandt's *The Return of the Prodigal Son*, which was proudly displayed on one of the walls. "Do you remember the parable behind that painting?"

Scott nodded slowly. He was in trouble.

❈ ❈

Julia sat bolt upright in bed, gasping for air.

It was only a nightmare. It was only a nightmare. You got away.

It took a moment to bring her frantic breathing under control. But once she realized that she was safe in the Clark's guest room and not underneath Simon on the floor of her old bedroom, she was able to relax. Somewhat.

She leaned over and turned on the lamp. The light dispelled the darkness of the room but did not cheer her. She picked up the glass of water and the pain pills that Gabriel left when he tucked her into bed several hours earlier. He'd curled around her, fully clothed, and held her until she fell asleep. But he was gone now.

I need him.

More than the pain pills or the light or the air, Julia needed Gabriel, to feel his body wrapped around hers, to hear his deep voice whisper words of comfort. He was the only person who could make her forget what had happened. She needed to touch him. She needed to kiss him in order to blot out her nightmare.

Julia took the pills to soothe the pain in her ankle. She hopped on one foot to Gabriel's room in order to soothe the pain in her heart. She was quiet as a mouse, listening for any stirring or footsteps in the other rooms. When she was satisfied that she would not be surprised, she silently opened Gabriel's door and closed it behind her.

It took a moment or two for her eyes to adjust to the semi-darkness. He'd neglected to pull the shades on the windows and was lying on what was normally her side of the double bed. She wondered if it was accurate to say that she had a side of the bed. She limped to the other side, pulled the covers back, and placed one knee on the mattress.

"Julianne." Gabriel's low whisper startled her.

She clapped a hand to her mouth so that she wouldn't cry out.

"Stop."

She froze. When her wits finally returned, she lowered her head. "Um, I'm sorry. I shouldn't have bothered you." Shame flooded through her, and she blinked back tears as she slowly turned to go.

"That's not what I meant. Wait."

Julia watched him throw off the covers and stand up, his back toward her. He was naked and the streaming starlight through the shades scattered across his back. It was an optical illusion of sorts, the delicate points of light dancing across his athletic form. She saw his shoulder blades and his spine, and the muscles of his lower back where the skin stretched as he leaned over to find his pajama bottoms.

And of course, the most beautiful backside and legs . . .

When he'd pulled on his pants, he turned to face her, his brilliantly sculpted chest and shoulders perfect in the dimness, the tattooed dragon slightly muted but ever present.

"Now you can crawl in with me." He chuckled. "I thought I'd make you nervous if you found me naked."

Julia rolled her eyes. She didn't like when he laughed at her, but she saw his point.

(Or rather, she didn't actually *see* it, but she understood what he meant.)

"Come here," he whispered, extending an arm and drawing her close so that when they reclined, her head rested naturally on his chest.

"I set my alarm so I could check on you. It would have gone off in fifteen minutes. How is your ankle?"

"It hurts."

"Did you take the pills I left for you?"

"Yes. They haven't kicked in yet."

Gabriel carefully shifted so that he could reach her hand and tenderly pressed his lips against her fingers. "My little warrior." He stroked her hair, caressing the waves with his fingertips. "Were you having trouble sleeping?"

"I had a nightmare."

"Do you want to talk about it?"

"No."

He squeezed her more closely just to indicate that he'd heard her and that if she changed her mind, he would listen.

"Would you kiss me?" she asked.

"I thought that after what happened you wouldn't want me to touch you."

Julia angled her head so that she could bring her lips up to his, ending their conversation.

Gabriel's mouth was soft and gentle, barely moving against hers. He could feel that her mouth was still tender, and he silently cursed Simon for making it that way. But Julia was having none of that. She wanted to drink him in, to let his fire engulf her, so that he was all she could feel or think about.

Opening her mouth, Julia traced his bottom lip with her tongue, savoring his sweetness. She pushed her tongue inside his mouth, laving his with hers and dancing, tangoing, tripping over it. Gabriel's fingers tightened in her hair, gently pulling her head back. Now his tongue pushed hers back, entering her and caressing her.

Julia began to hum at the sheer pleasure of his unhurried affection. While she was kissing him, she could think of nothing else. She kept her injured ankle away from him in order to protect it, and with her hands she found his hair, pulling and twisting it.

Gabriel groaned but didn't stop. She felt his body begin to stiffen next to her, pushing out against her bare thigh. He ran his right hand down her side, hovering over the swell of a breast before rubbing against her ribs and then her hip. He liked the way Rachel's tank top and yoga shorts fit Julianne's form, hugging her curves and exposing a great swathe of pale skin across her shoulders and above her breasts. She was beautiful, even in the semi-darkness. All of a sudden, she was on her back while he hovered over her, pressing his weight into his forearms. His knee came between her legs, and she parted them willingly.

She wanted more. She needed more. Her breathing was ragged and coming in gasps as she refused to loosen her hold on his hair, forcing their mouths together.

Gabriel responded by stroking her breasts over her tank top with his long fingers, applying just enough pressure to make her tingle and want more but not enough to satisfy her desires. Then he was pulling back, leaning on one forearm with eyes closed. This was her moment. Without even thinking about it, she grasped the hem of her tank top and tried to pull it off.

Gabriel's hand came to hers and halted her movement. He pressed their lips together, and soon they were teasing each other with their tongues, panting with warm and moist breaths. Julia freed her hands from underneath Gabriel's when he moved to stroke her upper thigh, dragging her leg around his hip as he pressed closer to her. Now that her hands were free, nothing prevented her from wresting off her top. She found the hem again and began to pull, twisting and writhing beneath his naked chest.

Both of Gabriel's hands clasped over hers. "Julianne," he gasped, for he was breathing hard. "Would you . . . please . . . stop." He rocked back on his heels and kneeled next to her, trying to catch his breath.

"Don't you want to?" Hers was the soft voice of an innocent, and it made Gabriel's heart clench.

He shook his head and closed his eyes. As his response sank in, so did something else. All of the cruel things Simon had ever said to her began to echo in her ears.

You're a stupid bitch. You're going to be a lousy lay. You're frigid. No other man is ever going to want you.

Julia rolled to her side, effectively sidestepping Gabriel, and swung her feet gingerly to the floor. She wanted to make it to the door before a sob ripped from her throat. But before she could put her weight on her good ankle, two long, strong arms wrapped around her waist, and she was trapped.

Gabriel placed his legs on either side of hers and pulled her so that their bare legs were dangling over the side of the bed together and her back was flush against his naked chest. She could feel his swift heartbeat and his breathing through her shoulder blades. It was an odd but especially erotic feeling.

"Don't leave," he whispered, pressing a light kiss to the edge of her ear. He leaned forward to bring his mouth to the right side of her neck, nuzzling her.

Julia sniffled.

"I didn't mean to upset you. Are you hurt very badly?" When she didn't answer, he kissed her ear again and squeezed her more tightly.

"Not physically," she managed, stifling a sob.

"Then tell me," he whispered. "Tell me how I hurt you."

Julia threw her hands up in desperate frustration. "You said that you wanted me, but when I finally work up the courage to throw myself at you, you reject me!"

Gabriel inhaled sharply, his breath making a whistling sound against her ear. She felt his arms stiffen and his tendons press into her skin. And something else, further down, pressing into the curve of her behind.

"Believe me, Julianne, I am not rejecting you. Of course I want you. You're so beautiful. So very lovely."

Gabriel reached down to kiss the side of her face. "We talked about this. Our time is coming. Do you really want our first time to be tonight?"

Julia hesitated, and that was the only answer he needed.

"Even if you were ready, darling, I wouldn't make love to you tonight. You're injured, which means you're going to be on the disabled list for a while. I need to make sure that you're fully recovered before we explore—ah—various *positions*."

She could hear his smile coloring his words. He was trying to make her laugh.

"But most importantly, there's this." He shifted so that he was leaning around her left side, gently tracing a finger around the angry bite mark on her neck.

She winced at his touch, and a flame of anger flared within him. He inhaled and exhaled several times to get his emotions under control, then he placed gentle kisses near the mark over and over again, until she sighed and let her head relax against his shoulder.

"You were fetal a couple of hours ago. I wouldn't be a very good lover if I capitalized on your vulnerability. Does that make sense?"

Julia thought about it, and nodded slowly.

"Something frightening happened to you tonight. Of course you want to feel safe and cared for. It's not a crime, Julianne. And I want to help you, my love, so badly. But there are many different ways to do that. You don't have to take your clothes off in order to capture my attention. You have it. Completely. You don't have to have sex with me in order for me to make you feel wanted."

"How?" Her voice was a tentative whisper.

"Like this." Gabriel pressed a kiss to her neck and shifted her so that she was reclining on her back.

He lay on his side next to her, propped up on his elbow, staring down into her wide, sad eyes. Starting with her hair, he began to touch her with gentle, unhurried caresses. He stroked her face to remove her tears. He traced her chin, her jaw line, her eyebrows. He moved to her neck and down to the lines of her collarbone.

She gasped when his fingers followed her sternum between her breasts to her abdomen, where he drew patterns on her naked skin. He placed his palm flat against her and leaned over to kiss the very tops of her breasts.

When he withdrew, her eyes were closed. "Darling?"

Her eyelids fluttered open.

"In this bed, there's only us. You and me. You are all that matters." He smoothed his hand across the curve of her waist and down to her left hip, where he gripped her loosely. "If you want to go back to your room, I'll walk you back. If you want to sleep alone, I'll let you be. I just need you to tell me what *you* want, and provided it's within my power, I'll give it to you. But please, darling, don't ask me to take your virginity. Not tonight."

She considered what he said and swallowed noisily. "I want to stay here. I don't sleep very well without you."

"I barely sleep at all without you. I'm glad the feeling is mutual." He kissed her lips and began to skim his hand lightly over her thigh and back to the curve of her bottom. "You know that I care for you, don't you?"

She nodded and touched his chest while he leaned forward, brushing his lips against her neck where the skin was unmarked.

"I'm sorry I did this." Gabriel circled the fading love bite from the day before.

Julia looked into guilty eyes. "Don't, Gabriel. That was different."

"I need to be more careful with you."

She sighed. "You are very careful with me."

"Roll over, darling."

Her eyes held a question, but she rolled onto her stomach and moved her head so that she could look at him, trusting him completely.

He kneeled beside her and gently brushed her hair aside. "Just relax. I want you to feel as beautiful as you are."

He began slowly, massaging her lightly with both hands, exploring every inch from head to toe. Then he stretched out by her feet and lifted them, paying special attention to her arches and her heels.

She moaned softly.

Gabriel chuckled. "Do you remember when you stayed with me after that disastrous seminar?"

Julia nodded, biting her lip.

His eyebrows knit together. "You were very suspicious of me. Of course, you were right to be suspicious, but even then I'd already decided that I . . . You're safe with me, love. I promise."

When Gabriel finished with her feet he crawled back up her body, allowing his lips to explore where his hands had been, nuzzling, kissing, nipping.

Julia searched his eyes and saw deep affection reflected back at her, and as he sank down by her side, she kissed him deeply.

"Thank you, Gabriel," she breathed.

He smiled in satisfaction, winding his fingers through her long hair.

It was in this space of peace and security that Julia realized her moment had come. They had already agreed that they would bare their souls before they bared their bodies. And there was a part of her that was weary of keeping secrets. Of keeping *his* secrets.

Gabriel had shared parts of his past with her already. Why had she withheld herself from him? It was going to be painful to speak the words aloud, but perhaps it would be more painful to have this thing between them remain unexplained. She inhaled deeply and shut her eyes, and without introduction, she began.

"I met him at a party my freshman year . . ." She cleared her throat a few times and continued in a whisper. "He went to the University of Pennsylvania. I'd heard of his father before, but that's not why I was interested in him. I liked him because he was funny and nice and we always had a good time together. That first Christmas, he showed up at my house to surprise me. He knew I liked Italian things, and so he bought me a candy-apple red Vespa. *Julia red*, he called it."

Gabriel raised his eyebrows.

"Of course, my love for all things Italian came from you. But I'd given up hope that I'd ever see you again. I thought you didn't care about me, and so I tried to move on. His parents approved of our relationship, and we were always being invited to Washington to visit them or to political events in Philadelphia. We dated casually for a few months, more like friends really, and then he told me he wanted more. I agreed.

"Things started to change after that. He wanted more of everything, and he became demanding." Julia's cheeks flushed deeply in the darkness.

Gabriel felt the temperature rise across her skin, and so he began to lightly rub her shoulders.

"He said that sex was his right as my boyfriend. When I said that I wasn't ready, he called me frigid. That simply reinforced my determination to wait. I wasn't really waiting for you, specifically, but I didn't want to be pressured into it. I know that sounds juvenile."

"Julianne, it's far from juvenile to assert that *you* should be the one to decide who you will and will not sleep with."

She smiled at him thinly. "The more he pushed, the more I tried to compensate by giving into him in other ways. He was extremely possessive. He didn't like me hanging out with Rachel, probably because she didn't like him. I did whatever I could to avoid conflict with him. And, um, he wasn't always pleasant."

She paused, trying to figure out how to say the next part.

"Did he hit you?" Gabriel forced himself to sound calm.

"Not really."

"That is not an answer, Julianne. *Did he hit you?*"

She could feel Gabriel's body begin to shake with anger. She wasn't about to lie to him, but she was worried about what he would say when she told him. So she chose her next words very carefully. "He pushed me around a couple of times. Natalie, my roommate, had to pull him off of me once."

"You do realize that him pushing you is still assault."

When Julia avoided his eyes, he continued. "I want to come back to this again. Another time."

"Honestly, the things he said to me were far worse than anything he ever did." She laughed softly. "He treated me better than my mother did, for the most part. Although there were times when I wanted him to hit me. I could have taken a punch, and it would have been over in seconds. That would have been preferable to having to listen to him tell me how frigid and worthless I was over and over again." She shuddered. "At least if he'd hit me, I could have told my dad. I could have shown him the bruise, and he would have believed me."

Gabriel was sickened by Julia's admission, which only increased his anger against Simon and her father. Despite his patient silence, she could almost hear the wheels turning in his mind.

"I never felt like I was good enough for him. And he certainly agreed. Since I wouldn't sleep with him, he demanded—um, other things. But I wasn't very good. He said if that was any indication of what I'd be like in bed, I'd be a lousy lay." She laughed again, and nervously played with her hair. "I wasn't going to tell you this, but I guess you have a right to know before I disappoint you. On top of being frigid, why would you want me if I can't even please a man in other ways?"

Gabriel unthinkingly let loose a string of profanities that would have curled a profane person's hair.

Julia remained very still, her nose twitching slightly, like a mouse. Or a rabbit.

"Julianne, look at me." He placed a light hand on her cheek, waiting until their eyes met. "Everything he said to you was a lie. You have to believe me when I tell you this. He said those things so that he could control you.

"Of course I want you. Look at you! You're beautiful and warm and intelligent. You're forgiving and gentle. You might not realize this, but you bring out those qualities in me. You make me *want* to be gentle and kind. And when we make love, that's how I will be with you."

He cleared his throat as his voice grew raspy. "Someone as giving and as passionate as you could *never* be terrible at anything sexual. You just need someone who will make you feel safe enough to express yourself. Then the tiger will emerge. He didn't deserve to see that side of you, and you were right not to show it to him. But we're different. Last night, the night in the museum, even earlier tonight, I've seen your passion. I've felt it. And it's breathtaking. *You* are breathtaking."

Julia looked into his earnest eyes in silent wonder.

"You told me you believe in redemption," he whispered. "So prove it. Forgive yourself for whatever you're ashamed of and let yourself be happy. Because really, Julianne, that's all I want for you. I want you to be happy."

She smiled and kissed him, reveling momentarily in his touch and his words. After a moment, she retreated, knowing that the worst of her story was yet to be told.

"I wanted to participate in the junior-year abroad program. He didn't want me to go. So I applied for it behind his back, and I didn't break the news to him until the beginning of the summer. He was furious, but he seemed to get over it.

"While I was in Italy, he would write these amazing e-mails and send me pictures. He told me he loved me." She swallowed hard. "No one ever loved me before."

She took a deep breath. "I didn't come home for Christmas or for the summer because I was taking extra courses and doing some traveling. When I came back at the end of August, Rachel took me shopping as a welcome home present. Grace had given her some money, and between the two of them they bought me a really pretty dress and a pair of Prada shoes."

She blushed.

"Um, you've seen those shoes before. I wore them on our first da— um, I mean when you took me out for steak."

He ran his fingers over the curve of her cheek. "It's all right, Julianne, you can call it our first date. That's how I think of it. Even though I was an ass."

She took another deep breath. "He made elaborate plans to celebrate my birthday. Rachel insisted on helping me get ready at her apartment, and I was supposed to drive to the Ritz-Carlton to meet him. But I forgot my camera. So I went to my dorm room first."

Now Julia began to shake. Every muscle, every part of her began shivering as if she was freezing cold.

Gabriel wrapped her in his arms. "You don't have to tell me anymore. I've heard enough."

"No." Her voice shook, but she continued. "I need to tell someone. Not even Rachel knows everything." She inhaled and exhaled a couple of times.

"I opened the door and the room was dark, except for the lamp on my roommate's desk. But Natalie's stereo was on. It was playing *Closer* by Nine Inch Nails. Stupidly, I thought she'd left the stereo on by mistake. I was going to turn it off, but before I could take another step, I saw them." Julia went very still. Still like a statue.

Gabriel waited.

"Simon was fucking Natalie in my bed. I was so shocked I couldn't move. At first, I thought it couldn't be him. And then I thought, it couldn't be her. But it was. And . . ."

Now her voice dropped to a whisper. "She'd been my roommate since we were freshmen. We were friends in high school. They saw me standing there, staring like an idiot. And he looked over at me and laughed, saying that they'd been fuck buddies since sophomore year. I just stood there because really, I couldn't understand what he was saying. Natalie walked over to me, naked, and said that I should join them."

Julia's mouth snapped shut. But it was too late. She'd pronounced the words. She'd said them aloud. And all of the agony and horror that she felt that day washed over her again. She moved to kneel and press her cheek against Gabriel's chest. But she did not cry.

Gabriel held her tightly, pressing his lips to the top of her head. *I should have killed him when I had the chance.*

He was silently glad that he hadn't known. He would have killed Simon, of that Gabriel had little doubt. *He's the Angelfucker. He was going to fuck my Julianne like an animal. Only he practiced on her roommate first.*

They sat in one another's arms for a while as she tried to push away her shame, and Gabriel sought to cast his murderous thoughts aside. When he felt her heartbeat slow, he began to whisper. He told her how much he cared for her. He told her she was safe with him. Then he asked her quietly if it would be okay if he talked to her a little.

She nodded.

"Julia, I'm sorry that happened to you." He shook his head. "I'm also sorry that you didn't grow up in a house with a man and a woman who shared a bed and loved each other. I had that benefit.

"You know what Richard and Grace were like, always touching one another, always laughing. I never heard him raise his voice to her. I never heard her say anything snide or rude. They were the perfect couple. And as much as it is embarrassing to think of one's parents having a sex life, it was obvious they were very passionate.

"When Richard gave me the infamous birds and the bees talk, he cited a line from the *Book of Common Prayer*, a vow that he'd made to Grace during their wedding ceremony, 'With this ring I thee wed, *with my body I thee worship,* and with all my worldly goods I thee endow.'"

"I've heard that before. It's beautiful."

"It is, isn't it? And in the context of my rather uncomfortable conversation with Richard, he pointed out that this vow is a pledge that the husband will make love to his wife, and not just use her for sex. He said that the vow expressed the idea that making love is an act of worship. The husband *worships* his wife with his body, by loving her and giving to her and moving with her toward ecstasy."

Gabriel cleared his throat, which was now hoarse. "I think it's safe to say that what you witnessed with your boyfriend was predatory and despicable. I know that you saw similar things when you were growing up in St. Louis, things that a little girl should never see. It's possible you thought that's just what intercourse is—and maybe you thought that all men were like *him*—malicious predators who use and abuse.

"Richard's description of lovemaking was completely different. He said that it is no less passionate than other pleasures, because the context provides the freedom and acceptance to explore one's desires in all of their various forms, whether they're desperate and needy, or slow and tender. The point is that the foundation that undergirds the act is one of mutual respect and giving—not taking or using."

Gabriel brought his lips to her ear so he could whisper to her. "I wandered far away from Richard's lifestyle, but I always wanted what he and Grace had. When I told you that I was intending to worship you with my body, I meant it. With all my heart. I will never take from you. I will only give. In my bed and outside of it."

Julia smiled against his chest.

"You and I are both starting over, and *behold, all things will become new.*"

She reached up and kissed him softly on the lips and whispered words of thanks to his mouth. His affirmation comforted her. It didn't take the pain away or erase the memories, but it relieved her to hear that he wouldn't hold her past weaknesses against her. For truly, one of the things she was most ashamed of was *allowing* herself to be treated so badly. It was why she had kept her secret. It was why she had feared exposure.

"Now I feel like an even bigger ass for joking with you about Nine Inch Nails when we were at Lobby. No wonder you were so upset when I mentioned that song."

Julia nodded slightly.

"As soon as I get back to Toronto, I'm going to change the presets on my radio. I won't be listening to that station anymore." He cleared his throat. "Love, you don't have to talk about it if you don't want to. But I'm wondering what you told your father. I owe you an apology for getting into a shouting match with him at the hospital. I said some things I shouldn't have."

She eyed him curiously.

"I told him he shouldn't have sent you back to live with your mother. That it was his job as a father to protect you, and that he failed."

Julia was surprised. No one, not even Rachel or Grace, had ever confronted Tom about his choices. No one. An expression of wonder spread across her pretty face.

"Aren't you angry with me?" He sounded surprised.

"I can't be. Thank you, Gabriel, for defending me. No one has ever done that before."

She took his hands in hers and kissed the slightly swollen knuckles and the places where the skin had split. His battle wounds were almost as dear to her as his beautiful, expressive eyes.

"I didn't tell my dad everything. Just that I caught *him* with Natalie, and that I couldn't live with her anymore. It created a problem since my dad was dating her mom. But he never complained."

"How very noble of him," said Gabriel sarcastically.

"I spent a few days in Selinsgrove trying to calm down, and Dad brought me back to school. He moved me out of the dorm and into a small studio apartment. You would have laughed at it, Gabriel. It was even smaller than the one I'm in now."

"I wouldn't laugh." He sounded hurt.

"It's just that you're so particular. You would have hated it even more than you hate my current apartment."

"Julianne, I don't hate your apartment. As I said before, I hate the fact that you have to live there. What happened next, after you went back to school?"

"I hid. They sort of became a couple after that, and I was afraid of running into them, so I avoided all of the places where I might be seen. I went to class, I worked on my Italian and my applications for grad school, and I stayed home. I kind of . . . retreated."

"Rachel mentioned something like that."

"I wasn't a good friend to Rachel. After that night, I stopped taking her calls. I wouldn't even speak to Grace, even though she wrote me the most beautiful letter. I sent your family a card at Christmas, but I was too humiliated to explain what happened. Rachel knows I caught *them* together because Natalie finally told her. But she doesn't know how bad it was. And I don't want her to know."

"Anything you tell me is strictly between us."

"I didn't want to admit that I had been so stupid as to get myself into that situation. That I gave in to him for so long. That I was blind to the fact that they were together. I wanted to pretend that it happened to someone else." She looked up into Gabriel's face, which was remarkably sympathetic.

"Please don't say that you are stupid ever again. Shame on them both for how they treated you. They're the villains in this story, not you." He kissed her forehead twice and buried his face in her long hair. "I think you need to get some sleep, sweetheart. It's been a long day, and we want you to heal."

"Won't it upset your family when they realize we're in here together?"

"They figured out we're a couple. And for the most part, I think they approve."

"For the most part?"

Gabriel sighed. "Richard doesn't object to us as a couple; he has conservative views on sex. So although I promised that we wouldn't be doing that under his roof, he would prefer we slept in separate rooms. Although I'm sure he'd turn a blind eye tonight and tomorrow night because of what happened to you."

"What about Rachel and Aaron? They share a room."

"Richard doesn't approve of that, but in his mind at least they're getting married. Rachel has always been supportive of me, and I think she's supportive of us."

"What about Scott?"

"Scott is very protective of you, and he knows that I've been a libertine, so . . ."

"You weren't a libertine. You were just lonely."

He kissed her softly. "That's very generous of you, but we both know it isn't true."

They both reclined, and Julia rested her head on his chest, running her fingers across his upper body. She hummed to herself as she mulled over his words, how he'd cared for her and wanted to worship her. They were, perhaps, the most important words she had ever heard. She traced a hesitant finger over his chest, outlining his tattoo.

Gabriel's hand quickly covered hers. "Don't," he breathed, pulling her hand away.

"I'm sorry. What's m-a-i-a?"

Julia heard him catch his breath. "I didn't mean to bring it up. But we were telling secrets. I thought . . ."

Gabriel began to rub his eyes with his free hand, but he didn't release her. "Maia is a name." His voice grew rough.

"Did you—love her?"

"Of course I loved her."

"Were you together long?"

He coughed. "It wasn't like that."

Julia squeezed him tightly and closed her eyes.

But Gabriel lay awake, staring at the ceiling for a very long time.

Chapter Twenty-nine

Julia awoke the next day to find Gabriel sitting on the edge of the bed, fully dressed and watching her. She yawned slightly and stretched in the rays of sunlight that streamed in from between the blinds.

"Good morning." She smiled.

He leaned over and pulled her into a warm embrace.

"I've been up and about, but I returned a little while ago to check on you. You're very peaceful when you sleep." He kissed her sweetly, then walked to the closet to retrieve a sweater.

Julia rolled onto her stomach and shamelessly ogled him, admiring the way his dress shirt skimmed across his shoulders. From her current vantage point, she could also admire his backside, hugged as it was by his black jeans.

Now that's a damn fine derrière, she thought.

Gabriel peered at her over his shoulder. "What was that?"

"I didn't say anything."

His lips pulled inward, as if he were restraining a grin. "Oh, really?"

He walked over and leaned down to whisper in her ear. "I didn't know that you were an *ass* girl."

"Gabriel!" Somewhat embarrassed at having been caught, she smacked his arm lightly, and they both began to laugh.

He caught her around the waist and pulled her onto his lap. "However, I would like to state unequivocally that my ass is quite flattered."

"Oh really?" She arched an eyebrow.

"Extremely. And he wishes for me to convey his very best greetings and—ah—he looks forward to making your acquaintance in a more *personal* manner when we're in Florence."

Julia shook her head at him and leaned forward, begging for a kiss.

She was rewarded with a brief but tender exchange before Gabriel pulled back.

He grew serious all of a sudden. "I need to talk to you about a couple of things."

She chewed at her lip and waited.

"Simon has been arrested and there are multiple charges. His father has dispatched the family attorney to save him, and there are rumors of a plea bargain."

"Really?"

"Apparently, the senator wishes to keep the sordid story out of the news. Scott placed a call to the prosecutor and received his assurance that your case will be given a very high priority. Scott emphasized that all of us would like to see the outcome include prison and not some sort of halfway house or treatment program. But given Simon's connections, I think prison is unlikely."

Julia made a mental note to thank Scott for speaking up for her. "What about you? Are you in danger?"

Gabriel grinned. "The Talbot family lawyer made noises about pressing charges. Thankfully, my brother had a short but illuminating conversation with him, pointing out that the press would be very interested in hearing my side of the story, as well as yours. I won't be charged. Needless to say, everyone involved is now sick of Scott."

Julia closed her eyes and exhaled slowly. The thought of something happening to Gabriel was painful, especially since she'd brought this trouble to them both.

"I need to take a shower and get dressed," she said, opening her eyes.

Gabriel gave her a heated look and trailed a single finger down the length of her arm. "I would dearly like to shower with you, but I'm afraid such an act would scandalize my relations."

Julia shivered. "Well, I can't have you scandalizing your relations, Professor Emerson."

"Indeed, Miss Mitchell. It would be most shocking. Most shocking. So in the interest of decorum, my very flattered ass and I will forego showering with you." He leaned forward, his eyes glowing. "*For now.*"

She laughed, and he left her to her daily ablutions.

When Julia returned to her bedroom after her shower, she found Gabriel hovering in the hallway. "Is something wrong?"

He shook his head. "I wanted to be sure you didn't trip or something. Where are your crutches?"

"In my room. I'm okay, Gabriel." She limped past him. When she found her hairbrush, she began to pull it awkwardly through her long, tangled tresses.

"Let me do that." Gabriel walked toward her and took the hairbrush from her hand.

"You're going to brush my hair?"

"Why not?" He pulled out a chair and encouraged her to sit down, and then he stood behind her and slowly began to run his fingers from crown to ends, disentangling her hair manually.

Julia closed her eyes.

Gabriel continued for a moment or two before bringing his lips to her ear. "Does this please you?"

She hummed at him, her eyes still closed.

He chuckled and shook his head. She was so sweet and easy to please. And he wanted to please her, desperately. When all the tangles had been removed, he gently stroked the brush through her hair, working slowly, section by section.

Never in her wildest dreams had Julia imagined Gabriel as a hairdresser. But there was something instinctual about the way he touched her, and the feeling of his long fingers coaxing her hair made her skin warm. She could only imagine the joys that awaited her in Florence when she would be able to enjoy all of him. *Naked.* She crossed her legs quickly.

"Am I enticing you, Miss Mitchell?" his honeyed voice whispered.

"No."

"Then I must not be doing this correctly." He restrained a chuckle and slowed his movements through her hair, pressing his lips to the edge of her ear. "Although my true purpose is to make you smile."

"Why are you so kind to me?"

His fingers stilled. "That's an extraordinary question to ask your lover."

"I mean it, Gabriel. Why?"

He moved his fingers through her hair again. "You've been kind to me since the first time I met you. Why wouldn't I be? Don't you think you deserve to be treated with kindness?"

Julia elected not to pursue her original question further. Despite the fact that she'd been overwrought the night before, she remembered confessing her love to him at the hospital. But her declaration had not been returned.

This is enough, she thought. *His actions, his kindness, his protection. This is more than enough. I don't need the words.*

Julia loved him so much it hurt; she'd always loved him, and her love had burned so brightly that even during her darkest days its luminosity had not died. But Gabriel didn't seem to return her love.

When he'd finished with her hair, he insisted on making her lunch. Afterward, they sat together in the kitchen, making plans for the evening, until the telephone rang and Richard walked in, carrying the cordless phone.

"It's your father," he said, handing the phone to Julia.

Gabriel intercepted it and covered the mouthpiece with his hand. "You don't have to talk to him. I'll take care of it."

"We'll have to talk eventually." Julia slipped off the bar stool and hobbled on her crutches into the dining room.

Richard shook his head at his son. "You can't get in between Julia and Tom."

"He hasn't been much of a father."

"He's the only father she has. And she is the light of his life."

Gabriel's eyes narrowed. "If he cared for her at all, he would have protected her."

Richard placed a hand on his shoulder. "Parents make mistakes. And sometimes, it's easier to place your head in the sand than to admit that your child is in trouble. And that it's your fault. I know this from personal experience."

Gabriel pursed his lips but said nothing.

Within ten minutes, Julia returned. Despite Richard's continued presence in the kitchen, Gabriel drew her into a hug and kissed her cheek. "Is everything okay?"

"My dad wants to take me to dinner tonight," she blurted.

Richard seemed to recognize her admission as his exit cue, so he retreated upstairs to his study.

"Do you want to see him?"

"It's going to be uncomfortable. But I said I would go."

"Julianne, you don't have to do anything. I'll take you to dinner, instead."

She shook her head. "He's trying, Gabriel. He's my father. I have to give him a chance."

Gabriel shook his head in frustration but elected not to argue with her.

At six o'clock sharp, Tom Mitchell appeared on the Clark's doorstep wearing a tie with a dress shirt and trousers. He tugged at his tie nervously. He wasn't used to wearing one. But for Julia . . .

Richard quickly welcomed him into the living room and entertained him while they waited for Julia to come downstairs.

"Are you sure you want to go?" Gabriel was reclining on his bed, watching Julia apply lipstick with the use of her compact.

"I'm not going to stand up my own father. Besides, Rachel is dragging Richard to see a chick flick, and you're going out with the guys. I'd end up sitting here all alone."

Gabriel pushed himself off the bed and walked over to her, wrapping his arms around her waist. "You wouldn't be alone. You'd be with me. And I do know how to keep a lady entertained." He began pressing wet kisses behind her ear to try to persuade her. "You're stunning," he whispered.

She blushed. "Thank you."

"Rachel found you a scarf." He fingered the edge of a blue silk Hermès design that his sister had artfully wrapped around Julia's neck to conceal her bite mark.

"It was Grace's," said Julia softly. "A gift from Richard."

"Richard liked to spoil her. Especially in Paris."

"You are very like him." She stood on tiptoe to press a kiss to his cheek.

"Wait till we arrive in Florence." He pulled her close and kissed her passionately before releasing her.

"So what will you be doing with the guys? Not a—strip club?"

She looked up at him through her eyelashes, looking a great deal too adorable.

Gabriel frowned. "Do you think I'd do that?"

"Isn't that what boys do on their nights out?"

He caressed her cheek with the back of his hand. "Do you think Rachel would approve of such an excursion?"

"No."

"And what about me, do you think that's what I want?"

Julia looked away and didn't answer.

"Why would I go look at other women when the most beautiful woman in the world shares my bed every night?" he protested, kissing her lightly. "The only woman I want to see naked is you."

Julia giggled. "What was my question? I can't remember what I was asking you."

He smirked. "Good. Come here."

※ ※

Later that evening, when the house was dark and everyone had retired, Julia slipped into Gabriel's room wearing a simple blue nightshirt. He was sitting in bed reading. He was shirtless and wearing his glasses, his knees bent up casually.

"Why, hello there." He smiled, placing *The End of the Affair* on his nightstand. "You look lovely."

She placed her crutches to one side and fingered her nightshirt gratefully. "Thanks for going to my dad's to pick up my things."

"You're welcome." He held out his hand, and she crawled into bed next to him.

He kissed her before he noticed that she was still wearing Grace's Hermès scarf. He tugged on one of the ends of it. "Why are you still wearing this?"

Julia lowered her eyes. "I don't want you to have to look at my scar."

He lifted her chin. "You don't need to hide from me."

"It's ugly. I don't want to remind you."

He stared deeply into her eyes, searchingly. Then he slowly undid the scarf. He pulled on it so that it gently brushed across the back of her neck and fell into his hand. She felt herself goose-pimple from the sensuous trail of silk across her skin, coupled with Gabriel's blazing gaze. He placed the scarf on his nightstand and leaned over to press his lips against the mark repeatedly.

"We both have scars, Julianne. Mine just aren't on the skin."

"I wish we didn't," she whispered. "I wish I was perfect."

Gabriel shook his head sadly. "Do you like Caravaggio?"

"Very much. His painting of *The Sacrifice of Isaac* is my favorite."

He nodded. "I always preferred *The Incredulity of St. Thomas*. Richard has a copy of it in his study. I was looking at it today."

"I always thought that painting was—strange."

"It is strange. Jesus appears to St. Thomas after the resurrection, and Thomas places his finger in the spear wound in Jesus' side. It's quite profound."

Julia did not see the profundity, so she remained quiet.

"If you want to wait until your scar disappears, Julianne, you'll wait forever. Scars never disappear. Caravaggio's painting made that point clear to me. Scars might heal and we might forget about them in time, but they're permanent. Not even Jesus lost his scars." Gabriel rubbed his hand across his chin thoughtfully.

"If I'd troubled myself to stop being selfish, I would have realized that. And I would have treated Grace and my family with greater care. I would have treated you with greater care in September and October." He cleared his throat. "I hope that you'll forgive me for the scars I've given you. I know that they're many."

Julia crawled into his lap and kissed him forcefully. "You were forgiven a long time ago and for far more than leaving scars. Please, let's not speak of this again."

The two almost-lovers shared a quiet moment before Gabriel asked her how her evening went.

Julia squirmed. "He cried."

Gabriel's eyebrows shot up. *Tom Mitchell cried? I don't believe it.*

"He described what he found at the house. And when I told him what happened before you rescued me, he cried. I told him about some of the fights and the things *he* used to say to me. And my Dad cried, right in the middle of a fancy restaurant." She shook her head. "We both cried. It was a mess."

Gabriel pushed her hair out of her face so that he could see her better. "I'm sorry."

"There were some things I needed to say, and he listened—maybe for the first time in my life. At least he's trying. That's a big step already. And when all of that was out of the way, we talked about you. He wanted to know how long we've been seeing one another."

"And what did you say?"

"I said that we hadn't been seeing one another for very long but that I . . . liked you. I told him that you'd done a lot for me and that I cared about you."

"Did you tell him how I feel about you?"

She wore a shy expression. "Well, I left out the part about you wanting to make love to me in Florence, but I said that I thought that you liked me."

Gabriel frowned. "I *like* you? Really, Julianne, is that the best you could do?"

She shrugged. "He's my dad. He doesn't want to hear the sentimental stuff. He wants to know if you're still doing drugs and getting into fights. And if you're monogamous with me."

Gabriel winced.

She hugged him tightly. "Of course, I told him that you were a model citizen and that you treated me like a princess. That I don't deserve you."

"Well, that's a lie." He kissed her forehead. "I don't deserve *you*."

"Nonsense."

They kissed softly for a moment or two, and Gabriel took off his glasses and placed them on top of his book. He turned out the light and spooned her blissfully.

Just as they were drifting off to sleep, Julia whispered, "I love you."

When he didn't respond, she assumed he was already dreaming. She sighed quietly and closed her eyes, snuggling backward against his chest. A strong arm flexed across her waist, pulling her tighter still.

She heard him inhale deeply and pause. "Julianne Mitchell, I love you too."

Chapter Thirty

Julia awoke the next morning to the feel of something warm pressed close to her heart and a gentle breeze of breath across her neck. Upon closer inspection, she realized that Gabriel's large hand was cupping her right breast as they spooned together. She giggled and shifted against his grasp.

He growled at her sudden movement.

"Good morning, Gabriel."

"Morning, beautiful." His lips found her cheek and kissed it.

"I take it you . . . slept well."

"Very well. And you?"

"Well, thank you."

"Does this bother you?" His hand caressed her gently through her nightshirt.

"No. It feels good." She rolled over to face him.

He slid his hand to the small of her back so he could pull her into a deep kiss.

"Julianne." He brushed a few wisps of hair out of her eyes. "There's something I would like to say to you."

Her brow furrowed.

He traced a single finger across her eyebrows, smoothing out the worry lines. "Don't frown. It's something nice. I think."

She looked up at him expectantly.

His eyes were large and dark and serious. *"I love you."*

She blinked twice and a smile slowly crept across her face. "I love you too. I thought I was hearing things when you said it last night."

He kissed her tenderly. "I wasn't sure you heard me, either."

"You know, you said it to me before."

"When?"

"The night I rescued you from Christa. I put you to bed, and you called me Beatrice. You said that you loved me."

He swallowed noisily. "Julianne, I'm sorry it took me so long to say it properly."

She wrapped her arms around his neck and pressed her forehead against the stubble on his chin. "Thank you."

"No, darling. I should be thanking you. I've—never felt this way before. It makes me realize how much time I've wasted." Gabriel's eyes grew sad.

Julia kissed him softly. "We both had a lot of growing up to do. It's better this way."

"I regret the way I treated those other women. And that I wasted my time with them. You know that, don't you?"

"I regret being with *him*. But there's nothing either of us can do about it now except be happy that we found each other."

"I wish we could spend the day in bed." His voice was suddenly wistful.

She laughed. "I think that would shock and scandalize your relations."

"Most likely. Damn them."

They both laughed until their laughter morphed into passionate kisses.

She was the first to retreat. "Can I ask you something?"

Gabriel's jaw set. "Of course." *Don't be too inquisitive this morning, Julianne. I can't tell you everything in Richard's house.*

"What kind of lingerie do you like on a woman?"

Gabriel's jaw immediately relaxed and his lips curled into a wicked smile. "You're asking this because—you're doing a survey?" He chuckled, taking her hand in his and pressing his lips against her knuckles.

She looked down at their conjoined hands. "I would like to go shopping before our trip. I was wondering what you—liked."

He gave her a heated look, heavy with desire. "Julianne, I am a man. If I were to tell you what lingerie I prefer, it would be *no lingerie*." He lifted her chin so that he could see her eyes. "You're very beautiful. When I think of being with you, I think of taking my time to admire your beauty—your face, your shoulders, your breasts, every part of you. Cream and pink and soft curves for my body to worship."

He pushed her gently so that she was on her back and he was kneeling on either side of her hips. "I want you to wear something that would make *you* feel comfortable and beautiful, because that's how I want you to feel when we're together." He captured her mouth and kissed her intently.

When he pulled back she eyed him impishly. "As comfortable as a Lululemon yoga outfit?"

He seemed puzzled. "I don't know what *lou lemons* are, but provided they make you comfortable, I'm sure I wouldn't object."

She arched her neck so that she could rub the tips of their noses together. "You're lovely, you know that? But I was serious when I asked you. I want to choose something you'll like."

"I'll like anything provided *you* are the one wearing it."

He kissed her again, and this time he allowed himself the luxury of lowering his naked chest so that it was close to but not touching hers. Heat and electricity jumped between their skin, and soon Julia was breathless.

"Color?" She gasped. "Style preference?"

Now he was chuckling, and stroking her cheek as it flushed beneath his fingers. "Well, not black or red."

"I thought those were the standard colors. They're supposed to be *seductive*."

He moved to the side so he could whisper in her ear. "You have already seduced me. I am enticed and tantalized and very, very excited."

Now the room grew warm, and she forgot what her next question was supposed to be. Finally, she remembered. "So no black or red. Any favorite colors?"

"You're stubborn, aren't you? I think you would look nice in light colors—white, pink, blue. I suppose I could say I envisioned you in something classic, with your hair cascading down your shoulders. But this isn't about me, this is about you. And I think you should choose." He grinned. "Of course, I might decide to purchase an item or two for you while we're there. But for our first time, it's all about what *you* want. What makes you feel special and sexy and cherished. That's what *I* want because I love you."

"I love you too."

She smiled up at him, and he thought his heart would melt. She took his face in her hand, running a thumb across his angular jaw, and he closed his eyes and leaned into her touch. When he opened his eyes, they were clear, bright, and very hungry.

She had to look away. "I need to get ready. What time do we have to leave for Philadelphia?"

He began to kiss across her collarbone from one shoulder to another. "After—*kiss*—breakfast—*kiss*. Our flight is around dinnertime—*kiss*—and we have to be at the airport early." *Double kiss.*

She kissed him once more and disappeared on her crutches into the hallway.

Downstairs, Richard was a whirling dervish of activity, making and serving Sunday breakfast for his hungry family. Scott was eating everything that wasn't nailed down or claimed by anyone else, and Rachel and Aaron were poring over pictures of Philadelphia wedding reception venues on Aaron's BlackBerry.

"There they are." Rachel greeted her brother and her best friend when they entered the kitchen.

"I need to give this back to you," Julia whispered as she began to undo the scarf she had knotted around her neck.

"Keep it. Mom would have wanted you to have it."

Julia pressed her friend into a grateful hug. Once again she was thankful for her generosity, and also for Grace, whose generous presence never seemed far away.

"You look happy this morning." Scott poured Julia a glass of orange juice as she sat down.

"I am. I really am."

"Make sure he treats you right," he whispered, his expression serious.

"He has changed, Scott. He . . . loves me." She spoke in a low voice so no one else could hear.

Scott gazed at her in surprise. "I'll be damned," he muttered. He shifted his weight uncomfortably, changing the subject.

"Simon was supposed to have a bail hearing yesterday. His lawyer was trying to have him released." He looked at Julia cautiously. "I haven't been able to find out what happened."

It took a moment for his words to register, but when they did, she was seized with anxiety. She knocked her orange juice over accidentally, turning her breakfast into a sticky, juice-soaked disaster.

She blinked rapidly as she tried to regain her composure, trying to mop up her latest mess, cursing herself for being such a bundle of nerves.

Gabriel has to be tired of watching me drop things. I am such an idiot.

Before she could stand to her feet, a hand appeared in front of her face. Julia looked up into a pair of concerned sapphire eyes. Gabriel moved his hand slightly, encouraging her to take it. He pulled her into his side and seated her on a different bar stool, kissing her forehead quickly.

"You're safe now," he whispered. "I won't let him near you." For good measure, Gabriel rubbed her arms up and down comfortingly.

While Richard prepared another waffle, Gabriel picked up her ruined breakfast and headed to the sink.

"I'll do that. Sit with your girl." Scott's voice was low and gruff at Gabriel's elbow. "And I'm sorry."

No one noticed the subtle exchange between the two brothers—the prodigal son and the son of constancy. Their eyes met and a look of understanding and perhaps even forgiveness passed between them. Gabriel nodded gratefully and took a seat by Julia, wrapping his arm around her waist and murmuring soothing words in her ear until she stopped shaking.

He had to get her out of Selinsgrove.

As they drove away, Julia closed her eyes and breathed a sigh of relief. It had been an emotional morning. Saying good-bye to her adoptive family was always difficult. And saying good-bye to her father after the weekend's events was exhausting.

"Are you sorry to leave?" Gabriel reached over to stroke her cheek.

She opened her eyes. "Part of me didn't want to leave. Part of me couldn't wait to put everything behind me."

"I feel the same way."

"What did my dad say to you when he shook your hand?"

Gabriel shifted in his seat. "He thanked me. He said he knew you could have been hurt a lot worse." Gabriel threaded his long fingers through Julia's, pulling her hand to his lips so that he could kiss it. "He asked me to keep an eye on his little girl. He said you were everything to him."

That made a tear run down Julia's cheek. She wiped it away and looked out the window. Things with her father had certainly changed.

On the flight back to Toronto, Julia cuddled up to Gabriel, eschewing her homework to rest her head on his shoulder.

"I need to make arrangements for our trip," he said, pressing a kiss to the top of her head.

"When will we leave?"

"I'd planned on leaving as soon as classes were over on Friday. But if you're coming, I'll need to wait until after Katherine turns in your grade. My lecture is on December tenth. Could we leave on the eighth?"

"I think so. I have to submit essays on Friday, and Katherine is expecting a draft of part of my thesis then too. I'm assuming she'll submit my grades within a few days, so I could probably leave on the eighth. When were you planning on coming back?"

Gabriel moved his arm so that it was wrapped around her and she was resting her head against his shoulder. "Rachel is adamant about having everyone home for Christmas. That includes you. So we would have to leave Italy on the twenty-third or the twenty-fourth and bypass Toronto for Philadelphia. Unless you'd rather spend Christmas in Italy, with me."

Julia laughed. "Not at the risk of incurring the wrath of Rachel. And my dad is expecting me, even though he knows I can't stay at his house." She shivered involuntarily.

Gabriel squeezed her. "Then you can stay with me. We'll reserve a room at a hotel. I'm not sleeping across the hall from you ever again."

She blushed at his remark and smiled.

"We'll have two weeks to enjoy Florence. Or we can travel to Venice and Rome, if you wish. We could rent a villa in Umbria. I know of a place near Todi that's very beautiful. I'd like to show it to you."

"As long as I'm with you, my love, I don't care where we are."

His lips tightened momentarily. "Bless you for that," he murmured. "Rachel is scheduling the wedding for late August, provided the

venue they want is available. I wonder why she wants to wait so long."
Julia was fishing to see if Gabriel had any information.

He shrugged. "Knowing Rachel, she'll need months to make sure
the proper people are notified and the wedding is featured on CNN."
They both chuckled.

"I think Rachel wants to start a family soon," said Julia. "I wonder
what Aaron thinks of that."

"He loves her. He wants to marry her. He's probably excited at the
thought of the love of his life carrying his child."

He paused for a moment, turning to face her. "Julianne, does it trouble you that I can't . . . ?"

"Not really, at least not right now. I want to finish my master's, then
work on my doctorate. I'd like to teach." She shrugged. "Perhaps this is
the benefit of dating a younger woman."

Gabriel snorted. "You make me sound antique. You realize that
when you're thirty you will probably change your mind, if not sooner.
And when that happens . . ."

She frowned and shook her head. "What do you expect me to say—
that I don't want you? I'm not going to say that. I love you, Gabriel, all
of you. Please don't push me away when we've finally gotten close." She
closed her eyes. "It hurts."

"Forgive me," he whispered, kissing the back of her hand.

She accepted his apology and tried to relax, weary from the day's
emotions.

Gabriel rubbed at his eyes so that he could think. But he soon realized that he needed space and time away from her in order to do that.

I won't need to push you away when I tell you about Paulina . . .

❋ ❋

The first week of December was the last week of classes. It was a quiet
week, for the most part. Gabriel and Julia dutifully kept their distance
from one another. Every evening he prepared his lecture for the Uffizi
Gallery in his spacious condominium while she worked tirelessly on
her essays and her thesis in her tiny hobbit hole.

They texted one another mercilessly:

> Darling, I miss you. Come over? Love, G

Julia smiled at the screen of her iPhone in such a way that even the iPhone blushed. Then she typed her reply:

> G, I miss you too. I'm finishing an essay for this crazy
> Dante seminar I'm taking. I'll probably be up all night.
> The professor is hot but demanding. I love you, Julia

She turned her attention back to her laptop as she continued editing her essay for Katherine. Within a few minutes, her iPhone was chirping again:

> Darling, You're in luck—I am a Dante specialist.
> Why don't you bring your essay over here
> and I will help you with it . . . all night . . . Love, G
> P.S. How hot?

Julia giggled at his message and hit *reply*:

> Dearest Dante Specialist, My professor is hot like fire,
> scotch bonnet peppers, and chicken vindaloo.
> I know what your all-nighter would include—
> and it wouldn't be finishing my essay.
> Rain check for Friday? Love, Your Julia. XO

Julia stared at her iPhone waiting for another text message. But it didn't come until she was in the bathroom:

> Darling Julia, That's pretty hot. Your rejection of my invitation
> has reduced me to a sea of loneliness, which I will now chase
> away with a shot of Scotch and two chapters of Graham Greene.
> Your X and O almost make up for it. I Love You, G.
> P.S. You are hot like the sun but far more lovely.

Julia smiled to herself and sent back a brief message, telling him how much she loved him. Then she spent the rest of her evening working.

They finally met in person at his last seminar on Wednesday, which was made all the more interesting by Christa Peterson's conspicuous behavior. She was quiet. She was still dressed fashionably, in an aubergine-colored cashmere sweater-dress that clung tantalizingly to her chest and derrière. Her makeup was flawless, her hair long and impeccably groomed. But her expression was sour, and she didn't take notes. Her arms remained crossed defensively across her ample breasts.

When Professor Emerson asked a question that she knew, she refused to raise her hand. When he looked over the rims of his glasses to see if he could coax her into participating, she scowled and looked away. Were it not for the fact that his mind was on Dante's *Paradiso*, he might have grown uneasy. But he didn't.

Christa was conspicuous not only in her silence but in her blatant hostility toward Julia, for whom she reserved the vilest of glares.

"What crawled up her butt?" Julia whispered to Paul as soon as the class was over.

He snickered. "Maybe she finally realized Emerson will never pass her dissertation proposal so she's contemplating a career change. There's a strip club on Yonge Street that's looking to hire. She might have what it takes to work there. Or not."

Now it was Julia's turn to snicker.

"By the way, I like your scarf. Very French." Paul grinned at her good-naturedly. "A gift from the boyfriend?"

"No. My best friend back home."

"Well, it looks nice on you."

Julia smiled at him, and they both packed up their books and walked home through the delicately cascading snow, telling (slightly edited) stories about their separate Thanksgivings.

Chapter Thirty-one

By Friday, Professor Emerson was in a foul mood. He'd spent almost an entire week without Julianne, and he'd had to watch her walk away with Paul after his seminar, without so much as a glance in his direction. He had to keep his distance when all he wanted to do was touch her and tell everyone she was his. Sleeping naked in the darkness, the demons had come and nightmares had taunted and oppressed him—nightmares normally held at bay by her very presence, a luminescence unequalled by the brightest star. A star he would soon have to live without.

He knew that he had to tell his secrets before they boarded the plane. Thus, he rued the fact that his (possibly) last week with Julianne had been spent alone. He'd changed his ticket and made all of the reservations for Julianne to accompany him to Florence, but he did so half-heartedly and not without investing in travel cancellation insurance, for he truly believed that she would leave him. He dreaded the moment when her wide, innocent eyes would darken and she would reject him as unworthy. But he would not allow her to gift her innocence to such a demon unknowingly. He would not play Cupid to her Psyche.

For that *would* be demonic.

Consequently, it was with undisguised coolness that he greeted her Friday evening when she arrived in time for dinner. He kissed her forehead fraternally and stepped aside, indicating that she should enter.

Abandon hope, he thought to himself.

Julia knew that something was wrong, and it wasn't solely because she could hear the strains of Puccini's *Madama Butterfly* wafting from the living room. Usually Gabriel greeted her with a hug and a few passionate kisses before removing her coat. Instead he stood there, not even making eye contact, waiting for her to speak.

"Gabriel?" She reached up to touch his face. "Is something wrong?"

"No," he lied, turning his face away. "Can I get you a drink?"

Julia resisted the urge to nag him for information and instead requested a glass of wine. She hoped he would be more forthcoming over dinner.

He wasn't. He served their dinner in silence, and when Julia tried to make polite small talk over the roast beef, he responded monosyllabically. She told him she'd completed all of her schoolwork for the semester and that Katherine Picton had agreed to turn her grades in before December eighth, but Gabriel only nodded in response, glaring into his soon to be empty wineglass.

Julia had never seen him drink so heavily. He was already drunk the night she rescued him at Lobby. But this night was different. He wasn't flirtatious and happy, he was tormented. With each glass, she grew more and more worried, but every time she opened her mouth to say something, she would catch a glimpse of fleeting sadness on his face, which made her refrain. He grew progressively cooler and more detached with each drink, so much so that by the time he served one of his housekeeper's homemade apple pies for dessert, Julia waved it aside and demanded that he silence Maria Callas so that they could talk.

That drew his attention, since the pie (and the *Butterfly*) was the culmination of his supper. His Last Supper.

"Nothing is wrong," he huffed, as he strode over to the stereo to stop the operatic performance.

"Gabriel, don't lie to me. It's obvious you're upset. Just tell me. Please."

The sight of Julianne, innocent Julianne, with her big brown eyes and her now furrowed brow almost undid him.

Did she have to be so sweet? So giving? Did she have to be compassionate? With a beautiful soul?

His guilt compounded. Perhaps it was a mercy that he hadn't seduced her. Her heart would mend more readily now, since they had not known each other sexually. They'd only been together for a few weeks. She would dry her tears quickly and maybe find a quiet, peaceful affection with someone good and constant, like Paul.

The thought made him violently ill.

Without a word, he walked over to the sideboard and grabbed one of the decanters and a crystal glass. He returned to his seat and poured two fingers' worth of Scotch. He drank half of it in one swallow and thumped his glass down roughly. He waited for the burning sensation in his throat to abate. He waited for the liquid courage to adhere to his insides, fortifying him. But it would take much more Scotch to dull the ache in his heart.

He took a deep breath. "I have some—unpleasant things to tell you. And I know that when I'm finished, I'll lose you."

"Gabriel, please. I—"

"Please, just let me say it." He tugged at his hair wildly. "Before I lose my courage."

He closed his eyes and inhaled once again. And when he opened them, he peered over at her like a wounded dragon. "You are looking at a murderer."

Sounds hit her ears but didn't sink into her consciousness. She thought she'd heard wrong.

"Not only am I a murderer, I took innocent life."

"If you can stand to remain in the same room with me for a few minutes, I'll explain how this came to be." He waited for her to react, but she sat quietly, so he continued. "I went to Magdalen College, Oxford, for my master's degree. You know this already. What you don't know is that while I was there I met an American girl called Paulina."

Julia inhaled sharply, and Gabriel paused. Every time she'd asked him about Paulina he'd always put her off. He'd tried to make her think that she was not a threat, but Julia hadn't believed him. Of course Paulina was a threat to their creeping closeness. Paulina had pulled him away in the middle of dinner back in October. And before he'd run away Gabriel had stood, haggard, quoting Lady Macbeth. Julia trembled slightly in anticipation.

"Paulina was an undergraduate. She was attractive, tall and regal with blond hair. She liked to tell people that she was related to the Russian aristocracy, an Anastasia of sorts. We became friends and would spend time together on occasion, but it wasn't physical. I was seeing other girls, and she was pining away for someone . . ."

He cleared his throat nervously.

"I graduated and moved to Harvard. We kept in touch via e-mail for a year or so, very casually, and she told me she'd been accepted to Harvard for her master's degree. She was studying to become a Dostoyevsky specialist. She needed help finding a place to live, so I told her about a vacancy in my building. She moved in that August."

He gazed at Julia searchingly. She nodded, trying to keep her trepidation from showing on her face.

"The year she arrived was my most difficult. I was working on my dissertation along with being a teaching assistant to a very demanding professor. I was staying up all hours writing and getting very little sleep. That was when I started doing cocaine." His gaze dropped, and he fidgeted with his hands, drumming atop the table.

"I used to go drinking with the guys from my program on the weekends. We'd get into fights, on occasion." He laughed. "I wasn't always on my best behavior, and sometimes we'd go out looking for trouble. It paid off, though, with Simon."

He leaned forward in his chair, resting his forearms on top of his knees. Julia watched his legs bounce nervously. With every sentence he grew more restless, indicating that he was approaching closer and closer to the edge of the abyss in which he had hidden his secret.

"One night someone passed around some coke. I wondered if it would help me stay up so I could work. That's how it started. I used it as a stimulant, and I alternated its use with alcohol. I thought because I went to Harvard, I was a respectable recreational drug user. I thought I could control it." He sighed deeply and the tone of his voice dropped. "I was wrong."

"Paulina was constantly around. She'd knock on my door at all hours because I was always awake. I'd write, and she'd sit on my couch and read or make Russian tea. She started cooking for me. Eventually, I gave her a key since she was over all the time. When I was doing coke, I didn't eat much. She was the only reason I ate anything nutritious at all."

Now Gabriel's voice took on a darker tone, as if the guilt inside him was clawing to get out. He read the question in her eyes and his jaw set.

"She knew about the cocaine. At first I tried to hide it, but she was always there. Finally, I gave up and started doing it in front of her. She didn't care."

Now he avoided Julia's gaze. He looked ashamed. "She'd lived a sheltered life. She was completely innocent about drugs and a lot of other things. I was a corrupting influence. One night, she stripped out of her clothes and suggested we snort lines off one another. I wasn't thinking straight, obviously, and she was naked . . ."

He exhaled slowly and shook his head, keeping his eyes on his fidgeting hands. "I won't make excuses. It was my fault. She was a nice girl who was used to getting what she wanted. And she wanted me—the drug addict downstairs." He rubbed at his chin with the back of his hand, and Julia suddenly realized he hadn't shaved that morning.

He squirmed in his chair. "The next morning I told her I'd made a mistake. I wasn't interested in being monogamous. The coke made me crave sex, although it eventually impaired my satisfaction. Karma, I suppose. I was used to being with different women every weekend. But when I told her all of this, she said she didn't care. No matter what I said or did, or how much of an asshole I was to her, she kept coming around. So that's how it was. She acted as if she was my girlfriend, and I acted as if she was a convenient lay. I didn't care about her, I only cared about myself and the drugs and the damned dissertation."

Julia felt her heart sink. She knew that Gabriel had never wanted for female companionship. He was a handsome man who was sensual in the extreme. Women fell all over themselves in order to attract his attention. Julia wasn't pleased about his past, but she'd accepted it and told herself that it didn't matter.

But Paulina was different. She'd known this intuitively from the first time she heard the name. Even though she believed Gabriel was no longer involved with her, what he was beginning to describe was much more serious than a one-night stand. The green specter of jealousy curled around her heart, squeezing it.

Gabriel stood up and started pacing, back and forth and back and forth. "Everything came to a crashing halt when she told me that she was pregnant. I accused her of trying to entrap me and told her to get rid of it." His face contorted with emotion, and he looked as if he were in pain.

"She cried. She got on her knees and said that she'd been in love with me since Oxford and that she wanted my baby. I wouldn't listen. I threw some money at her for an abortion and pushed her out of my apartment as if she were trash." Gabriel groaned—a twisted cry that seemed to come from the depths of his soul. He rubbed at his eyes with his fingers.

Julia placed a shaking hand to her mouth. She hadn't expected this. But as her mind raced ahead, a number of pieces of the puzzle that was Professor Emerson began to come together.

"I didn't see her again for a long time. I assumed she'd had the abortion. I didn't even bother to find out, that's how fucked up I was. A couple of months later, I stumbled into the kitchen one morning and found an ultrasound snapshot on my refrigerator. With a note."

He slumped back in his chair and placed his head in his hands. "She wrote, *'This is your daughter, Maia. Isn't she beautiful?'*" Gabriel's words were half strangled by the sob that escaped from his chest.

"I could see the outline of her little head and nose, her tiny arms and legs. Little hands and little feet. She was beautiful. This beautiful, fragile little baby. My little girl. *Maia.*" He swallowed another sob. "I didn't know. It wasn't real. *She* wasn't real until I saw her picture and . . ." Gabriel was crying.

Julia saw tears roll down his cheeks, and her heart ached. As her own eyes filled with tears she moved to go to him, but he raised a hand to stop her.

"I told Paulina I'd help with the baby. Of course, I was broke. I'd spent all my money on drugs and had already run up a tab with my dealer. Paulina knew that and somehow she still wanted me. We got back together, and she'd read on my couch while I wrote my dissertation. She stayed away from the drugs and tried to take care of herself and the baby. I tried to quit, but I couldn't."

He pulled his head up to look over at Julia. "Do you want to hear the rest? Or are you ready to leave now?"

She didn't hesitate. She walked over to him and wrapped her arms around his shoulders. "Of course I want to hear the rest."

He clung to her tightly, but only for a moment before he pushed her away and wiped his cheeks with the back of his hand. She stood to one side awkwardly while he continued his confession.

"Paulina's parents lived in Minnesota. They weren't wealthy, but they would send her money. Grace used to send me money too, whenever I called her. Somehow we were able to stay afloat. Or at least, delay the inevitable. But I used most of the money for drugs." He laughed darkly. "What kind of man takes money away from a pregnant woman and wastes it on cocaine?"

He quickly continued. "One night in September, I went on a bender. I was gone for a couple of days, and when I finally came home I collapsed on the sofa. I didn't even make it to the bedroom. I woke up the next morning completely hungover. I stumbled down the hall and saw blood on the floor."

Gabriel covered his eyes with his palms, as if he were trying to blot out the vision. Julia found herself holding her breath as she waited for his next revelation.

"I followed the trail and found Paulina lying on the bathroom floor in a pool of blood. I tried to find her pulse, but I couldn't. I thought she was dead." He was silent for a few minutes.

"If I'd checked on her when I got home, I could have called an ambulance. But I didn't. I was high, and I crashed, and I didn't care about anyone but myself. When they told me she lost the baby, I knew it was my fault. It was a completely preventable death. I might as well have killed her with my own hands."

He held his hands in front of his face and turned them slowly, as if he were regarding them for the first time. "I am a murderer, Julianne. A drug-addicted murderer."

She opened her mouth to contradict him, but he quickly cut her off.

"Paulina spent weeks in the hospital, first with physical problems, then with depression. I had to take a leave of absence from Harvard because I was too drugged up or drunk to work. I owed thousands of dollars to some dangerous people and had no way of coming up with the money. Paulina tried to kill herself in the hospital, so I wanted to check her into a private mental health facility, somewhere where they would be gentle with her. When I called her parents begging them to help, they told me I was a disgrace. That I needed to marry her, then they'd help us."

He paused. "I would have done it. But Paulina was too unstable to even discuss it. I made up my mind that I would discharge my duty to her, and then kill myself. That would put an end to all of our problems."

Gabriel looked up at her with cold, dead eyes. "So you see, Julianne, I am one of the damned. Through my own depraved indifference I caused the death of a child and the permanent destruction of a young woman's bright future. *It would have been better if I had had a millstone hung around my neck and been cast into the sea.*"

"It was an accident," said Julia quietly. "It wasn't your fault."

He laughed bitterly. "It wasn't my fault that I had sex with Paulina and made a baby? It wasn't my fault that I treated her like a whore, addicted her to drugs, and pressured her to have an abortion? It wasn't my fault that I stumbled in, high, and didn't even bother to check to see if she was in my apartment?"

Julia took his hands in hers and grasped them tightly. "Gabriel, listen to me. You contributed to the situation, yes, but it was an accident. If there was so much blood, then something was wrong with the baby. If you hadn't called the ambulance when you did, Paulina would have died. You saved her."

He wouldn't look up, but she moved her hand to his chin and forced him to look at her. "You saved her. You said yourself that you wanted the baby. You didn't want the baby to die."

He flinched beneath her touch, but she would not release him. "You are not a murderer. It was just a tragic accident."

"You don't understand." His voice was cold, listless. "I am just like *he* is. *He* used you, and I used her. I did more than use her. I treated her as if she were a plaything and gave her drugs, when I should have protected her. What kind of devil am I?"

"You are *nothing* like him," she hissed, her emotions getting the better of her. "He has no remorse for what he did to me, and given the opportunity he would do it again. Or worse."

She took a deep breath and held it. "Gabriel, you made some mistakes. You did terrible things. But you're sorry for them. You've been trying to make up for them for years. Shouldn't that count for something?"

"All the money in the world cannot pay for a life."

"A life you didn't take," she countered, eyes flashing.

He hid his face in his hands. This was not how he expected this conversation to go.

Why is she still here? Why hasn't she left me?

She stepped backward and watched him momentarily. She could feel the despair rolling off of him in waves as she frantically wracked her brain to find some way to reach him.

"Do you know Victor Hugo's *Les Misérables?*"

"Of course," he muttered. "What does that have to do with anything?"

"The hero abandons his sin and performs a penance; he looks after a young girl as if she were his own daughter. But all the while, a policeman hunts him, convinced that he hasn't reformed. Wouldn't you rather be the person performing penance than the policeman?"

Gabriel didn't answer.

"Do you think that you should have to suffer for your sin forever?"

No response.

"Because it seems that's what you're saying—you won't allow yourself to be happy. You won't allow yourself to have children. You think you've lost your soul. But what about redemption, Gabriel? What about forgiveness?"

"I don't deserve it."

"What sinner deserves it?" She shook her head. "When I told you about what happened with *him,* you told me to forgive myself and let myself be happy. Why can't you do the same thing?"

He looked down at the floor. "Because you were the victim. I'm the killer."

"Let's say that's true. What would be an appropriate penance, Gabriel? How would justice be served?"

"*An eye for an eye,*" he muttered.

"Fine. An eye for an eye would mean that you would have to save the life of a child. You're responsible for the death of a child, so justice requires that you give back a life. Not coins, not presents, but life."

He sat motionless, but she knew he was listening.

"You saved Paulina's life, but I know you won't count that. So you need to save the life of someone else's child. Wouldn't that pay for your sin? Or at least offer some kind of restitution?"

"It wouldn't bring Maia back. But it would be something. It would make me less—evil." Gabriel's shoulders hunched in his chair as he hung his head low.

The pain in his voice almost rent Julia's heart in two, but she continued bravely. "You would have to find a child who was in danger of dying and save her. And that would be atonement."

He nodded slightly, stifling a groan.

Julia sank down on her knees, taking his hands in hers. "Don't you see, Gabriel? I am that child."

He lifted his head and stared at her as if she were mad, his watery eyes boring into her own.

"Simon could have killed me. He was so angry when I slapped him, he was going to break through my bedroom door and kill me. Even if I had called nine-one-one, they never would have arrived in time.

"But you saved me. You pulled him away from my door. You kept him from going back into the house. I am alive now only because of you. I am Tom's baby girl, and you saved my life."

He remained motionless, entirely without words.

"A life for a life—that's what you said. You think you took a life, and now you've saved one.

"You have to forgive yourself. Ask Paulina to forgive you, ask God to forgive you, but you have to forgive yourself."

"It isn't enough," he whispered, his great, sad eyes still wet with tears.

"It won't bring your daughter back, that's true. But think about the gift you gave Tom—his only daughter. Turn our debt into penance. You are not a devil, you're an angel. My angel."

Gabriel stared at her quietly, trying to read her eyes, her lips, her expression. When he was finished, he held his hand out and drew her into his arms, settling her on his lap. He held her for what seemed like forever as his tears spilled onto her shoulder.

"I'm so sorry," he whispered. "I'm sorry I waited so long to tell you. I'm sorry my story is true. I've killed your faith in me. I know that."

"I still love you."

She tried to soothe him by murmuring in his ear, by letting him release his grief through his tears. And when his tears finally subsided, she touched the buttons of his white shirt and began undoing them quickly, before he could ask what she was doing. She peeled the shirt back from his naked chest and ran her fingers around his tattoo. Then slowly, very slowly, she lowered her lips to the dragon's mouth and kissed it.

When she sat back, Gabriel stared at her in silent wonder.

She removed her scarf and gently lifted his hand so that he was touching her bite mark, a mark that had faded slightly but not disappeared. And she placed her hand on top of his tattoo. He winced and closed his eyes.

"We both have scars. And maybe you're right, they won't disappear. But I am your atonement, Gabriel. My life is your gift to a father who could have lost his child forever. Thank you."

"I'm a hypocrite." His voice was rough. "I told Tom he was a terrible father. What kind of father was I?"

"A young one. An inexperienced one. You shouldn't have been taking drugs. But you wanted Maia. You said so yourself."

He shuddered as they clung to one another.

"Nothing I can say will bring her back. But if it would comfort you, I would say that I believe your little girl is singing with the blessed in Paradise. With Grace." She wiped his tears away. "I'm sure that Grace and Maia would want you to find love and forgiveness. They would pray for your redemption. They wouldn't think that you're evil."

"How can you be sure?" he whispered.

"I learned this from you. Canto thirty-two of Dante's *Paradiso* describes the special place God has for children. *Of such are the kingdom of heaven.* And in Paradise, there is only love and forgiveness. No hatred. No malice. Only peace."

He pulled her close and the couple, held one another tightly. Julia could not have imagined Gabriel's secret. And although she was distressed with the way his melancholy disposition had fashioned his grief, his grief was something she could not deny.

She hadn't loved a child only to see the child die. So she was moved with compassion for him and an abiding will to help him recognize his own self-worth and to accept that he was loveable, despite his past sins. Seated on his lap with his tears still dampening her blouse, the picture that was Gabriel Emerson became strikingly clear. In many ways, he was very much a frightened little boy, fearful that no one would forgive him his faults. Or love him in spite of them.

But she would.

"Gabriel, you can't be comfortable in this chair."

He nodded against her shoulder.

"Come." She stood up and took his hand, pulling him to his feet. She led him over to the sofa and encouraged him to sit down, while she flipped the switch for the fireplace.

He kicked off his shoes, and she coaxed him to stretch out lengthwise, resting his head in her lap. She traced his eyebrows and began running her fingers through his uncombed hair. He closed his eyes.

"Where is Paulina now?"

"In Boston. When I received my inheritance, I set up a trust fund for her and bought her an apartment. She has been in and out of rehab a couple of times. But she's well looked after, and she went back to Harvard part-time a year or two ago."

"What happened the night she called during our dinner?"

Gabriel gave her a puzzled look before recognition flashed across his face. "I forgot that you heard that call. She'd been drinking and got into a car accident. She was hysterical on the phone, and I thought I was going to have to fly down there. She only calls when she's in trouble. Or when she wants something."

"So what happened?"

"I ran back to my apartment, but before I left for the airport, I called my lawyer in Boston. He met her at the hospital and assured me that she wasn't as badly injured as she led me to believe. But she was charged a day or so later. There was nothing I could do but hire someone to defend her. She has been pretty good lately, but this happens from time to time."

Perhaps it was the flickering glow of the fire. Perhaps it was the stress of having revealed his darkest secret. But at that moment Gabriel looked remarkably old and weary for his thirty-something years.

"Do you love her?"

Gabriel shook his head. "I don't think my feelings count as love, although I feel something for her. She was never *familiar* to me, much to my shame. But I couldn't abandon her. Not when her family was so far away and they refused to help. I was the cause of her problems and the possibility that she'll never have another child." His voice grew uneven, and he shivered.

"Is that why you decided not to have children?"

"*An eye for an eye*, remember. When she cried in my arms and told me, I made the decision. I had a hard time convincing a doctor to agree to perform the procedure; they all argued that I was too young and that I would change my mind. But finally, I found someone to do it. Strangely, it comforted me at the time."

He reached his hand up to caress the curve of Julia's cheek. "I told her about you. She has always been jealous, but she knows I can't give her what she wants. Our relationship is—complicated. She will always be part of my life, Julianne. I need you to realize that. That is, if you still . . ."

She pressed their lips together. "Of course I still love you. You're supporting her and helping her whenever she gets into trouble. That's the honorable thing to do."

"Believe me, Julianne, I am far from honorable."

"Would you . . . tell me about your tattoo?"

He sat up so that he could remove his shirt, which he dropped unceremoniously onto the Persian carpet. He reclined on her lap and looked up into her eyes, which radiated acceptance and concern.

"I had it done in Boston after I was released from rehab."

Julia kissed the dragon once again, very, very gently.

Gabriel inhaled sharply at the feeling of her mouth against his naked flesh.

She moved her hands to stroke his hair, hoping it would comfort him. "What does the dragon represent?"

"The dragon is me or the drugs or both. The heart is mine, and it's broken, obviously. Maia will always be in my heart. You probably think it's horrible—to have such a morbid and ugly thing on my body. Permanently."

"No, Gabriel, I don't think that. It's like . . . a memorial."

"Paulina was about five months pregnant when she lost the baby. She was not in her right mind and neither was I, so we didn't have a funeral. A couple of years ago I had a headstone erected for Maia in Boston." He grasped Julia's hand in his and kissed her palm.

"She isn't buried there." His voice was pained.

"She wouldn't be there, anyway, Gabriel. She's with Grace now."

He paused and stared at her as his eyes filled with tears again. "Thank you for that," he whispered, pressing his lips to her hand once more. "There's a stone angel on either side of the headstone. I wanted it to be beautiful."

"I'm sure it's lovely."

"You've already received part of her memorial."

She looked puzzled.

"Your bursary. I named it for her—*Maia Paulina Emerson*."

Julia wiped a tear that sprang suddenly from her eye. "I'm so sorry I tried to give it back to you. I didn't know."

Gabriel reached up and kissed her nose. "I know that, my love. At the time, I wasn't ready to explain how significant the bursary was. I only wanted you to have it. No one else was worthy." He kissed her again softly.

"I should tell you that I asked Rachel about it. She had no idea."

"No one knows about Maia and Paulina except for Richard. And Grace. I was so ashamed of everything. They thought it would be enough for Scott and Rachel to know about the drugs. No one knows about the tattoo, however. You're the only one."

She tangled her fingers in his hair, willing him to find peace. "Your Puccini scared me," she whispered.

"It seemed . . . fitting."

She shook her head.

"The way I treated Paulina. She loved me for years, and I couldn't love her back." He shrugged awkwardly and shifted his gaze so that his intensity burned into hers. "I would never treat you like a butterfly, like something I've captured for my own amusement. I'd never pin you to a card and pull off your wings."

She shook her head as a pained look crossed her pretty face. "Gabriel, please. I trust you. *You* are not Puccini's Pinkerton. I know that."

In proof of her declaration, she kissed him, moving her mouth in concert with his until she had to pull back to draw breath.

"I don't deserve you," he whispered.

"Maybe we don't deserve each other, but I can choose who I love. And I choose you."

He frowned as if he didn't believe her.

"Please let me love you." Her voice cracked on the last two words, and a stray tear pushed down her cheek.

"As if I could even contemplate living without you." He drew her to him, the desperate passion of his tortured soul binding the two together.

She met him movement for movement, taking and giving all at once as she leaned over the beautiful man who rested his weary head in her lap. His mouth found her wrists as he kissed them with wet, open kisses, sucking gently at the delicate place where pale veins were covered by rice-paper skin.

"Forgive me, Julianne, but I need you. My sweet, sweet girl. So much." His eyes were a blue fire, and his voice was gravelly.

Before she knew what was happening, he'd repositioned himself so that he was sitting on the couch and she was straddling him. Their upper bodies pressed tightly together, his hands worshipping the gentle sway of her lower back and the curve of her behind through her wool trousers.

In the back of her mind, Julia recalled one of the black-and-white photographs from Gabriel's bedroom. And in that instant, she recognized its beauty and its passion from a first person perspective. It was want and need and desperation and deep, deep unconditional love now made free through the telling of dark, hidden secrets.

He felt her love in her kiss, her embrace, the way her fingers lightly brushed the back of his neck and the surface of his tattoo, coaxing open-mouthed kisses up and down the lines of his chest. She would give him everything. She would do anything to take away his pain, including offering up herself.

The Sacrifice of Isaac.

With trembling fingers, she undid the buttons of her blouse and slipped it from her shoulders. A faint gasp from Gabriel's mouth mirrored the sound of the silk sinking slowly to the floor.

She was his atonement.

Chapter Thirty-two

Julia awoke the next morning stark naked.

Or so she thought.

She was in Gabriel's bed with their bodies wrapped around each other. Her head rested on his shoulder while his left arm ran across her right hip, their legs scissored, their hips pressed close.

She moved a hand down his back until she found soft cotton covering his most beautiful of curves, which she explored surreptitiously. Then she looked in between them and realized she was wearing her pink bra and panties.

In her dream, they'd fallen into bed naked and made love for hours. Gabriel had placed his body over hers and held her gaze like a magnet as he entered into her slowly, until the two became one. An eternal circle with no end and no beginning. He'd worshipped her with his body and his words, and it was far more emotional and lovely than she'd ever dared hope.

But it was only a dream. She sighed and closed her eyes as the previous evening's events came flooding back. Sorrow and relief commingled and spread across her heart; sorrow for Gabriel's loss and tortured desperation, and relief that all their secrets had now been spoken.

Gabriel murmured her name, his eyes moving beneath his eyelids in deep REM sleep. He'd been so tired the night before. So broken. Julia kissed his cheek and quietly extricated herself from his arms, padding to the bathroom.

When she regarded herself in the mirror, she saw wild, rumpled hair, smeared eye makeup, and lips made fuller from kissing. Several love bites, mild in color and quite painless, dappled her neck and chest. He'd been a gentle but enthusiastic lover.

She washed her face and brushed her hair, taming her mane into a high ponytail and provocatively forsaking her purple bathrobe for one of Gabriel's button down shirts. She fetched the *Globe and Mail* from the exterior hallway and waved a shy good morning to Gabriel's nervous but not entirely unfortunate-looking next door neighbor, who stared through his rimless spectacles at her shapely bare legs before retreating like a frightened mouse into his apartment. He was not used to seeing such beauty so early in the morning, and he'd been clad only in Superman pajama bottoms of dubious origin.

When Julia entered the kitchen she was faced with a mess, for no one had cleaned up after dinner, their hands and minds too full for such pedestrian concerns. After indulging in a slice of apple pie with Vermont cheddar, Julia proceeded to return Gabriel's apartment to its formerly pristine condition. It took longer than she anticipated.

When the kitchen was spotless and Gabriel still had not emerged from his bed, she poured herself a very large mug of coffee and sat in his favorite chair by the fireplace with the newspaper. The sight of his Oxford shirt and her silk blouse lying on top of one another on the floor brought a blush to her cheeks and a smile to her lips.

"And this, alas! is more than we would do."

Gabriel had stopped her. She would have given herself to him gladly because she loved him. For her, it was not a matter of *if* she would make love with him, but *when*. But Gabriel had mumbled something against her naked breast and stopped.

He'd been so afraid that she would abandon him when she found out about his relationship with Paulina and the tragic loss of their child. But if anything, his confession had brought them closer. At least she'd been able to make that clear to him.

And in three days, perhaps, we will be as close as a couple can be. In two days they would leave for Italy, and she would accompany Gabriel to his lecture as his girlfriend. And when their time in Florence was ended, perhaps they would travel to Venice or Umbria as lovers.

Despite everything she and Gabriel had experienced, she felt very much at peace in his shirt and in his chair. They belonged to one another, she believed this. And as long as the Fates did not conspire against them, they would have their happiness. She hoped. However, the knowledge that Paulina had the ability to throw Gabriel into a tail-spin with a single telephone call troubled her deeply.

No less than an hour later, Gabriel strolled into the living room, scratching his head and yawning. His hair was messy with the exception of one perfect, errant curl that had taken a liking to his forehead. He was wearing a pair of faded blue jeans, his glasses, and nothing else. He wasn't even wearing socks. (Parenthetically, it should be noted that even Gabriel's feet were attractive.)

"Good afternoon, my love." He caressed her cheek with his fingers and leaned over to kiss her firmly. "I like your . . . outfit." His eyes took in the naked flesh that was visible below the edge of the shirttail.

"I like your outfit too. You're looking awfully *casual* this morning, Professor."

He leaned forward and gave her a heated look. "Miss Mitchell, you're lucky I decided to put on any clothes at all." He chuckled at her fierce blush and disappeared into the kitchen.

Oh, gods of all virgins who are planning to have sex with their sex-god (no blasphemy intended) boyfriends, please don't let me spontaneously combust when he finally takes me to bed. I really need a Gabriel-induced orgasm, especially after last night. Please. Please. Pretty please . . .

A few minutes later he reappeared and sank down on the couch with his coffee cup, scrubbing at his stubble with one hand. At length, he frowned in her direction.

"You're too far away." He patted his knee invitingly.

She grinned and walked over to him, allowing him to guide her so that she was seated comfortably on his lap. Gabriel crooked an appreciative arm around her hips, pulling her shirt up so that he could rest it comfortably against the lace of her boy shorts.

"And how is Miss Mitchell this morning?"

"Tired," she sighed. "But happy." Her eyes darted to his. "If it's okay for me to say that."

"It is. I'm happy too. And God, so relieved." He closed his eyes and leaned his head back, exhaling a very deep breath. "I was certain I'd lose you."

"Why?"

"Julianne, if one were doing a cost-benefit analysis, I would be a high-cost, high-risk, low-benefit venture."

"Nonsense. I don't see you that way at all."

He gave her a half-smile. "Only because you are the soul of forgiveness and compassion. Although I must admit, my best qualities and talents have heretofore remained hidden." Now his voice was husky, and the familiar spark of sensuality lit his blue eyes. "But I look forward to placing them entirely at your service again and again and again, *ad infinitum,* until you are weary of both them and me. And entirely, blissfully sated."

Julia swallowed. Hard.

He reached up to kiss her forehead, placing his coffee on the side table so that he could wrap her in his arms. "Thank you for staying."

"I love you, Gabriel. You have to accept the fact that I'm not going anywhere."

He hugged her in response, but remained silent.

"And you don't have to win me sexually. You've already won me," she whispered. "Your best quality is your heart, Gabriel, not your sexual prowess. It's your heart I fell in love with."

He was silent for so long, Julia thought she had upset him. Or insulted him.

Not a wise move to insult a prospective lover's lovemaking skills before *you've had the opportunity to sample them.* She opened her mouth to apologize, but he stopped her.

He kissed her firmly, a closed mouth kiss that quickly developed into the tugging of lips, the gentle play of tongues, and the caressing of cheeks.

When he pulled away, he crushed her to his chest and whispered in her ear. "You strip me bare. You see through everything. You are the only one who has ever known everything and still wanted me. Only you, my beloved."

She'd known intuitively that Gabriel used his sexuality as a shield to keep true intimacy and love at bay. But with his admission, she realized how painful and lonely it must have been for him all those years, and that was after the soul-crushing time in which he was invisible to his mother and the painful adjustment of becoming an adopted child. Having recognized all of this, in addition to his sorrow over Maia, she tried very hard to fight back tears, for she didn't want to upset him, but she couldn't stop them.

"Sssshhh, don't cry," Gabriel breathed. He wiped away her tears and kissed her forehead. "I love you. Please don't cry. Not because of me."

She snuggled in his arms and worked at stemming the flow of tears. He rubbed her back, gently petting her over and over. And when she was calm, she spoke.

"I love you, Gabriel. And I can't help but think that Grace would be very proud of you."

He frowned. "I'm not sure about that. But she would certainly be proud of you and all you've accomplished."

Julia smiled. "Grace had the gift of mercy."

"She did. Your choice of words is very interesting. *A Severe Mercy* was one of Grace's favorite books. She tried for years to get me to read it. I have a copy of it somewhere in the study. Maybe I should look for it."

"What's it about?"

"A young couple. The man ends up studying at Oxford, and I believe he becomes a protégé of C.S. Lewis. It's a true story."

"I'd love to go to Oxford, to see where the Inklings drank their beer and spun their tales. Katherine Picton talks about Oxford a lot."

Gabriel kissed her forehead. "I'd love to take you. I can show you the statues at Magdalen College that inspired Lewis to write about the stone animals in *The Lion, The Witch and the Wardrobe*. We could go in June, if you like."

Julia smiled and kissed him back. "If you lend me Grace's book, I'll take it to Italy. It might be nice to have something to read during our vacation."

He smirked at her and tapped a single finger to the end of her nose. "What makes you think I'll let you have time enough to read?"

She blushed and fumbled a vague response, but Gabriel continued, a grave expression on his face.

"I'm sorry we had to stop last night. It isn't right for me to tease you like that and just . . ." He searched her eyes for her reaction.

She wrapped her arms around him and embraced him tenderly. "It was an incredibly emotional evening. I was happy to be close to you and to fall asleep in your arms. I just wanted to comfort you any way I could. You don't need to apologize."

He cupped her face in both hands. "Julianne, your mere presence comforts me. But I was exhausted, and I'd been drinking . . . a recipe for disaster." He shook his head and looked ashamed. "I didn't want our first time together to have so much baggage, with all the ghosts of my past swirling in the air. I want us to go to a place that is ours alone and make some new memories. Some happy ones."

"Of course. Although I must say that I was pretty happy with our *interactions* last night." She laughed lightly and kissed him.

He returned her kiss eagerly. "So you aren't upset?"

"Gabriel, you are a gentleman worth waiting for. What kind of person would I be if I threw a tantrum because you said *stop*? If I were to say *stop*, I would hope that you would accept it and not get angry."

He frowned. "Of course, Julianne. You can always say *stop*."

"Well, what's good for the goose is good for the gander."

"So I'm a *gander* now, am I?" He kissed her once again.

"It's better than being a *geezer*."

"Oh, no." He squeezed her tightly. "No age jokes. I'm sensitive enough about our age difference."

She tossed her hair. "Our souls have to be about the same age. So who's counting?"

He tugged at her ponytail. "You're incredible. You're intelligent and funny, and damn, you're gorgeous. Last night, kissing your breasts . . ." He placed a hand reverently over her heart. "You rival Botticelli's muse."

"Botticelli?"

"Haven't you noticed how several of his paintings all feature the same woman? She is the topic of my lecture for the Uffizi Gallery—Botticelli's muse."

Julia smiled at him sweetly, placing a corresponding hand on his heart. "I can't wait."

"Neither can I."

After a lonely shower, Julia had a deuce of a time convincing Gabriel to let her out of his sight so that she could go shopping. He insisted on accompanying her. But when she finally explained that she wanted to shop for lingerie, *alone*, he relented.

"Promise me you'll stay with me until we leave for Italy." He looked at her through his eyebrows.

"I have to pack. My suitcase and all my things are at my apartment."

"When you've finished shopping, take a cab home and pack before you have the driver bring you back here. I have to run a few errands, but you have your own key and security card to let yourself in."

"And what kind of errands does Professor Emerson have to do today?"

He smiled at her seductively, and Julia felt her boy shorts slip along her hips as if they were intending to take a header to the floor.

"Perhaps I have my own shopping to do for—ah—*personal items*." He leaned forward to press his lips against her ear, his voice a smooth whisper. "I told you I was a good lover, Julianne. Trust me. I will anticipate your every need."

She shivered at the way his breath breezed across her neck, almost fluttering the omnipresent scarf she wore to hide her scar. She had no idea what he was implying, but she found herself tantalized by the way his words tripped off his tongue.

He owned her, body and soul.

❋ ❈

While Julia was pulling lingerie from the store racks to add to her ever expanding pile of items to try on, her iPhone chirped. She quickly checked it and found a text:

What are you looking at?—G

She giggled slightly and typed a short response:

Very tiny things.—Julia

Gabriel replied immediately:

How tiny?—G

P.S. Send pictures

Julia rolled her eyes as she hit *reply*:

Too tiny. No pictures—they'd ruin the surprise. Love, Julia

It took a little longer for Gabriel's next text to arrive:

Darling, No picture could ruin the experience of seeing you
in all your glory for the first time . . . You're that beautiful. Love, G

Julia's fingers couldn't type fast enough:

Thank you, Gabriel. I love you

Gabriel's final text message reached her just as she entered the
dressing room:

I love you too, sweetheart. Have fun . . . Hurry home to me.—G

The next two days were a whirlwind as Gabriel finished his administrative duties for the university, ensuring that all his grades were sub-
mitted. The semester was finally over.

Julia made a special trip to a spa for some pre-Italy pampering. In
keeping with her low pain tolerance and overall Mediterranean sensi-
bility, she politely declined the aesthetician's invitation to embrace all
things Brazilian.

Gabriel had kept most of their travel plans a secret, wishing to surprise her. So it was with amazement that their arrival in Florence on a
warmer than usual December day resulted in the happy couple walking
into the Gallery Hotel Art. The hotel was upscale, modern, and located
very close to the Ponte Vecchio, Julia's favorite bridge, and a few minutes from the Ponte Santa Trinita, which was featured in Holiday's
painting of Dante and Beatrice.

The concierge, Paolo, greeted them immediately. Although Gabriel
had not stayed in his hotel before, Paolo had been instructed by Dot-

tore Massimo Vitali, the Executive Director of the Uffizi Gallery, to extend every courtesy to Professor Emerson and his *fidanzata*. In fact, Paolo himself accompanied the bellhop and the lovers to their seventh-floor suite, which was called the Palazzo Vecchio Penthouse.

Julia gasped as the men parted like the Red Sea before her so that she could enter first. It was, perhaps, the loveliest room she'd ever seen. The floor was a dark hardwood offset with light-colored walls. The sitting room was graced with elegantly modern furniture and a sliding glass wall that partitioned it from the bedroom.

The bedroom itself was spacious and featured a large bed that was piled high with crisp, white linens. Mere steps away was a glass door that opened out onto the rooftop *terrazza*, which allowed bright sunlight to spill over the bed, illuminating it. One of the bathrooms boasted a huge pedestal bathtub, not unlike the tub Julia had enjoyed in their hotel in Philadelphia, while the other bathroom had a shower and two matching vanities. Gabriel took one look at the bathtub and decided that he needed to share it with Julianne that very evening.

But the crowning glory of the space was the *terrazza* itself, which offered breathtaking views of the Duomo, the Palazzo, and the surrounding hills. Julia envisioned curling up with Gabriel on the comfortable futon bed, which dominated the terrace, with a glass of Chianti, looking up at the stars. Or perhaps (she blushed), making love with him by candlelight underneath those same stars.

Orgasms with Gabriel by starlight . . .

Once they were alone, Julia hugged him tightly and thanked him over and over again for choosing such a beautiful room.

"It's all for you, my love." He kissed her softly. "All for you."

Truthfully, he would have liked nothing better than to spread Julianne out on the bed and make love to her immediately, but she hadn't slept well on the airplane, and he knew that she was tired. She yawned twice in a row and giggled when he tried to kiss her.

"I should clean up and pay a visit to the Uffizi. Would it be all right if I left you on your own? You can take a nap, if you like, or I could ask the concierge to book a massage for you in the spa."

Julia's eyes lit up at the latter offering, but she knew she was too sleepy to enjoy it. "A nap sounds good. I know it isn't the best strategy for overcoming jet lag, but I will be much better company over dinner and, um, *later on,* if I have a little more sleep." She blushed.

Gabriel traced a single finger around her jaw line. "I'll only say this once, Julianne. *There is no rush.* We can take our time tonight and just relax. Although I think it would be nice if we were to try out the bathtub. *Together.*" His lips curled up into a sexy half-smile.

"I'd like that," she said.

He kissed her nose, chuckling. "I requested special amenities from the *Farmacia di Santa Maria Novella.* See if any of the scents are to your liking, and we'll use them. In the meantime, I'll book our dinner reservations for nine or nine thirty."

"Sure. Where will we go?"

He smiled widely. "The Palazzo dell'Arte dei Giudici. Do you know it?"

"I've walked by it, but no, I didn't know they had a restaurant."

"I'm looking forward to showing it to you." He lifted her hand to his lips and kissed it softly. "I ordered a fruit basket and a few bottles of sparkling water. Charge what you like to the room." He grinned. "Although save the champagne to share with me later. *In the tub.*"

Julia looked down at her feet. "You're spoiling me."

He lifted her chin. "No, my love, not spoiling. Just treating you as you deserve to have been treated all along. You've been surrounded by fools your whole life. Of whom I was chief."

"Gabriel, you are many things, but a fool you are not." She leaned up on tiptoes to brush his lips with her own before leaving to take a shower.

A few hours later, Gabriel returned from a cordial meeting with his friend Massimo Vitali. Over espresso, the gentlemen discussed Gabriel's lecture the following evening and the plans for an elaborate banquet to be held inside the Uffizi in his honor. Gabriel was very grateful for the gesture, but more on behalf of Julianne than himself, for he thought only of how pleased she would be to participate in such a festive event. And in her favorite art gallery.

Entering the penthouse, Gabriel walked through the sitting room to the bedroom and found Julia asleep in the geographic center of the bed, on top of the covers. She was wearing champagne-colored satin pajamas, her long hair flowing around her head like a warm mahogany halo. She looked like a dark-haired Sleeping Beauty.

He watched her sleep for a moment and pressed a kiss to her cheek. When she didn't stir, he decided to pour himself a drink and sit out on the terrace until it was time to wake her. Truthfully, he was glad to have a moment to himself to plan and dream about the next few days. He felt as if the world had been lifted from his shoulders. Not only did she know the truth about Paulina and Maia, but she still loved him. And they'd escaped the wrath of the judicial committee and survived the academic semester together. He had much for which to be grateful. And most of all, he had his Julianne all to himself for two entire weeks.

Julia is not the kind of girl you screw around with. She's the kind of girl you marry. Scott's words resounded in his ears.

Scott was right. Julianne was special: an intelligent, compassionate beauty who loved deeply and gave freely. She deserved much more than just an affair, although Gabriel refused to consider their relationship an affair, no matter what people might say. He stealthily patted the small velvet box he'd hidden in his jacket pocket. The thought of being in a long-term relationship had always been so remote. Julianne had changed all that.

Tonight his plan was to show her how much he loved her. To adore her and to relax her. A bubble bath, a massage . . . anything he could do to make her comfortable with having him see her body. Julianne was still shy with him, and he wanted her to feel sexy and desirable. Simon had wrought deep fissures in her confidence. She thought she was frigid. She thought she was clumsy and sexually inadequate. She feared she would disappoint Gabriel when they eventually made love.

Gabriel knew that it would take a long time to dispel those lies and to heal those wounds. He was resolved to build her confidence incrementally, to help her see herself as he saw her—sexy, attractive, and passionate.

The only way he could do this would be to take his time and be patient and affirming. He was looking forward to demonstrating his love for her and subjecting all of his erotic arts to her service. She would never demand such things, such attention, which made the thought of giving everything to her so much more satisfying.

If their relationship was more advanced and Julianne was less shy, he would suggest that they make love on the terrace. The thought of

how Julianne's rose and cream skin would glow in the starlight made
his heart soar and his trousers twitch. But having sex outside would
likely be too nerve-wracking for her, and he'd be damned if he'd push
her to do anything that would make her even remotely uncomfortable.

We'll just have to come back . . .

Chapter Thirty-three

At eight o'clock that evening, Miss Julianne Mitchell put the finishing touches on her hair as her sweetheart gazed at her longingly from the doorway of the bathroom. He adored her. It was evident in every look, every touch, and the way he stared, unblinking, at her simplest actions.

She'd curled her hair and pinned it up, coaxing a few tendrils about her face, tendrils Gabriel longed to wrap around his fingers. Her aesthetician in Toronto had given her a small tube of industrial strength concealer, makeup that was designed to cover even the worst scars. It was so effective, Julia no longer had to wear a scarf to hide Simon's bite. Just being able to forget about the scar made Julia joyous, especially since Grace's lovely scarf would not have matched her new dress.

Her dress was a silky emerald green—long-sleeved and V-necked, as she preferred, its hem brushing the top of her knees. She wore sheer black stockings with a surprise attached to them and was about to step into her black Prada stilettos. As Gabriel watched her lean forward to put on her shoes, he vowed to purchase more of them. They did incredible things for her legs and to her cleavage as she leaned over.

"Allow me," he said, crouching in front of her in his freshly pressed navy suit. He took her hand and placed it on his shoulder, to aid her balance, while he lifted each foot and slipped on her shoes.

"Thank you," she murmured.

He smiled up at her and kissed her hand. "Anything for you, Cinderella."

Julia pulled her black three-quarter-length trench coat from the closet and was about to wriggle into it when Gabriel took it out of her hand.

"Let me," he protested. "I want to fuss over you."

"It's just a coat, Gabriel. No worries."

"Yes, I know it's a coat. But it's an opportunity for me to behave like a gentleman and honor you. Please don't deprive me, Julianne."

She flushed in embarrassment and nodded slowly. She wasn't used to such attention, of course, except from Gabriel. She wanted to be gracious and let him attend her, but it was far more than she ever expected or thought that she deserved. She reached up to kiss him and whispered her thanks against his lips. He took her arm and led her downstairs and toward the restaurant.

Julia and Gabriel walked slowly through the cobblestoned streets from the Palazzo Vecchio, over to the Palazzo dell'Arte dei Giudici e Notai, laughing and reminiscing about previous visits to Florence. They had to walk slowly, for navigating Florence in stilettos was more than a little challenging. Thankfully, Gabriel had taken Julia's arm to escort her properly, thus enabling her to walk upright and also to avoid much of the wolf whistles and catcalls of Florentine youths. The city had not changed that much since the days of Dante.

The restaurant Gabriel had chosen was called *Alle Murate*. It was located in a fourteenth-century guild hall a short walk from the Duomo, and it boasted incredible period frescoes, including a portrait of Dante himself. Julia was overwhelmed by the beauty of the artwork and found herself wandering slightly as the maître d' escorted them to their table.

Gabriel had reserved a quiet space on the loft floor overlooking the main room, just under the vaulted ceiling. It was the best table in the house, for it afforded the finest and closest views of the medieval illustrations. Four angels frozen in frescoes floated above them as Julia took Gabriel's hand and squeezed it. She was ecstatic.

"It's beautiful. Thank you. I had no idea these frescoes were here."

He smiled at her enthusiasm. "Tomorrow night will be even better. Massimo tells me that my lecture is scheduled after the museum closes and there will be a reception with local dignitaries and academics. Later on, there will be a banquet inside the Gallery. It will be a semi-formal affair, and we will be the guests of honor."

Julia smiled narrowly. "I didn't bring anything fancy enough for a semi-formal."

"I'm sure anything you brought would look beautiful. But I can understand not wanting to wear the same dress twice. So I will just have to take you shopping."

"Are you sure you wouldn't rather I left you to it? The banquet is a celebration of your lecture, so you'll be very busy. Maybe you'd be more comfortable if you could—mingle freely."

He reached over to push a curl away from her face. "Julianne, your presence is not only encouraged, it's required. I dislike going to social events alone. I always have. Having you at my side is the only pleasure the evening will afford, I assure you. Don't you want to join me?" His face took on a worried expression.

"I always enjoy your company. But people will ask me who I am and what I do . . . won't that be awkward for you?"

His features immediately darkened. "Of course not! I've been waiting for the end of the semester so I could enjoy your company in public and introduce you as my girlfriend. And there's nothing shameful about being a graduate student. Half the people at the banquet will have been graduate students at one time. You're a grown woman, you're intelligent and beautiful . . ."

He grinned wickedly. "*I* will have to stay close to *you* in order to keep my rivals at bay. They'll be circling around you like Etruscan wolves, vying for the attention of the prettiest woman at the party."

Julia smiled her gratitude and leaned over to kiss him. "Then I would be delighted to accompany you."

In answer, he pressed his lips to her hand, her palm, and her wrist, moving his lips gently to the sleeve of her dress. He pushed it up her forearm to expose her bare skin to his mouth. Julia's eyelids fluttered as he began kissing the delicate skin of her arm with wet, unhurried kisses. He dragged his lips to the sensitive space at the inside of her elbow and sucked lightly. For Gabriel knew, as Julia did not, that the inside of a woman's elbow was a particularly erogenous zone.

The sound of the waiter clearing his throat behind him merely slowed Gabriel's attentions. Julia blushed a brilliant red at being caught, which prompted him to release her arm reluctantly.

Over a bottle of Tuscan wine and a few *antipasti*, Gabriel asked about her study-abroad program, where she lived and what she did.

When she spoke of how she would visit the Uffizi on an almost daily basis to gaze at Botticelli's masterpieces, he wondered if there really was such a thing as destiny. And he wondered how he'd ever been fortunate enough to find her not once, but twice.

After they'd finished their main courses and were sitting quietly gazing into one another's eyes and exchanging chaste kisses, Gabriel released her hand and rummaged in his suit pocket.

"I have something for you."

"Gabriel, the trip is a gift in itself, and now you want to buy me a dress. I can't."

He shook his head. "This is different. Before I give it to you, I want you to promise that you won't refuse it."

Julia looked over into serious blue eyes. He wasn't joking. In fact, he was quite grave. She wondered what was hidden in the palm of his right hand.

"I can't promise something without knowing more about it."

He made a face. "Promise that you'll keep an open mind?"

"Of course."

"Hold out your hand."

Julia did as she was bidden, and Gabriel placed a small, black velvet box in her palm. She inhaled sharply.

"It isn't a ring. So you can start breathing again." His face was smiling, but his eyes were tense.

She opened the box and was stunned by what she saw. Nestled amongst black silk were two large, round, and perfect diamond solitaire earrings of about a carat each.

"Gabriel, I . . ." She searched for more words, but couldn't find any.

"Before you refuse them, I need to tell you their story. Will you listen? For me?"

She nodded, mesmerized by the glittering stones.

"They were Grace's. Richard gave them to her the first time he told her that he loved her. They weren't together very long before he fell for her completely. Legend has it that he sold his car to buy those earrings."

Julia's mouth hung open. Now she recognized them. Grace wore them almost constantly.

"I want you to have them."

She shook her head and gently, reverently closed the box. She held it out to him. "I can't. They were your mother's. You should keep them."

"No."

"Gabriel, please. They should go to Rachel or Scott."

"Rachel and Scott have other things. Richard gave these to me." As Gabriel began to panic, all he could do was focus on the small patch of velvet surrounded by her porcelain skin. His eyes narrowed a little. "If you refuse them, you will injure me." His words were barely above a whisper, but they hit Julia as if he had screamed.

She swallowed and took a minute to gather her thoughts. "I'm so sorry. They're lovely. And I can't express how wonderful I feel that you want me to have them, but this is wrong."

Julia saw that his mood was shifting from hurt to upset, and so she looked down at the tablecloth in front of her, hiding her eyes.

"You misunderstand me, Julianne. I'm not giving them to you because I think you should have something of Grace's. They aren't the equivalent of a scarf or a string of pearls."

She chewed at the inside of her mouth as she waited for him to continue.

He leaned across the table and pressed his palm against her cheek. "I am giving you these to commemorate the fact that I have already given you my heart." He swallowed thickly as his eyes searched hers. "This is my way of saying that you, Julianne, are the love of my life, and I want something of mine with you always. Don't you see? These diamonds represent my heart. You can't refuse them."

Julia saw in his eyes that he was absolutely serious. She knew that if he'd given her an engagement ring, she would have been shocked, but she would have accepted it. There was no other person in the world for her, just him. So why was she hesitating?

On the one hand, there was her pride, and on the other, there was the thought, the painful unacceptable thought, that she would hurt him by rejecting his gift. She didn't want to hurt him. She loved him, which meant that her decision had already been made.

"They're beautiful. The most beautiful gift I've ever received, next to your love. Thank you."

He kissed her fingers in gratitude. "Grace would be happy that we found one another. I believe that, Julianne. I believe that she's looking down on us and offering us her blessing. And she would be overjoyed that I was able to give her earrings to the woman I love."

He smiled, extending his hand and pulling her into a passionate embrace. "Thank you," he whispered.

After he'd kissed her, he took the box from her hand and helped her place the earrings in her ears. And he pressed a tender kiss to each earlobe. "*Meravigliosa*. Marvelous."

Julia laughed nervously. "Everyone downstairs is staring at us."

"Not everyone. The waiter is in the kitchen." He smirked at her, and they both laughed.

He caught her eye and leaned forward to whisper in her ear, "*Behold, thou art fair, my beloved.*"

Julia flushed deeply at Gabriel's erotic Hebrew poetry and murmured her reply against his neck, "*By night on my bed I sought him whom my soul loveth: I sought him, but I found him not. I will rise now, and go about the city in the streets, and in the broad ways I will seek him.*"

Gabriel responded with a slow, surprised smile and kissed her until the waiter returned.

When Julia declined dessert and the wine bottle was empty, the blissful couple floated in the direction of their hotel.

"How are your feet?" Gabriel gazed down wistfully at her beautiful high-heeled shoes.

She squeezed his hand. "I can't feel my feet. I can't feel anything at this moment except happiness."

He smiled at her tenderly. "My sweet girl."

He chose a single lock of hair and wound it gently around his finger before releasing it. "Can you tolerate a detour? The Duomo is beautiful by night, and I've never kissed you in its shadow."

She nodded, and he led her to the church so they could admire Brunelleschi's dome. It was an incredible feat of renaissance architecture, a great egg-shaped dome with a tiled roof soaring above a beautiful church. They walked to the front of the structure, near the Baptistery opposite, gazing at the façade and up at the roof. It was breathtaking, even at night.

Gabriel pulled her to his chest and kissed her lovingly, winding his fingers around the loose tendrils of her hair.

She half-moaned as he dragged his lips to her earlobe, drawing it into his mouth gently.

"You have no idea how it feels knowing that I gave you these." He nuzzled her earring with his nose. "Knowing that you wear my love for everyone to see."

Julia responded by kissing him eagerly.

With fingers entwined, they found themselves drawn to the Ponte Santa Trinita, the bridge where Dante saw Beatrice. Standing on the bridge, they looked down at the Arno, illuminated as it was at night by the lights of the buildings on the riverbanks.

"Julianne," he murmured, holding her in his arms as they watched the river flow.

"Gabriel." She smiled up at him and angled her face for a kiss.

He kissed her softly at first, but their kisses grew more and more intense. He pulled away, well aware of the fact that they were becoming a spectacle for the foot traffic across the bridge.

"I'm so glad I found you again. I've never been this happy." He stroked her cheek lazily and pressed his lips to her forehead.

Impulsively, she reached out and grabbed his silk tie, pulling him so that their faces were mere inches apart. "I want you," she breathed. And with that, Julia pulled him even closer and kissed him.

And what a kiss it was. Here was the tiger emerging from behind the façade of the kitten. Julia's passion, ignited by Gabriel's affection, poured into his mouth as she endeavored to show him how much she felt for him. Her hands, which had normally rested on either his shoulders or in his hair, left his tie to explore his chest and his back, feeling his muscles through his clothes, pressing him tightly against her.

Her aggression delighted him. He reciprocated within reason, well aware of the edge of the bridge at his back and the clusters of impertinent youths who continued to walk by.

When they were both panting for air, she brought her lips to his ear, "Make me yours. Now."

"Are you sure?" he rasped out, caressing her hips and her backside.

"With all my heart."

He brushed his thumb against her now swollen lower lip. "Only if you're ready."

"I've wanted you forever, Gabriel. Please don't make me wait any longer."

He chuckled softly. "Then we should get off this bridge."

He kissed her once more and excused himself to make a brief phone call. It was a quick exchange in Italian that sounded like Gabriel was confirming something with the concierge, but Julia couldn't hear everything. He turned his back on her deliberately and spoke in hushed tones.

When she asked him about it he grinned. "You'll see."

It took them a little longer than it should have to arrive at the hotel, for every few steps one of them would pull the other into a passionate kiss. There was laughter and gentle caresses; there were tender embraces and murmured words of seduction, and a tango or two against the wall of a darkened alley.

But really, the seduction was complete. For it had occurred in an old orchard years ago.

By the time Gabriel led Julia into the penthouse and out onto the *terrazza*, they were vibrating with shared electricity and very, very needy. Which meant that it took Julia a moment to notice the transformation. Pillar candles had been scattered around the space and contributed a warm, flickering luminosity to the starlight from above. The air was perfumed with jasmine. Pillows and a cashmere blanket beckoned them to recline on the futon banquette.

A bottle of champagne sat chilling in an ice bucket, and nearby, Julia saw a plate of chocolate-covered strawberries and what looked like tiramisu. And lastly, she noticed the music of Diana Krall.

Gabriel came up behind her and wrapped his arms around her waist, nuzzling her left ear with his nose. "Does this please you?"

"It's beautiful."

"I have plans for you this evening, my love. I'm afraid those plans don't include sleep until much, much later."

Julia shivered at the tone of his voice, low and sensual.

He held her more tightly. "Am I making you nervous?"

She shook her head.

He began to kiss her neck softly, floating his lips across her skin. "A declaration of desire," he murmured. "But tonight I will make good on my declaration when I take you to bed and make you my lover."

She trembled once again, and this time he crooked his arm across her collarbone, hugging her close. "Relax, darling. Tonight is all about pleasure. Your pleasure. And I intend to please you all evening."

He kissed her cheek, then spun her around slowly. "Foreplay is essential. And since this is new to both of us, there are a few things I'd like to do first." He searched her eyes for her reaction.

"I'm yours, Gabriel."

He smiled and embraced her softly. "I want to explore your senses— sound, taste, sight, touch. I want to take my time arousing and exciting you." He lowered his voice. "But most of all, I want to teach your body to recognize the man who worships you, just by my touch."

"I already recognize you, Gabriel. There's no one else."

He kissed her intensely and paused as *Besame Mucho* sounded in the air. "Will you dance with me?"

"Of course." *As if I'd ever refuse the chance to hold you in my arms . . .*

He pulled her close, and she pressed grateful lips to his jaw.

"Is this our song?" She stroked his lower lip with one of her fingers.

"It should be. I remember everything about that night. Your hair, your dress. You were a vision. And I was such a brute. The things I said." He shook his head. "How did you ever forgive me?"

Julia rebuked him with her eyes. "Gabriel, you're giving me the fairy tale I never thought I'd have. Please don't spoil it."

He kissed her lips repentantly and held her more tightly, running his hand across her ribs. For Gabriel knew, as Julia did not, that the ribs of a woman were another erogenous zone.

As they swayed to the music, he softly sang to her, pouring his soul into the Spanish words but changing them slightly so that she would know he would never let her go. He would give her nothing less than forever and hell itself could not prevent him from keeping his vow. He just hadn't spoken the words aloud.

Yet.

She lifted her head and stared at his mouth, memorizing its fullness and its curves, the way his bottom lip curled downward. She tugged it into her mouth unhurriedly, winding her fingers in his hair. He was sweetness and wet warmth, hunger and passionate need, love and devotion. And his kiss pressed itself to her very soul, so that even the tips of her toes felt his adoration and desire.

Two bodies pressed tightly together in a lover's dance, eager with anticipation.

Chapter Thirty-four

Julia reclined on her back on the terrace's banquette, staring up blissfully into Gabriel's sparkling eyes. He'd divested himself of his suit jacket and loosened his tie, but refused to remove it, remembering how arousing it had been when Julia tugged on it at the Ponte Santa Trinita.

She was captivated by him—his nose, his cheekbones, his angular jaw, his magnificent blue eyes under dark brows, and the chest hair that peeked out over the top of his white T-shirt beneath his open collar.

He was on his side facing her, resting his head on his upturned arm, his right leg crooked at the knee, pouring champagne. They toasted their love and partook of Gabriel's favorite vintage of Dom Pérignon before he leaned over to capture her lips with his.

"I'd like to feed you," he murmured.

"Yes, please."

"Close your eyes," he said. "Just taste."

Julia trusted him, so she shut her eyes and felt something nudge against her lower lip; then it was inside her mouth, all chocolate and juicy sweet strawberry and the feel of Gabriel's thumb brushing across her heated flesh. Opening her eyes, she grabbed him by the wrist, pulling his thumb slowly into her mouth.

His eyes widened, and he groaned. She drew his thumb across her tongue, touching it lightly, and sucking on it determinedly, before swirling across its tip to savor any remaining chocolate. Gabriel groaned a second time at the way Julia looked up at him through her eyelashes, staring down at her with a mixture of passion and surprise.

She released him and looked away. "I didn't mean to get your hopes up. Thumbs are one thing, but I'm terrible at—"

He interrupted her self-deprecation with his lips, kissing her almost roughly. He stroked up and down her neck with a single finger while he explored her mouth with his tongue. When he pulled back, his eyes had a fire in them.

"I don't want you to put yourself down anymore. I won't hear it. What we have is ours alone. Don't prejudge yourself or me or what the two of us can be together." He gave her a light peck on the cheek as if to soften his severe tone and brushed his lips against her ear.

"And I have no doubt that you are excellent at *that*. A mouth as gifted as yours could never disappoint." He winked at her impishly.

She flushed as red as the fruit but didn't respond.

He returned to feeding her strawberries dipped in chocolate, interspersed with small sips of champagne, until she declined any further dessert so that she could return the favor.

Picking up a fork, she loaded it with tiramisu and arched an expectant eyebrow at him. "Close your eyes."

Gabriel did as he was told, and she delicately slipped the fork between his lips. He hummed loudly, for the dessert was very good. Better still was the pleasure of being fed by his beloved. She was preparing to serve him another piece when he interrupted her.

"I think you forgot something, Miss Mitchell." His tongue swept across his lower lip.

He grasped her hand, dragging two of her fingers through a small portion of the dessert and drawing those same fingers languorously into his mouth. As usual he was unhurried, drawing gently on each finger, gliding his tongue up and down before sucking on them from root to tip.

As Gabriel adored her fingers with his mouth, Julia's body cried out for him. She couldn't help but imagine his most talented tongue dipping into her navel and lower down, where no one's mouth had ever been . . .

"Are you happy, love?"

Julia opened her eyes and blinked. "Yes." Her voice was shaky.

"Then kiss me."

She pulled him by his tie, just as he'd hoped, and he complied gladly, rolling so that he was almost on top of her, his knee between her thighs. He was warmth and wet kisses and long fingers that stroked up and down her ribs and down to her bottom, cupping it firmly. She felt the heat of his chest through his shirt as it pressed up against her breasts, and his hardness against her thigh, and she wanted more, more . . . on top, in between, *inside* . . .

Gabriel pulled back and took her hand in his, kissing the back of it. "Come to bed."

"You can have me here."

He furrowed his brow at first, and after his smile returned he kissed her nose. "Oh, no. I want you in my bed. Besides, it's chilly out here, and I can't have you catching pneumonia."

She looked slightly disappointed.

He hastened to comfort her. "If you still feel the same way, we'll revisit it tomorrow. But for tonight, we should be behind closed doors. I'll meet you inside. Take all the time you need."

He kissed her with restraint and watched her very fine derrière as she walked across the terrace and into the bedroom. He leaned back on the banquette and threw his arm over his face, unashamedly adjusting himself more than once through his navy wool trousers. The anticipation was killing him. He'd never been this excited before, so ready to spread her out before him and take her with abandon. But that was precisely what he would not allow himself to do.

Not tonight.

How had he ever thought that fucking some woman he didn't even know in one of the washrooms at Lobby was exciting? How had he believed that nameless, faceless orgasms would ever satisfy him? He'd spent his life worshipping at the altar of a silent, absent god who promised everything but delivered something fleeting that always left him wanting. He'd trafficked in lust masquerading as *eros*. But nothing had been further from reality.

Vanity of vanities. All is vanity.

Everything had changed since he found Julia again, and especially since he'd fallen in love with her. She'd broken him open and taken his emotional virginity, but she had done so patiently and gently. He would give her nothing less.

While Gabriel pondered the ways in which he could worship her, Julia was leaning against the vanity in the bathroom trying to catch her breath. Gabriel's sensuous foreplay was the equivalent of a scorched earth seduction. There was no going back. There was no slowing the tremendous, irresistible pull they felt toward each other.

Oh God, how I want him.

She studied herself in the mirror as she fixed her hair and makeup and brushed her teeth. Minty fresh and freshened up, she reached for her nightgown and robe, only to discover that in her passion-soaked haze, she'd entered the wrong room. Her lingerie was in the other bathroom.

Merda.

She could take off her clothes and wrap herself in one of the Turkish robes hanging behind the door. But that would rather defeat the purpose of purchasing lingerie. She could try to sneak into the other bathroom, but that would mean crossing through the bedroom, and Gabriel was sure to have come in from the terrace by now. No doubt he was reclining on the bed, like King Solomon in all his glory.

Julia trembled with anticipation at the mere idea. *Should I take a shower first and just wander out there in a towel? Should I strip down to my panties?*

As her brain stalled on how best to make her entrance, Gabriel tidied the terrace and moved everything inside. He placed the pillar candles around the room, grouping several of them by the bed. He adjusted the music so that a playlist he'd created solely for that night filled the air. He'd entitled the playlist Loving Julia and was more than a little proud of it. He placed a few personal items on the nightstand and turned out all the lights.

Then he waited.

And waited. But she didn't appear. He began to worry.

He walked over to the bathroom and pressed his ear against the door. He could hear nothing, not even the sounds of running water or the rustling of silk. His heart leaped into his throat. What if she was afraid? Or upset?

What if she locked me out?

He took a deep breath and knocked on the door.

"Come in."

He was surprised to be so invited. He opened the door carefully and peeked inside. Julia was standing in front of the mirror, looking shy. "Are you all right?"

"Yes."

He frowned. "What's wrong?"

"Nothing. I just—Gabriel, will you hold me? I had all these plans, and then I came in here and froze and . . ." She rushed over to him.

His face wore a concerned expression. "It's only me, love. Maybe I've overdone it."

She shook her head and pressed her face to his chest. "No, I'm over-thinking things, as usual."

"Then think about how much you are loved, my sweet, sweet girl. Tonight I will show you just how much."

He kissed her tenderly, and when she smiled up at him and nodded, he picked her up to carry her to the bed.

Julia wasn't afraid. She thought she might be, but as Gabriel held her in his arms, pausing with each step to kiss her, her nerves began to relax. She loved him. She wanted him. And she knew that he wanted her too.

He placed her on the edge of the bed and looked down on her with kindness. Julia's breathing stilled; that was the look he had given her in the orchard. In their orchard. Now she wanted him even more.

"You turned the lights out," she said.

"You have beautiful skin. It will be particularly alluring by candle-light." He kissed her forehead. "A figure such as yours would have in-spired cavemen to carve on walls." He kneeled in front of her and slowly removed her high heels.

"Are you sure?" she whispered.

He sat back and looked up at her, pushing a lock of hair out of her eyes. "Only if you are, love."

She smiled. "I meant—about the shoes. I could keep them on."

The thought thrilled him. He couldn't deny it. But he worried about her comfort, and there would be plenty of time for other, more playful moments.

"I shouldn't have let you navigate the cobblestones in such high heels. It had to be painful. No shoes tonight."

He caressed her feet slowly, running his thumb up and down the arch of her foot, a move designed to relax but also to arouse her. She began to whimper; it felt so good. She wondered briefly how his thumb would feel on other parts of her body, and a shiver coursed up and down her spine.

Gabriel paused. "You're quivering. We don't have to do this."

"It's a pleasant kind of quivering," she murmured.

He continued to caress her feet for a few minutes before his hands ascended the backs of her calves to rest behind her knees. His magical fingers teased the hidden erogenous zone, almost making her cry out. She couldn't keep her eyes open as her breathing came quicker.

He knows a woman's body the way . . . somebody knows something. What was I saying?

In truth, he knew her body better than she knew it herself, which was a regrettable state of affairs. Nevertheless, she trembled as she thought of what delights awaited her when he actually moved his hands a little higher.

As if he was reading her mind, he ceased his attentions to her knees and moved his hands up to her thighs, pressing and parting them slightly so he could run his thumbs up and down, pausing before coming to the tops of her stockings. He was trying his best to take his time, making sure that she enjoyed every movement, ensuring that he skipped nothing.

"Gabriel, please don't sit on the floor." She reached her hand out to him, and he kissed it.

"The whole evening is a gift. Simply accept it." A smile tugged at the edge of his oh-so-perfect lips. "St. Francis of Assisi would approve."

"But I want to make you happy too."

"You've already made me happy, Julia. More than you know. Would it help if I confessed that I'm nervous too?"

"Why would you be nervous?"

"I want to please you. I haven't been with a virgin since I lost my virginity and that was a long, long time ago. We're going to take this slowly. I want you to relax and be as comfortable as possible. And if you're ever—uncomfortable, I want you to tell me. Immediately. Can you do that for me?"

"Of course."

"I care for you—you're precious to me. And one of the most precious things to me is your voice. Please tell me what you want, what you need, *what you desire* . . ." His voice grew raspy on the final three words, and an involuntary tremor passed through Julia's body.

She leaned down to press her lips against his. "What I desire is for you to stop kneeling to me, Gabriel. So get up off the floor." She tried to look fierce, but he simply grinned at her.

Hello, Tiger . . .

"Give me a minute, and I'll be right back." He disappeared into the nearest washroom, and Julia could hear the sounds of the water running in the sink.

He returned momentarily to find her standing up and reaching around to the back of her dress. His hands immediately moved to cover hers.

"I'd like to do that." His voice was husky.

He unzipped her dress slowly, staring deeply into her eyes. Then he gently pushed the green silk off her shoulders. It made a sighing sound as it floated to the floor, as if it too, had been seduced by him.

Julia stood in an ivory satin slip, whose hem ghosted the top of her gartered black stockings. Gabriel gasped at the sight of her, for she looked like an angel. A brown-eyed angel with dark upswept hair against creamy white skin, wearing an ivory slip over black lace underthings. A juxtaposition of virtue and the possibility of *eros*.

He reached out an explorative finger to touch one of the garters. "I wasn't expecting this."

Julia blushed. "I know you didn't want black, but truthfully, I wasn't expecting you to see me in these. I thought I was going to change."

"Hey." He gently lifted her chin and caressed her colored cheek. "*You are stunning.* And I never said I didn't like black. But if you want to change, I'll wait."

He gazed down at her expectantly, but she shook her head. She'd waited long enough. She ran her hands up and down his powerful chest before pulling him toward her by his tie. She kissed him deeply and slowly unknotted it, trying to be as sinuous as possible, sliding it around the back of his neck and dropping it unceremoniously to the floor. She attended to the buttons on his shirt, making short work of them and

SYLVAIN REYNARD

placing it and his T-shirt on top of his tie. While he stood before her, half-naked, she pressed her mouth to his chest, wrapping both arms around his upper back so she could feel the muscles in his shoulders and lower down.

"I can feel your heart beating," she whispered.

"For you," he said, with a smoldering expression.

She smiled as she touched his abdominals and waist. His skin was warm, much warmer than hers, and oh, so inviting. Unbuckling his belt and unfastening his trousers was slightly nerve wracking, but he placed a steadying hand over hers and helped her when they refused to cooperate. When he stood in front of her in his boxer briefs, having already kicked off his shoes and socks, she took a deep breath, waited for his nod, and pushed his underwear over his hips.

She took a step backward to admire him. She licked her lips and grinned. Widely. Gabriel was gorgeous.

It was probably genetic, or maybe it was a gift from the gods, or a combination of both, enhanced by his diet and exercise. But as her eyes wandered over his muscular body and well-defined abdominal muscles, something inside her warmed and melted. She felt heat rushing to her womb and farther down, especially as she noticed the V that extended from his hips. He was a modern version of Michelangelo's *David*, but with far finer proportions and unspeakably beautiful hands. Perhaps it was in poor taste, but she was more than a little smug when she realized how much larger he was than *him*.

Karma . . . her conscience cheered. She fought back a giggle, biting her lip roughly so that she didn't behave like a schoolgirl in reaction to her momentous discovery.

Gabriel noticed her strange reaction but said nothing. He suppressed a smirk, telling himself that it was probably not the right time to joke with her about his size. He didn't want to overwhelm her, and he knew damn well how good he looked, particularly now as he strained at attention.

All because of her.

"May I?" He came closer and ghosted his fingers over her hair, pausing for permission.

She assented, and he began to remove the pins, one by one, spilling her curls onto her shoulders. Julia closed her eyes and drank in the feeling of Gabriel's fingers running through her hair. It reminded her of the day back at Richard's house when he played hairdresser.

He untangled each curl lovingly, crown to end, until her tresses hung about her face like a dark curtain. He grazed the curve of her neck before his fingers found the straps of her slip. He pushed them over her shoulders. Julia stood in a black lace bra, black lace boy shorts with attached garters, and black sheer stockings.

Erotic perfection paired with the blush of innocence.

She was truly lovely. But she was nervous under his watchful gaze. She didn't like being stared at for long periods of time; it made her self-conscious. So he gathered her to him and kissed her until he felt her shoulders soften.

"Julia, I would like to see all of you," he whispered.

She nodded, and he took his time removing her stockings, releasing the catches and slowly rolling them down her legs, pausing briefly to fondle the backs of her knees again. Her labored breathing in his ear assured him that he was doing it correctly. Then he stood behind her and pressed kiss upon kiss across her shoulders before gently unfastening her bra. She pulled it forward and dropped it at their feet, thinking to herself how sexy their clothes looked together on the floor.

He took a moment to cup her breasts from behind, bringing his body flush with hers. He caressed her lightly, brushing her nipples with his thumbs as he opened his mouth to pay homage to the skin beneath her ear. Then he slid his hands to her ribs, pausing to rub them up and down before hooking his fingers in the material at her hips. He continued teasing the skin beneath her ear with his tongue as he removed her panties.

Julia was finally, gloriously, nude.

He hugged her around the waist and moved her to face him, noting the way her eyes were bent to the floor, her plump lower lip worried between her teeth. She started to fidget with her hands, and Gabriel knew she was only a moment away from covering herself.

"You are a goddess." He freed her lip, pushing his thumb softly to the curve of her mouth before he lifted her chin. His eyes swept across her deliberately from head to toe and back up again so that she could see his admiration.

"When I am an old man and I can remember nothing else, I will remember this moment. The first time my eyes beheld an angel in the flesh.

"I will remember your body and your eyes, your beautiful face and breasts, your curves and this." He traced his hand around her navel before dragging it lightly to the top of her lower curls.

"I will remember your scent and your touch and how it felt to love you. But most of all, I will remember how it felt to gaze at true beauty, both inside and out. For you are fair, my beloved, in soul and in body, generous of spirit and generous of heart. And I will never see anything this side of heaven more beautiful than you."

He enveloped her in his arms, kissing her repeatedly with light kisses, trying to communicate with his lips how much he loved her. He fingered the diamonds in her ears and placed his mouth to her earlobe. "Having seen you naked, I should demand that the only thing you wear in my presence from now on are these earrings. Anything else is superfluous."

Julia pressed a quick kiss to his lips before moving to recline on the bed, peeking over at him shyly. Gabriel had to take a deep breath and release it in order to get his bearings, for the sight of Julia naked and inviting was almost his undoing.

"Why don't you lie on your stomach, darling? I'd like to admire your beautiful back."

She smiled and rolled over, folding her arms and resting her head on them so she could continue to stare. He hovered above her, a pleased look on his face as he pressed a kiss to each shoulder blade.

Just like my favorite black-and-white photograph, she thought.

"You're breathtaking, Julia, from all angles. A true work of art." He traced a finger down her spine, pausing as she shivered under his touch, then he smoothed a hand over one of her lower cheeks.

"You changed the music," she mused, recognizing Matthew Barber's romantic song *And You Give*.

"You inspired me."

He picked up a small bottle of sandalwood and satsuma scented massage oil and placed some of it in his hand, warming it, and began to rub her shoulders. Julia closed her eyes and sighed.

"Just feel." Gabriel kissed her cheek and continued his gentle movements, traveling down her back unhurriedly until he was exploring the two dimples above the curve of her peerless derrière.

"These are lovely." He pressed his lips to each dimple.

Julia flinched, so Gabriel paused. When he continued, she began to relax. After what seemed like an hour, he was whispering in her ear, coaxing her to roll over. She felt as if she was floating on a cloud. She blinked up at him, a lazy smile spreading across her face.

He reached down to nuzzle her nose with his as he moved over her, one leg between hers and one leg to the side, his elbows resting near hers.

"You're gorgeous," he whispered, lowering himself until their bodies whispered against one another. Then he slowly began to press angel-soft kisses up and down her neck and across her collarbone while he continued his massage of the front of her body with one hand.

Julia loved the way her breasts brushed up against his hard chest and the feel of his taut abdomen against her softness—the way his strong hand slid beneath her bottom, pulling her against his hips.

"You don't know how much I desire you," he murmured against her neck. "How sexy you are." He nuzzled the dip at the base of her throat, pausing to trace it with his tongue.

Without warning, Julia arched off the bed and cried out in pleasure. Her hands found his back, and she began tracing the muscles, coming to rest on his hips, pushing down on them.

"Not yet, love."

He worshipped her with his mouth, with lips, with the gentle nip of teeth, unhurriedly adoring his beloved's body. She tensed when he kissed her hip bone, tasting the skin with his tongue before drawing it into his mouth.

"What's wrong?" he murmured, as he nuzzled across her lower abdomen from one hip to the other.

"No one has ever . . ." She stopped, embarrassed.

He grinned wickedly against her hip, plying it with kisses and working her flesh with his tongue. *Of course he never did this for you. In addition to being a motherfucker, he was also a fool.*

"Sweetheart, spread your legs for me."

Her eyes were dark and slightly cautious, but she complied. She watched as he gazed at her appreciatively, his eyes darting up to meet hers. He smiled and gently began to pet her with his fingers. Julia moaned.

He touched her lightly at first, testing her with one finger, moving carefully. Then he stretched her with two fingers, curling them upward as his thumb began to rub tiny circles. He never took his eyes away from her face, watching for any sign of discomfort, listening to her breathing speed as his curled fingers found her spot inside. He bowed his head in admiration, bringing his lips to the top of her inner thigh, teasing her before taking the flesh into his mouth and sucking with abandon, while continuing the movements of his hand. It was an extraordinary combination.

Julia's body bowed off the bed as she came with a cry so loud it approximated a scream. He continued touching her, but lessened his suction until she thrashed and tried to close her legs. He brought his mouth up to hers and kissed her tenderly.

"Thank you," she whispered, feeling feather-light. *It should be a crime to have such gifted fingers . . . and what a mouth . . .*

"Did that please you?"

She nodded, breathing heavily, her eyes a little wild.

He doubted that the senator's son had ever found her spot, and the thought made his chest swell with pride. He was looking forward to introducing her to all of the places on her body that he could bring pleasure to, one by one. He dragged his finger from her neck, circling a breast, and down to the place on her thigh where there was now a fresh mark. He pressed the newly colored skin lightly.

"Does it hurt?"

"No. But how—?"

"This part of your thigh is very sensitive. Someone who is selfish or rushed would ignore it and touch here first." He moved his finger to pet her lightly between her legs.

She was still sensitive from her orgasm, and so she jumped. He withdrew his hand and traced her thigh again.

"Julia, the only thing that redeems my previous experiences is that I can place what I've learned at your service. The only woman I'm interesting in pleasing from now on is you."

She reached up to touch his face, and he leaned his cheek against her hand, closing his eyes. She pressed her thumb against his mouth, feeling his full lower lip, and tugged him forward into a passionate kiss. He responded by placing his body over hers, and her heart quickened, thinking the moment of their union was imminent.

Once again, she grasped his beautiful behind, urging him closer. He smiled patiently and pushed back on one arm. "This isn't a good position. I need to move you."

"I thought—me underneath you, isn't that right?"

"It's the worst position to lose your virginity in," he explained, planting baby kisses across her shoulder.

"I think I'll like it."

Gabriel pulled back. "Not for your first time; it would be too easy for me to hurt you without realizing it."

Hurt? she thought.

His heart stuttered at the worry that flitted across her eyes. He placed his hands on either side of her face. "I am not going to hurt you, Julianne. I am not a teenage boy. I'm not *him.* I'm going to be very, very gentle. That's why we can't do it like this."

"Why?"

"The angles. My weight on top of you, even if I'm distributing it to my knees. Gravity. If you're on top, you can control the movements, the depth of penetration. I'm giving the control to you. Trust me," he breathed, kissing her ear.

He continued to caress her, murmuring adorations against her smooth, almost translucent skin. Then he wrapped his arms around her back, lifting her from the bed and switching positions so that he was flat on his back and she lay on top of him.

As she rested on his chest, he whispered Dante's words to her in Italian:

"Color di perle ha quasi in forma, quale
convene a donna aver, non for misura;

ella è quanto de ben pò far natura;
per esemplo di lei bieltà si prova.
De li occhi suoi, come ch'ella li mova,
escono spirti d'amore inflammati,
che fèron li occhi a qual che allor la guati,
e passan sì che 'l cor ciascun retrova:
voi le vedete Amor pinto nel viso,
là 've non pote alcun mirarla fiso."

Gabriel praised her beauty and her goodness, comparing her to a pearl and declaring that Love, itself, was featured in her visage. Julia whispered her thanks for his beautiful words, stilling so that she could hear his heart beat under her ear. She was overwhelmed to think that she held this person, this man she had loved for so long, in her arms. She couldn't stop touching him, tracing every muscle, every sinew of taut perfection. She traced his eyebrows, the indentation above the center of his sensuous upper lip, his sideburns, his ears . . .

He reached up to kiss her, tracing her lips with his tongue and drawing her plump lower lip into his mouth. For a few moments there was skin on skin, two naked bodies flush and prone. Julia's hands continued to explore Gabriel's form, his face, his chest, his hips. She began to stroke his erection softly, hesitantly, pressing kiss after kiss to his neck and throat as she worked him with her hand.

He growled in her ear, signaling his pleasure. A surge of confidence propelled her to stroke him more surely, quickening her pace as she brought her lips to his chest, kissing his pectorals and his tattoo. He was panting now.

"Let me worship you with my body, Julia," he rasped, not wanting his impending satisfaction to take place in her hand.

She released him as he grasped her thighs, gently coaxing them apart so that they rested on either side of his narrow hips. She felt him beneath her, lifting of his own accord between her legs. She shifted slightly, and a worried look shadowed her lovely face.

Gabriel placed his hand on her heart. The little beating thing inside her spluttered frenetically at his touch and sped up. "Are you all right?"

She leaned forward, allowing her hair to hang about her face like a screen.

He reached up to push her hair behind her shoulders so that he could see her better. "Please don't hide. I want to watch you."

Julia bit her lower lip and looked away.

"What?"

She shook her head.

"Sweetheart, now is not the time to be shy. *Tell me.*"

She stared at his chest, trying very hard not to look at the dragon as it mocked her with its permanence. "This isn't how I imagined it," she whispered, so low he had to strain to hear her.

"Then tell me how."

"I thought you'd be . . . *over me.*" *His banner over me is love.*

"I like being on top, I won't deny it, but you're very small, sweetheart, and very delicate. I'm worried that—"

"I know I made you wait a long time, Gabriel." Her voice was just above a whisper. "It will be all right if you can't be careful with me. If you need to be . . . aggressive."

Her remark disturbed him deeply, for behind the words he recognized not her voice but Simon's. *Of course that's what she thinks—that's how* he *treated her. Men are dogs with no self-control, and she's just a plaything for their sexual release.* The idea sickened him, but he fought to keep revulsion from showing on his face. He placed his hand on her cheek and gently stroked her.

"Julia, I love you. If I were the kind of man who would be aggressive with you because you made me wait, then you shouldn't be going to bed with me. You're a person, not a toy.

"I don't want to use you. I want to please you. So much." At this he gazed up at her with large, dark eyes, dropping his voice to the merest whisper. "I want you forever, not just for tonight. So please, let me do this my way."

He begged her with his eyes to take him at his word. He didn't want to have to explain *why* he was concerned and what kind of outcome he was studiously avoiding. There would be time enough for that in the morning.

"All I ever wanted was for someone to love me," she said, quietly.

"You have that now."

He moved his mouth to her breasts, holding one gently in his hand while he nuzzled the other. They were perfect. Perfect in weight and size, natural and pretty. *Rosebuds and cream.* He thought back to the night he'd first seen one, peeking out from behind her purple robe in their hotel room in Philadelphia. How he'd longed to take her into his mouth. He flicked her with his tongue, licking softly, and gently drew on her nipple, feeling it peak still further in his mouth.

Julia threw her head back, making inarticulate noises. Gabriel measured her reaction carefully. He wanted her to be aroused, and if she orgasmed by this alone, so be it. It would make what followed much, much easier.

"Let go, love. You don't have to fight it," he spoke to her other breast, as he offered it his attention.

Julia shuddered at his words and began rocking against him, eyes closed, sliding back and forth. Within a few minutes he felt her tighten and release, her posture sagging as she finished. She opened her eyes, blinked, then smiled down at him almost languidly.

And thank you very much for orgasm number two . . .

She took the initiative to kiss him, murmuring her affection through swollen lips. When she retreated, he reached over to grab something from the nightstand. She watched as he freed himself from under her, squirting a clear substance into his right hand and rubbing it somewhat roughly up and down on himself.

He noticed the expression on her face and hastened to explain. "It will make things easier for you."

Julia flushed deeply. She knew about such things, although she had never had reason to use them before. She felt embarrassed that she hadn't thought to purchase it for herself. She had come to Florence unprepared.

"You're very kind."

His mouth curved up into his cocky half-smile. "I told you I'd anticipate your every need." He kissed her and reclined back on the pillow. "I can use a condom, if you've changed your mind."

"With all the tests you've had, I don't think we have anything to worry about."

"It's still your choice."

"I trust that you told me the truth about everything."

"I'm glad I'm your first."

She smiled widely at his declaration. "I want you to be my last, Gabriel." She kissed him passionately, her heart quick and full because of his words. Because of his actions. "But I want something from you now."

"Anything."

"I want you to be on top."

When his brow crinkled and he looked perilously close to a frown, she leaned over him in earnest. "You have already shown yourself to be a generous lover. But it isn't a good idea to put me in control when I don't know what I'm doing. It makes me nervous. I won't be able to relax and concentrate on how it feels. Please . . ." She added the last word as a half-hearted addendum, for she didn't want to have to plead with him. He'd asked her to voice her desires, and she was doing so.

He realized at that moment how stressful it would be for her to sit above him naked and exposed, responsible for what was to happen. Later on, perhaps, but not the first time. Despite his worries, he could not deny her. Gabriel nodded, a slight tension visible in his jaw, and in one fluid movement she was on her back and he was kneeling between her legs.

Her smile was like the rising sun. For this was how she had always imagined it.

"Thank you," she murmured against his mouth as he kissed her tenderly.

"It takes so little to make you happy."

"I wouldn't say *little*," she giggled as she rubbed her thigh against him.

He smirked at her, reveling in a moment of levity.

The music changed then, and Julia looked up at him with interest. "What's the name of this song?"

"*Lying in the Hands of God* by the Dave Matthews Band."

"I like it."

"Me too."

She regarded him curiously. "Why did you choose it?"

"The words, the music . . ." His smile widened as his eyes sparkled. "*The rhythm.*"

"Oh, really?"

"Feel it. Focus on the rhythm. It's perfect for making love." He gripped her hips and pressed himself up against her, sliding up and down in time to the music, knowing that she would enjoy the contact as much as he.

She moaned, all laughter gone, and began to push herself toward him.

"Take a deep breath, love," he whispered.

As she inhaled, he pressed inside her just a little. She closed her eyes and drank in the feeling.

Now that Gabriel had the merest hint of how she would feel around him, his body was tempting him to push in hard and fast. But he knew that any thrusting on his part would tear her. He wanted her. He wanted to be inside her. But he cast his desires aside for the moment and remained perfectly still, distributing his weight to his elbows on either side of her shoulders, lapping and sucking her breasts.

Now that she had an inkling of what it would be like to be connected to him, to be filled by him, she wanted more. Much, much more. She wanted all of him.

"Careful," he warned, as she lifted her hips, eager to entice him further. "The next part will be uncomfortable."

When she didn't open her eyes, he placed a hand to her face, running his thumb along her cheek.

"Look at me. Look into my eyes." His eyes fixed on hers as they fluttered open.

"I'll give you anything. My body, my soul, take them. Take everything."

They stared at one another as he pushed in a little deeper, nudging slowly, slowly . . .

Her eyes widened, and she inhaled roughly as he entered her.

Gabriel immediately froze, steadying her with a hand to her hip, ensuring that neither of them moved.

"I'm sorry, sweetheart," he crooned. He moved his hand to her face and began stroking her. "That's the worst of it, I promise. Are you all right?" He scanned her face eagerly for any signs of tears.

But there weren't any. It wasn't as painful as she thought it might be.

It wasn't completely comfortable, either, but the sensation of having him inside her, the emotions she saw on his face, in his eyes, distracted her from the twinges inside . . . it was almost too much.

She wanted more. More of him. More of *this* and *them* . . . she wanted to see him come apart above her and know that they had done this together. She wanted to find their own beautiful rhythm. The music swirled and rose about them, a tempting pace she was eager to match. She smiled, and he felt her smile travel all the way to his heart, allaying his worries. Without breaking eye contact, he began to move in and out maddeningly slowly.

She blinked rapidly at the feel of Gabriel inside her. Her hands slid down the tensing muscles in his back to his behind, smoothing over his curves and feeling his rhythmic thrusting beneath her touch. He balanced himself on one elbow, tracing sensual patterns up and down her ribs and over her shoulder. She was magnificent: her long, dark hair spread out across the white pillow, her brown eyes full and deep, locked on his, and her mouth, red and open, as she began to groan with every thrust.

Gabriel moved a hand to splay his long fingers across her ass, guiding and moving her, but following a gentle pace. He had waited so long. She watched his eyebrows come together and his teeth clamp down on his lower lip. They were moving, moving, not fast but with determination, the synchronized connection of two lovers who would not look away.

Julia saw so many emotions in his eyes: love, concern, passion, adoration, affection, *erotic desire* . . . He looked at her as if she was the only woman on earth, as if there was nothing else in their private universe but the two of them and the sensual music that floated in the air as Gabriel made love to her, punctuated as it was by the noises escaping their chests.

Julia heard herself moan and pant, casting aside any embarrassment at hearing sex sounds fly unbidden from her throat. Gabriel loved her cries, and they spurred him on, arousing him even more, as if that were possible. He reached in between them, and as his speed increased, he began to pet her in time to his thrusts. Her tightened grip on his ass indicated her pleasure, as she fought to keep her eyes open.

"*Look at me*. I want to see your eyes when you come." The intensity of his voice matched his expression.

Her eyes grew wide, and she cried out as his fingers sped. Julia tightened like a knot pulled just too tight and suddenly, gloriously fell.

Erotic whispers and murmured adorations filled her ears. He had not cursed. She was far too distracted to focus on this surprising fact. She could not know that he was a vocal lover who groaned and shouted expletives to match his urges and satisfactions. But in this space, sacred or otherwise, his spontaneous utterances had been clean and pure.

"I love you. I love you. I love you," he chanted above her, in time with his movements.

Julia was enjoying the feeling of intense, unparalleled *fulfillment* as it flowed through her. It was like nothing she had ever experienced before. And before she could find her way through her orgasm, she felt him push in deeply and cry out her name.

Gabriel collapsed, careful to distribute his weight to his elbows, a wave of emotion coursing through him as he came down from his climax. He held her close, whispering sweet words in Italian, waiting for her to open her eyes.

I love this woman. More than I love my own life . . .

His beautiful Beatrice was not a virgin anymore. He'd taken—and given—what Dante never had. He prayed silently that she wouldn't live to regret the decision that brought her to his bed, or her choice of first lover.

He shifted so that he was beside her and reached a finger to trace her chin. Only then did he notice the flush that had spread across her neck and chest and further down. The skin of her inside thighs had bloomed pinkish red, and Gabriel choked back a sick regret.

Oh God, I've hurt her.

"Julia?"

Now her eyelids opened. At first her gaze was wide and unfocused. Then in an instant it shifted. She saw him and the prettiest slow smile played across her lips, exposing her white teeth. She felt like she was a feather coasting on a summer breeze. It was so much better than anything else . . . to see and hear him, to touch and taste him and then finally, gloriously, the naked, raw, and rare climax.

He exhaled and kissed her deeply. "Are you all right?"

"Yes," she purred.

"I love you. I just want to make you happy, to watch you smile. Forever."

"You'll make me cry." Julia couldn't continue; she was beyond words. She kissed him, eyes closed, reveling in the arms of her lover. Her first. And last.

"Don't cry, my sweet, sweet girl." He kissed her eyelids, caressing her cheek with his hand.

Suddenly, he was gone, and Julia found herself alone in the large bed, made larger still and colder by his absence. The aching loss was immediate, but her mind was still slow, numbed as it was by her first taste of this ecstasy. Before she could slide a hand across the sheet to reach for him, he was pressing near her.

"Just let me look, darling." His whisper was hesitant.

She had no idea what he was asking, so she simply hummed her permission. Then tentative fingers grasped her knees and a gentle hand lifted one, angling and spreading her wide, but not too wide. Now her eyes were open.

Gabriel froze as their eyes made contact. "Just a quick look to make sure you're all right."

When he'd attended himself in the washroom, he hadn't noticed any blood. The realization had relieved him more than he could express. His eyes flickered down, and soon he was sighing, his shoulders relaxing. He pressed something warm and soft between her legs.

She flinched.

"I'm sorry." Again he pressed the damp cloth to her sensitive flesh. There were a couple of pinkish spots on it, but nothing alarming. In truth, he wished there had been no pink at all, but pink was infinitely better than red.

"I'm fine. You just surprised me." Julia's voice shook, but only because she was still floating, and the feeling of him touching her *there* had intensified her sensations.

Gabriel picked up a glass of water from the nightstand and placed it in one of her hands, shaking two a little white pills from a medicine bottle into the other.

"Ibuprofen," he explained, hastily. "For the pain."

"It's not that bad, Gabriel. I wouldn't call it *pain*."

"Please," he begged.

She was puzzled by his overreaction but elected not to be stubborn, popping the pills quickly into her mouth and downing the entire glass of water. She was thirsty.

When he'd soothed her and cleaned her up, he scooped her into his arms, kissing her forehead over and over. He carried her across the threshold of the bathroom.

Julia heard the water running before they walked through the door. "What's happening?" she managed, holding her head up.

"Let me care for you, baby." He kissed her forehead and gently placed her in the large and inviting bathtub.

The hot water and rose scented bubbles were comforting. She was still dreamy, but things were slowly coming into focus. She opened her eyes and saw Gabriel standing over her, still naked, still glorious, checking the temperature of the water with his fingers and adjusting the taps.

"Are you still thirsty?"

She nodded.

He disappeared for a moment and returned with a garnet-colored liquid in a wine glass.

"Cranberry with soda," he said. "It's good for you."

She arched an eyebrow at him, wondering how he became an expert at warding off female problems, but once again, decided not to pursue the question. She drank greedily and passed him the empty glass.

"You changed the music. What is it?"

"*Sogno* by Andrea Bocelli."

"It's pretty," she murmured.

"Not as pretty as you."

He turned off the water and climbed in behind her, placing his long legs on either side of her body, pulling her to his chest. They each sighed in contentment. She leaned her head back on his shoulder, and he stroked her hair, his touch light and gentle.

"Was it—okay for you?" she whispered.

That's an understatement, he thought.

"Like nothing I've ever experienced before. You were perfect. You are perfect." He pressed his lips to the top of her head, and she snuggled into his arms. "And very, very sexy. How about you?"

"It was even better than I imagined. Thank you."

He began to run his hands up and down the slick, wet skin around her ribs.

"Why the bath?" she asked, shifting against him slightly, feeling his new arousal against her backside.

His lips found her ear. "I wanted to care for you."

"Thank you, Gabriel, for your kindness to me. I know things would not have been as pleasant if I was with someone else."

He kissed her hair. "You deserve far more and far better than me, Beatrice," he whispered. *"La gloriosa donna della mia mente.* The glorious lady of my mind."

"My Dante." She turned to kiss his wet chest. "When can we do that again?"

Gabriel smiled. "Not until tomorrow. You need to heal first."

She squirmed slightly. "But it isn't that bad. You were very careful."

"After all that we've shared, I just want to hold you and be close. Rest in my arms and know that I love you. We'll be making love again very, very soon."

Julia felt comforted and let herself relax wholly against his body. She silently thanked the gods of large bathtubs, handsome, sexy lovers, and rose-scented bubble bath. (Not necessarily in that order.) And she thanked the gods of virgins who were about to have sex with their sex-god (no blasphemy intended) boyfriends for the mother of all orgasms. Thrice over.

In the wee hours of the morning, the Edenic lovers wound themselves around each other, flesh against flesh, sleepy and sated in a large, white bed. Lightness and darkness, innocence and experience, kissed and caressed in the warmth and acceptance created by their love. The dark angel whispered to his muse in Italian until she fell asleep in his arms, happier than she had ever been. She was loved.

Acknowledgments

I owe a debt to the late Dorothy L. Sayers, the late Charles Williams, Mark Musa, my friend Katherine Picton, and The Dante Society of America for their expertise on Dante Alighieri's *The Divine Comedy*, which informs my work. In this novel, I've used the Dante Society's conventions of capitalization for places such as Hell and Paradise.

I've been inspired by Sandro Botticelli's illustrations of the Comedy, which present Dante and Beatrice as I have always envisioned them.

In the course of writing this story I've found several electronic archives to be quite helpful, especially the Digital Dante Project of Columbia University, Danteworlds by the University of Texas at Austin, and the World of Dante by the University of Virginia. These portals will prove valuable to those readers who wish to delve more deeply into Dante's life and works. I've also consulted the Internet Archive site for its version of Dante Gabriel Rossetti's translation of *La Vita Nuova* along with the original Italian, which is cited in this book.

A debt of a different sort is owed to the University of Toronto and its city, both of which serve as a backdrop to this story.

I would like to thank Jennifer, who read the very first draft of this story and offered constructive criticism at every stage of the process. Her support and encouragement was invaluable, as was her keen eye. I am grateful also to Nina for her technical support, creative input, and wisdom.

Thanks are due to the fine staff of Omnific, especially Elizabeth, Lynette, CJ, Kim, Coreen, and Amy. It has been a pleasure working with you.

I would also like to thank those who read a previous version of my manuscript and offered criticisms, suggestions, and support, especially the Muses, Tori, Kris, and Erika.

Finally, I would like to thank my family. Sustained encouragement for the first-time novelist over the course of two years is no easy thing to offer, especially when there are other important things to be done. Without their support, this project would not be.

—SR

Lent 2011

Keep reading for a special preview of

GABRIEL'S RAPTURE

Available now from Berkley!

Professor Gabriel Emerson was sitting in bed, naked, reading *La Nazione*, the Florentine newspaper. He'd awoken early in the Palazzo Vecchio penthouse of the Gallery Hotel Art and ordered room service, but he couldn't resist returning to bed to watch the young woman sleep. She was on her side facing him, breathing softly, a diamond sparkling on her ear. Her cheeks were pink from the warmth of the room as their bed was bathed in sunshine from the floor-to-ceiling windows.

The bed covers were deliciously rumpled, smelling of sex and sandalwood. His blue eyes glimmered, traveling lazily over her exposed skin and long, dark hair. As he turned back to his newspaper, she shifted slightly and moaned. Concerned, he tossed the paper aside.

She brought her knees up to her chest, curling into a ball. Low murmurings came from her lips, and Gabriel leaned closer so he could decipher what she was saying. But he couldn't.

All of a sudden, her body twisted and she let out a heart-wrenching cry. Her arms flailed as she wrestled with the sheet that shrouded her.

"Julianne?" He placed a gentle hand on her bare shoulder, but she cringed away from him.

She began muttering his name, over and over again, her tone growing progressively more panicked.

"Julia, I'm here," he raised his voice. Just as he reached for her again, she sat bolt upright, gasping for air.

"Are you all right?" Gabriel moved closer, resisting the urge to touch her. She was breathing roughly, and under his watchful gaze, she fanned a shaking hand over her eyes.

"Julia?"

After a long, tense minute, she looked at him, eyes wide.

He frowned. "What happened?"

She swallowed loudly. "A nightmare."

"What was it about?"

"I was in the woods behind your parents' house, back in Selinsgrove."

Gabriel's eyebrows knit together behind his dark-rimmed glasses. "Why would you dream about that?"

She inhaled, drawing the sheet over her exposed breasts and up to her chin. The linen was full and white, swallowing her petite frame whole before billowing cloudlike over the mattress. She reminded him of an Athenian statue.

He ran his fingers gently over her skin. "Julianne, talk to me."

She squirmed under his piercing blue eyes, but he would not let her go. "The dream began beautifully. We made love under the stars, and I fell asleep in your arms. When I woke up you were gone."

"You dreamed I made love to you, then abandoned you?" His tone cooled to mask his discomfort.

"I woke up in the orchard without you once," she reproached him softly.

The fire in his belly was instantly quenched. He thought back to the magical evening six years ago when they first met, when they simply talked and held each other. He'd awoken the following morning and wandered away, leaving a sleeping teenage girl all alone. Surely her anxiety was understandable if not pitiable.

He unwound her clenched fingers one by one and kissed them repentantly. "I love you, Beatrice. I'm not going to leave you. You know that, right?"

"It would hurt so much more to lose you now."

With a frown he wrapped an arm around her shoulder, pressing her cheek to his chest. A myriad of memories crowded his mind as he thought back to what had transpired the evening before. He'd gazed on her naked form for the first time and initiated her into the intimacies of lovemaking. She'd shared her innocence with him, and he thought he'd made her happy. Certainly it had been one of the best evenings of his life. He pondered that fact for a moment.

"Do you regret last night?"

"No. I'm glad you were my first. It's what I wanted since we met."

He placed his hand on her cheek, tracing her skin with his thumb. "I'm honored to have been your first." He leaned forward, his eyes unblinking. "But I want to be your last."

She smiled and lifted her lips to meet his. Before he could embrace her, the chimes of Big Ben filled the room.

"Ignore it," he whispered fiercely, his arm stretching across her body, pushing her to recline beneath him.

Her eyes darted over his shoulder to where his iPhone lay on the desk. "I thought she wasn't going to call you anymore."

"I'm not answering, so it doesn't matter." He kneeled between her legs and lifted the sheet from her body. "In my bed, there's only us."

She searched his eyes as he began to bring their naked bodies into closer contact.

Gabriel leaned forward to kiss her, but she turned her head. "I haven't brushed my teeth."

"I don't care." He lowered his lips to her neck, kissing across her quickening pulse.

"I'd like to clean up first."

He huffed in frustration, leaning on one elbow. "Don't let Paulina ruin what we have."

"I'm not." She tried to roll out from under him and take the sheet with her, but he caught hold of it. He gazed over the rims of his glasses, his eyes sparkling with mischief.

"I need the sheet to make the bed."

Her eyes traveled from the white fabric that was clutched between her fingers, to his face. He looked like a panther waiting to pounce. She glanced over the side of the bed at the pile of clothes on the floor. They were beyond her reach.

"What's the problem?" he asked, stifling a grin.

Julia blushed and gripped the material more tightly. With a chuckle, he released the sheet and pulled her into his arms.

"You don't need to be shy. You're beautiful. If I had my wish, you'd never wear clothes again."

He pressed his lips to her earlobe, gently touching the diamond stud. He was certain his adoptive mother, Grace, would have been happy that her earrings found their way to Julia. With another brief kiss, he turned away, sliding over to sit on the edge of the bed.

She slipped into the washroom but not before Gabriel caught sight of her alluring back as she dropped the sheet just outside the door.

While brushing her teeth, she thought about what had transpired. Making love with Gabriel had been a very emotional experience, and even now her heart felt the aftershocks. That wasn't surprising considering their history. She'd wanted him since she spent a chaste night with him in an orchard when she was seventeen, but he'd been gone when she awoke the next morning. He'd forgotten her in the aftermath of a drunken, drug-induced haze. Six long years passed before she saw him again, and then, he didn't remember her.

When she encountered him again on the first day of his graduate seminar at the University of Toronto, he was attractive but cold, like a distant star. She hadn't believed then that she'd become his lover. She hadn't believed it possible that the temperamental and arrogant Professor would reciprocate her affection.

There were so many things she hadn't known. Sex was a kind of knowledge, and now she knew the sting of sexual jealousy in a manner she'd never experienced before. The mere idea of Gabriel doing what they'd done with some other woman, and in his case many other women, made her heart ache.

She knew that Gabriel's trysts were different from what they'd shared—that they were assignations not brought about by love or affection. But he'd undressed them, seen them naked, and entered their bodies. After being with him, how many of those women craved more? Paulina had. She and Gabriel had maintained contact over the years since they conceived and lost a child together.

Julia's new understanding of sex changed her view of his past and made her more sympathetic to Paulina's plight. And all the more guarded against losing Gabriel to her or to any other woman.

Julia gripped the edge of the vanity as a wave of insecurity washed over her. Gabriel loved her; she believed this. But he was also a gentleman and would never reveal that their union had left him wanting. And what of her own behavior? She'd asked questions and talked when she expected that most lovers would have been silent. She'd done very little to please him, and when she tried he'd stopped her.

Her ex-boyfriend's words came screaming back at her, swirling in her mind with condemnation:

You're frigid.

You're going to be a lousy lay.

She turned away from the mirror as she contemplated what might happen if Gabriel was dissatisfied with her. The specter of sexual betrayal reared its maleficent head, bringing with it visions of finding Simon in bed with her roommate.

She straightened her shoulders. If she could persuade Gabriel to be patient and to teach her, then she was confident she could please him. He loved her. He would give her a chance. She was his as surely as if he'd branded his name on her skin.

When she stepped into the bedroom she caught sight of him through the open door to the terrace. On her way, she was distracted by a beautiful vase of dark purple and paler, variegated irises sitting on top of the desk. Some lovers might have purchased long-stemmed red roses, but not Gabriel.

She opened the card that was nestled amongst the blossoms.

My Dearest Julianne,
Thank you for your immeasurable gift.
The only thing I have of value is my heart.
It's yours,
Gabriel.

Julia reread the card twice, her heart swelling with love and relief. Gabriel's words didn't sound like they were penned by a man who was dissatisfied or frustrated. Whatever Julia's worries, Gabriel didn't seem to share them.

Gabriel was sunning himself on the futon, his glasses off, his chest gloriously exposed. With his muscular, six-foot-two frame, it was as if Apollo himself had deigned to visit her. Sensing her presence on the terrace, he opened his eyes and patted his lap. She joined him, and his arms enveloped her as he kissed her passionately.

"Why, hello there," he murmured, brushing a stray tendril back from her face. He peered at her closely. "What's wrong?"

"Nothing. Thank you for the flowers. They're beautiful."

He brushed his lips against hers. "You're welcome. But you look troubled. Is it about Paulina?"

"I'm upset that she's calling you, but no." Julia's expression brightened. "Thank you for your card. It said what I desperately wanted to hear."

"I'm glad." He squeezed her more closely. "Tell me what's bothering you."

She toyed with the belt to her bathrobe for a moment, until he took her hand in his. She looked at him. "Was last night everything you'd hoped for?"

Gabriel exhaled sharply, for her question had taken him by surprise. "That's a strange question."

"I know it had to be different for you. I wasn't very . . . active."

"Active? What are you talking about?"

"I didn't do much to please you." She blushed.

He stroked the flushing skin lightly with the tip of his finger. "You pleased me a great deal. I know you were nervous, but I enjoyed myself tremendously. We belong to one another now—in every way. What else is troubling you?"

"I demanded that we switch positions when you would have preferred me on top."

"You didn't demand, you *asked*. Frankly, Julianne, I'd like to hear you demand things of me. I want to know that you want me as desperately as I want you." His expression relaxed, and he drew a circle or two around her breast. "You dreamed about your first time being a certain way. I wanted to give that to you, but I was worried. What if you were uncomfortable? What if I wasn't careful enough? Last night was a first for me too."

He released her, pouring coffee and steamed milk from two separate carafes into a latté bowl and spreading the tray of food between them on the banquette. There were pastries and fruit, toast and Nutella, boiled eggs and cheese, and several *Baci Perugina* Gabriel had bribed a hotel employee to run out and purchase along with the extravagant bouquet of irises from the *Giardino dell'Iris*.

Julia unwrapped one of the *Baci* and ate it, eyes closed with pure pleasure. "You ordered a feast."

"I awoke ravenous this morning. I would have waited for you but . . ." He shook his head as he picked up a grape and fixed her with a sparkling eye. "Open."

She opened her mouth, and he popped the grape inside, tracing his finger temptingly across her lower lip.

"And you must drink this, please." He handed her a wine glass filled with cranberry juice and soda.

She rolled her eyes. "You're overprotective."

He shook his head. "This is how a man behaves when he's in love and he wants his sweetheart healthy for all the sex he plans on having with her." He winked smugly.

"I'm not going to ask how you know about such things. Give me that." She grabbed the glass from his hand and downed it, her eyes focused on his, as he chuckled.

"You're adorable."

She stuck her tongue out at him before fixing herself a breakfast plate.

"How do you feel this morning?" Gabriel's face grew concerned.

She swallowed a piece of Fontina cheese. "Okay."

He pressed his lips together firmly, as if her answer displeased him.

"Making love changes things between a man and a woman," he prompted.

"Um, aren't you happy with, uh, what we did?" The pink of her cheeks faded immediately, leaving her pale.

"Of course I'm happy. I'm trying to find out if you're happy. And based upon what you've said so far, I'm worried that you aren't."

Julia picked at the fabric of her robe, avoiding Gabriel's probing gaze. "When I was at college the girls on my floor would sit around and talk about their boyfriends. One night they told stories about their first times." She nibbled at the tip of one of her fingers.

"Only a few of the girls had good things to say. The other stories were awful. One girl had been molested as a child. Some of the girls had been forced by a boyfriend or a date. Several of them said that their first times were completely awkward and unfulfilling—a boyfriend grunting and finishing quickly. I thought, if that's all I can hope for, I'd rather stay a virgin."

"That's horrible."

She fixed her eyes on the breakfast tray.

"I wanted to be loved. I decided it would be better to have a chaste affair of the heart and mind through letters than a sexual relationship. I had my doubts that I would ever find anyone who could give me both. Certainly, Simon didn't love me. Now I'm in a relationship with a sex god, and I can't give him anything like the pleasure he gives me."

Gabriel's eyebrows shot up. "Sex god? You've said that before, but believe me, I'm not—"

She interrupted him, looking him straight in the eye. "Teach me. I'm sure last night was not as, um . . . fulfilling as it usually is for you, but I promise that if you are patient with me, I will improve."

He cursed obliquely. "Come here." He pulled her around the breakfast tray and into his lap again, wrapping his arms around her. He was quiet for a moment, before sighing deeply.

"You assume that my previous sexual encounters were completely fulfilling, but you're wrong. You gave me what I've never had—love and sex together. You're the only one who has ever been my lover in the true sense."

He kissed her gently in solemn confirmation of his words. "The anticipation and the allure of a woman are crucial to the experience. I can safely say that your allurements and my anticipation were like nothing I've ever experienced before. Add to that the experience of making love for the first time . . . Words fail me."

She nodded but something about her movement disquieted him.

"I promise I'm not flattering you." He paused as if he were pondering his next words carefully. "At the risk of being *Neanderthal*, I should probably tell you that your innocence is tremendously erotic. The thought that I can be the one to teach you about sex . . . that someone so modest is also so passionate . . ." His voice trailed off as he looked at her intently. "You could become more skilled in the art of love by learning new tricks and new positions, but you can't become more attractive or more sexually fulfilling. Not to me."

Julia leaned over and kissed him. "Thank you for taking such good care of me last night," she whispered, her cheeks turning pink.

"As for Paulina, I'll deal with her. Please put her out of your mind."

Julia turned her attention back to her uneaten breakfast, resisting the urge to argue with him. "Will you tell me about your first time?"

"I'd rather not."

She busied herself with a pastry as she tried to think of a safer subject. The financial woes of Europe came readily to mind.

He rubbed at his eyes with both hands, covering them briefly. It would be far too easy to lie, he knew, but after all she'd given him, she deserved to know his secrets. "You remember Jamie Roberts."

"Of course."

Gabriel lowered his hands. "I lost my virginity to her."

Julia's eyebrows shot up. Jamie and her domineering mother had never been very pleasant to Julia, and she had always disliked them. She had no idea that Officer Roberts, who had investigated Simon's attack on her a month previous, had been Gabriel's first.

"It was not the greatest of experiences," he said quietly. "In fact, I would say it was scarring. I didn't love her. There was some attraction, of course, but no true affection. We went to Selinsgrove High School together. She sat next to me in History one year." He shrugged. "We flirted and messed around after school and eventually . . .

"Jamie was a virgin but lied and said she wasn't. I wasn't attentive to her at all. I was selfish and stupid." He cursed. "She said it didn't hurt much, but there was blood afterward. I felt like an animal and I've always regretted it." Gabriel cringed, and Julia felt the guilt radiating from him. His description made her almost ill, but it also explained a great deal.

"That's horrible. I'm so sorry." She squeezed his hand. "Is that why you were so worried last night?"

He nodded.

"She misled you."

"That's no excuse for my behavior, before or afterward." He cleared his throat. "She assumed we were in a relationship, but I wasn't interested. That made it worse, of course. I graduated from being merely an animal to being an animal *and* an asshole. When I saw her at Thanksgiving, I hadn't spoken to her in years. I asked her to forgive me. She was remarkably gracious.

"I've always felt guilty for treating her badly. I've stayed away from virgins ever since." He swallowed noisily. "Until last night.

"First times are supposed to be sweet, but seldom are. While you were worrying about pleasing me, I was worrying about pleasing you. Perhaps I was too careful, too protective, but I couldn't have borne it if I'd hurt you."

Julia put her breakfast aside and stroked his face. "You were very gentle and very generous. I've never known such joy, and that's because you loved me with more than just your body. Thank you."

As if to prove her point, he kissed her deeply. Julia hummed as his hands tangled through her hair, and she wrapped her arms about his neck. He slid his hands between them to the front of her robe, parting it hesitantly. He lifted his head, his eyes questioning.

She nodded.

He began whispering kisses against her neck and drew his mouth up to tug at her earlobe. "How do you feel?"

"Great," she whispered as his lips skimmed down to her throat.

He moved so he could see her face while one of his hands traveled to rest atop her lower abdomen. "Are you sore?"

"A little."

"Then we should wait."

"No!"

He laughed, his lips curling up into his signature seductive smile. "Did you mean what you said last night about making love out here?"

She shivered at the way his voice inflamed her but returned his smile, winding her fingers in his hair, tugging him closer. He opened her robe and began to explore her curves with both hands before dropping his mouth to kiss her breasts.

"You were shy with me this morning." He pressed a reverent kiss over her heart. "What changed?"

Julia brushed against the hint of a dimple in his chin. "I will probably always be a little shy about being naked. But I want you. I want you to look into my eyes and tell me you love me as you move inside me. I will remember that as long as I live."

"I'll keep reminding you," he breathed.

He divested her of her robe and positioned her on her back. "Are you cold?"

"Not when you're holding me," she whispered, smiling. "Wouldn't you rather have me on top? I'd like to try it."

He threw off his robe and boxer shorts quickly and covered her body with his own, placing a hand on either side of her face. "Someone might see you out here, darling. And I can't have that. No one gets to see this beautiful body except me.

"Although the neighbors and passersby might be able to *hear* you . . . for the next hour or so . . ." He chuckled as she inhaled sharply, a tremor of pleasure coursing all the way down to her toes.

He kissed her, pushing her hair away from her face. "My goal is to see how many times I can please you before I can't hold back anymore."

She grinned. "I like the sound of that."

"So do I. So let me hear you."

The blue sky blushed to see such passionate lovemaking, while the Florentine sun smiled down, warming the lovers despite the gentle breeze. Beside them, Julia's coffee and milk grew stone cold and sullen at being ignored.

❧ ❧

After a brief nap, Julia borrowed Gabriel's MacBook to send an email to her father. She had two important messages in her inbox. The first was from Rachel.

> Jules!
> How are you? Is my brother behaving himself? Have you slept with him yet? Yes, it is COMPLETELY inappropriate for me to ask that question, but come on, if you were dating anyone else you would have told me already.
> I'm not going to volunteer any advice. I'm trying not to think too much about it. Just let me know you're happy and he's treating you properly.

Aaron sends his best.
Love you,
Rachel.
PS. Scott has a new girlfriend. He's been secretive about her
so I'm not sure how long they've been dating. I keep bugging him
to introduce me but he won't.
Maybe she's a professor.

Julia snickered, glad that Gabriel was showering and not reading
over her shoulder. He'd be annoyed at his sister for posing such personal questions. She took a few moments to phrase her response before
typing her reply.

Hi Rachel,
The hotel is beautiful. Gabriel has been very sweet and gave
me your mother's diamond earrings. Did you know about that?
I feel guilty about it, so please let me know if this upsets you.
As to your other question, Yes. Gabriel treats me well, and I
am VERY happy.
Say hi to Aaron for me. Looking forward to Christmas.
Love, Julia. XO
PS. I hope Scott's girlfriend is a professor. Gabriel will never
let him hear the end of it.

Julia's second email was from Paul. It could be said that he pined for
her, but also he was grateful to have maintained their friendship. He
would rather keep his longings to himself than to lose her entirely. And
he had to admit that since she'd begun seeing her boyfriend Owen, her
very skin glowed.

(Not that he would have mentioned it.)

Hey Julia,
Sorry I didn't get the chance to say good-bye before you went
home. I hope you have a good Christmas. I have a gift for you.
Would you give me your address in Pennsylvania so I can send
it?

I'm back at the farm trying to find time to work on my dissertation in between large family gatherings and getting up early to help my dad. Let's just say my daily routine involves a lot of manure . . .

Can I bring you something from Vermont?

A Holstein of your very own?

Merry Christmas,

Paul.

P.S. Did you hear that Christa Peterson's dissertation proposal was accepted by Emerson?

I guess Advent really is the season of miracles.

Julia stared at the computer screen, reading and re-reading Paul's postscript. She wasn't sure what to make of it. It was possible, she thought, that Gabriel accepted Christa's proposal because she threatened him.

Julia didn't want to bring up such an unpleasant topic during their vacation, but the news troubled her. She typed a short reply to Paul, giving him her address, then she emailed her father, telling him that Gabriel was treating her like a princess. She closed the laptop and sighed.

"That doesn't sound like a happy Julianne." Gabriel's voice sounded behind her.

"I think I'm going to ignore my email for the rest of our trip."

"Good idea."

She turned to find him standing in front of her, wet from the shower, hair tousled, a white towel wound around his hips.

"You're beautiful," she blurted before thinking.

He chuckled and pulled her to her feet so he could embrace her. "Do you have a thing for men in towels, Miss Mitchell?"

"Maybe for one particular man."

"Are you feeling all right?" He raised his eyebrows expectantly, his expression hungry.

"I'm a little uncomfortable. But it was worth it."

His eyes narrowed. "You need to tell me if I'm hurting you, Julianne. Don't hide things from me."

She rolled her eyes. "Gabriel, it doesn't hurt; it's merely uncomfortable. I didn't notice it *during* because there were other things on my mind—*several* other things. You were very distracting."

He smiled and kissed her neck loudly. "You need to let me start distracting you in the shower. I'm tired of showering alone."

"I'd like that. How are you feeling?"

He pretended to ponder her question. "Let's see—loud, hot sex with my beloved inside and *outside* . . . Yes, I'd say I'm great."

He hugged her close, and the cotton of her robe absorbed some of the water droplets from his skin. "I promise it won't always be uncomfortable. In time, your body will recognize me."

"It already recognizes you. And misses you," she whispered.

Gabriel moved the top of her robe aside so he could kiss the slope of her shoulder. With a gentle squeeze, he walked to the bed, retrieving a bottle of ibuprofen and handing it to her.

"I have to run over to the Uffizi for a meeting, then I have to pick up my new suit at the tailor's." He appeared concerned. "Would you mind shopping for a dress by yourself? I'd go with you, but my meeting won't leave me with much time."

"Not at all."

"If you can be ready in half an hour, we can walk out together."

Julia followed Gabriel into the bathroom, all thoughts of Christa and Paul forgotten.

After her shower, she stood in front of one of the vanities, drying her hair while Gabriel stood at the other. She found herself glancing over at him, watching as he carried out his shaving preparations with military precision. Finally, she gave up putting on lipstick and simply leaned against the sink, staring.

He was still naked to the waist, the towel now low on his hips, as he painstakingly shaved in the classical style. His brilliant blue eyes narrowed in concentration behind his black glasses, his damp hair impeccably combed.

Julia suppressed a laugh at the degree to which his quest for perfection was manifested. Gabriel used a shaving brush with a black wooden handle to mix European shaving soap into a thick lather. After spreading the foam on his face with the brush, he shaved using an antiquated safety razor.

About the Author

Sylvain Reynard is a Canadian writer with an interest in Renaissance art and culture and an inordinate attachment to the city of Florence. (Parenthetically, it should be noted that the snarky narrator of *Gabriel's Inferno* was contracted to write this biographical description, and he can attest that SR is, in fact, real, and has an enviable collection of argyle socks.)

(For some professors, disposable razors simply aren't good enough.)

"What?" He turned, noticing that she was perilously close to ogling him.

"I love you."

His expression softened. "I love you too, darling."

"You're the only non-British person I've ever heard use the term *darling*."

"That isn't true."

"It isn't?"

"Richard used to call Grace that." Gabriel gave her a sad look.

"Richard is old-fashioned, in the best sense." She smiled. "I love the fact that you're old-fashioned too."

Gabriel snorted and continued shaving. "I'm not so old-fashioned, or I wouldn't be making mad passionate love with you outside. And fantasizing about introducing you to some of my favorite positions from the *Kama Sutra*." He winked at her. "But I *am* a pretentious old bastard and a devil to live with. You'll have to tame me."

"And how shall I do that, Professor Emerson?"

"Never leave." His voice dropped, and he turned to face her.

"I'm more worried about losing you."

He leaned over and kissed her forehead. "Then you have nothing to worry about."